THE IDIOT

Fyodor Dostoevsky

The Idiot

A new rendition by Anna Brailovsky,
based on the Constance Garnett translation

Introduction by Joseph Frank

THE MODERN LIBRARY

NEW YORK

2003 Modern Library Paperback Edition

LIBRARY OF CONGRESS CATALOGING-IN-PUBLICATION DATA
Dostoevsky, Fyodor, 1821–1881.
[Idiot. English]
The idiot / Fyodor Dostoevsky; a new rendition by Anna Brailovsky, based on the
Constance Garnett translation; introduction by Joseph Frank.
p. cm.
ISBN 0-679-64242-0
I. Brailovsky, Anna.   II. Garnett, Constance Black, 1862–1946.   III. Title.
PG3326. I3 2003
891.73'3—dc21   2002035699

Modern Library website address: www.modernlibrary.com

Printed in the United States of America

2 4 6 8 9 7 5 3

FYODOR DOSTOEVSKY

Great thinkers of the modern age from Nietzsche to Freud and Sartre have recognized Dostoevsky as a preeminent analyst of the human condition in the post-Enlightenment age. His pathbreaking novels, such as *Crime and Punishment* (1866) and *The Brothers Karamazov* (1879–80)—his last and crowning achievement—depicted the often devastating personal consequences of new political and social ideas by exploring his characters' internal struggles with the rapidly changing moral, social, economic, and religious order of the time. The remarkable depth of his analysis with respect both to individual psychology and to the complex fabric of human interaction has secured Dostoevsky his place as one the greatest and most widely read masters of the novel.

Dostoevsky was born in Moscow on October 30, 1821. His father, an army surgeon, was granted noble status in 1828 and purchased a small estate. In 1837, he sent his son to be educated at the Military Engineering Academy in St. Petersburg, where the latter remained even after his father's death to finish his education and receive his officer's rank. However, after just a year in government service, Dostoevsky retired to devote himself full-time to literature. His first work of fiction, *Poor Folk,* was published in 1846 to great acclaim and praised by one critic as the first "social novel" in Russia. Dostoevsky's early commitment to social problems was not limited to his fiction. He was a participant in several politically subversive groups that called for radical changes such as the emancipation of the serfs and reform of the judicial system. In 1849, he was arrested along with other members of the so-called Petrashevsky circle and condemned to death. Though the sentence was commuted, the prisoners were not informed of this until after they had been led in front of the firing squad. The anticipation of certain death left an indelible impression on Dostoevsky and he wrote about the experience at length in later works, such as *The Idiot* (1868–69).

Dostoevsky served four years of hard labor in Omsk followed by six years as a soldier in another Siberian town before being allowed to return to St. Petersburg, where he revived his literary reputation with the publication of his fictionalized prison memoir, *Notes from the Dead House* (1861–62). Two years later he published *Notes from the Underground,* a work that proved seminal in its use of an alienated anti-hero who anticipates Raskolnikov and Ivan Karamazov. Although he enjoyed literary success, Dostoevsky was continually plagued by a variety of personal troubles—worsening epilepsy, an unhappy marriage, a failed affair abroad, and the deaths of his wife and brother in the mid-sixties. In addition, there were great financial difficulties (compounded by gambling), at one point forcing him to complete his novel *The Gambler* (1866) in a mere twenty-six days. To flee his creditors, he went abroad again, where he remained with his second wife until 1871, writing *The Idiot* and much of *Demons* (1871–72)—a graphic condemnation of the nihilism prevalent among young Russian radicals in the 1860s, and a formally innovative work whose nonlinear narrative structure looks forward to the modernism of the twentieth century.

Upon his return to Russia, Dostoevsky lived a largely retiring life in a small town with his wife and young children. The last decade of his life was devoted chiefly to his "Diary of a Writer"—a series of journalistic essays and short fiction pieces published initially as a column in a reactionary journal and later as a monthly journal of its own—in which he developed at length his concerns with the disunity of contemporary Russian society and the messianic role of Russian Christianity. Dostoevsky's growing conservatism, religious focus, and scathing repudiation of the new generation of radicals had estranged some of his former associates. However, he was reconciled to his critics in June of 1880, when he delivered a rousing speech at the commemoration ceremonies of Russia's national poet, Alexandr Pushkin. The speech (published as a single issue of the Diary) declared the Russian character to have a unique genius for universality and affirmed Russia as the unifying force of Western civilization. In the wake of his electrifying proclamation of Russia's world mission, Dostoevsky was hailed as a prophet. When he died the following year, just two months after the completion of *The Brothers Karamazov*, his funeral was attended by fifty thousand mourners.

CONTENTS

THE IDIOT

INTRODUCTION

Joseph Frank

The final majesty, the ultimate freedom, and the perfect disinterestedness of divine love can have a counterpart in history only in a life which ends tragically.... It is impossible to symbolize the divine goodness in history in any other way than by complete powerlessness.

REINHOLD NIEBUHR, *THE NATURE AND DESTINY OF MAN*

Writing to a correspondent more than ten years after finishing *The Idiot,* Dostoevsky remarks that he is always particularly gratified to receive letters from people who consider this novel his finest creation. "All those who have spoken of it as my best work have something special in their mental formation," he writes, "that has always struck and pleased me."[1] Such a remark may easily be taken as little more than an epistolary flourish; but there is good reason to believe that Dostoevsky meant it seriously. For *The Idiot* is the most personal of all his major works, the book in which he embodies his most intimate, cherished, and sacred convictions. Readers who took this work to their hearts were, he must have felt, a select group of kindred souls with whom he could truly communicate.

In all his larger novels, Dostoevsky's positive convictions appear mainly as a foil and background for the noxious doctrines he wishes to undermine and destroy—or to depict as doomed to self-destruction. In *The Brothers Karamazov,* for example, though his religious ideal is extensively portrayed in Father Zosima, this ideal does not spring so directly from the living roots of his own personal experiences. It is only

---

1. F. M. Dostoevsky, *Polnoe Sobranie Sochinenii,* ed. and annotated by G. M. Fridlender et al., 30 vols. (Leningrad, 1972–1990), 29/Bk. 2: 139; February 14, 1877. This definitive edition of Dostoevsky's writings, which is now complete, contains his correspondence and provides an extensive and reliable scholarly apparatus.

in *The Idiot* that Dostoevsky includes an account of his ordeal before the firing squad, his own encounter with the imminence of death. This experience had given Dostoevsky a new apprehension of the meaning of life, and Prince Myshkin struggles to bring this revelation to a world mired in the sloth of the material and quotidian. Also afflicted with the epilepsy from which Dostoevsky suffered, the prince is overcome, at the onset of this disease, with the same ecstatic intuition of supernatural plenitude that his creator both cherished as a divine visitation and feared as the harbinger of madness.

The particular form assumed by the tragic fate of Prince Myshkin, quite aside from its general parallel with the Passion of Christ, is also linked with some other of Dostoevsky's most hallowed and sacrosanct beliefs. "To love man *like oneself,* according to the commandment of Christ, is impossible," Dostoevsky had written at the bier of his first wife. "The law of personality on Earth binds. The *Ego* stands in the way." In a passage of the deepest relevance for Prince Myshkin's unhappy fate, Dostoevsky continues: "Marriage and the giving in marriage of a woman is, as it were, the greatest deviation from humanism, the complete isolation of the pair from everyone else ... The family, that is the law of nature, but [it is] all the same abnormal, egotistical." Even that "most sacred possession of man on earth," the family, is thus a manifestation of the Ego, which prevents the fusion of individuals into an All of universal love. Only at the end of time—only when the nature of man has been radically transformed into that of an asexual, seraphic being—will the total realization of the Christian ideal of love become possible. Prince Myshkin approximates the extremest incarnation of this ideal that humanity can reach in its present unregenerate form; but he is torn apart by the conflict between the contradictory imperatives of his apocalyptic aspirations and his earthly limitations.

Although Prince Myshkin, the child of Dostoevsky's own theological musings, is certainly one of his author's most original creations, it is possible to construct a summary genealogy for him all the same. Myshkin can be related to all those romantic seekers for the absolute in Balzac—Louis Lambert, for example—whose absorption with the infinite wrecks their subliminal existence. From Balzac as well comes a perhaps closer analogue for Myshkin than any other character in the modern novel: the irresistibly attractive, androgynous hero-heroine of the fantastic *Seraphitus-Seraphita,* who ascends into a Swedenborgian heaven at the end of the book. Within Dostoevsky's own creative universe, Myshkin may be seen as prefigured by Colonel Rostanev in *The Village of Stepanchikovo* and Aleksey Valkovsky of *The Insulted and Injured.* The naïvely good-hearted Colonel also feels, if only sporadically, the same ecstatic apprehension of life that Myshkin struggles to impart to others; and the childlike ne'er-do-well Aleksey anticipates Myshkin's incapacity to live in time and his inability to choose between two women. Dostoevsky works out the character schema for Prince Myshkin by spiritualizing the spontaneous and whole-souled goodness of the Colonel and blending it with Aleksey's discontinuity and irresolution. The result is a discontinuity that springs from a total surrender of self in each human encounter, and an irresolution that becomes sublime in its aspiration toward a universality of love.

2

The first part of *The Idiot* was written at white heat, under the inspiration of Dostoevsky's decision to center a major work around the character of a "perfectly beautiful man"; and the singular spiritual fascination of Prince Myshkin derives very largely from the image of him projected in these early pages. Later in the book, Myshkin tends to be somewhat submerged by the flood of talk among the characters; and though he remains the implicit center of the action, his presence is much less strongly felt. In Part I, however, we see him in the clearest focus and receive the strongest impression of the Fra Angelico radiance that illuminates his personality.

The moral halo that surrounds the prince is conveyed in the very first scene, set in a railway carriage on the way to Petersburg, where he confronts the turbulent merchant's son Rogozhin and the amusingly cynical scrounger Lebedev. What strikes Rogozhin is the perfect unselfconsciousness with which the prince replies to his insolent questions, the complete lack of resentment toward his condescension. The prince's behavior is marked by a total absence of vanity or egoism; he simply does not seem to possess the self-regarding feelings on which such attitudes are nourished. Even more, he displays a unique capacity to take the point of view of his interlocutor—to such an extent, indeed, that he fully understands the other's view of himself. This does not mean that the prince necessarily agrees with these views (as when he rebukes Ganya Ivolgin for continuing to refer to him insultingly as "an idiot"); but he attributes their source to the strangeness of his appearance and behavior, and thus forgives them in advance. This explains the prince's failure to take umbrage at his reception by others; and his capacity to transcend himself in this way invariably disarms the first response of amused and superior contempt among those he encounters.

Max Scheler, in his admirable book *The Nature and Forms of Sympathy,* distinguishes what he calls "vicarious fellow feeling," which involves experiencing an understanding and sympathy for the feelings of others without being overcome by them emotively, from a total coalescence leading to the loss of identity and personality.[2] The underlying movement of *The Idiot* may be provisionally defined as the prince's passage from the first kind of fellow feeling to the second; but in Part I there are no indications of such a loss of identity. Rather, all the emphasis is placed on the prince's instinctive and undifferentiated capacity for completely lucid vicarious fellow feeling even under great stress. As an example, we may take the scene where the prince intervenes in the bitter altercation between Ganya Ivolgin and his sister, and himself receives the blow intended for the young woman. His response is to hide his face in his hands, turn to the wall, and say to Ganya in a breaking voice: "Oh, how ashamed you will be of what you've done."

This quality of the prince's character is not motivated psychologically in any way; but, in a suggestively symbolic fashion, it is linked with certain leitmotifs. On the one hand, the prince is much possessed by death: twice in these early pages he speaks of an execution he has recently witnessed; and he also recounts vividly the feelings and thoughts of a man first condemned to death by a firing squad and then unexpectedly reprieved. The first two descriptions dwell on the unutterable agony of the certainty of impending death—an agony mitigated only by the priest holding a cross to the lips of the condemned man as he mounts the scaffold. The third stresses the immense value assumed by each moment of existence as the end approaches, the infinite importance that suddenly seems to fill every precious instant of life.

2. Max Scheler, *The Nature of Sympathy,* trans. Peter Heath (London, 1954), chap. 2.

Despite the obsessiveness of the death motif in these early pages, the prince also admits to having been "happy" in the years just preceding his arrival in St. Petersburg; and the relation between these two motifs provides the deepest substratum of his values. The prince's "happiness," we learn, began with his recovery from a state of epileptic stupor. A sudden shock of awareness woke him to the existence of the world in the form of something as humble and workaday as a donkey. The donkey, of course, has obvious Gospel overtones, which blend with the prince's innocence and naïveté; and this patiently laborious animal also emphasizes, quite in accord with Christian kenoticism,[3] the absence of hierarchy in the prince's ecstatic apprehension of the wonder of life. The same point is made in the prince's remark that, in the early stages of his recovery, he had been consumed by restlessness and had thought to find "the key to the mystery of life" in his transcendent yearning to reach "that line where sky and earth meet," or in "some great town like Naples, full of palaces, noise, roar, life." But then, he adds, "I fancied that one might find a wealth of life even in prison."

Nothing arouses the suspicion and antagonism of the Epanchin sis-

---

3. *Kenosis* is a theological term defined in *Webster's International Dictionary* as "Christ's action of 'emptying himself' on becoming man, humbling himself even to suffering death; also, any of the various Christological theories based upon this, as that in becoming incarnate the Son surrendered all or something of the divine attributes." One of the distinguishing aspects of the Russian religious tradition, as defined by its greatest modern historian, G. P. Fedotov, is the stress placed on this aspect of the Christian faith. It is the suffering and humiliated Christ, according to Fedotov's generally accepted thesis, who lies at the heart of Russian spirituality.

Writing of the first Russian martyred saints, the princes Boris and Gleb, who were killed for political rather than religious reasons, Fedotov compares their meek acceptance of their fate with the teachings of the monk Theodosius, the founder of the Russian kenotic tradition. "Boris and Gleb followed Christ in their sacrificial deaths—the climax of His kenosis—as Theodosius did in His poverty and humiliations. . . . From the outside, it must give the impression of weakness as Theodosius' poverty must appear foolish to the outsider. Weak and foolish—such is Christ in his kenosis in the eyes of a Nietzsche just as he was in the eyes of the ancient pagan world." See G. P. Fedotov, *The Russian Religious Mind*, vol. 1 (New York, 1946), 130, and chap. 4 ("Russian Kenoticism").

Fedotov's reference to Nietzsche is by no means fortuitous. There is good reason to believe that Nietzsche was familiar with *The Idiot*, and that Dostoevsky's novel helped to shape his whole interpretation of Christianity. A convincing argument for this view, based on all the relevant material, has been advanced by the excellent German historian of religious philosophy Ernst Benz. See his *Nietzsches Ideen zur Geschichte des Christentums und der Kirche* (Leiden, 1956), 92–103.

ters more than this expression of what seem to them pious platitudes. The haughty and arrogant Aglaia tells Myshkin quite bluntly that he resembles the widow of a government clerk who comes to beg from her family and whose sole aim in life is "to live as cheaply as possible... that's your wealth of life in prison; perhaps, too, your four years of happiness in the country for which you bartered your Naples." The girls see in the prince's words only the utterances of a conventional "quietism" that complacently accepts evil and injustice as God's will and selfishly looks after its own creature comforts with a hypocritical sigh of commiseration. "If one shows you an execution or if one holds out one's finger to you," Aglaia bluntly tells Myshkin, "you will draw equally edifying reflections from both and be quite satisfied." This remark, however, leads to Myshkin's description of the agony of the condemned criminal kissing the cross; and the girls realize that no imputation of indifference or "quietism" can fairly be assigned as the source of his "happiness."

Far from being complacently indifferent to suffering—and particularly to the universal and ineluctable tragedy of death—Myshkin imaginatively re-experiences its tortures with the full range of his conscious sensibilities; but this does not prevent him, at the same time, from marveling in ecstasy before the joy and wonder of existence. Indeed, the dialectic of this unity is the point of the story about the man reprieved from execution—the story that embodies the most decisive and crucial event in Dostoevsky's own life. Most dreadful of all in those last moments, Myshkin says, was the regret of the poor victim over a wasted life and his frantic desire to be given another chance. "What if I were not to die? ... I would turn every minute into an age; I would lose nothing, I would count every minute as it passed, I would not waste one!" But on being asked what happened to this man after his reprieve, Myshkin ruefully admits that his frenzied resolution was by no means carried out in practice.

"Well, there you have it tried [says Alexandra Epanchin]. So it seems it's impossible really to live 'counting each moment.' For some reason it's impossible."

"Yes, for some reason it's impossible," repeated Myshkin. "So it seemed to me also ... and yet somehow I can't believe it."

Here is the point at which Myshkin's love of life fuses with his death-haunted imagination into the singular unity of his character. For Myshkin feels the miracle and wonder of life so strongly, he savors the inexpressible beauty and value of its every manifestation so deeply, precisely because he lives "counting each moment" as if it were the last. Both his joyous discovery of life and his profound intuition of death combine to make him feel each moment as one of absolute and immeasurable ethical choice and responsibility. The prince, in other words, lives in the eschatological tension that was (and is) the soul of the primitive Christian ethic, whose doctrine of totally selfless *agape* was conceived in the same perspective of the imminent end of time.

Very little is said about God or religion directly in Part I; but there is a constant play of allusion around the prince that places him in such a Christian context. Rogozhin, the merchant's son still close to the religious roots of Russian life, labels him a *yurodivi*, a holy fool; and though the gentlemanly and well-educated prince bears no external resemblance to these often extravagantly eccentric figures, he does possess their traditional gift of spiritual insight. The prince himself, speaking to General Epanchin's doorman of the inner suffering of a condemned man awaiting death, says passionately: "It was of this torture and of this agony that Christ spoke, too. No, you can't treat a man like that." Again, there is the mention of the cross, which the criminal going to the gallows kisses convulsively and which somehow helps him to sustain the torment. "But he was hardly aware of anything religious at this minute," the prince adds, meaning that the consolation of the cross operated instinctively, below any level of conscious awareness or doctrinal commitment. The idyllic New Testament note is struck very strongly in the prince's story of the poor, abused, consumptive Swiss peasant girl Marie, who had been reviled and mistreated as a fallen woman, and whose last days the prince and his band of children manage to brighten with the light of an all-forgiving love. In this way the figure of the prince is surrounded with a pervasive Christian penumbra that continually illuminates his character and serves to locate the exalted nature of his moral and spiritual aspirations.

The story concerning Marie also brings sharply to the foreground another leitmotif, one that may be called the "two loves"—the one

Christian, compassionate, nonpossessive, and universal, the other secular, ego-gratifying, possessive, and particular. Alexandra Epanchin's remark that the prince must have been in "love" prompts him to tell the story of Marie. But while the young woman was referring to the second kind of normal, worldly love, the prince's "love," as he takes care to explain, was only of the first type. Even the children clustered around the prince were confused by this difference and happily believed that the prince was in "love" with Marie when they saw him kissing her. But "I kissed her," he explains, "not because I was in love with her but because I was sorry for her, and because I had never, from the beginning, thought of her as guilty but only as unhappy." On first reading, one is tempted to take this inset story as a foreshadowing of what will redemptively occur in Myshkin's relations with Nastasya Filippovna; and it is possible—indeed, quite likely—that Dostoevsky may have initially meant it to be viewed as such. But the confusion of the children (and Myshkin is also a good bit of a child) will turn out rather to anticipate his own entrapment in the "two loves," whose mutually incompatible feelings and obligations will later result in the prince's disastrous inability to choose between Nastasya and Aglaia.

3

The world into which the prince is plunged upon his unexpected arrival in St. Petersburg is one that lives by standards directly opposite to those he embodies. It is a world locked in the grip of conflicting egoisms, a world in which the desire for wealth and social advantage, for sensual satisfaction, for power over others in one form or another, dominates and sweeps away all other humane and less self-centered feelings. All these motives are given full play in the intrigue, which parallels that of *La Dame aux camélias* by Dumas the younger, a work to which Dostoevsky alludes in the text and whose background presence serves to contrast the moral fiber of two different worlds: one French (and French-influenced Russian), the other purely Russian at its moral core. Part I of *The Idiot* turns on the plan to marry off Nastasya Filippovna with a handsome dowry, so as to allow Totsky—first her guardian, then her seducer—to wed the eldest Epanchin daughter. Much the same situation confronts the ex-courtesan Marguerite Gautier, *la dame aux camélias,* who, after being redeemed by love, is asked to abandon her devoted paramour so that his virginal sister can enter into a proper union. Marguerite "nobly" sacrifices herself on the altar of family pride and hypocritical virtue; but Nastasya refuses to be treated merely as a pawn in this sordid game of social chess. One can be sure that Dostoevsky, in thus reversing the situation, intends to contrast the moral superiority of Nastasya's inconsolable outrage at her violated human dignity with the docile acceptance of the tawdriest social prejudices by her French predecessor.[4]

No work of Dostoevsky's up to this time contains a comparable gallery of figures, among whom so many modulations and nuances of egoism are depicted with such vivid power. Every major character in the book (including the prince, though this point has invariably been missed) is susceptible to the imperative promptings of the ego inherent in the human condition; but, of course, definite degrees of moral value are assigned to its various manifestations in each character. Lowest of all on the moral scale is the pursuit of some personal utilitarian advantage or the satisfaction of some physical appetite. To this level belongs the greedy Ganya Ivolgin, ready to sell his soul to marry the abused Nastasya and thereby gain the dowry that will enable him to attain the wealth he craves. Here too belong the epicurean sensualist Totsky (who does not feel the slightest twinge of conscience at having ruined Nastasya forever, though he behaves well according to his lights in trying to arrange her future) and the harmless, hen-pecked General Epanchin, who also has abortive designs on Nastasya. The pompous general, though, is elevated a notch by his genuine devotion to his family and by the remorse he feels for having unknowingly berated an old woman on the point of death.

A significantly higher position on the moral scale is attained by those characters whose egoism, even though taking a self-destructive form, testifies to a genuine capacity for some sort of moral-spiritual

4. Totsky, of course, is a great admirer of Dumas the younger's book and declares that "it's a work which, in my opinion, is not destined to die or tarnish with age." Quite appropriately, the story he tells about "the worst of all the evil actions in his life" completely ignores his seduction of Nastasya and concerns the betrayal of a friend by obtaining a bouquet of camellias. It is no surprise that he is last seen becoming "fascinated by a Frenchwoman of the highest society, a marquise and a legitimist [royalist]."

experience. In this category we find the passion-mad Rogozhin, ready to squander a fortune and endure any suffering if only he can win Nastasya's love. And here is also Nastasya herself, whose plunge into degradation is the supreme example in Dostoevsky's work of what he called "the egoism of suffering," that is, the egoism of the insulted and injured, who revenge themselves on the world by masochistically refusing all attempts to assuage their sense of injury.[5] A place here can also be assigned to the dying young consumptive Ippolit Terentyev, whose rage against God parallels Nastasya's against society, and who refuses to reconcile himself with a Creator responsible for the supreme injustice of bringing human consciousness to birth and then condemning it to death.

On the next level may be placed such characters as Aglaia Epanchin and her mother Lizaveta Prokofyevna, Aglaia's wealthy and brilliant suitor Radomsky, and the prince himself. The egoism of all these characters does not assume any overtly aggressive form and is combined with admirable qualities of mind and heart; but each displays an egoistic trait in one form or another. Aglaia's besetting sin is the prideful arrogance and hauteur of her youthful beauty. Her mother—whose impulsive and childlike directness of vicarious fellow feeling brings her closest of all to the prince—still cannot resist giving way to the vanity of her birth and social position. Radomsky is the perfect model of a sympathetic and well-bred Russian gentleman, whose delicacy and courtesy is beyond reproach; but his worldly, skeptical intellect does not allow his emotions to go beyond the rules of decorum that protect his inner complacency. As for the prince, his "egoism" will consist in the purest and most chaste of earthly attachments to Aglaia and the desire to marry.

A. Skaftymov, in what is still the best Russian analysis of *The Idiot*, has pointed out that each of the major characters is caught in an inner struggle between his or her own particular manifestation of egoism

---

5. Dostoevsky first refers to this idea in *The Insulted and Injured* while depicting the character of little Nellie. The narrator speaks of her as having been "ill-treated," and "purposely trying to aggravate her wound by this mysterious behavior, this mistrustfulness of us all; as though she enjoyed her own pain, by this *egoism of suffering* [italics in text], if I may so express it. This aggravation of suffering and this revelling in it I could understand; it is the enjoyment of many of the insulted and injured, oppressed by destiny and smarting under the sense of injustice."

and a desire to overcome it in some appropriate form.[6] The role of the prince in Part I, who brings with him the atmosphere of a sublimely selfless moral ideal, is to serve as a catalyst for each in this secret struggle. Rogozhin spontaneously offers to clothe the prince properly on first meeting him. Even the busy financial operator General Epanchin cannot resist giving him twenty-five rubles, and he becomes concerned about the prince's future. Nastasya, witnessing the incident of Ganya slapping the prince, "was evidently stirred by a new feeling." A few moments later the prince addresses her: "Surely you are not what you are pretending to be now. It isn't possible!" he cries reproachfully. Under the influence of these words Nastasya, who had come to pay back with contemptuous mockery the resentment of Ganya and the disapproval of his family, kisses the hand of Ganya's mother with remorse. Ganya himself later comes to apologize to the Prince and confesses that, while he plans to go through with the disgraceful marriage, it makes him feel like a scoundrel. "Scoundrels love honest men," he tells the prince. "Don't you know that?"

The climax of the first part of the book is the tumultuous birthday party at Nastasya Filippovna's; all the characters gather here to await her decision on whether to accept Totsky's arrangement. Nastasya, of course, has carefully prepared the evening to culminate in the scandalous irruption of Rogozhin, whose brutal frankness in bidding for her favors (his hundred thousand rubles are wrapped in a copy of the *Stock Exchange News*) rips off the mask of hypocrisy from the whole sordid scheme. It is in the midst of this wild confusion that the moral appeal of the prince's presence also receives its strongest affirmation. Nastasya turns to him to decide the question of her marriage to Ganya because, as she says, the prince "is the first man I have met in my whole life that I believed in as a sincere friend. He believed in me at first sight and I in him." But while the prince's word stops her from marrying Ganya, his own offer of marriage, as she rises to a paroxysm of bitter self-hatred, is powerless to prevent her from running off with Rogozhin. The masochistic satisfaction of debasing herself, and thus of symbolically debasing Totsky and all her respectable "admirers" at the same time, proves stronger than the prince's appeal to

6. A. Skaftymov, "Tematicheskaya kompositsiya 'Idiot,'" *Nravstvennie Iskaniya Russkikh Pisatelei* (Moscow, 1972), 23–87. I am greatly indebted to this article for my own analysis.

her need for disinterested compassion and his recognition of her essential purity.

Nastasya is so majestic and overwhelming a figure in this early part of the book, and so much emphasis is placed on her victimization, that there has been an understandable tendency to see her only as a latter-day Iphigenia innocently doomed to destruction. It is quite clear, however, that Dostoevsky also wished to convey the festering and embittered pride that poisons all her relations with others, a pride that ultimately makes it impossible for her either to forgive herself or to accept the aid of the prince. This aspect of her character is indicated very explicitly in Myshkin's reaction to Nastasya's picture, which is repeated twice in the early chapters. His first response is to the traces of suffering that he sees in her features; but he immediately adds: "It's a proud face, awfully proud, but I don't know whether she's kind-hearted. Ah, if she were! That would rescue everything!" A second look at the photograph strengthens and sharpens this first impression: "There was a look of unbounded pride and contempt, almost hatred, in that face," Myshkin thinks, "and at the same time something confiding, something wonderfully simple-hearted. The contrast of these two features aroused a feeling of some sort of compassion." Both these aspects of Nastasya must always be kept in mind if we are to do justice to the complexity of Dostoevsky's artistic aims.

4

The first part of *The Idiot* was conceived and written as a self-contained unity and perhaps may best be read as an independent novella. It is clear from Dostoevsky's notebooks and letters that he had no satisfactory idea of how to continue. This uncertainty persists all through the middle sections of the book (Parts II and III), which are written from scene to scene with only the loosest thread of any central plot line. As a result, *The Idiot* possesses a kind of wayward charm and narrative spontaneity that is not artistically inharmonious with its thematic emphasis on the moral importance of impulsive sympathy and emotive frankness. However, the haphazardness of the action also makes this novel the most disorganized of Dostoevsky's longer works and the one most difficult to see in any unified perspective.

Essentially, the book now breaks down into three plot strands that alternate with one another more or less randomly. One continues the

Nastasya-Myshkin-Rogozhin relationship, though this rivalry sinks almost totally out of sight for long stretches. A second is the Aglaia-Myshkin love affair (with a new character, Radomsky, as the putative third in the triangle). Dostoevsky makes a feeble attempt to link these two plot lines by the device of Nastasya's unsolicited attempt to abet the Aglaia-Myshkin romance from the wings. This effort allows for Nastasya's return into the action from time to time and prepares for the crucial confrontation scene between the two women; but Dostoevsky's refusal to present more of Nastasya, except through indirect accounts, weakens the effect of her reappearances and makes them shrilly melodramatic. Moreover, neither of these narrative components is more than superficially related to a third, which roughly comprises the lengthy scenes involving a group of "young nihilists," the "Essential Explanation" of Ippolit Terentyev, the antic lucubrations of Lebedev, and the marvelous mendacities of that inspired liar, General Ivolgin.

One's problems with *The Idiot* are further increased by the curious intermezzo of the five chapters that begin Part II, which present Myshkin—as well as other characters like Rogozhin and Lebedev—in an unexpectedly new light. Nine months have elapsed between the end of Part I and the beginning of Part II, and important changes are supposed to have occurred in the prince during this period; but Dostoevsky evades the challenge of describing this inner evolution. It is clear, in any case, that Myshkin is now being seen from a perspective for which there was no earlier foreshadowing. This becomes obvious in Chapter 5 of Part II, where Dostoevsky depicts the prince in the state of mind engendered by an imminent epileptic fit. The contours of reality have here begun to cloud and blur for the poor prince, and he finds it difficult to distinguish between what he ardently longs for and what the true situation (as regards Rogozhin and Nastasya) really is. Under the influence of this confusion, he convinces himself that Rogozhin would be capable of compassion for Nastasya, despite the mountains of humiliation that she has heaped on him as revenge for accepting his attentions. "Compassion would teach even Rogozhin and awaken his mind. Compassion was the chief and perhaps the only law of all human existence." The Myshkin of Part I would certainly have subscribed to this sentiment; but there has been no previous indication that his outlook was a sublime illusion distorting a true vision of reality. The Myshkin of Part I, on the contrary, possessed an ideal that gave him uncanny insight into the hearts of all those whose lives he touched.

This change in Myshkin is a function of the new role that is now assigned to the prince's epilepsy. Epilepsy had no particular significance in Part I; Myshkin had awakened to the inestimable beauty of life—the foil for his universal compassion—only on *emerging* from his epileptic stupor. Now, however, it is in the "aura" of the moment before the epileptic onset that the prince experiences "gleams and flashes of the highest sensation of life and self-consciousness" and is filled with a feeling, "unknown and undivined till then, of completeness, of proportion, of reconciliation, and of ecstatic devotional merging in the highest synthesis of life." This quasi-supernatural revelation becomes the source of the prince's impassioned faith in a universal harmony; but this faith stands in absolute contradiction to the normal conditions of earthly existence. For the prince was well aware that, if his epileptic attacks resumed, "stupefaction, spiritual darkness, idiocy stood before him conspicuously as the consequence of these 'higher moments.' " Myshkin is thus inevitably doomed to catastrophe because the unearthly light of love and universal reconciliation cannot illuminate the fallen world of man for more than a dazzling and self-destructive instant.

From all the evidence, it is likely that Dostoevsky had no clear idea while writing Part I that the book was heading in this direction. The manner in which the prince overcomes incomprehension and hostility in the earlier pages, along with the foreshadowing provided by the story of Marie, would seem to indicate an original inclination to stress the regenerating effects of Christian love. But from the beginning of Part II, the prince is cast in a tragic (or, at least, self-sacrificial) role; the inner logic of his character now requires that the absolute of Christian love should conflict irreconcilably with the inescapable demands of normal human life. This new grasp of the prince very probably accounts for the change in the tonality of these chapters, with their menacing Gothic atmosphere of mystery and impending doom—a tonality that contrasts sharply with the even, unclouded, novel-of-manners lighting of Part I, despite the heightening of tension in certain scenes.

This altered projection of the prince also leads to the introduction of a new thematic motif, which first appears in the strange dialogue between Myshkin and Rogozhin about religious faith. Somewhat improbably, a copy of Holbein's *Dead Christ* turns up in Rogozhin's living room; and, with no transition whatever, the erstwhile drunken rowdy of Part I is shown as tormented, not only by Nastasya, but also by a crisis of religious doubt.[7] Holbein's picture, as we know, is an image of Christ after the Crucifixion as a bruised, bloody and broken man, without a trace of supernatural or spiritual transcendence, though it is described as such only much later in the book. All we learn here is that "a painting of our Savior who had just been taken from the Cross" has begun to undermine Rogozhin's religious faith; and Myshkin attempts to allay Rogozhin's disquietude by a lengthy and crucial speech.

This speech consists of four anecdotes grouped in pairs, which illustrate that the human need for faith and for the moral values of conscience based on faith transcends both the plane of rational reflection and that of empirical evidence. On the one hand, there is the learned atheist whose arguments Myshkin cannot refute; on the other, there is the murderer who utters a prayer for forgiveness before slitting his victim's throat. There is the drunken peasant soldier selling his cross; but there is also the peasant woman, perhaps the soldier's wife, comparing a mother's joy in her child with God's gladness at the heartfelt prayer of a sinner. The point of these stories is to show religious faith and moral conscience existing as an ineradicable attribute in the Russian people independent of reason, or even of any sort of conventional social morality. "The essence of religious feeling," Myshkin explains, "does not come under any sort of reasoning or atheism, and has nothing to do with any crimes or misdemeanors . . . But the chief thing is that you will notice it more clearly and quickly in the Russian heart than anywhere else."

This thematic motif is of key importance for understanding the remainder of the book. For in depicting religious faith and the stirrings of conscience as the totally irrational and instinctive needs of "the Russian heart," whose existence shines forth in the midst of everything that seems to deny or negate its presence, Dostoevsky is surely indicating the proper interpretation of Myshkin's ultimate failure and

---

7. Dostoevsky betrays his uneasiness at this unexpected metamorphosis by the awkward comment that "in Moscow they [the Prince and Rogozhin] had met frequently and spent a great deal of time together, and there were moments during their meetings which had left an indelible impression on their hearts."

tragic collapse. The values of Christian love and religious faith that Myshkin embodies are, in other words, too deep a necessity of the Russian spirit to be negated by his practical failure, any more than they are negated by reason, murder or sacrilege. If Holbein's picture and Myshkin's tirade are introduced so awkwardly and abruptly at this point, it is probably because Dostoevsky wished immediately to establish the framework within which the catastrophic destiny awaiting the prince would be rightly understood.

The action of these chapters, which serves as a coda to the central triangle of Part I, clearly dramatizes the prince's altered role. Myshkin's efforts to save the crazed Nastasya from destroying herself have placed him athwart the raging passion of Rogozhin, though the latter is fully aware that the prince's "love" for Nastasya is not carnal but Christian. The drama of Rogozhin's inner struggle is played out by the prince's obsession with Rogozhin's new knife, by the exchange of crosses between the two men, and by the blessing given the prince by Rogozhin's mother. Rogozhin thus tries to place the prince within a sacrosanct circle of religious awe that will shield him from the menacing knife; but it is the prince himself who provokes Rogozhin by breaking his promise not to seek out Nastasya. The euphoric influence of the pre-epileptic "aura" betrays Myshkin into a heinous breach of faith that uncovers the dangerous discrepancy between the real and the ideal; and Myshkin's neglect of this gap leads to the flash of Rogozhin's upraised blade. It is symbolically appropriate that the onset of the sacred illness, whose first symptoms are responsible for Myshkin's delusion, should save him from its fatal consequence when he collapses before Rogozhin can strike his blow.

5

The Idiot is filled with all sorts of minor characters who are related to the main plot lines only by the most tenuous of threads and who take over the book on the slightest of pretexts. The plethora of such digressions no doubt accounts for Dostoevsky's feeling that he had lost control of the novel; but it is not too difficult to see the thematic rationale of most of these episodes, even if, structurally, they come and go with very little motivation. Many of them have the function of the comic interludes in medieval mystery plays, which parody the holy events with reverent humor and illustrate the universality of their influence. Others serve to bring out facets of the Prince that Dostoevsky was unable to develop from the central romantic intrigue.

Lebedev, General Ivolgin and the "boxer" Keller make up a group with common characteristics—a group that affirms, sometimes in a grotesquely comic form, that the inner moral struggle precipitated by the Prince in the major figures also can be found among the smaller fry. To be sure, Dostoevsky abandons all attempts to maintain any psychological verisimilitude in the case of Lebedev and Keller; their mechanical shuttling between devotion to the Prince and petty swindling and skullduggery sometimes reaches the point of self-parody. This is particularly true of Lebedev, transformed from the randy scrounger of Part I into the compassionate figure who shares Myshkin's horror of capital punishment and prays for the soul of the guillotined Countess du Barry.

Without ceasing to be an unscrupulous scoundrel, ready to sell his soul for a ruble, Lebedev also piously interprets the Apocalypse and rails against the "materialism" of the modern world in drunken tirades. His long, mock-serious historical "anecdote" on the famines of the Middle Ages is manifestly a burlesque exemplum of the significance of his character and that of others like him. Similar to the starving medieval "cannibal"—who devoured sixty fat, juicy monks in the course of his life and then, despite the prospect of the most horrible tortures, voluntarily confessed his crimes—the behavior of Lebedev and his ilk testifies to the miraculous existence of conscience in the most unlikely places. Another example is the broken-down, Falstaffian General Ivolgin, whom Dostoevsky uses very effectively in Part I to parody the "decorum" surrounding Nastasya's life, and whose colossal mythomania is a protection against the sordid reality of his moral and social decline. The General dies of a stroke brought on by his torments over having stolen Lebedev's wallet, torments caused not so much by the theft itself—he returned the wallet untouched—but by the fear that he would henceforth be regarded as a thief in his own family.

The most extensive of these digressions is Prince Myshkin's encounter with the group of so-called Young Nihilists, an episode that, in the special key required by *The Idiot*, continues Dostoevsky's polemic with the ideology of the radicals of the mid-1860s. As already mentioned, this subplot provides a parodistic answer to attacks made on Dostoevsky in the past, and particularly a tit-for-tat riposte to

Saltykov-Shchedrin.[8] The young nihilists themselves are nothing but insolent little schoolboys, whose pathetic innocence and insecurity are strongly stressed as an implicit apologia for their aggressiveness. The point of this episode is to contrast the true selflessness of the prince, based on Christian love, with a doctrine of social justice blind to its own egoistic roots.

Dostoevsky's merciless caricature of the young nihilists was, of course, a calculated affront to the susceptibilities of the radicals; but it has not been sufficiently noticed that he depicts their motives as entirely honorable. The claim they advance to a share of the prince's fortune—on the ground that one of their number is the illegitimate son of the prince's deceased benefactor—has no basis in truth. But, as the prince points out, they had good reasons to believe they were rectifying a crying social injustice, and so no moral onus can be attached to their intent. What Dostoevsky attacks is not their aim to right a presumed social wrong but, rather, the unscrupulous means they adopt to attain their goal and the resulting inner contradiction in their position. For they scornfully reject all old-fashioned ideas of "morality," yet insist that the prince behave like "a man of conscience and honor"; and they always assume that their own motives, though deriving from a philosophy of egoistic self-interest, are perfectly pure and untainted, and do not require the moral self-scrutiny demanded from their opponents.

What distinguishes the prince, on the contrary, is precisely his capacity to respond in terms of the "other" and to avoid the pharisaism of the young nihilists' self-righteousness. He understands that the claimant to a share of his wealth, Burdovsky, has been downtrodden and humiliated all his life; and he forgives the young man's impossible behavior as a consequence of all the battering that his self-respect has been forced to endure. Instead of responding, like the other "respectable" characters, with contempt, outrage or indignation, the prince apologizes for having offended Burdovsky by offering in public to help him. Indeed, the figure of Burdovsky momentarily becomes a "double" for the prince, who remembers how pathetic and ridiculous a figure he has often cut himself. Confronted for the first time in his life with

8. For more information, see Joseph Frank, *Dostoevsky: The Stir of Liberation* (Princeton, N.J., 1986), 208–210.

truly active and selfless sympathy (the prince matches words with deed), Burdovsky finally acknowledges a feeling of gratitude inconsistent with his ideology ("I regard it as a weakness," he writes). By this admission, he overcomes the egoism of his resentments and enters the world of mutual moral obligations.

The acridly satirical scenes involving the young nihilists are perhaps too didactic to serve Dostoevsky's purpose successfully; and he is always least convincing when he offers his moral-religious point of view as an answer to concrete social dilemmas. Far more effective is the spotlight focused on the dying young consumptive Ippolit Terentyev, who detaches himself from the group of young nihilists to rise to major heights and become the first in Dostoevsky's remarkable gallery of metaphysical rebels. For Ippolit is revolting not against the iniquities of a social order but, anticipating Kirillov and Ivan Karamazov, against a world in which death, and hence immitigable human suffering, is an inescapable reality. With Ippolit, Dostoevsky picks up a major thematic motif of Part I and presents Myshkin with the strongest challenge to the "happiness" that the prince had declared himself to have discovered. Like Burdovsky, Ippolit is another quasi-double for Myshkin—one who shares his obsession with death and his ecstatic sense of life, yet lacks the prince's sustaining religious faith in an ultimate world-harmony. For this reason, Ippolit cannot achieve the self-transcendence that is the secret of the prince's moral effulgence and the response he evokes in others.

Ippolit's semi-hysterical "Essential Explanation" is carefully composed to contain all the main features of Myshkin's *Weltanschauung*, but combined with an *opposite* human attitude. His preoccupation with death does not lessen but strengthens his self-concern, and turns it into a pathetic megalomania, as can be seen from the touchingly incongruous epigraph, "après moi le deluge!," that he appends to his "Essential Explanation." He reveres the infinite beauty and value of life ("it is life, life that matters, life alone," he exclaims); but so precious does the gift of life *in itself* seem to the dying boy that he simply denies the existence of other evils and misfortunes less absolute than death. "I knew one poor fellow, who, I was told afterwards, died of hunger, and I remember that it made me furious: if it had been possible to bring the poor devil back to life, I believe I'd have him executed." Instinctively, Ippolit's feelings are on the side of the victims of social injustice (for example, the story of the starving doctor); and when he is carried on the current of such benevolent feelings, he admits "that I forgot my death sentence, or rather did not come to think of it and even did work." Only such concern with others can ease the tragedy of Ippolit's last days; but he finally abandons all such endeavors to brood over his own condition. Death, the universal portion, he comes to regard as a personal insult and "humiliation" aimed at him by "nature," or rather by the Creator of a world that requires the individual's consent to the indignity and injustice of being destroyed.

The thematic contrast between Ippolit and the prince is brought out most forcefully by their differing reactions to the key religious symbol of the book: Holbein's *Dead Christ*, whose unvarnished realism Ippolit finally expatiates on at length. Holbein's picture had led Myshkin to affirm the irrational "essence of religious feeling" as an ineradicable component of the human spirit; but for the young nihilist, it is only a confirmation of his own sense of the cruel meaninglessness of life. To Ippolit, the picture conveys a sense of nature "in the form of a huge machine of the most modern construction," which "has aimlessly clutched, crushed, and swallowed up a great priceless Being [Christ], a Being worth all of nature and its laws, worth the whole earth, which was created perhaps solely for the advent of that Being." Ippolit simply cannot grasp how the first disciples of Christ, who witnessed in reality what he sees only at the remove of art, could still have continued to believe in the triumph over death that Christ proclaimed; but this is precisely the mystery of faith to which Ippolit is closed, and whose absence poisons his last days with bitterness and despair.

Ippolit, like the other characters, instinctively regards the prince as the standard for his own conscience. The prince's "humility," however, is the ideological antithesis of Ippolit's "revolt," and it is Myshkin who must bear the brunt of the young nihilist's vituperative shifts of feeling. "Can't I simply be devoured without being expected to praise what devours me?" Ippolit asks caustically, in rejecting the prince's "Christian meekness." This question comes from such a depth of suffering in Ippolit that no offense on his part can lessen his right to an absolute claim on the indulgence of the other characters. For as Myshkin tells the ironically tolerant and distant Radomsky, it is not enough simply to be willing to overlook Ippolit's offensiveness out of condescending pity: "The point is that you, too, should be willing to accept forgiveness from him"—an unprecedented rebuke from the prince. "How do I come in?" asks the bewildered Radomsky. "What wrong have I done him?" None whatsoever, to be sure; but the prince understands that, for Ippolit, the untroubled possession of life by others is a supreme injustice, which should burden them with guilt and a sense of moral obligation.

The doomed and suffering Ippolit is thus entitled to boundless tolerance and compassion; but he too has an obligation to overcome his envy and resentment of those who, though now untouched, will eventually share his fate. Ippolit knows, as he tells the prince, that he is "unworthy" of what could be the purifying experience of his death; he uses its imminence only to harass and discomfit the living, and he is unable to conquer his malice up to the very last. Hence the prince's moving and beautiful reply to Ippolit's question on how best to die: "Pass by us and forgive us our happiness," says Myshkin in a low voice. Hence, too, the macabre quality of gallows humor in several of the scenes with Ippolit, the grating callousness that some of the characters display toward his plight. No pages of Dostoevsky are more original than those in which he tries to combine the utmost sympathy for Ippolit with a pitiless portrayal of what may be called "the egoism of dying." Dostoevsky wishes to show how the egocentricity that inspired Ippolit's "revolt" also impels him to a behavior that cuts off the very sympathy and love he so desperately craves. By turns pathetic and febrilely malignant, the unfortunate boy dies offstage, unconsoled and inconsolable, "in a state of terrible agitation."

6

The major action of *The Idiot* after Part I centers on the prince's budding romance with Aglaia Epanchin. The prince does not cease to preoccupy himself with Nastasya; but though he continues to pity her with all his heart, there is, nonetheless, a significant change in his attitude. Nastasya's behavior is now portrayed as alternating between extravagant displays of reverence for moral purity—revealed in the hysterical bathos of her letters to Aglaia, which deludedly idealize her rival as capable of the totally selfless love to which Myshkin aspires—and continual relapses into the masochistic cultivation of her own sense of depravity. "Do you know," the prince tells Aglaia, "that she seems to derive some dreadful unnatural pleasure from the continual consciousness of shame, a sort of revenge on someone." The prince at last becomes persuaded that Nastasya literally has gone mad, especially when he hears of her letters; and he speaks of them, almost on the point of tears, as "proof of her insanity." It is likely that Dostoevsky's continual later emphasis on Nastasya's "madness," which has the effect of absolving her of responsibility, is intended to hold the balance with this stronger stress on her self-destructive "egoism."

Prince Myshkin's note to Aglaia at the beginning of Part II clearly expresses his attraction for the haughty and high-spirited beauty; but it is only in Chapter 7 that their eccentric courtship is solidly established in the foreground. By reading Pushkin's poem "The Poor Knight" in the prince's presence, with obvious reference to his intervention on behalf of Nastasya, Aglaia reveals to what extent her lofty imagination has become inflamed by the prince's self-sacrificing magnanimity toward a victimized "fallen woman." This open display of admiration, which scandalizes the assembled company and terribly embarrasses the prince, strikes the note on which their relation will henceforth be depicted. Because the prince's humility and total lack of self-assertiveness make it impossible for him to act in his own interest, it is Aglaia who must take the initiative; and the manner in which she forces his hand, with a combination of girlish high spirits, temperamental petulance and true feminine instinct, results in some of Dostoevsky's most engaging scenes.

Aglaia's whole relation to the prince, however, is tainted with misunderstanding from the very start. To Aglaia, Myshkin is the Poor Knight of Pushkin's poem—a poem in which she sees united "in one striking figure the grand conception of the platonic love of medieval chivalry, as it was felt by a pure and lofty knight," a knight who was a "serious and not comic" Don Quixote. These words have usually been taken as objectively relevant to the prince; but although they apply to him in part, their more important function is to bring out the illusory nature of Aglaia's image of his character. Certainly one can say of Myshkin:

> He had had a wondrous vision:
> Ne'er could feeble human art

> Gauge its deep, mysterious meaning,
> It was graven on his heart.

But nothing could be less characteristic of the prince than the deeds of military valor performed during the Crusades by the Poor Knight in the service of the Christian faith:

> *Lumen coeli,* Sancta Rosa!
> Shouted he with flaming glance
> And the thunder of his menace
> Checked the Mussulman's advance.

The Poor Knight, in other words, represents the Christian ideal of the Catholic West in its days of glory and in all its corrupting confusion of spiritual faith and temporal power. The Russian Christian ideal, as Dostoevsky understood it, sharply splits off one from the other and accepts all the paradoxical and even demeaning social consequences of the prince's humility, meekness and all-forgiving love.

Aglaia's love for the prince is thus vitiated from the beginning by this misconception of the true nature of his values—a misconception that mirrors her own character, with its combination of ardent idealism and personal arrogance and pride. Aglaia is capable of loving the purity of spirit that she finds in the prince, but at the same time she wishes her ideal to be socially imposing and admired by the world. This fusion had attracted her to militant Catholicism, and she misguidedly seeks for it in the prince. By introducing the young nihilist scenes right after the "Poor Knight" reading, Dostoevsky forcefully dramatizes the opposition between Aglaia's image and the actual values that inspire the prince's conduct. The combative Aglaia welcomes the intrusion of the group because, as she says, "they are trying to throw mud at you, Prince, you must defend yourself triumphantly, and I am awfully glad for you." Far from emerging "triumphant," though, Myshkin reacts to insult and provocation with a docility and passivity that drive Aglaia into a towering rage. "If you don't throw out these nasty people at once, I shall hate you all my life, all my life!" she whispers to the prince "in a sort of frenzy."

Aglaia will continue to exhibit the same sort of dualism: irresistibly attracted by the prince's spiritual elevation and selflessness, she cannot reconcile herself to the ludicrous figure that he presents because of his lack of pride and normal social self-regard. When the prince, in defending Nastasya, insults an army officer who asks for his name, Aglaia automatically assumes that he will fight a duel and instructs him on how to load a pistol; but the prince never has any intention of engaging in such a conventionally heroic enterprise. Similarly, before the party scene at which he will be introduced officially as Aglaya's betrothed, she tries to have a "serious" talk with him to make sure that he will not commit any *faux pas.* Nonetheless, once more under the influence of the pre-epileptic "aura," the prince launches into a Slavophile attack on Roman Catholicism as "unchristian" because "Roman Catholicism believes that the Church cannot exist on earth without universal political power." He is thus denouncing in Roman Catholicism the very confusion of the temporal and the spiritual that, on the personal level, Aglaia wishes him to incarnate. It is no hazard that this speech appears precisely at the point where his personality is shown as most hopelessly incompatible with her requirements.

Myshkin's disastrous harangue also incorporates other motifs of great importance to Dostoevsky. The Russian need for religious faith is reasserted yet again as Myshkin describes the Russian proclivity to be converted to false faiths—such as Roman Catholicism or atheism. "Russian atheists and Russian Jesuits are the outcome not only of vanity," he declares, "not only of a bad, vain feeling but also of spiritual agony, spiritual thirst, a craving for something higher . . . for a faith in which they have ceased to believe because they have never known it! . . . And Russians do not merely become atheists, but they invariably *believe* in atheism, as though it were a new religion, without noticing that they are putting their faith in a negation." Myshkin here utters some of Dostoevsky's profoundest convictions, which the author well knew would be looked on by the majority of his compatriots with the same rather frightened and pitying incredulity as that displayed by the Epanchins' guests.

Despite the catastrophe of the prince's outburst and epileptic attack at the engagement party, Aglaia is still capable of conquering her dismay; for her the ultimate test of Myshkin will be his relation with Nastasya. No more than Rogozhin can Aglaia view the prince's "Christian love" for Nastasya—his boundless pity and sense of obligation—as anything but a threat to her own undisputed possession of the man she loves (though it was the prince's attitude toward Nastasya that had first stirred Aglaia's admiration). In the powerful confrontation scene between the two women, each tells the other some harsh truths; but Aglaia's cruel vindictiveness, from the height of her virtue and social position, is less forgivable than the delirious rage of Nastasya's self-defense in invoking her claim on the prince. The climax of the scene finds Myshkin called upon to choose between the two women and utterly unable to do so. Nastasya's "frenzied, despairing face" causes him to reproach Aglaia for her cruelty to the "unhappy creature"; Aglaia looks at him with "such suffering and at the same time such boundless hatred that, with a gesture of despair, he cried out and ran to her, but it was already too late." He is stopped by Nastasya's grasp, and remains to comfort the fainting and half-demented creature whose tortured face had once "stabbed his heart forever."

The prince thus finds himself helplessly caught in the rivalry of clashing egoisms, and he responds, on the spur of the moment, to the need that is most immediate and most acute. Each woman has a differing but equally powerful claim on his devotion; and his incapacity to make a choice dramatizes the profoundest level of Dostoevsky's thematic idea. For the prince is the herald of a Christian love that is nothing if not universal; yet he is also a man, not a supernatural being—a man who has fallen in love with a woman as a creature of flesh and blood. The necessary dichotomy of these two divergent loves inevitably involves him in a tragic imbroglio from which there is no escape, an impasse in which the universal obligation of compassion fatally crosses the human love that is the prince's morally blameless form of "egoism."

Three years earlier, sitting at the bier of his first wife, Dostoevsky had meditated on the situation to which he gives artistic life in Myshkin's tormented irresolution. "The family—this is the most sacred possession of man on earth," he had noted, "for by this law of nature man attains development (i.e., the succession of generations), the goal. But at the same time, by this very law of nature, in the name of the final ideal goal, man must unceasingly negate it (Duality)." In the same document, Dostoevsky states that Christ had given mankind only

one clue to the future nature of this "final ideal goal" of humanity—
a clue contained in the Gospel of Saint Matthew: "They neither marry,
nor are given in marriage, but are as angels in Heaven." The "final ideal
goal" of humanity is thus the total fusion of the individual Ego with
All in a mystic community literally (and not metaphorically) freed
from the constraints and limits of the flesh; it is the transcendent "synthesis" that Myshkin had glimpsed in the ravishment of the pre-
epileptic "aura."[9] Hence even the most chaste and innocent of earthly
loves constitutes an abrogation of the universal law of love, whose
realization, prefigured by Christ, is man's ultimate, supernatural goal.
The closing pages of *The Idiot* strikingly present this insoluble conflict
between the human and the divine that Dostoevsky felt so acutely, and
which could achieve its highest pitch of expressiveness and poignancy
only as embodied in such a "perfectly beautiful man" as Prince Myshkin.

7

The three concluding chapters that follow the confrontation scene
contain a significant shift in the narrative point of view; and this shift
is closely correlated with the unprecedented conflict focused through
Myshkin's remarkable character. Up until these chapters, the omni-
scient narrator has usually been able to describe and explain what the
prince is thinking and feeling. Now, however, the narrator confesses
that he is unable to understand Myshkin's behavior and must confine
himself to a "bare statement of facts"; "we find it difficult in many instances," he says, "to explain what occurred." The facts referred to are
these: on the one hand, Myshkin has become the fiancé of Nastasya,
and the plans for their wedding are going forward; but, on the other,
the prince still tries to visit Aglaia as if nothing had changed, and he
cannot comprehend why the impending marriage should affect his relation to her. "It makes no difference that I'm going to marry her [Nas-
tasya]," he tells Radomsky. "That's nothing, nothing." The strain of the
prince's impossible position has finally caused him to lose all touch
with reality. No longer able to distinguish between his vision of uni-

9. For a more extensive discussion of this diary entry, the only explicit and detailed
statement we have of Dostoevsky's religious convictions, see Frank, *Dostoevsky: The Stir of
Liberation* (Princeton, N.J., 1986), 296–309.

versal love and the necessary exclusions and limiting choices of life, he is presented as having passed altogether beyond the bounds of accepted social codes. To express this transgression, Dostoevsky adopts the guise of the baffled and puzzled narrator, whose bewilderment accentuates the impossibility of measuring the prince's comportment by any conventional standard.

This ever-widening distance between the prince and the world, the paradox of his behavior, is then placed at the center of a lengthy dialogue with Radomsky. The elegant man of the world gently but firmly criticizes Myshkin for having failed to side with Aglaia; and he analyzes the prince's behavior toward Nastasya both as the result of inexperience and as a consequence of "the huge mass of intellectual convictions which you, with your extraordinary honesty, have hitherto taken for real, innate, intuitive convictions." Radomsky detects an "element of *conventional democratic* feeling" in the prince's attitude toward Nastasya, "the fascination, so to say, of 'the woman question.'" The narrator, unexpectedly, prefaces such words by associating himself firmly with Radomsky's observations: "We are in complete sympathy with some forcible and psychologically deep words of Yevgeny Pavlovich, spoken plainly and unceremoniously . . . in conversation with Myshkin."[10]

How is one to interpret this disconcerting volte-face of the narrator? Certainly not as Dostoevsky's repudiation of his hero, but rather as a calculated shift in narrative stance from relative omniscience to ignorance and incomprehension; and this shift is meant to correspond with the inevitable trivialization of the prince's plight. For the ideas that Radomsky expresses are precisely the same as the wild rumors and ridiculous conjectures floating around Pavlovsk about the events in which the prince has been involved. Like Radomsky, who is even hinted to have aided the spread of such rumors, the gossips attribute the prince's conduct to "the gratification of marrying a 'lost' woman in sight of all the world and thereby proving his conviction that there

---

10. Robin Feuer Miller has argued that, in various ways, Dostoevsky begins to undermine the reader's trust in the narrator starting with Part III. This may well be so, and her perceptive analysis is of the greatest interest; but the narrator's earlier uncertainties and inconsistencies are qualitatively different from the adoption of Radomsky's belittling point of view. See Robin Feuer Miller, *Dostoevsky and "The Idiot"* (Cambridge, Mass., 1981), chap. 4.

were neither 'lost' nor 'virtuous' women ... [since] he did not believe in the old conventional division, but had faith only in 'the woman question'; that in fact a 'lost' woman was, in his eyes, somewhat superior to one not lost."

The moral profundities of the prince's conflict are thus distorted and reduced to the level of spiteful tittle-tattle and current clichés over female emancipation; and the narrator's declared agreement with Radomsky only adds to the melancholy irony of the prince's total isolation. Like Abraham in Kierkegaard's *Fear and Trembling,* who alone hears the secret commandment of God to sacrifice his son, the prince has now become a knight of faith whose obedience to the divine makes his conduct appear to others, more often than not, a sign of madness. Quite appropriately, Lebedev comes to this conclusion and tries to have the prince committed to a mental institution before the wedding ceremony. Radomsky too shares the same conviction that the prince "was not in his right mind"; but his thoughts come closer to Dostoevsky's thematic mark: "And how can one love two at once? With two different kinds of love? That's interesting ... poor idiot."

The closing pages show us the prince helplessly trapped between the conflicting claims of his human nature and his divine task, deprived of all comprehension and almost all sympathy, and overwhelmed by events over which he has no control. His grasp of the real world becomes weaker and weaker as all hope of human happiness for him vanishes irrevocably; he now lives at the mercy of the shifting moods of the unbalanced Nastasya, the spiteful whims of Ippolit and the antic machinations of Lebedev. At the end his personality simply dissolves, abandoning all claims for itself and becoming a function of the needs of others. The prince's final destruction is brought about by the murder of Nastasya, who, in a last access of remorse over having ruined his life, flees to the destruction she knows awaits her with Rogozhin. In the eerie and unforgettable death-watch scene over Nastasya's corpse, the prince loses himself completely in the anguish of the half-mad Rogozhin and sinks definitively into the mental darkness that he had long feared would be the price of his visionary illuminations. So ends the odyssey of Dostoevsky's "perfectly beautiful man," who had tried to live in the world by the divine light of the apocalyptic transfiguration of mankind into a universal harmony of love.

Two or three details in these final pages deserve a brief additional mention. One is the underscored reference to *Madame Bovary*, which Myshkin finds in Nastasya's room and insists on carrying away in his pocket. Are we not invited here to compare the agonies of Nastasya's tortured conscience with the despairing cynicism of Flaubert's French adulteress, who is driven to suicide by the ignominy of her life but not by any moral revulsion or change of heart? If so, this moment would reinforce the implied comparison already made with *La Dame aux camélias* to the detriment of the European moral consciousness. The anti-European note is struck again in relation to Aglaia, who continued to seek her ideal in the worldly and glamorous form she had been unable to find in the prince. It should be no surprise, if we have read *The Idiot* aright, to learn that Aglaia marries a shady Polish Catholic émigré-adventurer and quondam nobleman who "had fascinated [her] by the extraordinary nobility of his soul, which was torn with patriotic anguish" over the unhappy fate of his native land, but who then, appropriately, turns out to be a complete fake.

The last words, though, are given to Aglaia's mother, Lizaveta Prokofyevna, the character who has always been closest in spirit to the prince but has managed to keep her feet successfully on the ground. Her typically explosive and matronly denunciation of Europe—"they can't make decent bread; in winter they are frozen like mice in a cellar"—concludes the book with a down-to-earth affirmation of the same faith in Russia that Myshkin had expressed in the messianic eloquence of his ecstatic rhapsodies.

8

The Idiot is perhaps the most original of Dostoevsky's great novels, and certainly the most artistically uneven of them all. It is not hard to point out its flaws if we take the nineteenth-century conception of the well-made novel as a standard; more difficult is to explain why it triumphs so effortlessly over all the inconsistencies and awkwardnesses of its structure and motivation. One reason, perhaps, is that the very gaucheries and grotesqueness of its treatment of plot and character, after several readings, generate an intriguing quality of their own. Its appeal might be compared with the effects created by such artists as Rouault and Chagall, who also play fast and loose with realistic conventions and return to earlier naïve forms of folk art to revive feelings of religious awe and wonder. Moreover, as we have seen, Dostoevsky poured himself more personally and unconstrainedly into this book than into any other; readers sense they come very close in its pages to touching the quick of his own values, and so perhaps are inclined to overlook technical defects, or even to take them as a testimony of authenticity. Whatever its faults, *The Idiot* also contains some of the greatest scenes that Dostoevsky ever wrote: Nastasya Filippovna's birthday party; the black comedy, anticipating Beckett, of the reading of Ippolit's "Essential Explanation"; the tenderly touching tryst in the park between Myshkin and Aglaia; the haunting, dreamlike vigil of Rogozhin and the prince over Nastasya's corpse. Nor can any other Christ figure in modern literature rival Prince Myshkin in the purity of his appeal.

Taken in the perspective of Dostoevsky's work as a whole, *The Idiot* may also well be considered his most courageous creation. As we know, the inspiration for his most important works in this period was provided primarily by his antagonism to the doctrines of Russian nihilism. The underground man and Raskolnikov had assimilated its ideas into their hearts and minds, and Dostoevsky dramatized the disastrous aftermaths of such acceptance when taken to their ultimate limit in action. His next major novel will renew the same attack even more ferociously, and *The Idiot* is often contrasted with these works because Prince Myshkin, far from being a member of the intelligentsia spiritually infected by nihilism, is rather an iconic image of Dostoevsky's own highest Christian ideal. In fact, however, there is much less structural difference between *The Idiot* and these other works than may appear at first sight.

For with an integrity that cannot be too highly praised, Dostoevsky fearlessly submits his *own* most hallowed convictions to the same test that he had used for those of the nihilists—the test of what they would mean for human life if taken seriously and literally, and lived out to their full extent as guides to conduct. With exemplary honesty, he portrays the moral extremism of his own eschatological ideal, incarnated by the prince, as being equally incompatible with the normal demands of ordinary social life, and constituting just as much of a disruptive scandal as the appearance of Christ himself among the complacently respectable Pharisees. But whatever the tragedy that Prince Myshkin and those affected by him may suffer in *this* world, he brings with him the unearthly illumination of a higher one that all feel and respond to;

and it is this response to "the light shining in the darkness" that for Dostoevsky provided the only ray of hope for the future.

———

JOSEPH FRANK is Professor Emeritus of Slavic and Comparative Literature at Princeton University. The first volume of his definitive (and ongoing) biography, *Dostoevsky: The Years of Ordeal, 1850–1859*, won the 1984 National Book Critics Circle Award for Biography.

TRANSLATOR'S NOTE

Anna Brailovsky

In her translation of *The Idiot*, Constance Garnett's chief objective seems to have been to create an accessible English text that flowed with ease. To that end, she handled Dostoevsky's language with the authority of an editor, cutting lengthy sentences into shorter ones, substituting synonyms for frequently repeated words, and eliminating apparently redundant language. I have attempted to undo Garnett's drastic anglicization of the text by restoring the syntactical structure of the original as closely as the boundaries of English grammar would allow (at times, admittedly, perhaps pushing them). Wherever possible, I have also retained Dostoevsky's repetition of words or phrases, even where it may seem excessive to the English ear. (It must be noted that in the original, the repeated words may not always be exactly the same with each subsequent repetition. Because Russian declines all adjectives and nouns in accordance with three genders and six cases, the same word can have a number of different endings, which introduces a small measure of variety that is impossible to achieve in English.)

If my rendition is more difficult, more strange, more awkward than Garnett's, it is because I did not wish to create for the reader the illusion of a familiar Anglo-Saxon idiom. Rather, I set out to impart to the non-Russian-speaking reader some sense of the vast differences between Russian and English writing and of the unique cadence of Dostoevsky's prose. It does not seem natural in English to begin a sentence with a long series of parenthetical remarks that close in slowly to a central core, only to disperse again on the other side like ripples in a pond. But such plasticity is not simply a function of the fact that Russian lends itself far more readily than English to nonlinear constructions. Even native Russian speakers find that Dostoevsky's language demands some effort on the part of the reader. And this is all the more reason for the translator to avoid the temptation of unpacking Dostoevsky's dense constructions in order to make them fit more readily into the English mold. To break down a Dostoevsky sentence into shorter, more readable parts is not merely to turn Russian into English (in itself, an act of great linguistic violence), it is to turn Henry James into Ernest Hemingway (which is, of course, not at all to say that one has more or less literary merit, but only that the distinction must—and can—be maintained).

There are points in the novel, most notably in brief dialogues, where Garnett's uncomplicated phrasing is, in fact, well matched to the original, and readers familiar with her translation will see little, if any, difference between her rendition and mine. But many of the lengthier narrative passages—and especially the discursive chapters that introduce each of the novel's four parts—called for so much revision that the end result had little in common with Garnett's work. Additionally, I have Americanized the orthography and updated the transliteration of the names using, for the most part, the system recommended by the Modern Language Association for publications aimed at a general audience.

One notable exception to the MLA system is my transcription of the so-called "soft sign." This symbol, placed after a consonant, signals a short, nasal, palatal stop, very similar to the one produced by the tilde in the Spanish word *mañana,* or by the silent *g* in *peignoir.* In scholarly publications, the soft sign is indicated by the typographical mark ', but for general audiences, the MLA recommends simply leaving it out entirely. I found the former solution aesthetically unappealing in a novel, and the latter not always adequate to the task of guiding pronunciation. Therefore, I chose my transliterations somewhat unsystematically, according to what I thought might best approximate the original sound. For the most part, this led me to adopt Garnett's transliterations (which either left the sign out, as in *Nastasya* for *Nastas'ya,* or replaced it with the letter *y,* as in *Terentyev* for *Terent'ev*). My most un-orthodox choice was to transcribe the soft sign as the letter *j* wherever it occurs between two consonants—most notably Ganjka and Varjka, in the more derisive nicknames of Ganya and Varya Ivolgin (these names do not appear in Garnett at all; she simply used Ganya and Varya throughout). If the reader pauses after the first syllable as if about to pronounce the *j* and then goes on to say *ka* instead, the result-ing palatal stop should somewhat resemble the original.

Finally, although consistency with our system would dictate the spelling *Aglaya* (compare with Nastasya, Ganya, etc.), the name comes from ancient Greek mythology and is commonly spelled in English as *Aglaia.*

PART ONE

I

In late November, during a thaw, around nine in the morning, a train on the Petersburg–Warsaw railway line was approaching Petersburg at full blast. It was so damp and foggy that it had just barely grown light; within ten paces to the right and left of the rails, it was difficult to make out anything at all from the carriage windows. Among the passengers were some returning from abroad; but the third-class compartments were more crowded, mainly with common folk on business, from not too far away. As usual, everyone was tired, everyone's eyes had grown heavy in the night, everyone was chilled, all the faces were pale and yellow, matching the color of the fog.

In one of the third-class carriages, right by the window, two passengers had, from early dawn, been sitting facing one another—both were young people, both traveled light, both were unfashionably dressed, both had rather remarkable faces, and both expressed, at last, a desire to start a conversation. If they had both known, one about the other, in what way they were especially remarkable in that moment, they would naturally have wondered that chance had so strangely placed them face to face in a third-class carriage of the Warsaw–Petersburg train. One of them was a short man about twenty-seven, with almost black curly hair and small but fiery gray eyes. His nose was broad and flat, his cheekbones high; his thin lips continually curved into a sort of insolent, mocking and even malicious smile; but the high and well-shaped forehead redeemed the ignoble lines of the lower part of the face. What was particularly striking about the young man's face was its deathly pallor, which lent him an exhausted look in spite of his fairly sturdy build, and at the same time something passionate to the point of suffering, which did not harmonize with his insolent and coarse smile and his sharp and self-satisfied gaze. He was warmly dressed in a full, black, sheepskin-lined overcoat, and had not felt the cold at night, while his neighbor had been forced to endure all the pleasures of a damp Russian November night, for which he was evidently unprepared. He had a fairly thick and wide cloak with no sleeves and a huge hood, just like those frequently used by travelers in winter somewhere far abroad, in Switzerland or, for instance, Northern Italy, who do not reckon, of course, on such distances along the journey as from Eydt-kuhnen[1] to Petersburg. But what was entirely suitable and satisfactory in Italy turned out to be not quite fitting for Russia. The owner of the hooded cloak was a young man, also twenty-six or twenty-seven years old, somewhat above the average in height, with very fair thick hair, with sunken cheeks and a thin, pointed, almost white beard. His eyes were large, blue and intent; there was something calm, though somber, in their expression, something full of that strange look by which some can surmise epilepsy in a person at first glance. The young man's face was otherwise pleasing, delicate and lean, though colorless, and at this moment even blue with cold. From his hands dangled a meager bundle tied up in an old, faded raw-silk kerchief, which, it seemed, contained the entirety of his traveling effects. He wore thick-soled boots and spats—it was all very un-Russian. His dark-haired neighbor in the sheepskin observed all this, partly from having nothing to do, and at last, with that indelicate smile in which satisfaction at the misfortunes of others is sometimes so unceremoniously and casually expressed, he asked:

"Chilly?"

And he shuddered.

"Very," answered his neighbor, with extraordinary readiness, "and just think, it's thawing, too. What if there were a frost? I didn't even think it would be so cold at home. I've become unused to it."

"From abroad, eh?"

"Yes, from Switzerland."

"Phew! You don't say!" The dark-haired man whistled and burst into laughter.

They struck up a conversation. The readiness of the fair young man in the Swiss cloak to answer all his swarthy companion's inquiries was astonishing and without the merest suspicion of the absolute thoughtlessness, inappropriateness and idleness of some of the questions. In answering, he declared by the by that he had indeed not been in Rus-

---

1. A railway station on what was then the border between Russia and Prussia.

sia for a long time, a little over four years, that he had been sent abroad on account of an illness, some kind of strange nervous illness, like epilepsy or St. Vitus's dance, resulting in trembling fits and convulsions. The swarthy man chuckled several times as he listened; and he laughed particularly when, in answer to his inquiry, "Well, have they cured you?" the fair one answered, "No, they haven't."

"Ha! You must have wasted a lot of money over it, and we believe in them over here," the swarthy man observed sarcastically.

"That's the honest truth!" interposed a badly dressed gentleman sitting beside them, a petty official type, set in his crusty scrivener's ways, about forty, powerfully built, with a red nose and pimpled face—"That's the honest truth, sir,[2] they only absorb all the resources of Russia for nothing!"

"Oh, you are quite mistaken in my case!" the patient from Switzerland chimed in with a gentle and conciliatory voice. "Of course, I can't argue with you because I don't know all about it, but my doctor even shared his last penny with me for the journey here; and there, he supported me at his expense for nearly two years."

"Why, had you no one to pay for you?" asked the swarthy man.

"No; Mr. Pavlishchev, who used to pay for me there, died two years ago. I've since written to Generaless Epanchin,[3] a distant relation of mine, but I've had no answer. So I've come . . ."

"Where are you going then?"

"You mean, where am I going to stay? . . . I don't rightly know yet . . . Somewhere . . ."

2. In the spoken language of pre-Revolutionary Russia, one often finds the ending "-s" appended to any number of words in a phrase (here, it is appended to the word "truth"—"that's the truth-s"). This particle can signify a certain respect for the rank of one's listener or simply add emphasis to the words it follows. Rather than leave this untranslatable particle out, I have chosen to approximate its double function of respect and emphasis by an interjectional use of "sir" (as in the song lyric, "Yes, sir, that's my baby!")

3. Much like the wife of a count becomes a countess, all titles in Russian—whether military, civil service, or aristocratic—have a corresponding feminine form to designate the wife of the man holding the title. Since social status in nineteenth-century Russia is dependent as much, if not more, on service rank as on noble birth, I feel it important to preserve the titles of the female characters in translation, despite the initial awkwardness. It seems in any case less awkward than resorting to roundabout phrases such as "the general's wife." Where it is impossible to feminize a title by an "-ess" ending, I have placed "Madame" before the masculine form (e.g., Madame Collegial Secretary).

"You've not made up your mind yet?" And both his listeners burst out laughing again.

"And no doubt that bundle is all you've got in the world?" asked the swarthy man.

"I'm willing to bet on it," chimed in the red-nosed official with an exceptionally gleeful air, "and that he's got nothing else in the luggage van, though poverty is no vice, which, again, one mustn't neglect to note."

It turned out that this was the case, too; the fair-haired young man acknowledged it at once with extraordinary readiness.

"Your bundle has some value, anyway," the petty official went on, when they had laughed to their heart's content (remarkably, the owner of the bundle finally began to laugh himself, looking at them, which increased their mirth), "and though you could stake your head that it contains no golden rolls of foreign coin with Napoleons or Friedrichs, to say nothing of Dutch Arapchicks,[4] which may already be concluded merely from the spats covering those foreign boots of yours, yet . . . when we add to your bundle such a purported relation as, for example, Generaless Epanchin, then even the bundle takes on a certain different significance, needless to say, but only in the case that Generaless Epanchin is really your relation and you are not mistaken, out of absentmindedness . . . which a person is very, very wont to do, if only . . . from an excess of imagination."

"Ah, you've guessed right again," the fair young man chimed in. "It really is almost a mistake, that's to say, she is almost no relation; so much so that I really was not at all surprised back then, when I got no answer there. It was what I expected."

"You simply wasted the money for the postage. Hm! . . . Anyway, you are open-hearted and sincere, which is commendable. Hm! . . . As for General Epanchin, we know him, yes sir, for, actually, he is a man everyone knows; and I used to know the late Mr. Pavlishchev, too, who paid your expenses in Switzerland, that is if it was Nikolai Andreevich Pavlishchev, for there were two of them, cousins. The other lives in the Crimea. The late Nikolai Andreevich was a worthy man and well connected, and he'd four thousand serfs in his day . . ."

"Just so, Nikolai Andreevich Pavlishchev was his name."

4. A gold coin minted in Russia that resembled old Dutch ducats.

And having answered, the young man intently and searchingly scru-tinized the know-it-all gentleman. One encounters these know-it-all gentlemen sometimes, even fairly often, in a certain well-known social sphere. They know everything. All the restless curiosity and faculties of their mind are irresistibly bent in one direction, no doubt from lack of more important ideas and interests in life, as the contemporary thinker would put it. The phrase "they know everything," by the way, must be taken to apply to a rather limited sphere: where so-and-so serves, with whom he is acquainted, the amount of his net worth, where he was governor, to whom he's married, how much his wife brought in, who are his cousins, who twice removed, etc., etc., and so on in that vein. For the most part, these know-it-alls walk about with worn-out elbows and receive a salary of seventeen rubles a month. The people of whose lives they know every last detail would be at a loss to imagine their motives. Yet, in the meantime many of them are positively consoled by this knowledge, which amounts to a complete science, and derive from it self-respect and even their highest spiritual gratification. And indeed it is a fascinating science. I have seen learned men, literary men, poets, politicians, who sought and found in that very science their greatest worldly comforts and goals, indeed, posi-tively making their careers solely on that account. Throughout this entire conversation the swarthy young man had been yawning, looking aimlessly out of the window and impatiently expecting the end of the journey. He was somehow preoccupied, extremely preoccupied, al-most agitated; he was even becoming somewhat strange: at times he would both hear and not hear, look and not look, laugh and not know or understand what he was laughing at.

"Excuse me, whom have I the honor . . ." the pimply gentleman said suddenly, addressing the fair young man with the bundle.

"Prince Lev Nikolaevich Myshkin,"[5] replied the latter with prompt and unhesitating readiness.

"Prince Myshkin? Lev Nikolaevich? Don't know . . . Can't say I've ever heard . . ." the official responded thoughtfully. "I don't mean the name, that is, it's a historical name, it's to be found in Karamzin's *His-tory*,[6] as it should be; I mean you personally, and indeed there are no

5. The name derives from *mysh*, the Russian word for "mouse."

6. N. M. Karamzin's twelve-volume *History of the Russian State* (1816–29) was the first his-torical survey of Russia and a seminal literary work.

Prince Myshkins to be met with anywhere, one never hears of them anymore."

"I should think not," the prince answered at once, "there are no Prince Myshkins now except me; I believe I am the last of them. And as for our fathers and grandfathers, some of them had even been *odnodvortsy*.[7] My father, by the way, was a sublieutenant in the army, of the Junkers. But I don't in fact know how Generaless Epanchin also wound up being of the Myshkins, also the last in her line . . ."

"He-he-he! The last in her line! He-he! What a phrase you turn," giggled the official.

The swarthy man smirked, too. The fair man was rather surprised that he had managed to make a pun, and a pretty bad one at that.

"Imagine, I said it without thinking," he explained at last, wondering.

"To be sure, to be sure you did," the official assented good-humoredly.

"So then, Prince, and you've been studying the sciences out there too, with the professor, have you?" asked the swarthy man suddenly.

"Yes . . . I was studying."

"For my part, I've never studied anything."

"Well, I only did a little, you know," added the prince almost apologetically. "It wasn't possible to teach me systematically, because of my illness."

"Do you know the Rogozhins?" the swarthy man asked quickly.

"No, I don't know them at all. I know very few people in Russia. You're a Rogozhin, then?"

"Yes, my name is Rogozhin, Parfyon."

"Parfyon? That wouldn't be of those same Rogozhins . . ." the official began, with increased gravity.

"Yes, one of those, one of the same," interrupted the swarthy man quickly and with uncivil impatience. And indeed, he hadn't addressed the pimply official even once, but from the very start had spoken only to the prince.

"But . . . how is that?" The official froze with amazement and his eyes

7. In pre-Revolutionary Russia's feudal system, *odnodvortsy* were a subcategory of serfs belonging to the state (rather than to individual landowners); they owned their own small plot of land and were allowed to keep serfs themselves. Some impoverished minor aristocratic families also belonged to this group (literally, "one-yarders").

nearly popped out of his head, his whole face immediately beginning to assume a reverent and servile, almost frightened, expression. "Related to the same Semyon Parfyonovich Rogozhin, Hereditary Honorable Citizen,[8] what passed on a month since and left two and a half million in capital?"

"And how do you know he left a clear two and a half million?" the swarthy man interrupted, not deigning to glance toward the official now, either. "Just look! (he indicated him to the prince with a wink), and what do they possibly gain by sucking up to you at once? But it's true that my father has died, and as for me, a month later, I'm going home from Pskov practically barefoot. Neither my brother, that scoundrel, nor my mother have sent either money or word—I was sent nothing! Like a dog! I've spent the entire month lying in a fever in Pskov! . . ."

"And now you are coming in for a tidy million, at the lowest reckoning, oh Lord!" the official flung up his hands.

"What is it to him, tell me that?" said Rogozhin, nodding irritably and angrily toward him again. "Why, I am not going to give you a farthing of it, though you may walk on your hands before me, if you like."

"I will, I will."

"You see! But I won't give you anything, I won't, if you dance for a whole week."

"Well, don't! And I don't need it. Don't! But I shall dance. I shall leave my wife and children and dance before you. Only to flatter! To flatter!"

"Fie on you!" spat the swarthy man. "Five weeks ago, like you"—he addressed the prince—"with nothing but a bundle, I ran away from my father to Pskov, to my aunt; and there collapsed with fever, while he went and died without me. Kicked the bucket. Eternal memory to the deceased, but he almost killed me then! Would you believe it, Prince, yes, by God! Had I not run away then, he would have killed me on the spot."

"Did you do something to make him angry?" countered the prince, examining the millionaire in the sheepskin with some particular interest. But though there may have been something intrinsically remark-

---

8. A title conferred by the state as a reward for services; it was awarded to merchants and others of nonnoble birth.

able in the million and in receiving a legacy, the prince was surprised and interested by something else as well; and Rogozhin himself was for some reason especially keen to converse with the prince, though it seemed he was in need of conversation in a more mechanical than spiritual sense; rather more from preoccupation than frankness; from agitation and disquiet, for the sake of just looking at someone and prattling on about something. It seemed that he was still in a feverish state, and at the very least suffering from the chills. As for the official, well, he simply hovered over Rogozhin, didn't dare to breathe, hung on every word and weighed it, precisely as if looking for a diamond.

"Angry he certainly was, and perhaps with reason," answered Rogozhin, "but more than anything, my brother did me in. Nothing can be said against my mother, she's an old woman, reads the Lives of the Saints, sits with the crones, and whatever brother Senjka[9] resolves, so it shall be done. And why didn't he send word to me at the time, then? It's clear, sir! It's true I was unconscious at the time. They say a telegram was sent, too. But you just see if a telegram can get to my aunt. She's widowed going on thirty years now and keeps sitting with the holy fools from morning till night. A nun she isn't, but even worse. Well, the telegram gave her a fright, and without opening it, she went and presented it at the constable's station, where it still lies to this day. Only Konyov, Vassily Vassilielich, came to my rescue, wrote me all about it. At night my brother cut off the solid gold tassels from the brocaded pall on my father's coffin. 'Think what a lot of money they are worth,' he apparently said. Well, for that alone he can go to Siberia, if I like, for this is sacrilege. Hey there, you clown," he turned to the official, "what's the law say: is it sacrilege?"

"Sacrilege! Sacrilege!" the official at once concurred.

"Do they send you to Siberia for it?"

"To Siberia, to Siberia. At once to Siberia!"

9. A nickname for Semyon. There are a variety of ways to transform a name in Russian, and each sets its own emotional tone. In the case of Semyon, the common variations are as follows: Senya—simply a shortened form, implies familiarity but is otherwise neutral; Senechka—very affectionate, like an endearment, "dear little Senya"; Senjka—very chummy and colloquial, often used by schoolboys, in playful banter, or to express vexation (either mock or serious), frequently preceded by adjectives such as "bratty," "rascally," or "no-good." As the reader shall soon see, Dostoevsky makes frequent use of these emotional modulations throughout the text, particularly with the characters of Gavrila Ardalionovich (Ganya, Ganechka, Ganjka) and his sister Varvara (Varya, Varechka, Varjka).

"They think I am still ill," Rogozhin continued to the prince, "but without saying a word, on the quiet, still ailing, I got in the carriage and here I come: open the gates, dear brother Semyon Semyonovich! He told my late father tales about me, I know. But that I did actually irritate my father back then with Nastasya Filippovna, that's the truth. I'm alone on that one. Led down the wayward path."

"Over Nastasya Filippovna?" uttered the official fawningly, seeming to grasp something.

"Why, you don't know her!" Rogozhin shouted at him impatiently.

"And I do, too!" triumphantly answered the official.

"See here! As if there aren't lots of Nastasya Filippovnas! And what an insolent beastly creature you are, let me tell you! Well, I simply knew that some creature just like this would go and glom onto me at once!" he continued to the prince.

"But perhaps I do know, sir!" the official fidgeted. "Lebedev[10] knows! You are pleased to reproach me, your excellency, but what if I prove it? Yes, it's that very same Nastasya Filippovna over whom your father sought to teach you a lesson with a honeysuckle switch, and Nastasya Filippovna would be Barashkov,[11] a distinguished lady even, so to speak, and a princess in her own line, too, and connected with a certain Totsky, Afanasy Ivanovich, with him exclusively, with the landowner and financier, member of companies and societies and great friend of General Epanchin on that account..."

"Oho, so that's how it is!" Rogozhin was indeed surprised at last. "Phooey, the devil take him, but he really does know."

"He knows everything! Lebedev knows everything! I went about with young Alexandr Likhachev for two months, your excellency, and it was after his father's death too, and I know everything, that is, all the ins and outs, and it got to the point that without Lebedev he couldn't take a step. Lately he's residing in the debtor's prison, but back then I had the opportunity to know Armance and Coralie, and Princess Patsky and Nastasya Filippovna, and I had the opportunity to know much else besides."

"Nastasya Filippovna? Why, did she and Likhachev..." Rogozhin looked irately at him; his lips even turned white and trembled.

10. From *lebed'*, Russian for "swan."
11. From *barashek*, "little lamb."

"N-not at all! N-not at all! Not in the least!" the official caught himself and hurried on quickly. "N-not for all the money in the world could Likhachev land with her! No, she is not an Armance. There's only Totsky. And of an evening she sits in her own box at the Grand or the French Theatre. The officers say what they will between themselves, but even they can't prove anything. 'Look,' they say, 'that's Nastasya Filippovna, the very one,' but that's all; and regarding the details—nothing! Because there isn't anything."

"That's all true," gloomily confirmed Rogozhin, scowling. "Zalyozhev told me so at the time, too. At the time, Prince, I was running across the Nevsky in my father's three-year-old coat when she comes out of a shop and gets in her carriage. It set me all aflame on the spot. I run into Zalyozhev, I'm not in that one's league, goes around like a hairdresser's assistant, with an eyeglass in his eye, while at my father's house we wear tarred boots and are kept on Lenten soup. 'She's out of your league,' says he, 'she's a princess,' says he, 'name's Nastasya Filippovna, Barashkov by surname, and she lives with Totsky; and Totsky doesn't know how to get rid of her, for he's just reached the proper age, so to speak, fifty-five, and wants to marry the foremost beauty in Petersburg.' Then he convinces me that I could see Nastasya Filippovna that very day at the Grand Theatre, at the ballet; she'd be sitting in her box, in the *baignoire*.[12] Now at our house, with Father, just try going to the ballet—he'd make short work of you—he'd kill you! But I did slip in for an hour though, on the sly, and saw Nastasya Filippovna again; I didn't sleep all that night. Next morning the dear departed gives me two five percent bonds, five thousand a piece; 'Go,' he says, 'and sell them; take seven thousand five hundred to the Andreevs' office, pay the account, and as for the change from the ten thousand, bring it to me, and don't be stopping anywhere; I'll be waiting for you.' I cashed the bonds, took the money, but I didn't go to the Andreevs'. I went straight to the English shop, and for the whole lot, picked out a pair of earrings with a diamond nearly as big as a nut in each; I was left owing four hundred, but I gave them my name and they trusted me. With the earrings, I go to Zalyozhev: there you are, my good fellow, let's go to Nastasya Filippovna. And off we went. What was under my feet at the

___

12. Fr., box seats in the orchestra.

time, before me or around me—I neither know nor remember. We went straight into her drawing room, she came in to us herself. I didn't own up at the time that it was me, but Zalyozhev said, 'This is from Parfyon Rogozhin, in memory of his meeting you yesterday; will you kindly accept it?' She opened it, took a look and smirked: 'Thank your friend Mr. Rogozhin for his kind attention.' She bowed and went out. Well, why didn't I die on the spot! I went to her because I thought I wouldn't come back alive anyway. But what seemed to me most painful was that Zalyozhev, the beast, took all the credit. I'm short and dressed like a lackey, and I stood, silent, staring at her because I was ashamed, and he's in the height of fashion, curled and pomaded, rosy and in a check tie—he was all bows and graces, and no doubt just then she took him for me! 'Well,' I say as soon as we went out, 'don't you dare dream now of anything, do you understand?' He laughs. 'And how will you account for it with Semyon Parfyonovich now?' I must own, I wanted to jump in the water on the spot without going home, but I thought, 'It's all the same now,' and returned home like a damned soul."

"Ech! Uff!" The petty official wriggled, and was even seized with shivers. "Why, the deceased would have sent you to the next world for ten rubles, let alone ten thousand," he added, nodding to the prince. The prince scrutinized Rogozhin with interest; the latter seemed paler than ever at that moment.

"Sent you to the next world!" repeated Rogozhin. "What do you know about it? He found it all out at once," he went on, addressing the prince, "and Zalyozhev went gossiping about it to every Tom, Dick, and Harry. My father took me and locked me up upstairs and was at me for a whole hour. 'This is only a preface,' he said, 'but I'll come in to say good night to you!' and what do you think? The old man went to Nastasya Filippovna's, bowed down to the ground before her, wept and besought her; she brought out the box at last and flung it to him. 'Here are your earrings, you old graybeard,' she said, 'and they are ten times more precious to me now since Parfyon faced such a storm to get them for me. Greet Parfyon Semyonovich and thank him for me.' And meanwhile, with my mother's blessing, I'd obtained twenty rubles from Seryozha Protushin, and set off by train to Pskov, and I arrived in a fever. The old women took up reading the Lives of the Saints over me while I sat there drunk, and then I did the rounds of the taverns on my last farthing, spent the whole night sprawling senseless in the street, and by morning was delirious, on top of which, meanwhile, the dogs had gnawed me in the night. I barely just came to."

"Well, well, sir, now Nastasya Filippovna will sing another tune," the official chuckled, rubbing his hands. "What are earrings now, sir! Now we can make up for it with such earrings . . ."

"But if you say another word about Nastasya Filippovna, as there is a God above, I'll thrash you, though you used to go about with Likhachev!" cried Rogozhin, seizing him firmly by the arm.

"Well, if you thrash me, it means you won't reject me! Thrash away! By thrashing me, you'd be impressing me upon your mind . . . Why, here we are!"

They had in fact reached the station. Though Rogozhin said he had come away in secret, several men were already waiting for him. They shouted and waved their caps to him.

"I say, Zalyozhev here too!" muttered Rogozhin, gazing at them with a triumphant and almost malicious-looking smile, and turned suddenly to the prince. "Prince, I don't know why I've taken a liking to you. Perhaps I've met you at such a moment, though I've met him too (he indicated Lebedev) and I haven't taken a liking to him. Come and see me, Prince. We'll take off those little spats of yours, we'll put you into a first-rate fur coat; I'll get you a first-class dress coat, a white waistcoat, or whatever kind you like, I'll fill your pockets with money, and . . . we'll go see Nastasya Filippovna! Will you come, or won't you?"

"Listen, Prince Lev Nikolaevich!" Lebedev chimed in commandingly and solemnly. "Don't miss the chance, oh, don't miss the chance!"

Prince Myshkin stood up, courteously held out his hand to Rogozhin and said amiably:

"I will come with the greatest of pleasure and thank you very much for growing fond of me. I may come today, even, if I've time. For I tell you frankly I've taken a great liking to you myself, particularly when you were talking about the diamond earrings. I liked you before that, too, though you have a gloomy face. Thank you, too, for the clothes and the fur coat you promise me, for I certainly shall need clothes and a fur coat soon. As for the money, I have scarcely a farthing at the moment."

"There will be money, there will be money by the evening, come!"

"There will, there will!" the official chimed in, "by evening, before sunset there will be!"

"And women, Prince, are you very keen on them? Speak out sooner than later!"

"I, n-no! You see . . . you don't know, perhaps, but owing to my congenital illness, I don't even know women at all."

"Well, if that's how it is," exclaimed Rogozhin, "you're turning out to be a regular blessed innocent, Prince, and God loves such as you."

"And you, inkblot, follow me," said Rogozhin to Lebedev, and everyone got out of the carriage.

Lebedev ended up getting what he wanted. The noisy group soon disappeared in the direction of Voznesensky Prospect. The prince had to turn off toward Liteinaya. It was damp and rainy; the prince asked his way of passersby—it appeared that he had some three versts[13] to go, and he decided to take a cab.

II

General Epanchin lived in a house of his own a little off from Liteinaya, toward the Church of the Sacred Transfiguration. Besides this (magnificent) house—five-sixths of which was rented out—General Epanchin had another huge house in Sadovaya Street also bringing in an exceptional income. Aside from these two houses, he had a rather profitable and significant estate right near Petersburg; there was also some sort of factory in the Petersburg district. In former days the general, as everyone knew, had been a shareholder in government levies.[14] Now he had shares and a considerable influence in the control of some well-established companies. He had the reputation of being a man of significant fortune, with significant pursuits and significant connections. He had managed to make himself absolutely indispensable in certain places, among them also in his official position. Yet, too, it was well known that Ivan Fyodorovich Epanchin was a man of no education and came from soldier stock. The latter fact, no doubt, could only be to his credit; but the general, though he was an intelligent man, was not free of some rather pardonable little weaknesses and was not fond of certain allusions. But he was indisputably an intelligent and capable man. He made it a principle, for instance, not to put himself forward,

13. *Verst*—an old Russian unit of measure equal to .6629 miles.
14. In nineteenth-century Russia, the state sold to private individuals the exclusive right to collect certain government revenues. The system was abolished in 1863.

to efface himself where necessary, and many valued him specifically for his unpretentiousness, specifically because he always knew his place. But meanwhile, if only these observers could have seen what went on sometimes in the soul of Ivan Fyodorovich, who knew his place so well! Though he really had practical knowledge and experience in worldly matters and some very remarkable abilities, he liked to style himself more as the executor of the ideas of others than as the ruler of his own mind, a man "devoted without flattery," and—does not the spirit of the age demand it?—even Russian and sincere. With regard to the latter, he had even been embroiled in several amusing stories; but the general never lost heart, even in the face of the most amusing stories. Besides, he was always lucky, even at cards, and he played for very high stakes and far from attempting to conceal this little, as it were, weakness, which was materially and in other ways so profitable to him, he intentionally made a display of it. His society was mixed, but in any case obviously of the "bigwig" variety. But he had everything before him, he had plenty of time, plenty of time for everything, and everything was bound to come in due time and in its course. And with respect to years, General Epanchin was still, as they say, in his very prime, that is fifty-six and not a day more, which constitutes a flourishing age in any case, an age in which *real* life actually begins. His good health, his complexion, his sound though black teeth, his sturdy, solid figure, his preoccupied air at his office in the morning and his good-humored countenance in the evening at cards or at "his grace's"— all contributed to his success in the present and in the future, and strewed his excellency's path with roses.

The general had a flourishing family. Admittedly, all was not roses there, but there was also much on which his excellency's chief hopes and aims had long been earnestly and sincerely concentrated. And, after all, what aims are graver and more sacred than a father's? What should a man cling to, if not to his family? The general's family consisted of a wife and three grown-up daughters. The general had married many years before, when only a lieutenant, a girl of almost his own age, who was not distinguished by either beauty or education, and with whom he had received a dowry of only fifty souls—which did, however, serve to contribute to the foundation of his later fortune. But the general never in later years complained of his early marriage, never regarded it as the error of his improvident youth, and so respected his wife, and at times so feared her that, indeed, he positively loved her. The generaless was of the princely Myshkin line, a line rather ancient, although not brilliant, and she had a rather great opinion of herself on account of her birth. Some influential person at the time, one of those patrons whose patronage costs them nothing, had consented to interest himself in the young princess's marriage. He had opened the garden gate for the young officer and nudged him down the path; and the latter didn't even need a nudge, a glance alone sufficed— would not have been wasted in vain! With some few exceptions, the couple had spent the entirety of their long life together in harmony. At a very early age, the generaless had known—as a born princess and the last of her line, though perhaps also owing to personal qualities—how to secure certain very highly placed patronesses. Subsequently, in the face of the wealth and official importance of her spouse, she even began to feel somewhat at home in these highest circles.

It was in these last years that all three of the general's daughters— Alexandra, Adelaida and Aglaia—had grown up. It's true that all three were merely Epanchins, but of a princely line on the maternal side, with considerable dowries, with a father who aspired, in the future, to rise perhaps to a very high position indeed and, what is also rather important, all three were remarkably good-looking, including the eldest, Alexandra, who was already past twenty-five. The middle sister was twenty-three, while the youngest, Aglaia, had only just turned twenty. This youngest one was quite a beauty and was beginning to attract much attention in society. But that was not all: all three were distinguished in education, intelligence, and talent. It was well known that they were remarkably fond of each other and supported one another. There was even talk of some purported sacrifices on the part of the two eldest for the sake of the commonly held idol of the house—the youngest. In society, they not only did not like to show off, but were even too modest. No one could reproach them with haughtiness or conceit, yet everyone knew that they were proud and knew their worth. The eldest was a musician, the middle one a splendid painter; but virtually no one knew of this for many years, and it was found out only very recently, and by accident at that. In a word, an extraordinarily great deal was said in their praise. But there were also those bearing ill will. People spoke with horror of the number of books they had read. They were in no hurry to get married; a certain social sphere was dear to them, yet not very much so. This was all the more remarkable since everyone knew the attitude, character, aims, and desires of their father.

It was nearly eleven o'clock when the prince rang at the general's apartment. The general lived on the second floor and occupied premises that were modest for his means, though in proportion to his position. A liveried servant opened the door, and the prince had to explain himself at length to this man, who had, from the first, looked at him and at his bundle with suspicion. At last, on his repeated and definite assertion that he really was Prince Myshkin and that he absolutely must see the general on urgent business, the bewildered manservant conducted him into a little anteroom, before the actual waiting room adjoining the study, and handed him over to another servant who was on duty in this waiting room in the mornings and announced visitors to the general. This other servant wore a tailcoat, was past forty, had an anxious countenance, and was his excellency's special cabinet attendant and usher, as a result of which he knew his worth.

"Do wait in the waiting room, and leave your bundle here," he said, seating himself unhurriedly and with an air of importance in his armchair and looking with stern surprise at the prince, who had settled down on a chair right beside him with his bundle in his hands.

"If you'll allow me," said the prince, "I'd rather wait here with you; what am I to do in there alone?"

"You can't stay in the anteroom, for you are a visitor, in other words a guest. Do you want to see the general himself?"

The footman apparently could not come to terms with the thought of admitting such a visitor, and decided to question him once more.

"Yes, I have business . . ." began the prince.

"I'm not asking you what business—my business is just to announce you. But without the secretary, I've told you, I won't go and announce you."

The man's suspicion seemed to grow more and more; the prince was simply too much not the type of the ordinary visitor, and although it was rather often, virtually every day in fact, that the general, at a certain hour, had to receive—especially on *business*—some at times really quite checkered visitors, still, despite habit and the fairly wide latitude of his instructions, the attendant had grave doubts; the intercession of the secretary was essential before he showed him in.

"Are you really . . . from abroad?" he asked at last, as if involuntarily, and floundered; he wanted, perhaps, to ask: "Are you really Prince Myshkin?"

"Yes, I've just come directly from the train. It seems to me you wanted to ask: am I really Prince Myshkin? but didn't ask out of politeness."

"Hm . . ." the astounded footman remained silent.

"I assure you that I haven't lied to you, and you won't have to answer for me. As for my appearance and the bundle, there's nothing to wonder at there: at the moment, my circumstances are rather unimpressive."

"Hm! I have no apprehension on that score, you know. It's my duty to announce you, and the secretary will see you, excepting that you . . . Well, that's just it, excepting that . . . You're not seeing the general on account of need, if I may make bold to inquire?"

"Oh, no, you can rest assured of that. My business is different."

"You must excuse me, but I asked having looked at you. Wait for the secretary; his excellency himself is engaged with the colonel at present, and afterward the secretary . . . from the company . . . will come."

"In that case, if I've long to wait, I should like to ask: mightn't one have a smoke here somewhere? I've got a pipe and tobacco with me."

"Have . . . a . . . smoke?" the attendant glanced at him with scornful bewilderment, as if he still couldn't believe his ears. "Have a smoke? No, you're not allowed to smoke here, and furthermore, you ought to be ashamed to even think of it. Ha . . . if that isn't queer!"

"Oh, but I wasn't asking about this room; I know that; but I would have gone out somewhere, anywhere you might have told me, for I am used to it, and I haven't had a smoke some three hours now. Anyway, have it as you please, and, you know, there's a saying: when in Rome . . ."

"Well, and how am I going to announce a fellow like you?" muttered the attendant almost involuntarily. "In the first place, you shouldn't be here, but should be sitting in the waiting room because you're in the way of a visitor, in other words a guest, and I'll answer for it . . . You aren't aiming to live here, are you?" he added, once more glancing askance at the bundle, which evidently gave him no rest.

"No, I don't think so. Even if they invite me, I shan't stay. I've simply come to make their acquaintance, and nothing more."

"How's that? To make their acquaintance?" the attendant asked with amazement and redoubled suspiciousness. "Why did you say at first that it was business?"

"Oh, it's hardly business. That is, if you like, I do have one matter, but it is only to ask advice; chiefly, it's to introduce myself, for I am Prince Myshkin and Generaless Epanchin is also the last of the princess Myshkins, and aside from me and her, there are no Myshkins anymore."

"So you're a relation on top of it?" The footman, now positively alarmed, gave a start.

"Hardly that either. Still, if you stretch the point, then of course we're relations, but so distant that you can't really count it. I once addressed the generaless from abroad by letter, but she didn't answer me. Nonetheless, I considered it necessary to make her acquaintance on my return. I'm explaining all this to you now so that you may have no doubts, for I see that you are still uneasy: announce that Prince Myshkin is here, and in the announcement itself the reason for my visit will be clear. If I'm received—well and good; if not, it's perhaps just as well. But, I think, they can't refuse to see me: the generaless will surely want to see the eldest and only representative of her line, and she values her pedigree highly, as I have heard of her in detail."

It seemed the prince's conversation was quite ordinary; but as ordinary as it was, the more absurd did it become in the present case, and the experienced attendant could not but feel something that is utterly proper from man to man but utterly improper between guest and *man*.[15] And since *people* are far more intelligent than their masters generally suppose, it came into the attendant's head that it was a matter of two things: either the prince was some kind of sponger and had certainly come to beg, or the prince was simply a bit daft and had no self-respect, for an intelligent prince with self-respect would not sit in an anteroom and talk to a footman about his affairs, but be that as it may, in the one or the other case, wouldn't he still have to answer for him?

"Still, it would be better if you stepped into the waiting room," he remarked as insistently as possible.

"Well, had I been sitting there, I wouldn't have explained everything to you." The prince laughed good-humoredly. "And, no doubt,

---

15. "Man" as in manservant.

you would still have been anxious, looking at my cloak and bundle. But now, perhaps, you needn't wait for the secretary and can go and announce me yourself."

"I can't announce a visitor like you without the secretary, and besides, his excellency gave special orders just now that he was not to be disturbed for anyone while he is with the colonel, while Gavrila Ardalionovich goes in without being announced."

"An official, is he?"

"Who, Gavrila Ardalionovich? No. He is in the service of the company. You might at least put your bundle here."

"I'd been meaning to; if I may. And, you know, might I take off my cloak too?"

"Of course, you wouldn't go in with your coat, now, would you."

The prince stood up, hurriedly took off his cloak, and was left in a fairly decent, well-cut, though worn, suit jacket. A steel chain ran along his waistcoat. On the chain was a silver Geneva watch.

Although the prince was a bit daft—the footman had made up his mind about that—yet it seemed to the general's attendant, at last, unseemly to keep up a conversation with a visitor, despite the fact that for some reason he liked the prince, in his own way, of course. But from another point of view, he aroused in him a resolute and gross indignation.

"And the generaless, when does she see visitors?" asked the prince, sitting down again in the same place.

"That's not my business, sir. It varies, depending on the person. The dressmaker is even admitted at eleven. Gavrila Ardalionovich is also admitted before other people, he's even admitted to early lunch."

"Here in your rooms, it's warmer than abroad in winter," remarked the prince, "while there, it's warmer than here on the street, but in their houses in winter—a Russian person could hardly live there for not being used to it."

"They don't heat?"

"No, and the houses are set up differently, that is to say the stoves and windows."

"Hm! Have you been there long?"

"Four years now. But I was in the same place almost all the time, in the country."

"Grown unused to our ways, have you?"

"Yes, that's true. Would you believe it, I'm surprised to find I haven't forgotten how to speak Russian. As I'm talking to you now, I keep thinking: 'Why, I'm speaking quite well.' Perhaps that's why I talk so much. Indeed, I've been longing to speak Russian ever since yesterday."

"Hm! He! Used to live in Petersburg before, did you?" (As much as the footman resisted, it was impossible not to keep up such a polite and affable conversation.)

"In Petersburg? Scarcely at all, just briefly, in transit. I knew nothing of it before, and now I hear so much is new that they say whoever knew it has to learn how to get to know it all over again. People talk a great deal about the courts[16] here now."

"Hm! . . . The courts. The courts, it's true, there are courts. And abroad, how is it in the courts, more fair than ours or not?"

"I don't know. I've heard a great deal that's good about ours. For instance, we have no capital punishment."[17]

"Do they execute people there, then?"

"Yes. I saw it in France, in Lyons. Schneider took me with him there."

"Do they hang them?"

"No, in France they're still cutting off their heads."

"And do they scream?"

"How could they! It's done in an instant. They make the man lie down and this wide blade comes down heavy and powerful, brought down by a machine, the guillotine it's called . . . The head pops off before you can bat an eyelash. The preparations are hard. When they read the sentence, get the machine ready, bind the man, lead him up the scaffold—that's what's horrible. The people come running, even the women, though they don't like it there when the women look on."

"It's no business for them."

"Of course! Of course! Such suffering! . . . The criminal was an intelligent man, fearless, strong, up there in years, Legros by name. But I tell you, whether you believe me or not, when he mounted the

16. In 1864, the court system underwent substantial reforms; under the new system, cases were tried in open hearings, argued by defense attorneys, and decided by jury.

17. Although capital punishment was abolished in 1754, it was reinstated soon after for treason and other crimes against the state. It was, in reality, quite common, and Dostoevsky himself had a narrow escape in 1849 (see note 18 on page 24).

scaffold—he was crying, and was white as a sheet. Is it possible? Isn't it awful? Who cries for fear? I'd no idea that a grown man could cry for fear, not a child, a man who'd never cried before, a man of forty-five. What must be happening in the soul, to what anguish is it brought? It's an outrage on the soul and nothing else! It is written: 'Thou shalt not kill,' so because he has killed, we should kill him too? No, it mustn't be. It's been a month since I saw it, and to this day it seems to stand before my eyes. I've dreamt of it a half a dozen times."

The prince even became animated as he spoke, a faint color rose in his pale face, although his voice was still quiet. The attendant followed him with sympathetic interest, as if, it seemed, he did not wish to take his eyes off him; perhaps he was also a man with imagination and an attempt at thought.

"It's a good thing at least that there is not much torment," he remarked, "when the head falls off."

"You know what?" the prince took up warmly, "you've noted that, and everyone notes it just the same as you, and the machine, the guillotine, was invented for that object. But at the time, one thought occurred to me: what if it is even worse? This will seem absurd, it will seem wild to you, but with some imagination, even such a thought will occur to you. Consider: if, for instance, we take torture; there is suffering and wounds, torment of the flesh, and, no doubt, all this distracts the mind from spiritual suffering, so that you are tormented only by the wounds until you die. But the chief, the most terrible, pain is perhaps not in the wounds, but in the fact that you know for certain that in an hour, and then in ten minutes, and then in half a minute, and then now, this very moment—your soul will leave your body and you won't be a person anymore, and it's certain; the main thing is, it's *certain*. When you lay your head down right under the knife and hear the knife slide over your head, that very quarter of a second is the most terrible of all. Do you know that this isn't my fancy, that many people have said the same? I believe that so thoroughly that I'll tell you what I think right off. To kill for murder is a punishment immeasurably greater than the crime itself. Murder by legal sentence is immeasurably more terrible than brigandly murder. A person murdered by brigands, stabbed at night in the woods or something, no doubt still hopes to be saved until the very last moment. There have been instances when a man's throat's been cut, yet he still hopes, or runs, or begs for mercy.

But here, all that last hope, which makes dying ten times easier, is taken away *for certain;* here, there is a sentence, and the whole awful torture lies in the fact that there is certainly no escape, and there is no torture in the world more terrible. Lead a soldier out and set him right opposite the cannon in battle and fire at him, he will still hope, but read the same soldier a sentence of *certain* death, and he'll lose his mind or burst into tears. Who says that human nature is able to bear this without madness? Why this outrage, so hideous, unnecessary, useless? Perhaps there exists such a man, one who's been read the sentence, allowed to suffer, and then told: 'You can go, you've been pardoned.'[18] Such a man, perhaps, could tell us. It was of this suffering and this horror that Christ spoke, too. No, you can't treat a man like that!"

Although the attendant would not have been able to express all this like the prince, he understood the most important part of it, if not all, which was evident from the softened expression on his face.

"If you really want so much," he declared, "to have a smoke, it may perhaps be possible, if you make haste about it. For they may ask for you suddenly, and you wouldn't be here. Just here under the little stairs, you see, there's a door. Go through the door, there's a closet to the right: you can do it there, but open the casement, for it's against the rules."

But the prince didn't have time to go and smoke. A young man with papers in his hands suddenly came into the anteroom. The attendant began helping him off with his furs. The young man cast a sidelong glance at the prince.

"This gentleman, Gavrila Ardalionych,"[19] the attendant began confidentially and almost familiarly, "announces himself as Prince Myshkin and a relation of the mistress, has come by train from abroad with bundle in hand, just . . ."

18. Dostoevsky is here referring to himself. In the 1840s, he was associated with an underground socialist group led by Mikhail Vasilyevich Petrashevsky. The *petrashevtsy* were arrested and sentenced to death by firing squad in 1849, but a reprieve was issued at the very last minute, after all the preparations for the execution were completed. Dostoevsky was sentenced to hard labor instead.

19. The last two syllables of a patronymic, "-ovich" or "-evich," are often shortened in speech by swallowing the "-ov" or "-ev," especially when the speaker is not making a conscientious effort to be overly formal.

The prince did not hear the rest because the attendant began to whisper. Gavrila Ardalionovich listened attentively and glanced with great curiosity at the prince. At last, he ceased listening and approached him impatiently.

"You are Prince Myshkin?" he asked with extreme graciousness and politeness. He was a very handsome young man, also some twenty-eight years old, a slim blond, of medium height, with a small Napoleonic beard, with an intelligent and very handsome face. Only his smile, for all its graciousness, was a trifle too refined; the teeth it displayed were a trifle too pearly and even; in spite of his gaiety and apparent sincerity, there was something a trifle too intent and searching in his gaze.

"He must gaze quite differently when he's alone, and perhaps he never laughs," the prince sensed somehow.

The prince explained all he could, in brief, almost the same as he had already explained before to the attendant, and before that to Rogozhin. Meanwhile Gavrila Ardalionovich appeared to be recollecting something.

"Wasn't it you," he asked, "about a year ago, or even less, who pleased to send a letter, from Switzerland I think, to Elizaveta Prokofyevna?"

"Just so."

"Then they know about you here and will certainly remember you. You're here to see his excellency? I'll announce you at once . . . He will be at liberty directly. Only you ought . . . You had better step into the waiting room in the meantime . . . Why is the gentleman here?" He turned sternly to the attendant.

"I've told him, he didn't want to . . ."

At that moment the door from the study was suddenly opened and some sort of military man, with a portfolio in his hand, speaking loudly and making his bows, emerged from it.

"You there, Ganya?" cried a voice from the study, "come here, would you!"

Gavrila Ardalionych nodded to the prince and went hastily into the study.

Some two minutes later the door was opened again and the clear and affable voice of Gavrila Ardalionych was heard:

"Prince, please come in."

III

The general, Ivan Fyodorovich Epanchin, stood in the middle of his study and looked with extreme curiosity at the prince as he entered, even took two steps toward him. The prince approached and gave his introductions.

"Well, sir," answered the general, "how can I be of service?"

"I have no pressing business; my object was simply to make your acquaintance. I should be sorry to disturb you, as I don't know your arrangements, nor when you see visitors . . . But I have just come off the train . . . arrived from Switzerland . . ."

The general was on the point of smirking, but on second thought he checked himself; then he thought again, narrowed his eyes, scrutinized his visitor once more from head to foot, then rapidly motioned him to a chair, sat down himself a little to the side, and turned to the prince with impatient expectation. Ganya stood in the corner of the study, next to the bureau, and sorted papers.

"I have little time for making acquaintances as a rule," said the general, "but as you have no doubt some object . . ."

"I had a feeling," interrupted the prince, "that you would undoubtedly see some special object in my visit. But, upon my word, except for the pleasure of making your acquaintance, I have no personal object of any kind."

"It is of course an extraordinary pleasure for me too, but life is not all play, from time to time, you know, there are also matters of business . . . Moreover, I still haven't been able to discover anything in common between us . . . any reason, so to speak . . ."

"There certainly is no reason, and of course very little in common. Because if I am Prince Myshkin and your wife is of our line, that, to be sure, is no reason. I quite understand that. Still, that is all that my object consists in. It's more than four years since I was in Russia; and the state I left in: nearly out of my mind! I knew nothing then, and even less now. I have need of good people; I even have one matter of business and don't know where I can turn. The thought struck me back in Berlin: 'They're almost relations, I'll start with them; perhaps we may be useful to each other, they to me and I to them—if they are good people.' And I had heard that you were good people."

"Much obliged, sir," the general said in wonderment, "allow me to inquire, where are you staying?"

"I am not staying anywhere as yet."

"That means you've come straight from the train to me? And . . . with luggage?"

"Well, all the luggage I have is one small bundle of linen, and nothing else; I usually carry it in my hand. I shall have time to take a hotel room this evening."

"So you still have the intention of taking a room?"

"Oh yes, of course."

"Judging by your words, I nearly thought that you had come to stay here."

"That might have been, but only at your invitation. For my part, I confess, I would not have stayed even with an invitation, not for any reason, but simply . . . It's my nature."

"Then, it seems, it's for the best that I haven't invited you, and won't invite you. Allow me, Prince, so as to make things clear once and for all: since we have just agreed that there can be no talk of relationship between us—although, of course, it would have been very flattering for me—then, it would seem . . ."

"Then, it would seem, I should get up and leave?" The prince started to get up, even laughing gaily somehow, despite the evident difficulty of his position. "And upon my word, General, although I know absolutely nothing, practically, neither of the custom here, nor in general of how people here live, yet I imagined that things with us would inevitably turn out exactly as they have. What of it, perhaps that's how it should be . . . And back then, too, there was no answer to my letter . . . Well, good-bye, and forgive me for troubling you."

The prince's gaze was so affectionate in that moment, and his smile so free from the slightest shade of anything like concealed ill will, that the general was suddenly stayed and suddenly looked at his guest somehow in a different light; the entire change of attitude occurred in a single instant.

"But you know, Prince," he said in an almost completely different tone, "I don't know you, after all, and Elizaveta Prokofyevna will perhaps like to have a look at someone who shares her family name . . . Wait, if you have the time."

"Oh, I have the time; my time is entirely my own" (and the prince immediately placed his soft, round-brimmed hat on the table). "I confess, I was counting on it that, perhaps, Elizaveta Prokofyevna would remember that I wrote to her. Just now your servant, while I was waiting out there for you, suspected I'd come to beg for a handout; I noticed it, and no doubt you've given strict orders on that subject. But, honestly, I haven't come for that, but only to get to know people. Only I think, a bit, that I'm in your way, and that worries me."

"Here's the thing, Prince," said that general with a good-humored smile, "if you really are the sort of person you seem to be, then, it appears, it will be pleasant to make your acquaintance; only, you see, I'm a busy man, and I'll sit down again directly to look through and sign some things, and then I'm going to his grace's, and then to the office, and that's how it happens that, though I'm glad to see people . . . good ones, that is . . . still . . . But I am so convinced that you are a man of excellent breeding that . . . And how old are you, Prince?"

"Twenty-six."

"Uff! And I thought you were much younger."

"Yes, they say my face looks young for my age. And I shall soon learn not to be in your way, for I very much dislike being in the way . . . And, ultimately, I fancy, we seem such different people . . . Through various circumstances, that, perhaps, we cannot have many points in common, but you know, I don't believe in that last idea myself, for very often it only seems that there are no points in common, while they are very much there . . . it just happens on account of human laziness that people sort themselves by appearances and fail to find anything . . . But perhaps I'm starting to bore you? You seem . . ."

"Two words, please: have you any means at all? Or do you intend to take up some kind of occupation, perhaps? Forgive me, that I . . ."

"Oh, mercy, I quite appreciate and understand your question. I have at the moment no means and no occupation either, though, sir, I must. The money I've just had was not my own, Schneider gave it to me, my professor, who was treating me and teaching me in Switzerland; he gave it to me for the journey, and gave me just enough, so that now, for instance, I have only a few farthings left. I do have one matter, in fact, and I need advice, but . . ."

"Tell me, how do you intend to live meanwhile, and what were your plans?" interrupted the general.

"I wanted to get work of some sort."

"Oh, so you're a philosopher; and by the by ... are you aware of any talents, any abilities, if only a few, that is, of the bread-winning sort? Forgive me, again ..."

"Oh, please don't apologize. No sir, I fancy I've no talents or special abilities; quite the contrary in fact, for I am an ill man, and did not get a proper education. As for the bread, it seems to me ..."

The general interrupted again, and again began to question him. The prince once more recounted all that had already been recounted. It turned out that the general had heard of the late Pavlishchev and had even known him personally. Why Pavlishchev took an interest in his upbringing, the prince could not explain himself either—but, possibly, it was simply from a friendship of long standing with his late father. The prince was left still a small child after his parents were gone, and spent his entire life growing up in country villages, as his health required the country air. Pavlishchev had entrusted him to some old ladies with an estate, relations of his; there was at first a governess, and later a tutor, hired for him; he declared, incidentally, that although he remembered everything, there was little that he could satisfactorily explain, for there was much that he had not realized. Frequent attacks of his illness had made him almost an idiot (the prince said it just like that: "idiot"). He recounted, finally, that Pavlishchev had once, in Berlin, met Professor Schneider, a Swiss, who specialized in precisely these illnesses, had an institution in Switzerland, in the canton of Valais, treated patients by his own method with cold water and exercise, treated both idiocy and madness, and, in the bargain, educated and took charge of general mental development; that Pavlishchev sent him to him in Switzerland nearly five years ago, and had died two years ago himself, suddenly, having made no provisions; that Schneider kept and continued to treat him for two more years; that he did not cure him, but had helped him greatly and that, finally, upon his own wish and upon a certain chance circumstance, he had now sent him to Russia.

The general was very much surprised.

"And you have no one in Russia, absolutely no one?" he asked.

"No one now, but I hope ... Plus, I have received a letter ..."

"At the least," interrupted the general, not having heard the bit about the letter, "you've been trained for something, and your illness will not prevent you from taking, for instance, some easy post, in some kind of service?"

"Oh, it would certainly not prevent me. And as for the post, I should be more than glad of it, for I want to see what I am fit for. I have, after all, been studying steadily all these four years, though not quite properly, but following his special system, and in the process I managed to read a great many Russian books."

"Russian books? Then, you know grammar and can write without mistakes?"

"Oh, I can, very much so."

"Excellent, sir; and your handwriting?"

"My handwriting is outstanding. There, perhaps, is where my talent lies after all; there, I am simply a calligraphist. Here, let me write you something as a sample," the prince said eagerly.

"Do me the favor. Indeed, it's quite essential. . . . And I like this readiness of yours, Prince, you are very nice, I must say."

"You've got such lovely writing implements, and what a lot of pencils, what a lot of quills, and what thick, lovely paper . . . And what a lovely study you have! I know that landscape, it's a Swiss scene. I'm sure the artist painted it from nature, and I'm sure that I've seen the place: it's in the canton of Uri . . ."

"Very probably, though it was bought here. Ganya, give the prince some paper; here are quills and paper, here, use this little table if you please. What's this?" The general turned to Ganya, who had meanwhile taken from his portfolio and handed him a large photograph. "Ah! Nastasya Filippovna! Was it she herself, she sent it to you herself, was it she?" he asked Ganya eagerly and with great curiosity.

"Just now, when I went with my good wishes, she gave it to me. I've been asking for it a long time. I don't know whether it wasn't a hint on her part at my coming empty-handed, without a gift, on such a day," added Ganya, smiling unpleasantly.

"Oh, no," interrupted the general with conviction. "Honestly, what a way of thinking you have! As if she'd hint . . . And she's not at all mercenary. Besides, what would you give her: why, you'd need thousands! Unless perhaps your portrait? Speaking of which, hasn't she asked you for a portrait yet?"

"No, not yet; and maybe she never will. You remember about this evening, of course, Ivan Fyodorovich? You are one of those particularly invited, after all."

"I remember, I remember, of course, and I'll be there. I should think so, her birthday, twenty-five years old! Hm! . . . Do you know, Ganya, I'll let you in on it, be prepared. She promised Afanasy Ivanovich and me that at the party this evening she would say the final word: to be or not to be! So mind you, be ready."

Ganya was suddenly so abashed that he even turned a little pale.

"Did she say that positively?" he asked, and his voice seemed to quiver.

"She gave her word these three days ago. We both pressed her so much that we got it out of her. Only she asked not to tell you beforehand."

The general examined Ganya intently; Ganya's embarrassment, evidently, did not please him.

"Remember, Ivan Fyodorovich," Ganya said uneasily and hesitantly, "that she has given me complete freedom of choice until the moment she decides her own affairs, and that even then I have the last word . . ."

"Then do you mean . . . then do you mean . . ." The general was suddenly alarmed.

"I don't mean anything."

"Mercy, what do you intend to do to us?"

"But I'm not refusing. Perhaps I haven't put it right . . ."

"The idea of you refusing!" the general uttered with vexation, not even caring to check the vexation. "It's not a question of your *not* refusing, dear fellow, rather, it's a question of your readiness, of the pleasure, the happiness with which you will receive her promise . . . What's going on with you at home?"

"What does that matter? At home, everything is under my control, only Father is playing the fool as usual, but he's become a perfect disgrace, you know; I don't speak to him anymore, but still, I have him firmly in grip, and honestly, if it were not for Mother, I'd show him the door. Mother does nothing but cry, of course; my sister's fuming, but I told them straight out at last that I'm master of my fate and that at home, I want . . . obedience. At least, I spelled that all out for my sister, in front of Mother."

"Dear fellow, I still fail to grasp," observed the general thoughtfully, shrugging his shoulders somewhat and spreading his hands a bit. "Recently, Nina Alexandrovna, too—when she came, remember?—keeps sighing and moaning. 'What's the matter?' I ask. Turns out, it seems like *dishonor* to them. Now where's the dishonor, may I ask? Who can reproach Nastasya Filippovna with anything or bring anything against her? Surely not that she was together with Totsky? But that's such nonsense, under the well-known circumstances, especially! 'You wouldn't allow her in the company of your daughters?' she says. Well! There's a thing! That's Nina Alexandrovna for you! I mean, how can she not understand, how can she not understand . . ."

"Her own position?" Ganya prompted the embarrassed general. "She understands; don't be angry with her. Incidentally, I let her have it right there about sticking her nose in other people's business. But, still, the only thing that's kept it all together at home till now is that the last word hasn't been said yet, but the storm's coming. If the last word is said today, it would seem, it'll all come out."

The prince heard this entire conversation sitting in the corner writing his calligraphic sample. He finished, approached the table, and presented his page.

"So that's Nastasya Filippovna!" he uttered, looking attentively and with curiosity at the photograph. "Remarkably good-looking!' he added immediately with warmth. Indeed, the portrait showed a woman of exceptional beauty. She had been photographed in a black silk dress of an extremely simple and elegant cut; her hair, which appeared to be dark auburn, was arranged in a simple, homespun way; her eyes were dark and deep, her brow pensive; the expression of her face passionate and as if disdainful. She was rather thin in the face, perhaps, and pale . . . Ganya and the general looked at the prince in surprise.

"How's that, Nastasya Filippovna? Surely you don't know Nastasya Filippovna already?" asked the general.

"Yes; only one day in Russia, but I already know a beauty like that," answered the prince, and at once told of his encounter with Rogozhin and recounted his whole story.

"There's news for you!" again fretted the general, having listened to the story with the greatest attention, and looked searchingly at Ganya.

"Most likely nothing but disgraceful tomfoolery," muttered Ganya, who was also somewhat disconcerted. "A merchant's pup out carousing. I've heard something about him before."

"And so have I, dear fellow," put in the general. "At the time, after the earring incident, Nastasya Filippovna told the whole story. But it's a different matter now. There may really be a million there and ... passion, a disgraceful passion perhaps, but there's still a whiff of passion about it, and it's well known what these gentlemen are capable of in their intoxication! ... Hm! ... I hope no sort of funny episode will come of it!" the general concluded thoughtfully.

"Are you afraid of the million?" Ganya grinned.

"And you're not, of course?"

"How did he strike you, Prince," Ganya suddenly addressed him, "is he a serious person or simply a rogue? Your own opinion?"

There was something peculiar taking place in Ganya as he asked this question. Just as if some new and peculiar idea was kindled in his brain and flashed impatiently in his eyes. For his part, the general, who was genuinely and sincerely worried, also looked sideways at the prince, though apparently not expecting much from his answer.

"I don't know, how shall I put it," answered the prince, "only it seemed to me that there was a great deal of passion in him, and even a sort of unhealthy passion. And he himself seems still quite ill, too. It's quite possible that he'll be laid up again in the first few days in Petersburg, especially if he goes carousing."

"Really? That's what it seemed to you?" the general latched on to this idea.

"Yes, so it seemed."

"And yet, episodes of that kind may happen not just in a few days, but even before the evening, this very day, perhaps, something may yet occur," said Ganya to the general with a wry laugh.

"Hm! ... Of course ... Very likely, and then it will all depend on how it strikes her," said the general.

"And you do know what she's like sometimes?"

"Like what do you mean?" The general again reared up, having reached a level of extreme perturbation. "Listen, Ganya, please don't contradict her much today and do try to be, you know ... in a word, pleasing ... Hm! ... Why are you making that wry face? Listen, Gavrila Ardalionovich, it would now be to the point, and very much to the point, to say: what is it that we're taking the trouble for? You understand, as regards any personal benefit of my own that is at stake here, I'm long since taken care of; one way or the other, I'll settle the matter to my advantage. Totsky has made up his mind once and for all and I am perfectly secure. And so if there's anything I want now, it's simply your own advantage. Judge for yourself; don't you trust me? Besides, you're a man . . . a man . . . in a word, a man of sense, and I was counting on you . . . and in the present case . . . that's . . . that's . . ."

"That's the main thing," Ganya finished, again coming to the assistance of the general in his difficulty and twisting his lips into a most malignant smile, which he no longer wished to conceal. He looked with his feverish gaze straight into the general's eyes, as though wanting the latter to read in his gaze everything that was in his mind. The general turned crimson and exploded.

"That's right, sense is the main thing!" he concurred, looking sharply at Ganya. "Well, you're a funny person, Gavrila Ardalionovich! You seem downright pleased, I see, about this little merchant boy, as a way out for you. But it's precisely by your good sense that you ought to have been guided here from the outset; you ought to understand here and . . . and act honestly and straightforwardly with both sides, or else . . . give warning beforehand, so that others aren't compromised, especially since there was plenty of time for it, and even now there's still plenty (the general raised his eyebrows significantly), despite the fact that there are only a few hours left . . . Do you understand? Understand? Do you want to or don't you, when it comes down to it? If you don't want to, then say so—you're welcome to it. No one, Gavrila Ardalionovich, is holding you back, no one is dragging you against your will into a trap, if you see a trap here, that is."

"I want to," uttered Ganya in a low but firm voice, dropped his eyes and sullenly fell silent.

The general was satisfied. He had lost his temper, but, evidently, already regretted having gone so far. He turned suddenly to the prince and his face seemed to betray an uneasy consciousness that the prince had been there and had heard everything. But he was instantly reassured: one glance at the prince was enough to reassure anyone perfectly.

"Oho!" exclaimed the general, looking at the calligraphic specimen proffered by the prince, "why, that's a model copy! And an exceptional one! Take a look, Ganya, what talent!"

On the thick sheet of vellum the prince had written in medieval Russian script the phrase: "The humble Abbot Pafnuty has put his hand thereto."

"This," the prince explained with extraordinary pleasure and eagerness, "this is the Abbot Pafnuty's own signature, copied from a fourteenth-century manuscript. Our old abbots and bishops used to sign their names beautifully, and with what taste at times, with what effort! Don't you at least have the Pogodin edition,[20] General? And here, I've written in another script: this is the large round French script of the last century, some letters were even written differently, it was the script of the marketplace, the script of the professional scribes, which I've taken from their samples (I had one)—you'll admit that it is not without its merits. Look at these round *d*'s and *a*'s. I have transposed the French character onto the Russian letters, which is very difficult, but it turned out well. And here is another splendid and original script, this here phrase: 'Diligence overcomes all obstacles.'[21] It's a Russian script, a scrivener's, or if you will, a military scribe's. This is how one writes an official state letter to an important person, also a round script, a nice, *black* script, written thickly but with what wonderful taste. A calligrapher would never allow such flourishes, or, better said, these attempts at flourishes, these unfinished half-tails—notice—but on the whole, you see, it does give it character, and indeed, the very soul of the military scribe comes through: he would like to let himself go, and his talent is crying out for it, but the military collar is tightly buttoned, the discipline comes out in the handwriting—it's lovely! I was amazed recently by such a specimen. I found it by chance, and fancy where—in Switzerland! Now this is a simple, ordinary English

20. An album of lithographs published in 1840 by the historian M. P. Pogodin containing the reproductions of samples of Old Church Slavonic scripts from the eleventh to the eighteenth centuries.

21. As would have been common knowledge to Dostoevsky's contemporaries, this motto was printed on a medal issued in 1838 in honor of General Kleinmikhel after he had supervised the rebuilding of the fire-damaged Winter Palace. In the 1840s, Kleinmikhel was responsible for building Russia's ambitious railway network (at the cost of many lives). Like General Epanchin, he was an uneducated man who had risen through the ranks on sheer drive, and his name virtually stood for zeal in the civil service.

script of the purest kind: elegance can go no further, it's all exquisiteness, tiny beads, pearls; it's finished; but here's a variation, and again a French one, I got it from a French commercial traveler: the same script as the English but the black strokes are a trifle blacker and thicker than in the English, and so the proportion of light and dark is spoiled; and notice too: the oval is different, a trifle rounder and plus the flourish is allowed, and a flourish—that's a most perilous thing! A flourish requires extraordinary taste; but if only it's successful, if only the right proportion is found, then such a script is so incomparable that you can even fall in love with it."

"Oho! What fine points you go into," laughed the general, "why, my good fellow, you are not simply a calligrapher, you are an artist! Eh, Ganya?"

"Marvelous," said Ganya, "and even with a cognizance of his vocation," he added, laughing derisively.

"Go on, laugh, but there's a career here," said the general. "Do you know, Prince, to what personage we'll get you to write now? Why, you can count on thirty-five rubles a month from the start. But it's half-past twelve," he concluded, glancing at the clock. "To business, Prince, for I must make haste and perhaps I may not see you again today. Sit down for a minute; I've already explained that I'm not able to receive you often; but I sincerely wish to help you a little, a little, of course, meaning in the most essential form, and then for the rest you must do as you please. I'll find you a little post in the office, not a hard one, but needing accuracy. Now, sir, for the next thing. In the home, that is to say the family, of Gavrila Ardalionovich Ivolgin, this young friend of mine here with whom I have the pleasure of acquainting you, his dear mother and sister have cleared two or three furnished rooms in their apartments and let them, with board and servants, to lodgers with excellent references. I am sure Nina Alexandrovna will accept my recommendation. For you it will be more than a godsend, Prince, for one thing, because you will not be alone, but, so to speak, in the bosom of a family, and in my view, you ought not to be alone at first in such a metropolis as Petersburg. Nina Alexandrovna, the dear mother, and Varvara Ardalionovna, the dear sister of Gavrila Ardalionovich, are ladies for whom I have the greatest respect. Nina Alexandrovna is the wife of a retired general who was a comrade of mine when I was first in the service, but with whom, owing to certain circumstances, I've broken off relations, which, however, does not prevent me from respecting him in his way. I tell you all this, Prince, so you may understand that I recommend you personally, so to speak, and consequently am responsible for you, as it were. The terms are extremely moderate, and I hope that your salary will soon be quite sufficient to meet them. Of course, a man needs pocket-money too, if only a little, but you won't be angry with me, Prince, if I tell you that you would do better to avoid pocket-money, and indeed, money in your pocket in general. I say this on the basis of my impression of you. But as your purse is completely empty now, allow me, for a start, to offer you these twenty-five rubles here. Of course, we will settle accounts, and if you are as sincere and genuine a person as you appear from your words, then no difficulties could arise between us on that account. And if I take such an interest in you, it is because I actually have a certain aim in mind for you; you will know of it later. You see, I am perfectly straightforward with you; I hope, Ganya, that you have nothing against installing the prince in your apartments?"

"Oh, on the contrary! And dear Mother will be delighted . . ." affirmed Ganya politely and obligingly.

"You've only one room occupied, I think. That, what's his name, Ferd . . . Fer . . ."

"Ferdyshchenko."

"That's right; I don't like your Ferdyshchenko, he is some kind of sleazy clown. And I can't understand why Nastasya Filippovna encourages him so. Is he really a relation of hers?"

"Oh no, that's only a joke! There's not a whit of relationship."

"Well, the devil take him! Well, what of it, Prince, are you satisfied?"

"I thank you, General, you have acted like an exceptionally kind man in your treatment of me, especially since I did not even ask for help; I don't say that out of pride; I really didn't know where to lay my head. Although, to tell the truth, I'd been invited by Rogozhin just now."

"Rogozhin? Oh, no; I would give you some fatherly, or if you prefer, friendly, advice, to forget about Mr. Rogozhin. And altogether, I would advise you to stick to the family that you're about to enter."

"Since you are so kind," the prince began, "I have one piece of business. I have received the news . . ."

"Well, excuse me," interrupted the general, "I haven't a minute more now. I'll tell Elizaveta Prokofyevna about you presently: if she wishes to receive you at once (I will try to recommend you in that light) I advise you to make use of the opportunity and gain her good graces, for Elizaveta Prokofyevna can be of great use to you; you share the name, after all. If she doesn't wish to, don't seek it, some other time, perhaps. And you, Ganya, take a look at these bills in the meantime. Fedoseev and I were struggling with them recently. You mustn't forget to include them . . ."

The general went out, and so the prince did not have a chance to tell him of his business, about which he had tried in vain to speak for practically the fourth time. Ganya lit a cigarette and offered another to the prince; the prince accepted it, but refrained from conversation for fear of disturbing him, and began to survey the study. But Ganya scarcely glanced at the sheet covered with figures, which the general had indicated to him. He was preoccupied; Ganya's smile, his expression, his pensiveness weighed on the prince even more when they were left alone. Suddenly, he approached the prince; at that moment, the latter was again standing over the portrait of Nastasya Filippovna and examining it.

"So you like a woman like that, Prince?" he asked him suddenly, looking at him piercingly. And it seemed as if he had some peculiar intention.

"It's a wonderful face!" answered the prince, "and I am sure her fate is not of the ordinary sort. The face is cheerful, but she has suffered terribly, hasn't she? Her eyes tell one that, these two little bones, two points under her eyes at the top of the cheeks. It's a proud face, terribly proud, and I don't know whether she is kind. Ah, if she were! That would redeem it all!"

"And would *you* marry such a woman?" Ganya went on, his feverish gaze fixed upon him.

"I can't marry anyone, I am not healthy," said the prince.

"And would Rogozhin marry her? What do you think?"

"Well, why not? One could get married tomorrow, I think; he'd marry her, and after a week, perhaps, he'd cut her throat."

The prince had no sooner uttered this than Ganya shuddered so violently that the prince nearly cried out.

"What's the matter?" he asked, seizing his arm.

"Your excellency! His highness begs you to come to her highness," the footman announced, appearing in the doorway. The prince went off after the footman.

IV

All three Epanchin daughters were healthy young ladies, blooming, tall, with magnificent shoulders, well-developed chests, strong, almost masculine arms, and, naturally, as a consequence of their strength and healthiness, they were sometimes fond of a good meal, which fact they had no desire of concealing. Their mamma, Generaless Elizaveta Prokofyevna, sometimes looked askance at the frankness of their appetite, but since some of her views, for all the outward show of respect with which they were received by her daughters, had long since lost the initial and unquestioned authority they once had among them—even to the point that the established unanimous conclave of three girls had begun thoroughly to gain the upper hand—the generaless found it, in consequence, more expedient, for the sake of her own dignity, to yield without argument. Admittedly, her temperament was fairly often disobedient and did not follow the dictates of her good sense; with every year, Elizaveta Prokofyevna was becoming more capricious and impatient, she had even become somewhat eccentric, but as her rather well-trained and submissive husband always remained at hand, any excess and pent-up sentiment was vented upon him, after which domestic harmony was restored again and all went better than one could wish.

The generaless, incidentally, had not lost her appetite herself, and as a rule, at half past twelve, partook with her daughters of an ample lunch that was almost like a dinner. The young ladies each drank a cup of coffee in their beds even earlier, at exactly ten o'clock, upon waking. They had become fond of it and it became a custom for all. At half past twelve the table was laid in the little dining room next to their mamma's rooms, and occasionally, even the general himself appeared at this familial and intimate lunch, time allowing. Besides tea, coffee, cheese, honey, butter, a special sort of pancake beloved by the generaless, cutlets, and so on, strong, hot bouillon was also served. On the morning our story began, the whole family was gathered together in the dining room waiting for the general, who had promised to appear at half past twelve. If he had been even a moment late, he would have been sent for immediately; but he made his appearance punctually. Going up to greet his wife and kiss her hand, he noticed something excessively peculiar in her face. And although he had already had a presentiment the night before that it would be just so today on account of an "incident" (as he was wont to put it himself), and had been uneasy on this score as he fell asleep yesterday, nonetheless he now felt trepidation again. His daughters went up to kiss him; and though they were not angry with him, still, there seemed to be something peculiar here, too. Admittedly, the general had, owing to certain circumstances, become excessively suspicious of late; but as he was an experienced and adept father and husband, he promptly took measures.

We will perhaps do little harm to the vividness of our story if we pause here and resort to the aid of some clarification in order to establish directly and most precisely those relations and circumstances in which we find General Epanchin's family at the beginning of our tale. We have just said that the general, though not a man of much education, but on the contrary, as he personally described himself, a "self-taught man," was nonetheless an experienced husband and adept father. For instance, he made it a principle not to hurry his daughters into marriage—that is, not to "hover over" them and not to bother them unduly with the anguish of his parental desire for their happiness, as so unwittingly and naturally happens everywhere you look, even in the most sensible families in which grown-up daughters are accumulating. He even succeeded in bringing over Elizaveta Prokofyevna to this principle, though it was a difficult business—difficult because it was unnatural; but the general's arguments were exceedingly weighty and founded on palpable facts. Moreover, left entirely to their own will and decision, the maidens, naturally, would be bound, finally, to realize their position for themselves, and then the business would take off, for they would set to it willingly, putting aside their caprices and excessive discrimination; all that would be left for the parents to do would be to keep an unflagging and, as far as possible, unnoticeable watch over them, that they might make no strange choice and show no unnatural inclination, and then, seizing a fitting moment, help with all their strength and guide the business with all their influence. Finally, there was the mere fact that, with every year, for instance, their fortune and social consequence grew in geometrical progression; consequently, the more time went by, the more the advantage the girls gained as brides. But amongst all these incontestable facts appeared another fact: the eldest daughter, Alexandra, suddenly and almost quite unexpectedly (as these things always happen) reached the age of twenty-five. Almost at the same moment Afanasy Ivanovich Totsky, a man of the best society, with the highest connections, and extraordinary wealth, again discovered his long-cherished desire to marry. He was a man of five-and-fifty, of a refined temperament and extraordinarily exquisite taste. He wanted to marry well; he was an exceptional admirer of feminine beauty. As he had been for some time on terms of most extraordinary friendship with General Epanchin, especially strengthened by their joint involvement in certain financial enterprises, he had broached the subject, so to speak, by asking his friendly advice and guidance: would a proposal of marriage to one of his daughters be considered? The quiet and happy course of General Epanchin's family was about to experience a conspicuous upheaval.

The beauty of the family was, as we have said already, indisputably the youngest, Aglaia. But even Totsky, a man of extreme egoism, realized that it was useless for him to look in that direction and that Aglaia was not for him. Perhaps the somewhat blind love and the over-ardent affection of the sisters exaggerated the state of affairs, but they had settled among themselves, in the most sincere fashion, that Aglaia's fate was not to be an ordinary fate, but the highest possible ideal of earthly bliss. Aglaia's future husband was to be a paragon of all perfections and achievements, not to mention the possessor of vast wealth. The sisters had even considered between themselves, without wasting many words over it, the possibility, if need be, of a sacrifice on their parts for the sake of Aglaia: her dowry was to be colossal and beyond comparison. The parents knew of this compact on the part of the two elder sisters, and so when Totsky asked advice, they had hardly any doubts that one of the elder sisters would certainly not refuse to crown their hopes, especially as Afanasy Ivanovich would not make difficulties on the score of the dowry. As for Totsky's proposal, the general, with his usual understanding of life, immediately attached the greatest value to it. Since, owing to certain special circumstances, Totsky was obliged to be extremely circumspect in his behavior, and was merely sounding out the matter, the parents also presented their daughters with only the remotest suppositions for their consideration. In response to this they received the announcement—at the very least, reassuring, if equally indefinite—that the eldest, Alexandra, would, perhaps, not refuse. Though she was a young lady of strong will, she was kind, sensible, and exceptionally easygoing; it was conceivable that she might be perfectly happy to marry Totsky, and if she gave her word, she would keep to it honorably. She was not fond of show, and not only posed no threat of fuss and violent upheaval, but could even have brought sweetness and peace into her husband's life. She was very handsome, though not particularly striking. What could be better for Totsky?

And yet the matter still continued to be managed tentatively. It had been mutually and amicably agreed between Totsky and the general that any formal and irrevocable steps were to be avoided. Even the parents had not yet begun to speak with their daughters quite openly; and there seemed to be some initial signs of disharmony: Generaless Epanchin, the matriarch of the family, was for some reason becoming dissatisfied, and that was very important. There was a circumstance that stood in the way of everything, one intricate and troublesome happenstance, which might irrevocably ruin the whole business.

This intricate and troublesome "happenstance" (as Totsky himself expressed it) had begun a very long time ago, some eighteen years back. In the neighborhood of one of Afanasy Ivanovich's most prosperous estates, in one of the central provinces, lived in poverty one petty landowner and most wretched country squire. This was a man remarkable for his incessant and absurd bad luck—a certain retired officer from a good aristocratic family, even finer than Totsky's own in this respect, by the name of Filip Alexandrovich Barashkov. In debt and mortgaged to the hilt, he finally managed, after some excruciating, almost heroic efforts, to bring his small household into a more or less satisfactory state. At the smallest success he was extraordinarily heartened. Having taken heart and radiant with hope, he absented himself for a few days to his little district town to see and, if possible, come to an understanding with one of his chief creditors. On the third day after his arrival in the town, the elder of his little village appeared before him, on horseback, with a singed cheek and a scorched beard, and announced that "the homestead had burned down" the day before, at the height of midday, and moreover "it has pleased the lady to burn too, while the little children were unhurt." Even Barashkov, accustomed as he was to the buffeting of fortune, could not bear this surprise; he went out of his mind and died in delirium a month later. The burned-down property, with its peasants wandered off to the four corners of the earth, was sold to pay his debts; as for the two little girls, six and seven years old, Barashkov's children, Afanasy Ivanovich Totsky, in the generosity of his heart, undertook their maintenance and upbringing. They were brought up with the children of Totsky's steward, a retired civil servant with a large family, and moreover a German. Soon, only one girl, Nastasya, was left, for the younger one died of whooping cough; as for Totsky, he lived abroad and soon completely forgot about both of them. Once, some five years later, it occurred to him on his way elsewhere to look in on his estate, and he suddenly noticed, in his country house, in the family of his German, a charming child, a girl about twelve, playful, sweet, clever and promising to become extremely beautiful; on that subject Afanasy Ivanovich was an unerring connoisseur. That time, he only spent a few days on his estate, but he had time to leave some instructions; a significant change took place in the girl's education: a respectable and elderly Swiss governess, experienced in the higher education of young ladies, cultivated and competent to teach various subjects besides French, was engaged. She was installed in the country house, and the education of little Nastasya took on extraordinary dimensions. Exactly four years later this education came to end; the governess left, and a lady came for Nastya—also some sort of landowner and also a neighbor of one of Mr. Totsky's estates, but in another remote province—and took Nastya away with her, on the instructions and authority of Afanasy Ivanovich. On this small estate there happened to be a wooden house, just recently built, though it was small; it was particularly elegantly furnished, and the little village, too, was appropriately, as it were, called Delightful Wick. The landed lady brought Nastasya straight to this quiet little house, and as she was a childless widow, living less than a verst away, she installed herself in the house with Nastasya. Besides Nastasya, there arrived an old housekeeper and an experienced young maid. In the house she found musical instruments, a choice library for a young girl, pictures, engravings, pencils, paints and brushes, a marvelous thoroughbred lapdog, and within a fortnight, Afanasy Ivanovich himself made his appearance . . . From that time on, he became somehow particularly fond of this remote little thorp of his in the steppes, visited every summer, would stay two, even three months at a stretch, and a fairly long time passed in that manner, some four years, in tranquillity and happiness, with elegance and taste.

It happened once at the beginning of winter, four months after one of Totsky's summer visits to Delightful Wick, which had on that occasion lasted only a fortnight, that a rumor was circulated, or, better said, a rumor somehow reached Nastasya Filippovna, that Afanasy Ivanovich was going to be married in Petersburg to a beauty, a rich and highborn one—in a word, that he was in fact making a substantial and brilliant match. The rumor later turned out to be not quite correct in all the details: the marriage was then only a project, and everything was still very indefinite, but nonetheless, from that point on, Nastasya Filippovna's fate somehow took a drastic turn. She suddenly displayed extraordinary determination and discovered quite unexpected strength of will. Without wasting time on reflection, she left her little rural house and suddenly came to Petersburg, straight to Totsky, all by her little lonesome. He was amazed, and would have spoken to her; but he found suddenly, almost from the first word, that it was necessary to abandon completely the language, the intonations, the logic, the past themes of agreeable and refined conversation that had been made use of hitherto with such success—everything, everything, everything! Before him was an entirely different woman, not in the least resembling the one he had known till then and had left only that July in Delightful Wick.

This new woman turned out, in the first place, to know and understand an extraordinarily great deal—so much so that one had to marvel deeply about where she might have acquired such information, developed such definite ideas. (Could it really have been from her young girl's library?) And if that wasn't enough, she even understood an extraordinarily great deal from the legal point of view and had a positive knowledge, if not of the world, at least of how certain things in the world are done; secondly, this was an entirely different temperament from before, that is to say, it was not something timid, schoolgirlishly indeterminate, sometimes charming in its original playfulness and naïveté, sometimes melancholy and pensive, astonished, mistrustful, tearful and agitated.

No: here was an extraordinary and surprising creature who laughed in his face and stung him with the most venomous sarcasms, openly declaring that she had never had any feeling in her heart for him ex-

cept the deepest contempt, contempt to the point of nausea, which
had come upon her immediately after her first surprise. This new
woman announced that it was, in the full sense of the expression, a
matter of absolute indifference to her if he at once married anyone he
chose, but that she had come to prohibit this marriage, to prohibit it
from spite, simply because she wanted to, and, consequently, it must be
so—"well, if only that I may have a good laugh at you, because I, too,
finally, want to laugh now."

That at least was how she expressed herself; she did not perhaps
utter all that was on her mind. But while this new Nastasya Filippovna
laughed and spelled all this out, Afanasy Ivanovich was deliberating
the matter to himself, and, as far as he could, bringing his somewhat
shattered thoughts to order. This deliberation took him some no little
time; he was weighing things and making up his mind for almost a fortnight; but at the end of the fortnight he had reached a decision. The
thing was that Afanasy Ivanovich was at the time already nearing fifty,
and he was, to the highest degree, an established and settled man. His
standing in the world and in society had been long, long ago secured
on the most firm foundations. He loved and prized himself, his peace
and comfort, above everything in the world, as befits a man who is upstanding to the highest degree. Not the least disturbance, not the least
instability could be admitted into that which had taken an entire life to
establish and obtained such magnificent form. On the other hand, his
experience and deep insight told Totsky very quickly and exceptionally correctly that he had to do with a creature entirely beyond the
pale, that it is just such a creature who would not only threaten but
certainly act, and, what was most important, would decidedly stop at
nothing, especially as there was decidedly nothing in life that was dear
to her and so it would not even be possible to tempt her. Evidently,
there was something else at work here, one suspected something
churning within her spirit and her heart—something like romantic indignation, God knows at whom and over what, some kind of an insatiable feeling of contempt, entirely out of all bounds—in a word,
something highly ridiculous and inadmissible in upstanding society,
the encounter with which would constitute a true scourge from above
for any upstanding person. Of course, with Totsky's wealth and connections, one might have committed some trifling and entirely innocent piece of villainy in order to rid oneself of the unpleasantness. On

the other hand, it was evident that Nastasya Filippovna was hardly in a position to do much harm, in a legal sense, for instance; she could not even create a scandal of any consequence, because it was so easy to contain her. But all that was only applicable in the case that Nastasya Filippovna decided to behave like everyone, and like one behaves generally in such cases, without falling too eccentrically out of the norm. But it was just here that Totsky's unfailing eye served him well: he managed to perceive that Nastasya Filippovna herself fully realized how harmless she was in the juridical sense, but that there was something very different on her mind and ... in her flashing eyes. Valuing nothing, least of all herself (it needed much intelligence and insight to perceive in that moment that she had long ceased to value her fate, and for him, skeptic and worldly cynic such as he was, to believe in the earnestness of this feeling), Nastasya Filippovna was quite capable of ruining herself, irrevocably and disgracefully, with Siberia and a sentence of hard labor, only to humiliate the man for whom she cherished such an inhuman aversion. Afanasy Ivanovich never concealed the fact that he was somewhat of a coward, or, better put, in the highest degree conservative. If he had known, for instance, that he would be murdered at the altar on his wedding day, or that anything of that sort, exceedingly unseemly, ridiculous, unpleasant in society, would happen, he would certainly have been afraid; however, not so much of being killed or wounded, or of having someone spit in his face in public, etc., etc., but of its happening to him in such an unnatural and unpleasant form. But that was just what Nastasya Filippovna portended, though she still said nothing about it; he knew that she had studied him and understood him thoroughly, and she knew with what to strike him a blow. And as his marriage was still at the stage of a mere intention, Afanasy Ivanovich came to terms with it and gave way to Nastasya Filippovna.

His decision was helped by one other circumstance: it was difficult to imagine the degree to which this new Nastasya Filippovna did not resemble the former one in face. Formerly, she had been only a very pretty young girl, but now ... For a long time Totsky could not forgive himself the fact that he had gazed for four years and failed to discern. Admittedly, it is also a significant factor when, on both sides, all of a sudden, a radical inner change takes place. He remembered, however, that there had also been moments in the past when strange ideas had sometimes come into his head, at the sight, for instance, of those eyes: there was as if a presentiment in them of some kind of deep and mysterious darkness. Those eyes gazed—just as if they were asking a riddle. In the last two years, he had often wondered at the change in the color of Nastasya Filippovna's face; she was becoming terribly pale and—strange to say—was even handsomer for it. Totsky—who, like all gentlemen who have lived freely in their day, had initially viewed with contempt how cheaply he had obtained this inexperienced soul—had lately felt rather doubtful of his attitude. In any case, he had already made up his mind in the previous spring to lose no time in marrying Nastasya Filippovna off, in an excellent match and with a good dowry, to some sensible and upstanding gentleman serving in another province. (Oh, how horribly and how maliciously Nastasya Filippovna now laughed at this idea!) But now Afanasy Ivanovich, fascinated by the novelty, even imagined that he might again exploit this woman. He decided to settle Nastasya Filippovna in Petersburg and to surround her with luxurious comfort. If not one thing, he would have the other: with Nastasya Filippovna, one might cut a dash and even wax vainglorious in a certain known circle. And Afanasy Ivanovich did so greatly prize his reputation in that line.

Five years of life in Petersburg had passed since then, and of course much became clear in that time. Totsky's position was not a comforting one; the worst of it was that, having been once intimidated, he could never quite put his mind at ease afterward. He was afraid—and did not even know himself of what—he was simply afraid of Nastasya Filippovna. For some time, during the first two years, he almost began to suspect that Nastasya Filippovna wanted to marry him herself, but did not speak from her extraordinary pride and was obstinately waiting for his proposal. It would have been a strange pretension; Afanasy Ivanovich furrowed his brow, frowned and brooded heavily. To his great and (such is the heart of man!) somewhat unpleasant surprise, he was suddenly convinced by something that happened that, even if he made the offer, he would not be accepted. For a long time he did not understand this. It seemed to him that there was only one possible explanation, that the pride of the "offended and fantastic woman" had reached such a frenzied pitch that she would rather once express her contempt by refusing him than secure her position forever and attain inaccessible heights of grandeur. The worst of it was that Nastasya Filippovna had gained the upper hand to a terrible extent. She was not susceptible to mercenary considerations either, not even very large ones, and though she accepted the luxury offered her, she lived very modestly and had accumulated almost nothing during those five years. Afanasy Ivanovich ventured upon very subtle tactics to break his chains: imperceptibly and artfully, by means of adroit assistance, he began to tempt her with a variety of the most ideal temptations. But these paragons in the flesh—princes, hussars, secretaries from the embassies, poets, novelists, even Socialists—none of them made the least impression on Nastasya Filippovna, as though she had a stone in place of a heart and her feelings had been withered and dried up once and for all. She lived a rather secluded life, read, even studied, and was fond of music. She had few acquaintances; she was wont to associate with some poor and ridiculous wives of petty officials, knew a couple of actresses of some sort and some old women, was very fond of the large family of a respectable teacher, and in this family she was much loved and given a warm reception. Quite often, in the evenings, five or six acquaintances would gather at her house, and no more. Totsky took care to visit her very frequently. Recently, not without some effort, General Epanchin had made Nastasya Filippovna's acquaintance. At the same time, quite easily and with no effort whatsoever, a young civil servant named Ferdyshchenko, a very unseemly and sleazy clown who affected to be merry and was wont to drink, had made her acquaintance as well. Another acquaintance was a strange young man called Ptitsyn, modest, neat, and highly polished, who had risen from poverty and become a moneylender. And, at last, Gavrila Ardalionovich made her acquaintance too . . . In the end, Nastasya Filippovna gained a strange reputation: everyone had heard of her beauty, but that was all; no one had anything to boast of, no one had anything to tell. Such a reputation, her education, her elegant manners, her wit, all this confirmed Afanasy Ivanovich definitively in a certain plan of his. And here begins the moment at which General Epanchin began to take so active and exceptional a part in this story.

When Totsky had so courteously turned to him for his advice as a friend in regard to one of his daughters, he made a full and candid confession on the spot, in the most noble way. He revealed that he had made up his mind not to stop *at any means whatsoever* to gain his freedom; that he would not rest even if Nastasya Filippovna assured him herself that she would leave him entirely in peace for the future; that words were not enough for him, that he needed the fullest guarantees. They talked things over and determined to act together. Initially, it was decided to try the gentlest means and to play, so to speak, upon the "noble chords of her heart." They went together to Nastasya Filippovna, and Totsky began most directly by announcing the intolerable misery of his position; he blamed himself for everything; he said frankly that he could not repent of his original offense, for he was an inveterate sensualist and could not control himself, but that now he wanted to marry, and the whole fate of this highly respectable and socially distinguished marriage was in her hands; in a word, that he rested all his hopes on her noble heart. Then General Epanchin, in his role as the father, began to speak and he talked reasonably, avoided sentimentality, mentioned only that he fully admitted her right to decide Afanasy Ivanovich's fate, cleverly displayed his own humility, pointing out that the fate of his daughter, and perhaps of his two other daughters, now depended on her decision. To Nastasya Filippovna's question what it was, exactly, they wanted of her, Totsky with his previous, entirely bald directness confessed to her that she had given him such a scare five years before that he could not feel entirely at ease even now until Nastasya Filippovna married somebody herself. He added at once that his request would, of course, be absurd on his part, if he had not some foundation for it. He had observed quite well and ascertained for a fact that a young man of very good birth, living in the most respectable family, namely, Gavrila Ardalionovich Ivolgin, with whom she was acquainted and whom she received in her house, had long loved her with all the strength of his passion and would of course give half his life for the mere hope of winning her affection. Gavrila Ardalionovich himself had confessed as much to him, Afanasy Ivanovich, long ago, from friend to friend and in the purity of his young heart, and Ivan Fyodorovich, who had taken the young man under his wing, had long known of his passion as well. Finally, if only he, Afanasy Ivanovich, is not mistaken, the young man's love was long since known to Nastasya Filippovna herself, and he fancied indeed that she looked on it indulgently. Of course, it was harder for him than anyone to speak of this. But if it pleased Nastasya Filippovna to allow that aside from selfishness and a desire to arrange for his own comfort, he, Totsky, had at least some thought for her well-being, she would realize that it had for some time been strange and even painful for him to see her loneliness: that this was nothing but a vague gloom, a complete disbelief in the renewal of life, which might reawaken so wonderfully in love and in family, and thus take on new aims; that it was throwing away talents perhaps of the most brilliant kind, a willful reveling in melancholy, in a word, even a sort of romantic sentiment worthy neither of the good sense nor the noble heart of Nastasya Filippovna. Repeating once more that it was harder for him than for anyone else to speak of it, he concluded by saying he could not relinquish the hope that Nastasya Filippovna would not respond with contempt if he expressed his genuine desire to guarantee her future and offered her the sum of seventy-five thousand rubles. He added in explanation that the sum was already secured to her in his will in any case; in a word, that this was nothing like compensation of any sort . . . and, finally, why not allow and forgive in him a human desire to do something to ease his conscience, etc., etc., all that is usually said on the topic in such circumstances. Afanasy Ivanovich spoke at length and eloquently, filling in, so to speak, in passing, the very interesting information that he had not dropped a word about the seventy-five thousand before, and that not even Ivan Fyodorovich, sitting right there, had known of it; in a word, *no one* knew.

Nastasya Filippovna's answer astounded the two friends.

Not only did she show not even the slightest trace of her former derision, her former hostility and hatred, her former laughter, the mere recollection of which sent a cold shiver down Totsky's spine, but on the contrary, she seemed glad of the opportunity, finally, to speak with someone frankly and friend to friend. She confessed that she had long been wanting to ask for friendly advice and that only her pride had hindered her, and that now, when the ice had been broken, nothing could be better. With a melancholy smile at first, and then with a gay and boisterous laugh, she confessed that there could in any case be no such storm as in the past; that she had long since changed her view of things to some extent and although there was no change in her heart, still she had been compelled to admit many things as accomplished facts; what's done is done, the past is the past, and so she even found it strange that Afanasy Ivanovich still continued to be so apprehensive. Here she turned to Ivan Fyodorovich and with the air of deepest respect announced that she had long ago heard a great deal about his daughters and had long been in the habit of having deep and sincere respect for them. The mere thought that she could be in any way of service to them would seem to be a source of pride and happiness for her. It was true that she was heavy at heart and dreary, very dreary; Afanasy Ivanovich had guessed her dreams; she would have liked to find new life, if not in love then in family, having realized a new aim; but she could say practically nothing about Gavrila Ardalionovich. She fancied it was true that he loved her; she felt that she too might come to love him if she could believe in the firmness of his attachment. Incidentally, what she liked best of all was the fact that he worked, toiled, and supported the entire family by himself; but he was very young, even if sincere; the decision was a hard one. She had heard that he was a man of energy and pride, eager to have a career, eager to make it. She had heard too that Nina Alexandrovna Ivolgin, Gavrila Ardalionovich's mother, was an excellent and highly respected woman; that his sister, Varvara Ardalionovna, was a very remarkable and energetic young woman; she had heard much about her from Ptitsyn. She had heard that they bear their misfortunes cheerfully; she would very much like to make their acquaintance, but there was still the question, would they receive her into the family gladly? In general, she had nothing to say against the possibility of this marriage, but it would require a great deal of thinking about; she would beg them not to hurry her. As for the seventy-five thousand, there was no need for Afanasy Ivanovich to make such difficulties talking about it. She knew the value of money and would certainly take it. She thanked Afanasy Ivanovich for his delicacy, for the fact that he had kept it even from the general, and not just from Gavrila Ardalionovich, but then, why should he not know of it beforehand too? There was no need for her to be ashamed of this money on entering their family. In any case, she had no intention of apologizing to anyone for anything, and wished they should know it. She would not marry Gavrila Ardalionovich until she was certain that neither he nor his family had any hidden feeling on that account. In any case, she did not consider herself to blame in any way, and it would be better for Gavrila Ardalionovich to find out on what footing she had been living these five years in Petersburg, in what relation she stood to Afanasy Ivanovich, and whether she had put aside much capital. Finally, if she accepted the money now, it was not at all in payment for the dishonor of her maidenhood, for she was not to blame, but simply as a compensation for her disfigured fate.

Toward the end, she even grew so hot and angry laying all this out (which, indeed, was quite natural) that General Epanchin was very pleased and considered the matter settled; but Totsky, having once been frightened, did not entirely believe it now, and was for a long time afraid whether there might not be some snakes in the grass. However, the negotiations had begun: the point on which the whole scheme of the two friends rested, namely, the possibility of Nastasya Filippovna's becoming taken with Ganya, began gradually to grow clearer and be borne out, so that even Totsky began to believe at times in the possibility of success. Meanwhile, Nastasya Filippovna came to an understanding with Ganya; few words were said, as if her virtue suffered by it. She allowed him his love, however, and even sanctioned it, but announced insistently that she would not bind herself in any way; that up until the very day of the wedding (if a wedding should take place) she reserved for herself the right to say "no," even if it were in the very last hour; and she granted the exact same right to Ganya. Soon afterward, Ganya learned, through a helpful happenstance, that the ill will harbored by his entire family toward this marriage and toward Nastasya Filippovna, which manifested itself in unpleasant domestic scenes, was known to Nastasya Filippovna in great detail; she did not take up the subject with him, although he expected it daily. Indeed, we might say much more still of all the incidents and complications arising on account of this match and the negotiations for it; but we have gotten ahead of ourselves as it is, considering, all the more, that some of these complications appeared in the form of rumors that were far too vague. For instance, purportedly Totsky had found out from somewhere that Nastasya Filippovna had entered into some indefinite and secret understanding with the Epanchin girls—a wildly improbable rumor. But there was another rumor that he unwillingly believed, and he feared it to the point of nightmares: he had heard for certain that Nastasya Filippovna was supposedly aware to the fullest that Ganya was only marrying her for money; that Ganya had a black soul, mercenary, impatient, envious, and immeasurably, out of all proportion, vain; that though Ganya had really been passionately striving to conquer Nastasya Filippovna before, after the two friends had decided to exploit this passion—which had been initiated on both sides—for their own purposes, and to buy Ganya by selling Nastasya Filippovna to him for a lawful wife, he began to hate her like his own nightmare. Passion and hatred seemed to mingle strangely in his soul, and although after painful hesitation he finally gave his consent to marry the "foul woman," he vowed in his soul to make her pay bitterly for it and to "finish" her afterward, as he had supposedly put it himself. Nastasya Filippovna supposedly knew all this and was secretly hatching something. Totsky was in such a panic that he even gave up confiding his worries to Epanchin; but there were moments when, like a weak man, he would decidedly take heart again and quickly regain his spirits: extremely so, for instance, when Nastasya Filippovna finally gave her word to the two friends that in the evening, on her birthday, she would say her last word on the matter. On the other hand, the strangest and most improbable rumor, concerning the honorable Ivan Fyodorovich himself, appeared, alas!, to be more and more well-founded.

At first glance, it appeared to be the wildest drivel. It was difficult to believe that Ivan Fyodorovich, in his venerable old age, with his excellent sense and his thorough knowledge of the world, and all the rest of it, could have been tempted by Nastasya Filippovna himself—and, it would seem, to such an extent that this caprice had almost become a passion. But what he was hoping for in this situation—it was hard to even imagine; possibly for the complicity of Ganya himself. Totsky suspected something of the kind, at any rate; he suspected the existence of some almost tacit agreement, founded on a mutual insight, between the general and Ganya. Besides, it is well known that a man carried away by passion, especially if he is getting on in years, becomes completely blind and is ready to find hope where there is none; what's more, he loses his judgment and acts like a foolish child, though he be wise as Solomon. It was known that for Nastasya Filippovna's birthday, the general had procured some marvelous pearls, costing an immense sum, as a present from himself, and had a great deal of interest in this present, though he knew that Nastasya Filippovna was not a mercenary woman. On the eve of Nastasya Filippovna's birthday he was as if in a fever, though he ably concealed his state. It was of those very pearls that Generaless Epanchin had heard. Admittedly, Elizaveta Prokofyevna had begun to experience her husband's flightiness a long time ago, and had even partly grown accustomed to it; but it was impossible to let such an incident pass: the rumor of the pearls interested her in the extreme. The general detected this ahead of time; certain little words had been said the night before; he foresaw a momentous discussion and was afraid of it. That was why he was particularly unwilling, on the morning on which our story begins, to go have lunch in the bosom of his family. Even before the prince's appearance, he had meant to excuse himself on the pretext of business and to escape. To escape, in the general's case, sometimes meant, quite simply, to run away. He wanted to gain at least that day, and above all that evening, without unpleasantness. And suddenly, the prince had so expediently turned up. "A perfect godsend!" thought the general to himself as he went in to meet his wife.

V

The generaless was jealously possessive of her origins. What must it have been for her to hear, without the slightest preparation, that this Prince Myshkin, the last of the line, of whom she had already heard something, was nothing more than a pitiful idiot and practically a pauper and accepted charity? The general was precisely counting on the effect, so as to interest her at once, deflect all her attention somehow in another direction.

In extraordinary situations, the generaless would usually pop her eyes out to an extreme extent and, throwing back her whole body somewhat, would stare vaguely before her without uttering a word. She was a tall woman, the same age as her husband, with dark hair, greatly streaked with gray, but still thick, with a somewhat aquiline nose, a lean build, sunken yellow cheeks, and thin, drawn-in lips. Her forehead was high, but narrow; her gray, rather large eyes sometimes had the most unexpected expression. She had once had the weakness to fancy that her gaze was particularly effective: this conviction remained indelible in her.

"Receive him? You say, receive him now, at once?" and the generaless popped her eyes out with all her might at Ivan Fyodorovich, fidgeting before her.

"Oh, as far as that goes, there's no need of ceremony, if only you see fit to see him, my dear," the general hastened to explain. "He is quite a child, and such a pathetic one; he has some sort of sickly fits; he has just arrived from Switzerland, came straight from the train, queerly dressed, in some German way, and to boot, he hasn't a farthing, literally; he's close to crying. I gave him twenty-five rubles and want to find him some kind of little scrivener's post in our office. And you, *mesdames*, I beg you to offer him victuals, for I fancy he is hungry, too . . ."

"You amaze me," the generaless went on as before. "Hungry and fits! What sort of fits?"

"Oh, they don't occur that frequently, and besides, he is almost like a child, although educated. I should like to ask you, *mesdames*"—he addressed his daughters again—"to give him an examination; it would be good, after all, to find out what he is fit for."

"An ex-am-in-a-tion?" the generaless drawled out and in the utmost astonishment again began to roll her eyes back and forth between her daughters and her husband.

"Ah, my dear, don't take it in that sense . . . But anyway, it's just as you please; I had in mind to treat him kindly and take him in, for it is almost a good deed."

"Take him in? From Switzerland?"

"Switzerland won't stand in the way here; but anyway, I repeat, it's as you like. I only said, you know, because, firstly, he is a namesake, and might even be a relation, and secondly, he doesn't know where to lay his head. I even thought that it would be rather interesting for you, since he comes from our family."

"Of course, *maman*, if one needn't stand on ceremony with him; besides, he'll want to eat after the journey, why not feed him if he doesn't know what to do with himself?" said the eldest, Alexandra.

"And on top of it, he's a perfect child, you could still play blind man's buff with him."

"Blind man's buff! How do you mean?"

"Oh, *maman*, do leave off the pretense, please," Aglaia interrupted with vexation.

The middle daughter, Adelaida, who was given to mirth, could not restrain herself and burst out laughing.

"Send for him, Papa, *maman* gives you leave," Aglaia decided. The general rang and ordered that the prince be called.

"But on the condition that he absolutely must have a napkin tied round his neck when he sits at table," decided the generaless, "call for

Fyodor, or let it be Mavra . . . to stand behind his chair and look after him while he eats. Is he at least quiet during his fits? Does he gesture about?"

"On the contrary, he is very nicely brought up and has wonderful manners. He is sometimes a little too simple . . . But here he is himself! There you are, my ladies, may I commend to you, the last Prince Myshkin of the line, your namesake, and, perhaps, even relation, receive him, treat him kindly. They will go in to lunch directly, Prince, so do us the honor . . . As for me, excuse me, I'm late, I must rush . . ."

"We all know where you're rushing off to," the generaless uttered meaningfully.

"I rush, I rush, my dear, I'm late! Do give him your albums, *mesdames,* let him write something there for you, to show what a calligrapher he is, just as a rarity! What talent; you should see how he wrote out for me just now, in old-fashioned handwriting: 'The Abbot Pafnuty put his hand thereto . . .' Well, good-bye."

"Pafnuty? Abbot? But stop a minute, stop, where are you going, and who is this Pafnuty?" the generaless called out with insistent vexation and on the point of agitation to her hastily departing spouse.

"Yes, yes, my dear, there was this abbot in the olden days . . . and I'm going to the count's, he's expecting me, long ago, and, what's more, he fixed the hour himself . . . Prince, good-bye!"

The general departed with rapid steps.

"I know what count he's going to see!" Elizaveta Prokofyevna pronounced sharply, and irritably turned her eyes to the prince. "Well, now!"—she began, recollecting vexedly and with distaste—"well, what was it! Ah, yes: well, what about this Abbot?"

"Maman," began Alexandra, and Aglaia even stamped her little foot.

"Don't interfere with me, Alexandra Ivanovna," snapped the generaless. "I want to know too. Sit down right here, Prince, here, in this easy chair, opposite me, no, here, near the sun, move nearer the light, so that I can see. Well, what abbot?"

"The Abbot Pafnuty," answered the prince attentively and seriously.

"Pafnuty? That's interesting. Well, what about it?"

The generaless asked her questions impatiently, rapidly, sharply, not taking her eyes off the prince, and when the prince answered, she nodded her head at every word.

"The Abbot Pafnuty, of the fourteenth century," began the prince, "he headed a monastery on the Volga, in what is now the province of Kostroma. He was famous for his holy life, went to the Tartars, helped run affairs at the time, and signed some document; I've seen a copy of this signature. I liked the handwriting and I learned it. When the general wanted to see how I write just now so as to find me a job, I wrote several phrases in different scripts, and among them, 'The humble Abbot Pafnuty put his hand thereto' in the abbot's own handwriting. The general liked it very much, and so he mentioned it just now."

"Aglaia," said the generaless, "remember: Pafnuty, or better write it down, else I always forget. Incidentally, I thought it would be more interesting. Where is this signature?"

"I think it was left in the general's study, on the table."

"Send at once and fetch it."

"Oh, better, I'll write it for you again, if you'd like."

"Of course, *maman*," said Alexandra, "but now it would be better to have lunch; we're hungry."

"Quite so," decided the generaless. "Come, Prince; are you very hungry?"

"Yes, I've begun to be very hungry now, and I am very grateful to you."

"It's a very good thing that you are polite, and I notice you are not at all such a . . . queer creature as you were deigned to be described. Come. Sit here, facing me," she fussed, seating the prince when they arrived in the dining room. "I want to look at you. Alexandra, Adelaida, help the prince to something. He is really not such an . . . invalid at all, is he? Perhaps the napkin is not even necessary . . . Did they used to tie a napkin under your chin at mealtimes, Prince?"

"Long ago, when I was about seven, I fancy, they did, but now I usually put the napkin in my lap when I eat."

"So it should be. And your fits?"

"Fits?" The prince was somewhat surprised. "My fits are very rare now. Although I don't know; they say the climate here is bad for me."

"He speaks well," observed the generaless, addressing her daughters and continuing to nod her head at the prince's every word. "I didn't expect it. It would seem it was all stuff and nonsense as usual. Help yourself, Prince, and do tell: where were you born, where were you brought up? I want to know everything; you interest me extremely."

The prince expressed his thanks and, eating with excellent appetite, again began recounting all that he had been obliged to speak about already more than once this morning. The generaless grew increasingly more and more pleased. The girls also listened rather attentively. They reckoned up the kinship; it turned out that the prince knew his family tree rather well; but no matter how they tallied it, there turned out to be hardly any relation between him and the generaless. One might have still figured some distant relation between the grandfathers and grandmothers. This dry subject was particularly to the liking of the generaless, who scarcely ever had a chance to speak of her pedigree, for all her desire to do so, and thus she got up from the table in an excited state of mind.

"Let us all go to our gathering room," she said, "and they'll bring the coffee there. We have this common room here," she turned to the prince, leading him away, "simply, my little drawing room, where we gather when we are alone, and each of us does her own thing: Alexandra, here, my eldest daughter, plays the piano, or reads, or sews; Adelaida paints landscapes and portraits (and can never finish anything), while Aglaia sits doing nothing. I can't take anything up either: nothing comes out right. Well, here we are; sit down, Prince, here, by the fireplace, and do tell. I want to know how you tell things. I want to be fully convinced, and when I see Princess Belokonsky, the old lady, I shall tell her all about you. I want them all to become interested in you too. Well, speak, then."

"*Maman*, but it's very strange to relate things that way," observed Adelaida, who had in the meantime straightened up her easel, taken up brushes and palette, and set about copying a landscape, begun long ago, from an engraving. Alexandra and Aglaia sat down together on a little sofa and, folding their hands, prepared to listen to the conversation. The prince observed that particular attention was directed toward him from all sides.

"I would never tell anything if I were ordered to like that," observed Aglaia.

"Why? What's so strange about it? Why shouldn't he tell us things? He's got a tongue. I want to know how well he can speak. Come, about anything at all. Tell us how you liked Switzerland, your first impression. You'll see, he'll begin directly, and begin splendidly, too."

"The impression was strong . . ." began the prince.

"There, you see," chimed in the impatient Elizaveta Prokofyevna, addressing her daughters, "he has begun after all."

"Do, at least, then, *maman*, let him speak," Alexandra checked her. "This prince may be a great swindler, and not an idiot at all," she whispered to Aglaia.

"Certainly so, I've seen that a long while," answered Aglaia. "And it's vile on his part to play up the role. Does he want to gain something by it, do you suppose?"

"The first impression was a very strong one," repeated the prince. "When I was brought from Russia through various German towns, I merely looked about in silence and, I remember, I didn't even ask about anything. This was after a series of violent and painful attacks of my illness, and whenever my illness intensified and the fits came several times in a row, I would always sink into complete stupefaction and lose my memory completely, and while my mind did function, the logical flow of thought was as if broken off. I couldn't connect more than two or three ideas together. So it seems to me. But whenever the fits calmed down, I would become healthy and strong again, like I am now. I remember there was an unendurable melancholy in me; I even wanted to cry; I was constantly amazed and uneasy: it affected me terribly that everything was foreign; I understood that much. The foreignness was killing me. I was entirely roused from this gloom, I remember, in the evening, in Basel, upon entering Switzerland, and I was wakened by the bray of an ass in the marketplace. The ass astonished me and for some reason I was extraordinarily pleased with it, and at the same time suddenly everything seemed to clear up in my head."

"An ass? That's odd," observed the generaless. "But on the other hand, there's nothing odd about it, any one of us may even fall in love with an ass," she observed, looking wrathfully at the laughing girls. "It's happened in mythology. Continue, Prince."

"I've been awfully fond of asses ever since. It's even some kind of affinity in me. I began to ask about them because I'd never seen them before, and immediately confirmed for myself that this was the most useful animal, industrious, strong, patient, cheap, long-suffering; and through this ass, I suddenly began to like all of Switzerland, so that my former melancholy passed completely."

"This is all very strange, but we can leave out the bit about the ass;

let's move on to another subject. Why do you keep laughing, Aglaia? And you, Adelaida? The prince told us splendidly about the ass. He saw it himself, but what have you seen? You haven't been abroad, have you?"

"I've seen an ass, *maman*," said Adelaida.

"And I've heard one, too," chimed in Aglaia. All three laughed again. The prince laughed with them.

"That's very wicked on your part," observed the generaless, "you must excuse them, Prince, but they are kindhearted. I am always quarreling with them, but I love them. They are flighty, frivolous, out of their minds."

"But why?" laughed the prince. "I wouldn't have missed the chance in their place either. But all the same, I stand behind the ass: the ass is a kind and useful person."

"And are you kind, Prince? I ask out of curiosity," asked the generaless.

Everyone laughed again.

"There's that accursed ass again; I wasn't even thinking of it!" exclaimed the generaless. "Believe me, please, Prince, I did not at all mean to . . ."

"Intimate? Oh, I believe you, without a doubt!"

And the prince laughed ceaselessly.

"It's a good thing that you're laughing. I see that you're a most kindhearted young man," said the generaless.

"Sometimes not kind," answered the prince.

"But I am kind," the generaless put in unexpectedly, "and if you like, I am always kind, and this is my only failing, for one oughtn't always be kind. I am very often angry, with them for instance, and with Ivan Fyodorovich especially, but the rotten thing is that I am kindest of all when I am angry. Just now, before you came in, I was angry and pretended that I didn't understand anything, and couldn't understand it. I am like that sometimes; just like a child. Aglaia gave me a lesson; thank you, Aglaia. But it's all nonsense. I'm not quite so foolish as I seem and as my daughters would like to make me out. I have a will of my own and I'm not easily embarrassed. Incidentally, I say this without malice. Come here, Aglaia, give me a kiss, there . . . Well, that's enough affection," she observed when Aglaia kissed her with feeling on the lips and on the hand. "Go on, Prince. Perhaps you will remember something more interesting than an ass."

"I still don't understand how one can relate anything so directly," observed Adelaida again, "I could never find my bearings."

"But the prince will find his bearings, because the prince is extremely smart, and is ten times smarter than you at least, and maybe even twelve times. I hope you will perceive it after this. Prove it to them, Prince; go on. You really can pass over the ass now. Well, what, besides the ass, did you see abroad?"

"Oh, it was smart about the ass too," observed Alexandra, "the prince related his episode of illness and how he came to like everything through one external impetus in a very interesting way. I always found it interesting how people go out of their minds and then get well again. Especially if it happens all of a sudden."

"Isn't that the truth? Isn't that the truth?" The generaless reared up. "I see that you can be smart sometimes too; well, come, stop laughing! You left off at the Swiss scenery, I think, Prince, well?"

"We arrived in Lucerne, and I was taken to the lake. I sensed how lovely it was, but at the same time, I felt terribly heavy-hearted," said the prince.

"Why?" asked Alexandra.

"I don't understand it. I always feel heavy-hearted and uneasy looking at such natural scenery for the first time; both happy and uneasy; come to think of it, this was all still while I was ill."

"No, really, I would very much like to see it," said Adelaida. "And I don't see when we're going to manage to make it abroad. I haven't been able to find subjects for painting these last two years now: 'The East and South have long since been described.'[22] Find me a subject for a picture, Prince, do."

"I don't know a thing about it. It seems to me you only need to look and paint."

"I don't know how to look."

"Well, why are you talking in riddles? I don't understand a thing!" interrupted the generaless. "What do you mean, you don't know how to look? You've got eyes, so look. If you don't know how to look here,

22. This is an inexact quote from a poem by Lermontov.

you won't learn abroad either. Better tell us how you looked at things yourself, Prince."

"Yes, that would be better," added Adelaida. "After all, the prince learned to how to look abroad."

"I don't know; I merely mended my health abroad; I don't know if I learned how to look at things. Incidentally, I was very happy almost the entire time."

"Happy! You know how to be happy?" cried Aglaia. "Then how can you say that you didn't learn to look at things? You might teach us, even."

"Teach us, please," laughed Adelaida.

"I can't teach you anything." The prince laughed too. "I spent almost all my time abroad in this rural Swiss village; I rarely traveled anywhere far; so what could I teach you? At first, it was merely not dreary for me; soon I began to regain my health; then every day became precious for me, and more precious as time went on, so that I began to notice it. I would go to bed very satisfied, and would get up even happier still. But why all this is so—it's rather difficult to recount."

"So you didn't even want to go anywhere, there was no longing for any place?" asked Alexandra.

"At first, at the very outset, yes, there was a longing, and I would fall into a state of great restlessness. I kept thinking of how I would live; I wanted to know my fate, and was particularly restless in those moments. You know, there are such moments, especially in solitude. We had a waterfall there, a small one; it fell from high up in the mountain and in such a thin thread, almost perpendicular—white, noisy, foamy; it fell from high up, but it seemed rather low, it was half a verst away but seemed fifty paces off. I used to like listening to the sound of it at night; it was in those moments that I was sometimes overcome with great restlessness. Sometimes also at midday, when you wandered into the mountains somewhere, you stood by yourself in the middle of the mountain, pines all around you, ancient, big, full of sap; up above on the cliff, an old medieval castle, ruins; our little village far below, barely visible; the sun bright, the sky blue, the stillness terrible. Well then, indeed, I would feel drawn away somewhere, and I kept fancying that if you went straight ahead, walked a long, long way, and got beyond that line, the very one where the sky meets the earth, that the whole key to the mystery would be there, and directly, you would see a new life, a thousand times more vivid and tumultuous than ours; I kept dreaming of a big city, such as Naples, all full of palaces, tumult, thundering noise, life . . . Indeed, what didn't I dream of! But afterward I fancied that even in prison, you could find tremendous life."

"That last laudable thought I had already read in my Bible reader when I was twelve years old," said Aglaia.

"That's all philosophy," remarked Adelaida, "you are a philosopher and have come to edify us."

"You may be right," smiled the prince, "I am really, perhaps, a philosopher, and who knows, maybe I do in fact have a notion to edify . . . It may be; truly, it may be."

"And your philosophy is exactly like that of Yevlampia Niko-laevna," Aglaia chimed in again, "she's a civil servant's wife, a widow, comes to see us, a bit like a sponger. The entire object of her life is— cheapness; only to live as cheaply as possible, she only talks of farthings, and, take note, she has money, she's a swindler. And your tremendous life in prison is exactly like that, and maybe your four years of bliss in the country, too, in exchange for which you sold your city of Naples, and with clear profit, too, it would seem, though it was for a trifle."

"As regards life in prison, one might argue the point," said the prince. "I heard an account from one man who spent some twelve years in prison; this was one of the invalids in the care of my professor. He had fits, he was at times restless, wept, and even tried to kill himself once. His life in prison had been a very sad one, I assure you, but by no means trifling. And his entire acquaintance consisted of a spider and a little tree that grew under the window . . . But it's better I tell you about another encounter I had last year with a certain man. There was a very strange circumstance about it—strange, namely, in that such things happen very rarely. This man had once been led, together with some others, up the scaffold, and they read him his sentence of death by firing squad, for a political offense. Some twenty minutes later they read out a reprieve and another punishment was set instead; however, in the interim between these two sentences, twenty minutes or at least a quarter of an hour, he lived in the fullest conviction that he would die suddenly in the next few minutes. I was terribly eager to listen whenever he would occasionally recall his impressions at the time, and I would start to question him about it again several times. He remembered it all with extraordinary vividness and used to say that he would never forget anything of those minutes. Some twenty paces from the scaffold, around which a crowd and some soldiers were standing, there were three posts stuck in the ground, as there were several criminals. They led the first three to the posts, bound them, put the death-dress on them (long white gowns), shoved white hoods over their eyes so they wouldn't see the rifles; then a company of several soldiers was drawn up opposite each post. My acquaintance was the eighth in the line, so he would have to go to the posts in the third turn. The priest went to each in turn with the cross. By the reckoning, there were five minutes left to live, no more. He would say that these five minutes seemed to him an infinite term, a vast wealth; he fancied that in these five minutes he would live so many lives that there was no need yet to think of the last moment, so that he even made various arrangements: worked out the time for taking leave of his comrades, set aside some two minutes for it, then set aside two minutes more for thinking to himself for the last time, and then, for looking around him one last time. He remembered very well that he made precisely those three arrangements and worked it out precisely like that. He was dying at twenty-seven, strong and healthy; taking leave of his comrades, he remembered, he asked one of them a somewhat irrelevant question and was even very interested in the response. Then, when he had taken his leave of his comrades, came those two minutes that he had set aside for *thinking to himself;* he knew beforehand what he would think about; he kept wanting to picture to himself, as quickly and vividly as possible, just how it could be: now he exists and is living, but in three minutes he will be *something else,* someone or something—but what, then? Where, then? He meant to decide all that in those two minutes! Not far off there was a church, and the top of the cathedral with the gilt roof glittered in the bright sun. He remembered that he stared very persistently at that roof and the rays of light flashing from it; he could not tear himself from the rays: it seemed to him that those rays were his new nature, that in three minutes he would somehow merge with them . . . The uncertainty and the repulsion from this new thing that would be and would come momentarily were dreadful; but he said that nothing had been more difficult for him at that time than the incessant thought: 'What if I were not to die! What if life were returned to me— what eternity! And it would all be mine! I would turn every minute into an entire age, I wouldn't lose a thing, I would count every minute, and wouldn't waste a thing for nothing!' He said that this thought finally mutated in him into such outrage that he longed to be shot quickly."

The prince suddenly fell silent; everyone waited for him to go on and draw a conclusion.

"Have you finished?" asked Aglaia.

"What? I'm finished," said the prince, emerging from a momentary pensiveness.

"But what did you tell that story for?"

"Oh . . . it came to mind . . . just for conversation . . ."

"You are very disconnected," observed Alexandra, "probably, Prince, you wanted to show that not one instant can be valued at a trifle, and sometimes five minutes are more precious than a treasure. That's all very laudable, but let me ask, however, what of this friend who told you such horrors . . . After all, they changed his sentence and, it would seem, presented him with that 'eternal life.' Well, and what did he do with this wealth afterward? Did he live counting every moment?"

"Oh, no, he told me himself—I've already asked him about it—he didn't live like that at all, and wasted many, many moments."

"Well, it would seem, there you have it, it would seem one couldn't truly live 'counting each moment.' For some reason, you just can't."

"Yes, for some reason you just can't," repeated the prince, "I thought so myself . . . and yet I somehow can't believe it . . ."

"You mean, you think you will live more wisely than anyone?"

"Yes, I have thought that too sometimes."

"And you think so still?"

"And . . . I think so still," responded the prince, continuing to look at Aglaia with a gentle and even timid smile; but he laughed again at once and looked gaily at her.

"That's modest," said Aglaia, becoming almost irritated.

"But how brave you are, however, that you laugh; for my part, I was so struck by everything in his story that I dreamt of it afterward, I dreamt precisely of those five minutes . . ."

He searchingly and earnestly surveyed his listeners once more.

"You are not angry with me for anything?" he asked suddenly, as if embarrassed, but looking all of them straight in the eye.

"What for?" exclaimed all three girls in amazement.

"Well, because I seem to be preaching the whole time . . ."

They all laughed.

"If you are angry, then don't be angry," he said, "I'm quite aware myself that I've lived less than others and understand less than anyone about life. Perhaps I talk very queerly sometimes . . ."

And he was overwhelmed with confusion.

"If you say that you were happy, then it would seem you've lived not less but more; so why are you making pretenses and apologies?" Aglaia began sternly and persistently. "And don't worry, please, that you are preaching to us, there is no pomp about it on your part. With your quietism, one might fill a hundred years of life with happiness. One can show you an execution or hold out one's little finger, you will draw an equally edifying thought from the one and from the other, and will remain quite satisfied to boot. One can surely get through life like that."

"I can't make out what you're so cross about," chimed in the generaless, who had been watching the speakers' faces for some time, "and I can't make out what you're talking about either. What finger, and what kind of nonsense is this? The prince talks splendidly, only rather sadly. Why are you discouraging him? When he began, he was laughing, and now he is quite glum."

"It's all right, *maman*. But it's a pity you haven't seen an execution, Prince, I should like to have asked you one thing."

"I have seen an execution."

"You have?" cried Aglaia. "I should have guessed it! That crowns the whole business. If you've seen it, how can you say that you've lived happily the whole time? Well, didn't I tell you the truth?"

"But do they have executions in your village?" asked Adelaida.

"I saw it in Lyons, I went there with Schneider, he took me with him. We chanced upon it directly as we arrived."

"Well, did you like it? Was there much that was edifying in it? Educational?" asked Aglaia.

"I did not like it at all and I was rather ill afterward, but I admit that I was riveted to the spot, I could not take my eyes off it."

"I couldn't have taken my eyes off it either," said Aglaia.

"They dislike it very much there when women come to look, they even write about such women in the papers afterward."

"Then, since they find that it's no affair for women, they thus wish to say (and, it would seem, justify) that it's a men's affair. I congratulate them on their logic. And you think so too, no doubt?"

"Tell us about the execution," interrupted Adelaida.

"I wouldn't feel at all inclined to now . . ." The prince became confused and appeared to frown.

"You seem to grudge telling us about it," taunted Aglaia.

"No, it is because I've just been telling the story of this very execution earlier."

"Telling whom?"

"Your attendant, while I was waiting . . ."

"What attendant?" resounded from all sides.

"Why, the one that sits in the entry, with the gray streak and ruddy face; I was sitting in the entry waiting to see Ivan Fyodorovich."

"That's odd," remarked the generaless.

"The prince is a democrat," Aglaia rapped out. "Well, if you told Alexei about it, you can't refuse us."

"I simply must hear about it," said Adelaida.

"Just now, in fact," the prince turned to her, taking heart again somewhat (it seems he was wont to take heart very quickly and trustingly), "I did, in fact, have a thought, when you asked me for a subject for a picture, to give you a subject: to paint the face of a condemned man the moment before the guillotine strikes, when he is still standing on the scaffold before lying down on that plank."

"How do you mean the face? Just the face?" asked Adelaida. "It would be a strange subject, and what sort of picture would it make?"

"I don't know, and why not?" the prince insisted fervently. "Recently, in Basel, I saw such a picture. I should like very much to tell you . . . Some day I'll tell you . . . It struck me very much."

"You shall certainly tell us about the Basel picture afterward," said Adelaida, "but now, explain to me the picture from this execution. Can you tell me how you imagine it to yourself? How is one to draw the face? Only the face, just like that? What kind of face is it then?"

"It's literally a minute before death," the prince began with perfect readiness, carried away by the recollection and to all appearances immediately forgetting everything else, "that very moment when he has just mounted the ladder and has just stepped onto the scaffold. Here, he glanced in my direction; I looked at his face and understood everything . . . But then, how can you recount it! I would like terribly, so terribly, for you, or someone else, to draw it. It would be best if it were you! I thought at the time that a picture of it would do good. You know, here it is necessary to imagine everything that has gone before, everything, everything. He had been living in prison and expecting his execution not for another week at the least; he had been counting on the usual formalities, that an order would have to be forwarded somewhere and would only come back in a week. But here, suddenly, by some chance, the business was shortened. At five in the morning, he was sleeping. It was in late October; at five o'clock it is still cold and dark. The prison superintendent came in quietly, with a guard, and carefully touched him on the shoulder; the latter sat up, leaning on his elbow—he sees the light: 'What is it?'—'The execution is at ten o'clock.' Just roused from sleep, he did not believe it, began to argue that the order wouldn't be ready for a week, but when he came fully to his senses, he ceased arguing and fell silent—that's how they told it— then he said: 'But it's hard it should be so sudden . . .'—and fell silent again, and didn't want to say anything more. The next three or four hours are spent on the usual things: the priest, breakfast, at which he is given wine, coffee and beef (isn't that a mockery? Only think how cruel it is, but on the other hand, God's truth, these innocent people do it out of the goodness of their hearts and are convinced that it's humane), then the toilet (do you know what the toilet of a criminal is like?), and finally, they take him through the town to the scaffold . . . I think that here, too, it must seem that there is still an eternity left to live, while they're taking you along; I fancy he must have thought along the way: 'There's a long time left, three streets more; I shall pass by this one, then there'll still be that one left, and then that one, with the baker on the right . . . It'll be a long time before we get to the baker's!' There are crowds of people all around, shouting, clamor, ten thousand faces, ten thousand eyes—you have to bear it all, but the main thing is the thought: 'There's ten thousand of *them,* and they're not executing any of them, but they're executing me!' Well, that is all preparatory. There is a little ladder leading to the scaffold; here, before the ladder, he suddenly began to cry, and this was a strong and manly person, a great villain, they say, he was. The priest never left him for a moment, and rode with him in the cart and kept talking all the while— I doubt that he heard: he'd start to listen, but after two words he'd no longer comprehend. So it must have been. At last he began going up the ladder; his legs were tied together so that he could only move with tiny steps. The priest, who must have been an intelligent man, left off speaking and only kept giving him the cross to kiss. At the foot of the ladder he was very pale, and when he got to the top and stood on the scaffold, he became white as paper, as white as writing paper. His legs must have been growing weak and wooden, and he must have felt nauseous—as though something were choking his throat and it almost tickled—have you ever felt that when you were frightened, or in very terrifying moments when all your reason remains but has no more control? It seems to me that if one is faced with inevitable destruction, for instance, a house is falling on you, then you would suddenly feel a terrible longing to sit down and close your eyes and wait—come what may! Well, in that very moment, whenever this weakness began, the priest would hastily, with a rapid gesture and in silence, put a cross all of a sudden to his very lips, a little silver cross, four-pointed—he kept putting it up frequently, every minute. And the moment the cross touched his lips, he would open his eyes and seem to come alive again for a few seconds, and his feet would move. He kissed the cross greedily, made haste to kiss it, as if he was in haste not to forget to grab some kind of provision, just in case, but I doubt that he was cognizant of anything religious at the time. And so it went until he was laid on the plank . . . It's strange that people rarely faint at these last moments! On the contrary, the head is terribly alive and must be working with such mighty, mighty, mighty force, like an engine at full speed; I imagine there's a continual throbbing of various thoughts, all unfinished, and perhaps even absurd, such irrelevant thoughts: 'That one there keeps looking—he has a wart on his forehead, see, one of the executioner's bottom buttons is rusty' . . . and in the meantime, you know everything and remember everything; there is this one point that you simply can't forget, and you can't lose consciousness, and everything moves and turns about it, this one point. And to think that it is like that up to the very last quarter of a second, when your head is already lying on the plank, and waits, and . . . *knows,* and suddenly hears above how the steel starts to glide! You'd hear that for certain! If I were lying there, I should listen on purpose and hear! It may only be one tenth of a moment, but you'd hear it for certain! And just imagine, it's still argued that, maybe, when the head flies off, then for one more second, it may be that it knows that it's flown off—what a concept! And what if it's five seconds! . . . Paint the scaffold so that only the last step can be seen distinctly and up close; the criminal has stepped upon it: his head, his face white as paper, the priest holds up the cross, the former greedily holds out his blue lips and looks, and—*knows everything*. The cross and the head—that's the picture, the face of the priest, the executioner, his two attendants, and a few heads and eyes below—all that might be painted in the background, in a haze, for embellishment . . . That's the picture."

The prince fell silent and looked at them all.

"That's nothing like quietism, certainly," muttered Alexandra to herself.

"Well, now tell us about how you were in love," said Adelaida.

The prince looked at her with astonishment.

"Listen," Adelaida seemed to hasten, "you still owe us the story of the Basel picture, but now I want to hear about how you were in love; don't deny it, you were. Besides, once you start telling a story, you cease being a philosopher."

"No sooner do you finish telling us a story than you are immediately ashamed of what you've told," Aglaia suddenly observed. "Why is that?"

"How utterly foolish that is," snapped the generaless, looking indignantly at Aglaia.

"It's not clever," Alexandra assented.

"Don't believe her, Prince," the generaless addressed him, "she does it on purpose from some sort of malice; she is not at all so foolishly brought up; don't think anything of their pestering you so. No doubt, they are up to something, but they are fond of you already. I know their faces."

"And I know their faces," said the prince, placing a particular emphasis on his words.

"What do you mean?" asked Adelaida with curiosity.

"What do you know about our faces?" the other two inquired curiously too.

"I'll tell you afterward," he said quietly and earnestly.

"You are decidedly trying to pique our interest," cried Aglaia, "and what solemnity!"

"Very well, then," Adelaida hastened again, "but if you're such a connoisseur of faces you certainly must have been in love, so it seems I guessed right. Well, tell us about it."

"I haven't been in love," answered the prince just as quietly and earnestly, "I . . . was happy in a different way."

"How, then, in what?"

"Very well, I'll tell you," uttered the prince, as though deep in thought.

VI

"And now," began the prince, "you are all looking at me with such curiosity that were I not to satisfy it, you might, perhaps, be angry with me after all. No, I'm joking," he added quickly with a smile. "In that place . . . in that place, there were children everywhere, and I was always with children there, with nothing but children. These were the children of the village, the whole gang that went to school. It was not that I taught them; oh, no, there was a schoolmaster for that—Jules Thibaut; though perhaps I did teach them, but for the most part I was simply with them, and all those four years went by in that way. I had no need of anything else. I used to tell them everything, I concealed nothing from them. Their fathers and relations were all cross with me, for the children couldn't get on without me finally and were always flocking round me, and the schoolmaster finally even became my chief enemy. I made many enemies there, and all on account of the children. Even Schneider reproved me. And what were they so afraid of? Children can be told everything—everything; I've always been astonished by the thought of how little grown-ups understand children, even fathers and mothers their own children. Nothing should be concealed from children on the pretext that they are little and that it is too early for them to understand. What a sad and unfortunate idea! And how readily the children themselves detect that their fathers consider that they are too little and understand nothing, though they understand everything. Grown-ups do not know that even in the most difficult case a child can give exceedingly important advice. Oh, Lord! when that pretty little bird looks at you, happy and trusting, you should be ashamed to deceive it! I call them birds because there's nothing better than a bird in the world. But actually, everyone in the village was angry with me more because of one incident . . . while Thibaut was simply envious of me; at first he used to shake his head and wonder how it was the children understood everything with me and practically nothing

with him, and then he began laughing at me when I told him that neither of us could teach them anything, but that they can teach us. And
how could he be envious of me and say things against me, when he
spent his life with children himself! The soul is healed through children . . . There was one patient in Schneider's institution, one very
miserable man. It was such a terrible misery that there could hardly be
anything like it. He had been brought to be treated for derangement.
In my opinion he was not deranged, it was simply that he was terribly
miserable—that was all that was the matter with him. And if only you
knew what our children became to him in the end . . . But I'd better tell
you about that patient another time; now, I'll tell you how it all began.
At first the children didn't take to me. I was so big, I am always so
clumsy; I know I am ugly too . . . And then, too, I was a foreigner.
The children used to laugh at me at first, and they even began throwing stones at me after they saw me kiss Marie. And I only kissed her
once . . . No, don't laugh"—the prince made haste to check the smile
on the faces of his listeners—"there was no love at all involved. If only
you knew what a miserable creature this was, you would be very sorry
for her yourselves, as I was. She was from our village. Her mother
was a very old woman, and in their tiny, utterly ramshackle little two-
window house, one window was set apart by permission of the village
authorities; from this window, the old woman was allowed to sell laces,
thread, tobacco and soap, all for the slightest pittance, and that was
what she lived on. She was sick and her legs kept swelling up so that
she always sat in one place. Marie was her daughter, some twenty years
old, weak and skinny; she had been consumptive for a long time, but
she kept on going from house to house hiring herself out to do hard
work by the day—scrubbing floors, washing linens, sweeping out yards
and minding cattle. A French commercial traveler seduced her and
took her away, and a week later left her alone on the road and went off
on the sly. She came home begging, all filthy, in rags, with her boots in
pieces; she had gone on foot the whole week, slept in the fields and
caught a dreadful cold; her feet were covered in wounds, her hands
were swollen and chapped. Though, actually, she wasn't comely before
that, either; only her eyes were gentle, kind, innocent. She was terribly
silent. Once, before that, she suddenly began to sing while working,
and I remember everyone was surprised and began laughing: 'Marie is
singing! What? Marie is singing!'—and she was terribly abashed and

fell silent forever then. Back then, they were still kind to her, but when she came back, sick and worn out, there was no sympathy for her from anyone! How cruel they are in that! What hard ideas they have about such things! Her mother was the first to receive her with anger and contempt: 'Now you've dishonored me.' And she was the first to abandon her to her disgrace: as soon as they heard in the village that Marie had come home, everyone went to have a look at Marie, and virtually the whole village ran to assemble in the old woman's cottage: old men, children, women, girls, everyone, in a hurrying, eager crowd. Marie was lying on the ground at the old woman's feet, hungry and in rags, and she was crying. When they all ran in, she covered herself in her disheveled hair and lay prone on the floor. Everyone around her stared at her as though she were a reptile; the old men condemned and upbraided, the young people even laughed, the women upbraided her, condemned, and looked at her with such loathing, as though at some kind of spider. Her mother allowed it all, sat there herself, nodding her head and approving. At the time, the mother was very ill and almost dying; two months later she did in fact die; she knew she was dying, but still, up to the time of her death she didn't give a thought to being reconciled with her daughter, didn't even speak one word to her, turned her out to sleep in the entry, scarcely gave her anything to eat. She often had to soak her bad legs in hot water; Marie bathed her legs every day and waited on her. She accepted all her services in silence and never said a kind word to her. Marie put up with everything and afterward, when I made her acquaintance, I noticed that she approved it all herself, and looked on herself as the lowest of the low. When the old woman became completely bedridden, the old women of the village came to take care of her in turns, as is the custom there. Then they gave up feeding Marie altogether; and in the village everyone drove her away and no one even wanted to give her work as before. Everyone spat on her, as it were, and the men even ceased considering her as a woman; they would say all sorts of nasty things to her. Sometimes, very rarely, when the drunkards got drunk on Sunday, they would throw pennies to her for laughs, just like that, on the ground; Marie would pick them up without a word. She had begun to cough up blood by that time. At last her rags were torn to absolute tatters, so that she was ashamed to show herself in the village; and she had gone barefoot since she came back. And it was then, particularly, that the children, the

whole gang of them—there were a little over forty schoolchildren—
began jeering, and even throwing dirt at her. She asked the cowherd to
let her look after the cows, but he drove her away. Then she began
going off for the whole day with the flock of her own accord, without
permission. As she was of great use to the cowherd, and he noticed it,
he no longer drove her away, and sometimes even gave her the leftovers from his dinner, cheese and bread. He considered this as a great
kindness on his part. And when her mother died, the pastor did not
scruple to heap shame on Marie in church before all the people. Marie
stood behind the coffin, as she was, in her rags, and cried. A crowd of
people had collected to see how she would cry and walk behind the
coffin; then the pastor—he was still a young man, and his whole ambition was to become a great preacher—turned to them all and pointed
to Marie. 'Here you see the cause of this worthy woman's death' (and
it was not true, for the woman had been ill for two years); 'here she
stands before you and dares not look at you, for she has been marked
out by the finger of God; here she is, barefoot and in rags—a warning
to all who lose their virtue! Who is she? Her daughter!' and so on in
that vein. And, imagine, this infamy pleased almost everyone! But . . .
here the story took a certain turn; the children interfered, for by then
the children were all on my side, and had begun to love Marie. This
was how it happened. I wanted to do something for Marie; she was
badly in need of money, but I never had a farthing at that time. I had a
little diamond pin, and I sold it to a peddler; he went from village to
village buying and selling old clothes. He gave me eight francs, and it
was certainly worth forty. I was a long time trying to meet Marie alone;
at last we met by a hedge outside the village, on a bypath to the mountain, behind a tree. Then I gave her the eight francs and told her to take
care of it, because I should have no more, and then I kissed her and
said that she mustn't think I had any evil intent, and that I kissed her
not because I was in love with her, but because I was very sorry for her,
and that I had never, from the very beginning, thought of her as guilty
but only as unhappy. I wanted very much to comfort her at once and to
persuade her that she shouldn't consider herself below everyone, but I
think she didn't understand. I saw that at once, though she scarcely
spoke all the time and stood before me with downcast eyes and horribly abashed. When I had finished, she kissed my hand, and I at once
took her hand and would have kissed it, but she hastily pulled it away.

Suddenly, in that moment, the children saw us, a whole crowd of them; I learned afterward that they had been keeping watch on me for some time. They began whistling, clapping their hands and laughing, and Marie ran away. I tried to speak to them, but they began throwing stones at me. The same day everyone knew of it, the whole village; the whole brunt of it fell on Marie again: they began to dislike her more than ever. I even heard that they wanted to have her punished by the authorities, but, thank goodness, that didn't come off. But the children gave her no peace: they teased her more than ever, and flung dirt; they would chase her, she would run away from them with her weak lungs, gasping for breath, and them after her, shouting and reviling. Once I even jumped in to fight with them. Then I began talking to them; I talked to them every day as much as I could. They sometimes stopped and listened, though they still abused me. I told them how unhappy Marie was; soon they left off abusing me and walked away in silence. Little by little, we began talking together, I concealed nothing from them; I told them everything. They listened with great interest and soon began to pity Marie. Some of them, when they met her, began greeting her kindly; it's the custom there when you meet people— whether you know them or not—to bow and wish them good morning. I can fancy how astonished Marie was. One day two little girls got some things to eat and brought them to her; they came and told me of it. They told me that Marie started crying, and that now they loved her very much. Soon all of them began to love her, and at the same time they suddenly began to love me too. They took to coming to see me often, and always asked me to tell them stories; I think I must have told them well, for they were very fond of listening to me. And subsequently I studied and read solely so I could tell them of it afterward, and for the remaining three years I used to tell them stories. Later on, when everybody blamed me—including Schneider—for talking to them like grown-ups and concealing nothing from them, I would answer that it is shameful to lie to them, and that they know everything anyway, however much you try to conceal things from them, and that they might learn it in a nasty way, but they wouldn't learn it in a nasty way from me. One need only remember one's own childhood. They did not agree ... I had kissed Marie a fortnight before her mother died; by the time the pastor delivered his sermon, all the children were already on my side. I at once related and explained the pastor's act to them; they were all angry with him, and some of them to such an extent that they broke the glass in his windows with stones. I stopped them, for that was wrong; but everyone in the village heard of it at once, and that was when they began to accuse me of corrupting the children. Then they all found out that the children loved Marie, and were terribly alarmed; but Marie was already happy. The children were even forbidden to meet her, but they would run out on the sly to where she kept the herds, pretty far away, nearly half a verst from the village; they brought her dainties, and some simply ran out to hug and kiss her, say '*Je vous aime, Marie,*'[23] and then run back as fast as their legs would carry them. Marie was almost beside herself at such unlooked-for happiness; she had never even dreamt of such a thing; she was chagrined and delighted, and the main thing was that the children, especially the girls, liked to run to her to tell her that I loved her and had talked to them a great deal about her. They told her that I had told them all about her, and that now they loved her and pitied her and would always do so. Then they would run to me, and with such happy, concerned little faces tell me that they had just seen Marie and that Marie sent her greetings. In the evenings I used to walk to the waterfall; there was one spot there quite hidden from the village and surrounded by poplars; that's where they would gather round me in the evening, some even coming secretly. I think they got immense enjoyment out of my love for Marie, and on this one point, in my entire stay there, I did deceive them. I did not assure them that I did not love Marie at all, that is to say, was not in love with her, that I was simply very sorry for her; I saw by all the signs that they would rather have it as they imagined it and had settled it among themselves, and so I said nothing and let it seem that they guessed right. And what delicacy and tenderness were shown by those little hearts: incidentally, it seemed to them impossible that their dear Léon loved Marie so, while Marie was so badly dressed and without shoes. Imagine, they managed to get her shoes and stockings and linen, and even some kind of dress; how they contrived to do it I can't make out; the whole troop worked on it. When I questioned them, they only laughed merrily, and the girls clapped their hands and kissed me. I sometimes went to see Marie secretly too. She was becoming very ill already and could scarcely walk; in the end,

23. Fr., I love you, Marie.

she gave up working for the herdsman entirely, but still went out every morning with the cattle. She used to sit a little apart. There was a nearly vertical overhanging cliff there with a ledge jutting out; she used to sit in the very corner on the rock, out of sight of everyone, and she sat there almost without moving all day, from early morning till the cattle went home. She was by then so weak from consumption that she sat most of the time with her eyes shut and her head leaning against the rock and dozed, breathing heavily; her face had grown thin as a skeleton's, and the sweat stood out on her brow and temples. That was how I always found her. I used to come for a moment, and I too did not want to be seen. As soon as I appeared, Marie would start, open her eyes and fall to kissing my hands. I no longer tried to take them away, for it was a joy to her; all the while that I sat with her she trembled and wept; she did, it's true, try to speak a few times, but it was difficult to understand her. She seemed like a crazy creature, in a state of terrible excitement and ecstasy. Sometimes the children came with me. In that case, they would usually stand a little way off and keep watch to protect us from someone or something, and that was an extraordinary pleasure for them. When we went away, Marie was left alone again, motionless as before, with her eyes shut and her head leaning against the rock; perhaps she was dreaming of something. One morning she could no longer go out with the cows and remained at home in her empty house. The children heard of it at once, and almost all of them went to visit her that day; she lay in bed, all by her lonesome. For two days she was tended only by the children, who ran in to see her by turns, but later, when they had heard in the village that Marie was really dying, the old women from the village started going to her, to sit and keep watch. I think they had begun to pity Marie in the village; at least, they did not prevent the children from seeing her and did not scold them, as they had done before. Marie was drowsy all the time, her sleep was fitful—she coughed terribly. The old women drove the children away, but they ran under the window sometimes only for a moment, just to say '*Bonjour, notre bonne Marie.*'[24] No sooner would she catch sight of them or hear them than she would revive and, not heeding the old women, would try to raise herself on her elbow, nod to them and thank them. They continued to bring her dainties, but she

24. Fr., Good day, our good Marie.

scarcely ate anything. I assure you that, thanks to them, she died almost happy. Thanks to them, she forgot her bitter trouble; as if she received forgiveness from them, for up to the very end she looked upon herself as a great sinner. They were like little birds beating their wings against her window and calling to her every morning, '*Nous t'aimons, Marie.*'[25] She died very soon. I had expected her to last much longer. The day before her death, before the sun went down, I went to see her; I think she knew me, and I pressed her hand for the last time; how her hand had wasted away! And next morning they came to me and said that Marie was dead. Then the children could not be restrained: they decked her coffin with flowers and put a wreath on her head. The pastor no longer vilified the dead woman in the church, and anyway, there were not many people at the funeral, only a few came out of curiosity; but when the coffin had to be carried out, the children all rushed forward to carry it themselves. Since they were not able to bear the weight, they helped; all of them ran after the coffin, and all of them were crying. Ever since, Marie's little grave has been constantly honored by the children; they deck it with flowers every year and planted roses round it. But it was after the funeral that I was most persecuted by the villagers on account of the children. The main instigators were the pastor and the schoolmaster. The children were strictly forbidden even to meet me, and Schneider even made it his duty to enforce this. But we did see each other all the same; we communicated from afar by signs. They used to send me little notes. In the end it was all smoothed over, and then things were going very well: this persecution even brought me nearer to the children than ever. In the last year I was almost reconciled to Thibaut and the pastor. And Schneider talked to me a great deal and argued with me about my pernicious 'system' with children. As if I had a system! At last Schneider expressed to me a very strange thought of his—it was just before I went away. He told me that he had become fully convinced that I was a complete child myself, that is, altogether a child; that I was like an adult only in face and figure, but that in development, in spirit, character, and perhaps even intelligence, I was not grown up, and that so I should remain, if I lived to be sixty. I laughed very much: he was wrong, of course, for I'm not little, now am I? But one thing really is true, I don't in fact like being with

25. Fr., We love you, Marie.

adults, with grown-up people—and I noticed that a long time ago—I don't like it because I don't know how. Whatever they say to me, however kind they are to me, for some reason I always feel weighed down with them, and I am awfully glad when I can get away to my companions; and my companions have always been children, not because I am a child myself, but simply because I was always drawn to children. When I was first in the village—at the time when I used to go off into the mountains to pine by myself—when I, rambling by myself, sometimes, especially at midday when school let out, began to meet the whole troop of them, noisy, running with their satchels and slates, with shouts and games and laughter, my whole soul would suddenly long to go out to them at once. I don't know, but I began to feel some kind of extremely intense and happy sensation at every meeting with them. I would stop and laugh with happiness, looking at their little legs flashing and ever running along, at the boys and girls running together, at their laughter and their tears (for many of them managed to fight, cry, make up, and begin playing again on the way home from school), and then I forgot all my pining. Afterward, in all those three years, I couldn't even understand how and why people are sad. My whole fate was centered on the children. I never reckoned on leaving the village, and it did not enter my mind that I should one day come back here to Russia. I fancied that I would always stay there, but I saw at last that Schneider couldn't go on keeping me after all; and then a piece of business turned up, so important apparently that Schneider himself urged me to go, and sent word here on my behalf. I shall look into it and seek advice. Perhaps my lot will change completely; but all that's not to the point, and not the main thing. What does matter is that my whole life has changed already. I left a great deal there—too much. It's all gone. As I sat in the train, I thought: 'Now I am going among people; I know nothing, perhaps, but a new life is beginning for me.' I determined to perform my business resolutely and honestly. I may find it dull and difficult among people. In the first place, I resolved to be courteous and open with everyone; after all, no one will expect more than that of me. Perhaps here, too, they will take me for a child—well, let them. Everyone takes me for an idiot, too, for some reason. I was indeed so ill at one time that I really did resemble an idiot then; but how can I be an idiot now, when I can see for myself that people take me for an idiot? I come into places and think, 'I see I'm taken for an idiot, but

I'm intelligent after all, and they don't surmise it.' . . . I often have that thought. It was only in Berlin, when I got a few little letters from there, which they had already managed to write me, that I realized how much I love them. It's very hard getting the first letter! How downcast they were seeing me off! They'd begun seeing me off for a month beforehand: *'Léon s'en va, Léon s'en va pour toujours!'*[26] We gathered every evening at the waterfall, as we had before, and kept talking of how we would part. Sometimes we were as merry as before; only when we separated at night they began to kiss and hug me fervently, which they had not done before. Some of them ran in to see me by themselves, in secret from the others, simply to kiss and hug me alone, not before all the others. When I was setting off on the journey, they all, the whole flock of them, went with me to the station. The railway station was about a verst from our village. They restrained themselves to keep from crying, but many of them couldn't do it and cried aloud, especially the girls. We made haste so as not to be late, but one or another of them would suddenly rush out of the crowd at me in the middle of the road, throw his little arms around me and kiss me, and would stop the whole crowd simply for that; and although we were in a hurry, still everyone stopped and waited while he said good-bye. When I'd taken my seat in the train-car and the train had started, they all shouted 'Hurrah!' at me and stood on the spot a long time, until the train was out of sight. I gazed at them too . . . Listen, when I came in here and looked at your sweet faces—I scrutinize faces very closely now—and heard your first words, for the first time since then my heart felt light. I thought then that perhaps I truly was one of the lucky people: you see, I know that one doesn't often meet people whom one likes from the first, yet here I've come straight from the railway station and I meet you. I know very well that one ought to be ashamed to talk of one's feelings to everyone, but here I am talking to you and I'm not ashamed. I am an unsociable person and perhaps will not come to you again for a long time. Only don't take that as a nasty thought: I said it not because I don't value your friendship, and don't think either that I have taken offense at something. You asked me about your faces and what I noticed in them. I shall tell you that with great pleasure. You, Adelaida

26. Fr., Leon is going, Leon is going forever!

Ivanovna, have a happy face, the most likable of the three. Besides the fact that you are very good-looking, one looks at you and says, 'She has a face like a kind sister.' You approach one simply and gaily, but you are also quick to see into the heart. That's what I imagine about your face. You, Alexandra Ivanovna, have a wonderful and very sweet face too, but perhaps you have some secret sorrow; you have, without a doubt, the kindest soul, but you are not gay. You have some kind of peculiar nuance in your face, similar to the one of Holbein's Madonna in Dresden. Well, so much for your face: am I a good guesser? You yourselves took me for one. But about your face, Elizaveta Prokofyevna," he turned suddenly to the generaless, "about your face I not only imagine, but I am positively certain that you are a perfect child in everything, in everything, in everything good and everything bad, in spite of your age. You are not angry with me for saying so, are you? You know what I think of children, don't you? And don't think it's from simplicity that I have so frankly said all this just now about your faces: oh no, not at all! Perhaps I have my own idea, too."

VII

When the prince fell silent, everyone was looking at him gaily, even Aglaia, but particularly Lizaveta Prokofyevna.

"Now, there's an examination for you!" she exclaimed. "Well, dear ladies, you thought that you were going to patronize him like a poor relation, but he himself scarcely deigns to choose you, and with the proviso, to boot, that he'll come by only rarely. Well, we've been left for fools, and I am glad of it; and Ivan Fyodorovich most of all. Bravo, Prince, we were bid just now to put you through an examination. And as for what you said about my face, it's perfectly true: I am a child, and I know it. I knew about it even before you told me; you've expressed my very thoughts in a word. I consider your character entirely in accord with mine, and am very glad: like two peas in a pod. Only you are a man and I am a woman, and haven't been to Switzerland; there's the entire difference."

"Don't be hasty, *maman,*" exclaimed Aglaia. "The prince says that he had a particular thought behind all his admissions and did not speak just so."

"Yes, yes," laughed the others.

"Don't chaff him, my dears, he may be cleverer that all the three of you together. You'll see. Only how come, Prince, you have said nothing of Aglaia? Aglaia is waiting, and I am waiting."

"I can't say anything right now; I'll say it later."

"Why? I would think she is conspicuous."

"Oh, yes, she is conspicuous; you are extremely beautiful, Aglaia Ivanovna. You are so lovely that one is afraid to look at you."

"Is that all? What about her qualities?"

"It's difficult to judge beauty; I am not ready yet. Beauty is—a riddle."

"That means that you've posed Aglaia a riddle," said Adelaida. "Solve it, Aglaia, won't you. But is she lovely, Prince, is she?"

"Extremely," answered the prince with warmth, casting an enthusiastic glance at Aglaia, "almost like Nastasya Filippovna, though the face is quite different! . . ."

Everyone looked at one another in surprise.

"Like who-o-o?" drawled the generaless. "How do you mean Nastasya Filippovna? Where have you seen Nastasya Filippovna? What Nastasya Filippovna?"

"Just now, Gavrila Ardalionovich was showing her portrait to Ivan Fyodorovich."

"What, he brought Ivan Fyodorovich her portrait?"

"To show it. Nastasya Filippovna had given Gavrila Ardalionovich her portrait today, and the latter brought it to show."

"I want to see it!" The generaless reared up. "Where is this portrait? If she gave it to him, then he must have it, and he is, of course, still in the study. On Wednesdays, he always comes to work and never leaves before four. Have Gavrila Ardalionovich called at once! No, I am not exactly dying to see him, in fact. Do me a favor, Prince, my pet, go to the study, take the photograph from him and bring it here. Tell him we want to look at it. Please."

"He is nice, but a bit too simple," said Adelaida when the prince had left.

"Yes, a bit too much," Alexandra agreed, "so that he is even a little absurd."

Neither the one nor the other seemed to utter their entire thought to the end.

"Still, he wriggled out of it very well with our faces," said Aglaia, "he flattered everyone, even *maman*."

"None of your barbs, please," exclaimed the generaless. "He did not flatter me, rather I was flattered."

"You think he was putting on airs?" asked Adelaida.

"I fancy he's not quite so simple."

"Now, there you go!" chafed the generaless. "Well, as I see it, you're even more absurd than he is. He's a bit simple, but he's got all his wits about him, in the most honorable sense, obviously. Exactly like me."

"Of course, it's disagreeable that I let it slip about the portrait," the prince was realizing to himself as he walked to the study feeling some gnawings of conscience. "But ... perhaps it was a good thing that I let it slip ..." A certain strange thought was beginning to dart through his mind, though it was still not entirely clear.

Gavrila Ardalionovich was still sitting in the study and was absorbed in his papers. It would seem that he indeed did not receive his salary from the joint-stock company for nothing. He was terribly disconcerted when the prince asked him for the portrait and recounted the way they had come to know of the portrait.

"Eh-eh-eh! And what did you have to go blabbering for!"—he exclaimed with ill-natured vexation—"You don't know anything . . . Idiot!" he muttered to himself.

"It's my fault, I did it entirely without thinking; it happened to come up. I said that Aglaia was almost as beautiful as Nastasya Filippovna."

Ganya asked him to relate it in more detail; the prince related it. Ganya again looked at him derisively.

"Well, you had to go and get stuck on Nastasya Filippovna . . ." he muttered, but, breaking off, sank into thought.

"Listen, Prince," Ganya said suddenly, as if an unexpected thought had struck him, "I have a great favor to ask of you . . . Though, in all honesty, I don't know . . ."

He became discomfited and didn't finish; he was making up his mind on something and seemed to be struggling with himself. The prince waited in silence. Ganya scanned him again with a searching, intent gaze.

"Prince," he began again, "right now, in there, they . . . due to one completely strange circumstance . . . and an absurd one . . . for which I am not to blame ... well, in a word, that's irrelevant—in there, I fancy, they are rather cross with me, so that for some time I haven't wanted to go in there without being called. I must urgently speak with Aglaia Ivanovna at present. I've written a few words, in the event (a tiny folded paper appeared in his hand), but, you see, I don't know how to give it to her. Won't you undertake, Prince, to give it to Aglaia Ivanovna at once, but only Aglaia Ivanovna alone, in such a way, that is, so that no one sees it, you understand? It's no very terrible secret, nothing of that sort ... but ... Will you do it?"

"I'm not entirely comfortable with it," answered the prince.

"Oh, Prince, it's an extreme necessity for me!" Ganya began to plead, "she will perhaps answer ... Believe me, it's only in the worst case, in the absolute worst case, that I could have turned to you ... But with whom could I send it? ... It's very important ... terribly important for me ..."

Ganya was terribly afraid that the prince would not consent, and looked into his eyes with cringing supplication.

"Very well, I'll give it to her."

"But only so that no one notices," entreated Ganya, delighted. "And another thing, Prince, I may rely on your word of honor, can't I?"

"I won't show it to anyone," said the prince.

"The note is not sealed, but ..." Ganya began to utter, fretting too much, and stopped in embarrassment.

"Oh, I won't read it," the prince answered quite simply, took the portrait and left the study.

Left alone, Ganya clutched at his head.

"One word from her, and I ... truly, perhaps, I will break it off! ..." He could not sit down to his papers again for excitement and suspense, and began pacing from one corner of the study to the other.

The prince pondered as he went; he was unpleasantly struck by the errand, and unpleasantly struck by the thought of a letter from Ganya to Aglaia, too. But coming within two rooms of the drawing room, he suddenly stopped, as though recollecting something, looked around him, went to the window, nearer to the light, and began looking at the portrait of Nastasya Filippovna.

He wanted, as it were, to decipher something hidden in that face that had recently astonished him. The recent impression it had made had scarcely left him, and now he was in a hurry as if to verify something again. This face, extraordinary in its beauty and in something else, astonished him even more now. There was something like immeasurable pride and contempt, almost hatred, in that face, and at the same time something trusting, something wonderfully simple-hearted; these two contrasting elements aroused a feeling almost of compassion at the sight of these features. Her dazzling beauty was positively unbearable, the beauty of a pale face, almost sunken cheeks and glowing eyes; a strange beauty! The prince gazed at it for a minute, then suddenly recollected himself, looked around him, hastily raised the portrait to his lips and kissed it. When he walked into the drawing room a minute later, his face was perfectly calm.

But he had hardly entered the dining room (which was separated by one more room from the drawing room) when Aglaia, who was coming out, nearly collided with him in the doorway. She was alone.

"Gavrila Ardalionovich asked me to give you this," said the prince, handing her the note.

Aglaia came to a stop, took the note, and looked somewhat strangely at the prince. There was not the slightest embarrassment in her expression, perhaps only a shade of surprise in her eyes, and even that seemed only to refer to the prince. In her gaze, Aglaia seemed almost to demand that he account for himself—however did he wind up mixed up in this affair with Ganya?—and to demand it calmly and haughtily. They looked at one another for two or three seconds; finally, something mocking barely took shape in her face; she smiled slightly and walked past him.

The generaless gazed for some moments, silently and with a certain shade of nonchalance, at the photograph of Nastasya Filippovna, which she held before her in her outstretched hand, distancing it from her eyes excessively for effect.

"Yes, good-looking," she pronounced at last, "very good-looking indeed. I've seen her twice, only from afar. That's the sort of beauty you appreciate, then?" she suddenly said to the prince.

"Yes, that sort . . ." answered the prince with some effort.

"You mean, this very sort of beauty?"

"This very sort."

"Why?"

"In that face . . . there is so much suffering," answered the prince, as though involuntarily, as though he were talking to himself rather than answering a question.

"Anyway, perhaps you are talking drivel," the generaless concluded, and with a haughty gesture she flung the photograph away from her onto the table.

Alexandra took it, Adelaida approached her, and they looked at it together. At that moment Aglaia came back into the drawing room.

"What power!" Adelaida cried suddenly, looking eagerly over her sister's shoulder at the portrait.

"Where? What power?" Lizaveta Prokofyevna asked sharply.

"Such beauty is power," said Adelaida heatedly. "With beauty like that one might turn the world upside down!"

She walked pensively away to her easel. Aglaia only glanced cursorily at the portrait, narrowed her eyes, stuck out her little lower lip, walked away and sat down to the side, folding her hands.

The generaless rang the bell.

"Call Gavrila Ardalionovich here; he is in the study," she ordered the servant who came in.

"*Maman!*" exclaimed Alexandra significantly.

"I want to say a few words to him—that's enough!" her mother snapped quickly, cutting short her protest. She was evidently irritated. "We have nothing but secrets here now, Prince, you see. Nothing but secrets! It has to be so, it's a sort of etiquette, it's foolish. And in such a matter, which above everything demands frankness, clarity and honesty. There are marriages being arranged. I don't like these marriages . . ."

"*Maman,* what are you saying?" Alexandra again made haste to check her.

"What is it, dear daughter? Do you like it yourself, then? As for the prince's hearing it, we are friends. He and I are, in any case. God seeks good men, of course, but He has no need of wicked and capricious ones; especially capricious ones, who decide one thing today, and say something else tomorrow. Do you understand, Alexandra Ivanovna? They say I'm a bit queer, Prince, but I can tell what's what. For the heart is the main thing, and the rest is all nonsense. One must have sense too, of course . . . Perhaps sense is the main thing after all. Don't smirk, Aglaia, I am not contradicting myself: a foolish woman with a heart and no sense is just as much an unhappy fool as a foolish woman with sense and no heart. It's an old truth. You see, I am a fool with a heart and no sense, and you are a fool with sense and no heart; and so we are both unhappy, and we both suffer."

"And what makes you so unhappy, then, *maman*?" Adelaida could not resist asking. She seemed the only one of the company who had not lost her good humor.

"Learned daughters, for one thing," snapped her mother, "and as that's enough of itself, there's no need to trumpet the rest. There's been enough loquaciousness. We shall see how you two (I don't count Aglaia) will get out of it with your sense and loquaciousness, and whether you, most admirable Alexandra Ivanovna, will be happy with an honorable gentleman? . . . Ah! . . ." she exclaimed, seeing Ganya enter, "here comes another matrimonial alliance. Good day!" she said in response to Ganya's bow, not inviting him to sit down. "You are embarking upon matrimony?"

"Upon matrimony? . . . How? . . . What matrimony? . . ." muttered Gavrila Ardalionovich, dumbfounded. He was terribly disconcerted.

"Are you getting married? I ask you, if you prefer that expression?"

"N-no . . . I . . . N-no," lied Gavrila Ardalionovich, and a flush of shame washed over his face. He stole a glance at Aglaia, who was sitting off to the side, and quickly looked away. Aglaia gazed coldly, intently, and calmly at him, not taking her eyes off him, and observed his confusion.

"No? You said no?" the merciless Lizaveta Prokofyevna persistently continued to interrogate. "Enough, I shall remember that today, Wednesday morning, in answer to my question, you said: 'no.' What is it today, Wednesday?"

"I think Wednesday, *maman*," answered Adelaida.

"They never know the days. What day of the month is it?"

"The twenty-seventh," answered Ganya.

"The twenty-seventh? That is good, by a certain reckoning. Goodbye. You have a great deal to do, I think, and it's time for me to dress and be on my way; take your photograph. Give my regards to poor Nina Alexandrovna. Good-bye, Prince, my pet! Come and see us often, and I will go see old lady Belokonsky on purpose to tell her about you. And listen, my dear: I believe it was precisely for me that God brought you to Petersburg from Switzerland. Perhaps you'll have other business, but it's mainly for me. That was precisely God's design. Good-bye, dears. Alexandra, come to my room, my friend."

The generaless went out. Ganya, knocked off-balance, disoriented, angry, picked up the photograph from the table and with a twisted smile turned to the prince.

"Prince, I am heading home now. If you've not changed your mind about boarding with us, I will take you, for you don't even know the address."

"Wait a moment, Prince," said Aglaia, suddenly rising from her chair. "You must write in my album. Papa said you were a calligraphist. I'll bring it to you at once . . ."

And she went out.

"Good-bye, Prince, I am going too," said Adelaida.

She pressed the prince's hand firmly, smiling at him affably and kindly, and went out. She did not look at Ganya.

"It was you," snarled Ganya, suddenly falling upon the prince as soon as everyone had gone. "You're the one who babbled to them that I'm getting married!" he muttered in a rapid half-whisper, with an enraged face and an angry gleam in his eyes. "You shameless little chatterbox, you!"

"I assure you, you are mistaken," the prince answered calmly and politely. "I didn't even know you were going to be married."

"You heard Ivan Fyodorovich before, how he said that everything would be settled tonight at Nastasya Filippovna's, and that's what you repeated! You're lying! Where could they have found out from? Damn it all, who could have told them, except you? Wasn't the old woman hinting to me?"

"You must know best who told them, if you really fancy you were getting hints; I didn't say a word about it."

"Did you deliver the note? An answer?" Ganya interrupted with feverish impatience. But at that very moment Aglaia returned and the prince didn't have time to answer anything.

"Here, Prince," said Aglaia, laying her album on the little table, "choose a page and write me something. Here is a quill, still a new one, too. Is it all right that it's a steel one? I heard that calligraphists don't write with steel ones."

Speaking with the prince, she seemed not even to notice that Ganya was right there. But while the prince was fixing the quill, looking for a page, and making ready, Ganya went up to the fireplace where Aglaia was standing, just to the right, near the prince, and in a quavering, breaking voice said almost in her ear:

"One word, only one word from you—and I am saved."

The prince turned around quickly and looked at them both. There was real despair in Ganya's face; he seemed to have uttered those words without thinking, at great speed. Aglaia looked at him for a few seconds with exactly the same calm surprise with which she had recently looked on the prince, and it seemed that this calm surprise of hers, this bewilderment, as if from a complete incomprehension of what was being said to her, was more terrible for Ganya at this moment than the strongest contempt.

"What am I to write?" asked the prince.

"I will dictate to you," said Aglaia, turning to him. "Are you ready? Then write: 'I do not enter into bargains.' Then write the date and month underneath. Show me."

The prince handed her the album.

"Excellent! You've written it wonderfully; you have exquisite hand-writing! I thank you. Good-bye, Prince . . . Wait," she added, as if suddenly recollecting something, "come along, I want to give you something for a keepsake."

The prince followed her; but upon entering the dining room, Aglaia stopped.

"Read this," she said, handing him Ganya's note.

The prince took the note and looked at Aglaia in bewilderment.

"But I know that you haven't read it, and you couldn't be that man's confidant. Go on, read, I want you to read it."

The note had evidently been written in haste:

Today my fate will be decided, you know in what way. Today I must give my word irrevocably. I have no right to your sympathy, I dare not have any hopes; but once you uttered a word, just a single word, and this word brought light into the whole dark night of my life and be-came my beacon. Speak one such word again now—and you will save me from ruin! Only say to me: *break off everything,* and I will break it all off this very day. Oh, what would it cost you to say that! In that word, I ask only for a sign of your sympathy and pity for me—and only that, *only that!* And nothing else, *nothing!* I dare not dream of any kind of hope, for I am not worthy of it. But after a word from you, I will accept my poverty again, and will begin to endure my desperate situation with joy. I shall face the struggle, I shall be glad of it, I shall be resurrected in it with new strength!

So send me that word of compassion (only compassion *alone*, I swear!). Do not be angry with the audacity of a desperate and drowning man for daring to make a last effort to save himself from ruin.

G.I.

"This man assures me," said Aglaia sharply, when the prince had finished reading, "that the words 'break off everything' will not compromise me and will bind me to nothing, and gives me, as you see, a written guarantee of it in this very note. Notice how naïvely he hastened to underline certain little words, and how coarsely his secret thought shows through it. And incidentally, he knows that if he broke it all off, but by himself, not waiting for a word from me and without even telling me about it, without resting any hopes on me, then I should have changed my feelings toward him, and perhaps might have become his friend. He knows that for certain! But he has a dirty soul; he knows but cannot bring himself to do it; he knows, and still asks for a guarantee. He is not capable of acting on faith. He wants, in the place of the hundred thousand, for me to give him hopes of my hand. And as for the previous word, of which he speaks in the note and which supposedly brought light into his life, it is a bold-faced lie. I simply took pity on him once. But he is insolent and shameless: he immediately had the thought at the time that hope was possible; I understood it at once. Ever since then, he has been angling for me; and he is angling now. But enough. Take the note and give it back to him, right away, as soon as you leave our house, obviously, not before."

"And what shall I say to him in answer?"

"Nothing, of course. That's the best answer. But, it would seem, you intend to live in his house?"

"Ivan Fyodorovich himself advised me to this morning," said the prince.

"Then be on your guard against him, I warn you; he won't forgive you now for returning his note to him."

Aglaia pressed the prince's hand lightly and went out. Her face was grave and sullen; she did not even smile when she nodded to the prince in parting.

"I'll be right there, I'll only get my bundle," said the prince to Ganya, "and we'll leave."

Ganya stamped his foot from impatience. His face had positively turned black with fury. At last, both went out into the street, the prince with his bundle in his hand.

"The answer? The answer?" Ganya pounced upon him. "What did she say to you? Did you deliver the letter?"

The prince gave him the note without a word. Ganya froze.

"What! My letter!" he cried, "he didn't even deliver it! Oh, I should have guessed it! Oh, acc-ccu-cursed . . . It's clear that she understood nothing just now! But how, how, how could you not deliver it, oh, acc-ccu-ccursed . . ."

"Excuse me, on the contrary, I succeeded in delivering your note at once, the very minute you'd given it to me, and exactly as you had asked. It has come into my hands again because Aglaia Ivanovna gave it back to me just now."

"When? When?"

"As soon as I'd finished writing in her album, when she invited me to follow her. (You heard her?) We went into the dining room, she handed me the note, bid me to read it, and bid me to give it back to you."

"Re-eee-ead it!" Ganya shouted practically at the top of his lungs, "read it! You've read it?"

And he stood stock still again in stupefaction in the middle of the sidewalk, so astounded that he positively gaped.

"Yes, I've read it, just now."

"And it was she, she herself gave it to you to read? Herself?"

"She herself, and believe me, I would not have read it unless she asked me to."

Ganya was silent for a minute and was trying to work something out with painful effort, but suddenly he exclaimed:

"It can't be! She could not have bid you to read it. You are lying! You read it on your own!"

"I am speaking the truth," answered the prince in the same, utterly unruffled tone, "and believe me: I am very sorry that it has made such an unpleasant impression upon you."

"But, you miserable creature, did she at least say anything to you at the time? Didn't she make some answer?"

"Yes, of course."

"Well, speak then, speak, oh, damn it!"

And Ganya stamped on the pavement twice with his right foot, which was clad in a galosh.

"As soon as I read it, she told me that you were angling for her; that you would like to compromise her so that she might give you hopes, so that, supported by this hope, you might break without a loss with the other hope of a hundred thousand. That if you had done this without bargaining with her, had broken everything off yourself, without asking for a guarantee from her beforehand, then she would have perhaps become your friend. That's everything, I think. Oh, something more: when I asked, after I'd already taken the letter, what was the answer, she said that no answer would be the best answer of all—I think that's how it was; excuse me if I've forgotten her exact words and only repeat it as I understood it."

Ganya was overcome by immeasurable fury, and his rage burst forth without any restraint.

"Ah! So that's how it is!" he snarled, "so my notes are thrown out the window! Ah! She won't enter into bargains—then I will! And we'll see! I've still got more to fall back on ... We'll see! ... I'll make her knuckle under! ..."

He grimaced, turned pale, foamed at the mouth; he shook his fist. In this manner, they walked a few steps. He stood on not the least bit of ceremony with the prince, just as if he were alone in his room, for he looked upon him as absolutely of no consequence. But suddenly he realized something and came to his senses.

"But how is it," he suddenly turned to the prince, "how is it that you (idiot!—he added to himself), that you are suddenly trusted with such confidences two hours after you were first acquainted? How is it?"

Envy was just what he needed on top of all his suffering. It suddenly stung him in the very heart.

"That I wouldn't be able to explain," answered the prince.

Ganya looked at him wrathfully.

"Can it be to make you a present of her confidence that she called you into the dining room? Didn't she intend to give you something?"

"That's just how I understand it."

"But what for, devil take it! Whatever did you do there? How have you made them like you? Listen," he was all aflutter (everything in him in that moment was somehow scattered and boiling in disorder, so that he could not gather his thoughts)—"listen, couldn't you remember somehow, and work it out properly, just what you were talking about in there, all the words, from the very beginning? Didn't you notice anything, won't you recollect?"

"Oh, certainly I can," answered the prince. "At the very beginning, when I first came in and made their acquaintance, we began talking about Switzerland."

"Oh, to hell with Switzerland!"

"Then, about capital punishment..."

"Capital punishment?"

"Yes; something occasioned it... Then I told them about how I lived there for three years, and one story to do with a poor village girl..."

"Oh, to hell with the poor village girl! And further?" Ganya was wild with impatience.

"Then how Schneider told me his opinion of my character and compelled me..."

"Hang Schneider, and damn his opinions! Further!"

"Further, something occasioned my speaking of faces, that is to say, of facial expressions, and I said that Aglaia Ivanovna was almost as beautiful as Nastasya Filippovna. And that was when I let it slip about the portrait..."

"But you didn't repeat, did you, you didn't repeat what you heard lately in the study? No? No?"

"I tell you again, I did not."

"Well, where the devil, then... Bah! Did Aglaia show the note to the old lady, I wonder?"

"In that regard, I can assure you positively that she did not show it. I was there the entire time; and she didn't have the time to do it, anyway."

"But perhaps you missed something... Oh! Acc-ccu-cursed idiot," he exclaimed, completely beside himself now, "he can't even tell anything properly."

Ganya, having once begun to be abusive and meeting no resistance, lost all restraint, as it is always wont to happen with certain people. A little more, and he might have even begun to spit, to such a point was he enraged. But precisely this rage made him blind; otherwise he would have long since taken note of the fact that this "idiot," whom he was disparaging this way, was indeed at times only too quick and subtle in understanding everything and could give an extremely satisfactory account of things. But suddenly, something unexpected happened.

"I must tell you, Gavrila Ardalionovich," the prince suddenly said, "that earlier, I had in fact been so unwell that I really was almost an idiot; but now I have been well again a long time, and so I rather dislike it when people call me an idiot to my face. Though you might be excused in consideration of your misfortunes, in your vexation, you've given me a tongue-lashing twice already. I don't like that at all, especially so sudden, as you've done it, at the first acquaintance; and since we are presently standing at a crossing, wouldn't it be better if we went our separate ways: you go to the right, to your house, and I to the left. I've got twenty-five rubles, and I am certain to find some lodging house."

Ganya was terribly disconcerted and even flushed with shame.

"Excuse me, Prince," he exclaimed warmly, suddenly exchanging his vituperative tone for extreme politeness, "for heaven's sake, excuse me! You see what trouble I'm in! You still know nearly nothing, but if you knew it all, you would certainly excuse me just a little; though, naturally, it's inexcusable . . ."

"Oh, I don't need such big apologies," the prince hastened to answer, "I do understand, after all, that it is very unpleasant for you, and that's why you've been railing. Well, let's go to your house. I'll come with pleasure . . ."

"No, I can't let him go like that now," thought Ganya to himself, casting spiteful glances at the prince along the way, "this swindler has dragged it all out of me, and then suddenly took off the mask . . . There's something significant in it. But we shall see! Everything will be resolved, everything, everything! This very day!"

They were already standing right by the house.

VIII

Ganya's apartment was on the third floor, on a very clean, light, and spacious staircase, and consisted of six or seven rooms, large and small, admittedly of the most ordinary kind, but in any case, not quite within the means of a civil servant and family man, even with an income of two thousand rubles. However, it was suited to the keeping of lodgers, with board and service, and had been taken by Ganya and his family no more than two months ago, to the greatest distaste of Ganya himself, upon the insistence and pleading of Nina Alexandrovna and Varvara Ardalionovna, who wished in turn to be useful and increase the family's income if only a little. Ganya scowled and called keeping lodgers a disgrace; after this, he began to feel as if ashamed in society, where he had been accustomed to appear as a young man with a certain brilliance and a future. All these concessions to fate and all this vexatious constriction—all these were his deep psychic wounds. For some time past he had become extremely and quite disproportionately irritable over every trifle, and if he still consented to yield for a time and put up with it, it was only because he was resolved to change and undo it all in the nearest possible future. But meanwhile, that very change, that very same way out on which he had determined, constituted a formidable problem—a problem the impending solution to which threatened to be more troublesome and agonizing than all that had gone before.

The apartment was divided by a hallway that began right at the entryway. On one side of the hallway were the three rooms that were intended to be let, to "specially recommended" lodgers; aside from that, on the same side of the hallway, at its farthest end, next to the kitchen, was a fourth room, more cramped than the rest, which was occupied by retired General Ivolgin himself, the father of the family, who slept on a wide sofa and was obliged to go in and out of the flat through the kitchen and by the back stairs. This same little room was also occupied by Gavrila Ardalionovich's thirteen-year-old brother, the schoolboy Kolya; he was also fated to be crammed in here, to do his lessons, sleep on another, rather old, narrow, and short little sofa, on torn sheets, and, above all, to wait on and *keep an eye* on his father, who was more and more incapable of doing without it. The prince was given the middle of the three rooms; the first, on the right, was occupied by Ferdyshchenko, and the third, to the left, was still empty. But Ganya first led the prince into the family's side of the apartment. These family quarters consisted of a drawing room, which, when necessary, turned into a dining room; a sitting room, which, actually, was a sitting room only in the mornings, and in the evenings turned into Ganya's study and his bedroom; and, finally, of a third room, cramped and always shut up: this was the bedroom of Nina Alexandrovna and Varvara Ardalionovna. In a word, everything in this apartment was cramped and hemmed in; Ganya could only grind his teeth to himself; though he was and wished to be respectful to his mother, one could see upon setting foot in their house that he was a great despot in his family.

Nina Alexandrovna was not alone in the sitting room, Varvara Ardalionovna was sitting with her; they were both busy with some kind of knitting and talked with a guest, Ivan Petrovich Ptitsyn. Nina Alexandrovna seemed to be about fifty, with a thin, sunken face and very dark rings under her eyes. She looked unwell and somewhat doleful, but her face and expression were rather pleasant; from the first word, an earnest disposition full of genuine dignity made itself evident. In spite of her doleful air, one could sense that she had firmness and even determination. She was dressed with exceeding modesty, in something dark, and entirely like an old woman, but her attitude, her conversation, her entire manner revealed a woman who had been in better society.

Varvara Ardalionovna was a girl of twenty-three, of medium height, rather thin, with a face that was not what one would call beautiful, but that contained the secret of being likeable without beauty and arousing feelings for herself approaching passion. She was very like her mother and was even dressed in almost the same way as her mother, out of a complete lack of desire to get dressed up. Her gray eyes might have at times been very merry and kind, if they had not as a rule looked grave and pensive, sometimes even too much so, especially in recent times. Firmness and determination were visible in her face, too, but one could sense that this firmness might even be more vigorous and enterprising than her mother's. Varvara Ardalionovna was rather hot-tempered, and her brother was sometimes even afraid of this hotheadedness. The guest sitting with them now, Ivan Petrovich Ptitsyn, was a bit afraid of it, too. He was still a fairly young man, just shy of thirty, modestly but elegantly dressed, with a pleasant but somehow a bit too solemn manner. His dark, reddish-brown little beard marked him as a man not engaged in affairs of civil service.[27] He could talk cleverly and well, but was more often silent. He made a pleasant impression on the whole. He was obviously not impartial toward Varvara Ardalionovna, and did not conceal his feelings. Varvara Ardalionovna treated him amicably, but put off answering certain of his questions and did not even like them; Ptitsyn, however, was far from being discouraged. Nina Alexandrovna was kind to him, and lately had even began to confide much in him. Moreover, it was known that he was engaged in trying to make his fortune by lending money at high interest on more or less good security. He was a great friend of Ganya's.

After a detailed but disjointed introduction given by Ganya (who greeted his mother rather dryly, did not greet his sister at all, and immediately drew Ptitsyn out of the room), Nina Alexandrovna said some kind words to the prince and bid Kolya, who peeped in at the door, to conduct him to the middle room. Kolya was a boy with a merry and rather sweet face, with a trusting and simple manner.

"And where is your luggage?" he asked, ushering the prince into the room.

"I have a bundle; I left it in the entryway."

"I'll bring it to you at once. We have but cook and Matryona for servants, so I help out too. Varya looks after everything and gets cross. Ganya says you've come from Switzerland today?"

"Yes."

"And is it nice in Switzerland?"

"Very."

"Mountains?"

27. In 1698, as part of an effort to westernize Russian society, Peter the Great outlawed beards for all but the clergy. According to Orthodox belief, however, shaving was a sin, and many devout men who were not in military or civil service refused. They were allowed to keep their beards upon paying a special tax. While the rules were relaxed somewhat by subsequent rulers, the prohibition on beards in the state service remained in place until the 1860s.

"Yes."

"I'll haul in your bundles at once."

Varvara Ardalionovna came in.

"Matryona will make your bed at once. Do you have a trunk?"

"No, a bundle. Your brother has gone for it; it's in the entryway."

"There's no bundle there except this little one; where did you put it?" asked Kolya, coming back into the room.

"Oh, there isn't but that," explained the prince, accepting his bundle.

"A-ah! And I was wondering whether they hadn't been carried off by Ferdyshchenko."

"Don't make up silly nonsense," sternly said Varya, who spoke even with the prince somewhat tersely and just barely with civility.

"*Chère Babette*,[28] you could treat me more tenderly, I'm not Ptitsyn after all."

"You could get a whipping, too, Kolya, you're still that stupid. You can ask Matryona for anything you need; dinner is at half past four. You can dine with us or in your own room, as you prefer. Let's go, Kolya, don't get in his way."

"Let's go, you determined character!"

On their way out, they ran into Ganya.

"Is Father home?" Ganya asked Kolya, and on Kolya's affirmative reply whispered something in his ear. Kolya nodded and followed his sister out.

"Two words, Prince; I forgot to mention it with all this . . . business. I have a request: do me a favor—if it won't be a great bother to you—don't gossip here of what has just passed between Aglaia and me, nor *there* of what you'll find here; because there's plenty of disgrace here too. The devil take it, anyway . . . At least, restrain yourself for today."

"I assure you that I gossiped much less than you think," said the prince with some irritation at Ganya's reproaches. Their relations were evidently becoming more and more strained.

"Well, I've endured enough today through you. In a word, I'm asking you."

---

28. Fr., dear Babette. Varvara is the Russian variant of Barbara, of which Babette is a diminutive form in French.

"And keep this in mind, too, Gavrila Ardalionovich, in what way was I actually bound of late, and why shouldn't I have spoken of the portrait? After all, you didn't ask me."

"Phooey, what a horrid room," remarked Ganya, looking around him contemptuously. "Dark, and the windows to the yard. In all respects, you've come to us at the wrong time. . . . Well, that's not my business; I don't let the rooms."

Ptitsyn peeked in and called Ganya; the latter left the prince hastily, despite the fact that he had something he still wanted to say, but he was evidently ill at ease and seemed ashamed to begin; and he seemed to have sniped about the room in confusion, too.

No sooner had the prince washed and managed to get fixed up somewhat than the door opened again and a new figure appeared.

This was a gentleman of some thirty years, not insignificant height, broad-shouldered, with a huge, curly, reddish head of hair. His face was fleshy and ruddy, his lips thick, his nose broad and flat, eyes small, swollen, and mocking, as if they were incessantly winking. On the whole, it made a pretty insolent impression. He was a bit grimily dressed.

He first opened the door exactly far enough to poke his head in. The head, having been poked in, surveyed the room about five seconds, then the door began to open slowly, the whole figure came into view in the doorway, but the guest still did not come in, and instead continued, squinting his eyes, to scrutinize the prince from the doorway. At last, he closed the door behind him, came nearer, sat down on a chair, took the prince firmly by the arm, and sat him down across from him on the sofa.

"Ferdyshchenko," he said, looking intently and inquiringly into the prince's face.

"And what of it?" answered the prince, almost bursting out in laughter.

"A lodger," Ferdyshchenko spoke again, continuing his scrutiny as before.

"Did you want to make my acquaintance?"

"Heh!" said the guest, ruffling up his hair and sighing, and began to stare in the opposite corner. "Have you got money?" he asked suddenly, turning to the prince.

"A little."

"How much, exactly?"

"Twenty-five rubles."

"Show me."

The prince took the twenty-five-ruble note out of his waistcoat pocket and handed it to Ferdyshchenko. The latter unfolded it, looked at it, then turned it over to the other side, then held it to the light.

"Rather strange," he said, as if lost in reflection, "why ever would they turn brown? These twenty-fivers sometimes brown terribly, while others, on the contrary, fade completely. Take it."

The prince took his note back. Ferdyshchenko got up from the chair.

"I've come to warn you: in the first place, not to lend me money, because I will be sure to ask you to."

"Very well."

"Do you intend to pay here?"

"I intend it."

"Well, I don't; thanks. I'm the next door to your right, did you see? Try not to come and see me too often; I shall come and see you, don't worry. Have you seen the general?"

"No."

"Nor heard him, either?"

"Of course not."

"Well, you'll see him and hear him then; what's more, he tries to borrow money even of me. *Avis au lecteur.*[29] Good-bye. Is it possible to live with the name Ferdyshchenko? Eh?"

And he went to the door. The prince later learned that this gentleman felt it incumbent upon him to amaze everyone by his originality and merriment, but somehow could never carry it off. He even made an unpleasant impression on some people, which he sincerely lamented, but still he did not abandon his self-appointed task. At the door he managed to recover, as it were, having stumbled against a gentleman who was coming in; after letting this new visitor, who was a stranger to the prince, into the room, he winked at him warningly several times behind his back and, in this manner, left not without some aplomb after all.

The new gentleman was tall, about fifty-five or even more, rather

29. Fr., note to the reader (i.e., be warned!).

corpulent, with a purple-red, fleshy and flabby face, framed by thick gray sideburns, sporting a mustache, and with large eyes that popped out to some great extent. He would have cut a rather imposing figure if there had not been something slovenly, threadbare, even grimy about it. He was dressed in plain house-clothes—an old frock coat with practically tattered elbows; his linen was also sullied. At close quarters he smelled not a little of vodka; but his manner was impressive, somewhat studied, and with a visibly jealous desire to astound with his dignity. The gentleman approached the prince unhurriedly, with an affable smile, took him silently by the hand and, keeping it in his, peered into his face for some time, as if recognizing familiar features.

"It's he! It's he!" he pronounced softly, but solemnly. "As he lives and breathes! I heard them utter a dear and familiar name, and it brought back the irretrievable past ... Prince Myshkin?"

"Precisely so, sir."

"General Ivolgin, retired and unfortunate. Your name and patronymic, may I be so bold to ask?"

"Lev Nikolaevich."

"Yes, yes! Son of my friend, the companion of my childhood, one might say, Nikolai Petrovich?"

"My father's name was Nikolai Lvovich."

"Lvovich," the general corrected himself, but without haste, and with absolute self-assurance, as though he had not in the least forgotten it, but had uttered the wrong name by accident. He sat down, and also taking Myshkin by the arm, seated him beside him. "I used to carry you in my arms."

"Is that so?" asked the prince. "My father has been dead some twenty years now."

"Yes; twenty years; twenty years and three months. We went to school together; I went straight into the army ..."

"My father was in the army too, sublieutenant in the Vassilkovsky regiment."

"In the Belomirsky. His transfer to the Belomirsky occurred almost just before his death. I stood there and blessed him for eternity. Your dear mother ..."

The general paused, as if arrested by a sad memory.

"And she died six months later, too, from a chill," said the prince.

"Not from a chill. Not from a chill—believe an old man. I was there, and I buried her too. It was grief for her prince, and not a chill. Yes, sir, I remember the princess too! Youth! It was on her account that the prince and I, childhood friends, almost came to murder each other."

The prince was beginning to listen with some mistrust.

"I was passionately in love with your mother when she was betrothed—betrothed to my friend. The prince observed it and was dumbfounded. He comes to me early in the morning, before seven o'clock, wakes me up. I get dressed in amazement; there's silence on both sides; I understood it all. He takes two pistols out of his pocket. Across a handkerchief. Without witnesses. Why have witnesses when in five minutes we're sending each other into eternity? We loaded, stretched the handkerchief, took position, placed the pistols at each other's hearts, and were looking each other in the face. Suddenly, both had tears gushing from our eyes, our hands trembled. Both, both at once! Well, here, naturally, followed embraces and a battle of mutual generosity. The prince cries: she's yours! I cry: she's yours! In a word . . . in a word . . . have you come . . . to live with us?"

"Yes, for a little time, perhaps," said the prince, seeming to stammer somewhat.

"Prince, Mother asks you to come to her," called out Kolya, looking in at the door. The prince would have risen to go, but the general put his right palm on his shoulder and amiably pulled him down to the couch again.

"As a true friend of your father's I want to warn you," said the general, "you can see for yourself, I have suffered, through a tragic catastrophe; though without a trial! Without a trial! Nina Alexandrovna is an uncommon woman. Varvara Ardalionovna, my daughter, is an uncommon daughter! Circumstances force us to take in boarders—an unheard-of downfall! . . . I, who was on the eve of becoming governorgeneral! . . . But you, we shall always be glad to receive. And in the meantime, there is a tragedy in my house!"

The prince looked at him inquiringly and with great curiosity.

"A marriage is being arranged, and an uncommon one. A marriage between a woman of dubious character and a young man who could have been a *kammerjunker*.[30] That woman is to be brought into the same

---

30. Ger., a minor noble title involving low-level duties at court.

house with my daughter, and with my wife! But as long as I breathe, she shall not enter it! I will lie down on the threshold and let her step over me! . . . Ganya, I scarcely speak to now, even avoid meeting him. I warn you on purpose; if you are to live with us, then you'll be witness to it in any case. But you are the son of my friend, and I have the right to hope . . ."

"Prince, do me a favor, come into the sitting room," called Nina Alexandrovna, now appearing in the doorway herself.

Nina Alexandrovna glanced reproachfully at the general and searchingly at the prince, but did not say a word. The prince set off after her; but no sooner had they entered the sitting room and sat down, and no sooner had Nina Alexandrovna begun, very rapidly and in an undertone, to apprise the prince of something, than it suddenly pleased the general himself to appear in the sitting room. Nina Alexandrovna fell silent at once and, with evident vexation, bent over her knitting again. The general perhaps observed this vexation, but continued to be in the most excellent spirits.

"The son of my friend!" he exclaimed, addressing Nina Alexandrovna. "And so unexpectedly! I'd long ceased to even imagine. But, my dear, you can't say you don't remember the late Nikolai Lvovich? You were in time to meet him alive . . . in Tver?"

"I don't remember Nikolai Lvovich. Is that your father?" she asked the prince.

"Yes; but he died, I think, not in Tver but in Elizavetgrad," the prince observed timidly to the general. "I heard it from Pavlishchev . . ."

"In Tver," maintained the general, "the transfer to Tver came just before his death, and even before his illness developed. You were still too little, and could not remember either the transfer or the journey; as for Pavlishchev, he may have been mistaken, though he was a most excellent man."

"You knew Pavlishchev, too?"

"He was an uncommon person, but I witnessed it in person. I blessed him on his deathbed . . ."

"But my father died awaiting trial," observed the prince again, "although I was never able to find out exactly for what; he died in a hospital."

"Oh, that was in the matter of Private Kolpakov, and there is no doubt that the prince would have been acquitted."

"Was that so? You know it for certain?" asked the prince with particular interest.

"I should think so!" exclaimed the general. "The court broke up without coming to a decision. It was an impossible case! A mysterious case, even, one might say: Staff Captain Larionov, the company commander, dies; the prince is appointed for a time to carry out his duties; good. Private Kolpakov commits a theft—boot-leather from a comrade—and spends it on drink; good. The prince—and take note, this was in the presence of the field-sergeant and the corporal—rakes Kolpakov over the coals and threatens to have him flogged. Very good. Kolpakov goes to the barracks, lies down on the cot and, after a quarter of an hour, dies. Excellent, but the case is unexpected, almost impossible. One way or another, Kolpakov is buried; the prince reports it, and then Kolpakov is stricken from the lists. What could be better, it seems? But exactly half a year later, at the brigade review, Private Kolpakov turns up, as though nothing had happened, in the third company of the second battalion of the Novozemlyansky infantry regiment,[31] in the same brigade and in the same division!"

"How!" exclaimed the prince, beside himself with astonishment.

"It's not so, it's a mistake!" Nina Alexandrovna suddenly addressed him, looking at him almost in anguish. *"Mon mari se trompe."*[32]

"But, my dear, *se trompe*, that's easily said, but try and solve such a case yourself! Everyone was dumbfounded. I should have been the first to say *qu'on se trompe.*[33] But, unhappily, I was a witness and was on the commission myself. All eyewitness reports showed that this was the same Private Kolpakov, absolutely the very same one, who had been buried half a year ago with the usual parade and drum-beating. The case is indeed uncommon, almost impossible, I agree, but . . ."

"Father, they've served your dinner," announced Varvara Ardalionovna, entering the room.

"Ah, that's capital, excellent! I am certainly hungry . . . But the case, one might say, was even psychological . . ."

"The soup will be cold again," said Varya with impatience.

"I'm coming, I'm coming," muttered the general leaving the room.

31. This regiment is fictional. The name is taken from Griboedov's seminal play *Woe from Wit.*

32. Fr., My husband is mistaken.

33. Fr., that there was a mistake.

"And in spite of all the inquiries" could still be heard from the corridor.

"You will have to excuse a great deal in Ardalion Alexandrovich if you remain with us," said Nina Alexandrovna to the prince. "But, anyway, he won't bother you very much; he even dines alone. You will agree, everyone has his failings and his . . . peculiarities, and some others, perhaps, have even more than those who usually have the finger pointed at them. I would ask you for one thing most particularly: if my husband ever applies to you about payment for the room, then tell him that you have given it to me. That is to say, anything you give to Ardalion Alexandrovich would count toward your bill in any case, but I ask you solely for the sake of accuracy . . . What is this, Varya?"

Varya came back into the room and without speaking handed her mother the portrait of Nastasya Filippovna. Nina Alexandrovna started and scrutinized it for some time, at first as if with dismay, and then with an oppressively bitter feeling. At last, she looked inquiringly at Varya.

"A present to him today, from herself," said Varya, "and in the evening, everything shall be settled between them."

"This evening!" Nina Alexandrovna repeated in a low voice, as though in despair. "Well, then. There is no more doubt about it anymore, and no hope left either: she has proclaimed it all with her portrait . . . But did he show it to you himself?" she added with surprise.

"You know that we've hardly spoken a word for the last month. Ptitsyn told me all about it, and the portrait was lying on the floor there, by the table; I picked it up."

"Prince," Nina Alexandrovna turned to him suddenly, "I wanted to ask you (that was, namely, why I asked you to come here), have you known my son long? I believe he said that you've only just arrived from somewhere today?"

The prince gave a brief account of himself, leaving out the greater part. Nina Alexandrovna and Varya heard him out.

"I am not trying to pry anything out about Gavrila Ardalionovich by questioning you," remarked Nina Alexandrovna, "you must make no mistake on that account. If there is something he cannot admit to me himself, I don't even want to find it out behind his back. I bring it up, namely, because earlier, while you were here, and afterward, when you had gone out, Ganya answered to my question about you: 'He knows everything, there's no need to stand on ceremony with him!' What does this mean? That is, I should like to know to what extent . . ."

Ganya and Ptitsyn suddenly came in; Nina Alexandrovna fell silent at once. The prince remained in the chair next to her, while Varya moved away; the portrait of Nastasya Filippovna lay in the most conspicuous place, on Nina Alexandrovna's worktable, right in front of her. Seeing it, Ganya frowned, took it from the table with annoyance, and flung it on his writing-table, which stood at the other end of the room.

"Is it today, Ganya?" Nina Alexandrovna asked suddenly.

"Is what today?" Ganya almost started, and suddenly flew at the prince. "Ah, I understand, you're here already! . . . Well, what is it with you, finally, some kind of disease? Can't you restrain yourself? Well, can't you get it, finally, your excellency . . ."

"I'm at fault here, Ganya, and no one else," interrupted Ptitsyn.

Ganya looked at him inquiringly.

"But it's better so, Ganya, especially since the business is settled, on one side," muttered Ptitsyn, and, moving away, sat at the table, took out of his pocket some piece of paper covered with penciled writing, and began to examine it intently. Ganya stood sullenly and waited with unease for the family row. It did not occur to him to apologize to the prince.

"If everything is settled, then Ivan Petrovich is naturally right," said Nina Alexandrovna. "Don't scowl, please, and don't get irritated, Ganya, I'm not going to ask you about anything you don't care to tell me yourself, and I assure you that I am completely resigned, do me a favor, don't get agitated."

She pronounced this without taking her attention from her work and, it seemed, with genuine calm. Ganya was surprised, but was cautiously silent and kept looking at his mother, waiting for her to explain herself more clearly. Domestic quarrels had cost him much too dearly already. Nina Alexandrovna noticed this caution and added with a bitter smile:

"You are still skeptical and don't believe me; don't worry, there shall be no tears, no entreaties, as before, on my part, at least. My only desire is that you may be happy, and you know that; I submit to the inevitable, but my heart will always be with you, whether we remain together or whether we part. Of course, I answer only for myself; you can't demand the same thing of your sister..."

"Ah, her again!" exclaimed Ganya, looking mockingly and with hatred at his sister. "Mamma! I swear to you again what I have promised you already: no one shall ever dare to be heedless of you as long as I am here, as long as I live. Whoever may be concerned, I shall insist on the utmost respect being shown to you from anyone who enters our doors..."

Ganya was so happy that he looked at his mother with an almost conciliatory, almost affectionate, expression.

"I wasn't afraid of anything on my account, Ganya, you know that; it's not for myself that I've worried and suffered all this time. They say everything will be settled between you today? What will be settled, then?"

"This evening, at her house, she promised to announce whether she agrees or not," answered Ganya.

"For almost three weeks we have avoided speaking of it, and it has been better so. Now that everything is settled, I will allow myself to ask just one thing: how could she have given you her consent and even give you her portrait when you don't love her? Can you really ... with a woman so ... so ..."

"Well, experienced, you mean?"

"I didn't mean to put it that way. Can you really have hoodwinked her to such an extent?"

An extraordinary exasperation was suddenly audible in this question. Ganya stood still awhile, thought for a minute and, not disguising his derision, said:

"You've gotten carried away, Mamma, and couldn't restrain yourself again, and that's just how everything always began and heated up with us. You said there would be neither interrogations nor reproaches, and they've begun already! We'd better drop it; truly, let's drop it; at least, you had the intention ... I will never leave you for anything; another man would have run away from such a sister, at the least—See how she's looking at me now! Let's put an end to it here! And I was starting to feel so happy ... And how do you know that I am deceiving Nastasya Filippovna? As for Varya—she can please herself, and—enough. Well, that's really quite enough now!"

Ganya was becoming hotter under the collar with every word and paced aimlessly about the room. Such conversations went straight to the sore spot of every member of the family.

"I said that if she comes into the house, I shall leave it, and I'll keep my word too," said Varya.

"Out of obstinacy!" cried Ganya. "And it's out of obstinacy that you won't be married, either! What are you snorting at me for? I don't give a damn about it, you know, Varvara Ardalionovna; if it please you— you can carry out your intentions at once. I'm quite sick of you. What! You've made up your mind, at last, to leave us, Prince!" he cried to the prince, having seen that the latter was rising from his place.

Ganya's voice betrayed that stage of irritation in which a man almost revels in this irritation, gives himself up to it without any restraint, and virtually with growing delight, no matter where it may lead. The prince nearly looked around in the doorway in order to give some reply, but seeing from the aggrieved expression on his assailant's face that only the proverbial drop was lacking here to make the bucket overflow, he turned and went out in silence. A few minutes later he heard, by the echoes coming from the sitting room, that the discussion had become even noisier and more candid since his absence.

He crossed the drawing room into the entryway in order to get to the hall, and from it, to his room. Passing close to the front door to the stairs, he heard and noticed that outside the door, someone was making desperate efforts to ring the bell; but the bell, it seemed, must have had something wrong with it: it barely shuddered, but there was no sound. The prince undid the bolt, opened the door and—stepped back in amazement, even shuddered from head to toe: before him stood Nastasya Filippovna. He knew her at once from her portrait. Her eyes flashed with vexation when she saw him; she walked quickly into the entry, pushing him out of the way with her shoulder, and said indignantly, flinging off her fur coat:

"If you're too lazy to mend the bell, then you should at least sit in the entry when people knock. There, now he's dropped my coat, the oaf!"

The coat was indeed lying on the floor. Nastasya Filippovna, without waiting for the prince to take it off for her, had flung it off herself into his arms, not looking, from behind, but the prince was not quick enough to receive it.

"You should be turned out. Go along and announce me."

The prince was about to say something, but was so disconcerted that he did not get a word out and, carrying the coat, which he had picked up off the floor, went toward the sitting room.

"There, now he's taking the coat with him! What are you taking the coat for, eh? Ha-ha-ha! Why, are you a lunatic?"

The prince came back and stared at her as though he were petrified; when she burst out laughing, he chuckled too, but he still couldn't get his tongue going. In the first moment, when he had opened the door to her, he was pale; now the color suddenly rushed to his face.

"Well, what kind of idiot is this?" Nastasya Filippovna cried out in indignation, stamping her foot at him. "Well, where are you going now? Well, who are you going to announce now?"

"Nastasya Filippovna," muttered the prince.

"Why do you know me?" she asked him quickly. "I've never laid eyes on you! Go along, announce me . . . What's all that shouting?"

"They're quarreling," answered the prince, and went off to the sitting room.

He entered at a rather critical moment: Nina Alexandrovna was on the point of entirely forgetting that she was "resigned to everything": she was, however, defending Varya. At Varya's side, Ptitsyn was standing, too, having now left his pencil-scribbled paper. Varya herself did not draw back, indeed, she was not a girl of the timid sort; but her brother's abuse was becoming ruder and more insufferable with every word. In such circumstances she usually ceased to speak and only looked silently, mockingly, at her brother, not taking her eyes off him. This maneuver, as she knew, was capable of driving him beyond all bounds. In this very minute, the prince stepped into the room and pronounced:

"Nastasya Filippovna!"

IX

Universal silence prevailed; everyone looked at the prince as if not understanding him and—not wishing to understand. Ganya was numb with horror.

The arrival of Nastasya Filippovna, and especially at the present moment, was for everyone the strangest and most troublesome surprise. Just the fact that Nastasya Filippovna had pleased to call on them for the first time was in itself enough; hitherto she had carried herself so haughtily that in her conversations with Ganya she had not even expressed the desire to make the acquaintance of his family, and most recently, she had made no mention of them at all, just as if they did not exist. Though Ganya was to some extent even glad to see a discussion that would be so troublesome to him put off, yet in his heart he still tallied this haughtiness against her. In any case, he had sooner expected mockery and barbed remarks about his family from her, and not a visit to his house; he knew for a fact that she was informed of everything that was going on in his home with regard to his engagement and of the view his family took of her. Her visit, now, after the present of the portrait and on her birthday, the day on which she had promised to decide his fate, was almost equivalent to the decision itself.

The bewilderment with which everyone looked at the prince did not last long: Nastasya Filippovna herself appeared at the sitting room door and again slightly pushed the prince aside as she entered the room.

"At last, I've managed to get in . . . Why do you tie up the bell?" she said merrily, giving her hand to Ganya, who rushed headlong to meet her. "Why is your face so discomposed? Introduce me, please . . ."

Ganya, utterly disconcerted, introduced her first to Varya, and the two women exchanged strange looks before holding out their hands to each other. Nastasya Filippovna, however, laughed and masked her feelings with merriment; but Varya did not wish to mask hers and looked at her grimly and intently; not even a trace of a smile, which simple politeness alone demands, showed on her face. Ganya became paralyzed with fear; there was nothing left to entreat, and no time for it, and he cast such a menacing look at Varya that she understood, by the power of this look, what the moment meant for her brother. Then she seemed to make up her mind to give in to him and gave Nastasya Filippovna a slight smile. (All of them in the family still loved each other too much.) The business was improved somewhat by Nina Alexandrovna, whom Ganya, hopelessly confused, introduced after his sister, even leading her to Nastasya Filippovna first. But no sooner was Nina Alexandrovna about to speak of her "particular pleasure" than

Nastasya Filippovna, not hearing her out to the end, turned hurriedly to Ganya and, sitting down (even without being asked) on a little sofa in the corner by the window, exclaimed:

"Where's your study, then? And . . . and where are the lodgers? You take lodgers, don't you?"

Ganya flushed terribly and was about to stammer some answer, but Nastasya Filippovna added at once:

"Wherever could you keep lodgers here? You don't even have a study. Is there profit in it?" She suddenly turned to Nina Alexandrovna.

"It's somewhat troublesome," the latter began to reply, "it stands to reason, there should be profit. But, in fact, we've only just . . ."

But Nastasya Filippovna was again no longer listening: she was looking at Ganya, laughing, and shouting to him:

"What a face you're making! Oh, my goodness, what a face you have at this moment . . ."

There passed some moments of this laughter, and Ganya's face, indeed, became very distorted: his stupefaction, his comic, timid confusion suddenly left him; but he turned terribly pale; his lips twisted in convulsion; silently, intently, and with an evil gaze, he looked steadily into the face of his visitor, who went on laughing.

There was also another observer here who had yet to throw off his virtual stupefaction at the sight of Nastasya Filippovna; but though he stood rooted to the spot, in his former place in the doorway of the sitting room, still he had had the time to notice the pallor and the ominous change in Ganya's face. That observer was the prince. Almost in fright, he suddenly instinctively stepped forward.

"Drink some water," he whispered to Ganya. "And don't look like that . . ."

It was evident that he spoke with no forethought, with no particular intention of any kind, but just so, on first impulse; but his words produced an extraordinary effect. All Ganya's spite seemed suddenly to turn on the prince; he seized him by the shoulder and looked at him in silence, vindictively and hatefully, as if unable to utter a word. There was a general commotion: Nina Alexandrovna even uttered a faint cry, Ptitsyn stepped forward in concern, Kolya and Ferdyshchenko, who appeared at the door, stopped short in amazement; only Varya continued to look on with a scowl, but she watched attentively. She did not sit down, but stood to the side, near her mother, with her arms folded across her bosom.

But Ganya caught himself at once, almost in the first moment of his movement, and burst out in nervous laughter. He regained his self-possession completely.

"Why, Prince, are you a doctor?" he cried as merrily and benevolently as he could. "He positively frightened me; Nastasya Filippovna, may I introduce—this is a most treasured person, though I myself have only known him since the morning."

Nastasya Filippovna looked at the prince in bewilderment.

"Prince? He's a prince? Only fancy, and just now, in the entry, I took him for a footman and sent him in to announce me! Ha-ha-ha!"

"No harm done, no harm done!" chimed in Ferdyshchenko, approaching hurriedly and relieved that they had begun to laugh. "No harm: *se non è vero* . . . "[34]

"And I even virtually abused you, Prince. Forgive me, please. Ferdyshchenko, how do you come to be here at such an hour? I thought I would at least not meet with you. Who? What prince? Myshkin?" she questioned Ganya, who had in the meantime, still holding the prince by the shoulder, managed to introduce him.

"Our boarder," repeated Ganya.

It was obvious that they presented the prince as a rarity (and one that came in handy for everyone as a way out of a false position); they nearly thrust him at Nastasya Filippovna, and the prince even clearly heard the word "idiot" being whispered behind him, apparently by Ferdyshchenko, by way of explanation to Nastasya Filippovna.

"Tell me, why didn't you undeceive me just now, when I was so terribly . . . mistaken about you?" Nastasya Filippovna went on, scanning the prince from head to foot in a most unceremonious fashion; she waited with impatience for an answer, as though entirely convinced that the answer would invariably be so stupid that one would have to laugh.

"I was surprised at seeing you so suddenly . . ." muttered the prince.

"And how did you know it was I? Where have you seen me before? Could it be? Really, it's as though I have seen him somewhere

---

34. It. proverb: *se non è vero, è ben trovato*—though it may not be true, 'tis well devised.

before. And might I ask, why were you frozen to the spot just now? What is so stupefying about me?"

"Come now, come!" Ferdyshchenko went on simpering. "Well, come now! Oh, Lord, the things I'd say in answer to such a question! Well, come now . . . A real blockhead you'd be, Prince, after that!"

"And I should say them too, in your place," laughed the prince to Ferdyshchenko. "I was very struck of late by your portrait," he went on to Nastasya Filippovna, "then I talked to the Epanchins about you . . . And early this morning, even before arriving in Petersburg, in the train, Parfyon Rogozhin was telling me a lot about you . . . And at the very minute I opened the door to you, I was thinking about you too, and suddenly there you are."

"And how did you recognize that it was I?"

"From the portrait and . . ."

"And what else?"

"And because I had imagined you just like that . . . It's as though I've seen you somewhere too."

"Where? Where?"

"I seem to have seen your eyes somewhere . . . But it's impossible! I'm just going on . . . I've never been here before. Perhaps, in a dream . . ."

"Attaboy, Prince!" exclaimed Ferdyshchenko. "No, I take back my *se non è vero*. But anyway . . . anyway, he does it all in innocence!" he added regretfully.

The prince had uttered his few phrases in an uneasy voice, breaking off and often pausing for breath. Everything about him suggested extreme agitation. Nastasya Filippovna looked at him with curiosity, but she was no longer laughing. At that very moment, suddenly, a loud new voice was heard from behind the crowd that had closed around the prince and Nastasya Filippovna, and, so to speak, parted the crowd and split it in two. Before Nastasya Filippovna stood the head of the family himself, General Ivolgin. He wore an evening coat and had a clean shirtfront; his mustaches were dyed . . .

This was more than Ganya could endure.

Narcissistic and vain to a morbid, splenetic degree; searching in these last two months for anything at all that offered a more upstanding means of support and presented him in a more honorable light; sensing that he was still a novice in his chosen path and, perhaps, wouldn't survive; at last, in despair, taking up an attitude of complete insolence at home, where he was a despot, but not daring to try it in front of Nastasya Filippovna, who continued to confuse him to the last minute and mercilessly maintained the upper hand over him; "the impatient pauper," as Nastasya Filippovna herself put it, of which he had already been informed; having sworn by every oath to make her pay bitterly for it afterward and at the same time dreaming like a child of reconciling all oppositions—now he was forced to drink even of this terrible cup too, and, above all, in such a moment! One more unforeseen torture, most dreadful for a vain man, had fallen to his lot—to blush for his kindred, in his own house. "And is the reward itself worth it, after all!" flashed through Ganya's mind at that instant.

What was happening in that very moment was what he had seen these two months only in his dreams at night, in the form of a nightmare, what had frozen him with horror and made him burn with shame: the meeting had come at last between his father and Nastasya Filippovna. At times, tormenting and agitating himself, he would try to imagine the general at the marriage ceremony, but was never able to complete the agonizing picture and made haste to abandon it. Perhaps he exaggerated his misfortune out of all proportion; but that is always so with vain people. In the course of these two months he had had time to consider the matter thoroughly and make up his mind, and had promised himself at all costs to curb his parent, if only for a time, and if possible even to get him out of Petersburg, whether his mother consented to it or not. Ten minutes earlier, when Nastasya Filippovna made her entrance, he was so taken aback, so dumbfounded, that he forgot the possibility of Ardalion Alexandrovich's appearance on the scene and had made no arrangement. And behold, here was the general before them all, and solemnly got up for the occasion too in an evening coat, at the very moment when Nastasya Filippovna was "only seeking some pretext to cover him and his family with ridicule." (He was convinced of that.) And, indeed, what could her visit mean if not that? Had she come to make friends with his mother and sister, or to insult them in his own house? But judging by the position taken up by both sides, there could no longer be any doubt: his mother and sister were sitting to the side like outcasts, while Nastasya Filippovna seemed positively to have forgotten that they were in the same room with her ... and if she behaved like that, then it was certain she had her own object!

Ferdyshchenko took hold of the general and led him up.

"Ardalion Alexandrovich Ivolgin," pronounced the general with dignity, bowing and smiling. "An old unhappy soldier and father of a family that is happy in the hopes of including such a charming . . ."

He did not finish. Ferdyshchenko quickly set a chair behind him and the general, who was rather weak on his legs in that moment, so soon after dinner, positively plopped or, better said, fell onto the chair; but this, incidentally, did not disconcert him. He sat directly opposite Nastasya Filippovna and, with an agreeable simper, slowly and with great effect raised her little fingers to his lips. By and large, it was rather difficult to disconcert the general. Except for a certain slovenliness, his appearance was still fairly presentable, a fact of which he was quite well aware. In the past, he had had occasion to move in very good society, from which he had been finally excluded only two or three years before. It was since that time that he had devoted himself with far too great a lack of restraint to certain of his weaknesses; but he still retained to that day his adroit and pleasant manner. Nastasya Filippovna, it seemed, was highly delighted at the advent of Ardalion Alexandrovich, of whom of course she had known through hearsay.

"I've heard that my son . . ." began Ardalion Alexandrovich.

"Yes, your son! And you're a pretty one, too, his papa! Why do you never come to see me? What, are you hiding, or is your son hiding you? You at least might come to see me without compromising anyone."

"Children of the nineteenth century and their parents . . ." the general tried to begin again.

"Nastasya Filippovna, please excuse Ardalion Alexandrovich for a moment, someone is asking for him," said Nina Alexandrovna loudly.

"Excuse him! Mercy, I've heard so much about him, I've been wanting to see him for so long! And what business could he have? Isn't he retired? You won't leave me, General, you won't go away?"

"I give you my word that he shall come to see you himself, but now he is in need of rest."

"Ardalion Alexandrovich, they say you are in need of rest!" exclaimed Nastasya Filippovna, making a displeased and offended face, just like a vapid little fool who's had her toy taken away from her. The general, as if on cue, did his best to make his position even more foolish.

"My dear! My dear!" he said reproachfully, solemnly turning to his wife and laying his hand on his heart.

"Will you not come away from here, Mamma?" Varya asked loudly.

"No, Varya, I'll sit it out to the end."

Nastasya Filippovna could not have failed to hear the question and the answer, but it seemed only to increase her mirth. She at once began to shower the general with questions again, and after five minutes the general was in the most festive mood and holding forth amidst the loud laughter of the present company.

Kolya pulled at the prince's lapel.

"Well, can't you get him away somehow! Is there no way? Please!" And there were even tears of indignation burning in the poor boy's eyes. "Oh, cursed Ganjka!" he added to himself.

"I used indeed to be a great friend of Ivan Fyodorovich Epanchin's," the general babbled on in reply to Nastasya Filippovna's questions. "He, I, and the late Prince Lev Nikolaevich Myshkin, whose son I have embraced today after twenty years' separation, we three were inseparable, a regular cavalcade, so to speak: Athos, Porthos, and Aramis.[35] But, alas, one is in the grave, struck down by slander and a bullet; another is before you and is still battling with slanders and bullets . . ."

"With bullets!" exclaimed Nastasya Filippovna.

"They are here, in my breast, and were received under the walls of Kars,[36] and in bad weather I feel them. In all other respects, I live like a philosopher, walk, go out, play checkers at my café like any bourgeois retired from business, and read the *Indépendance*.[37] But as for our Porthos, Epanchin, after the incident on the railway, more than two years ago, on account of the Bolognese lapdog, I've finished with him completely."

"A lapdog! And what is this?" asked Nastasya Filippovna with particular interest. "About a lapdog? Let me see, and on the railway! . . ." she repeated, as though recollecting it.

"Oh, it was a stupid incident, not even worth repeating; because of

35. The three musketeers of Dumas's novel.

36. During the course of the Crimean War (1853–56), Kars, a fortified city in northeast Turkey, was besieged by Russian troops from May to November 1855.

37. *Indépendance Belge*, a newspaper covering politics and society in Western Europe, published in Brussels from 1830 to 1937.

Princess Belokonsky's governess, Mistress Schmidt, but . . . it's not even worth repeating."

"But you simply must tell it!" cried Nastasya Filippovna merrily.

"And I haven't heard it yet!" remarked Ferdyshchenko, *"c'est du nouveau."*[38]

"Ardalion Alexandrovich!" came again the beseeching voice of Nina Alexandrovna.

"Papa, someone's asking for you!" shouted Kolya.

"It's a stupid story, and can be told in two words," began the general with a self-satisfied air. "Two years ago, yes! nearly two, just after the opening of the new ――― railway (I was already in civilian dress), while I was troubling about some extremely important matters in connection with my giving up the service, I took a ticket, first class: I go in, sit down, have a smoke. That is to say, I continue smoking, I had lit up before. I'm alone in the compartment. Smoking isn't prohibited, nor is it allowed; it's sort of half-allowed, as a rule; well, and depending on the person. The window is down. Suddenly, just before the whistle sounded, two ladies with a lapdog seat themselves directly opposite; they're late; one dressed up in the most sumptuous manner, in pale blue; the other more modestly, in black silk with a little cape. Not bad-looking, with a disdainful air, speaking English. I take no notice, of course; go on smoking. That is, I almost think the better of it, but since the window is open, I keep on smoking out the window. The lapdog is resting on the pale-blue lady's knee, a tiny thing, no bigger than my fist, black, with white paws, a rarity even. Silver collar with a motto on it. I pay no mind. Only, I notice that the ladies, it seems, are angry, about the cigar, of course. One of them stared at me through her lorgnette, a tortoiseshell one. I pay no mind again: for, after all, they said nothing! If only they had said something, warned me, asked me— well, there's such a thing as human language, after all! But here, they keep silent . . . and suddenly—and this is without the slightest, I must tell you, warning, really, without the very slightest, as though she had suddenly taken leave of her senses—the pale-blue one goes and snatches the cigar out of my hand and flings it out the window. The train races along, I'm staring at her like I'm half mad. The woman was

38. Fr., this is something new.

savage; a savage woman, yes, positively in a savage state; but incidentally, a portly woman, plump, tall, blond, with rosy cheeks (too much so, in fact), her eyes flashing at me. Without uttering a word and with extraordinary courtesy, the most perfect courtesy, with the most refined, so to speak, courtesy, I approach the lapdog with two fingers, take it delicately by the scruff of the neck and whoosh, fling it out the window after the cigar! It lets out just one squeal! The train keeps racing on . . ."

"You are a monster!" exclaimed Nastasya Filippovna, laughing and clapping her hands like a little girl.

"Bravo, bravo!" cried Ferdyshchenko. And Ptitsyn—for whom the appearance of the general was also extremely unpleasant—smirked too; even Kolya laughed and also cried out: "Bravo!"

"And I'm right, I'm right, I'm right thrice over!" the triumphant general continued with fervor, "for if cigars are forbidden in a railway carriage, then dogs are even more so."

"Bravo, Papa!" cried Kolya gleefully. "Splendid! I should certainly, certainly have done the same."

"But what about the lady?" Nastasya Filippovna inquired impatiently.

"Her? Well, that's just where the whole unpleasantness resides," the general went on, frowning. "Without uttering a word and without the slightest warning, as it were, she goes and slaps me on the cheek! A savage woman; entirely in a savage state!"

The general dropped his eyes, raised his eyebrows, shrugged his shoulders, pursed his lips, flung up his hands, paused, and suddenly pronounced:

"I got taken away!"

"And hard? Hard?"

"By God, not hard! A scandalous scene ensued, but it wasn't hard. I only waved her away once, solely just to wave her away. But the devil himself had a hand in it: the pale-blue one turned out to be an Englishwoman, a governess or even some sort of family friend of Princess Belokonsky, and the one in the black dress, she was the eldest of the princess's daughters, an old maid of thirty-five. And you know on what terms Generaless Epanchin stands with the house of Belokonsky. All the princesses in a faint, tears, mourning for the favorite pet lapdog, howls of the six princesses, howls of the Englishwoman—a perfect Bedlam! Of course, I went to express remorse, begged forgiveness, wrote a letter, but no reception—not for me, nor for the letter; and with Epanchin, there were quarrels, ostracizing, banishment!"

"But allow me, how can that be?" Nastasya Filippovna asked suddenly. "Five or six days ago I read in the *Indépendance*—I always read the *Indépendance*—exactly the same story! But precisely the same! It happened on one of the Rhine railways, in a carriage, with a Frenchman and an Englishwoman: the cigar was snatched in the same way, the lapdog was thrown out the window the same way, and finally, everything ended in the same way as with you. Even the dress was pale blue!"

The general blushed terribly. Kolya blushed too and pressed his head between his hands; Ptitsyn quickly turned away. Only Ferdyshchenko went on guffawing as before. There's no need to even speak of Ganya: he had been standing the entire time, enduring a mute and insufferable agony.

"I assure you," muttered the general, "that the very same thing happened to me . . ."

"Father really had some trouble with Mistress Schmidt, the governess at the Belokonskys'," cried Kolya, "I remember it."

"What! Alike to a T? One and the same story at the opposite ends of Europe, and the same to a T in all its details, down to the pale-blue dress!" persisted the merciless Nastasya Filippovna. "I'll send you the *Indépendance Belge*!"

"But note," the general still insisted, "that it happened to me two years earlier . . ."

"Ah, well there is that, if anything!"

Nastasya Filippovna roared with laughter, as if in hysterics.

"Papa, I beg you to come out and have a word," said Ganya in a shaking, tormented voice, mechanically seizing his father by the shoulder. An infinite hatred seethed in his gaze.

In that very moment there was an exceptionally loud ring at the front door. Such a ringing might have pulled down the bell. It portended an extraordinary visit. Kolya ran to open the door.

X

The entryway was suddenly extremely full of noise and people; from the sitting room, it sounded as though several people had come in from the yard and were continuing to come in. Several voices were talking and shouting at once; there was talking and shouting, too, on the staircase, the door to which from the entryway, as one could hear, had not been closed. The visit was turning out to be extremely strange. Everyone exchanged looks; Ganya rushed into the drawing room, but several people had already entered it.

"Ah, here he is, the Judas!" cried a voice familiar to the prince. "Greetings, Ganjka, you villain!"

"It's he, it's he himself, indeed!" affirmed another voice.

The prince could have no doubts: the first voice was Rogozhin's, and the second, Lebedev's.

Ganya stood as if in a stupor on the threshold to the sitting room and gazed at them in silence, not hindering the entrance into the drawing room of some ten or twelve people, who came in one after the other in Parfyon Rogozhin's wake. The company was extremely mixed, and was distinguished not only by its variety, but also by its disgraceful conduct. Some of them walked in off the street as they were, in overcoats and furs. There was no one completely drunk, actually; however, they all seemed highly tipsy. They all, it seemed, had need of one another to enter; not one would have had the courage on their own, but it was as if they all pushed one another in. Even Rogozhin walked cautiously at the head of the crowd, but he had some intention, and he seemed glumly and irritably preoccupied. The others only constituted a chorus, or, better said, a gang for reinforcement. Besides Lebedev, there was Zalyozhev, who had flung off his fur in the entry and walked in swaggering and raffish, with a wave in his hair, and two to three other gentlemen of the same sort, evidently of the petty merchant class. Some fellow in a semimilitary coat; some short and extremely fat person who kept laughing continually; some immense gentleman about six and a third feet tall, also unusually fat, extremely glum and taciturn, who evidently relied much on his fists. There was a medical student; there was a smarmy Pole. Standing on the landing, peeping into the entryway but not venturing to come in, were two ladies of some sort; Kolya slammed the door in their faces and latched it.

"Greetings, Ganjka, you villain! You didn't expect Parfyon Rogozhin, did you?" repeated Rogozhin, reaching the sitting room and stopping in the door opposite Ganya. But at that moment he suddenly discerned within the sitting room, directly opposite himself, Nastasya Filippovna. Evidently, he had not even conceived that he might meet her here, for the sight of her had an extraordinary effect on him; he turned so pale that even his lips went blue. "So then it's true!" he uttered quietly, as if to himself, looking completely forlorn. "It's the end! . . . Well . . . you shall pay for it now!" he suddenly snarled, looking at Ganya with violent rage. "Well . . . ach!"

He even gasped for breath, even spoke with difficulty. Mechanically, he continued to move toward the sitting room, but having crossed the threshold, he suddenly saw Nina Alexandrovna and Varya and stopped, somewhat embarrassed, in spite of his agitation. After him came Lebedev, who stuck to him like a shadow and was very drunk, then the student, the gentleman with the fists, Zalyozhev, bowing to the right and left, and finally the short little fat man squeezed himself in. The presence of the ladies still restrained them somewhat and evidently severely hampered them, but of course, only until the *beginning*, until the first pretext arose to shout and to *begin* . . . Then, all the ladies in the world would not have hampered them.

"What, you here too, Prince?" Rogozhin said absently, surprised in part at meeting the prince. "Still in your little spats, e-ech!" he sighed, already forgetting about the prince and transferring his gaze again to Nastasya Filippovna, continuing to move and to be drawn toward her, as to a magnet.

Nastasya Filippovna also looked with uneasy curiosity at the guests.

Ganya came to himself at last.

"But allow me, finally, what does this mean?" he began loudly, sternly surveying the newcomers and addressing himself principally to Rogozhin. "You haven't come to a stable, I believe, gentlemen, my mother and sister are here . . ."

"We can see that your mother and sister are here," muttered Rogozhin through his teeth.

"That can be seen, that your mother and sister are here," Lebedev confirmed for emphasis.

The gentleman with the fists, probably figuring that the moment had arrived, began growling something.

"Now, wait a minute!" Ganya raised his voice, exploding suddenly, and somehow out of measure. "Firstly, I beg you all to leave here and go into the drawing room, and secondly, be so kind as to inform me ..."

"Picture that, he doesn't recognize me." Rogozhin grinned maliciously, not budging from the spot. "Don't you recognize Rogozhin?"

"I believe I've met you somewhere, but ..."

"Picture that, met me somewhere! Why, just three months ago, I lost two hundred rubles of my father's money to you; the old man died before he found it out; you dragged me into it, and Kniff finagled it. Don't recognize me? Ptitsyn witnessed it! Why, if I were to show you three rubles out of my pocket now, you'd crawl on all fours to Vassilevsky for them—that's the sort you are! That's what your soul is! And I've come here now to buy you for money, you never mind that I've come with such boots on, I've got money, brother, a lot of it, I can buy the whole of you, lock, stock and barrel ... I'll buy all of you, if I like! I'll buy everything!" Rogozhin grew more and more hot under the collar and seemed to be getting more and more drunk. "E-eh!" he cried, "Nastasya Filippovna! Don't chase me off, say a little word: are you going to marry him or not?"

Rogozhin asked his question like a lost man, as if appealing to some deity, but with the courage of a man condemned to death, who has nothing left to lose. In deadly anguish, he awaited her reply.

Nastasya Filippovna measured him with a mocking and haughty gaze, but glanced at Varya and Nina Alexandrovna, looked at Ganya, and suddenly changed her tone.

"Not at all, what's the matter with you? And whatever has put it into your head to ask such a question?" she answered quietly and gravely, and as if in some surprise.

"No? No!" exclaimed Rogozhin, becoming almost frantic with happiness. "Then you're not?! But they told me ... Ach! Well! ... Nastasya Filippovna! They say that you are engaged to Ganjka! To him? But could it be possible? (I tell them all!) Why, I can buy him up for a hundred rubles, if I give him a thousand, well, three, to yield, he'll run off on the eve of his wedding day, and leave his bride to me. Isn't that right, Ganjka, villain! You'd take the three thousand, wouldn't you!

Here they are, here! That's what I came for, to get such a written agreement from you; I said I'll buy him—and I'll buy him!"

"Get out of here, you're drunk!" shouted Ganya, turning red and pale by turns.

Upon his outburst, there was a sudden explosion of several voices at once; Rogozhin's entire crew had long been awaiting the first provocation. Lebedev was at extreme pains to whisper something in Rogozhin's ear.

"That's true, official!" answered Rogozhin, "that's true, drunken soul! Ech, here goes nothing. Nastasya Filippovna!" he exclaimed, gazing at her like a half-wit, growing timid and then suddenly taking heart to the point of audacity. "Here's eighteen thousand!" And he flung on the table before her a packet wrapped in white paper and tied crosswise with string. "Here! And . . . and there's more to come!"

He did not have the courage to finish saying what he wanted.

"No-no-no!" whispered Lebedev to him again with a terribly frightened air; one could guess that he was frightened by the magnitude of the sum and was proposing to try it with an incomparably smaller one.

"No, brother, when it comes to that, you're a fool, you don't know what you've gotten yourself into . . . and, evidently, I'm a fool right along with you!" Rogozhin suddenly caught himself and started under the flashing gaze of Nastasya Filippovna. "E-ech! I've muddled it, listening to you," he added with deep regret.

Nastasya Filippovna peered into Rogozhin's crestfallen face and suddenly burst into laughter.

"Eighteen thousand, for me? Well, now the peasant comes out!" she added suddenly with insolent familiarity and rose slightly from the sofa as if intending to leave. Ganya observed the whole scene with a sinking heart.

"Forty thousand, then, forty, not eighteen!" shouted Rogozhin. "Vanjka Ptitsyn and Biskup promised to get me forty thousand by seven o'clock. Forty thousand! Cash down."

The scene was turning out to be extraordinarily disgraceful, but Nastasya Filippovna went on laughing and did not leave, just as if she were actually prolonging it intentionally. Nina Alexandrovna and Varya also rose from their seats and, silently, in dismay, waited to see how much further it would go; Varya's eyes glittered, but for Nina Alexandrovna, it all had a painful effect; she trembled and seemed on the point of fainting.

"And if that's how it is—a hundred! This very day, I'll give you a hundred thousand! Ptitsyn, help me out, it'll be worth your while!"

"You've gone out of your mind!" whispered Ptitsyn suddenly, going up to him quickly and seizing him by the arm. "You're drunk, they'll send for the watchmen. Where do you think you are?"

"He's talking rubbish from the drink!" pronounced Nastasya Filippovna, as though taunting him.

"I'm not talking rubbish, it will be here! It will be here by evening. Ptitsyn, help me out, you profiteering soul, charge what you will, get me a hundred thousand by evening; I'll prove that I'll stop at nothing!" Rogozhin suddenly became animated to the point of rapture.

"But, just a moment, what is the meaning of this?" Ardalion Alexandrovich, angered, menacingly and suddenly cried out, approaching Rogozhin. The suddenness of the previously silent old man's outburst made it highly comic. Laughter was heard.

"Where did this come from?" laughed Rogozhin, "come on, old man, we'll get you drunk!"

"Now, that's just vile!" exclaimed Kolya, downright crying from shame and vexation.

"Why, is there really not one to be found among you to take this shameless woman out of here!" suddenly cried Varya, quivering all over with rage.

"That's me they're calling shameless!" parried Nastasya Filippovna with contemptuous gaiety, "and I came like a fool to invite them to my party this evening! That's how your sister treats me, Gavrila Ardalionovich!"

For some time, Ganya stood as though thunderstruck at his sister's outburst; but seeing that Nastasya Filippovna really was going this time, he rushed frantically at Varya and seized her arm in fury.

"What have you done?" he cried, looking at her as though wanting to wither her on the spot. He had utterly lost his bearings and was not thinking clearly.

"What have I done? Where are you dragging me? Surely not to beg her pardon for having come to insult your mother and dishonor your home, you base creature?" cried Varya again in triumph, looking at her brother with defiance.

For a few moments, they stood like this, opposite one another, face to face. Ganya was still holding her arm in his hand. Varya pulled once, twice, with all her might, but couldn't bear it and suddenly, completely beside herself, spat in her brother's face.

"What a girl!" cried Nastasya Filippovna. "Bravo, Ptitsyn, I congratulate you!"

Everything went dark before Ganya's eyes, and, completely forgetting himself, he struck at his sister with all his might. The blow would have certainly landed on her face. But suddenly, another hand checked Ganya's hand in midflight.

Between him and his sister stood the prince.

"That'll do, now, enough!" he uttered insistently, though he was also shaking all over, as if from an extremely violent shock.

"Why will you be eternally getting in my way?" roared Ganya, letting go of Varya's arm, and with his now freed hand, at the ultimate peak of fury, winding up for all he could, he gave the prince a slap in the face.

"Ach!" Kolya flung up his hands. "Ach, my God!"

Exclamations were heard on all sides. The prince went pale. With a strange and reproachful gaze, he looked Ganya straight in the eyes; his lips quivered and tried to articulate something; they were twisted into some kind of strange and utterly unsuitable smile.

"Well, let it fall on me . . . but her . . . I won't allow it!" he uttered softly at last; but suddenly he couldn't bear it, left Ganya, hid his face in his hands, moved away to a corner, stood with his face to the wall and uttered in a breaking voice:

"Oh, how ashamed you shall be of what you've done!"

Ganya was, indeed, standing there as if completely crushed. Kolya rushed to hug and kiss the prince; after him, pressing together in a crowd, came Rogozhin, Varya, Ptitsyn, Nina Alexandrovna, everyone, even the old man, Ardalion Alexandrovich.

"Never mind, never mind!" muttered the prince in all directions, with the same unsuitable smile.

"And he will regret it!" cried Rogozhin. "You shall be ashamed, Ganya, that you've insulted such a . . . sheep (he could not find another word)! Prince, my heart, leave them; curse them, come along! You'll see what Rogozhin's love can be!"

Nastasya Filippovna was also very much astounded, both by Ganya's action and the prince's response. Her usually pale and pensive face, which had been so out of keeping with her seemingly affected laughter just before, was now visibly stirred by a new feeling; yet, nonetheless, she seemed reluctant to betray it and the mocking smile seemed to be at pains to remain on her face.

"Truly, I have seen his face somewhere!" she said, suddenly serious now, abruptly recalling her former question again.

"And you, aren't you ashamed? Surely you are not like that, like you were just pretending to be. Why, it isn't possible!" cried the prince with deep and heartfelt reproach.

Nastasya Filippovna was surprised, chuckled, but, seeming to hide something under her smile, in some confusion, glanced at Ganya and walked out of the sitting room. But even before reaching the entry, she suddenly turned back, went quickly up to Nina Alexandrovna, took her hand and raised it to her lips.

"I really am not like this, he guessed it," she whispered quickly, fervently, suddenly flushing hotly, and, turning around, left so quickly this time that no one even had time to realize what she had come back for. They only saw that she had whispered something to Nina Alexandrovna and, it seemed, kissed her hand. But Varya saw and heard everything and followed her out with her eyes, in wonderment.

Ganya came to himself and rushed to see Nastasya Filippovna out, but she had already gone out the door. He overtook her on the stairs.

"Don't see me out!" she shouted to him. "Good-bye, till this evening! You must come, do you hear!"

He returned chagrined and pensive; uncertainty weighed heavy on his heart, even heavier than before. The prince haunted him too ... He was so preoccupied that he scarcely noticed as the whole of Rogozhin's crowd pressed past him and even shoved against him in the doorway, hurriedly making their way out of the apartment after Rogozhin. They were all discussing something loudly, at the top of their voices. Rogozhin himself was walking with Ptitsyn, going on insistently about something important and, evidently, urgent.

"You've lost, Ganjka!" he shouted as he went by.

Ganya looked after them uneasily.

XI

The prince left the sitting room and shut himself up in his room. Kolya ran in to him at once to console him. The poor boy seemed unable to tear himself away from him now.

"You've done well to come away," he said, "there'll be a bigger hullabaloo there now than before, and it's like that every day with us, and it was all stirred up on account of that Nastasya Filippovna."

"A lot of different things have festered and accumulated here at your place, Kolya," observed the prince.

"Yes, they've festered. It's not even worth talking about with us. We're to blame for everything ourselves. But I have a great friend, he's even more unfortunate. Would you like to meet him?"

"Very much. Is he a comrade of yours?"

"Yes, almost like a comrade. I'll explain it all to you later . . . But is Nastasya Filippovna good-looking, do you think? I've never seen her before, you know, and I've tried to desperately. She simply dazzled me. I'd forgive Ganjka everything if he were doing it for love; but why is he taking the money, that's the trouble!"

"Yes, I don't much like your brother . . ."

"Well, I should think not! As if you could, after . . . But you know, I can't endure these differences of opinion. Some madman, or fool, or scoundrel, in a fit of madness, slaps you in the face and a man is disgraced for life, and can't wipe out the insult any other way except in blood, unless the other begs for pardon on his knees. In my view, that's absurd and despotic. That's what Lermontov's drama *The Masquerade* is based on, and—it's stupid, in my view. That is, I mean to say, unnatural. But then he wrote it almost in his childhood."

"I liked your sister very much."

"The way she spat Ganjka in the mug! She's plucky, Varjka! But you didn't spit, and I'm sure it was not for want of pluck. But here she is—speak of the devil. I knew she'd come; she's gracious, though she has faults."

"And you've no business here," Varya pounced upon him first of all, "go off to Father. Is he bothering you, Prince?"

"Not at all, quite the contrary."

"Well, now, elder sister, there you go! That's just what's rotten about her. And, by the way, I thought that Father'd be sure to go off with Rogozhin. He is penitent now, I expect. I should see what he's about, I suppose," added Kolya, going out.

"Thank God, I got Mother away and put her to bed, and there was no fresh trouble. Ganya is disconcerted and quite deep in thought. And he's got plenty to think about. What a lesson! . . . I've come to thank you again and to ask you, Prince: have you not known Nastasya Filippovna before?"

"No, I haven't."

"Then why on earth did you tell her to her face that she was 'not like that'? And it seems you guessed right. It turns out that she is perhaps not like that, in fact. Although I can't make her out! Of course, her object was to insult us, that's clear. But if she came to invite us, how could she start behaving with Mother like that? Ptitsyn knows her exceptionally well, and he said he would hardly have known her just now. And with Rogozhin? It's impossible for anyone with self-respect to talk like that in the house of one's . . . Mother is very worried about you, too."

"Never mind that!" said the prince with a wave of his hand.

"And how was it that she obeyed you . . ."

"Obeyed what?"

"You told her she ought to be ashamed of herself and she changed at once. You have an influence over her, Prince," added Varya, giving off a slight laugh.

The door opened, and, completely unexpectedly, Ganya entered.

He did not even hesitate at the sight of Varya; for a moment, he stood on the threshold, and then resolutely approached the prince.

"Prince, I behaved badly, forgive me, dear man," he said suddenly and with great feeling. The look on his face expressed great pain. The prince looked on in amazement and did not answer at once. "Come, forgive me, come, forgive me!" Ganya urged impatiently. "Come, if you like, I'll kiss your hand now!"

The prince was exceedingly astounded and silently embraced Ganya with both arms. They kissed each other with sincere feeling.

"I never, ever thought that you were like this!" said the prince at last, catching his breath with difficulty. "I thought that you were . . . incapable of it."

"Of owning my fault? . . . And what made me think lately that you were an idiot! You notice what other people would never notice. One could talk to you, but . . . better not talk!"

"Here is someone else whose pardon you ought to ask," said the prince, pointing to Varya.

"No, they are all my enemies. You may be sure, Prince, there've been many attempts; they don't forgive sincerely here," broke hotly from Ganya, and he turned away from Varya.

"Yes, I'll forgive!" said Varya suddenly.

"And you'll go to Nastasya Filippovna in the evening?"

"I'll go, if you bid me, but you'd better judge for yourself: is it at all possible for me to go now?"

"But she's not like that, you know. You see what riddles she sets us! It's all tricks!" And Ganya laughed viciously.

"I know for myself that she's not like that, and full of tricks, but what tricks? And another thing, Ganya, look what she herself takes you for. Let her kiss Mother's hand. Let it all be trickery of some sort, but all the same, you know, she was laughing at you! It's not worth seventy-five thousand, God's truth, brother! You're still capable of honorable feeling, and that's why I tell you this. Hey, don't you go either! Hey, beware! It can't end well!"

Having said this, full of agitation, Varya quickly left the room . . .

"That's how they all are," said Ganya, smirking, "and can they suppose I don't know that myself? Why, I know much more than they do."

Having said this, Ganya sat down on the sofa, evidently disposed to prolong the visit.

"If you know it yourself," asked the prince rather timidly, "how can you have chosen such torment, knowing that it really is not worth seventy-five thousand?"

"I'm not talking about that," muttered Ganya. "But, by the way, tell me, what do you think, I want to know your opinion particularly: is such 'torment' worth seventy-five thousand or isn't it?"

"In my view, it's not worth it."

"Well, I knew it! And is such a marriage shameful?"

"Very shameful."

"Well, then let me tell you, I'm going to marry her, and there's no doubt about it now. Just lately I was still vacillating, but not now! Don't speak! I know what you want to say . . ."

"I wasn't going to say what you think, but I'm greatly surprised by your extraordinary confidence..."

"In what? What confidence?"

"In the fact that Nastasya Filippovna will invariably marry you and that all of this is already settled, and secondly, even if she does marry you, that the seventy-five thousand will wind up in your pocket, just like that. But of course, there's a great deal here I don't know."

Ganya gave a great start in the prince's direction.

"Of course, you don't know everything," he said, "and why else would I accept this whole burden?"

"It seems to me that it happens left and right: people marry money, but the money's with the wife."

"N-no, it won't be that way with us... There are... there are some circumstances here..." muttered Ganya, uneasily pensive. "And as for her answer, there's no doubt about it anymore," he added quickly. "What makes you conclude that she'll refuse me?"

"I know nothing except what I've seen; and then Varvara Ardalionovna was saying just now..."

"Eh! That's just the way they are, they don't know what to say anymore. As for Rogozhin, she was laughing at him, rest assured, I made that out. That was obvious. Before, I was frightened, but now, I've made it out. Or maybe it's the way she behaved to Mother, and to Father, and to Varya?"

"And to you."

"Perhaps; but that's just good old-fashioned womanish vindictiveness, and nothing more. This is a terribly irritable, touchy and vain woman. Just like a civil servant passed over in service rank! She wanted to show herself and all her contempt for them... well, and for me too; that's true, I don't deny it... But all the same, she'll marry me. You have no idea the sorts of tricks human vanity is capable of: you see, she considers me a villain for taking her, another man's mistress, so openly for her money, and doesn't know that another man would dupe her even more vilely: would have come on to her and started spouting liberal-progressive stuff, and drawing it out of the various women questions, and she'd go in for it like a thread through a needle. He would have convinced the vain little fool (and it's so easy!) that he was only taking her for her 'nobility of heart and her misfortune,' but would have married her for money all the same. I don't find favor here because I don't care to sham; but that's what I ought to do. But what is she doing herself? Isn't it just the same? Then what reason has she after that to despise me and get up these games? Because I don't give in myself, and I show some pride. Well, we shall see!"

"And can you really have loved her before this?"

"I loved her in the beginning. But that's enough . . . There are women who are only good for being mistresses, and for nothing more. I'm not saying that she has been my mistress. If she'll want to behave quietly, I'll behave quietly too; but if she's mutinous, I'll leave her at once, and take the money with me. I don't want to be ridiculous; above all, I do not want to be ridiculous."

"I keep thinking," observed the prince cautiously, "that Nastasya Filippovna is smart. Why should she go into the trap, sensing what torment it would be? Why, she could have married someone else, too. That's what's so surprising to me."

"Ah, well, that's where the calculation lies! You don't know everything here, Prince . . . It's . . . And besides, she's convinced that I love her madly, I swear, and, you know, I strongly suspect that she loves me too, in her own way, that is, you know the saying: 'You always hurt the ones you love.' Her whole life, she'll take me for a knave (and perhaps that's what she needs) and, all the same, she'll love me in her own way; she's preparing for it, that's her nature. She is an extremely Russian woman, I tell you; but I've got a little surprise of my own in store for her. That scene with Varya lately happened accidentally, but to my advantage; now she's seen my devotion and is convinced of it, and that I'd break all ties for her. So, we're not such fools either, rest assured. By the way, you don't think I am usually such a blabbermouth, do you? Perhaps, Prince, my dear man, I really am doing wrong by confiding in you. But it's precisely because you're the first honorable man I've come across that I pounced on you, only don't take 'pounce' for a pun. You are not angry for what happened lately, are you? This is the first time in the last two years, perhaps, that I have spoken from my heart. There are terribly few honest people here; none more honest than Ptitsyn. Why, I fancy you're laughing, no? Villains love honest people—you didn't know this? And of course I . . . But then again, in what way am I a villain, tell me, on your conscience? Why do they all follow her lead in calling me a villain? And, do you know, I follow their lead and hers, and call myself a villain too! That's what's vile, so vile!"

"I shall never take you for a villain now," said the prince. "Lately, I took you entirely for a fiend, and suddenly you've made me so happy—there's a lesson: don't judge without experience. Now I see that one can't take you for a fiend, and what's more, not for an overly rotten person, either. In my opinion, you are simply the most ordinary man that could possibly be, if only perhaps very weak and not at all original."

Ganya smirked sarcastically to himself, but kept silent. The prince saw that his response displeased him, became embarrassed, and fell silent too.

"Has Father asked you for money?" Ganya inquired.

"No."

"If he does, don't give it to him. But he once was a decent person, I remember. He was received by people of good standing. And how quickly is it all over with them, these old decent people! The slightest change of circumstances and there's nothing left of what was previously there, it's all gone in a flash. Before, he used not to tell such lies, I assure you; before, he was just an overenthusiastic person, and—see what it's come to! Of course, the wine's to blame. Do you know that he keeps a mistress? He's become more than simply a harmless little liar now. I can't understand my mother's long-suffering patience. Has he told you about the siege of Kars? Or how his gray trace-horse began to talk? He'll even go as far as that."

And Ganya suddenly roared with laughter.

"Why are you looking at me like that?"

"Why, I'm surprised that you laughed so genuinely. Truly, you still have the laugh of a child. Just now, you came in to make up with me and said: 'If you like, I'll kiss your hand'—that's just how children would make up. So it seems you are still capable of such words and such impulses. And then suddenly you begin a regular harangue about this black business and about these seventy-five thousand. Truly, this is all somehow absurd and impossible."

"And what do you want to conclude from that?"

"That, could it be you're acting too heedlessly, shouldn't you look about you first? Varvara Ardalionovna is right, perhaps."

"Ah, morality! That I'm still a silly boy, I know that myself," interrupted Ganya hotly, "if only from having started such a conversation with you. I'm not entering into this marriage out of calculation, Prince," he continued, blurting it out like a young man injured in his pride. "In calculation, I should certainly make a mistake, for I am not yet firm of mind and character. I'm going into it out of passion, carried away, for I have one capital aim. Now, you think that I'll get seventy thousand and run out to buy a carriage. No, sir, I shall wear out my old frock coat of the year before last and drop all my club acquaintances. There are few people of perseverance among us, though we are all money-grubbers, and I want to persevere. The main thing here is to carry it through to the end—that's all there is to it! Ptitsyn used to sleep in the street at seventeen, peddled penknives and began with a farthing; now he has sixty thousand, but after what contortions! Well, I shall skip all those contortions and begin straight off with capital; in fifteen years they will say: 'There's Ivolgin, king of the Jews.' You tell me I am not an original person. Take note, dear prince, that nothing offends a man of our day and our race more than to tell him that he is not original, that he is weak-willed, has no particular talents, and is an ordinary person. You haven't even deigned to consider me a good villain, and, do you know, I wanted to devour you for it just now! You've insulted me more than Epanchin, who considers me (and with no discussion, without offering temptations, in the simplicity of his heart, take note of that) capable of selling him my wife! This, my friend, has driven me wild with rage for a long time now, and I want money. When I have acquired money, you should know, I shall be a highly original man. What is most vile and hateful about money is that it even grants you talents. And will grant them until the end of the world. You will say that this is all childish or perhaps poetical—well, what of it, it'll make it all the merrier for me, but the business shall be done all the same. I'll carry it through and persevere. *Rira bien qui rira le dernier.*[39] Why does Epanchin insult me like that? From spite, is it? Never, sir. It's simply because I am of too little consequence. Well, sir, but in that case . . . However, that's enough, and it's time. Kolya has poked his nose in twice already: he's calling you to dinner. And I was on my way out. I'll mosey in to see you sometimes. You'll be all right with us; they'll take you right into the family now. Mind you, don't give me away. I fancy you and I shall either be friends or enemies. And what do you think, Prince, if I had kissed your hand before (as I sincerely offered to) would I have become your enemy for it in consequence?"

39. Fr., He who laughs last laughs best.

"You certainly would have, but not forever; later, you wouldn't have been able to bear it and you'd forgive," the prince decided, having reflected and laughed.

"Oho! Why, one must be more on one's guard with you. Hell's bells, you've put some venom in it here, too. And who knows, perhaps you're an enemy to me after all? By the way, ha-ha-ha! I forgot to ask: was I right in fancying that you like Nastasya Filippovna just a little too much, eh?"

"Yes . . . I like her."

"In love, are you?"

"N-no."

"But he's turned all red and anguished. Well, never mind, never mind, I won't laugh; good-bye. But do you know, she's a virtuous woman, can you believe it? You think she's living with that man, with Totsky? Not a bit of it! And a long time since. And did you notice that she is terribly awkward herself, and before, at certain moments, was embarrassed? Truly. It's just that sort who are fond of dominating others. Well, good-bye!"

Ganechka went out far more relaxed than he had come in, and in good humor. The prince remained motionless some ten minutes, thinking.

Kolya poked his head in at the door again.

"I don't want any dinner, Kolya; I had a good lunch at the Epanchins' before."

Kolya came through the door completely and handed the prince a note. It was from the general, folded and sealed. It was evident from Kolya's face how difficult it was for him to deliver it. The prince read it, stood up, and took his hat.

"It's just two steps," said Kolya, growing sheepish. "He's sitting there now over a bottle. And how he managed to get credit there, I can't conceive. Prince, be a dove, please, don't tell on me afterward to my people, that I've given you the note! I've sworn a thousand times not to deliver those notes, but I'm sorry for him; and I say, please, don't stand on ceremony with him: give him some trifle and let that be the end of it."

"I had the thought myself, Kolya; I need to see your father . . . on account of a certain circumstance . . . Well, let's go . . ."

XII

Kolya led the prince not too far off, to Liteinaya Street, into a café–cum–billiards room, on the ground floor, with a street entrance. Here, to the right, in the corner, in a separate room, Ardalion Alexandrovich was installed, like an old regular, with a bottle in front of him on the little table, and, in point of fact, with the *Indépendance Belge* in his hands. He was awaiting the prince; he had no sooner laid eyes on him than he immediately laid aside the newspaper and began a fervent and long-winded explanation, of which, however, the prince could make out almost nothing, for the general was fairly well into his cups.

"I haven't got ten rubles," interrupted the prince, "but here's twenty-five, change it and give me fifteen back, for I am left without a farthing myself."

"Oh, without a doubt; and rest assured, that I'll at once . . ."

"But aside from that, I've come to you with a request, General. Have you never been to Nastasya Filippovna's?"

"Me? Me never been? You say that to me? Several times, my dear fellow, several times!" exclaimed the general in a fit of self-satisfied and triumphant irony. "But in the end, I broke it off myself, for I don't wish to encourage an unseemly alliance. You saw yourself, you were a witness this morning: I've done everything that a father can do, but a mild and indulgent father; and now, a father of a different sort will come on the scene, and then—we'll just look and see whether the distinguished old warrior masters the intrigue or the shameless cocotte enters into the most honorable family."

"And I had wanted, actually, to ask whether you—as an acquaintance—could take me to Nastasya Filippovna's this evening. I must invariably go today; I have business; but I have no idea how to get in. I was introduced lately, but all the same, not invited: there's a party there this evening. However, I'm ready to skip over certain proprieties, and let them even laugh at me, if only I could get in somehow."

"And you've hit upon my idea precisely, precisely, my young friend," exclaimed the general delightedly, "I didn't ask you to come on account of that trifle!" he continued, snatching up the money, however, and putting it in his pocket. "I sent for you precisely to invite you to accompany me on an expedition to Nastasya Filippovna, or, better said, an expedition against Nastasya Filippovna! General Ivolgin and Prince Myshkin! How will that strike her? As for me, on the pretext of a civility on her birthday, I shall finally announce my will—obliquely, not directly, but it will all be as if directly. Then Ganya will see himself what he must do: whether his father, distinguished and . . . so to speak . . . and so on, or . . . But whatever will be, will be! Your idea is extremely productive. At nine o'clock we shall start, we still have time."

"Where does she live?"

"From here, it's far: by the Grand Theater, in Mitovtsov's house, almost on the square, on the second floor . . . She won't have a large gathering, birthday or no, and it will break up early . . ."

It was long since evening; the prince still sat listening and waiting for the general, who had begun countless stories and not finished a single one of them. On the prince's arrival, he had asked for another bottle and had only finished it an hour later, then he asked for another, and finished that too. It may be supposed that in that time the general had managed to narrate almost the whole of his history. At last, the prince got up and said he could not wait any longer. The general emptied the last dregs out of the bottle, stood up, and walked out of the room, stepping rather unsteadily. The prince was in despair. He could not understand how he could have entrusted himself so foolishly. As a matter of fact, he had never actually entrusted himself; he had simply counted on the general as a means of getting in to see Nastasya Filippovna somehow, even if it caused a bit of a scene, but he had certainly not counted on an exceptionally great scene: the general turned out to be decidedly drunk, in a most eloquent state, and talked ceaselessly, with feeling, on the verge of tears. The topic of his incessant talk was how through the bad behavior of all the members of his family everything was falling into ruin and how it was high time, at last, to put a stop to it. At last they came out onto Liteinaya Street. It was still continuing to thaw; a dreary, muggy, foul wind whistled up and down the streets, the carriages splashed in the mud, the shoes of the trotters and hacks struck the road with a resounding ring. Pedestrians drifted over the sidewalks in a dejected and wet crowd. Here and there, they came across a drunk.

"Do you see those second stories lit up?" said the general. "My old comrades live all about here, and I, I, who's seen the most service and the most suffering of all of them, I trudge on foot to the Grand Theater, to the lodging of a woman of suspect reputation! A person who has thirteen bullets in his chest . . . You don't believe it? And in the meantime, it was solely on my account that Pirogov telegraphed to Paris and abandoned besieged Sevastopol for a time, and Nelaton, the court doctor in Paris, managed to procure a letter of free passage in the name of science and appeared in besieged Sevastopol in person to examine me.[40] The very highest authorities know all about it: 'Ah, that's the Ivolgin who has thirteen bullets in him! . . .' That's what they say, sir! Do you see that house, prince? On the second floor there lives an old comrade, Sokolovich, with his most honorable and numerous family. That house, and three more houses on the Nevsky and two in the Morskaya—that's the whole of my present circle of acquaintance, that is to say, my own personal acquaintance. Nina Alexandrovna resigned herself to circumstances long ago. But I still continue to remember . . . and, so to speak, refresh myself in the cultured society of my former comrades and subordinates, who adore me to this day. That General Sokolovich (incidentally, I haven't been to see him for some little time, and haven't seen Anna Fyodorovna) . . . You know, dear prince, when you yourself don't entertain, you somehow unintentionally stop visiting others. But by the way . . . hm . . . it seems you don't believe me . . . But why don't I introduce the son of my closest friend and comrade of my childhood into this delightful family circle? General Ivolgin and Prince Myshkin! You will see an exquisite girl, and not one, but two, even three, ornaments of the city and society: beauty, culture, enlightenment . . . the woman question, poetry—all this has combined into a happy, heterogeneous mix, not counting at least eighty thousand rubles dowry, in hard cash, for each, which is never a drawback, regardless of any feminist and social questions . . . in a word, I certainly, certainly must, it is my duty, to introduce you. General Ivolgin and Prince Myshkin!"

"At once? Right now? But you've forgotten," began the prince.

"I've forgotten nothing, nothing, come along! Here, up this magnificent staircase, how now, no porter, but . . . it's a holiday, and the porter

---

40. Pirogov was a prominent Russian surgeon in charge of care of the wounded in the seige of Sevastopol; Nelaton was a famous French surgeon and member of the Paris Academy. He had never been to Russia.

has taken himself off. They haven't turned that drunkard out yet. This Sokolovich is indebted for the whole happiness of his life and career to me, to me and no one else, but . . . here we are."

The prince had stopped protesting against the visit and submissively followed the general, so as not to irritate him, in the firm hope that General Sokolovich and all his family would evaporate little by little like a mirage and turn out to be nonexistent, so that they could quietly retrace their steps down the staircase. But, to his horror, he began to lose this hope: the general led him up the stairs like a man who really had acquaintance here, and every minute he would put in some biographical or topographical detail full of mathematical precision. At last, when, having already reached the second floor, they stopped on the right before the door of a luxurious apartment and the general took hold of the bell, the prince finally made up his mind to flee; but one strange circumstance held him for a moment.

"You've made a mistake, General," he said, "the name on the door is Kulakov, but you are ringing for Sokolovich."

"Kulakov . . . Kulakov proves nothing. The apartment is Sokolovich's and I'm ringing for Sokolovich; hang Kulakov . . . Why, here is someone to open the door."

The door was opened indeed. A footman peered out and announced that "the masters are not at home, sirs."

"What a pity, what a pity, and as if by design!" Ardalion Alexandrovich repeated several times with profound regret. "Tell them, dear fellow, that General Ivolgin and Prince Myshkin wished to present their respects in person and regret extremely, extremely . . ."

At that moment, another face peered out of the rooms into the open doorway, apparently belonging to a housekeeper, perhaps even a governess, a lady of about forty in a dark dress. She approached inquisitively and mistrustfully, hearing the names of General Ivolgin and Prince Myshkin.

"Marya Alexandrovna is not at home," she pronounced, scrutinizing the general particularly. "She has gone out with the young lady, Alexandra Mikhailovna, to her grandmother's."

"Alexandra Mikhailovna, too, good heavens, what misfortune! Would you believe it, madam, I always have such misfortune! I humbly beg you to give my compliments, and beg Alexandra Mikhailovna to remember . . . in a word, convey to her my heartfelt wishes for what she herself wished on Thursday evening, to the sounds of a Chopin ballad; she will remember . . . My heartfelt wishes! General Ivolgin and Prince Myshkin!"

"I won't forget, sir," bowed the lady, becoming more trusting.

Going down the stairs, the general, with unabated fervor, continued to regret that they had found no one at home and that the prince had been denied such charming acquaintance.

"Do you know, my dear fellow, I am somewhat of a poet in my soul, have you noticed that? But incidentally . . . incidentally, it seems we called at altogether the wrong place," he concluded suddenly and quite unexpectedly. "The Sokoloviches, I recollect now, live in a different house and, I fancy, they are even in Moscow now. Yes, I was slightly mistaken, but . . . no matter."

"I would like to know just one thing," the prince remarked disconsolately. "Must I cease to count on you entirely and hadn't I better go alone?"

"Cease? To count on? Alone? But what in the world for, when, for me, this constitutes the most capital undertaking on which so much depends in the fate of my entire family? But, my young friend, you don't know Ivolgin. To say 'Ivolgin' is to say 'a rock': depend on Ivolgin like a rock, that's what they used to say in the squadron where I began my service. I have only just to call in for one little minute on the way at the house where, for some years now, my soul finds rest after my trials and tribulations . . ."

"You want to go home?"

"No! I want . . . to go see Captainess Terentyev, Captain Terentyev's widow, one of my former subordinates . . . and even friend . . . Here, at the captainess's, I am refreshed in spirit and here is where I bring my daily cares and my family troubles . . . And as today I particularly have a heavy moral burden, I . . ."

"It seems, even without that, I've made a terribly foolish mistake," muttered the prince, "in having troubled you lately. And besides, you're now . . . Good-bye!"

"But I cannot, I really cannot let you go, my young friend!" the general reared up. "A widow, mother of a family, and draws from her heart the strings that echo through my entire being. A visit to her—it's a matter of five minutes, I don't stand on ceremony in that house, I almost live there; I'll wash, take only the most necessary steps to freshen up, and then we'll set off to the Grand Theater in a hackney. Rest assured that I have need of you for the entire evening . . . Here, in this house, and we've arrived . . . Ah, Kolya, you here already? What, is Marfa Borissovna at home, or have you only just come yourself?"

"Oh, no," answered Kolya, who had just run into them at the gates of the house, "I've been here a long while, with Ippolit; he's worse, was in bed this morning. I've just been down to the shop to get some cards. Marfa Borissovna is expecting you. Only, Papa, uff! You're in a state! . . ." concluded Kolya, intently scrutinizing the way the general walked and stood. "Well, then, let's go!"

The meeting with Kolya induced the prince to accompany the general to Marfa Borissovna, but only for one minute. The prince had need of Kolya; as for the general, he had decided to abandon him in any case and could not forgive himself that he had lately had the notion of relying on him. They climbed for a long time, up to the fourth floor, and by the back stair.

"You want to introduce the prince?" asked Kolya on the way.

"Yes, my dear, to introduce him: General Ivolgin and Prince Myshkin, but what . . . how . . . Marfa Borissovna . . ."

"Do you know, Papa, you'd better not go! She'll give it to you! You've not shown head or tail for three days, and she's expecting money. Why did you promise her money? You're always doing things like that! Now go and deal with it."

On the fourth floor, they stopped before a low door. The general was evidently losing heart and kept pushing the prince in front of him.

"I'll stay here," he muttered, "I want to surprise her . . ."

Kolya went in first. Some lady, heavily made-up and rouged, in slippers, in a scanty negligee, with her hair plaited in little braids, about forty, peered out from the doorway, and the general's surprise suddenly burst like a bubble. No sooner had the lady seen him that she promptly screamed:

"There he is, the base and venomous man, just as my heart anticipated!"

"Let's come in, it's nothing," muttered the general to the prince, still laughing it off with a guileless air.

But it was not nothing. They had hardly come in, through a dark and low-pitched entryway, into a narrow drawing room furnished with half a dozen rush-bottomed chairs and two card tables, when the lady

of the house immediately continued in some kind of affectedly lachry-
mose and common tone:

"And aren't you ashamed, aren't you ashamed, you savage and
tyrant of my family, you savage and monster! You've robbed me of
everything, sucked me dry, and are still not content. And how long am
I to put up with you, you shameless and dishonorable man!"

"Marfa Borissovna, Marfa Borissovna! This . . . is Prince Myshkin.
General Ivolgin and Prince Myshkin," muttered the general, trembling and discombobulated.

"Would you believe it," the captainess suddenly turned to the
prince, "would you believe that this shameless man has not spared my
orphan children! He's robbed us of everything, carried off everything,
sold and pawned everything and left us nothing. What am I to do with
your IOUs, you sneaky and unscrupulous man? Answer, you sneak, answer me, you insatiable heart: how, how am I to feed my orphan children? And here he shows up drunk and can't stand on his legs . . . What
have I done to call down the wrath of God, you heinous and disgraceful sneak, answer me?"

But the general was not up to it.

"Marfa Borissovna, twenty-five rubles . . . All I can, thanks to a generous friend. Prince! I was cruelly mistaken! Such is . . . life . . . But
now . . . excuse me, I feel weak," continued the general, standing in the
middle of the room and bowing in all directions. "I am weak, excuse
me! Lenochka, a pillow . . . my dear!"

Lenochka, an eight-year-old girl, ran at once to fetch a pillow and
put it on the hard and tattered sofa covered in oilcloth. The general sat
down upon it, with the intention of saying much more, but as soon as
he touched the sofa he immediately leaned over on his side, turned to
the wall and sank into the sleep of the just. Marfa Borissovna mournfully and ceremoniously motioned the prince to a chair at the card
table, sat down herself facing him, propping her right cheek on her
hand, and began to sigh silently, looking at the prince. Three little children, two girls and a boy, of whom Lenochka was the eldest, went up
to the table, laid their arms on it, and all three also began intently to
scrutinize the prince. Kolya made his appearance from the next room.

"I am very glad I've met you here, Kolya," the prince turned to him,
"could you help me? I absolutely must be at Nastasya Filippovna's. I
had asked Ardalion Alexandrovich before, but you see he's fallen

asleep now. Take me there, please, for I don't know the streets, nor the way. Though I have the address: by the Grand Theater, Mitovtsov's house."

"Nastasya Filippovna? Why, she's never lived by the Grand Theater, and father's never been at Nastasya Filippovna's, if you want to know; it's strange that you expected anything of him. She lives near Vladimirsky, at the Five Corners, it's much nearer here. Do you want to go now? It's half past nine. If you'll allow, I'll take you there."

The prince and Kolya went out at once. Alas! The prince had nothing with which to pay for a cab, so they had to go on foot.

"I wanted to introduce you to Ippolit," said Kolya, "he's the eldest son of that scantily clad captainess and was in the other room; he's ill and was lying down all day today. But he's so queer; he's frightfully touchy, and I fancied he'd feel ashamed in front of you, since you came at such a moment... Still, I am not as ashamed as he is, because it's my father, but his mother, there's still a difference, for there's no dishonor for the male sex in such cases. But then again, maybe it's a prejudice about the hierarchy of the sexes in such cases. Ippolit is a splendid lad, but he's a slave to certain prejudices."

"You say he has consumption?"

"Yes, it seems the best thing for him would be to die soon. If I were in his place, I should certainly want to die. He feels sorry for his brother and sisters, those little ones you saw. If it were possible, if only the money were there, he and I would have rented a separate apartment and renounced our families. That's our dream. And do you know, when I told him just now what happened to you, he even flew into a regular rage and said that the man who accepts a blow without fighting a duel, he's the scoundrel. But then, he's terribly irritated, and I've given up arguing with him. So then, it seems, Nastasya Filippovna invited you to her at once?"

"That's just it, she didn't."

"How can you go then?" exclaimed Kolya, and even stopped short in the middle of the sidewalk. "And ... and in such clothes, and there's an evening party?"

"Goodness knows, I've no idea how I'll get in. If they receive me—good; if not—then forget the whole business. And as for the clothes—what is to be done?"

"But do you have business? Or are you going just like that, *pour passer le temps*[41] in 'noble society'?"

"No, actually, I . . . that is, I have business . . . It's difficult for me to put into words, but . . ."

"Well, what exactly your business is, let that be as you please, the main thing for me is that you're not simply cadging an invitation to spend the evening in the charming society of cocottes, generals, and moneylenders. If it had been so, excuse me, Prince, I would have laughed at you and despised you. There are frightfully few honest people here, to the point that there's absolutely nobody you can respect. One can't help looking down on people, and they all insist on respect; Varya first of all. And have you noticed, Prince, in our age, everyone's a speculator! And particularly among us, in Russia, in our well-mannered fatherland. And how did it all come about—I don't understand it. It was standing so firmly, it seems, and what's happening now? Everyone says it, and it's written up everywhere. Exposed. In Russia, everyone is exposing things. Our parents are the first to go back on themselves and are ashamed themselves of their old morals. Why, in Moscow, you had a father persuading his son to stop *at nothing* to obtain money; it was reported in the press. Just look at my general. Well, what has he come to? And yet, you know, it seems to me that my general is an honest man; by God, it's so! It's nothing but disorder and wine. By God, it's so! I even feel sorry for him; only, I'm afraid to say so because everyone laughs; but, by God, I feel sorry for him. And what is there in them, then, the sensible people? They're all usurers, every last one of them! Ippolit justifies usury, he says it's how it should be, economic upheaval, ebb and flow or something, to hell with them. It vexes me to hear it from him, but he's resentful. Imagine, his mother, the captainess, gets money from the general and then hands it out to him at high interest; terribly shameful! And do you know that Mother, my mother that is, Nina Alexandrovna, the generaless, helps Ippolit with money, clothes, linens, and everything, even helps the children in part, through Ippolit, because she neglects them. And Varya too."

"There, you see, you say that there are no honest and strong people and that everyone's just a usurer; but there you have strong people,

41. Fr., to pass the time.

your mother and Varya. Isn't helping here and in such circumstances a sign of moral strength?"

"Varjka does it from vanity, to show off, so as not to fall behind Mother; but as for Mother, she really . . . I respect it. Yes, I respect that and approve of it. Even Ippolit feels it, and he's become almost completely embittered. At first, he would laugh and called it low on my mother's part; but now he's starting to feel it sometimes. Hm! So you call that strength? I shall make note of that. Ganya doesn't know, or he would call it indulgence."

"Ganya doesn't know, then? There seems to be a great deal Ganya still doesn't know," blurted out the prince, who had become pensive.

"Do you know, Prince, I like you very much. I can't get that recent incident of yours out of my mind."

"And I like you very much too, Kolya."

"Listen, how do you intend to live here? I shall soon find employment for myself and will start earning something; let's live together, all three, me, you, and Ippolit, we'll rent an apartment; and we'll receive the general at our place."

"With the greatest pleasure. But we'll see. I feel very . . . very upset. What? Are we there already? In this house . . . what a magnificent entrance! And a hall-porter. Well, Kolya, I don't know what will come of it."

The prince stood there as if at a loss.

"You'll tell me about it tomorrow. Don't be timid. God grant you success, for I share your convictions in everything! Good-bye. I'll go back there and tell Ippolit. As for your being received, there's no doubt of it, have no fear. She's terribly original. Up this staircase on the first floor, the porter will show you."

XIII

The prince was very uneasy as he went up and tried with all his might to give himself courage. "The worst that can happen," he thought, "is that they won't receive me and think something bad of me, or, perhaps, receive me and then start laughing in my face . . . Eh, it's nothing!" And indeed, this did not alarm him very much, but the question "What would he do there and why was he going?"—to that question, he certainly could find no comforting answer. Even if it were possible in some way, catching a favorable opportunity, to say to Nastasya Filippovna: "Don't marry this man and don't destroy yourself, he doesn't love you, it's your money he loves, he told me so himself, and Aglaia Epanchin told me so too, and I've come to relate it to you," this would have hardly turned out right and proper in all respects. And another unresolved question presented itself, and such a vital one that the prince was even afraid to consider it, could not and dared not even admit it, did not know how to formulate it, flushed and trembled at the mere thought of it. But in the end, despite all these doubts and apprehensions, he went in all the same and asked for Nastasya Filippovna.

Nastasya Filippovna occupied a not very large but, indeed, magnificently furnished apartment. In these five years of her life in Petersburg, there had been a time, in the beginning, when Afanasy Ivanovich had particularly spared no expense for her; he still had hopes of her love in those days, and had thought to tempt her, chiefly, with comfort and luxury, knowing how easily habits of luxury are acquired and how difficult it is to give them up afterward, when luxury, little by little, turns into necessity. In this respect, Totsky clung to the good old tradition, without modifying it in any way, having an unbounded respect for the supreme power of the appeal to the senses. Nastasya Filippovna did not refuse luxury, she was even fond of it, but—and this seemed extremely strange—she would not succumb to it in the least, as if she could have always done without it; she even made an effort to announce this fact a few times, which was an unpleasant surprise for Totsky. However, there was much in Nastasya Filippovna that surprised Afanasy Ivanovich unpleasantly (subsequently, even to the point of contempt). To say nothing of the inelegance of the sorts of people she sometimes attracted to herself and, it would seem, had a tendency to attract, discernible in her were also some other utterly strange tendencies: some kind of barbaric mixture of two tastes manifested itself, a capacity for making do and being satisfied with things and means the mere existence of which, it would seem, a well-bred and refined person could not even admit. In fact, if, for example, Nastasya Filippovna had suddenly displayed some sweet and charming ignorance, such as, for instance, that peasant women were not in a position to wear the batiste undergarments that she wore, Afanasy Ivanovich would probably have been extremely pleased. It was to such results that the whole of Nastasya Filippovna's education had been from the beginning directed, following the plan of Totsky, who was a man of very great understanding in that regard; but, alas! the results turned out to be very strange. Nonetheless, in spite of that, there still was and remained in Nastasya Filippovna something that at times astonished even Afanasy Ivanovich himself with its extraordinary and fascinating originality, some kind of power, and sometimes enchanted him even now, when all of his former designs on Nastasya Filippovna had collapsed.

The prince was met by a girl (Nastasya Filippovna's servants were always female) and, to his surprise, she heard his request to announce him without a trace of perplexity. Neither his dirty boots, nor his wide-brimmed hat, nor his sleeveless cloak, nor his flustered appearance caused her to hesitate in the slightest. She took off his cloak, asked him to wait in the reception room and went off at once to announce him.

The company gathered at Nastasya Filippovna's consisted of the most ordinary and usual circle of her acquaintance. The guests were few in number, indeed, compared with previous annual gatherings on the same occasion. Present, first and most important, were Afanasy Ivanovich Totsky and Ivan Fyodorovich Epanchin; both were amiable but both were secretly somewhat uneasy on account of an ill-disguised anticipation of the promised declaration in regard to Ganya. Aside from them, of course, there was Ganya, too—he was also very gloomy, very pensive, even almost entirely unforthcoming, standing off to the side for the most part, at some distance, and keeping silent. He had not ventured to bring Varya, and Nastasya Filippovna made no mention of her; however, immediately after greeting Ganya, she alluded to his scene with the prince. The general, who had not heard of it, was much interested. Then Ganya, dryly, with restraint, but with perfect frankness, related everything that had happened lately, and how he had already gone to the prince to beg his pardon. At that, he fervently expressed his opinion that it had been very strange and, God knows, unaccountable to call the prince an idiot, that he thinks quite the opposite of him, and that, most certainly, this man is in full possession of his mind. Nastasya Filippovna listened to this dictum with great attention and watched Ganya with curiosity, but the conversation passed immediately to Rogozhin as a leading figure in the morning's scene, and one in whom Afanasy Ivanovich and Ivan Fyodorovich also began to take an extraordinary interest. It appeared that the person who could relate the most particulars about Rogozhin was Ptitsyn, who had been with him, plugging away on account of his business, practically till nine o'clock in the evening. Rogozhin insisted most strenuously on their obtaining a hundred thousand rubles that very day. "He was, of course, drunk," observed Ptitsyn, "but difficult as it may be, it seems the hundred thousand will be procured for him, only I don't know whether today, and whether all at once; but many are working on it, Kinder, Trepalov, Biskup; he's agreeing to any kind of interest, of course it's all in a drunken stupor and in the first flush of fortune . . ." Ptitsyn concluded. All this information was received with interest, in part gloomy interest; Nastasya Filippovna kept silent, evidently not caring to say what she felt. Ganya, too. General Epanchin worried to himself almost more than all the others; the pearls, which had already been presented that morning, had been accepted with a rather too frigid politeness, and even with some kind of peculiar smirk. Of all the guests, Ferdyshchenko alone was in a merry and festive mood and howled loudly with laughter at times for no discernible reason, and that was only because he had imposed on himself the role of the jester. Afanasy Ivanovich himself, who had the reputation of a refined and elegant storyteller, and who had in past times led the conversation at these parties, was evidently out of humor and even in some kind of state of confusion entirely unlike him. The remaining guests—who were, however, few in number (one pitiful old teacher, invited for God knows what reason; some unknown and very young man, fearfully timid and continually silent; one sprightly lady of forty, of the actress type; and one exceedingly beautiful, exceedingly well and richly dressed, and extraordinarily taciturn young lady)—were not merely incapable of particularly enlivening the conversation, but at times simply did not even know what to talk about at all.

And so the appearance of the prince actually turned out to be just what was wanted. The announcement of his name caused bewilderment and a few queer smiles, especially when it became clear from Nastasya Filippovna's surprised air that she had not dreamed of inviting him. But after her surprise, Nastasya Filippovna suddenly displayed so much pleasure that the majority promptly prepared to meet the incidental guest with laughter and mirth.

"It may be this has happened on account of his innocence," concluded Ivan Fyodorovich Epanchin, "and in any case it is rather dangerous to encourage such tendencies, but at the present moment, truly, it's not at all bad that he's taken it into his head to turn up, even if it is in such an original manner: he may, perhaps, amuse us, as far as I can judge of him at least."

"Especially as he has invited himself!" Ferdyshchenko put in at once.

"Well, what of that?" dryly asked the general, who detested Ferdyshchenko.

"Why, he will pay for his entrance!" explained the latter.

"Well, sir, Prince Myshkin is not Ferdyshchenko, at any rate," the general could not resist saying; he still hadn't been able to reconcile himself to the thought of being in the same company and on an equal footing with Ferdyshchenko.

"Ay, General, spare Ferdyshchenko," replied the latter, grinning. "You see, I've got special privileges."

"And what special privileges are those?"

"Last time I had the honor of explaining it in detail to the company; for the sake of your excellency, I'll repeat it again. If it will please you to note, your excellency, everyone has wit, but I have no wit. To make up for it, I have successfully sued for leave to speak the truth, for everyone knows that the truth is told only by those who have no wit. In addition, I am a very vindictive man, and that is also because I'm without wit. I humbly bear any insult, but only until my offender encounters misfortune; at the very first misfortune, I remember it at once and at once avenge myself in some way, I kick out, as was said of me by Ivan Petrovich Ptitsyn, who, of course, never kicks anyone himself. Do you know Krylov's fable,[42] your excellency: 'The Lion and the Ass'? Well, there you have it, that's you and me, it's written about us."

"I think you've gone off spewing nonsense again, Ferdyshchenko," sputtered the general, boiling over.

"But what is it, your excellency?" took up Ferdyshchenko, who had reckoned on being able to take it up and spread it on even thicker. "Don't worry, your excellency, I know my place. If I say that you and I are the lion and ass from Krylov's fable, then the part of the ass I, of

---

42. Ivan Andreevich Krylov (1768–1844), a widely read author of Aesopian fables.

course, take on myself, while your excellency is the lion, as it says in Krylov's fable:

> The mighty lion, terror of the woods
> With growing years has lost his youthful strength

And I, your excellency, am the ass."

"With the latter, I'm in agreement," incautiously blurted out the general.

All this was, of course, performed coarsely and with deliberation, but it was the accepted thing that Ferdyshchenko was allowed to play the fool.

"Why, they only keep me and receive me here for the sole purpose," Ferdyshchenko had once exclaimed, "that I may talk precisely in this vein. Well, really, is it possible to receive a person such as myself? You see, I do understand that. Well, is it possible to take me, such a Ferdyshchenko, and seat me beside such a refined gentleman as Afanasy Ivanovich? Unwillingly, one is left with only one explanation: they seat me there precisely for the reason that it is not even imaginable."

But though it was coarse, all the same, it could be quite cutting, and at times very much so, and, it seemed, that was just what Nastasya Filippovna liked. For those who wanted, without fail, to spend time at her house, there was no choice but to make up their minds to put up with Ferdyshchenko. It may be that he had even guessed the whole truth when he supposed that he had been received to begin with because his presence had from the first been insufferable to Totsky. Ganya, for his part, endured an endless series of torments from him, and in that respect, Ferdyshchenko had managed to be of great use to Nastasya Filippovna.

"As for the prince, I will have him begin by singing us a fashionable romance," concluded Ferdyshchenko, looking to see what Nastasya Filippovna would say.

"I don't think so, Ferdyshchenko, and please don't get too heated up," she said dryly.

"A-ha! If he's under special protection, then I will relent, too . . ."

But Nastasya Filippovna rose, not listening to him, and went to meet the prince herself.

"I regretted," she said, suddenly appearing before the prince, "that lately, in my haste, I forgot to invite you to me, and am very glad that you yourself now give me the opportunity to thank you and praise you for your decisiveness."

As she said this, she scrutinized the prince intently, endeavoring to make at least some sense of his action.

The prince would perhaps have made some reply to her gracious words, but was so dazzled and astonished that he could not even utter a word. Nastasya Filippovna noticed this with satisfaction. That evening she was in full evening dress and made an extraordinary impression. She took him by the hand and led him to the company. Just before the entrance to the drawing room, the prince suddenly stopped and with extraordinary agitation hurriedly whispered to her:

"Everything is perfection in you . . . even that you are thin and pale . . . One wouldn't even wish to imagine you any other way . . . I had such a longing to come to you . . . I . . . forgive me . . ."

"Don't apologize," laughed Nastasya Filippovna, "that would destroy all the strangeness and originality. But it seems it's true what they say about you, that you're a strange man. So you consider me to be perfection, do you?"

"Yes."

"Though you are a master at guessing, still you are mistaken. I'll remind you of that this very evening . . ."

She introduced the prince to the guests, to more than half of whom he was already known. Totsky immediately made some polite remark. Everyone seemed to revive somewhat, everyone began to talk and laugh at once. Nastasya Filippovna seated the prince beside her.

"But after all, what is so remarkable in the prince's appearance?" Ferdyshchenko shouted louder than all the rest. "The case is clear, the case speaks for itself!"

"The case is too clear and speaks for itself too much," Ganya, who had been silent, suddenly chimed in. "I've been observing the prince today almost continuously, from the very instant, before, when he looked for the first time upon the portrait of Nastasya Filippovna on Ivan Fyodorovich's table. I remember quite well that I thought even then of something that I am now utterly convinced of, and, by the way, which the prince himself confessed to me."

Ganya uttered this whole speech extremely seriously, without the slightest trace of playfulness, even glumly, which appeared somewhat strange.

"I made no confessions to you," answered the prince, flushing, "I simply answered your question."

"Bravo, bravo!" shouted Ferdyshchenko. "At least it's sincere, both crafty and sincere!"

Everyone laughed loudly.

"Don't shout, Ferdyshchenko," Ptitsyn admonished him in an undertone, with disgust.

"I should not have expected such feats of prowess from you," uttered Ivan Fyodorovich, "why, do you know who would be up to that? And I had taken you for a philosopher! Oh, you quiet ones!"

"And to judge from the way the prince blushes at an innocent jest like an innocent young girl, I conclude that, like an honorable lad, he harbors in his heart the most laudable intentions," suddenly and entirely unexpectedly uttered, or, better said, champed, the toothless, septuagenarian old teacher, who had been entirely silent till that time, and of whom no one could have expected that he would even begin to speak that evening. Everyone laughed more than ever. The little old man, probably imagining that they were laughing at his wit, started to laugh even more heartily, looking at everyone, at which he broke out in a violent coughing fit, so that Nastasya Filippovna, who for some reason was extremely fond of all such odd little old men and women and even lunatics, at once undertook to coddle him, kissed him, and bade that he be brought more tea. She asked the maidservant who had come in for a cloak, in which she wrapped herself, and ordered more wood to be put on the fire. Upon the question what time it was, the maid answered that it was already half past ten.

"Ladies and gentlemen, would you like to have some champagne?" Nastasya Filippovna suddenly suggested. "I have it ready. Perhaps it will make you more merry. Please, no ceremony."

The offer of drink, and especially in such naïve turns of phrase, made a very strange impression coming from Nastasya Filippovna. Everyone knew the extraordinary standard of decorum maintained at her previous parties. In general, the party was becoming merrier, but not in the same way as usual. The wine, however, was not turned down, first of all, by the general himself, secondly, by the sprightly lady, the little old man, Ferdyshchenko, and after them, by the rest. Totsky also took his goblet, hoping to play down the new tone taking over the company by lending it as far as possible the character of an agreeable jest. Only Ganya drank nothing. As for the strange and at times very sharp and quick sallies of Nastasya Filippovna—who had also taken some wine and declared that she would drink three glasses—and her hysterical and objectless laughter, alternating suddenly with a silent and even morose contemplation, it was difficult to make anything of them. Some suspected that she was feverish; they began, at last, to notice that she too seemed to be waiting for something herself, frequently looked at the clock, and was becoming impatient and preoccupied.

"You seem to be a little feverish?" asked the sprightly lady.

"Not a little, but very much; that's why I wrapped myself up in my cloak," replied Nastasya Filippovna, who really had turned more pale and seemed at times to be suppressing a violent shiver.

Everyone began to fret and spring into motion.

"But shouldn't we let our hostess rest?" said Totsky, looking at Ivan Fyodorovich.

"Absolutely not, ladies and gentlemen! I particularly beg you to stay. Your presence, especially today, is indispensable to me," Nastasya Filippovna suddenly declared insistently and emphatically. And as almost all the guests knew that a very important decision was meant to be made that evening, these words seemed exceedingly loaded. The general and Totsky exchanged glances once more. Ganya twitched convulsively.

"It would be good to play some *petit-jeu*,"[43] said the sprightly lady.

"I know a most splendid and new *petit-jeu*," put in Ferdyshchenko, "or at the least, one that has been played only once in all the world, and even then, it didn't come off."

"What is it?" asked the sprightly lady.

"A party of us were together one day—well, we'd had a bit to drink, it's true—and suddenly someone made the suggestion that each of us, without leaving the table, should tell something about himself, but something that he himself, in his own good conscience, considered the worst of all the evil deeds in the entire course of his life; but with the point that it's sincere, that's the main thing, that it be sincere, no lying!"

43. Fr., parlor game.

"A strange idea!" said the general.

"Why, what could be stranger, your excellency, but that's the best of it."

"A funny idea," said Totsky, "but then again, an understandable one: a special kind of bragging."

"Perhaps that's just what was wanted, Afanasy Ivanovich."

"Why, that would set you crying, not laughing, with such a *petit-jeu*," observed the sprightly lady.

"The thing is quite impossible and absurd," Ptitsyn chimed in.

"And did it come off?" asked Nastasya Filippovna.

"That's just it, it didn't, it came out badly; everyone really did tell something, many told the truth, and just imagine, some even told it with pleasure, but afterward, everyone was ashamed, they couldn't keep it up! On the whole, though, it was highly amusing, in its own way, that is."

"But truly, it would be good!" observed Nastasya Filippovna, suddenly becoming animated. "Truly, let's try it, ladies and gentlemen! Indeed, we are not very merry, somehow. If each of us would consent to tell something . . . of that sort . . . of course, voluntarily, there's complete freedom here, how about it? Perhaps we could keep it up? It would be awfully original, in any case . . ."

"It's a stroke of genius!" took up Ferdyshchenko. "Ladies are excluded, however, the men must start; the thing is determined by lots, as it had been before! Invariably, invariably! Anyone who really doesn't want to, of course, needn't tell anything, but you'd have to be particularly disagreeable! Let's have your lots, gentlemen, here, give them to me, in my hat, the prince shall draw. The object is most simple, to describe the worst thing you've ever done in your life—it's awfully easy, gentlemen! You'll see! If anyone forgets, I undertake on the spot to remind him!"

The idea appealed to no one. Some frowned, some smiled slyly. Some protested, but not too much; Ivan Fyodorovich, for instance, who was loath to oppose Nastasya Filippovna and had noticed how taken she was by this strange idea. In her desires, Nastasya Filippovna was always unrestrainable and merciless once she had made up her mind to express them, though they might be the most capricious desires, and useless even to herself. And now she was as if hysterical; she fussed, laughed spasmodically, in fits, especially at the protests of the uneasy Totsky. Her dark eyes glittered, two red spots appeared on her pale cheeks. The dejected and disgusted air of some of her guests possibly may have inflamed even more her mocking desire; it may be she was particularly attracted by the cynicism and cruelty of the idea. Some were even convinced that she had some special object in it. Anyway, they began to assent: in any case, it aroused their curiosity, and for many, it was very alluring. Ferdyshchenko fussed more than anyone.

"And what if it's something that's impossible to tell . . . before the ladies?" timidly remarked the silent youth.

"Why, don't tell it then: as if there aren't enough wicked deeds without that," answered Ferdyshchenko. "Oh, you youngster!"

"Well, and I don't know which of my actions I should consider the worst," put in the sprightly lady.

"Ladies are exempted from the obligation to tell of anything," repeated Ferdyshchenko, "but only from the obligation; anything of their own inspiration will be admitted with gratitude. And as for the men, if they are really too much disinclined, they are exempt as well."

"But what proof is there that I shan't tell lies?" asked Ganya, "and if I lie, the whole point of the game is lost. And who wouldn't tell lies? Everyone would invariably lie."

"Why, that in itself is fascinating, to see just how a person would lie here. And as for you, Ganechka, there's no particular danger of your telling lies, for we all know your worst action as it is. But just think, gentlemen," exclaimed Ferdyshchenko suddenly with some kind of inspiration, "just think, with what eyes we shall all look at one another afterward, tomorrow, for instance, having told our tales!"

"But is this possible? Can it really be in earnest, Nastasya Filippovna?" asked Totsky with dignity.

"If you're afraid of wolves—don't go in the forest!" observed Nastasya Filippovna with a smirk.

"But allow me, Mr. Ferdyshchenko, is it possible to make a *petit-jeu* out of this?" Totsky went on, becoming more and more uneasy. "I assure you that such things never come off; why, you said yourself that it had already not come off once."

"How, not come off! Why, last time I told the story of how I stole three rubles, I simply went and told it!"

"That may be. But surely there was no possibility of your having told it so that it resembled the truth and you were believed? But

Gavrila Ardalionovich has observed entirely justly that with the slightest hint of falsehood, the whole point of the game is lost. The truth is only possible accidentally, through a particular sort of boastful frame of mind in exceedingly bad taste, which is inconceivable and utterly unseemly here."

"But what a subtle person you are, Afanasy Ivanovich, you positively amaze me!" cried Ferdyshchenko. "Imagine, gentlemen, by observing that I couldn't tell the story of my thieving in such a way that it would resemble truth, Afanasy Ivanovich hints in the subtlest way that I couldn't in fact have stolen (for it is unseemly to say so out loud), though perhaps he is in private completely convinced that Ferdyshchenko might very well be capable of thieving! But to business, gentlemen, to business, the lots have been collected, and you've put in yours too, Afanasy Ivanovich, so it seems no one refuses. Prince, draw!"

The prince silently put his hand into the hat and drew the first lot—Ferdyshchenko's; the second—Ptitsyn's; the third—the general's; the fourth—Afanasy Ivanovich's; the fifth—his own; the sixth—Ganya's, and so on. The ladies had not put in lots.

"Good heavens, what misfortune!" exclaimed Ferdyshchenko. "And I had thought that the first would fall to the prince, and the second to the general. But, thank God, at least Ivan Petrovich comes after me, and I shall be rewarded. Well, gentlemen, of course, I am obliged to set a good example, but what I regret most of all at the present moment is that I am so insignificant and not distinguished in any way; even my rank is of the lowest; well, and what is there, indeed, of interest in the fact that Ferdyshchenko has done a wicked deed? Why, and what is my worst deed? It's a case of *embarras de richesse*.[44] Shall I tell of the same theft, to convince Afanasy Ivanovich that one may steal without being a thief?"

"You are also convincing me, Mr. Ferdyshchenko, that it is indeed possible to find pleasure, even to thrill, in describing one's sleazy deeds, though no one has asked about them . . . But in any case . . . Excuse me, Mr. Ferdyshchenko."

"Begin, Ferdyshchenko, you are chattering too much and will never finish!" Nastasya Filippovna ordered irritably and impatiently.

Everyone noticed that after her recent fit of laughter, she sud-

44. Fr., embarrassment of riches.

denly became positively morose, peevish, and irritable; nonetheless, she stubbornly and despotically insisted on her impossible caprice. Afanasy Ivanovich was in terrible anguish. He was also infuriated by Ivan Fyodorovich: he sat at his champagne as if nothing were the matter and, perhaps, even reckoned on telling something in his turn.

XIV

"I've no wit, Nastasya Filippovna, that's what makes me chatter too much!" cried Ferdyshchenko, beginning his story. "Had I the same wit as Afanasy Ivanovich or Ivan Petrovich, I should have sat still and held my tongue tonight, like Afanasy Ivanovich and Ivan Petrovich. Prince, let me ask you, what do you think; you see, it seems to me that there are many more thieves in the world than non-thieves, and that there isn't a single man, even the most honest one, who hasn't stolen something, if only once in his life. That's my idea, from which, incidentally, I don't at all conclude that there's nothing but thieves left and right, although, goodness knows, one is terribly tempted to conclude that sometimes. What do you think?"

"Phooey! how stupidly you tell your story," commented Darya Alexeevna, "and what nonsense, it can't be that everyone should have stolen something; I've never stolen anything."

"You've never stolen anything, Darya Alexeevna; but what will the prince say, who's suddenly gone all red?"

"It seems to me what you say is true, only you exaggerate very much," said the prince, who had indeed turned red for some reason.

"And you, Prince, have you never stolen anything yourself?"

"Phooey! how absurd this is! Come to your senses, Mr. Ferdyshchenko," interposed the general.

"Quite simply, when it came down to it, you were too ashamed to tell it, and now you want to drag the prince in with you, because he's meek," snapped out Darya Alexeevna.

"Ferdyshchenko, either tell your story or keep silent and don't speak for others. You put one out of all patience," said Nastasya Filippovna sharply and with annoyance.

"In a minute, Nastasya Filippovna; but since the prince has confessed—for I insist that the prince has as good as confessed—what would, for instance, someone else (to mention no names) say, if he wanted to tell the truth sometime? As for me, gentlemen, there isn't anything more to tell: it's very simple, and stupid, and nasty. But I assure you that I am not a thief; I don't know how I came to steal. It happened the year before last, at Semyon Ivanovich Ishchenk's dacha on a Sunday. He had some guests to dinner. After dinner, the men remained sitting over their wine. It occurred to me to ask Marya Ivanovna, his daughter, a young lady, to play something on the piano. As I walk through the corner room, on Marya Ivanovna's worktable there are three rubles, a green note: she'd taken it out to spend on something for the household. There's not a soul in the room. I took the note and put it in my pocket, what for—I don't know. What came over me— I don't understand it. Only I hastily returned and sat down at the table. I kept sitting there and waiting for something, in a state of rather great agitation, chattered away without stopping, told anecdotes, laughed; then I sat down with the ladies. About a half an hour later they missed it and began questioning the maids. They suspected a maid called Darya. I showed extraordinary interest and sympathy, and I remember that, when Darya became completely flustered, I began persuading her to confess, vouching my head for Marya Ivanovna's kindness, and all this aloud, before everyone. Everyone looked on, and I felt extraordinary pleasure precisely in the fact that I was preaching while the note lay in my own pocket. I spent those three rubles that very evening on drink at a restaurant. I went in and asked for a bottle of Lafitte; I had never before asked for just a bottle like that, by itself; I wanted to spend it as fast as possible. I felt no particular pangs of conscience, not then, nor later. I should certainly not repeat it another time; you may believe that or not, as you like, I don't care. Well, sirs, that's all."

"Only, of course, that's not the worst deed you've committed," said Darya Alexeevna with aversion.

"That's a psychological incident, and not a deed," commented Afanasy Ivanovich.

"And the maid?" asked Nastasya Filippovna, not disguising her most horrified aversion.

"The maid was turned out the very next day, it stands to reason. It's a strict household."

"And you allowed it?"

"Now that's wonderful! Why, should I really have gone and told on myself?" giggled Ferdyshchenko, though he was partly astonished by the overly unpleasant general impression made by the story.

"How filthy that is!" exclaimed Nastasya Filippovna.

"Bah! You want to hear of a man's foulest deed and expect to shine in the process! The most foul deeds are always very filthy, we shall hear that in a minute from Ivan Petrovich; and aren't there all sorts that shine on the outside and want to seem virtuous because they have their own carriage. Aren't there all sorts who keep their own carriage . . . And by what means . . ."

In a word, Ferdyshchenko lost his patience entirely and suddenly flew into a rage, positively forgetting himself and overstepping all bounds; even his whole face became twisted. Strange as it seems, it was very possible that he expected his story to produce an entirely different result. These "blunders" of bad taste and "particular sort of boasting," as Totsky had put it, happened rather frequently with Ferdyshchenko, and were entirely in his character.

Nastasya Filippovna even shuddered with rage and looked intently at Ferdyshchenko; the latter immediately lost heart and fell silent, almost going cold with fright: he had gone too far.

"But shouldn't we put an end to it altogether?" Afanasy Ivanovich asked artfully.

"It's my turn, but I make use of my exemption and shall not speak," said Ptitsyn resolutely.

"You don't want to?"

"I can't, Nastasya Filippovna; and on the whole, I consider such a *petit-jeu* impossible."

"General, I believe it's your turn," said Nastasya Filippovna, addressing him. "If you refuse too, then it shall all come apart after you, and I shall be sorry, for I was counting on describing, in conclusion, a deed 'from my own life,' only I wanted to do it after you and Afanasy Ivanovich, for you must give me courage," she concluded, laughing.

"Oh, if you promise to as well," cried the general fervently, "then I am ready to recount my whole life to you; but, I confess, while waiting my turn, I have already prepared my story . . ."

"And from his excellency's air alone one may conclude with what particular literary pleasure he worked up his little anecdote,"

Ferdyshchenko—though still somewhat abashed—ventured to remark, smiling venomously.

Nastasya Filippovna gave the general a cursory glance and also smiled to herself. But it was evident that her glumness and irritability were growing more and more. Afanasy Ivanovich was doubly alarmed hearing of the promised story.

"I have had, ladies and gentlemen, like everyone, occasion to commit actions in my life that were not very pretty," began the general, "but strangest of all is that I myself regard the brief incident I am about to relate as the basest incident in my entire life. Almost thirty-five years have passed since then; yet in recollecting it, I have never been able to rid myself of a certain sensation grating at my heart, so to speak. The business, incidentally, was exceedingly foolish: I had just recently been made lieutenant and was toiling away in the army. Well, we all know what a lieutenant is—his blood's all aboil, but his housekeeping's not worth a farthing; I had an orderly in those days, Nikifor, who troubled himself an awful lot about my housekeeping, scrimped, mended, scrubbed and cleaned, and even stole right and left anything that wasn't nailed down, all just to augment the household; he was a most faithful and honest man. I was strict, of course, but just. We happened to be stationed for some time in a little town. I was given quarters in the suburbs, in the house of a retired sublieutenant's widow. The old lady was eighty years old, or near enough, at least. Her little house was dilapidated, rotten, made of wood, and she was so poor that she didn't even keep a servant. But the main thing that distinguished her was that she had at one time had a large family and numerous relations; but some had died in the course of time, some went away, and yet others forgot about the old woman; as for her husband, she had buried him four, five years before. Some years previously, a niece used to live with her, hunchbacked and mean as a witch, it was said; she had even bitten the old woman on the finger, but she had died too, so that the old lady had already been struggling on for some three years all by her lonesome. I was bored to distraction there, and she was so empty-headed you could get nothing out of her. In the end, she stole a rooster of mine. The business has remained murky to this day, but there was no one else to do it besides her. We quarreled over the rooster, quarreled seriously, and here it happened that, at my very first request, I was transferred to other quarters, to a suburb on the other side of town, in the house of a merchant with a large family and a big beard, as I remember him. Nikifor and I were delighted to move, and left the old lady with indignation. Three days go by, I come in from drill and Nikifor reports that 'it was a mistake, your honor, to leave our bowl at the old landlady's, for there's nothing to serve the soup in.' I was astounded, of course. 'How's that, how did our bowl come to be left behind at the landlady's?' Nikifor, surprised, goes on to report that the landlady, when we were leaving, did not give him back our bowl for the reason that since I had broken her own pot, she was keeping our bowl in place of her pot, and supposedly I had suggested this to her myself. Such meanness on her part naturally enraged me beyond all bounds; my blood boiled, I leapt up and flew off. I get to the old lady's entirely beside myself, so to speak; I look, there she is sitting in the entry hall, all by her lonesome, in the corner, just as if she were hiding from the sun, her cheek propped on her hand. Right away, you must know, I went and poured all my wrath over her. 'Why you,' I said, 'you so and so!' and so on, you know, in the regular Russian style. Only, I look, and there's something strange in the scene: she's sitting, her face trained at me, eyes bulging out, and not a word in reply, and she's looking out strangely, so strangely, and seems to be swaying. At last, I calmed down, peered in her face, questioned her, not a word in reply. I stand there indecisively; the flies are buzzing, the sun is setting, everything is still; completely disconcerted, I finally leave. I had not yet reached the house when I was summoned to the major's, then I had to go to the company, so that I didn't return home till it was quite evening. Nikifor's first words: 'Do you know, your honor, our landlady has died.'— 'When?'—'Why, this evening, some hour and a half ago.' So, that means at precisely the time I was abusing her, she was passing away. I was so struck by this, let me tell you, that I could barely collect myself. The thought of it even began to haunt me, I even dreamt of it at night. Of course, I am not superstitious, but on the third day, I went to the church for the funeral. In a word, the more time goes on, the more it comes to mind. Not exactly, but just from time to time, you picture it, and you feel unwell. And the main thing, as I finally decided, was what? In the first place, a woman, so to speak, a human creature, what they call in our time a humane creature, she lived, lived a long time, and finally outlived herself. At one time she had had children, a husband, family, relations, all of this, so to speak, seethed around her, all of these, so to speak, smiles, and suddenly—a complete blank, everything out the window, she was left alone, like . . . some kind of fly accursed from the beginning of time. And then, at last, God had brought her to the end. With the setting of the sun, on a still summer evening, my old woman flies away too—it's not without its moral idea, to be sure; and then, in this very moment, instead of a tear to see her off, so to speak, a young, reckless lieutenant, arms akimbo and swaggering, escorts her from the surface of the earth to the Russian tune of knavish swearing over a lost bowl! There is no doubt, I am at fault, and though, due to the distance in time and the change in my nature, I have long since looked upon my action as if it were another man's, nonetheless, I still continue to regret it. So that, I repeat, it seems positively strange to me, all the more so since, if I am at fault, then still not entirely: why should she have taken it into her head to die at that moment? Of course, there is only one excuse: that the act was in a certain sense psychological; all the same, I could not find peace until, some fifteen years ago, I began to maintain at my expense two chronically ill old ladies in the almshouse, so as to soften the last days of their earthly existence with a decent upkeep. I'm thinking of turning it into a perpetuity, bequeathing the capital. Well, there it is, ladies and gentlemen, that's all of it. I repeat that I may have been at fault in many things in my life, but this incident, upon my conscience, I consider the basest action of my entire life."

"And instead of the basest, your excellency has described one of the good deeds of your life; you've cheated Ferdyshchenko!" concluded Ferdyshchenko.

"Indeed, General, I never imagined that you had such a good heart after all; it's even a pity," Nastasya Filippovna said carelessly.

"A pity? Why, then?" asked the general with an obliging laugh and, not without some self-satisfaction, took a sip of champagne.

But it was Afanasy Ivanovich's turn, who had prepared himself too. Everyone anticipated that he would not refuse, like Ivan Petrovich, and for certain reasons awaited his story with particular curiosity; at the same time, they were stealing glances at Nastasya Filippovna. With an extraordinary air of dignity entirely in keeping with his stately appearance, Afanasy Ivanovich began in his quiet, polite voice to tell one of his "charming anecdotes." (By the way, he was a man of fine appearance, stately, tall, a little bald, a little gray, and rather stout, with soft, rosy, and somewhat sagging cheeks, and false teeth. He dressed in loose and elegant clothes, and wore exquisite linen. His plump, white hands were a sight to behold. On the index finger of his right hand was a costly diamond ring.) All the while he was telling his story, Nastasya Filippovna intently examined the lace frill of her sleeve and kept pinching it with two fingers of her left hand, so that she did not have a chance to look even once at the speaker.

"What makes my task easier most of all," began Afanasy Ivanovich, "is the absolute obligation of recounting nothing other than the very worst deed of my whole life. In that case, of course, there can be no hesitation: conscience and the heart's memory at once dictate just what must be told. I confess with bitterness that among all the innumerable, thoughtless and perhaps . . . frivolous actions of my life there is one the impression of which has lain almost too heavily on my mind. It happened nearly twenty years ago; I was staying then in the country with Platon Ordyntsev. He had just been elected marshal of nobility and come down with his young wife to spend the winter holidays. It was just around the time of Anfisa Alexeevna's birthday, and two balls had been arranged. At that time, that charming novel of Dumas *fils, La Dame aux camélias,* was in the height of fashion and was just making a great sensation in society—it is a poetic work that, in my opinion, is destined neither to die nor to go out of date. In the provinces, all the ladies were in ecstasies over it—those, at least, who had read it. The charm of the story, the originality of the principal character's situation, that tantalizing world analyzed in every subtlety and, finally, all those fascinating particulars scattered throughout the book (for instance, the circumstances of the use of the nosegays of white and pink camellias alternately), in a word, all these charming details, and all of it together, had nearly created shock waves. Camellias became extraordinarily fashionable. Everyone demanded them, everyone was trying to get them. I ask you: is it possible to get many camellias in a country district when everyone is asking for them for the balls, even when there aren't many balls? Petya Vorkhovsky was pining away at the time, poor fellow, for Anfisa Alexeevna. Although I honestly don't know whether there was anything between them, that is, I mean to say, whether he could have had some serious hope. The poor fellow was going out of his mind to get camellias for Anfisa Alexeevna by the night of the ball. The Countess Sotsky, from Petersburg, a guest of the governor's wife, and Sofia Bezpalov, as it became known, would certainly come with nosegays, white ones. Anfisa Alexeevna longed, for the sake of a certain special effect, to have red ones. Poor Platon was almost run into the ground; the usual story—he's the husband; he promises that he'll obtain the flowers, and—what happens? On the very eve of the ball they were snapped up by Katerina Alexandrovna Mytishchev, a terrible rival of Anfisa Alexeevna in everything; they were at daggers. Naturally, there are hysterics and fainting fits. It was all over with Platon. Clearly, if Petya had been able to contrive a bouquet somehow at that interesting moment, his business might have been furthered quite a bit; a woman's gratitude in such cases is boundless. He flew about like a madman; but the business was impossible, and no use even talking about it. Suddenly, I run into him at eleven o'clock at night, on the eve of the birthday and the ball, at Marya Petrovna Zubkov's, a neighbor of Ordyntsev's. He's beaming. 'What's the matter with you?'—'I've found them! Eureka!'—'Well, friend, you do surprise me! Where? How?'—'In Yekshaisk (that's a little town there, only twenty versts away, and not in our district), there's a merchant there, Trepalov, wears a long beard and has a lot of money, lives with his old lady, and instead of children they've got nothing but canaries. They've both got a passion for flowers, and he has camellias.'—'Mercy, but it's not true, well, and what if he doesn't give them to you?'—'I'll get on my knees and will grovel at his feet till he does, and I shan't go away without them!'—'When are you going, then?'—'Tomorrow as soon as it's light, at five o'clock.'—'Well, God be with you!' And, you know, I was so happy for him; I go back to Ordyntsev's; finally, it's past one o'clock and I still can't get it out of my mind, you know. I was about to go to bed when, suddenly—the most original thought! I make my way immediately to the kitchen, wake Savely, the coachman, give him fifteen rubles, 'Have the horses ready in half an hour!' In half an hour, naturally, the sledge was at the gate; Anfisa Alexeevna, I was told, had a migraine, was feverish and in delirium—I get in and drive off. A little after four, I'm at Yekshaisk, at the inn; I waited till daybreak, but only till daybreak: after six o'clock, I was at Trepalov's. I said this and that, and 'Have you got camellias? My good kind sir, I ask you like my own father, help me, save me, I'll bow down at your feet!' The old man, I see, is tall, gray-haired, severe—a terrifying old man. 'No, no, on no account! I won't consent!' I plumped down at his feet! I actually prostrated myself! 'What is it, my good sir, what is it, dear fellow?' He was even alarmed. 'Why, a human life is at stake!' I shout at him. 'Well, take them, if that's so, in God's name.' Well, did I cut the red camellias then! They were a wonder, exquisite, he had a whole little greenhouse. The old man sighed. I pull out a hundred rubles. 'No, dear sir, don't you go and insult me in that way.' 'Well, in that case,' I say, 'honorable sir, donate these hundred rubles to the local hospital for the betterment of the upkeep and the food.' 'Well, that, my good man,' he says, 'is a different matter, good, and noble, and charitable; I'll present it in the name of your good health.' And you know, I liked that Russian old man, a real Russian, so to speak, to the backbone, *de la vraie souche*.[45] Delighted at my success, I set off on the home journey at once; I went back a roundabout way to avoid meeting Petya. As soon as I arrived, I sent the bouquet to Anfisa Alexeevna, to greet her as she waked. You can imagine the delight, the gratitude, the tears of gratitude! Platon, beaten and lifeless just the day before, that Platon is sobbing at my breast. Alas! All husbands are this way since the creation of . . . lawful matrimony! I dare not add any more, only that for poor Petya, the business collapsed definitively with that episode. At first, I thought that he would murder me when he found out, and even made ready to meet him, but what happened was something that even I wouldn't have believed: a fainting fit, delirium by evening, brain fever by morning; he's sobbing like a baby, in convulsions. A month later, as soon as he was well again, he volunteered for the Caucasus; it turned out quite the romantic novel! He ended by being killed in the Crimea. At that time, his brother, Stepan Vorkhovsky, was in command of a regiment and earned distinction. I admit, I suffered for many years afterward from pangs of conscience: why, with what object, had I dealt him such a blow? And well and good if I'd been in love myself at the time. But it was simple mischief, for the sake of simple flirtation, nothing more. Had I not snatched that bouquet from him, who knows, the man might have been alive to this day, might be happy, successful, and it would not have even entered his head to go fight the Turks."

Afanasy Ivanovich fell silent with the same stately dignity with

---

45. Fr., of genuine stock (i.e., the real McCoy).

which he had begun his story. The company noticed that Nastasya Filippovna's eyes flashed somewhat strangely and even her lips quivered when he finished. Everyone kept glancing at both of them with curiosity.

"They've cheated Ferdyshchenko! How they have cheated him! No, really, how they've cheated him!" exclaimed Ferdyshchenko in a tearful tone, realizing that he could and must put in a little word.

"And who told you to misunderstand the business? Well, now take a lesson from the clever people!" Darya Alexeevna (an old and faithful friend and ally of Totsky) quipped at him, almost triumphantly.

"You are right, Afanasy Ivanovich, the *petit-jeu* is most tiresome, and we must end it quickly," Nastasya Filippovna negligently pronounced. "I'll tell you myself what I promised, and let us all have a game of cards."

"But the promised anecdote first of all," fervently assented the general.

"Prince," Nastasya Filippovna suddenly addressed him sharply and unexpectedly, "my old friends here, the general and Afanasy Ivanovich, keep wanting to marry me off. Tell me, what do you think: shall I get married or not? I will do as you tell me."

Afanasy Ivanovich turned pale; the general froze; everyone stared and craned their necks. Ganya stood rooted to the spot.

"To . . . to whom?" asked the prince in a halting voice.

"To Gavrila Ardalionovich Ivolgin," continued Nastasya Filippovna sharply, firmly, and distinctly, as before.

Several seconds of silence went by; the prince seemed to make an effort but could not get the words out, as if a terrible weight was pressing on his chest.

"N-no . . . don't marry him," he whispered at last, and drew a breath with effort.

"So it shall be, then! Gavrila Ardalionovich!" She turned to him sovereignly and ceremoniously, as it were. "Have you heard how the prince decided? Well, that is my answer; and let it be the end of this matter once and for all!"

"Nastasya Filippovna!" muttered Afanasy Ivanovich in a trembling voice.

"Nastasya Filippovna!" pronounced the general in a persuasive but agitated voice.

There was a general stir and commotion.

"What's the matter, friends?" she went on, scrutinizing the guests as if in surprise, "what have you gotten so unnerved about? And what faces you all have!"

"But . . . recollect, Nastasya Filippovna," mumbled Totsky, faltering, "you made a promise . . . quite voluntarily, and might have partly spared . . . I'm at pains and . . . of course, disconcerted, but . . . In a word, now, at such a moment, and before . . . before people, and it's all . . . to end by such a *petit-jeu* a serious matter, a matter of honor and of the heart . . . on which depends . . ."

"I don't understand you, Afanasy Ivanovich; you really are becoming entirely muddled. In the first place, what do you mean 'before people'? Are we not in the lovely company of intimate friends? And why *petit-jeu*? I really did want to tell my anecdote, and, well, there you have it, I've told it; isn't it good? And why do you say that it's not serious? Isn't this serious? You heard that I said to the prince, 'I will do as you tell me'; had he said yes, I would have given my consent at once, but he said no, and I refused. My whole life was hanging by a hair; what could be more serious?"

"But the prince, what's the prince to do with it? And what is the prince, after all?" muttered the general, almost unable to restrain his indignation at the prince's having such authority, which was even offensive.

"Why, the prince, for me, is this: he is the first man in my entire life in whom I have believed as a sincerely faithful friend. He believed in me at first sight, and I believe in him."

"I have only to thank Nastasya Filippovna for the extraordinary delicacy with which she . . . has treated me," at last articulated Ganya, pale and with a quivering voice and twitching lips. "It was, of course, the way it should be . . . But . . . the prince . . . In this matter, the prince . . ."

"Is reaching for the seventy-five thousand, do you mean?" Nastasya Filippovna suddenly broke him off. "That's what you wanted to say? Don't clam up, you certainly meant to say that! Afanasy Ivanovich, I had forgotten to add: take that seventy-five thousand for yourself and you should know that I set you free for nothing. It's enough! You must catch your breath, too! Nine years and three months! Tomorrow—a new leaf; but today—I'm the birthday girl and I'll be all for myself, for the first time in my whole life! General, you too, take back your pearls, give them to your wife, here they are; and tomorrow, I shall move out of this apartment for good. And there will be no more parties, ladies and gentlemen!"

Having said this, she suddenly rose, as if intending to leave.

"Nastasya Filippovna! Nastasya Filippovna!" was heard on all sides. Everyone became agitated, everyone rose from their seats; everyone surrounded her, everyone listened with unease to these impetuous, feverish, frantic words; everyone felt some kind of disturbance, no one could get to the bottom of it, no one could make out a thing. At that moment, there was suddenly a loud, violent ringing of the bell, exactly as there had been lately at Ganechka's apartment.

"A-ha! And here's the denouement! At last! Half past eleven!" cried Nastasya Filippovna. "I beg you to be seated, ladies and gentlemen, here's the denouement!"

Having said this, she sat down herself. A strange laugh quivered on her lips. She sat silently, in feverish expectation, and looked at the door.

"Rogozhin and his hundred thousand, not a doubt of it!" muttered Ptitsyn to himself.

X V

Katya, the maid, came in much alarmed.

"Goodness knows what's going on out there, Nastasya Filippovna, some ten people have piled in, and all drunk, ma'am, asking to be shown in here; they say it's Rogozhin and that you know."

"That's true, Katya, let them all in at once."

"You don't mean . . . all of them, Nastasya Filippovna, ma'am? Why, they're utterly disgraceful. It's ghastly!"

"All of them, all of them, Katya, let them all in, don't be afraid, every last one of them, or they'll come in without you. What an uproar they're making, just like before. Ladies and gentlemen, you are perhaps offended"—she turned to the guests—"at my receiving such company in your presence? I deeply regret it and beg your pardon, but it's necessary, and I would really, really like for all of you to consent to be my witnesses at this denouement, although, of course, you must please yourselves . . ."

The guests continued being astonished, whispering and exchanging looks, but it became perfectly clear that all this had been calculated and arranged beforehand, and that Nastasya Filippovna—though she had certainly gone out of her senses—could not be put off her course now. Everyone was horribly tormented by curiosity. Besides, there was no one there to be particularly alarmed. There were only two ladies: Darya Alexeevna, a sprightly lady who had seen all sorts of sights and who was not easily disconcerted, and the lovely but silent stranger. But the silent stranger could hardly have understood anything: she was a German visitor and knew not a word of Russian; besides, it seemed, she was as stupid as she was lovely. She was a novelty, and it had become a fashion to invite her to certain parties, sumptuously attired, with her hair done up as though for a show, and to seat her in the drawing room like a charming picture to adorn the evening, just as people sometimes borrow from their friends for a special occasion a painting, a vase, a statue, or a screen. As for the men, Ptitsyn, for instance, was a friend of Rogozhin's; Ferdyshchenko was in his element, like a fish in water; Ganechka still could not recover himself, yet he felt—however vaguely, but irresistibly—a feverish need to stick it out by his whipping post to the end; the old teacher, who had only a dim notion of what was the matter, was close to tears and literally trembled with fear, noticing some kind of exceptional agitation around him and in Nastasya Filippovna, whom he adored like his own grandchild; but he would sooner have died than have deserted her at such a moment. As for Afanasy Ivanovich, he could not, of course, compromise himself in such adventures; but he was too much interested in the matter, though it was taking such a crazy turn; moreover, Nastasya Filippovna had dropped for his benefit two or three words of such a kind that it was absolutely impossible to leave without resolving the matter for good. He determined to sit it out to the end and to keep perfectly silent and remain just an observer, as was, indeed, demanded by his dignity. Only General Epanchin, who had just before been offended by such an unceremonious and ridiculous return of his gift, might, of course, feel still more offended by all these strange eccentricities or, for instance, by the entrance of Rogozhin; and a man such as himself had, even without all that, already demeaned himself too far by resolving to sit down beside Ptitsyn and Ferdyshchenko; however, what the strength of passion was capable of doing could, at last, be conquered by the sense of obligation, the feeling for duty, rank, and importance, and self-respect in general, so that Rogozhin and company were, in the presence of his excellency, in any case, inadmissible.

"Ah, General," Nastasya Filippovna interrupted him at once, as soon as he had turned to her with his protest, "I had forgotten! But be assured that I had foreseen it about you. If it's such an offense to you, I won't insist on keeping you, though I would have very much wanted to see you, particularly, beside me at this moment. In any case, I thank you very much for your acquaintance and your flattering attention, but if you fear..."

"Allow me, Nastasya Filippovna," exclaimed the general in a fit of chivalrous generosity, "to whom are you saying this? Why, I will remain at your side now out of sheer devotion, and if, for instance, there is any danger... Besides, I must confess, I am extremely curious. I only meant to say that they will spoil the carpets and, perhaps, break something... And it's best not to have them at all, in my view, Nastasya Filippovna!"

"Rogozhin himself!" proclaimed Ferdyshchenko.

"What do you think, Afanasy Ivanovich," the general managed to whisper to him hastily, "hasn't she gone out of her mind? That is, not allegorically, but in the real medical manner, eh?"

"I've told you that she's always been disposed that way," Afanasy Ivanovich whispered back slyly.

"And a fever on top of that..."

Rogozhin's company consisted of almost the same configuration as that morning; there was only the addition of some dissipated old man, in his time a former editor of some kind of disreputable, libelous little paper, of whom the story went that for drink he had once pawned his false gold teeth; and one retired sublieutenant, decidedly a rival and competitor, by trade and calling, of this morning's gentleman with the fists; he was utterly unknown to all Rogozhin's party, and had been picked up in the street, on the sunny side of Nevsky Prospect, where he had been stopping the passersby and begging for alms in the diction of Marlinsky,[46] on the guileful pretext that he himself "had given mendicants as much as fifteen rubles in his own time." Both rivals at once

---

46. The pseudonym of a novelist and Decembrist (i.e., participant in the December Revolution of 1825) whose Romantic prose was extremely popular in the 1820s and '30s, especially among military men.

took up a hostile attitude to one another. After the admittance of the "mendicant" into the company, the gentleman with the fists considered himself affronted and, being silent by nature, he merely growled at times like a bear and looked with profound contempt on the approaches and playful overtures made to him by the "mendicant," who turned out to be a worldly and diplomatic man. Judging by appearances, the sublieutenant promised to get his own in "the business" more by dexterity and agility than strength, and he was shorter than the fisted gentleman, too. Tactfully, without entering into an open argument, but boasting terribly, he had already hinted several times at the superiority of English boxing; in a word, he turned out to be a thoroughgoing champion of the West. At the word "box," the fisted gentleman only smiled contemptuously and huffily, and, in his turn, not deigning to contradict his rival openly, he would from time to time, silently, as if unintentionally, show or, better said, thrust into view one utterly national matter—a huge fist, sinewy, gnarled, covered with a sort of reddish fuzz; and it became perfectly clear to everyone that if this deeply national matter were accurately brought to bear on any object, it would reduce it to a pulp.

Again, as before, none of them were absolutely "smashed," thanks to the efforts of Rogozhin himself, who had kept his visit to Nastasya Filippovna in mind all day long. He himself had managed to sober up almost completely, but was almost stupefied from all the impressions he had endured on this outrageous day, unlike anything in his whole entire life. One thing only had remained constantly in his mind and his heart at every minute, every instant. For the sake of that *one thing* he had spent the whole time between five o'clock in the afternoon right through to eleven in continual misery and anxiety, occupied with the Kinders and the Biskups, who had also nearly gone out of their minds rushing about like mad on his errands. But, after all, the hundred thousand in ready cash, about which Nastasya Filippovna had dropped a mocking and utterly vague hint in passing, had managed to materialize, at a rate of interest that even Biskup himself did not discuss with Kinder out loud, but only in a whisper, out of shame.

As before, Rogozhin stepped out before everyone, the rest moved forward behind him, somewhat timidly, though fully conscious of their advantages. Mainly, and God knows why, they were timid of Nastasya Filippovna. Some of them even thought they would all be promptly "kicked downstairs"; among those who thought this, incidentally, was the dandy and lady-killer Zalyozhev. But others, and chiefly the fisted gentleman, felt in their hearts, though it was unspoken, the deepest contempt and even hatred for Nastasya Filippovna, and had come to her as to a siege. But the magnificent decoration of the first two rooms, the objects that they had never seen or heard of before, the choice furnishings, the paintings, the huge statue of Venus—all of this made on them an irresistible impression of respect and almost of fear. This did not, of course, prevent them all, despite their fear, from crowding in, little by little and with insolent curiosity, into the drawing room after Rogozhin; but when the fisted gentleman, the "mendicant" and some of the others noticed General Epanchin among the guests, they were in the first moment so crestfallen that they even began to retreat a bit, back into the other room. Only Lebedev was among the more heartened and resolute, and stepped forward almost beside Rogozhin, having grasped the true significance of a million and four hundred thousand clear capital, and one hundred thousand right here and now, in the hand. It must be noted, however, that all of them, not even excluding the knowing Lebedev, were somewhat muddled with respect to ascertaining the precise bounds and limits of their powers and whether everything, indeed, was now allowed to them or not. Lebedev was ready to swear at certain moments that everything was, but at other moments, he felt an uneasy need to remind himself, just in case, of certain preeminently heartening and reassuring articles of the legal code.

As for Rogozhin himself, the impression Nastasya Filippovna's drawing room made on him was the reverse of that made on all his companions. As soon as the curtain over the door was raised and he saw Nastasya Filippovna—everything else ceased to exist for him, as it had that morning, and even more powerfully than it had that morning. He turned pale, and for an instant stopped short; one could surmise that his heart was beating violently. Timid and flustered, he gazed for some seconds at Nastasya Filippovna, not taking his eyes off her. Suddenly, as though he had lost all his reason and nearly staggering, he approached the table; on the way, he stumbled against Ptitsyn's chair and trod with his great big dirty boots on the lace trimming of the silent German beauty's magnificent light blue dress; he neither apologized nor noticed. Coming to the table, he laid upon it a strange object with which he had come into the drawing room, holding it before him with both hands. It was a thick packet of paper, some six inches high and eight long, firmly and thickly wrapped in a copy of the *Financial News*, and tied extra tight on all sides and twice across with string, like the kind used to tie up blocks of sugar. Then he stood still, not saying a word and letting his hands hang down, as if awaiting his sentence. He was dressed exactly as before, except for a new silk scarf around his neck, bright green and red, with a huge diamond pin in the form of a beetle, and a massive diamond ring on a dirty finger of his right hand. Lebedev stopped short three paces from the table; the rest, as was said, were gradually gathering in the drawing room. Katya and Pasha, Nastasya Filippovna's maids, had run up also, to look in from behind the partly lifted curtains with great amazement and alarm.

"What is this?" asked Nastasya Filippovna, scanning Rogozhin intently and with curiosity, and indicating the "object" with her eyes.

"One hundred thousand!" answered the other almost in a whisper.

"Ah, so he's kept his word! What a man! Sit down, please, here, on this chair; I shall have something to say to you later. Who is with you? All your previous company? Well, let them come in and sit down; there, they can sit on that sofa, and here's another sofa. Here are two armchairs . . . What is it, don't they want to?"

Indeed, certain of them had become positively disconcerted, beat a hasty retreat and settled down to wait in the other room, but others remained and took their seats as they were invited to, only as far as possible from the table, mostly in the corners—some of them still wishing to efface themselves, and others taking heart increasingly, and somehow with unnatural rapidity, as time went on. Rogozhin also sat down on the chair he had been shown, but he didn't sit down for long; he soon stood up and did not sit down again. Little by little, he began to distinguish and scrutinize the visitors. Seeing Ganya, he smiled malignantly and whispered to himself: "Well, see here!" He glanced at the general and at Afanasy Ivanovich without embarrassment and even without any particular curiosity. But when he noticed the prince beside Nastasya Filippovna, he could not tear his eyes away from him for a long time in extreme amazement, as if at a loss to explain this encounter. It may well have been that he was at moments in a state of actual delirium. Aside from all the upheavals of that day, he had spent all the previous night in the train and had not slept for almost forty-eight hours.

"This, ladies and gentlemen, is one hundred thousand rubles," said Nastasya Filippovna, turning to everyone with a kind of feverishly impatient defiance, "here, in this dirty packet. Earlier today, he shouted like a madman that he would bring me a hundred thousand this evening, and I've been waiting for him all the time. He was bidding for me: he began at eighteen, then he suddenly jumped to forty, and then to this hundred here. He's kept his word after all! Phoo, how pale he is! . . . It all happened at Ganechka's earlier: I went to pay a visit to his mother, to my future family, and there his sister shouted to my face: 'Won't anyone turn this shameless creature out!' And as for Ganechka, her brother, she spat in his face. She's got character, that girl!"

"Nastasya Filippovna!" the general pronounced reproachfully. He was beginning to understand the business somewhat, in his own way.

"What's the matter, General? Is it unseemly? Come, let's drop the farce! What if I used to sit in a box at the French Theater like an inaccessible paragon of virtue, and ran like a wild thing from everyone who's been pursuing me for five years, and looked upon them like proud innocence itself; why, that was all a folly that overtook me! There, before your very eyes, he's come and put a hundred thousand on the table, after five years of innocence, and no doubt they've got troikas outside waiting for me. He's priced me at a hundred thousand! Ganechka, I see you are still angry with me? Why, could you really have meant to bring me into your family? Me, Rogozhin's woman! What was it the prince said lately?"

"I didn't say that you were Rogozhin's, you're not Rogozhin's!" the prince brought out in a shaking voice.

"Nastasya Filippovna, that's enough, dear girl, that's enough, love," Darya Alexeevna said suddenly, unable to restrain herself. "If they make you so miserable, then why pay them any mind! And can you really mean to go off with such a one, though it be for a hundred thousand! Truly, a hundred thousand—it's nothing to sneeze at! But you take the hundred thousand, do, and send him packing, that's the way to deal with them; ech! if I were you I'd take them all and . . . What's in it, after all!"

Darya Alexeevna became positively irate. She was a very good-natured and impressionable woman.

"Don't be angry, Darya Alexeevna," Nastasya Filippovna chuckled to her, "why, I didn't say it to him in anger, you know. I didn't reproach him, did I? I simply can't understand how this folly possessed me to want to enter an honorable family. I've seen his mother; I kissed her hand. And as for my jeering at your house today, Ganechka, that was on purpose, to see for myself for the last time how far you could go. But you surprised me, truly. I expected a good deal, but not that! Why, could you really have taken me, knowing that he was giving me such pearls, practically on the eve of your wedding, and I was accepting them? And what about Rogozhin? Why, he was bargaining for me in your own home, before your mother and sister, and all the same, after that, you've come here to make the match and nearly brought your sister! Can Rogozhin really have been right when he said that you'd crawl on all fours to Vassilevsky Island for three rubles?"

"He would," Rogozhin suddenly uttered quietly, but with an air of profound conviction.

"And if you had been dying of hunger, fine, but then you get a good salary, they say! And on top of all that, besides the disgrace, to bring a hateful wife into your house! (For you do hate me, I know that!) No, now I believe that such a man could murder for money! Why, they're all seized with such greed nowadays, so torn apart for money, that they seem to have gone mad. Still a child, and already striving to be a moneylender! Or he'll wind some silk around a razor, fasten it, come up quiet from behind and slaughter his friend like a sheep, as I read recently.[47] Well, you are a shameless fellow! I'm shameless, and you're even worse. I won't even say anything about that other bouqueteer ..."

"Is this you, is this you, Nastasya Filippovna!" the general flung up his hands in genuine distress. "You, so tactful, with such refined ideas, and now! Such language! What expressions!"

"I am tipsy now, General." Nastasya Filippovna laughed suddenly. "I want to have my fling! This is my day, my holiday, my red-letter day, I've been waiting for it a long time. Darya Alexeevna, do you see this bouqueteer, this *monsieur aux camélias*?[48] There he sits laughing at us ..."

47. This is a reference to a murder that took place in Moscow in 1867: the merchant Mazurin killed a jeweler using a razor that he had wrapped with some cord to keep it from wobbling. Like Rogozhin, Mazurin came from a well-known merchant family, had inherited a large fortune and a Hereditary Honorable Citizen title from his father, and lived in the ancestral house with his mother.

48. Fr., gentleman of the camellias (a play on the title of the Dumas novel).

"I am not laughing, Nastasya Filippovna, I am only listening with the greatest attention," parried Totsky with dignity.

"Well, and why did I torment him for five whole years and not let him go? Was he worth it? He is simply what he ought to be . . . And he'll likely think I've done him wrong, too: why, he's given me an education, kept me like a countess, and the money, how much money's been spent, and he'd already picked out an honest husband for me back in the country, and Ganechka here; and would you believe it: I didn't live with him these five years, but I took his money, and thought that I was in the right! Why, I've muddled myself up completely! You say, take the hundred thousand and send him packing if it's revolting. And it's true, that it's revolting . . . I might have been married long ago, and not to Ganechka either, but, you see, it would have been quite loathsome too. And for what have I wasted five of my years in this bitterness! Believe it or not, four years ago I thought for a time: shouldn't I go and marry my Afanasy Ivanovich outright? I thought it out of spite back then; goodness knows what was going through my head back then; but you know, truly, I would have made him! He pressed it on me himself, believe it or not. Of course, he was lying, but he falls easily to temptation, he can't restrain himself. But afterward, thank God, I thought: is he worth such bitterness? And I suddenly became so revolted by him then that, if he had besought me himself, I would not have accepted him. And all these five years I've been keeping up this farce! No, it's better to go out on the street, where I belong! Either have a spree with Rogozhin, or go be a washing-woman tomorrow! For I'm wearing not a stitch of my own; I'll go away—and leave him everything, I shall leave every last rag, and who'll take me with nothing? Ask Ganya there if he'll have me. Why, even Ferdyshchenko wouldn't take me! . . ."

"Perhaps Ferdyshchenko wouldn't take you, Nastasya Filippovna, I'm a candid man," interrupted Ferdyshchenko, "but the prince would! You sit there lamenting, but you take a look at the prince! I've been watching him a long time . . ."

Nastasya Filippovna turned with curiosity to the prince.

"Is that true?" she asked.

"It's true," whispered the prince.

"Will you take me as I am, with nothing?"

"I will, Nastasya Filippovna . . ."

"Well, here's a new development!" muttered the general. "I might have expected it."

The prince looked with a mournful, stern and penetrating gaze into the face of Nastasya Filippovna, who continued to scan him.

"Here's another one!" she suddenly said, addressing Darya Alex-eevna again. "But, you see, it's straight out of the goodness of his heart, I know him. I've found a benefactor! However, perhaps it's true what they say about him, that he's ... *not quite*. What are you going to live on, then, if you're so in love that you'll take Rogozhin's woman for a wife—you, a prince? ..."

"I take you as an honest woman, Nastasya Filippovna, and not Ro-gozhin's," said the prince.

"Me? I'm an honest woman?"

"You."

"Well, all that's straight ... out of a novel! Those are old-fashioned fancies, Prince, my pet; nowadays the world has grown wiser, and it's all nonsense! And how'd you reckon getting married, when you still need a nursemaid to look after you, yourself!"

The prince got up and in a shaking, timid voice, but with the air of a deeply convinced man, pronounced:

"I don't know a thing, Nastasya Filippovna, I haven't seen a thing, you're right, but I ... I will consider that you will be doing me an honor, and not I. I am nothing, and you have suffered and have come pure out of such hell, and that is a great deal. Why then are you ashamed, and want to go off with Rogozhin? That's the fever ... You've given Mr. Totsky back seventy thousand and say that you will give up everything that is here, everything, no one here would do that. I ... Nastasya Filippovna ... I love you. I would die for you, Nastasya Fil-ippovna. I won't allow anyone to say a word about you, Nastasya Filippovna ... If we shall be poor, I will work, Nastasya Filippovna ..."

At the last word, a snigger was heard from Ferdyshchenko and Lebedev, and even the general seemed to quack to himself with great displeasure. Ptitsyn and Totsky could not help smiling, but restrained themselves. The rest simply gaped with astonishment.

"... But perhaps we shan't be poor, but very rich, Nastasya Filip-povna," the prince went on in the same timid voice. "Although I don't know for certain, and it's a pity that I still have not been able to find anything out about it this whole day, but in Switzerland, I received a letter from Moscow from a certain Mr. Salazkin, and he informs me that it seems I may receive a very large inheritance. This here is the letter . . ."

The prince did in fact produce a letter from his pocket.

"Why, is he raving perhaps?" muttered the general. "This is a perfect madhouse!"

For an instant, some silence ensued.

"I believe you said, Prince, that the letter to you was from Salazkin?" asked Ptitsyn. "That is a man very well known in his own circle; he's a very distinguished solicitor, and if it is really he who apprises you of it, you may believe it entirely. Fortunately, I know his hand, for I had some business recently . . . If you would let me have a look, perhaps I might be able tell you something . . ."

Silently, with a shaking hand, the prince held out the letter to him.

"Why, what's this, what's this?" the general suddenly harkened, looking at everyone like a half-wit, "why, could it really be an inheritance?"

Everyone fixed their eyes on Ptitsyn, who was reading the letter. The general curiosity had received a new and exceedingly strong impetus. Ferdyshchenko could not keep still; Rogozhin looked on in bewilderment and with terrible agitation cast his gaze back and forth between the prince and Ptitsyn. Darya Alexeevna was on pins and needles in expectation. Even Lebedev could not bear it, came out of his corner and, bent over double, started peeping at the letter over Ptitsyn's shoulder with the air of a man fearing that he'll get a wallop for it directly.

XVI

"It's a genuine thing," Ptitsyn announced at last, folding up the letter and handing it to the prince. "By the uncontested testament of your aunt, you will receive, without any difficulties, an exceedingly large fortune."

"It can't be!" exclaimed the general, just like a pistol shot.

Everyone gaped again.

Ptitsyn explained, addressing himself chiefly to Ivan Fyodorovich, that five months previously, the prince had lost an aunt, whom he had never known personally, the elder sister of the prince's mother, daughter of a Moscow merchant of the third guild called Papushin, who had died in poverty and bankruptcy. But this Papushin's own elder brother, also recently deceased, was a well-known rich merchant. About a year before, he had lost, almost in the same month, both his two sons. This shocked him to such an extent that not long afterward the old man took ill himself and died. He was a widower, with not a single heir except for the prince's aunt, Papushin's own niece, a rather poor woman living in the house of strangers. At the time she came into the inheritance, this aunt was already almost dying of dropsy, but she had at once begun to search for the prince, entrusting the matter to Salazkin, and had had time to make her will. Apparently, neither the prince nor the doctor with whom he was living in Switzerland wanted to wait for official notification or make inquiries, and instead, the prince, with Salazkin's letter in his pocket, decided to set off himself . . .

"I can only tell you one thing," concluded Ptitsyn, turning to the prince, "that all this must be incontestable and true, and everything Salazkin writes to you about the incontestability and legality of your business you may consider as good as hard cash in your pocket. I congratulate you, Prince! Perhaps you will receive a million and a half as well, and possibly even more. Papushin was a very wealthy merchant."

"Bravo! Prince Myshkin, the last of the line!" squealed Ferdyshchenko.

"Hurrah!" croaked Lebedev in a drunken little voice.

"Why, and I lent him twenty-five rubles of late, the poor fellow, ha-ha-ha! It's phantasmagorical, that's just what it is!" pronounced the general, almost stupefied with amazement. "Well, congratulations, congratulations!" And, rising from his seat, he went up to the prince to embrace him. In his wake, the others also began to get up and also thrust themselves upon the prince. Even those who had retreated behind the curtain began to appear in the drawing room. A vague murmur began, there were exclamations, even demands for champagne were heard; everyone milled about and fussed. For an instant they almost forgot Nastasya Filippovna and that she was, after all, the hostess of her party. But gradually the idea occurred to almost everyone at once that the prince had just proposed to her. The affair, it seemed, was turning out to be three times more crazy and extraordinary than before. Totsky, deeply amazed, kept shrugging his shoulders; he was almost the only one sitting; the rest of the crowd, all in disorder, pressed around the table. Everyone asserted afterward that it was at this moment that Nastasya Filippovna went mad. She continued to sit and for some time scanned everyone with some kind of strange and wondering gaze, as though not comprehending and straining to think straight. Then she suddenly turned to the prince and, menacingly furrowing her brow, scrutinized him intently; but this was only for a moment; perhaps she suddenly fancied that this was all a joke, a mockery; but the prince's appearance immediately reassured her. She pondered, then smiled again, as if not clearly cognizant of the cause ...

"Then I really am a princess!" she whispered to herself, as if mockingly, and, glancing by chance at Darya Alexeevna, she laughed. "The denouement is an unexpected one ... I ... expected something different ... But why are you all standing, ladies and gentlemen, pray, do sit down, congratulate me and the prince! Someone, it seems, asked for champagne; Ferdyshchenko, go and order it. Katya, Pasha"—she suddenly caught sight of her maids in the doorway—"come here, I'm going to be married, did you hear? To the prince, he has a million and a half, he's Prince Myshkin and is marrying me!"

"And a good thing, too, my dear, it's high time! It's not a chance to miss!" cried Darya Alexeevna, tremendously moved by what had passed.

"Well, sit down beside me, then, Prince," Nastasya Filippovna went on. "Just so, and here they are bringing the wine, congratulate us, then, friends!"

"Hurrah!" shouted a multitude of voices. Many crowded around the wine; among them were almost all of Rogozhin's followers. But though they shouted and were prepared to shout, yet many of them, in spite of the strangeness of the circumstances and the surroundings, realized that a different stage was being set. Others were flustered and waited mistrustfully. And many whispered to one another that this was quite an ordinary affair, that princes marry all sorts of women, even girls out of gypsy camps. Rogozhin himself stood still and stared, having twisted his face into an immutable, perplexed smile.

"Prince, dear fellow, come to your senses!" the general whispered with horror, coming up from the side and pulling the prince by his sleeve.

Nastasya Filippovna noticed and burst out laughing.

"No, General! I am a princess myself now, did you hear?—the prince won't let me be insulted! Afanasy Ivanovich, you congratulate me; I can sit down beside your wife everywhere now; what do you think, is it advantageous having a husband like that? A million and a half, and a prince as well, and, they say, an idiot to boot, what could be better? Only now does real life begin! You're too late, Rogozhin! Take away your packet, I'm marrying the prince and am richer than you are myself!"

But Rogozhin had grasped the heart of the matter. Unspeakable suffering inscribed itself in his face. He flung up his hands and a groan broke from his breast.

"Give way!" he shouted to the prince.

There was laughter all around.

"For you, he should give way, then?" Darya Alexeevna chimed in triumphantly. "Just look, he's dumped his money on the table, the lout! Why, the prince is taking her in marriage, while you've shown up to make a disgrace of yourself!"

"And I take her! I take her at once, this very minute! I'll give everything . . ."

"Just look, a drunk from the tavern, you should be turned out!" Darya Alexeevna repeated indignantly.

The laughter was louder than before.

"Do you hear, Prince?" Nastasya Filippovna turned to him. "That's how a peasant is bargaining for your bride!"

"He is drunk," said the prince. "He loves you very much."

"And won't you feel ashamed later that your bride nearly went off with Rogozhin?"

"That was when you were in a fever, and you are in a fever now, almost delirious."

"And you won't be ashamed when they tell you afterward that your wife used to live with Totsky and was kept by him?"

"No, I shan't be ashamed . . . You were not with Totsky by your own will."

"And you will never reproach me with it?"

"I won't reproach you."

"Well, take heed, don't answer for your whole life!"

"Nastasya Filippovna," said the prince softly and as if with compassion, "I told you before that I would take your consent as an honor, and that you are doing me an honor, not I you. You smirked at those words, and all around, I heard, they were laughing too. I may have put it very absurdly, and was absurd myself, but it seemed to me all the time that I . . . understand where the honor lies, and I am certain I spoke the truth. You wanted to ruin yourself just now, irrevocably, for you'd never have forgiven yourself for it afterward: but you are not to blame for anything. It cannot be that your life is already altogether ruined. What does it matter that Rogozhin's come to you and Gavrila Arda-lionovich wanted to deceive you? Why do you bring it up incessantly? What you've done, very few are capable of, I tell you that again, and as for your meaning to go off with Rogozhin, you decided that in a fit of illness. And you are having a fit now, and you had much better go to bed. You would have gone off to be a washerwoman the very next day, you wouldn't have stayed with Rogozhin. You are proud, Nastasya Fil-ippovna, but perhaps you are unhappy to such an extent that you really do consider yourself to blame. You need a lot of looking after, Nastasya Filippovna. I will look after you. I saw your portrait before, and it was just as if I had recognized a face that I knew. It seemed to me at once as if you were already calling to me . . . I . . . I shall respect you all my life, Nastasya Filippovna," the prince suddenly concluded, seeming to suddenly recollect himself, flushing, and realizing in front of what sorts of people he was saying this.

Ptitsyn bent his head, as if chastened, and looked on the ground. Totsky thought to himself: "He's an idiot, but he knows that flattery is the best way to get at people; it's instinct!" The prince also noticed, in the corner, Ganya's glittering gaze, with which the latter seemed to want to reduce him to ashes.

"There's a kindhearted man!" pronounced Darya Alexeevna, much touched.

"An educated man, but doomed to ruin!" whispered the general in an undertone.

Totsky took his hat and made ready to slip away quietly. He and the general exchanged glances, meaning to leave together.

"Thank you, Prince, no one has ever talked to me like that before," said Nastasya Filippovna. "They were all striking bargains for me, but no man who was decent had ever courted for my hand before. Did you hear, Afanasy Ivanych? What did you think of all that the prince said? Why, it was almost improper . . . Rogozhin! Don't you go yet. But you're not going anyway, I see. Perhaps I shall come with you after all. Where did you mean to take me, then?"

"To Ekaterinhof,"[49] Lebedev reported from the corner, while Rogozhin only started and gazed wide-eyed, as though he could not believe his senses. He was completely stupefied, just as if he had had a violent blow on the head.

"But what are you saying, what are you saying, my dear! You're truly having fits; have you taken leave of your senses?" Darya Alexeevna reared up, alarmed.

"What, did you seriously think it?" Nastasya Filippovna jumped up from the sofa, roaring with laughter. "To ruin such a child? Why, that's just in Afanasy Ivanovich's line: he's fond of children! Come along, Rogozhin! Get your packet ready! Never mind about wanting to marry me, let me have the money all the same. Perhaps I shan't marry you after all. You thought, since you meant to marry me, that the packet would stay with you? Wrong! I'm a shameless hussy myself! I was Totsky's concubine . . . Prince! you need Aglaia Epanchin now, and not Nastasya Filippovna, and not—Ferdyshchenko here pointing fingers at you! You may not be afraid, but I shall be afraid that I have ruined you, and that you shall reproach me afterward. As for your proclaiming that I am doing you an honor, Totsky knows all about it. And as for Aglaia Epanchin, Ganechka, you've missed your chance with her; did you know that? If you hadn't haggled with her, she would have certainly married you! That's what you all are like: keep company with disreputable women or honest ones—make your choice! Or you are sure to get mixed up . . . Look how the general is staring, with his mouth open . . ."

"This is Sodom, Sodom!" repeated the general, tossing his shoulders. He too got up from the sofa. Everyone was on their feet again. Nastasya Filippovna seemed in a perfect frenzy.

"Is it possible?" moaned the prince, wringing his hands.

"And you thought not? I am proud myself, perhaps, though I am a shameless hussy. You called me perfection before; a fine sort of perfection that goes into the gutter, simply to boast of trampling on a million and a princedom! What sort of wife should I make you after that?

49. Ekaterinhof was a royal palace and park on the outskirts of Petersburg, situated on the banks of the Neva by Finland Sound. The Vauxhall there was a favorite destination for winter revelers on sleigh-rides out of town.

Afanasy Ivanovich, but I really have flung a million out the window, you know! How could you think I would be happy to marry Ganya and your seventy-five thousand? The seventy-five thousand you take for yourself, Afanasy Ivanych (and you didn't even get up to a hundred, Rogozhin topped you!); and as for Ganechka, I'll comfort him myself, I've had an idea. But now I want to go out on the town, for I'm a street wench, you know! I've spent ten years in prison, now my happiness has come! Well, what is it, Rogozhin? Get ready, we're going!"

"We're going!" roared Rogozhin, almost frantic with delight. "Hey, you . . . all around . . . wine! Ough!"

"Have the wine ready, I shall be drinking. And will there be music?"

"Yes, yes! Don't come near her!" squealed Rogozhin in a frenzy, seeing Darya Alexeevna approaching Nastasya Filippovna. "Mine! All mine! My queen! The end!"

He was gasping with joy; he kept walking around Nastasya Filippovna and shouting at everyone: "Don't come near her!" The whole company had by now pressed into the drawing room. Some were drinking, some were shouting and laughing, all of them were in the most excited spirits and completely at their ease. Ferdyshchenko began to try to insinuate himself into their company. The general and Totsky again made a move to quickly slip away. Ganya also had his hat in his hand, but he stood in silence and still seemed as if unable to tear himself away from the scene developing before him.

"Don't come near her!" Rogozhin was yelling.

"Well, what are you shouting for?" Nastasya Filippovna laughed at him. "I am still the mistress of my house; if I like, I can still kick you out. I haven't taken your money yet, there it lies still; give it here, the whole packet! This is the packet with the hundred thousand, then? Phooey, how revolting! What's the matter with you, Darya Alexeevna? Would you really have me ruin him?" (She pointed to the prince.) "How can he be married, he still wants a nanny himself; the general there will be his nanny—see how he is hanging upon him! Look, Prince, your bride has taken the money because she is a dissolute woman, and you wanted to marry her! Well, what are you crying for? Does it pain you? You ought to laugh, in my view," continued Nastasya Filippovna, who had two large tears glittering on her cheeks herself. "Trust to time—it will all pass! Better to think twice now than later . . . Well, what are you all crying for? Here's Katya crying too! What is it, Katya, dear? I'm leaving you and Pasha a great deal, I've settled it already; and now good-bye! I've made you, an honest girl, wait on me, a dissolute woman ... It's better so, Prince, it's truly better, you'd have despised me later on, and we should not have been happy! Don't swear, I don't believe it! And how stupid it would have been! ... No, better part as friends, for you know, I'm a dreamer myself, and no good would have come of it! Haven't I dreamed of you myself? You're right there, I dreamed of you long ago, even back on his country estate, the five years I lived all by my lonesome; you think and you think, there were times, and you dream and you dream—and I kept imagining someone like you, kind, honest, good, and also so foolish that he would come suddenly and say: 'You are not to blame, Nastasya Filippovna, and I adore you!' Well, you'd lose yourself in daydreams like that sometimes until you nearly went out of your mind ... And then this one would show up: he'd stay two months of the year, disgrace me, insult me, provoke me, corrupt me, and go away—I wanted to fling myself in the pond a thousand times, but I was too base and hadn't the heart; well, and now ... Rogozhin, are you ready?"

"Ready! Don't come near her!"

"Ready!" shouted several voices.

"The troikas are waiting, with bells!"

Nastasya Filippovna snatched the packet up in her hands.

"Ganjka, I've had a thought: I want to compensate you, for why should you lose everything? Rogozhin, would he crawl on all fours to Vassilevsky for three rubles?"

"He would."

"Well, then listen, Ganya, I want to see into your soul for the last time; you tortured me yourself for three whole months; now it's my turn. You see this packet, there's a hundred thousand in it! I'm going to throw it in the fireplace right now, onto the fire, before everyone, all are witnesses! As soon as the fire has caught it all around—reach into the fireplace, only without gloves, with your bare hands, and turn up your sleeves, and pull the packet from the fire! If you pull it out—it's yours, the whole hundred thousand is yours! You'll only burn your fingers a bit—but it's a hundred thousand, just think! It won't take long to pull it out! And I shall get a good look at your soul, seeing how you climb into the fire after my money. Everyone's a witness that the packet will be yours! And if you don't go after it, then it will burn; I won't let anyone near it. Get away! Everyone, get away! It's my money! I took it for a night with Rogozhin. Is it my money, Rogozhin?"

"Yours, my joy! Yours, my queen!"

"Well, then, everyone, get away, I'll do what I like! Don't interfere! Ferdyshchenko, make up the fire."

"Nastasya Filippovna, I can't raise my hands to it!" answered Ferdyshchenko, dumbfounded.

"E-ech!" cried Nastasya Filippovna, snatched up the tongs, dug out two smoldering chunks of wood, and as soon as the fire flared up, flung the packet into it.

There was an outcry all around; many even crossed themselves.

"She's gone out of her mind, out of her mind!" they shouted all around.

"Oughtn't we . . . oughtn't we . . . to tie her up?" whispered the general to Ptitsyn, "or send for the . . . Why, she's gone out of her mind, hasn't she? Hasn't she?"

"N-no, perhaps this is not quite madness," whispered Ptitsyn, white as a handkerchief and trembling, unable to take his eyes off the smoldering packet.

"Is she mad? She's mad, isn't she?" the general persisted to Totsky.

"I have told you that she's a *colorful* woman," muttered Afanasy Ivanovich, who had also gone somewhat pale.

"But, after all, it's a hundred thousand, you know! . . ."

"Oh Lord, oh Lord!" was heard on all sides. Everyone crowded around the fireplace, everyone pressed forward to see, everyone exclaimed. Some even jumped on chairs to look over each other's heads. Darya Alexeevna whisked away into the other room and, in alarm, whispered about something with Katya and Pasha. The beautiful German had fled.

"Dear lady! Our queen! Almighty!" wailed Lebedev, crawling on his knees in front of Nastasya Filippovna, stretching out his hands to the fire. "A hundred thousand! A hundred thousand! I saw them myself, they were packed up before me! Dear lady! Merciful! Order me into the fire: I'll go in entire, I'll put my whole gray head in! . . . My sick wife, bedridden, thirteen children—all orphans, I buried my father last week, he's had nothing to eat, Nastasya Filippovna!" And, having finished wailing, he started to crawl to the fire.

"Get away!" cried Nastasya Filippovna, shoving him away. "Stand back, all of you! Ganya, why are you standing still? Don't be ashamed! Reach for it! Your happiness!"

But Ganya had already endured too much on that day and that evening, and was not ready for this last unexpected ordeal. The crowd parted before him into two halves, and he was left face to face with Nastasya Filippovna, within three steps of her. She was standing right by the fireplace and waiting, with her fiery, searching gaze fixed upon him. Ganya, in his evening dress, with his hat in his hands, and his gloves, stood before her silently and meekly, with his arms folded, and looked at the fire. A mad smile strayed over his face, which was white as a handkerchief. It's true, he could not take his eyes off the fire, off the smoldering packet; but something new seemed to have risen up in his soul, as if he had vowed to endure the ordeal; he did not move from the spot; after a few moments, it became clear to everyone that he was not going to go after the packet, that he didn't want to go.

"Hey, they'll burn, and it'll be shame upon your own head," Nastasya Filippovna shouted to him, "you'll hang yourself afterward, you know, I'm not joking!"

The fire, which had in the beginning flamed up between two smoldering brands, at first nearly died out when the packet had fallen on it and smothered it. But a little blue flame continued to cling underneath to one corner of the lower brand. At last, a long, thin, blue tongue of flame licked the bundle too, the fire caught and ran up the paper, around the edges, and suddenly the whole packet flared up in the fireplace, and a bright flame shot up. Everyone drew a deep breath.

"Dear lady!" Lebedev was still wailing, rushing forward again, but Rogozhin dragged him off and pushed him away once more.

Rogozhin himself turned into nothing but a fixed stare. He could not tear himself away from Nastasya Filippovna, he was drunk with delight, he was in seventh heaven.

"That's the way, queen!" he repeated every minute, addressing himself to anyone who happened to be around him. "That's the style!" he kept crying, beside himself. "Well, and which of you pickpockets would do a thing like that, eh?"

The prince looked on mournfully and silently.

"I'd pull it out with my teeth for a mere thousand!" offered Ferdyshchenko.

"I could do it with teeth, too!" the fisted gentleman groaned in the rear in a fit of genuine despair. "D-damn it all! It's burning, it will all burn up!" he exclaimed, seeing the flame.

"It's burning, it's burning!" they all cried with one voice, almost everyone also making a dash for the fireplace.

"Ganya, quit your posturing, I'm saying it for the last time!"

"Reach for it!" roared Ferdyshchenko, rushing to Ganya in a positive frenzy and pulling him by the sleeve. "Reach for it, you conceited little jackanapes! It'll burn! Oh, ac-cc-ccursed!"

Ganya pushed Ferdyshchenko violently away, turned, and walked to the door; but before he had taken two steps, he staggered and fell in a heap on the floor.

"A fainting spell!" they cried all around.

"Dear lady, it'll burn up!" wailed Lebedev.

"It'll burn for nothing!" they roared from all sides.

"Katya, Pasha, bring him water, spirits!" yelled Nastasya Filippovna, grabbing the tongs and snatching out the packet.

Almost all the outer wrapping had been burnt and was smoldering, but it could be seen at once that the inside was untouched. The packet was wrapped threefold in newspaper, and the notes were unhurt. Everyone breathed more freely.

"Only a poor little thousand spoiled perhaps, and the rest are all unhurt," Lebedev pronounced with tenderness.

"It's all his! The whole packet is his! Do you hear, gentlemen?" Nastasya Filippovna declared, laying the packet near Ganya. "And he didn't do it after all, he endured it! So, his vanity is even greater than his craving for money. It's nothing, he'll come to! But he might have murdered, perhaps . . . There, he is coming to himself. General, Ivan Petrovich, Darya Alexeevna, Katya, Pasha, Rogozhin, do you hear? The packet is his, Ganya's. I'm giving it over entirely into his possession, as compensation for . . . well, for whatever it may have been! Tell him. Let it lie there by him . . . Rogozhin, march! Farewell, Prince, it's the first time I've seen a man! Farewell, Afanasy Ivanovich, *merci!*"[50]

The whole Rogozhin band rushed with tumult, with thunder, with shouts through the rooms to the front door after Rogozhin and Nasta-

50. Fr., thank you.

sya Filippovna. In the hall, the maids gave her her fur coat; the cook, Marfa, ran in from the kitchen. Nastasya Filippovna kissed them all.

"But can it be, dear lady, that you are leaving us altogether? Why, where will you go? And on your birthday, too, such a day!" the weeping girls asked, kissing her hands.

"To the gutter, Katya, you heard that's where my place is, or else to be a washerwoman! I've done with Afanasy Ivanovich! Send him my regards, and don't think badly of me . . ."

The prince rushed headlong toward the street entrance, where everyone was taking their seats in four troikas with bells. The general managed to overtake him on the staircase.

"Pray, Prince, come to your senses!" he was saying, seizing his arm. "Give it up! You see what she is like! I speak as a father . . ."

The prince looked at him, but without uttering a word broke away and ran downstairs.

In front of the entrance, from which the troikas had just pulled away, the general saw the prince grabbing the first driver and shouting him on to Ekaterinhof, after the troikas. Then the general's gray trotter pulled up and took the general home, with new hopes and calculations and the pearls, which the general had, in spite of everything, not forgotten to take with him. Once or twice, between the calculations, the tantalizing figure of Nastasya Filippovna flitted through his mind, too; the general sighed . . .

"It's a pity! A genuine pity! A lost woman! A mad woman! . . . Well, well, as for the prince, it's not Nastasya Filippovna he needs now . . ."

In that same vein, some edifying words were also uttered in parting by two other companions among Nastasya Filippovna's guests, who had determined to go a little way on foot.

"Do you know, Afanasy Ivanovich, they say something of that sort happens among the Japanese," Ivan Petrovich Ptitsyn was saying. "Apparently, an injured party there goes to the one who injured him and says to him: 'You have wronged me, and for that, I have come to rip open my stomach before your very eyes,' and with those words actually does rip open his stomach before the eyes of the offender and probably must feel extraordinary satisfaction, as though he had in fact had his revenge. There are strange temperaments in the world, Afanasy Ivanovich!"

"And you think there was something of the sort here too?" Afanasy

Ivanovich responded with a smile. "Hm! . . . That's clever, though . . . and you've made an excellent comparison. You've seen for yourself, though, my dear Ivan Petrovich, that I've done all I could; I can't do more than what's possible, you'll admit? Though you must admit, too, that there were some capital features in that woman . . . brilliant qualities. Earlier, I even wanted to cry out to her, if I could only have allowed myself to do so in that Sodom, that she herself is my best vindication for all her accusations. Well, and who wouldn't have been captivated sometimes by that woman to the point of forgetting all reason and . . . everything? Just look, that lout, Rogozhin, came to her hauling a hundred thousand! Let us say, everything that just happened there was—ephemeral, romantic, unseemly; but for all that, it was colorful, for all that, it was original, you must admit that. My God, what might have become of such a temperament, and with such beauty! But, in spite of all efforts, and even education—it's all lost! A diamond in the rough—I've said it several times . . ."

And Afanasy Ivanovich sighed deeply.

PART TWO

I

Two days after the strange adventure at Nastasya Filippovna's party, with which we concluded the first part of our story, Prince Myshkin hurried away to Moscow, on business concerning the receipt of his unexpected inheritance. It was said at the time that there might be other reasons for the hastiness of his departure; but of this, as well as of the prince's adventures in Moscow and in the duration of his absence from Petersburg in general, we can give relatively little information. The prince was away exactly six months, and even those who had certain reasons to be interested in his fate could find out far too little about him in all that time. It's true, rumors of a sort did reach, though very rarely, one or another person, but for the most part they were strange ones and they almost always contradicted one another. Of course, the most interest in the prince was shown in the home of the Epanchins, of whom he had not even had time, upon departure, to take his leave. The general, actually, did see him at the time, and even two or three times; they had conversed seriously about something. But though Epanchin himself saw him, he did not inform his family about it. And at first, that is to say for almost a whole month after the prince's departure, it was on the whole not comfortable to speak of him in the home of the Epanchins. Only the general's wife, Lizaveta Prokofyevna, pronounced at the very beginning "that she had been cruelly mistaken in the prince." Then, two or three days later, she added, no longer naming the prince, but rather vaguely, that "the chief feature of her life was being continually mistaken in people." And, at last, some ten days later, concluded, in the form of a sententious pronouncement, having been irritated on some account with her daughters, that "there's been enough mistakes! There'll be no more of them." In addition, we can't neglect to mention that for a rather long time, a kind of unpleasant mood hung about their house. There was something oppressive, strained, unspoken, discordant; everyone scowled. The general was busy day and night, taking care of affairs; they had rarely seen him more busy and active—especially in his official work. His people hardly managed to get a glimpse of him. As for the young Epanchin ladies, of course, nothing was said by them openly. Perhaps even when they were alone with one another, too little was said. These were proud girls, haughty, and sometimes reserved even with one another, though they understood each other not only at a word but at a glance, so that at times there was no need to say much.

Only one thing might have been concluded by a disinterested observer, if there had happened to be one there: that, judging by all the above-mentioned facts, few as they were, the prince had nonetheless managed to make a particular impression on the Epanchin family, though he had appeared among them only once, and briefly at that. Perhaps the impression was a feeling of simple curiosity, justified by certain eccentric adventures of the prince. However it may be, the impression remained.

Little by little, the rumors that had circulated about the town had had time to be veiled in the darkness of obscurity. True, there were stories told about some little prince and simpleton (no one could be sure of his name) who had suddenly come into a vast inheritance and married a visiting Frenchwoman, a notorious cancan dancer at the Château-des-Fleurs in Paris. But others said that the fortune was inherited by some general, and the one who had married the visiting Frenchwoman and notorious cancan dancer was a young Russian merchant of untold wealth, and at his wedding, drunk and from pure boasting, he had burned over a candle some lottery tickets worth exactly seven hundred thousand. But all these rumors very soon died away, a result much aided by circumstances. The whole of Rogozhin's company, for instance, many of whom might have told a few things, went off, the whole heap of them, with Rogozhin himself at their head, to Moscow, almost exactly a week after the terrible orgy at the Ekaterinhof Vauxhall, at which Nastasya Filippovna was present too. From some rumors, it had become known to one or another person, the very few who were interested, that on the very next day, Nastasya Filippovna had run off and disappeared, and that apparently they had finally traced her as having gone to Moscow; so that Rogozhin's departure to Moscow was also found to have a certain correspondence with this rumor.

There were also the beginnings of rumors on account of Gavrila Ardalionovich Ivolgin, who was also pretty well known in his own circle. But something happened to him, too, which quickly cooled and consequently completely obliterated all the unkind stories about him: he became very sick and was unable to appear not only anywhere in society, but even at work. After a month's illness, he recovered, but for some reason resigned his position in the office of the joint-stock company and his place was taken by another. He had not once been to the house of General Epanchin, either, so that another civil servant started coming to the general as well. Gavrila Ardalionovich's enemies might have supposed that he was to such an extent discomfited by everything that had happened to him that he was even ashamed to go out into the street; but he was indeed taken ill somehow: he had even sunk into a splenetic state, grown pensive and irritable. That very winter, Varvara Ardalionovna was married to Ptitsyn; everyone who knew them directly ascribed this marriage to the circumstance that Ganya was unwilling to return to his duties and not only had ceased maintaining the family, but even began himself to be in need of assistance, and almost of looking after.

Let us note in parenthesis that in the Epanchin house, no mention was ever made of Gavrila Ardalionovich either—as though there had been no such man in the world, and not only in their house. But in the meantime, everyone there had learned (and even rather quickly) one very remarkable circumstance, namely: on that same fatal night, after the unpleasant adventure at Nastasya Filippovna's, Ganya, having returned home, did not go to sleep but began to await the return of the prince with feverish impatience. The prince, who had gone to Ekaterinhof, returned from there after five o'clock in the morning. Then Ganya went into his room and laid on the table before him the scorched packet of money presented to him by Nastasya Filippovna while he was lying in a faint. He begged the prince persistently to give this present back to her at the first opportunity. When Ganya went in to see the prince, he was in a hostile and almost desperate mood; but it appeared that some words were exchanged between him and the prince, after which Ganya sat with the prince for two hours and sobbed bitterly the entire time. They parted on friendly terms.

This information, which had reached all the Epanchins, turned out, as was later confirmed, to be entirely accurate. Of course, it was strange that information of this sort could reach them and be known so soon; all that had happened at Nastasya Filippovna's, for instance, became known at the Epanchins' virtually the very next day, and even in fairly accurate detail. As regards the information about Gavrila Ardalionovich, it might have been supposed that it had been carried to the Epanchins by Varvara Ardalionovna, who had somehow suddenly appeared as a visitor to the Epanchin girls, and had even very quickly come to be on a very good footing with them, which amazed Lizaveta Prokofyevna exceedingly. But though Varvara Ardalionovna had thought fit for some reason to become so intimate with the Epanchins, yet she certainly would not have talked to them about her brother. She too was a rather proud woman, in her own way, despite the fact that she had made friends in the place from which her brother had almost been turned out. Before that, although she had been acquainted with the Epanchin girls, they had seen each other rarely. And actually, even now she hardly ever showed herself in the drawing room, but went in, or more like slipped in, from the back porch. Lizaveta Prokofyevna had never cared for her, neither before nor now, though she greatly respected Nina Alexandrovna, Varvara Ardalionovna's mother. She wondered, got angry, ascribed the acquaintance with Varya to the whims and willfulness of her daughters, who "no longer knew what to think up to spite her," but nonetheless, Varvara Ardalionovna continued to visit them, both before and after her marriage.

But a month had passed since the prince's departure, and Generaless Epanchin received from old Princess Belokonsky, who had gone a fortnight before to Moscow to stay with her eldest married daughter, a letter, and this letter produced a visible effect on her. Although she relayed nothing of it either to her daughters or to Ivan Fyodorovich, still, from various signs, it became evident to the family that she was somehow particularly excited, even agitated. She began talking rather strangely to her daughters and always of such extraordinary subjects; she was evidently longing to talk it out, but for some reason she restrained herself. On the day she received the letter, she was affectionate to everyone, even kissed Adelaida and Aglaia, repented of some fault with regard to them in particular, but what, namely, it had been they could not make out. Even to Ivan Fyodorovich, whom she had kept in disgrace the entire month, she had suddenly become indulgent. Naturally, the very next day, she was extremely angry at her sentimentality of the day before, and managed to quarrel with everyone even before dinner, but toward evening the horizon cleared again. On the whole, she continued to be in fairly good humor the entire week, which had not happened for quite some time.

But another week later a second letter came from Belokonsky, and this time the generaless made up her mind to speak out. She announced solemnly that "old lady Belokonsky" (she never called the princess anything else when she spoke of her behind her back) sent her rather comforting news about that "queer fellow, well, about that prince, you know!" The old lady had ferreted him out in Moscow, had inquired about him, had found out something very good; the prince, at last, had come to see her himself and had made an impression on her that was almost extraordinary. "It is evident from the fact that she had invited him to visit her every day, in the afternoons, between one and two, and that he has been hanging about there every day and she is not sick of him yet," concluded the generaless, adding that through the "old lady" the prince had been received in two or three good houses. "It's a good thing that he's not sitting around on his hands and being bashful, like a fool." The girls, to whom all this was being imparted, noticed at once that Mamma concealed rather a great deal of her letter from them. Perhaps they learned this from Varvara Ardalionovna, who might have known and, of course, did know everything that Ptitsyn knew about the prince and his stay in Moscow. And Ptitsyn may have been even more informed than anyone else. But he was an exceedingly closemouthed man in regard to business, though, naturally, he did keep Varya apprised. The generaless at once conceived a greater dislike than ever for Varvara Ardalionovna on account of it.

But however that may be, the ice was broken, and it became suddenly possible to speak of the prince aloud. Moreover, the extraordinary impression and that quite disproportionately great interest that the prince had left and aroused about himself in the Epanchin household once more became apparent. The generaless was indeed astonished at the effect produced on her daughters by the news from Moscow. And the daughters, too, were astonished at their mamma, who had so solemnly proclaimed to them that "the chief feature of her life was being continually mistaken in people," and at the same time entrusted the prince to the attentions of the "powerful" old Princess Belokonsky in Moscow, whereby, of course, her attentions had to be cajoled out of her with much begging and pleading, for the "old lady" was not easily moved in such cases.

But as soon as the ice was broken and a fresh wind was blowing, the general too hastened to speak out. It turned out that he too took an extraordinary interest. However, he informed them only of "the business aspect of the question." It turned out that, in the interests of the prince, he had charged two very trustworthy and, in their own way, influential gentlemen in Moscow with the task of keeping an eye on him, and especially on Salazkin, who was guiding him in the matter. Everything that had been said about his inheritance, "about the fact of the inheritance, so to speak," turned out to be correct, but the inheritance itself in the end turned out to be not nearly as considerable as had been rumored at first. The assets were half entangled; there turned out to be debts, there turned out to be other claimants of some kind, and the prince, despite all guidance, was behaving in a most unbusinesslike way. "God bless him, of course!" Now that the "ice of silence" was broken, the general was glad to declare it "in all sincerity," for though "the lad was a bit *lacking*," still, he was worth it. But in the meantime, he had done something stupid all the same: for instance, creditors of the late merchant had shown up with questionable, worthless documents, and some, getting wind of the prince's character, even without any documents at all—and what do you think? The prince satisfied almost all of them, in spite of his friends' representations that all of these wretched little people and creditors had absolutely no claim at all; and he satisfied them only because it turned out, in fact, that some of them had actually been done an injury.

At that, the generaless responded that Belokonsky had written something of the sort to her too, and she added harshly that "it was stupid, very stupid; there's no curing a fool," but it was evident from her face how pleased she was at the conduct of this "fool." In the end, the general observed that his wife had taken an interest in the prince just as if he were her own son and had begun to be awfully affectionate to Aglaia for some reason; seeing this, Ivan Fyodorovich assumed for a time a rather businesslike mien.

But, after all, this pleasant atmosphere did not last long. A mere fortnight had passed, and something suddenly changed again, the generaless took on a black look, and the general, shrugging his shoulders a few times, once again submitted to the "ice of silence." The fact of the matter was that only a fortnight before, he had privately received some news, though brief and therefore not entirely clear, but still accurate, that Nastasya Filippovna, who had at first disappeared in Moscow, then had been found there by Rogozhin, then disappeared somewhere again and was found by him again, had, at last, almost given him her word to marry him. And behold, only a fortnight later his excellency had suddenly received news that Nastasya Filippovna had run away for the third time, practically from under the veil, and this time had disappeared somewhere in the provinces, and in the meantime, Prince Myshkin had vanished from Moscow too, leaving all his business in Salazkin's care, "whether with her, or simply in pursuit of her—that's not clear, but there's something in it," the general concluded. Lizaveta Prokofyevna, too, had received some unpleasant information from her quarter. At long last, two months after the prince's departure, almost every rumor about him in Petersburg died down for good, and in the Epanchin house, there was no more breaking of the "ice of silence." Varvara Ardalionovna, however, still visited the girls nonetheless.

To make an end of all these rumors and explanations, we will add that there were many changes in the Epanchin household by the spring, so that it was difficult not to forget the prince, who sent no news of himself and perhaps did not care to do so. In the course of the winter, little by little, they had finally decided to go abroad for the summer, that is, Lizaveta Prokofyevna with her daughters; the general, naturally, could not allow himself to waste his time on "frivolous diversion." The decision came about at the particular and persistent urging of the girls, who were thoroughly persuaded that their parents did not want to take them abroad because they were incessantly concerned with giving them away in marriage and finding them husbands. Possibly the parents were convinced, at last, that husbands might be met with abroad too, and that a trip for one summer, far from upsetting anything, might even perhaps "be conducive." It would be to the point here to mention that the project of the marriage of Afanasy Ivanovich Totsky and the eldest Epanchin girl had fallen apart altogether, and his formal proposal had never taken place. This had somehow happened of itself, without big discussions and without any family struggle. Since the time of the prince's departure, everything had suddenly died down on both sides. And this circumstance, too, had been among the number of causes of the oppressive atmosphere in the Epanchin family at the time, though the generaless did declare right then that she was so glad she was ready "to cross herself with both hands at once." The general, though he was in disfavor and knew that he was to blame, still sulked for a long time; he was sorry about Afanasy Ivanovich: "Such a fortune and such a clever man!" Not long afterward the general learned that Totsky had become captivated with a visiting Frenchwoman of the highest society, a marquise and a *légitimiste*,[1] that the marriage was taking place and that Afanasy Ivanovich was to be taken to Paris and then somewhere in Brittany. "Well, with the Frenchwoman, he's gone," concluded the general.

So the Epanchins were preparing to set off before the summer. And suddenly a circumstance occurred that again changed everything, and again the trip was put off, to the great delight of the general and the generaless. A certain prince had come to Petersburg from Moscow, Prince Shch.,[2] a well-known man, by the way, and well known in a rather good respect. He was one of those men, and one might even say one of those activists, of modern times, honest and modest, who sincerely and thoughtfully yearn for the public weal, are always working, and are distinguished by that rare and happy quality of always being able to find work. Not thrusting himself into the limelight, avoiding the zealotry and empty rhetoric of the parties, not counting himself among the leading ranks, the prince had still rather thoroughly understood much of what had happened in recent times. He had been in government service earlier, and then had begun to take an active part in the affairs of the *Zemstvo*.[3] Moreover, he was a correspondent of several Russian learned societies. In collaboration with a well-known technical expert, he had been instrumental, with his collected facts and researches, in the more accurate placement of one of the most important projected railway lines. He was thirty-five years old. He was a man "of the highest society" and, moreover, with a "good, serious, indisputable" fortune, in the words of the general, who had the opportunity, on account of some rather serious business, to come together and become acquainted with the prince at the house of the count, his superintendent. The prince, out of a certain particular curiosity, never

---

1. A supporter of the Bourbon family as the legitimate heirs to the French throne (restored after the defeat of Napoleon, the Bourbons were once again overthrown in the July Revolution of 1830).

2. The series of letters *Shch.* is the transliteration of a single Russian initial.

3. The local elected assembly (with a predominantly aristocratic membership) of a rural district.

avoided acquaintance with Russian "men of business." It came to pass that the prince was introduced to the general's family, too. Adelaida Ivanovna, the second of the sisters, made a rather strong impression on him. Toward the spring, the prince had proposed. Adelaida liked him extremely; Lizaveta Prokofyevna liked him too. The general was very happy. The trip, it stands to reason, was put off. The wedding was fixed for spring.

In fact, the trip might have still come off in the middle of the summer, or toward the end of it, if only in the form of a brief tour for a month or two taken by Lizaveta Prokofyevna and the two daughters remaining with her, to dispel their sadness at the loss of Adelaida. But once again, something new happened: toward the end of the spring (Adelaida's wedding plans had been slowed somewhat and it was put off until the middle of the summer), Prince Shch. introduced into the house of the Epanchins one of his distant relations, who was, however, rather well known to him. This was a certain Yevgeny Pavlovich R., still a young man, some twenty-eight years old, an imperial aide-de-camp, extremely handsome, "highborn," a witty, brilliant, "new" man of "exceeding education" and far too unheard-of wealth. With regard to the last point, the general was always very careful. He made inquiries: "Indeed, it does turn out to be something of the kind—though, of course, it must still be confirmed." This young and promising aide-de-camp was greatly raised in status by the testimonial sent by old lady Belokonsky from Moscow. There was only one rather ticklish aspect to his reputation: several liaisons and, as it was asserted, "conquests" of various broken hearts. Seeing Aglaia, he became extraordinarily assiduous in his visits to the Epanchins'. It's true, nothing had been said yet, no hint even had been dropped, but it still seemed to the parents that it would be out of the question to go abroad that summer. Aglaia herself, perhaps, was of a different opinion.

All this was happening just before the second appearance of our hero on the scene of our story. By that time, to judge by appearances, poor Prince Myshkin had been completely forgotten in Petersburg. If he were to suddenly appear now among those who had known him, he would have seemed to fall out of the sky. But in the meantime, we will, after all, reveal one other fact, and so complete our introduction.

Kolya Ivolgin, after the prince's departure, had at first continued his previous life, that is to say, he went to school, visited his friend Ippolit, looked after the general, and helped Varya around the house, that is, was her errand-boy. But the boarders had soon vanished: Ferdyshchenko moved out somewhere three days after the adventure at Nastasya Filippovna's and soon disappeared completely, so that nothing more was heard of him; it was said that he was drinking somewhere, but not on good authority. The prince had gone away to Moscow; it was all finished with the boarders. Later on, when Varya was married, Nina Alexandrovna and Ganya moved with her to Ptitsyn's house, to Izmailovsky Polk;[4] and as for General Ivolgin, a quite unforeseen event befell him about the same time: he was put in the debtors' prison. He was conveyed there by his friend the captainess, on account of some drafts he had given her at various times to the value of two thousand rubles. All this was a complete surprise to him, and the poor general was "undoubtedly the victim of his immeasurable faith in the generosity of the human heart, speaking generally." Having adopted the soothing habit of signing promissory notes and bills of exchange, he had not even supposed the possibility of their having any repercussions, if only at some later date, and kept thinking that it was *all right*. It turned out not to be all right. "How can you put your faith in people after that? How can you demonstrate a generous trustingness?" he used to exclaim bitterly, sitting with his new companions in Tarasov House[5] over a bottle of wine and telling them anecdotes of the siege of Kars and the soldier who rose from the dead. But actually, he took to this new life superbly. Ptitsyn and Varya said that this was indeed the very place for him; Ganya agreed with them entirely. Only poor Nina Alexandrovna shed bitter tears in secret (at which her household positively wondered) and, forever ailing, dragged herself just as often as she could to see her husband in Izmailovsky Polk.

But from the time of the "general's mishap," as Kolya expressed it, and in fact from the time of his sister's marriage, Kolya had gotten almost entirely out of hand and gone so far that recently he rarely even showed up to sleep at home. Hearsay had it that he had made a great number of new acquaintances; moreover, he had become far too well known in the debtors' prison as well. Nina Alexandrovna could not get along there without him; and at home they did not even pester him

---

4. A section of Petersburg, so named because it housed the Izmailovsky Regiment.

5. The name of the debtors' prison in Petersburg.

now with their curiosity. Varya, who had treated him so severely before, did not subject him to the slightest interrogation about his wanderings now; and Ganya, to the surprise of the rest of the household, talked with him and was sometimes even intimate with him on entirely comradely terms, in spite of his hypochondria, which had never happened before, since the twenty-seven-year-old Ganya had naturally never taken the slightest friendly interest in his fifteen-year-old brother, had treated him rudely, demanded that the whole household should be nothing but strict with him, and was constantly threatening to "box his ears," which drove Kolya "beyond the utmost limits of human endurance." One might have imagined that Kolya was now becoming positively indispensable to Ganya at times. He had been very much struck by Ganya's returning the money back then; for that, he was ready to forgive him a great deal.

Three months had passed since the prince's departure, when the Ivolgin family heard that Kolya had suddenly made the acquaintance of the Epanchins and had been very well received by the young ladies. Varya soon learned of this; Kolya, however, did not become acquainted with them through Varya, but "of his own accord." Little by little, they grew fond of him at the Epanchins'. The generaless was at first very displeased at him, but soon she began to make much of him "for his frankness and because he doesn't flatter." That Kolya did not flatter was perfectly correct; he managed to get on a perfectly equal and independent footing with them, though he sometimes read books and papers to the generaless; but he had always been ready to be of use. Once or twice, however, he quarreled violently with Lizaveta Prokofyevna, announced to her that she was a despot and that he would not set foot in her house again. The first time the quarrel arose on account of "the woman question," and the second time on account of the question of what the best time of the year is for catching green-finches. As unlikely as it may appear, on the third day after the quarrel, the generaless sent a note round to him by a footman asking him to come without fail. Kolya did not put on airs and went at once. Aglaia alone was, for some reason, continually not well disposed toward him and treated him haughtily. Yet it was to her lot that it fell to be astonished by him. One time—it was at Easter—seizing a moment when they were alone, Kolya handed Aglaia a letter, saying only that he was told to give it to her alone. Aglaia menacingly looked the "conceited little puppy" up and down, but Kolya did not wait and went out. She opened the note and read:

> Once you honored me with your confidence. Perhaps you have quite forgotten me now. How has it happened that I am writing to you? I don't know; but I felt an irresistible desire to remind you of me, and you in particular. How often I have had need of all three of you, but of all three I saw only you. I need you, I need you very much. I have nothing to write to you about myself, nothing to tell. And that's not what I wanted; I would like terribly that you should be happy. Are you happy? That was all I wanted to say to you.
>
> YOUR BROTHER, PR. L. MYSHKIN.

Having read that brief and rather incoherent note, Aglaia suddenly flushed all over and fell to thinking. It would be difficult for us to convey the course of her thoughts. Among other things, she asked herself whether she should show it to anyone. She felt somehow ashamed. She ended, however, by throwing the letter onto her little table with a mocking and strange smile. The next day she took it out again and put it into a thick, strongly bound book (she always did this with her papers so that she might find them more readily when she wanted them). And only a week after did she happen to discern what the book was. It was *Don Quixote de la Mancha*. Aglaia burst out in great peals of laughter—for some unknown reason.

It was unknown, too, whether she had shown her acquisition to any one of her sisters.

But even while she was reading the letter it had suddenly occurred to her: can that conceited and boastful little puppy really have been chosen by the prince as a correspondent, and perhaps, what's more, his only correspondent here? Though with a show of extraordinary disdain, but nonetheless, she did put Kolya to an interrogation. But the ever-touchy "puppy" did not pay the least attention this time to her disdain; somewhat briefly and rather dryly he explained to Aglaia that, although he had given the prince his permanent address, just in case, just before the prince's departure from Petersburg and had offered him his services, this was the first commission he had received from him, and his first note to him; and in support of his words he produced the letter that he had received himself. Aglaia did not scruple and read it. The letter to Kolya ran as follows:

> Dear Kolya, will you be so kind as to give the enclosed and sealed note to Aglaia Ivanovna. Be well.
>
> YOUR LOVING PR. L. MYSHKIN.

"Still, it's ridiculous to trust such a chit," Aglaia pronounced huffily, giving Kolya back the note, and walked by him contemptuously.

This was more than Kolya could endure: after all, he had even begged of Ganya, on purpose, and just for the occasion and without telling him the reason, to wear his absolutely new green scarf. He was bitterly offended.

I I

It was the first days of June, and the weather in Petersburg had been uncommonly fine for a whole week. The Epanchins had their own luxurious dacha at Pavlovsk. Lizaveta Prokofyevna became suddenly excited and roused herself, and after not two days of bustle they moved there.

Two or three days after the Epanchins' move, Prince Lev Nikolaevich Myshkin arrived by the morning train from Moscow. No one met him at the station; but as he got out of the carriage he suddenly fancied that he saw the strange, fervent gaze of two eyes belonging to someone in the crowd that surrounded the passengers arriving with the train. When he looked more attentively, he could not discern anything more. Of course, he had only fancied it; but it left an unpleasant impression. And apart from that, the prince had already been sad and pensive and seemed worried about something.

The cab drove him to a hotel not far from Liteinaya. The hotel was shabby. The prince took two small rooms, dark and badly furnished, washed, dressed, asked for nothing, and went out hurriedly, as though afraid of losing time or of not finding someone at home.

If anyone had seen him now of those who had known him half a year before in Petersburg, on his first arrival, he might well have concluded that he had changed in appearance much for the better. Yet this was scarcely the case. It was solely in his dress that the entire change resided: his entire outfit was different, made in Moscow and by a good tailor; but there was something wrong even with his clothes: they were sewn rather too much in accordance with fashion (as conscientious but not very talented tailors are always wont to sew), and, on top of that, made for a man who was not the least bit interested in it, so that upon closer examination of the prince anyone too eager to laugh might, perhaps, have found something to smile at after all. But people will laugh at all sorts of things.

The prince took a cab and set off to Peski. In one of the Rozhdestvensky streets,[6] he soon found a small wooden house. To his surprise it turned out to be a pretty little house, clean, kept in excellent order, and with a front garden in which flowers were growing. The windows on the street were open, and from them came the continuous sound of a harsh voice, almost a shouting, as though someone were reading aloud or even making a speech; the voice was infrequently interrupted by a chorus of ringing laughter. The prince went into the yard, mounted the steps to the little porch and asked for Mr. Lebedev.

"Why, there he is," answered the cook, who opened the door with her sleeves tucked up to her elbows. She jabbed her finger at the "drawing room."

In this drawing room—covered with dark-blue wallpaper and furnished quite neatly and with certain pretensions, that is to say, with a round table and a sofa, with a bronze clock under a glass case, with a narrow mirror on a wall panel, and with the most old-fashioned little chandelier with glass pendants suspended by a bronze chain from the ceiling—in the middle of the room stood Mr. Lebedev himself, with his back to the entering prince, in a waistcoat, but without a topcoat, in accordance with the summer weather; and, beating his own breast, he was declaiming bitterly on some subject. His listeners were: a boy of fifteen with a merry and not unintelligent face and a book in his hands; a young girl about twenty, dressed in mourning and carrying a baby in her arms; a girl of thirteen, also in mourning, who was laughing a great deal and opening her mouth awfully wide while doing it; and, finally,

6. In Petersburg, it is not uncommon for streets of the same name to be grouped together in a numbered series (First Rozhdestvensky, Second Rozhdestvensky, etc.). The Rozhdestvensky streets in the Peski district were at the time populated by people of low rank and means.

one very strange-looking listener, a lad of about twenty lying on the sofa, rather handsome, on the swarthy side, with thick long hair, large black eyes, and with a slight inclination to sideburns and a little beard. This listener, it seemed, frequently interrupted and contradicted Lebedev in his oration; this, most likely, was what provoked the laughter of the rest of the audience.

"Lukyan Timofeich, I say, Lukyan Timofeich! Looky here! Do glance this way!... Well, confound you!"

And the cook went out with an exasperated wave of her hands, so infuriated that she flushed red all over.

Lebedev looked around and, seeing the prince, stood for some time as though thunderstruck; then he rushed to him with an obsequious smile, but seemed to freeze again along the way, murmuring:

"Il-il-illustrious prince!"

But suddenly, as though still unable to assume the proper mien, he turned around and, out of the blue, rushed first at the girl in mourning with the baby in her arms, so that she was startled and drew back; but, leaving her at once, he flew at the thirteen-year-old girl, who was hanging about the threshold to the next room and continuing to smile with the remnants of her recent laughter. She was scared by his shout and bolted at once to the kitchen; Lebedev even stamped his feet at her to add to her alarm, but meeting the eye of the prince, who looked on embarrassed, he brought out in explanation:

"To show . . . respect. He-he-he!"

"There is no need of all this . . ." the prince was beginning.

"One minute, one minute, one minute . . . like a whirlwind!"

And Lebedev vanished quickly from the room. The prince looked with surprise at the girl, at the boy, and at the figure on the sofa; they were all laughing. The prince laughed too.

"He's gone to put his frock coat on," said the boy.

"How vexing this is," the prince began, "and I would have thought . . . Tell me, is he . . ."

"Drunk, you think?" cried the voice from the sofa. "Not a bit of it! Three or four glasses, well, perhaps some five; but what's that, after all—the regular thing."

The prince turned to the voice from the sofa, but the girl began speaking, and, with a most candid air on her charming face, she said:

"He never drinks much in the morning; if you have come to see him on business, you had better speak to him now. It's the best time. When he comes back toward evening, mayhap, he is intoxicated; though now he more often cries at night and reads aloud to us from the holy scriptures, for it's only five weeks since our mother died."

"He ran away because it was no doubt hard for him to answer you," laughed the young man on the sofa. "I'll bet anything that he is cheating you already and is hatching something now."

"Only five weeks! Only five weeks!" Lebedev took up, coming back in his frock coat, blinking and pulling his handkerchief out of his pocket to wipe his tears. "Orphaned!"

"But why have you come out all in tatters?" said the girl. "Why, behind the door there lies your new coat, didn't you see it?"

"Hold your tongue, you chit!" Lebedev shouted at her. "Oo, you!" he stamped his feet at her. But this time she only laughed.

"Why are you trying to frighten me? I am not Tanya, you know, I shan't run. But you might wake Lyubochka here and she'll have convulsions, too . . . What are you shouting for?"

"God forbid! Bite your tongue, bite your tongue!" Lebedev was terribly frightened all at once, and flying up to the baby, who was asleep in his daughter's arms, made the sign of the cross over it several times with a frightened air. "God save her, God preserve her! That's my own baby daughter, Lyubov," he turned to the prince, "born in most lawful wedlock of my newly departed wife, Yelena, who died in childbirth. And this unappealing little snipe is my daughter Vera, in mourning. And this, this, oh, this . . ."

"What, have you lost your voice?" cried the young man. "Go on, don't be bashful."

"Your excellency!" Lebedev cried suddenly with a sort of rush, "have you been following in the papers about the murder of the Zhemarin family?"[7]

"I've read of it," said the prince with some surprise.

"Well, that's the veritable murderer of the Zhemarin family, he's the very one!"

"What do you mean?" said the prince.

---

7. The merchant Zhemarin, his wife, mother, son, and another relation, along with two servants, were murdered during the course of a robbery by an eighteen-year-old student employed to tutor Zhemarin's eleven-year-old son. The murder occurred not long before Dostoevsky began work on *The Idiot*.

"That is, allegorically speaking, the future second murderer of a future second Zhemarin family, if there turns out to be such a one. He is preparing himself for it . . ."

Everybody laughed. It occurred to the prince that Lebedev really might be dithering and playing the fool because, anticipating the questions he would ask, he did not know how to answer them, and was trying to gain time.

"He is a rebel! He hatches plots!" shouted Lebedev, as though unable to restrain himself any longer. "Tell me, can I, have I the right to recognize such a slanderer, such a prodigal, so to speak, and monster, as my own nephew, the only son of my deceased sister Anisya?"

"Oh, do stop it, you drunken fellow! Would you believe it, Prince, he's taken it into his head now to be an advocate, pleads cases in the court; he's become so eloquent, he talks in high-flown language to his children at home. He made a speech before the justices of the peace five days ago. And whom do you think he undertook to defend: not the old woman who begged and pleaded with him, and who'd been robbed by a rogue of a moneylender who appropriated five hundred rubles from her, all she had in the world, but that very moneylender, a certain Zaidler, a *zhid*,[8] just because he promised him fifty rubles . . ."

"Fifty rubles if I won the case, only five if I lost it," Lebedev explained suddenly in an entirely different tone from the one he had used till then, as though he had never shouted at all.

"Well, he bungled it, of course—it's not the old order after all; they only laughed at him. But he was awfully pleased with himself. Remember, says he, O judges who are no respecters of persons, that a sorrowful, bedridden old man living by his honest toil is losing his last crust of bread; remember the wise words of the lawgiver: 'Let mercy prevail in the courts.' And believe it or not, every morning he recites that very speech to us here, exactly as he spoke it there; just before you came in, he was reading it for the fifth time today, he was so pleased with it. He licks his chops over himself. And now he's planning to defend someone else. You are Prince Myshkin, I believe? Kolya told me about you, that he had never met anyone smarter than you in the world . . ."

"And there's no one! There's no one! There's no one smarter in the world!" Lebedev took up at once.

8. A derogatory term for a Jew.

"Well, for his part, let's assume he's lying. The one loves you, and the other wants to ingratiate himself with you; but I don't intend to flatter you at all, just so you know. You're not without sense: you be the judge between him and me. Well, would you like for the prince here to judge between us?" he turned to his uncle. "I'm glad, indeed, Prince, that you've turned up."

"I would!" cried Lebedev resolutely, and involuntarily looked around at the audience, which began to close in again.

"Well, what have you got here, then?" uttered the prince, furrowing his brow.

He did, in fact, have a headache, and furthermore, he was becoming more and more convinced that Lebedev was duping him and that he was glad to see the business put off.

"Statement of the case. I am his nephew, that was not a lie, though he's always lying. I haven't finished my studies, but I mean to, and I'll get my way, for I have character. But in the meantime, for subsistence, I've taken a job on the railway at twenty-five rubles a month. I admit, moreover, that he has helped me two or three times already. I had twenty rubles, and I gambled them away. Would you believe it, Prince, I was so base, so low, that I lost them gambling!"

"To a miscreant, a miscreant who ought not to have been paid!" yelled Lebedev.

"Yes, to a miscreant, but one who ought to have been paid," continued the young man. "As for the fact that he's a miscreant, I'll bear witness to that, and not only because he beat you up. He's an officer who's been turned out of the army, Prince, a discharged lieutenant from Rogozhin's former gang, and teaches boxing. They're all scattered now since Rogozhin sent them off. But the worst of it is that I knew he was a miscreant, a blackguard, and a petty thief, and yet I sat down to play with him anyway, and that, gambling away my last ruble (we were playing *palki*[9]), I thought to myself: If I lose, I'll go to Uncle Lukyan and bow down to him—he won't refuse me. That was low, that there was really low! That there was conscious baseness!"

"That there was certainly conscious baseness!" repeated Lebedev.

"Well, don't crow over it, wait a bit," his nephew cried testily. "He's only too pleased. I came here to him, Prince, and owned up to every-

9. A card game.

thing; I acted honorably, I did not spare myself. I abused myself before him all I could—all here are witnesses. In order to take that job on the railway, I absolutely must rig myself out somehow, for I'm all in rags. Just look at my boots! Otherwise, I couldn't turn up for my job, and if I don't turn up at the proper time, my job will be taken by someone else, and I shall be high and dry, and when would I find another job again? Now I am only asking him for fifteen rubles and promise that I will never ask him for anything else again and, what's more, in the course of the first three months I'll pay him back the entire loan down to the last farthing. I'll keep my word. I can live on bread and *kvas*[10] for months together, for I have character. For three months, I shall get seventy-five rubles. With what I borrowed before, I shall owe him only thirty-five rubles, and so it would seem I shall have something to pay him with. Well, let him fix what interest he likes, damn it! Doesn't he know me? Ask him, Prince; when he has helped me before, haven't I paid him back? Why doesn't he want to now, then? He's angry that I paid that lieutenant; there's no other reason! That's the sort of person he is—a regular dog in the manger!"

"And he won't go away!" exclaimed Lebedev. "He lies there and won't go away."

"That's just what I told you. I won't go till you give it to me. What are you smiling at, Prince? It seems you find me in the wrong?"

"I am not smiling, but to my mind, you really are somewhat in the wrong," the prince answered unwillingly.

"Well, say straight out that I am altogether wrong, don't shuffle: what is this 'somewhat'?"

"If you like, you are altogether wrong."

"If I like! Ridiculous! Why, can you suppose that I don't know myself that it's rather a ticklish way to act, that it's his money, his discretion, while from my end it's coercion. But you, Prince . . . don't know much of life. If you don't educate them, nothing will come of it. You have to educate them. My conscience is clear, you know; on my conscience, he shall suffer no loss by me, I'll pay him back with interest. He has got moral satisfaction out of it too: he has seen my humiliation. What more does he want? What would be the use of him if he contributes no good? Pray, what does he do himself? Ask him, then, what

10. A popular drink made of fermented rye and sugar.

he contrives to do with others and how he dupes people. Why, I'll give my head if he hasn't already duped you and hasn't already contemplated how to dupe you some more! You're smiling, you don't believe it?"

"It seems to me that all this hasn't much to do with your business," observed the prince.

"I've been lying here for the last three days, and what goings on I've seen!" cried the young man, not listening. "Just imagine, he suspects this angel, this young girl here, now an orphan, my cousin, his daughter, and every night he searches her room for paramours! He comes in here on the sly and looks under my sofa, too. He has gone out of his mind with suspiciousness; he sees thieves in every corner. He jumps up every minute in the night, sometimes he looks at the windows to see if they are properly fastened, sometimes he tries the doors, peeps into the oven, and he'll do this half a dozen times in the night. At the court, he speaks for swindlers, but as for himself, he gets up three times a night to pray, right here, in the drawing room, on his knees, and bangs his forehead on the floor for half an hour at a time; and who doesn't he pray for, what laments doesn't he sing, in his drunkenness? He prayed for the soul of the Countess du Barry, I heard it with my own ears; Kolya heard it too: he's gone completely out of his mind!"

"Do you see, do you hear how he slanders me, Prince!" exclaimed Lebedev, flushing and truly beside himself. "And he doesn't know that, though I may be a drunkard and sponger, a thief and blackguard, the one thing in my life I can stand up for was that I took that grinning rascal, when he was still an infant, and wrapped him in his swaddling clothes, and washed him in the trough, and at my widowed, penniless sister's, I—just as penniless—sat up nights, didn't sleep a wink, attended to them both when they were sick, stole wood from the porter downstairs, used to sing him songs and snap my fingers, all with an empty belly, and this is what my nursing has come to! Here he lies, laughing at me now! What business is it of yours if I really did cross myself once for the soul of the Countess du Barry? Three days ago, Prince, I read the story of her life for the first time in the lexicon. And you, do you know what she was, du Barry? Speak up, do you know or not?"

"Oh, of course, you're the only one that knows?" the young man muttered mockingly, but unwillingly.

"She was a countess who, having risen from shame, ruled in the position of a queen, and to whom a great empress wrote in a letter, in her own handwriting, *'ma cousine.'*[11] A cardinal, a *nuntius*[12] at a *levée du roi*[13] (do you know what a *levée du roi* was?) offered himself to put the silk stockings on her bare little feet, and even thought it an honor—a lofty and sacred personage like that! Do you know that? I see from your face you don't. Well, and how did she die? Answer if you know!"

"Get away with you! Pestering me like that."

"The way she died was that after such honors this former wielder of power was dragged to the guillotine by the executioner, Sampson, guiltless, for the diversion of the Parisian *poissardes*,[14] and she didn't even understand what was happening to her, from terror. She saw that he was bending her neck down under the knife and shoving her along with kicks—while the people laughed—and she started screaming: *'Encore un moment, monsieur le bourreau, encore un moment!'* which means, 'Wait one little minute, Mr. Bourreau,[15] only one!' And perhaps for the sake of that little minute, God will forgive her, for one cannot imagine a greater *misère* for the human soul than that. Do you know the meaning of the word *misère*? Well, that's what *misère* is. When I read about that countess's cry for one little minute, I felt as though my heart had been pinched with a pair of tongs. And what is it to you, you worm, if I did, getting ready for bed, think of mentioning that great sinner in my prayers? And perhaps the reason I mentioned her was that, ever since the beginning of the world, probably no one has crossed himself for her sake, nor even thought of doing so. And it may be pleasant for her to feel in the other world that there is a sinner like herself who's prayed for her just once on this earth. What are you laughing at? You don't believe, atheist. Well, how do you know? And you told a lie if you did eavesdrop on me: I wasn't simply praying just for the Countess du Barry; my supplication went like this: 'Lord, give rest to the soul of that great sinner the Countess du Barry and all like her,' and that's a different matter altogether; for there are many such great sinners and examples of the mutability of fortune, who have suffered much, and who writhe yonder now, and moan, and wait; why, at the time, you too,

11. Fr., my cousin.
12. Lat., papal legate.
13. Fr., the king's morning dressing ceremony (lit. "rising of the king").
14. Fr., fishmongers.
15. Fr., executioner.

and people like you, of your ilk, insolent and hurtful, were also in my prayers, since you've troubled to eavesdrop on how I pray . . ."

"Well, enough, that'll do, pray for whom you like, damn you, screaming your head off!" the nephew interrupted with vexation. "He is mightily well-read, you see. You didn't know it, did you, Prince?" he added with an awkward grin. "He is always reading different books and memoirs of that sort nowadays."

"Your uncle is, anyway, not . . . a heartless man, after all," the prince observed reluctantly. The young man was beginning to be rather repugnant to him.

"Why, you're likely to puff him up with praise like that! Look, he's got his hand on his heart and his mouth pursed up—he licks it up at once. He's not heartless, perhaps, but he's a swindler, that's the trouble; and he's drunk besides, he's come apart at the seams, like any man who's been drunk for a few years, and that's why nothing comes together for him. He loves his children, we'll give him that, respected my late aunt . . . He even loves me and you know, upon my word, he's left me a share in his will . . ."

"I-I won't leave you anything!" cried Lebedev with embitterment.

"Listen, Lebedev," said the prince firmly, turning away from the young man. "I know from experience that you can be a businesslike man when you choose . . . I have very little time now, and if you . . . Excuse me, what is your name and patronymic, I've forgotten?"

"Ti-ti-timofei."

"And?"

"Lukyanovich."

Everyone in the room laughed again.

"He's lying!" cried the nephew. "He's lying even here! His name is not Timofei Lukyanovich at all, Prince, but Lukyan Timofeevich! Come, tell us, why did you lie? Isn't it just the same to you if it's Lukyan or Timofei, and what does it matter to the prince? You know, he tells lies simply from habit, I assure you."

"Can that be true?" asked the prince impatiently.

"Lukyan Timofeevich, indeed," Lebedev concurred and grew flustered, dropping his eyes humbly and again putting his hand on his heart.

"But my God, why would you do it?"

"Out of self-deprecation," whispered Lebedev, bending his head lower and more humbly.

"Nonsense, what self-deprecation! If only I knew where to find Kolya now!" said the prince and turned as if to go.

"I'll tell you where Kolya is," the young man put himself forward again.

"No, no, no!" Lebedev flared up and flew into a great excitement.

"Kolya slept here, but in the morning he went out to look for his general, whom you, Prince, have bought out of the debtors' prison, God only knows why. The general was promising only yesterday to come here to sleep, but he did not come. Most likely he slept in the hotel the Pair of Scales very close by here. Kolya is probably there, or in Pavlovsk at the Epanchins'. He had the money, he wanted to go yesterday. So, it would seem, either at the Scales or in Pavlovsk."

"In Pavlovsk, in Pavlovsk! . . . And we'll go this way, this way, into the garden and . . . have some coffee . . ."

And Lebedev started dragging the prince by the arm. They went out of the room, crossed the little yard, and went through a gate. Here there was in fact a very tiny and charming garden in which, owing to the fine weather, all the trees were already in leaf. Lebedev seated the prince on a green wooden bench by a green table fixed in the ground, and took a seat himself across from him. A minute later the coffee did, in fact, appear as well. The prince did not refuse it. Lebedev continued, obsequiously and eagerly, to look into his eyes.

"I didn't know you had such an establishment," said the prince, with the air of a man thinking of something completely different.

"O-orphans," Lebedev almost began, stooping over, but checked himself: the prince was looking absently before him and had no doubt forgotten his question. Another minute passed; Lebedev watched carefully and waited.

"Where were we?" said the prince, as if coming to. "Oh, yes! Why, you know yourself, Lebedev, what our business is. I have come in response to your letter. Speak."

Lebedev became disconcerted, wanted to say something, but only stuttered: no words came out. The prince waited and smiled mournfully.

"I think I understand you perfectly, Lukyan Timofeevich. You thought that I wouldn't rouse myself from the remote depths where I was at your first message, and wrote to clear your conscience. But I did come after all. Well, enough, don't deceive me! That's enough serving two masters. Rogozhin has been here for three weeks, I know everything. Have you had time to sell her to him, as you did last time, or no? Tell the truth."

"The monster found it out himself—himself."

"Don't abuse him; he has treated you badly, of course . . ."

"He beat me, he beat me up!" Lebedev took up with terrifying fervor, "and set his dog on me in Moscow, chased me the whole length of the street, a borzoi bitch. A most fearsome bitch."

"You take me for a child, Lebedev. Tell me, did she leave him now in earnest, that time in Moscow?"

"In earnest, in earnest, again practically at the altar. He was already counting the minutes, while she made off here to Petersburg, and straight to me: 'Save me, protect me, Lukyan, and don't tell the prince . . .' She is even more afraid of you, Prince, than of him, and—it's an enigma!"

And Lebedev slyly put his finger to his forehead.

"And now you've brought them together again?"

"Most illustrious prince, how could I . . . how could I have prevented it?"

"Well, that's enough, I'll find it all out myself. Only tell me, where is she now? With him?"

"Oh, no! No-no! She is still by herself. I'm free, she says, and you know, Prince, she insists strongly on that, I'm still perfectly free, she says! She is still living at my sister-in-law's on Petersburg Street, like I wrote you."

"And she is there now?"

"There, unless she is at Pavlovsk, on account of the fine weather, at Darya Alexeevna's dacha. I am, she says, perfectly free; she was boasting of her freedom only yesterday to Nikolai Ardalionovich. A bad sign!"

And Lebedev grinned toothily.

"Is Kolya often with her?"

"He is heedless and unfathomable, and not secretive."

"Is it long since you were there?"

"Every day, every day."

"Then you were there yesterday?"

"No sir, three days ago."

"What a pity you've been drinking, Lebedev! Or I might have asked you."

"No, no, no, not a bit of it!"

And Lebedev positively drew himself up.

"Tell me, how did you leave her?"

"S-searching..."

"Searching?"

"She seems to keep looking for something, as if she had lost something. And as for the impending marriage, she is sick at the very thought of it and takes it for an insult. And as for *him,* she thinks of him as of a bit of orange rind and no more, that is, actually, more, with fear and trembling; she has forbidden all mention of him, even, and they meet only when it's absolutely necessary ... and he feels it only too well! But there's no getting out of it, sir! ... She's agitated, mocking, double-talking, belligerent..."

"Double-talking and belligerent?"

"Belligerent; for she almost pulled my hair last time over one conversation. I took to admonishing her with the Apocalypse."

"How, now?" asked the prince, thinking that he had misheard.

"By reading the Apocalypse. She is a lady with an agitated imagination, he-he! And moreover, I've made the observation that she is too partial to serious subjects, however remote. She is fond of them, quite fond, and even considers it a mark of particular respect toward herself. Yes, sir. And the exegesis of the Apocalypse is my strong suit, I've been interpreting it for the last fifteen years. She agreed with me that we are now living in the age of the third horse, the raven one, and of the rider who has the balance in his hand, seeing that everything in the present age is measured out and subject to bargain, and all the people are looking for nothing but their own rights: 'a measure of wheat for a dinar and three measures of barley for a dinar' ... And yet they want to keep a free spirit, and a pure heart, and a sound body, and all the gifts of God while they're at it. But by rights alone they won't keep them, and afterward will follow the pale horse and he whose name was Death and after him will come hell ... And that's what we talk about when we meet, and ... it had a great effect."

"That is what you believe yourself?" asked the prince, scanning Lebedev with a strange look.

"I believe it and interpret it. For I am destitute and naked, and an atom in the vortex of humanity. And who will show Lebedev respect? He is fair game for everyone's wit, and they are all ready to give him a kick. But here, in the exegesis of it, I am equal to the grandest of men. For I have intellect! And a grand gentleman trembled before me . . . sitting in his armchair, trying to grasp it in his mind. His illustrious excellency Nil Alexeevich, two years back, just before Easter week, had heard it said—when I was still serving in his department—and purposely called me up from the office to his study, through Pyotr Zakharich, and questioned me in private: 'Is it true that you expound the Antichrist?' And I made no secret of it: 'Aye, that I do,' I say, and set it out, and presented it, and did not soften the horror, but intentionally increased it, unfolding the allegory, and fitted dates to it. And he smirked, but at the dates and correspondences began to tremble, and asked me to close the book and go away, and rewarded me at Easter, but by St. Thomas's day[16] he gave up his soul to God."

"What are you saying, Lebedev?"

"So it was. He fell out of his carriage after dinner . . . knocked his head against a post, and like a little babe, like a little babe, passed away on the spot. Seventy-three years old he was; ruddy, gray-haired, sprinkled all over with scent, and he used to be all smiles, just like a little child. Pyotr Zakharich recalled it at the time: 'You foretold it,' he said."

The prince began getting up. Lebedev was surprised and even perplexed that the prince was already rising.

"You've become rather indifferent, sir, he-he!" he ventured to observe obsequiously.

"Truly, I don't feel quite well; my head is heavy, from the journey perhaps," answered the prince, frowning.

"You ought to take a little dacha, sir," Lebedev broached timidly.

The prince stood pondering.

"I myself am off, three days hence, to my dacha with all my household, to preserve my newborn nestling, and to fix up everything in this little house in the meantime. And to Pavlovsk, too."

"You are going to Pavlovsk, too?" asked the prince suddenly. "Why,

---

16. The day, shortly after the Resurrection, on which Christ appeared to the apostle Thomas (or Doubting Thomas) and allowed him to touch his wound.

what is this, is everyone here going to Pavlovsk? And you have a dacha of your own there, you say?"

"Not everyone is going to Pavlovsk, no sir. As for me, Ivan Petrovich Ptitsyn has let me have one of the dachas he's acquired for cheap. It's nice, and high up, and green, and cheap, and *bon ton*,[17] and musical, and that's why everyone goes to Pavlovsk. I'm actually in the little annex, and the dacha itself . . ."

"You've let it?"

"N-n-no. Not . . . quite, sir."

"Let it to me," the prince proposed suddenly.

That seemed to be just what Lebedev had been leading up to. The idea had entered his head three minutes before. And yet he no longer had need of a tenant; he already had a summer renter who had himself apprised him that he might, perhaps, take the dacha. And Lebedev knew for a fact that he would take it not "perhaps" but certainly. But now he was suddenly struck with an idea—by his reckoning, a very fruitful one—to give the dacha to the prince, taking advantage of the fact that the previous tenant had expressed himself vaguely. "A complete coming together and a completely new turn of things" suddenly rose before his imagination. He received the prince's proposition virtually with delight, so that he even waved away his direct question about the price.

"Well, as you like; I'll make inquiries; you shan't lose your due."

They were both already coming out of the garden.

"And I could . . . I could . . . if you liked, I could tell you something rather interesting, highly honored prince, relating to the same subject," muttered Lebedev, squirming with glee at the prince's side.

The prince paused.

"Darya Alexeevna has a dacha at Pavlovsk too, sir."

"Well?"

"And a certain person is a friend of hers and evidently intends to visit her frequently in Pavlovsk. With an object."

"Well?"

"Aglaia Ivanovna . . ."

"Ach, that's enough, Lebedev!" the prince interrupted, with some

17. Fr., distinguished and tasteful.

sort of unpleasant sensation, as though he had been touched on his sore spot. "That's all . . . wrong. I'd rather you tell me, when are you moving? The sooner the better for me, as I am at a hotel . . ."

As they talked, they left the garden and, without going into the rooms, crossed the yard and reached the gate.

"But what could be better?" Lebedev hit upon at last. "Come straight here to me from the hotel today, and the day after tomorrow we will all go to Pavlovsk together."

"I'll see," said the prince pensively and went out the gate.

Lebedev looked after him. He was struck by the prince's sudden absentmindedness. Going out, he had even forgotten to say good-bye, didn't even nod his head, which was not in keeping with what Lebedev knew of the prince's courtesy and consideration.

I I I

It was already past eleven. The prince knew that at the Epanchins' city residence, he would now find no one at home but the general, there on business, and even that was unlikely. It occurred to him that the general might perhaps take him at once to Pavlovsk, and before then he particularly wanted to make one call. At the risk of being late to the Epanchins' and putting off his trip to Pavlovsk till the next day, the prince decided to go and seek the house at which he so particularly wanted to call.

This visit was, however, risky for him to some extent. He was having difficulties and wavered. He knew that the house was found on Gorokhovaya Street, not far from Sadovaya, and resolved to go there, hoping that on the way to the spot, he would succeed, at last, in making up his mind.

As he approached the corner of Gorokhovaya and Sadovaya, he was surprised himself at his extraordinary excitement; he had not expected his heart to throb so painfully. One house attracted his attention even from a distance, no doubt from its peculiar physiognomy, and the prince remembered afterward that he had said to himself: "That must be the very house." With extraordinary curiosity, he approached it to verify his conjecture. The house was large, gloomy, three stories high, without any architectural elements whatsoever, and a dirty-green color. A certain—though very small—number of houses of this sort, built at the end of the last century, have survived particularly in these streets of Petersburg (where everything changes so quickly) almost unchanged. They are built solidly, with thick walls and extraordinarily few windows; on the ground floor, the windows sometimes have gratings. For the most part, there is a money changer's shop below. The Skopets[18] who runs the shop rents rooms above it. Without and within, the house is somehow inhospitable and frigid, everything appears to be hiding and secreting itself away, and why it seems so from the mere physiognomy of the house—it would be hard to explain. Architectural lines have, of course, a secret of their own. These houses are occupied almost entirely by traders. Coming up to the gates and glancing at the inscription, the prince read: "House of the Hereditary Honorable Citizen Rogozhin."

Ceasing to waver, he opened the glass door, which slammed noisily behind him, and began to climb the main staircase to the second floor. The staircase was dark, made of stone, coarsely designed, and its walls were covered with red paint. He knew that Rogozhin with his mother and brother occupied the whole second floor of this dreary house. The servant who opened the door to the prince led him in without taking his name, and led him a long way; they passed through a grand parlor the walls of which were "faux marble," with an oak block floor and furnishings from the twenties, coarse and heavy; they passed also through some little cells, winding and zigzagging, mounting two or three steps and going down as many, till at last they knocked at a door. The door was opened by Parfyon Semyonovich himself; seeing the prince, he turned so pale and was so frozen to the spot that for a time he resembled a stone idol, looking with his fixed and frightened gaze and twisting his mouth into some kind of utterly bewildered smile—as though he found something impossible and almost miraculous in the prince's visit. Though the prince had expected something of the sort, he was surprised.

"Parfyon, perhaps it's inopportune, I can go away, you know," he uttered at last with embarrassment.

"It's opportune! It's opportune!" Parfyon recovered himself at last. "You're welcome. Come in!"

18. *Skoptsy* were a particularly extreme sect of Old Believers (see note 21) who practiced self-immolation as a way to escape what they perceived to be the reign of the Antichrist.

They said *ty* to each other.[19] In Moscow, they had had occasion to get together often and at length, and there had even been several moments in their meetings that had been impressed only too memorably in each other's hearts. But now, they had not met for over three months.

The pallor and a kind of slight, fleeting trembling had still not left Rogozhin's face. Though he had welcomed his guest, his extraordinary discomfiture persisted. While he led the prince to the armchairs and seated him at the table, the latter happened to turn to him and stood still at the impression made by his extraordinarily strange and heavy gaze. Something seemed to transfix the prince and at the same time some memory came back to him—something recent, painful, gloomy. Not sitting down and remaining motionless, he looked Rogozhin straight in the eyes for some time; at the first moment, they seemed to gleam more brightly. At last, Rogozhin smirked, but somewhat discomfited and as if at a loss.

"Why are you giving me such an intent look?" he muttered. "Sit down!"

The prince sat down.

"Parfyon," he said, "tell me straight out, did you know that I was coming to Petersburg today or not?"

"That you were coming—I did think so; and, you see, I was not mistaken," the latter added, with a caustic smile, "but how should I know that you would come today?"

A certain harsh abruptness and strange irritability in the question that was contained in the answer amazed the prince even more.

"And even if you knew that it was *today*, why be so cross about it?" uttered the prince softly, in confusion.

19. Russian has two forms of addressing others. The familiar address, *ty* (like the French *tu*), is reserved for family members and close friends; for everyone else—and most especially for anyone superior in age, rank, or social position—the formal address, *vy* (like the French *vous*), is used. When the familiar form is used by two people upon mutual consent, it is a sign of great friendship and intimacy; the familiar address is also used to address servants and children, and often among the lower classes and students, where strict decorum is not always maintained. In any other context, its use is rude and disparaging. I should like to note here, too, that unlike the English reader, the reader of the original does not actually need to be *told* that Myshkin and Rogozhin are using the *ty* form—since he can clearly see its use for himself in the previous two sentences, and throughout the rest of the dialogue. Thus, this statement of the obvious has a far more emphatic function for the Russian reader than for the English.

"Well, why do you ask, anyway?"

"Earlier, getting out of the train, I saw a pair of eyes that looked at me exactly like the way you've looked at me just now from behind."

"So that's it! Well, whose eyes were they, then?" Rogozhin muttered suspiciously. The prince fancied that he shuddered.

"I don't know; I almost think that I was seeing things in the crowd; I'm beginning to see things everywhere somehow. Parfyon, my friend, I feel almost as I did five years ago, back when the fits were still coming over me."

"Well, perhaps you were seeing things; I don't know . . ." muttered Parfyon.

The affectionate smile on his face was very unbecoming to him at that moment, just as if something in that smile had broken and it did not seem at all in Parfyon's power to patch it together, no matter how he tried.

"So, would you go abroad again, then?" he asked, and suddenly added: "And do you remember how we came from Pskov in the same carriage together last autumn? I was coming here, and you . . . in your cloak, remember, and those little spats?"

And Rogozhin suddenly laughed, this time with some kind of open malice, and positively relieved that he had succeeded in expressing it in some way.

"Have you settled here for good?" asked the prince, looking around the study.

"Yes, I'm at home. Where else should I be, then?"

"It's a long time since we've met. I've heard such things about you, not like yourself."

"What tales wouldn't people tell," remarked Rogozhin dryly.

"But you've sent away all your gang; and here you sit in your ancestral home and don't get up to any mischief. Well, and that's a good thing. Is it your own house, or does it belong to all of you in common?"

"The house is my mother's. That's the way to her rooms across the corridor."

"And where does your brother live?"

"My brother, Semyon Semyonych, is in the annex."

"Is he a family man?"

"Widowed. What do you need to know that for?"

The prince looked at him and did not answer; he suddenly grew thoughtful and, it seemed, did not hear the question. Rogozhin did not insist and waited. They were silent awhile.

"I guessed it was your house just now, as I approached it, from a hundred paces," said the prince.

"How so?"

"I don't know at all. You house has the physiognomy of your whole family and your whole Rogozhin way of life; but ask me how I concluded that—I have nothing to explain it. It's raving nonsense, of course. I'm even anxious that it troubles me so. Before, I would have never even imagined that you live in such a house, but as soon as I saw it, it occurred to me at once: 'Why, that's just the sort of house he ought to have!'"

"Well, whatdya know!" Rogozhin smirked indeterminately, not quite understanding the prince's unclear thought. "This house was built by my grandfather," he remarked. "It was always occupied by Skoptsy, the Khludyakovs, and they still rent from us now."

"What gloom. You sit here rather gloomily," said the prince, looking around the study.

It was a big room, lofty, somewhat dark, filled with all sorts of furniture—for the most part, big office desks, bureaus, cupboards, in which business books and papers of some sort were kept. A wide sofa covered in red morocco evidently served Rogozhin as a bed. The prince noticed two or three books lying on the table at which Rogozhin had seated him; one of them, Solovyev's *History*,[20] was open and had a bookmark in it. On the walls, in dull gilded frames, there were a few oil paintings, dark and covered with soot, upon which it was very difficult to make anything out. One full-length portrait attracted the prince's attention: it represented a man of fifty, in a frock coat of German cut, but with long tails, with two medals around his neck, with a very sparse, short, graying little beard, with a wrinkled and yellow face, with a suspicious, secretive and doleful gaze.

"That wouldn't be your father, would it?" asked the prince.

"The very same," answered Rogozhin with an unpleasant grin, as though girding himself for some unceremonious jest at his dead father's expense to follow at once.

20. A twenty-nine-volume history of Russia published between 1851 and 1879; seventeen volumes had appeared by 1867.

"He wasn't one of the Old Believers,[21] was he?"

"No, he used to go to church; but it's true, he used to say that the old form of belief was truer. He had a great respect for the Skoptsy, too. This used to be his study. Why do you ask if he was an Old Believer?"

"Will you have your wedding here?"

"H-here," answered Rogozhin, almost starting at the unexpected question.

"Will you have it soon?"

"You know yourself it doesn't depend on me."

"Parfyon, I'm not your enemy and have no intention of interfering with you in any way. I tell you that again as I've told you before, once, in almost such a moment. When your wedding was arranged in Moscow, I didn't interfere with you, you know that. The first time *she* rushed to me herself, practically from before the altar, begging me to 'save' her from you. It's her own words I am repeating to you. Afterward, she ran away from me too. You found her again and were leading her to the altar, and now they tell me she ran away from you again here. Is that true? Lebedev told me so; that's why I've come. But that you'd come together again I learned for the first time only yesterday in the train, from one of your former friends, Zalyozhev, if you care to know. I came here with a purpose: I wanted to persuade *her*, finally, to go abroad, for the sake of her health; she is rather broken down, both in body and soul, and in her mind especially, and in my view, she needs great care. I did not intend to accompany her abroad myself, but had in mind to arrange it all without me. I'm telling you the honest truth. If it's absolutely true that you've made up again, I shan't even show myself to her, and I'll never come again to see you either. You know yourself I'm not deceiving you, because I've always been open with you. I've never concealed from you what I think about it, and I have always said that to marry you would be *her* certain perdition. Your perdition, too . . . perhaps even more than hers. If you were to part again, I

21. In the seventeenth century, the leaders of the Russian Orthodox establishment, with the backing of the state, instituted a series of church reforms, setting off vehement protest that resulted in the Great Schism. The schismatics refused to accept the authority of the new church and considered any changes in the old rituals and liturgies as corrupting foreign influence; hence, they were known as the Old Believers. After a brief period of severe persecution and martyrdom, communities of Old Believers came to be tolerated by the state and gained a reputation for being sober, hardworking and prosperous people.

should be very glad; but I have no intention of breaking you up and coming between you myself. Be assured and don't suspect me. Why, you know yourself whether I was ever *really* your rival, even when she ran away to me. Now you are laughing; I know what you are laughing at. Yes, we lived apart and in different towns, and you know all that *for certain*. But I've explained to you before that I don't love her with love but with pity. I believe I define it exactly. You said at the time that you understood my words; is that true? Did you understand? See how hatefully you are looking at me! I've come to reassure you, for you are dear to me too. I am very fond of you, Parfyon. But now I shall leave and never come again. Farewell."

The prince got up.

"Sit with me a little," said Parfyon softly, not rising from his place and resting his head on the palm of his right hand. "It's a long time since I've seen you."

The prince sat down. Both fell silent again.

"Whenever you are not before me, I feel anger against you at once, Lev Nikolaevich. In these three months that I have not seen you, I have been angry with you every minute, upon my word. I could have gone and poisoned you, just like that! That's how it is. And now, you've been sitting with me for a quarter of an hour and all my anger is passing away and you are dear to me again as you used to be. Sit with me a little . . ."

"When I am with you, you believe me, but when I am away, you leave off believing me at once and begin to suspect me again! You take after your father!" answered the prince with a friendly chuckle and trying to hide his emotion.

"I believe your voice when I am with you. I understand, you know, that we can't be put on a level, you and I . . ."

"Why did you add that? And now you are irritated again," said the prince, wondering at Rogozhin.

"Well, our opinion's not been asked for here, brother," answered the other. "It's been surmised without us. Why, we even love in different ways, too, there's a difference in everything," he continued softly after a pause. "You say you love her with pity. I have not an ounce of such pity for her in me. And she hates me too, more than anything. I dream of her every night now: always that she is laughing at me with other men. And that's just how it is, brother. She's going to the altar with me, but she has neglected to even give me a thought, as though she were changing a shoe. Would you believe it, I haven't seen her for five days, because I don't dare to go to her; she'll ask: 'What have you come for?' As if she hasn't shamed me enough ..."

"How shamed you? What are you saying?"

"As if he didn't know! Why, it was with you she ran away from me, 'before the altar,' you said so yourself just now."

"Why, you don't believe yourself that ..."

"Didn't she shame me in Moscow with that officer, Zemtyuzhnikov? I know for certain she did, and even after she had fixed the wedding day herself."

"It can't be!" exclaimed the prince.

"I know it for a fact," Rogozhin confirmed with conviction. "Why, isn't she that sort of woman? It's no good, brother, even saying that she isn't. That's nothing but nonsense. With you, she won't be that sort, and will be horrified at the business herself, perhaps, but with me, she is precisely that sort. That's how it is, you know. She looks upon me as the lowest refuse. I know for a fact that she took up with Keller, that officer, the one who boxes, just to make a laughingstock of me ... And you don't even know yet the things she pulled with me in Moscow! And the money, how much money I've wasted ..."

"But ... how can you marry her now! ... What will you do afterward?" asked the prince in horror.

"I haven't been to see her in five days now," he went on after a minute's pause. "I keep fearing she'll turn me out. 'I am still mistress of myself,' she says, 'if I choose, I'll cast you out altogether and go abroad.' It was she who told me that she'd go abroad," he observed as if parenthetically, looking in a peculiar way into the prince's eyes; "sometimes, it's true, she's only scaring me, she keeps finding me funny for some reason. But another time she really scowls, becomes sullen, won't say a word; that's what I'm afraid of. The other day, I thought: I won't go empty-handed when I go to see her—but it only made her laugh, and afterward she even went into a rage. She gave her parlor-maid, Katya, one of my shawls, the likes of which she may never have seen before, though she did live in luxury. And as to when our wedding is to be, I dare not open my lips. Well, what sort of bridegroom is it that's afraid just to go see her? So here I sit, and when I can bear it no longer, I steal past her house and go creeping about on the street, or hide behind some corner. The other day, I kept watch near her gate almost till daybreak—I fancied something was going on. And she must have looked out the window: 'What would you have done to me,' she says, 'had you seen me deceiving you?' I couldn't bear it, and I said: 'You know yourself.'"

"What does she know?"

"Well, and how do I know, then!" Rogozhin laughed maliciously. "In Moscow, I couldn't catch her out with anyone, though I was a long time on the track. I took her aside then once and said: 'You promised to go to the altar with me, you're entering an honest family, and do you know what you are now? That,' I said, 'is what you are!'"

"You told her?"

"I did."

"Well?"

"'I wouldn't care to take you for a footman now, perhaps,' she says, 'let alone be your wife!' 'And I won't go away with that,' I say, 'it's all one end!' 'And I,' she says, 'I'll go call Keller now, I'll tell him, and he'll boot you out the gate.' I flew at her right there, and beat her black and blue."

"It can't be!" exclaimed the prince.

"I tell you, it was so," Rogozhin confirmed quietly, but with flashing eyes. "For thirty-six hours on end, I didn't sleep, nor eat, nor drink, didn't leave her room, was on my knees before her: 'I'll die,' I say, 'I won't leave till you forgive me, and if you have me taken out—I'll drown myself; for what should I do now without you?' She was like a madwoman all that day, she would weep, then plan to kill me with a knife, then rail at me, by turns. She called Zalyozhev, Keller, Zemtyuzhnikov, and everyone, showed me to them, put me to shame. 'Come, gentlemen, let's all go to the theater tonight, the whole company, let him stay here if he won't go, I'm not bound by him. And they'll bring you tea here, Parfyon Semyonych, while I'm out, you must have worked up quite a hunger today.' She came back from the theater alone: 'They are all little cowards and knaves,' she says, 'they're afraid of you and they try to put the fear in me: they say, he won't leave after all, and will cut your throat, maybe. But I'll go into my bedroom and not even lock the door after me; that's how afraid of you I am! Just so you know and see it! Have you had any tea?' 'No,' I say, 'and I won't.' 'Well, so long as it was offered, but this behavior is very unbecoming to you.' And she did as she said, she didn't lock her door. In the morning she comes out and laughs: 'Have you gone out of your mind or something?' she says. 'Why, you'll die of hunger!' 'Forgive me,' I say. 'I don't want to forgive you. I won't marry you, I've said so. Have you really been sitting in that chair all night, have you not slept?' 'No,' I say, 'I haven't slept.' 'How clever! And you won't have tea or dinner again?' 'I said I won't—forgive me!' 'If only you knew how ill it suits you! It's like a saddle on a cow. You haven't got it into your head to scare me, have you? What a misfortune for me, that you go hungry; there's a fright!' She grew angry, but not for long, she took to gibing at me again. I wondered at her there, how it was that there was no rancor in her at all? For, you know, she'll keep a grudge, with other people, she'll keep a grudge a long time! And then it occurred to me that she considers me so lowly that she can't even bear me a grudge that much. And that's the truth! 'Do you know,' she says, 'what the Roman pope is?' 'I've heard,' I say. 'You've never learned any general history, Parfyon Semyonych,' she says. 'I never learned anything,' I say. 'Well,' she says, 'I'll give you something to read: there was a pope once, and he got angry with an emperor, and the latter stood before his palace for three days, without drinking, without eating, barefoot, on his knees, until he forgave him; what do you suppose that emperor thought to himself in those three days, standing on his knees, and what vows did he take? . . . But wait,' she says, 'I'll read it to you myself!' She jumped up and brought the book: 'It's poetry,' she says, and began reading to me in verse how that emperor had vowed during those three days to avenge himself on that pope. 'Don't you like that, Parfyon Semyonovich?' she says. 'That's all true,' I say, 'what you've read.' 'Aha! you say yourself that it's true, so you, too, perhaps, are making vows that "when she is married to me, I'll make her remember it all, then I'll have my fun with her!"' 'I don't know,' I say, 'perhaps I'm thinking that.' 'What do you mean, you don't know?' 'I just don't know,' I say, 'I have no thoughts for that now.' 'What are you thinking of now, then?' 'Well, you'll get up and walk past me, and I'm looking at you and watching you; your dress rustles and my heart sinks; and when you go out of the room, I remember every little word of yours, what you said and in what tone; and all last night I didn't think of anything; I listened all the while how you were breathing in your sleep, and how, twice, you stirred . . .' 'And I dare say,' she laughed, 'you don't think and don't remember about the fact that you beat me?' 'Perhaps I do think of it,' I say, 'I don't know.' 'And if I don't forgive you and won't marry you?' 'I told you, I'll drown myself.' 'Perhaps you'll murder me first...' she said, and grew thoughtful. Then she got angry and went out. An hour later she comes in to me, all gloomy. 'I will marry you, Parfyon Semyonovich,' she says, 'and not because I'm afraid of you, for I'll come to ruin anyway. And where's it better, then? Sit down,' she says, 'they'll bring you dinner directly. And if I marry you,' she added, 'then I'll be a faithful wife to you, have no doubt of that and don't be uneasy.' Then she was silent and said: 'And after all, you're not a flunky; I used to think that you were the very image of a flunky.' And she fixed the wedding day on the spot, and a week later she went and ran away from me here, to Lebedev. When I arrived, she said: 'I'm not repudiating you altogether; I only want to wait some more, as long as I like, because I am still my own mistress. You can wait too, if you like.' That's how it is between us now... What do you think of all that, Lev Nikolaevich?"

"What do you think yourself?" the prince questioned back, looking sorrowfully at Rogozhin.

"Do you suppose I think?" broke from the latter. He would have added something, but remained silent in hopeless dejection.

The prince stood up and wanted to take leave again.

"I won't hinder you, in any case," he said softly, almost pensively, as though replying to some secret inner thought of his own.

"Do you know what I'll tell you!" Rogozhin suddenly grew animated, and his eyes kindled. "How is it that you yield to me like that, I don't understand it? Have you stopped loving her completely? Before, you were still pining, at least; I saw it, you know. Then what did you come here for, at such breakneck speed? From pity?" (And his face twisted with malicious mockery.) "He-he!"

"You think I'm deceiving you?" asked the prince.

"No, I believe you, but I don't understand any of it. Most likely, your pity is perhaps greater than my love!"

Something spiteful and urgently desiring to express itself at once flared up in his face.

"Well, there's no distinguishing your love from fury," smiled the prince, "and once it passes, the trouble may perhaps be worse. I tell you this, brother Parfyon..."

"That I'll cut her throat?"

The prince shuddered.

"You will hate her bitterly for this very love you feel now, for all this torture you are undergoing now. What is strangest of all to me is, how she can again mean to marry you? When I heard it yesterday, I scarcely believed it, and my heart grew heavy. Why, she has repudiated you twice already, and has flown from the altar, that means she has some foreboding! . . . What does she find in you now, then? Not your money, surely? That's nonsense. And no doubt you've spent a good deal of it already. Can it be simply to get a husband? Why, she could have found plenty of others besides you. Any man would be better than you, for you really may cut her throat, and she understands that only too well now, perhaps. Is it that you love her so passionately? It's true, there's that . . . I have heard there are such women, who are looking just for that kind of love . . . only . . ."

The prince stopped and sank into thought.

"Why are you chuckling at my father's portrait again?" asked Rogozhin, who was observing with extraordinary intentness every change, every fleeting expression on the prince's face.

"Why, did I chuckle? Oh, it came into my head that if this misfortune had not happened to you, had this love not come over you, you would most likely have become exactly like your father, and in a very short time too. You would have settled in silently by yourself in this house with an obedient and submissive wife, stern and sparing of words, trusting no one and having no need of it, only accumulating your money in silent gloom. At the most, you would sometimes have praised the old books and become interested in the two-fingered sign of the cross,[22] and that only in your old age . . ."

"Laugh away. And here she was saying the exact same thing recently, when she was looking at that portrait! Queer, how you are of a mind in everything now . . ."

"Why, has she been in your house?" asked the prince with curiosity.

"She has. She looked a long time at the portrait and questioned me about the late gentleman. 'You'd be just like that, too,' she chuckled to me at last. 'You have strong passions, Parfyon Semyonovich,' she says, 'such passions that you might have been carried off with them straight

22. One of the more controversial church reforms concerned the manner of crossing oneself. The Old Believers extended two fingers to symbolize the dual nature of Christ while the reformed church used three fingers for the Holy Trinity.

to Siberia, to hard labor, if you weren't intelligent, too; for you have a great deal of intelligence,' she says. (That's just what she said, do you believe it? It's the first time I heard such a thing from her!) 'You would have soon given up all your present silliness. And as you are an entirely uneducated man, you would have begun saving money, and would have settled in, like your father, in this house with your Skoptsy; perhaps you would have gone over to their faith in the end yourself, and would have grown so fond of your money that you would have heaped up not two but ten million, perhaps, and would have died of hunger on your bags of money, for you are passionate in everything, you push everything to a passion.' That was just how she talked, almost in those very words. She had never talked to me like that before! You know, she always talks of trivialities with me, or jeers at me: and she began laughing this time, too, but then grew so gloomy; she went looking around all over the whole house, and seemed just like she was frightened of something. 'I'll change all this,' I say, 'and do it up, or, perhaps, even buy another house before the wedding.' 'No-no,' she says, 'nothing must be changed here, we'll live like this. I want to live at your mother's side,' she says, 'when I become your wife.' I took her to my mother—she was respectful to her, as if she had been her own daughter. Even before this, some two years now, Mother had not been entirely in her right mind (she's ill), and since my father died, she's become quite like a baby: she can't talk, she can't walk, and only bows from her place to everyone she sees; it seems if we didn't feed her, she wouldn't notice it for three days. I took Mother's right hand, folded her fingers: 'Bless her, Mother,' I say, 'she's going to the altar with me'; she kissed my mother's hand with such feeling then; 'Your mother,' says she, 'must have had a great deal of sorrow to bear.' She saw this book here in my room: 'What, have you begun reading *Russian History*?' (And she had said to me herself once, in Moscow: 'You should civilize yourself at least in some way, you might at least read Solovyev's *Russian History*, why, you know nothing at all.') 'That's a good thing you're doing,' she says, 'keep at it, read. I'll write you a list myself of the books you ought to read first of all; do you want me to?' And never, never before had she talked to me like that, so that she even amazed me; for the first time I breathed like a living man."

"I am very glad of that, Parfyon," said the prince with sincere feeling, "very glad. Who knows, after all perhaps God will bring you together."

"That will never be!" Rogozhin cried hotly.

"Listen, Parfyon, if you love her so, wouldn't you want to gain her respect? And if you want to, then don't you have some hope? I said before that it's a strange riddle to me: why is she marrying you? But though I can't solve it, I have no doubt that there must be a sufficient, sensible reason. She is convinced of your love; but she must be convinced of some of your good qualities also. Why, it can't be otherwise! What you said just now confirms this. You told me yourself that she has found it possible to speak to you in quite a different way from how she has spoken and behaved to you before. You are suspicious and jealous, and that has made you exaggerate everything you've noticed amiss. Of course she doesn't think so ill of you as you say. Otherwise it would mean that in marrying you she was deliberately throwing herself in the river or under the knife. Is that possible? Who throws themselves deliberately in the river or under the knife?"

Parfyon heard out the prince's fervent words with a bitter smile. His conviction, it seemed, had already been unshakably established.

"How dreadfully you look at me now, Parfyon!" broke from the prince with a feeling of dread.

"In the river or under the knife!" uttered the other at last. "Ha! Why, that's just why she is marrying me, because she expects the knife from me! Why, can it be, Prince, that you still haven't grasped what it's all about?"

"I don't understand you."

"Well, perhaps you really don't understand, he, he! They do say about you that you're . . . *not quite right*. She loves another—take that in! Just as I love her now, she loves another man now. And do you know who that other man is? It's *you*! What, you didn't know?"

"Me!"

"You. She has loved you ever since that day—her birthday. Only she thinks it's impossible to marry you, because supposedly she would disgrace you and ruin your whole life. 'Everyone knows what I am,' she says. She still harps on that herself to this day. She told me all this straight to my face. She's afraid of ruining and disgracing you, but as for me, it seems, that's no matter, she can marry me—that's how much she honors me, take note of that too!"

"But why did she run away from you to me and . . . from me . . ."

"And from you to me! Ha! Why, who knows what will come into her head all of a sudden! She is always in a sort of fever now. One day she'll cry out: 'Marrying you is like drowning myself. Let's make haste with the wedding!' She hurries things on herself, fixes the day, but when the time comes near—she takes fright, or her thoughts take a different course—God knows, you've seen it yourself: she weeps and laughs and shakes with fever. And what is there strange in her having run away from you? She ran away from you then because she realized herself how much she loves you. It was too much for her with you. You said just now that I sought her out in Moscow; that's not true—she ran from you straight to me herself: 'Fix the day,' she says, 'I'm ready! Break out the champagne! Let's go to the gypsies! . . .' she cries! . . . Why, if it were not for me, she would have thrown herself in the river long ago; that's the truth. She hasn't thrown herself in because, perhaps, I'm even more dreadful than the water. It's from spite that she's marrying me . . . If she marries me, I tell you for sure, it will be *from spite*."

"But how can you . . . how can you! . . ." exclaimed the prince, but did not finish. He looked at Rogozhin with horror.

"Well, why don't you finish?" added the other, grinning. "If you like, I'll tell you what you're thinking to yourself at this very moment: 'And how can she be his wife now? How can she be allowed to come to that?' It's clear what you're thinking . . ."

"It was not for that I came here, Parfyon, I tell you, that's not what I had in my mind . . ."

"It may be it was not for that and not with that in mind, but only now it has certainly become for that, he-he! Well, enough! Why have you gotten so upset? Why, can you really not have known it? You amaze me!"

"That's all jealousy, Parfyon, it's all sickness, you've exaggerated it all immeasurably . . ." muttered the prince in extreme agitation, "what's with you?"

"Leave it," said Parfyon, and quickly snatched from the prince's hand a little knife, which the latter had picked up from the table, and put it down again in its former place, beside the book.

"It's as if I had known as I was approaching Petersburg, as though I had a presentiment . . ." the prince went on. "I didn't want to come here! I wanted to forget everything here, to root it out of my heart! Well, farewell . . . But what's with you!"

While he was speaking, the prince had absentmindedly again

grabbed from the table the same little knife, and again Rogozhin took it out of his hands and threw it on the table. It was a rather simple form of knife, with a buck-horn handle, nonfolding, with a blade some six inches long and a corresponding width.

Seeing that the prince had given particular attention to the fact that this knife had been twice torn from his hands, Rogozhin snatched it up in angry vexation, put it in the book and flung the book on another table.

"You cut the pages with it, do you?"[23] asked the prince, but somehow absentmindedly, as if still in a state of deep contemplation.

"Yes, the pages . . ."

"But it's a garden knife, you know."

"Yes, it's a garden knife. Can't one cut a book with a garden knife?"

"But it's . . . quite new."

"Well, and what of it that it's new? Can't I buy a new knife now?" Rogozhin exclaimed at last in some kind of frenzy, becoming more irritated with every word.

The prince shuddered and looked at Rogozhin intently.

"Ach, look at us!" he laughed suddenly, recovering himself completely. "Excuse me, brother, when my head is as heavy as it is now, and this illness . . . I become so utterly, utterly absentminded and ridiculous. I wanted to ask you about something entirely different . . . I don't remember what. Farewell . . ."

"Not that way," said Rogozhin.

"I've forgotten!"

"This way, this way, come, I'll show you."

I V

They went through the same rooms that the prince had already passed through; Rogozhin walked a little ahead, the prince behind him. They came into a big room. Here, on the walls, were several pictures, all of them portraits of bishops and landscapes in which nothing could be distinguished. Over the door leading into the next room there hung a picture rather strange in shape, about two yards long and no more than

23. In the nineteenth century, books were sold with uncut pages, so that readers of a new volume would have to cut the edges open as they read.

a foot high. It was a painting of our Savior who had just been taken from the cross. The prince glanced at it briefly, as if recalling something, but he did not stop and wanted to pass through the door. He felt very heavy at heart and wanted to get out of this house as soon as possible. But Rogozhin suddenly stopped before the picture.

"All these pictures here," he said, "my late father, who bought them for a ruble or two at auctions, was fond of. A connoisseur looked them all over; rubbish, he said, but that one—that painting over the door, which was bought for a couple of rubles too, that, he says, is not rubbish. When my father was still alive, a man turned up that offered three hundred and fifty rubles for it, and Ivan Dimitrich Savelyev, a merchant with a hankering for pictures, went up to four hundred for it, and last week he even offered my brother Semyon Semyonych five hundred. I've kept it for myself."

"Why, it's . . . it's a copy of a Hans Holbein," said the prince, having had time to examine the picture, "and though I'm no great expert, it seems to be an excellent copy. I saw the picture abroad and I can't forget it. But . . . what's the matter . . ."

Rogozhin suddenly left the picture and went on along his previous path. No doubt his preoccupation and the peculiarly irritable mood that had so suddenly manifested itself in Rogozhin might have, perhaps, explained this abruptness; still, the prince found it rather strange that the conversation, which had not even been started by him, after all, should have been broken off so suddenly, and that Rogozhin did not even answer him.

"But what I've long wanted, Lev Nikolaevich, to ask you is, do you believe in God or not?" Rogozhin suddenly spoke up again after having gone a few steps.

"How strangely you ask and . . . stare!" observed the prince involuntarily.

"But I like looking at this picture," Rogozhin muttered after a moment's silence, just as if he had forgotten his question again.

"At this picture!" the prince suddenly exclaimed, struck by a sudden thought. "At this picture! Why, that picture might make some people lose their faith!"

"Well, that's just what it's doing," Rogozhin assented unexpectedly. They had already reached the front door.

"What?" the prince stopped short. "Why, what are you saying! I was almost joking, and you are so serious! And what did you ask me for, whether I believe in God?"

"Oh, nothing, just like that. I meant to ask you before. Many people don't believe nowadays, you know. And say, is it true (you've lived abroad, after all)—some fellow in his cups told me that here, in Russia, there are more such people what don't believe in God than in all other lands? 'It's easier for us,' he says, 'than for them, because we have gone further than they have . . .'"

Rogozhin chuckled caustically; having spoken his question, he suddenly opened the door and, holding on to the handle of the lock, waited for the prince to go out. The prince wondered at this, but went out. The other went out after him onto the landing of the stair and closed the door behind him. They both stood facing one another with such a look about them that it seemed both had forgotten where they were and what they had to do next.

"Farewell, then," said the prince, holding out his hand.

"Farewell," uttered Rogozhin, firmly but entirely mechanically pressing the hand that was held out to him.

The prince went down one step and turned around.

"As to the question of faith," he began, smiling (evidently not wishing to leave Rogozhin like that) and, in addition, brightening up at a sudden recollection, "as to the question of faith, last week I had four different encounters in two days. One morning I was riding a new railway line and talked for four hours with a certain Mr. S—— in the carriage, made his acquaintance on the spot. He really is a very learned man, and I was delighted at the prospect of talking to a really learned man. On top of that, he is a most unusually well-bred man, so that he talked to me quite as if I were his equal in knowledge and understanding. He doesn't believe in God. Only, one thing astounded me: that it was as if he were not talking about that at all, the whole time, and it astounded me precisely because previously, too, whenever I have met with unbelievers before, or read such books, it always seemed to me that they speak and write in their books not about that at all, although at first glance it may seem to be about that. I said so to him at the time, but it must be that I expressed myself unclearly or did not know how to do it, for he understood nothing in the end . . . In the evening, I stopped for the night at a provincial hotel, and a murder had just been committed there the night before, so that everyone was talking about it when I arrived. Two peasants, of considerable age, and not drunk either, who had known each other for a long time, were pals, had been drinking tea and were meaning to go to bed together in the same little room. But one had noticed during those last two days that the other had a watch, a silver one on a yellow bead chain, which he had apparently not seen on him before. The man was not a thief, was even an honest man, and by a peasant's standard not at all poor. But he was so taken by this watch, and it tempted him to such an extent, that, at last, he could not stand it: he took a knife, and when his friend had turned away, he approached him cautiously from behind, took aim, cast his eyes heavenward, crossed himself and, praying bitterly to himself—'Lord, forgive me for Christ's sake!'—he cut his friend's throat in one stroke like a lamb, and took his watch."

Rogozhin broke out in peals of laughter. He roared as if he were in some kind of fit. It was positively strange to see such laughter after such a gloomy recent mood.

"Why, I love it! No, but that beats everything!" he cried out convulsively, practically gasping for breath. "The one doesn't believe in God at all, while the other believes so much that he even murders men with a prayer ... No, my dear prince, you can't make that up! Ha-ha-ha! No, that beats everything! ..."

"Next morning, I went out to wander about the town," the prince went on as soon as Rogozhin quieted down, though the laughter still quivered spasmodically and convulsively on his lips. "I see staggering along the wooden pavement a drunken soldier in an utterly disordered state. He comes up to me: 'Buy a silver cross, sir, I'll give it to you for a mere *dvugrivennyi*;[24] it's silver!' In his hand I see a cross—and he must have just taken it off his own neck—on a very worn-out blue little ribbon, only it was really just a tin one, you could see it at first glance, large in size, eight-cornered, covered in a Byzantine pattern. I took out a *dvugrivennyi* and gave it to him, and put the cross around my neck at once—and it was evident from his face how pleased he was that he had pulled one over on a stupid gentleman, and he went off immediately to drink his cross away, there was no doubt about that. At that time, brother, I was quite carried away by the rush of impressions that burst upon me in Russia; I had understood nothing of her before, grew up

24. A twenty-kopeck coin.

just like a senseless mute, and recollected her in some fantastic way during those five years abroad. Well, I walked on then and thought: no, I'll wait before I judge this Christ-seller. God only knows what's hidden in those drunken and weak hearts. An hour later, when I was going back to the hotel, I came upon a peasant woman with an infant. The woman was still quite young, the baby about six weeks old. The baby smiled at her, the first time since its birth by the looks of it. I saw her suddenly cross herself with great devoutness. 'What is it, my child?' I say (I was always asking questions then, you know). 'Why,' she says, 'just as there's a mother's joy when she notices her baby's first smile, that's just the joy that God has too, every time he sees from heaven that a sinner is praying to him with all his heart.' That was what the woman said to me almost in those words, and such a deep, subtle and truly religious thought, such a thought, in which all the essence of Christianity is expressed at once, that is, the whole conception of God as our own Father and of the joy God takes in man, like a father in his own child—the most fundamental idea of Christ! A simple peasant woman! . . . True, she was a mother . . . and who knows, perhaps that woman was the wife of that same soldier. Listen, Parfyon. You asked me a question before, here is my answer: the essence of religious feeling does not fall under the province of any reasoning, or any crimes and misdemeanors, or any atheist doctrines; there's something else here, and it will always be something else; there is something that the atheist doctrines will eternally glide over and they will eternally be speaking *of something else.* But the chief thing is that you will notice it more clearly and quickly in the Russian heart, and here is my conclusion! This is one of the foremost of my convictions, which I take away from our Russia. There is work to be done, Parfyon! There is work to be done in our Russian world, believe me! Remember how we used to get together in Moscow and talk once, you and I . . . And I didn't want to come back here at all now! And it was not at all, not at all like this that I thought to meet with you! Oh, well! . . . Good-bye, till we meet again! May God be with you!"

He turned and went down the stairs.

"Lev Nikolaevich!" Parfyon shouted from above when the prince had reached the first half-landing, "that cross, the one you bought from the soldier, is it on you?"

"Yes, it's on me."

And the prince stopped again.

"Let's have a look at it."

Here was another new oddity! He thought a moment, went upstairs again, and pulled his cross out for him to see without taking it off his neck.

"Let me have it," said Rogozhin.

"What for? Why would you . . ."

The prince would not have liked to part with this cross.

"I'll wear it, and give mine to you, you wear it."

"You want to exchange crosses? Certainly, Parfyon, if that's so, I'm delighted; we'll be brothers!"

The prince took off his tin cross, Parfyon his gold one, and they exchanged them. Parfyon was silent. With heavy-hearted surprise, the prince noted that the former mistrustfulness, the former bitter and almost mocking smile still did not seem to leave the face of his adopted brother; at moments, at least, it plainly manifested itself. In silence, Rogozhin at last took the prince's hand and stood for some time as if unable to make up his mind about something; at last, he suddenly drew him after himself, uttering in a scarcely audible voice, "Come along." They crossed the landing of the first floor and rang at the door facing the one they had come out of. It was soon opened to them. An old woman, all hunched over and wearing a black knitted kerchief, bowed down to Rogozhin deeply and silently; the latter quickly asked her something, and not stopping for the answer led the prince on through the rooms. Again there was a series of dark rooms, of an extraordinarily cold cleanliness, coldly and severely furnished with old-fashioned furniture under clean white covers. Without announcing himself, Rogozhin led the prince straight into a smallish room resembling a drawing room, partitioned by a polished mahogany screen with doors at each end, behind which was probably a bedroom. In the corner of the drawing room, by the stove, a little old lady was sitting in an armchair, not exactly very old in appearance, and even with a fairly healthy, pleasant round face, but already gone completely gray and (it could be seen at first glance) fallen back completely into childhood. She was wearing a black woolen dress, a large black kerchief around her neck, and a neat white cap with black ribbons. Her feet were resting on a footstool. Next to her sat another neat little old lady, rather older than she, also in mourning and also wearing a white cap—no doubt some sort of companion—who was silently knitting a stocking. The two of them, no doubt, were always silent. The first little old lady, seeing Rogozhin and the prince, smiled to them and nodded her head several times kindly as a sign of her pleasure.

"Mother," said Rogozhin, kissing her hand, "this is my great friend, Prince Lev Nikolaevich Myshkin. We've exchanged crosses, he and I; he was like my own brother to me in Moscow for a time, did a great deal for me. Bless him, Mother, as you would bless your own son. Wait, dear old lady, like this, let me fold your hand . . ."

But the little old lady, before Parfyon had time to touch her, raised her right hand, put her two fingers against her thumb and three times devoutly made the sign of the cross over the prince. Then she kindly and affectionately nodded her head to him again.

"Well, let's go, Lev Nikolaevich," said Parfyon, "I only brought you here for that . . ."

When they came out onto the staircase again, he added:

"You know, she understands nothing that's said to her, and understood nothing of my words, but she blessed you; that means she wanted to do it herself . . . Well, good-bye, it's time to be going, for me and you both."

And he opened his door.

"Well, at least let me embrace you in parting, you strange fellow!" exclaimed the prince, looking at him with tender reproach, and would have embraced him. But Parfyon had scarcely raised his arms when he let them fall again at once. He could not bring himself to it; he turned away so as not to look at the prince. He did not want to embrace him.

"Have no fear! Though I've taken your cross, I won't murder you for your watch!" he muttered indistinctly, laughing suddenly in some strange way. But suddenly his whole face changed; he turned horribly pale, his lips quivered, his eyes glowed. He raised his arms, embraced the prince firmly and, gasping for breath, uttered:

"Well, take her then, since it's fate! She's yours! I yield! . . . Remember Rogozhin!"

And, turning from the prince, without looking at him, he hurriedly went into his apartment and slammed the door after him.

V

It was by now late, almost half past two, and the prince did not find Epanchin at home. Leaving a card, he made up his mind to go to the hotel Scales and inquire for Kolya there; and if he were not there, to leave a note for him. At the Scales they told him that Nikolai Ardalionovich "had gone out still in the morning, sir, but upon going out had left word that in case anyone came asking for him, they were to say that by three o'clock he might be back, sir. And if he were not here by half past three, it would mean that he had gone to Pavlovsk by train, to Madame Epanchin's dacha, sir, and would therefore dine there, sir." The prince sat down to wait for him and, as he was there, asked for dinner.

By half past three and even by four, Kolya had not made an appearance. The prince went out and headed mechanically wherever his eyes would lead him. At the beginning of the summer in Petersburg there are sometimes exquisite days—bright, still and hot. As if by design, this day was one of those rare days. For some time, the prince wandered aimlessly. The city was little known to him. He stopped sometimes at street crossings in front of certain houses, in squares, on bridges; once he went into a confectioner's to rest. Sometimes he would begin to examine the passersby with great curiosity, but most often he noticed neither the passersby nor just where he was going. He was in a torturous state of tension and agitation and at the same time felt an extraordinary craving for solitude. He longed to be alone and to give himself up quite passively to this agonizing tension, without seeking the slightest way out. He was utterly averse to resolving the questions that had rushed in a flood into his heart and his mind. "How then, am I to blame for all this?" he muttered to himself, almost unconscious of his own words.

Toward six o'clock he found himself on the platform of the Tsarskoe Selo railway line. The solitude had soon become unbearable for him; a new impulse fervently seized his heart, and for a moment, the darkness in which his soul languished was illuminated with a bright light. He took a ticket to Pavlovsk and was in an impatient hurry to set off; but, of course, he was pursued by something, and this was a reality and not a fantasy, as he may have been inclined to believe. He had almost taken his seat on the train when he suddenly flung the ticket he had only just taken on the floor and went back out of the station, confused and pensive. Some time later, in the street, he seemed suddenly to recall something, he seemed all at once to grasp something very strange, something that had long worried him. He suddenly happened to consciously catch himself engaged in a certain pursuit that had already been occupying him for a long time, but of which he had not been aware till that minute: for some hours previously, even at the Scales, and it would seem even before the Scales, he had suddenly, at intervals, begun looking around him for something. And he would forget it, even for a long while, half an hour at a time, and then suddenly turn about again and search all around uneasily.

But he had no sooner observed in himself this morbid and till then quite unconscious impulse, which had taken hold of him for so long, when there flashed before him another recollection that interested him extremely: he remembered that in the same moment when he noticed that he kept looking for something all around him, he was standing on the sidewalk before a shop window examining with great interest the wares displayed in the window. He wanted now, without fail, to verify: had he really stood just now, perhaps only five minutes before, in front of the window of that shop, had he not imagined it, had he not mixed something up? Did that shop and those goods in fact exist? Indeed, he was in fact in a particularly morbid frame of mind that day, almost in the same frame of mind that used to come over him formerly, at the onset of the attacks of his former illness. He knew that at such times, before the attacks, he would be exceptionally absent-minded, and often even mixed up things and faces, if he did not look at them with particular, strained attention. But there was also a particular reason why he wanted so much to verify whether he really had been standing then before that shop: among the things laid out on display in the shop window, there was one thing he had looked at, and had even put the price of it at sixty kopecks silver; he remembered this in spite of all his absentmindedness and agitation. Consequently, if that shop existed and that thing really was displayed among the wares, he must have stopped specifically to look at that thing. So this thing must have held such a great interest for him that it attracted his attention even at the time when he was in such terrible confusion, just after he had come out of the railway station. He walked looking to the right, almost in misery, and his heart beat with uneasy impatience. But here was the shop, he had found it at last! He had already been five hundred paces from it when he had gotten it into his head to turn back. And there was the article worth sixty kopecks; "certainly, sixty kopecks, it's not worth more!" he confirmed now and laughed. But he laughed hysterically; he became very heavy-hearted. He remembered clearly now that on this very spot, standing here before this window, he had suddenly turned around, just as he had done earlier when he caught Rogozhin's eyes fixed upon him. Having assured himself that he was not mistaken (of which, actually, he had felt quite sure even before he verified it), he left the shop and walked quickly away from it. All this had to be pondered over as soon as possible, without fail; it was clear now that it had not been his fancy at the station either, that, without fail, something real had happened to him, and, without fail, it was related to all of his previous unease. But some kind of insuperable inner loathing prevailed again: he did not want to ponder over anything, and he did not ponder; he fell to musing on something quite different.

He mused among other things about the fact that in his epileptic state, there was one stage, almost right before the fit itself (only if the fit came on while he was awake), when suddenly, in the midst of sadness, spiritual darkness and oppression, his brain seemed at moments to become aflame, and with an extraordinary burst, all his vital forces suddenly exerted themselves to the utmost all at once. The sense of life, the consciousness of self, were multiplied almost tenfold at these moments, which passed like a flash of lightning. His mind, his heart were suffused with extraordinary light; all his uneasiness, all his doubts, all his anxieties were as if put to rest at once, resolving themselves in a kind of higher serenity, full of luminous, harmonious joy and hope. But these moments, these flashes, were only the presentiment of that final second (never more than a second) with which the fit itself began. That second was, of course, unendurable. Thinking of that moment later, when he was well again, he often said to himself that all these lightning bolts and flashes of the highest self-awareness and self-consciousness, and, so it would seem, of the "highest form of existence" as well, were nothing but disease, the disturbance of a normal state; and if so, it was not at all the highest form of existence, but on the contrary must be considered among the very lowest. And yet, after all, he came at last to an extremely paradoxical conclusion: "What of it, if it is disease?" he decided at last. "What does it matter that this intensity is abnormal, if the result, if the minute of sensation, remembered and analyzed afterward in a healthy state, turns out to be the acme of harmony and beauty, and gives a heretofore unheard-of and undivined feeling of completeness, of proportion, of reconciliation, and of ecstatic worshipful fusion with the highest synthesis of life?" These vague expressions seemed to him very comprehensible, though still too weak. That it really was "beauty and worship," that it really was the "highest synthesis of life" he could not doubt, and could not admit the possibility of doubt. Why, it was not as though he dreamt visions of some sort at that moment, abnormal and unreal, as from hashish, opium or wine, debasing the reason and distorting the soul. He was quite capable of judging that when the attack was over. These moments were nothing but an extraordinary intensification of self-consciousness—if the state was to be expressed in one word—of self-consciousness and at the same time of the most direct possible sensation of self. If at that second, that is at the very last conscious moment before the fit, he had time to say to himself clearly and consciously: "Yes, for this moment one might give one's whole life!" then, certainly, that moment in itself was really worth the whole of life. However, he did not insist on the dialectical part of his conclusion: stupefaction, spiritual darkness, idiocy stood before him as vivid consequences of these "higher moments"; seriously, of course, he could not have disputed it. In his conclusion—that is in his estimate of that minute—there was undoubtedly a mistake, but the reality of the sensation still somewhat perplexed him. What, indeed, was he to make of that reality? For, after all, the very thing had happened; he had actually had time to say to himself in that very second that this second, for the infinite happiness he had fully felt, might well be worth the whole of life. "At that moment," as he once told Rogozhin in Moscow, at the time when they used to get together there, "at that moment I seem somehow to understand the extraordinary saying that *there shall be no more time.* Probably," he added, smiling, "this is the very second in which the epileptic Mohammed's upset pitcher of water had not had time to spill, though he had had the time, in that same second, to survey all the habitations of Allah."[25] Yes, he and Rogozhin had often gotten together in Moscow, and they had not talked only of this. "Rogozhin said earlier that I had been a brother to him then; he said that for the first time today," the prince thought to himself.

He thought this, sitting on a bench under a tree in the Summer Garden. It was about seven o'clock. The Garden was empty; something dark covered up the setting sun for an instant. It was sultry; it looked like there was a distant presaging of a thunderstorm. In his present contemplative mood it was a kind of lure for him. He latched on to every external object about him with his recollections and his mind, and he found pleasure in it: he kept wanting to forget something present and vital; but at the first glance about him he was aware again at once of his gloomy thought, the thought he was so longing to get away from. He started to recall that he had talked at dinner to the waiter at the restaurant of a recent, extremely strange murder, which had caused a great stir and much talk. But he had no sooner recollected it than something peculiar happened to him again.

An extraordinary, irresistible desire, almost a temptation, suddenly paralyzed all his will. He got up from the bench and walked from the Garden straight toward the Petersburg side.[26] Earlier, on the bank of the Neva, he had asked some passerby to point out to him across the river the Petersburg side. It was pointed out to him; but he had not gone there then. And in any case it would have been useless to go that day; he knew that. He had long had the address; he could easily find the house of Lebedev's relation; but he knew almost for certain that he would not find her at home. "She is gone to Pavlovsk for sure, or Kolya would have left some word at the Scales, as agreed." And so, if he went there now, then, of course, it was not in order to see her. A different, dark, tormenting curiosity tempted him now. A new, sudden idea had come into his mind . . .

But it was more than enough for him that he had set off and that he

25. This is a reference to an incident in the life of the Prophet Mohammed, the founder of Islam, in which Mohammed was visited in the night by the Archangel Gabriel and taken on a wondrous journey from Mecca to Jerusalem and then to heaven, where he conversed with God. Upon his return, he managed to catch and stop from spilling a pitcher of water that Gabriel had knocked over with his wings.

26. The part of St. Petersburg that lies on the north bank of the Neva, in the vicinity of the Peter and Paul Fortress.

knew where he was going: a minute later he was walking along again taking almost no notice of the way. Further consideration of his "sudden idea" became at once terribly distasteful to him and almost impossible. He peered with torturously strained attention at everything that his eye happened upon, gazed at the sky, at the Neva. He started to speak to a little boy he encountered. Perhaps his epileptic condition was also growing more and more acute. The storm, it seemed, was actually gathering, though slowly. It was beginning to thunder far away. It was becoming very sultry . . .

For some reason, Lebedev's nephew, whom he had seen earlier, kept popping into his mind now, as an incessant and stupidly tiresome musical motif can sometimes pop into one's mind. What was strange was that he kept popping into his mind in the form of that murderer, whom Lebedev himself had mentioned earlier while introducing his nephew to him. Yes, he had read about that murderer only a little while ago. He had read and heard much about such things since he had been in Russia; he followed all this persistently. And earlier, he had been almost too interested in his talk with the waiter about just that same murder of the Zhemarins. The waiter agreed with him, he remembered that. He remembered the waiter, too; he was not a dumb lad, staid and fastidious; but "on the other hand, God only knows what he is like. It's hard to make new people out in a new land." In the Russian soul, however, he was beginning to have a passionate faith. Oh, there was much, much he had endured in those six months that had been quite new to him, unguessed, unheard-of and unexpected! But the soul of another is a dark place, and the Russian soul is a dark place; a dark place for many. He had long been close with Rogozhin, for instance, intimately close, close like "brothers"—but did he know Rogozhin? And actually, what chaos, what a muddle, what hideousness is found here sometimes in all this! And what a repulsive and self-satisfied little pimple that nephew of Lebedev's was! But then, what am I saying? (the prince went on dreaming), was it he who killed those creatures, those six people? I seem to be mixing it up . . . How strange it is! My head seems to be spinning . . . But what a charming, what a sweet face Lebedev's eldest daughter had—the one who was standing with the baby—what an innocent, what an almost childish expression and what an almost childish laugh! Strange that he had nearly forgotten that face and only remembered it now. Lebedev, who stamped his feet at them, probably adored them all. But what was most certain, like two times two, was that Lebedev adored his nephew too!

But then again, how could he venture to judge them so finally, he who had only arrived that day; how could he pronounce such verdicts? Why, hadn't Lebedev posed a riddle to him that day: well, had he expected such a Lebedev? Had he known a Lebedev like that before? Lebedev and du Barry—heavens! Anyway, if Rogozhin did commit murder, at least he would not murder with such disorder. There would not be such chaos. A weapon made to order after a pattern[27] and six people mowed down in complete delirium . . . Why, had Rogozhin a weapon made to order after a pattern . . . He had a . . . but . . . had it been decided that Rogozhin would commit murder?! The prince suddenly started. "Isn't it a crime, isn't it baseness on my part to make such a supposition with cynical openness!" he exclaimed, and a flush of shame instantly flooded his face. He was astounded, he stood in the road as if rooted to the spot. He remembered all at once the Pavlovsk station earlier and the Nikolaievsky station earlier, and the question asked right to Rogozhin's face about the *eyes,* and Rogozhin's cross, which he was wearing now, and the blessing of his mother, to whom Rogozhin had taken him himself, and that last convulsive embrace, Rogozhin's last renunciation, earlier, on the stairs—and after all that, to catch himself on an incessant search for something about him, and that shop and that object . . . what baseness! And, after all that, he was going now with a "particular purpose," with a particular "sudden idea"! Despair and anguish seized his entire soul. The prince wanted to turn back immediately and go home to the hotel; he even turned around and began walking, but a minute later he stopped, reflected, and went back again along his previous path.

Yes, he was already on the Petersburg side, he was near the house; but you see, it was not with that same purpose he was going there now; it was not with that "particular idea"! And how could it be? Yes, his illness was returning, there was no doubt of that; perhaps he would even have the fit that very day. All this darkness was owing to the fit; "the idea," too, was owing to the fit! Now the darkness was dispelled, the demon driven away, doubt did not exist, there was joy in his heart!

---

27. In preparation for the crime, the murderer of the Zhemarin family had a weapon—something like a mace—made to order to his specific design.

And—it was so long since he had seen *her,* he needed to see her, and . . . Yes, he would have liked to meet Rogozhin now; he would have taken him by the hand and they would have gone together . . . His heart was pure; he wasn't Rogozhin's rival, was he? The next day he would go himself and tell Rogozhin that he had seen her; why, he had flown here, as Rogozhin said earlier, simply to see her! Perhaps he would find her there; why, it was not certain after all that she was at Pavlovsk!

Yes, all this must be established clearly now, so that all might read clearly into one another, so that there might be no more such gloomy and passionate renunciations like the recent renunciation of Rogozhin's; and let all this be realized freely and . . . in the light. Hadn't Rogozhin the capacity for light? He said he did not love her like that, that he had no compassion, "not an ounce of such pity in me." It's true he had added afterward that "your pity is perhaps greater than my love"—but he had been slandering himself. Hm! . . . Rogozhin at a book—was not that "pity," was it not the beginning of "pity"? Did not the very presence of that book demonstrate that he was fully conscious of his attitude to *her?* And the story he told earlier? No, that was deeper than mere passion. And does her face instill no more than passion? Why, can that face indeed instill passion now? It instills suffering, it clutches the whole soul, it . . . and a burning, agonizing memory suddenly passed through the prince's heart.

Yes, agonizing. He remembered how he had agonized not long ago when first he had noticed in her signs of insanity. Then he had been almost in despair. And how could he have left her when she ran away from him back then to Rogozhin? He ought to have run after her himself instead of waiting for news of her. But . . . was it possible Rogozhin had not yet noticed the insanity in her? Hm . . . Rogozhin sees other causes in everything, passionate causes! And what insane jealousy! What did he mean to say by that supposition of his earlier? (The prince suddenly flushed and something seemed to shudder in his heart.)

But anyway, what use was it to remember that? There was insanity on both sides here. And for him, the prince, to love that woman passionately—it was almost unthinkable, it would have been almost cruelty, inhumanity. Yes, yes! No, Rogozhin was slandering himself; he had a great heart that could suffer and be compassionate. Once he finds out the whole truth, and once he is convinced what a piteous creature that broken, half-mad woman was—wouldn't he forgive her then all the past, all his agonies? Wouldn't he become her servant, her brother, her friend, her Providence? Compassion would teach even Rogozhin and awaken his mind. Compassion is the chief and perhaps only law of all humanity. Ah, how unpardonably and dishonorably he had wronged Rogozhin! No, it was not that "the Russian soul was a dark place," but that in his own soul there was darkness, if he could imagine such horrors. Because of a few warm words from the heart in Moscow, Rogozhin had called him his brother, while he ... But that was sickness and delirium! That would all resolve itself! ... How gloomily Rogozhin had said earlier that he was "losing his faith"! That man must be suffering terribly. He said that he "liked looking at that picture"; he does not like it, rather, it means that he feels a need. Rogozhin is not merely a passionate soul; he is a fighter, after all: he wants to get back his lost faith by force. He needs it now to an agonizing point ... Yes! to believe in something! To believe in someone! But how strange that picture of Holbein's was, though ... Ah, here is the street! And that must be the house, so it is, No. 16, "the house of Madame Collegial Secretary Filisov."[28] Here! The prince rang and asked for Nastasya Filippovna.

The mistress of the house herself answered him that Nastasya Filippovna had gone to Pavlovsk that morning to stay with Darya Alexeevna, "and it might even come to pass, sir, that she will stay there some days." Filisov was a little, sharp-eyed, sharp-faced woman, about forty, with a sly and watchful expression. When she asked for his name—a question to which she seemed intentionally to lend an air of secrecy—the prince was at first unwilling to answer; but he turned back at once and asked her urgently to give his name to Nastasya Filippovna. Filisov received this insistence with increased attention and an extraordinary air of secrecy, by which she evidently wished to announce, "Set your mind at rest; I understand, sir." The prince's name obviously made a very great impression on her. The prince looked absentmindedly at her, turned, and went back to his hotel. But he left with quite a different look from the one he wore when he rang at Filisov's door. Once again, and as if in a single instance, an extraordinary change had come over him: he walked along once more pale, weak,

28. Collegial Secretary: level X civil service rank (in Imperial Russia, all military and civil service posts were ranked according to a table of fourteen ranks, with I being the lowest and XIV the highest).

suffering, agitated; his knees trembled and a vague bewildered smile hovered about his blue lips: his "sudden idea" had suddenly been confirmed and justified, and—he believed in his demon again!

But was it confirmed? But was it justified? Why that shiver again, that cold sweat, that darkness and chill in his soul? Was it because he had again, just now, seen those *eyes*? But he had gone out of the Summer Garden for the sole purpose of seeing them! That was, indeed, what his "sudden idea" consisted in. He had insistently desired to see "those eyes of late," so as to be ultimately convinced that he would meet them *there*, at that house. He had desired it feverishly, and why was he so crushed and astounded now by the fact that he had actually just seen them? As though he had not expected it! Yes, those were the *same eyes* (and there could be no doubt now that they were the *same eyes*) that had gleamed at him in the morning, in the crowd, when he was getting out of the train on the Nikolaevsky railway; they were the same (absolutely the same!) whose gaze he had caught later on, behind his back, just as he was sitting down at Rogozhin's recently. Rogozhin had denied it at the time: he had asked with a twisted and chilling smile, "Whose eyes were they?" And the prince had had an intense desire, not long ago, at the station of the Tsarskoe Selo railway—when he was getting into the carriage to go down to see Aglaia, and suddenly caught sight of those eyes again, for the third time that day—to go up to Rogozhin and tell *him* "whose eyes" they were! But he had run out of the station and had come to himself only in front of the cutler's shop, at the moment when he was standing there and pricing at sixty kopecks a certain object with a buck-horn handle. A strange and dreadful demon had got hold of him for good and would not let him go again. That demon had whispered to him in the Summer Garden, as he sat lost in thought under a linden tree, that if Rogozhin had felt such a need to follow him from early morning and to dog his every footstep, then, having found that he was not going to Pavlovsk (which was, of course, a fatal bit of news for Rogozhin), Rogozhin would, without fail, go *there*, to that house on the Petersburg side, and would, without fail, lie in wait there for him, the prince, who had given him his word of honor only that morning that he would "not see her" and that he had not come to Petersburg "for that." And here was the prince hurrying feverishly to that house, and what is there in it if he really did meet Rogozhin there? He had seen only an unhappy man whose state of mind was gloomy, but very easy to understand. That unhappy man did not even conceal himself now. Yes, earlier Rogozhin had for some reason refused to confess it and told a lie, but at the station he stood almost without concealing himself. Indeed, it was rather he, the prince, who had concealed himself, and not Rogozhin. And now, at the house, he stood on the other side of the street, some fifty paces away catercorner, on the opposite sidewalk, with his arms folded, and waited. Here, he was already entirely in plain view and, it seemed, wanted to be in plain view on purpose. He stood like an accuser and a judge and not like . . . But not like what?

And why had he, the prince, not gone up to him now himself, and instead turned away from him, as though having noticed nothing, though their eyes had met? (Yes, their eyes had met! and they had looked at one another.) Why, hadn't he himself wanted, just recently, to take him by the hand and go *there* together with him? Why, hadn't he himself meant to go to him next day and tell him he had been to see her? Why, hadn't he himself renounced his demon while still heading there, halfway along the way, when joy had suddenly flooded his soul? Or was there really something in Rogozhin—that is, in the whole image of the man *that day*, in all his words, movements, actions, looks, taken in their entirety, that could justify the prince's awful misgivings and the outrageous whisperings of his demon? Something of the sort that is evident all of itself, but is difficult to analyze and describe, impossible to justify on sufficient grounds, but which nonetheless makes, despite all this difficulty and impossibility, an utterly complete and irresistible impression that passes involuntarily into absolute conviction? . . .

Conviction—of what? (Oh, how the prince was tortured by the monstrosity, the "baseness" of this conviction, of "that base foreboding," and how he condemned himself!) "Say, then, if you dare, of what?"—he kept telling himself incessantly with reproach and challenge—"formulate, dare to express your entire thought, clearly, precisely, without faltering! Oh, I am ignoble!"—he repeated with indignation and a flush on his face—"and with what eyes shall I look upon that man now for the rest of my life! Oh, what a day! Oh, God, what a nightmare!"

There was a moment at the end of that long and agonizing way back from the Petersburg side when an irresistible desire seized the prince—to go straightaway to Rogozhin, to wait for him, to embrace him with shame, with tears, to tell him everything and to end it all at once. But he was already standing at his hotel . . . How he had disliked that hotel before, those corridors, that whole house, his room—he disliked them at first sight; several times that day he had recollected with some kind of particular disgust that he would have to return here . . . "Why, what is it with me today that I believe every presentiment, like a sick woman!" he thought with an almost irritable smirk, stopping at the gate.[29] A new unbearable flood of shame, almost of despair, held him rooted to the spot, just outside the gate. He stood still for a minute. It happens to people sometimes that way: sudden and unbearable memories, especially when they are associated with shame, usually hold them, for a moment, in place. "Yes, I am a man of no heart and a coward!" he repeated gloomily, and abruptly moved to go on, but . . . He stopped short again . . .

Under the gateway, which was dark as it is, it was particularly dark at that moment: the storm cloud had crept over the sky and engulfed the evening light, and at the same time that the prince approached the house the storm suddenly broke and there was a downpour. At the time when he abruptly moved from his place after his momentary halt, he was at the start of the gateway, by the very entrance to the gateway from the street. And suddenly, in the depths of the gateway, in the semidarkness, just by the entry to the stairs, he saw a man. This man seemed to be waiting for something, but he moved like a flash and vanished at once. The prince was not able to get a clear look at this man, and, of course, could not have said for certain who he was. Besides, there were so many people who might be passing through here; there was a hotel here, and people were continually passing through and running in and out of the corridors. But he suddenly felt a complete and overwhelming conviction that he recognized the man and that this

---

29. The following passage from the 1868 edition was deleted in the version published in 1874: *One circumstance that had happened that day rose particularly before his imagination at that moment, but he imagined it "coldly," with "full possession of his reason," "without nightmare now." He suddenly recalled the knife of late on Rogozhin's table. "But why, indeed, shouldn't Rogozhin have as many knives as he likes on his table?" he wondered greatly at himself and, on the spot, frozen with amazement, suddenly pictured to himself his recent stop at the cutler's shop. "But what connection can there finally be in that! . . ." he started to exclaim, and broke off.*

man was certainly Rogozhin. A moment later, the prince rushed after him up the stairs. His heart froze. "Everything will be decided now!" he uttered to himself with strange conviction.

The staircase up which the prince ran from the gateway led to the corridors of the first and second floors, on which were the rooms of the hotel. This staircase, as in all old houses, was of stone, dark and narrow, and it turned around a thick stone column. On the first half-landing there turned out to be a hollow in the column, like a niche, not more than a pace wide and half a pace deep. Yet there was room for a man to stand there. Dark as it was, upon reaching the half-landing the prince still discerned at once that here, in this niche, a man was for some reason hiding. The prince suddenly wanted to pass by without looking to the right. He had taken one step already, but he could not resist and turned around.

Those two eyes of late, *the very same ones,* suddenly met his gaze. The man hidden in the niche had also already had time to take a step out of it. For one second they both stood facing one another and almost touching. Suddenly, the prince seized him by the shoulders and turned him back toward the staircase, nearer to the light; he wanted to see his face more clearly.

Rogozhin's eyes flashed and a rabid smile contorted his face. His right hand raised itself and something gleamed in it; the prince did not think of checking it. He only remembered that, it seemed, he had cried out:

"Parfyon, I don't believe it!"

Then suddenly something seemed torn asunder before him: his soul was suffused with intense *inner* light. The moment lasted perhaps half a second; yet, nonetheless, he clearly and consciously remembered the beginning, the very first sound of his terrible scream, which broke of itself from his breast and which he could not have checked by any effort. Then his consciousness was instantly extinguished and complete darkness followed.

He was having an attack of epilepsy, of which he had been free for a very long time now. It is well known that attacks of epilepsy, that is the seizure itself, come on in an instant. In this instant, the face is suddenly horribly distorted, especially the gaze. Convulsions and spasms overwhelm the whole body and all the features of the face. A terrible, inconceivable scream that is unlike anything else breaks forth from the breast; in that scream everything human seems suddenly to vanish and it is impossible, or at the least very difficult, for the observer to conceive and admit that it is the very same man screaming. One even imagines that someone else who was inside this man was screaming. That is, at least, how many people have described their impression, while for many, the sight of a man having a seizure fills them with positive and unbearable horror, in which there is even something mystical. It must be supposed that such a feeling of sudden horror, combined with all the other terrible impressions of the moment, had suddenly paralyzed Rogozhin on the spot and so saved the prince from the inevitable blow of the knife that was already falling on him. Then, before he had time to grasp that it was a fit, and seeing that the prince had staggered away from him and suddenly fallen backward downstairs, knocking his head violently against the stone step, Rogozhin flew headlong downstairs, ran around the prostrate figure and, almost not knowing what he was doing, ran out of the hotel.

From the convulsions, thrashings and shudders, the body of the sick man slipped down the steps, of which there were no more than fifteen, to the bottom of the staircase. Very soon, not more than five minutes later, people noticed the prone man and a crowd collected. A whole pool of blood by his head instilled perplexity: had the man hurt himself, or "was there some foul play?" Soon, however, some recognized the epileptic sickness; one of the people at the hotel recognized the prince as having arrived that morning. The confusion was finally resolved, somewhat luckily, due to one lucky circumstance.

Kolya Ivolgin, who had promised to be at the Scales at four o'clock and had instead gone to Pavlovsk, had, upon a certain sudden consideration, refused to dine at Generaless Epanchin's, and had come back to Petersburg and hurried to the Scales, where he had turned up about seven o'clock. Learning from the note that had been left for him that the prince was in town, he hastened to find him at the address given in the note. Being informed at the hotel that the prince had gone out, he went downstairs to the dining rooms and waited for him there, having his tea and listening to the organ. Chancing to overhear a conversation about a fit that someone had had, he ran out to the spot, following an accurate presentiment, and recognized the prince. Suitable steps were taken at once. The prince was carried to his room; though he had come to, he did not fully regain consciousness for a rather long time. A doctor who was sent for to look at his injured head gave him a medicated compress and pronounced that there was not the least danger from the bruises. And an hour later, when the prince began to be able to understand pretty well what was going on around him, Kolya moved him in a covered carriage from the hotel to Lebedev's. Lebedev received the sick man with extraordinary warmth and with bows. For his sake, too, he hastened his removal to his dacha; by the third day they were all at Pavlovsk.

VI

Lebedev's dacha was not large, but comfortable and even pretty. The part of it which was to let was especially spruced up. On the rather spacious terrace, by the entrance from the street into the rooms, orange, lemon and jasmine trees had been placed in large green wooden tubs, which in Lebedev's opinion gave the place the most charming appearance. Some of these trees he had acquired together with the dacha, and he was so enchanted by the effect they produced on the terrace that he resolved to take advantage of an opportunity to buy some more of the same kinds of trees in tubs at an auction. When all the trees had at last been brought to the dacha and put in their places, Lebedev had several times that day run down the terrace steps to the street, and from the street admired his property, each time mentally increasing the sum which he proposed to ask from his future tenant. The prince, weakened, sick at heart, and physically shattered, liked the dacha immensely. Actually, on the day of arriving at Pavlovsk—that is, on the third day after the fit—the prince had, on the surface, the look of an almost well man, though inwardly he felt that he was still not over it. He was glad of everyone who was about him those three days, glad of Kolya, who hardly left his side, glad of the whole Lebedev family (without the nephew, who had disappeared somewhere); he was glad of Lebedev himself; and he even received with pleasure General Ivolgin, who had visited him while he was still in the city. On the day of their arrival, which had occurred toward evening, a good many guests had assembled about him on the terrace: the first to arrive was Ganya, whom the prince hardly recognized—he had changed so much and grown so much thinner in all that time. Then came Varya and Ptitsyn, who also summered at Pavlovsk. As for General Ivolgin, he was almost invariably found in Lebedev's quarters, and, so it seemed, had even moved in with him. Lebedev made an effort not to let him in to the prince and to keep him in his own part of the house; he treated the general like a friend; by all appearances, they had known each other a long time. The prince noticed that in those three days they sometimes engaged in long conversations together, not infrequently shouted and argued, even, it seemed, about learned subjects, which evidently was a source of pleasure for Lebedev. One might have even thought that the general was necessary to him. But from the time they moved to Pavlovsk, Lebedev had begun to exercise with respect to his own family the same precautions he had taken with respect to the general; on the pretext of not disturbing the prince, he would not let anyone in to see him, stamped his feet, rushed at his daughters and chased them, not excluding Vera with the baby, at the least suspicion that they were going to the terrace, where the prince was, in spite of all the prince's entreaties not to send anyone away.

"In the first place, there will be no respect shown if you let them do what they like; and in the second place, it's really improper for them . . ." he explained at last in reply to the prince's direct question.

"But why so?" protested the prince. "Really, you only torment me with all this attention and watchfulness. It's dull for me alone, I've told you so several times; and you yourself, with your incessant arm-waving and tiptoeing around, depress me all the more."

The prince was hinting at the fact that, though Lebedev chased away all his household on the pretext that quiet was necessary for the invalid, he himself had been coming in all those three days practically every minute, and each time he first opened the door, poked his head in, surveyed the room, just as though he wished to make sure—was he there? had he not run away?—and then slowly, on tiptoe, with stealthy steps, approached the armchair, so that he sometimes unintentionally startled his lodger. He was continually inquiring if he wanted anything, and when the prince began asking him at last to leave him alone, he turned away obediently without a word, made his way on tiptoe back to the door, waving his hands as he walked, as though to make it known that he had only just looked in, that he would not say a word, that he had already gone out and would not come back, and yet within ten minutes, or at most a quarter of an hour, he would reappear. Kolya, who had free access to the prince, aroused by that very fact the deepest sorrow and even resentful indignation in Lebedev. Kolya noticed that Lebedev would stand at the door for half an hour at a time and eavesdrop on what he and the prince were talking about, and of course he informed the prince.

"It's just as if you've appropriated me, since you keep me under lock and key," the prince protested. "At the dacha, anyway, I want it to be different; and rest assured, I shall receive anyone I like and go anywhere I choose."

"Without the faintest doubt!" Lebedev waved his hands.

The prince scanned him intently from head to foot.

"Say, Lukyan Timofeevich, the little cupboard that was hanging at the head of your bed, have you brought it here?"

"No, I haven't."

"What, have you left it there?"

"Impossible to bring it, it would have to be wrenched from the wall . . . firmly, firmly."

"But perhaps there's another one just like it here?"

"Even better, even better, I bought the dacha together with it."

"A-ha! Who was it you wouldn't admit to see me earlier? An hour ago."

"It . . . it was the general, sir. It's true I didn't let him in, and he has no business coming to you. I have a great respect for that man, Prince, he . . . he is a great man, sir; don't you believe me? Well, you will see; but all the same . . . it would be better, illustrious prince, if you did not receive him, sir."

"But why so, allow me to ask? And why are you standing on tiptoe now, Lebedev, and why do you always approach me as though you wanted to whisper a secret in my ear?"

"I am abject, abject, I feel it," Lebedev replied unexpectedly, striking himself on the chest with feeling. "But won't the general be too hospitable for you, sir?"

"Too hospitable?"

"Yes, sir, hospitable. To begin with, he is intending to live with me now; well, let that be, sir, but he is so eager, he insists at once on being related. He and I have figured out the relationship several times already; it turns out that we are connected by marriage. You, too, turn out to be a nephew of his twice removed, on the mother's side; he explained it to me only yesterday. If you are a nephew, then you and I must be relations too, illustrious prince. That would be all right, sir, it's a trifling weakness; but he assured me just now that all his life, ever since he was an ensign up to the eleventh of June last year, he had never had less than two hundred people to dinner at his table. He went so far at last as to say they never got up, so they had dinner and supper and tea for fifteen hours out of four-and-twenty for thirty years on end without the slightest break, so that they scarcely had the time to change the tablecloths. One would get up and go and another would come, and on holidays there would be as many as three hundred. And on the day of Russia's thousandth anniversary he counted seven hundred people. That's a passion, you know, sir; such assertions are a very bad sign, sir. One is quite afraid even to receive such hospitable people in one's house, and so I thought: won't such a hospitable person be too much for the two of us?"

"But you are on rather good terms with him, it seems?"

"We are like brothers, and I take it as a joke; let us be family: what is it to me—all the more honor. Even through the two hundred people at dinner and the thousandth anniversary of Russia I can discern that he is a very remarkable man. I mean it sincerely, sir. You brought up secrets just now, prince—that is, that I seem to approach you as if I wanted to tell a secret; and as it happens there is a secret: a certain person has just made it known that she would very much like to have a secret rendezvous with you."

"Why in secret? Not at all. I'll go and see her myself; why, even today."

"Not at all, not at all!" Lebedev waved his hands. "It's not what you suppose that she is afraid of. By the way, the monster comes each and every day to ask after your health. Did you know that?"

"You call him 'monster' so often it makes me quite suspicious."

"You can feel no sort of suspicion—no sort of suspicion at all," Lebedev hurried to dismiss. "I only wanted to explain that a certain person is not afraid of him, but of something very different, very different."

"But of what, then, tell me quickly," the prince questioned impatiently, looking at Lebedev's mysterious contortions.

"Therein lies the secret." And Lebedev snickered.

"Whose secret?"

"Your secret. You forbade me yourself, most illustrious prince, to speak of it before you . . ." Lebedev muttered; and having thoroughly enjoyed the fact that he had taken his hearer's curiosity to the point of painful impatience, he suddenly concluded: "She is afraid of Aglaia Ivanovna."

The prince furrowed his brow and was silent for a minute.

"Upon my word, Lebedev, I'll leave your dacha!" he said suddenly. "Where are Gavrila Ardalionovich and the Ptitsyns? In your rooms? You've enticed them over to your place too."

"They are coming, sir, they're coming. And even the general after them. I'll open all the doors and I'll call my daughters too—everyone, everyone, at once, at once," Lebedev whispered in alarm, brandishing his arms and rushing from one door to the other.

At that moment Kolya appeared on the terrace, having come from the street, and announced that visitors were coming in his wake, Lizaveta Prokofyevna with her three daughters.

"Shall I admit the Ptitsyns and Gavrila Ardalionovich, or not? Shall I admit the general or not?" Lebedev jumped up, astonished by the news.

"Why not? Anyone who likes. I assure you, Lebedev, you've misunderstood something about my attitude from the very beginning; you've made some kind of perpetual mistake. I have not the slightest reason for hiding and concealing myself from anyone," laughed the prince.

Looking at him, Lebedev felt it his duty to laugh too. Lebedev, in spite of his great agitation, was also, evidently, extremely pleased.

The news brought by Kolya was true; he had come only a few steps in advance of the Epanchins to announce their arrival, so that the visitors suddenly arrived on the terrace from both sides; from the terrace—the Epanchins; and from the rooms—the Ptitsyns, Ganya, and General Ivolgin.

The Epanchins had found out just now, from Kolya, about the prince's illness and about the fact that he was in Pavlovsk; till then the generaless had been in painful perplexity. More than two days before, the general had passed on the prince's card to his family; this card awakened in Lizaveta Prokofyevna a firm conviction that the prince himself would arrive in Pavlovsk to see them promptly following this card. It was in vain that the girls assured her that a man who had not written for half a year would perhaps be far from being in such a hurry now, and that he perhaps had a great deal to do in Petersburg apart from them—how should they know his business? The generaless was decidedly angry at these remarks and was ready to wager that the prince would make his appearance next day at the latest, though "even that would be rather late." The next day she waited away all the morning; they awaited him to dinner, and toward evening, and when it got quite dark Lizaveta Prokofyevna became cross with everything and quarreled with everyone, making of course no mention of the prince as the occasion of the quarrels. No mention was made of him on the third day either. When Aglaia incidentally let drop at dinner that *maman* was angry because the prince had not come—at which the general immediately remarked that he "was not to blame for that, you know"—Lizaveta Prokofyevna got up and left the table in wrath. At last, toward evening, Kolya arrived with all the news and accounts of all the prince's adventures so far as he knew them. Lizaveta Prokofyevna was triumphant, but in any case Kolya came in for a good scolding: "He hangs about here for days together and there's no getting rid of him, and now he might at least have let us know, if he did not think fit to come himself." Kolya was on the point of being angry at the words "no getting rid of him," but he put it off for another time, and if the phrase had not been just too hurtful, then, perhaps, he would have forgiven it altogether, for he was so pleased with Lizaveta Prokofyevna's agitation and anxiety on hearing of the prince's illness. She insisted for a long time on the necessity of sending a special messenger to Petersburg to get hold of some medical celebrity of the first magnitude and to rush him over by the first train. But her daughters talked her out of it; they were, however, unwilling to be left behind by their mamma when she instantly got ready to visit the invalid.

"He is on his deathbed," said Lizaveta Prokofyevna in a fluster, "and fancy our standing on ceremony! Is he a friend of the family or not?"

"But it's not right to stick your head in before you know the lay of the land, either," observed Aglaia.

"Very well, then, don't come. You will do well indeed; if Yevgeny Pavlovich comes, there will be no one to receive him."

At those words Aglaia, of course, set off at once after the others, which indeed she had intended to do in any case. Prince Shch., who had been sitting with Adelaida, at her request instantly agreed to escort the ladies. Even earlier, at the very beginning of his acquaintance with the Epanchins, he had been much interested when he heard from them of the prince. It turned out that he was acquainted with him; that they had met somewhere lately and had spent a fortnight together in some little town. That was some three months before. Prince Shch. had even told them a great deal about Myshkin and on the whole gave a rather nice report of him, so it was now with genuine pleasure that he went to call on his old acquaintance. General Ivan Fyodorovich was not at home that evening. Yevgeny Pavlovich had not yet arrived either.

It was not more than three hundred paces from the Epanchins' to Lebedev's dacha. Lizaveta Prokofyevna's first unpleasant impression at the prince's was to find a whole company of visitors around him, to say nothing of the fact that this company included two or three persons for whom she had a positive hatred; the second was her amazement at the sight of the young man who came to meet them, to all appearances in perfect health, fashionably dressed, and laughing, instead of the dying man on his deathbed whom she had expected to find. She actually stopped short in bewilderment, to the intense delight of Kolya, who of course might perfectly well have explained before she had even set out from her dacha that no one was dying and there was no deathbed of any sort, but he had not explained it, slyly foreseeing the comic wrath of the generaless when, as he reckoned, she would certainly be angry at finding the prince, her genuine friend, in good health. Kolya was so tactless, indeed, as to speak his surmise aloud, in order to completely irk Lizaveta Prokofyevna, with whom he was continually, and sometimes very viciously, sparring, in spite of the bonds of friendship that tied them.

"Wait a bit, my solicitous friend, don't be in a hurry, don't spoil your triumph!" answered Lizaveta Prokofyevna, sitting down in the armchair that the prince set for her.

Lebedev, Ptitsyn and General Ivolgin rushed to pull up chairs for the young ladies. General Ivolgin gave Aglaia a chair. Lebedev set a chair for Prince Shch. too, even managing, by the very curve of his back, to express extraordinary deference as he did so. Varya greeted the young ladies as usual with delight and whispers.

"It's the truth, Prince, that I expected to find you[30] almost in bed, so much did I exaggerate things in my fright, and not for anything would I lie, I felt dreadfully vexed just now by your happy face, but I swear it was only for a minute, before I had had time to think. When I have thought things out, I always act and speak more sensibly; I think it's the same with you. But in reality, I would perhaps be less pleased at my own son's recovery, if I had one, than I am at yours; and if you don't believe me, then shame on you, and not on me. And this malicious boy allows himself to play worse jokes than this at my expense. I believe he is a protégé of yours; so I warn you that one fine morning, believe me, I shall deny myself the pleasure of enjoying the honor of his further acquaintance."

"But how am I to blame?" cried Kolya. "However much I would have assured you that the prince was almost well again, you would not have been willing to believe me, because to imagine him lying on his deathbed was much more interesting."

"Have you come to us for long?" Lizaveta Prokofyevna turned to the prince.

"The whole summer, and perhaps longer."

"You are alone, aren't you? Not married?"

"No, not married." The prince smiled at the naïveté of the barb.

"There's nothing to smile at; it does happen. I was thinking of this dacha; why didn't you move in with us? We have a whole wing empty, but anyway, do as you like. Have you hired it from him? That person?" she added in an undertone, nodding at Lebedev. "Why is he simpering like that?"

At that moment Vera came out of the house onto the terrace, as was her wont, with the baby in her arms. Lebedev, who was wriggling about near the chairs decidedly at a loss what to do with himself but desperately anxious not to go, immediately flew at Vera, waving his arms at her and chasing her off the terrace and, forgetting himself, even stamping his feet.

"Is he out of his mind?" added Generaless Epanchin suddenly.

30. From this moment on, Lizaveta Prokofyevna addresses the prince with the familiar *ty*. General Epanchin also begins to do so later on in this chapter. The prince continues to address them both with the polite *vy* form throughout the novel.

"No, he is . . ."

"Drunk perhaps? But your company is not attractive," she snapped, encompassing the remaining guests in her gaze as well. "But what a sweet girl, though! Who is she?"

"That's Vera Lukyanovna, the daughter of Lebedev here."

"Ah! . . . She is very sweet. I want to make her acquaintance."

But Lebedev, overhearing Lizaveta Prokofyevna's words of approval, was already dragging his daughter forward himself to present her.

"Orphans, orphans!" he wailed, approaching. "And this baby in her arms—an orphan, her sister, my daughter Lyubov, and born in most lawful wedlock from my recently departed wife, Yelena, who died six weeks ago in childbirth, by the will of God . . . Yes'm . . . She takes her mother's place, though she is a sister and no more . . . no more, no more . . ."

"And you, dear fellow, are no more than a fool, if you'll excuse me! Well, enough, you know it yourself, I suppose," Lizaveta Prokofyevna rapped out suddenly in extreme indignation.

"Perfectly true!" Lebedev bowed deeply and with the greatest deference.

"Listen, Mr. Lebedev, is it true what they say, that you interpret the Apocalypse?" asked Aglaia.

"Perfectly true . . . for fifteen years now."

"I've heard about you. And there was something in the newspapers about you, I think?"

"No, that was about another interpreter, another one, ma'am; but he is dead, and I've succeeded him," said Lebedev, beside himself with delight.

"Be so good as to interpret it to me sometime, soon, as we are neighbors. I don't understand anything in the Apocalypse."

"I can't neglect to warn you, Aglaia Ivanovna, that all this is mere charlatanism on his part, believe me," quickly and all of a sudden put in General Ivolgin, who had been waiting as if on pins and needles and wanting with all his might to start a conversation somehow. He sat down beside Aglaia Ivanovna. "Of course, a summer house has its own privileges," he went on, "and its own pleasures, and to receive such an extraordinary poseur for the interpretation of the Apocalypse is a diversion like any other, and even a diversion remarkable in its cleverness, but I . . . You are looking at me with surprise, I think? General Ivolgin. I have the honor to introduce myself. I used to carry you in my arms, Aglaia Ivanovna."

"Very glad to meet you. I know Varvara Ardalionovna and Nina Alexandrovna," Aglaia muttered, straining to the utmost not to burst out laughing.

Lizaveta Prokofyevna flushed angrily. Something that had been accumulating for a long time in her heart suddenly demanded an outlet. She could not endure General Ivolgin, with whom she had once been acquainted, but very long ago.

"You are lying, dear fellow, as is your wont. You have never carried her in your arms," she snapped indignantly.

"You've forgotten, *maman,* upon my word, he did, at Tver," Aglaia suddenly confirmed. "We were living at Tver then. I was six years old then, I remember. He made me a bow and arrow and taught me to shoot, and I killed a pigeon. Do you remember we killed a pigeon together?"

"And you brought me a helmet made of cardboard, and a wooden sword, I remember too!" cried Adelaida.

"I remember it too," confirmed Alexandra. "You quarreled then over the wounded pigeon, and you were put in separate corners; Adelaida stood there as she was, in the helmet and with the sword."

The general, who had told Aglaia that he had carried her in his arms, had said it just like that, merely to begin the conversation, and solely because he almost always began a conversation in that way with all young people, if he found it necessary to make their acquaintance. But this time it turned out, as if by design, that he was speaking the truth, and, as if by design, he had forgotten it himself. So when Aglaia suddenly confirmed that they had shot a pigeon together, his memory cleared all at once, and he recalled it all himself, down to the very last detail, as people often do remember in their old age something in the remote past. It is difficult to convey what there was in this reminiscence that could have produced such a strong effect on the poor and—as was his wont—slightly tipsy general; but he was all at once extraordinarily moved.

"I remember, I remember it all!" he cried. "I was a captain then. You were such a pretty little mite . . . Nina Alexandrovna . . . Ganya . . . I used to be . . . a guest in your house. Ivan Fyodorovich . . ."

"And see what you've come to now!" put in the generaless. "So you haven't drunk away all your better feelings, if it affects you so much? But you've tormented your wife to death. Instead of taking your children in hand, you sit in the debtors' prison. Go away, my friend, go in somewhere and stand behind the door in a corner and have a cry; remember your former innocence, and mayhap God will forgive you. Go along, go along, I mean it seriously. There is nothing better for reforming yourself than remembering former times with contrition."

But to repeat that she was speaking seriously was unnecessary: General Ivolgin, like all people who are continually drunk, was very sensitive, and, like all drunk people who have had too great a fall, he did not easily bear memories of the happy past. He got up and walked humbly to the door, so that Lizaveta Prokofyevna was at once sorry for him.

"Ardalion Alexandrovich, my dear man!" she called after him. "Stop a minute; we are all sinners; when you feel your conscience does not reproach you so much, come and see me; we'll sit and chat over the past. I dare say I am fifty times as great a sinner myself, perhaps. But now, good-bye, go along, it's no use your staying here ..." she suddenly grew alarmed that he would come back.

"You'd better not go after him just now," the prince stopped Kolya, who was about to run after his father, "or he will be vexed in a moment and this whole moment will be spoiled."

"That's true; don't disturb him; go in half an hour," Lizaveta Prokofyevna decided.

"See what comes of speaking the truth for once in his life; it reduced him to tears!" Lebedev ventured to put in.

"Well, and you, my man, must be another pretty one if what I've heard is true," Lizaveta Prokofyevna immediately pounced upon him.

The mutual relations of all the guests who had gathered at the prince's gradually became evident. The prince was of course able to appreciate and did appreciate the full degree of the interest shown in him by the generaless and her daughters, and, of course, he told them sincerely that he himself, that very day, even before their visit, had intended without fail to call on them, despite his illness and the late hour. Lizaveta Prokofyevna, looking at his visitors, responded that one might still carry this out now. Ptitsyn, who was a very polite and accommodating person, rose very soon and retreated to Lebedev's quarters, rather anxious to take Lebedev away with him. The latter promised to follow him quickly; Varya, meanwhile, had got to talking with the girls, and remained. She and Ganya were rather glad of the general's departure; Ganya himself also went off soon after Ptitsyn. And in the few minutes that he had been on the terrace in the presence of the Epanchins, he had conducted himself modestly and with dignity, and was not in the least disconcerted by the determined looks thrown his way by Lizaveta Prokofyevna, who had twice scanned him from head to foot. Indeed, anyone who had known him before might have thought that he had greatly changed. Aglaia was very much pleased at it.

"That was Gavrila Ardalionovich who went out, wasn't it?" she asked suddenly, as she was fond of doing sometimes, loudly, sharply, interrupting the conversation of others by her question, and addressing no one in particular.

"Yes," answered the prince.

"I hardly recognized him. He is very much changed and ... greatly for the better."

"I am very glad for him," said the prince.

"He has been very ill," added Varya, happily commiserating.

"How has he changed for the better?" Lizaveta Prokofyevna asked in angry bewilderment and almost in dismay. "Where do you get that from? There's nothing better. What is it, namely, do you see that's better?"

"There is nothing better than the 'poor knight'!" suddenly proclaimed Kolya, who had been standing by Lizaveta Prokofyevna's chair all the while.

"That's what I think myself, too," said Prince Shch., and he laughed.

"I am precisely of the same opinion," Adelaida declared solemnly.

"What 'poor knight'?" asked the generaless, scanning all the speakers with bewilderment and vexation, but seeing that Aglaia flushed hotly, she added with anger, "What stuff and nonsense! What 'poor knight'?"

"Is it the first time that urchin, your favorite, happens to twist other people's words?" answered Aglaia, with haughty indignation.

In every one of Aglaia's furious outbursts (and she was often furious), almost every time, in spite of all her evident seriousness and implacability, there were still so many glimpses of something childish, impatiently schoolgirlish and badly disguised, that it was sometimes impossible not to laugh when one looked at her, much to the extreme vexation of Aglaia, incidentally, who did not understand what people were laughing at, and "how they could, how they dared, laugh." Her sisters and Prince Shch. began laughing now too, and even Prince Lev Nikolaevich, who had also flushed for some reason, smiled himself. Kolya roared with laughter and was triumphant. Aglaia became angry in earnest, and looked twice as pretty. Her confusion was very becoming to her, and on top of that, her vexation at her own confusion.

"As though he hasn't twisted so many of your words, too!" she added.

"I based it on your own exclamation!" cried Kolya. "A month ago you were looking through *Don Quixote*, and you cried out those very words, that there was nothing better than the 'poor knight.' I don't know whom you were talking of at the time: of Don Quixote or of Yevgeny Pavlych or of some other person; but you were talking of someone and the conversation was a long one."

"I see you allow yourself far too much, my dear, with your conjectures," Lizaveta Prokofyevna checked him with vexation.

"Why, am I the only one?" Kolya did not desist. "Everyone said so at the time, and they are saying it now; why, just now, Prince Shch. and Adelaida Ivanovna and everyone declared that they stood up for the 'poor knight,' so, it must be, there is a 'poor knight' after all, and he certainly exists, and, as I see it, if it were not for Adelaida Ivanovna, we should all have known long ago who the 'poor knight' was."

"How am I at fault?" laughed Adelaida.

"You wouldn't draw his portrait, that's how you're at fault! Aglaia Ivanovna asked you then to draw the portrait of the 'poor knight,' and described the whole subject of the picture, which she had made up herself, you remember the subject, don't you? You didn't want to . . ."

"But how could I draw it, whom should I draw? According to the subject, the 'poor knight'

> . . . no more in sight of any
> Raised the visor from his face.[31]

---

31. These are lines from a Pushkin poem. The poem is read in its entirety on pages 272–73.

What sort of face could have come out, then? What was I to draw: the visor? An anonymous figure?"

"I don't understand any of it, what visor?" The generaless was piqued, and she was beginning to have a very clear idea in her own mind who was meant by the title (probably agreed upon long ago) of the "poor knight." But what made her go off especially was that Prince Lev Nikolaevich was also disconcerted, and became at last completely abashed like a boy of ten. "Well, will there be an end to this foolishness or not? Will they explain to me this 'poor knight'? Is it some kind of secret or something, so awful that one can't approach it?"

But everyone only went on laughing.

"It's quite simply that there is this strange Russian poem," Prince Shch. intervened at last, evidently anxious to suppress and change the subject, "about a 'poor knight,' a fragment without a beginning or an end. About a month ago we were all laughing after dinner once and trying as usual to find a subject for Adelaida Ivanovna's next picture. You know that the common task of the family has long consisted in finding a subject for Adelaida Ivanovna's picture. That's when we hit on the 'poor knight,' which of us first I don't remember."

"Aglaia Ivanovna!" exclaimed Kolya.

"Perhaps, I don't dispute it, only I don't remember," Prince Shch. went on. "Some of us laughed at the subject, others declared that nothing could be loftier, but in order to paint the 'poor knight,' in any case, we needed a face; we began to go over the faces of all our acquaintances; not one was suitable, and that's where the business was left, that was all. I don't understand why Nikolai Ardalionovich got it into his head to recall it all and bring it up again. What was amusing and appropriate at the time is quite uninteresting now."

"Because some fresh foolishness is implied, hurtful and offensive," Lizaveta Prokofyevna snapped out.

"There's no foolishness in it, nothing but the deepest respect," suddenly pronounced Aglaia—completely unexpectedly, in a grave and earnest voice—who had managed to recover herself completely and to suppress her previous confusion. What's more, one might, looking at her, have supposed from certain signs that she was positively glad that the jest kept going further and further; and this entire turnaround took place in her at the very moment when the prince's embarrassment, which had been growing greater and greater and had reached an extraordinary degree, had become all too clearly evident.

"At one time they are laughing like half-wits, and here they suddenly turn up with deepest respect! Lunatics! Why respect? Tell me at once, why it is that, out of the blue, you've so suddenly got the deepest respect?"

"Deepest respect," Aglaia went on as gravely and earnestly in response to her mother's almost spiteful question, "because in that poem a man is represented who is capable of having an ideal and, secondly, having once set this ideal before him has faith in it, and having faith in it, of blindly giving up his entire life to it. This does not always happen in our day. There, in that poem, it doesn't say just in what, exactly, the 'poor knight's' ideal consisted, but it's evident that it was some radiant image, some image of 'pure beauty,' and, in love, the knight even puts a rosary around his neck instead of a scarf. Of course, there is also some obscure device of which we are not told in full, the letters A.N.B., which he has inscribed on his shield . . ."

"A.N.D.," Kolya corrected her.

"Well, I say A.N.B., and that's what I want to say," Aglaia interrupted with vexation. "However that may be, it's clear that for this 'poor knight' it had ceased to matter whoever his lady was or whatever she might do. It was sufficient that he had chosen her and put faith in her 'pure beauty,' and then did homage to her forever; therein lies his merit, that even if she became a thief afterward, he would still be bound to believe her and be ready to break a spear for her pure beauty. The poet seems to have wanted to unite in one extraordinary figure the whole grand conception of the medieval, chivalrous, platonic love of some pure and lofty knight; of course, all that's an ideal. And in the 'poor knight,' that feeling is taken to the extreme, to asceticism; it must be admitted that the capacity for such feeling means a great deal, and that such feelings leave behind a profound impression and, from one point of view, are rather laudable, to say nothing of Don Quixote. The 'poor knight' is the same Don Quixote, only serious, not comic. I didn't understand at first and laughed, but now I love the 'poor knight' and, most important, respect his exploits."

This was how Aglaia concluded, and, looking at her, it was difficult to tell whether she was in earnest or laughing.

"Well, he must have been some kind of fool anyway, he and his exploits!" decided the generaless. "And you too, my girl, are speaking nonsense, a regular lecture; it's not quite fitting, in my view, on your part. In any case, it's unacceptable. What poem? Recite it; no doubt you know it! I want to hear this poem without fail. My whole entire life, I could never stand poetry, as if I'd had a foreboding about it. For goodness' sake, put up with it, Prince! You and I have got to put up with things together, it seems," she added, addressing Prince Lev Nikolaevich. She was vexed out of all patience.

Prince Lev Nikolaevich tried to say something, but could get nothing out due to his continuing embarrassment. Only Aglaia, who had taken such liberties in her "lecture," was not in the least disconcerted, and seemed even glad. She got up at once, still grave and earnest as before, looking as though she had been preparing herself for this and was only waiting to be asked, stepped into the middle of the terrace, and stood facing the prince, who was still sitting in his armchair. Everyone looked at her with some amazement, and almost all of them, Prince Shch., her sisters, and her mother, looked with an uncomfortable feeling at this new, impending prank, which had in any case ventured somewhat too far. But it was evident that what Aglaia liked was precisely all that affectation with which she was beginning the ceremony of reciting the poem. Lizaveta Prokofyevna was on the point of sending her off to her seat, but at the very moment when Aglaia was about to begin declaiming the well-known ballad, two new guests stepped onto the terrace from the street, talking loudly. These were General Ivan Fyodorovich Epanchin and a young man who followed him. There was a slight commotion.

VII

The young man who accompanied the general was about twenty-eight, tall and well proportioned, with a beautiful and intelligent face and with a gleaming look, full of wit and mockery, in his big black eyes. Aglaia did not even look around at him and went on reciting the poem, continuing with affectation to look at no one but the prince and addressing him alone. It became clear to the prince that she was doing all this with some particular design. But, at least, the new arrivals offered some corrective to his awkward situation. Seeing them, he stood up, nodded his head cordially to the general from a distance, signed to them not to interrupt the recitation, and succeeded in retreating behind his armchair, where, leaning with his left elbow against its back, he continued listening to the ballad, now, so to speak, in a more comfortable and less "absurd" position than sitting in the chair. For her part, Lizaveta Prokofyevna motioned twice to the visitors with a peremptory gesture to stand still. The prince was, incidentally, much interested in his new visitor accompanying the general; he clearly surmised that he must be Yevgeny Pavlovich Radomsky, of whom he had heard a good deal already, and thought of more than once. He was stymied only by his civilian dress; he had heard that Yevgeny Pavlovich was a military man. A mocking smile played about the new visitor's lips all the time the poem was being recited, as though he too had already heard something about the "poor knight."

"Perhaps it was his idea," thought the prince to himself.

But it was quite different with Aglaia. All of the initial affectation and pompousness with which she had stepped forth to recite the poem she now covered up with such earnestness and insight into the spirit and meaning of the poetic work, pronounced each word of the poem with such significance, spoke the lines with such noble simplicity that by the end of the recitation she had not only captured everyone's attention, but also, by conveying the lofty spirit of the ballad, she had, as it were, to some extent justified that exaggerated, affected gravity with which she had so solemnly stepped into the middle of the terrace. In that gravity, one might now discern only the immeasurability and, perhaps, even the simplicity of her respect for that which she had taken upon herself to convey. Her eyes shone and a faint, scarcely perceptible shiver of inspiration and ecstasy passed once or twice over her beautiful face. She recited:

> Lived a knight once, poor and simple,
> Pale of face with glance austere,
> Spare of speech, but with a spirit
> Proud, intolerant of fear.
> He had had a wondrous vision:
> Ne'er could feeble human art
> Gauge its deep, mysterious meaning,
> It was graven on his heart.
> And since then his soul had quivered

With an all-consuming fire,
Never more he looked on women,
Speech with them did not desire.
But he dropped his scarf thenceforward,
Wore a chaplet in its place,
And no more in sight of any
Raised the visor from his face.
Filled with purest love and fervor,
Faith which his sweet dream did yield,
In his blood he traced the letters
A.M.D.[32] upon his shield.
When the Paladins proclaiming
Ladies' names as true love's sign
Hurled themselves into the battle
On the plains of Palestine,
Lumen coeli, Sancta Rosa![33]
Shouted he with flaming glance,
And the fury of his menace
Checked the Mussulman's advance.
Then returning to his castle
In far distant countryside,
Silent, sad, bereft of reason,
In his solitude he died.

Recalling that moment later, the prince long after agonized in extreme discomfiture over a question that remained unresolved for him: how was it possible to unite such a genuine, noble feeling with such unmistakable and malicious mockery? That it was mockery he did not doubt; he understood that clearly and had grounds for it: in the course of the recitation Aglaia had taken the liberty of changing the letters A.M.D. into the letters N.F.B. That this was not a mistake or mishearing on his part—of this he could have no doubt (it was proven afterward). In any case, Aglaia's stunt—a joke, of course, though too ruthless and thoughtless—was premeditated. Everyone had been talking (and "laughing") about the "poor knight" a whole month ago. And yet, whenever the prince recalled it afterward, it turned out that Aglaia

32. *Ave, Mater Dei* (Hail, mother of God).
33. Lat., light of heaven, holy rose.

had pronounced those letters without any trace of jest or sneer, without even any special emphasis on those letters to bring their hidden significance into higher relief, but, on the contrary, with such unchanged gravity, with such innocence and naive simplicity, that one might have supposed that those very letters were in the ballad and printed in the book. Something weighty and unpleasant seemed to sting the prince. Lizaveta Prokofyevna, of course, did not understand or notice either the change in the letters or the allusion. General Ivan Fyodorovich understood only that a poem was being recited. Of the other listeners, many understood and were surprised both by the boldness of the stunt and by the intention, but they kept silent and tried to show nothing. But Yevgeny Pavlovich (the prince was even ready to wager) not only had understood, but was even trying to show he had understood: he smiled with too mocking an air.

"How splendid!" cried the generaless in genuine delight, as soon as the recitation was over. "Whose poem is it?"

"Pushkin's, *maman*, don't put us to shame, it's disgraceful!" exclaimed Adelaida.

"Why, one might be even more of a fool with you all!" Lizaveta Prokofyevna responded bitterly. "It's a disgrace! Give me that poem of Pushkin's as soon as we get home."

"But I don't believe we've got a Pushkin at all!"

"Since time immemorial," added Alexandra, "there have been two dog-eared volumes of some sort lying about."

"We must send someone, Fyodor or Alexei, by the first train to town to buy one—Alexei would be best. Aglaia, come here! Kiss me, you recited it splendidly, but if you recited it sincerely," she added almost in a whisper, "I am sorry for you; if you recited it to mock him, I do not approve of your feelings, so that in any case it would have been better not to recite it at all. Do you understand? Go along, miss, I shall have a talk with you yet, but we've stayed too long here."

Meanwhile the prince was exchanging greetings with General Epanchin, and the general was introducing Yevgeny Pavlovich Radomsky to him.

"I picked him up on the way here, he had just come by train; he heard that I was coming here and all the rest were here . . ."

"I heard that you were here too," Yevgeny Pavlovich interrupted, "and as I had long meant to seek out not only your acquaintance but also your friendship, I didn't want to lose any time. You are unwell? I have only just heard . . ."

"I am perfectly well and very glad to make your acquaintance; I've heard a great deal about you, and even talked about you with Prince Shch.," answered the prince, holding out his hand.

Mutual courtesies were exchanged, they pressed each other's hands and looked intently into each other's eyes. At that moment the conversation became general. The prince noticed (and he was noticing everything now, rapidly and eagerly, and possibly what was not even there at all) that Yevgeny Pavlovich's civilian dress excited universal and exceptionally great surprise, so much so that for a time all other impressions were effaced and forgotten. One might have thought that this change of dress constituted something of great consequence. Adelaida and Alexandra questioned Yevgeny Pavlovich in bewilderment, Prince Shch., his relation, even with great uneasiness; the general spoke almost with agitation. Only Aglaia looked with curiosity, but perfect composure, at Yevgeny Pavlovich for a moment, as though she were simply trying to compare, was it the civilian dress or the military that suited him best, but a minute later she turned away and did not look at him again. Lizaveta Prokofyevna, too, did not care to ask any questions about anything, though perhaps she, too, was somewhat uneasy. The prince fancied that Yevgeny Pavlovich did not seem to be in her good graces.

"He has surprised me, amazed me!" Ivan Fyodorovich maintained in answer to all inquiries. "I didn't want to believe him when I met him lately in Petersburg. And why so suddenly, that's the riddle! Isn't he always the first to shout himself that there's no need to break the furniture?"[34]

From the talk that arose, it emerged that Yevgeny Pavlovich had long ago announced his intention of resigning his commission; but each time he had spoken of it so flippantly that it had been impossible to believe him. Why, indeed, he always talked of serious things with such a jesting air that it was impossible to make him out, especially if he didn't want to be made out.

34. A reference to Gogol's famous comedy *The Government Inspector* (1836), in which a character says, "It's true, of course, that Alexander the Great is a hero, but why break the furniture?" The quote became a household phrase meaning roughly that there's no need to make a tempest in a teacup.

"But it's only for a time, you know, for some months, a year at most, that I shall be on the retired list," laughed Radomsky.

"But there is no need of it whatever, from what I know of your affairs, at least." The general was still growing excited.

"But to visit my estates? You advised it yourself; besides, I want to go abroad . . ."

The subject, anyway, was soon changed; but the exceedingly unusual and still persistent unease seemed to go, in the opinion of the prince as he observed it, beyond reasonable bounds, and there must have been something unusual in it.

"So the 'poor knight' is on the scene again," Yevgeny Pavlovich started to ask, approaching Aglaia.

To the prince's amazement, she surveyed him with bewilderment and a questioning air, as though wishing to give him to understand that there could have been not the least discussion of the "poor knight" between them, and that she did not even comprehend his question.

"But it's too late, too late to send to town for Pushkin now, too late!" Kolya argued with Lizaveta Prokofyevna, at the end of his tether. "I've told you three thousand times: it's too late."

"Yes, it really is too late to send to town now," Yevgeny Pavlovich intervened here, too, hurriedly leaving Aglaia. "I believe the shops are shut by now in Petersburg, it's past eight," he affirmed, looking at his watch.

"You've waited so long without missing it, you can wait it out till tomorrow," put in Adelaida.

"And anyway, it's not the proper thing," added Kolya, "for people of the best society to be too much interested in literature. Ask Yevgeny Pavlych. It's more proper to be interested in a yellow charabanc with red wheels."

"You're quoting from books again, Kolya," observed Adelaida.

"But he never speaks except in quotations," chimed in Yevgeny Pavlovich, "he takes whole phrases out of critical reviews. I've long had the pleasure of knowing Nikolai Ardalionovich's conversation, but this time he is not quoting from books. Nikolai Ardalionovich is plainly alluding to my yellow charabanc with red wheels. But I have exchanged it already, you're behind the times."

The prince listened closely to what Radomsky was saying . . . It seemed to him that he bore himself in a wonderful, modest, cheerful manner, and he particularly liked the fact that he spoke on such perfectly equal and friendly terms with Kolya, who was taunting him.

"What is this?" asked Lizaveta Prokofyevna, addressing Vera, Lebedev's daughter, who was standing before her with some large, almost new and finely bound volumes in her hands.

"Pushkin," said Vera, "our Pushkin. Father bade me to offer it to you."

"How's that? How is that possible?" cried Lizaveta Prokofyevna in surprise.

"Not as a present, not as a present! I wouldn't take the liberty!" Lebedev jumped out from behind his daughter's back. "At cost price, ma'am. This is our very own family Pushkin, Annenkov's edition[35], which you can't even find nowadays—at cost price, ma'am. I offer it with veneration, wishing to sell it and so to satisfy the honorable impatience of your excellency's most honorable literary feelings."

"Well, if you're selling it, thank you. You won't be a loser by it, no doubt; only stop simpering, please, my man. I've heard about you; they say you are very well read; we'll have a talk one day; will you bring them yourself, then?"

"With veneration and . . . deference!" Lebedev simpered with extraordinary satisfaction, snatching the books from his daughter.

"Well, just mind you don't lose them! Take them, even without deference, but only on condition," she added, surveying him intently, "that I only admit you to the door and don't intend to receive you today. Your daughter Vera you may send at once, if you will, I like her very much."

"Why don't you tell him about those people?" Vera turned to her father impatiently. "Why, they'll come in of themselves, if you don't: they've begun to be noisy. Lev Nikolaevich," she turned to the prince, who had already taken his hat, "there are some people come to see you, they came some time ago, four of them, they're waiting in our rooms and being abusive, but Father won't let them in to you."

"What visitors?" asked the prince.

"They've come on business, they say, only they're of the sort, if you don't let them in now, they'll be sure to stop you on the way. You'd bet-

---

35. The seven-volume collected works of Pushkin edited by P. V. Annenkov appeared in 1855–57. It was the first collected edition to rely on the author's original manuscripts.

ter see them, Lev Nikolaevich, and then they'll be off your back. Gavrila Ardalionovich and Ptitsyn are reasoning with them in there, but they're paying no heed."

"The son of Pavlishchev, the son of Pavlishchev! It's not worth it, not worth it!" Lebedev waved his hands. "It's not even worth listening to them, sir; and it's not proper for you to disturb yourself on their account, most illustrious prince. There you have it, sir. They aren't worth it . . ."

"The son of Pavlishchev! Good heavens!" cried the prince, extremely disconcerted. "I know but . . . you see, I . . . I entrusted that matter to Gavrila Ardalionovich. Gavrila Ardalionovich told me just now . . ."

But Gavrila Ardalionovich had already come out of the house to the terrace; Ptitsyn came after him. In the next room there were sounds of uproar and the loud voice of General Ivolgin, who seemed to be trying to shout down several others. Kolya ran to the noise at once.

"This is very interesting!" observed Yevgeny Pavlovich aloud.

"So he must know of the matter!" thought the prince.

"What son of Pavlishchev? And . . . what son of Pavlishchev can there be?" General Ivan Fyodorovich was asking in bewilderment, surveying all the faces with curiosity, and observing with amazement that he was the only one who knew nothing about this new development.

Indeed, the excitement and expectation were universal. The prince was profoundly amazed that such an entirely personal affair of his could already have roused so much interest in everyone here.

"It will be a very good thing if you put a stop to this at once and *yourself*!" said Aglaia, going up to the prince with particular earnestness, "and allow us all to be your witnesses. They are trying to throw mud at you, Prince, you must vindicate yourself triumphantly, and I am awfully glad for you in advance."

"I want this disgusting claim to be stopped at last, too," cried the generaless. "Give it to them, Prince, don't spare them! My ears have been tingling with this business, and I've spoiled much humor on your account. Besides, it will be interesting to look at them. Call them in and we'll sit down meanwhile. It's a good idea of Aglaia's. Have you heard something about it, Prince?" She turned to Prince Shch.

"Of course I have: why, it was in your house. But I am particularly anxious to have a look at these young people," answered Prince Shch.

"They are those nihilists, aren't they?"

"No, ma'am, they are not like those nihilists." Lebedev stepped forward, almost shaking with excitement as well. "They are different, ma'am, a special sort, my nephew said they have gone far beyond nihilists, ma'am. You are wrong if you think you'll abash them by your presence, your excellency; they won't be abashed, no, ma'am. Nihilists are, all the same, sometimes well-informed people, even learned, but these—they've gone further, they have, ma'am, for they are above all men of action, ma'am. This, actually, is a sort of sequel to nihilism, though not in a direct line, but obliquely, by hearsay, and they don't announce themselves in little newspaper articles of some sort, but directly in action, ma'am. It's not, for instance, about the meaninglessness of a Pushkin,[36] nor, for instance, of the necessity of Russia's breakup into parts;[37] no, ma'am, now they consider it directly a right that if one wants anything very much, one is to stop at no obstacles, even though one might have to do in eight people in the process, so it is, ma'am. But all the same, Prince, I should not advise you . . ."

But the prince had already gone to open the door to the visitors.

"You are slandering them, Lebedev," he uttered, smiling, "your nephew has hurt your feelings very much. Don't believe him, Lizaveta Prokofyevna. I assure you that the Gorskys and the Danilovs[38] are only exceptions, and these are only . . . mistaken . . . Only I would be loath to see them here, before everyone. Excuse me, Lizaveta Prokofyevna, they'll come in, I'll show them to you and then take them away. Come in, gentlemen!"

He was more worried by another thought that was painful to him. He fancied: had not someone arranged this business now, precisely for that hour and time, beforehand, precisely for these witnesses and perhaps in anticipation of his shame rather than his triumph? But he felt too sad at the thought of his "monstrous and wicked suspiciousness."

36. Some radical writers championed realism and social critique in literature to such an exclusive extent that they wholly repudiated Pushkin's poetry as irrelevant, though he was clearly considered a national treasure by the general public.

37. A utopian program published in 1862 envisioned Russia as a federation of republics.

38. Gorsky was the murderer of the Zhemarin family. Danilov was a nineteen-year-old university student who robbed and murdered a moneylender and his maid in Moscow around the same time.

He felt he would have died if anyone found out that he had such an idea in his head, and at the moment when his new guests walked in, he was genuinely ready to consider himself as the lowest of the low, of everyone around him, in a moral sense.

Five persons entered, four new arrivals, and the fifth in their wake, General Ivolgin, in a state of heated excitement, in agitation, and in a fit of most violent eloquence. "This one is on my side, most certainly!" thought the prince, with a smile. Kolya slipped in along with everyone; he was talking hotly to Ippolit, who was one of the visitors; Ippolit was listening and smirking.

The prince made his visitors sit down. They were all such young people, having scarcely reached majority, even, that one might have wondered at the incident, and at all the ceremony it had caused. Ivan Fyodorovich, for instance, who knew nothing about this "new development" and could not make it out, was quite indignant at the sight of their youthfulness, and would certainly have made some sort of protest had he not been checked by his wife's unaccountable fervor with respect to the prince's private affairs. However, he remained, partly out of curiosity and partly from kindheartedness, even hoping to help, or in any case to be of use by dint of his authority. But General Ivolgin's bow to him, from a distance, roused his indignation again; he frowned and made up his mind to maintain a persistent silence.

Among the four very young visitors, however, there was one man of about thirty, the retired lieutenant from Rogozhin's gang, the boxer, "who had in his time given as much as fifteen rubles each to beggars." It could be guessed that he had accompanied the others to lend them courage, as a sincere friend, and, if necessity arose, to support them. Of the remainder, the foremost and most prominent position was taken by the young man to whom the designation "son of Pavlishchev" had been given, though he introduced himself as Antip Burdovsky. He was a young man poorly and untidily dressed, in a jacket with sleeves sullied to the point of a mirror shine, with a greasy waistcoat buttoned up to the neck, with linen that had disappeared somewhere, with an impossibly soiled black silk scarf that was twisted like a rope, with unwashed hands, with an extremely pimply face, fair hair and, if one may so express it, with an innocently insolent gaze. He was about twenty-two, thin and tallish. There was not a trace of irony or reflection in his face; on the contrary, there was a complete, obtuse intoxication with his own rights and, at the same time, something like a strange and incessant craving to be and feel constantly offended. He spoke with agitation, hurrying and stumbling over his words, as if not enunciating them completely, just as though he were tongue-tied or even a foreigner, though he was, in fact, entirely of Russian origin.

He was accompanied, first of all, by Lebedev's nephew, already known to the reader, and, second, by Ippolit. Ippolit was a very young man, seventeen or possibly eighteen, with an intelligent but continually irritated expression on his face, on which illness had left terrible signs. He was thin as a skeleton, pale and yellow, his eyes gleamed and two red spots blazed on his cheeks. He coughed incessantly; every word, almost every breath, was followed by a wheeze. It was evident the consumption was at a rather advanced stage. It seemed that he had not more than two or three weeks left to live. He was very tired and sank into a chair before everyone else. The rest stood somewhat on ceremony upon entering, and were nearly on the point of being flustered, but they had an important air all the same, and were obviously afraid of somehow losing their dignity, which was strangely out of harmony with their reputation for disavowing all useless worldly trivialities, conventions, and almost everything in the world except their own interests.

"Antip Burdovsky," pronounced the "son of Pavlishchev," hurrying and stumbling over his words.

"Vladimir Doktorenko," Lebedev's nephew introduced himself, clearly, distinctly, indeed, as though boasting of the fact that his name was Doktorenko.

"Keller!" muttered the retired lieutenant.

"Ippolit Terentyev," squealed the last of the party in an unexpectedly squeaky voice. They all took their seats at last, sitting in a row on chairs opposite the prince; having introduced themselves, they all frowned at once and, to give themselves heart, shifted their caps from one hand to the other; they all got ready to speak, but nonetheless kept silent, waiting for something with a defiant air, which seemed to say, "No, my friend, you are wrong there, you won't pull one over on us!" One felt that someone had only to utter one single first word for a start, and they would all begin talking at once, interrupting and tripping each other up.

VIII

"Gentlemen, I did not expect any of you," the prince began, "I've been ill until today, and as for your business (he turned to Antip Burdovsky), I entrusted it to Gavrila Ardalionovich Ivolgin a month ago, of which I informed you at the time. Still, I do not eschew a personal explanation, only, you must admit, at such a time ... I suggest you go with me into another room, if you won't keep me long.... My friends are here now, and believe me ..."

"Friends ... as many as you like, but all the same, allow us," Lebedev's nephew suddenly broke in, in a rather reproving tone, though still not raising his voice very much, "allow us to point out that you might have treated us with more consideration, and not have made us wait two hours in your servants' hall ..."

"And of course ... I too ... This is princely behavior! ... And this is ... And you must be the general! But I am not your servant! And I, I ..." Antip Burdovsky suddenly began to mutter in extraordinary excitement, with trembling lips, with an aggrieved tremor in his voice, with spittle flying from his mouth, just as if he had burst or ruptured, but he was suddenly in such a hurry that ten words later one could no longer understand him.

"It was princely behavior!" Ippolit cried in a shrill, cracked voice.

"If I were treated like that," growled the boxer, "that is, if it were directly related to me, as a man of honor, if I were in Burdovsky's place ... I ..."

"Gentlemen, I only heard this minute that you were here, upon my word," the prince repeated again.

"We are not afraid of your friends, Prince, whoever they may be, for we are within our rights," Lebedev's nephew declared again.

"But what right had you, let me ask," Ippolit squeaked again, by now growing extremely hot under the collar, "to put Burdovsky's case to the judgment of your friends; it's all too plain what the judgment of your friends might mean!"

"But after all, if you don't wish to speak here, Mr. Burdovsky," the prince finally managed to squeeze in, staggered by such an opening, "then I tell you, let us go into another room at once, and I tell you again that I only heard of you all this very minute . . ."

"But you've no right to, you've no right, you've no right! . . . Your friends . . . So there!" Burdovsky suddenly began gabbling again, looking wildly and apprehensively about him, and the more he mistrusted and shied away, the more heated he became. "You have no right!" And having uttered those words he stopped abruptly, breaking off, as it were, and mutely opening wide his shortsighted, extremely bulging and thickly bloodshot eyes, he stared questioningly at the prince, bending forward with his whole upper body. This time the prince was so surprised that he fell silent himself, and also gazed at him, wide-eyed and without uttering a word.

"Lev Nikolaevich!" Lizaveta Prokofyevna called suddenly. "Here, read this at once, this minute, it has directly to do with your business."

She hurriedly held out to him a weekly of a satirical variety, and pointed with her finger at the article. Lebedev, while the visitors were still coming in, had skipped sideways up to Lizaveta Prokofyevna, whose favor he was trying to curry, and without uttering a word, having pulled this paper out of his sidepocket, had put it just before her eyes, pointing to a marked column. What Lizaveta Prokofyevna had already had time to read had astounded and agitated her terribly.

"But wouldn't it be better not aloud," murmured the prince, very much embarrassed. "I could read it alone . . . afterward . . ."

"Then you had better read it, read it at once, aloud! Aloud!" Lizaveta Prokofyevna turned to Kolya, impatiently snatching from the prince's hand the paper, which the latter had barely had a chance to touch. "Read it aloud to all, so that everyone may hear."

Lizaveta Prokofyevna was an excitable lady, and readily carried away, so that suddenly and all at once she would, without stopping to think, sometimes heave all anchors and launch into the open sea, not bothering about the weather. Ivan Fyodorovich stirred uneasily. But while everyone involuntarily stopped for the first minute and waited in perplexity, Kolya opened up the newspaper and began aloud at the passage that Lebedev had darted up to point out to him:

"Proletaria and scions, an episode of daily and everyday robbery! Progress! Reform! Justice!

"Strange things happen in our so-called holy Russia, in our age of reforms and of joint-stock enterprises, the age of national movements and of hundreds of millions of rubles carried abroad every year, the age of encouraging big industry and of the paralysis of working hands! etc., etc., one cannot enumerate all, gentlemen, and so—straight to the point. Here is a strange anecdote about a scion of our washed-up landed gentry (*de profundis!*),[39] one of those scions, incidentally, whose grandfathers were utterly ruined at the roulette wheel, whose fathers were obliged to serve as lieutenants and ensigns in the army, and usually died charged with some innocent misuse of public money, while their children, like the hero of our story, either grow up idiots, or are even mixed up in criminal cases, in which, however, they are acquitted by the jury with a view to edification and reformation; or else, ultimately, they end up pulling one of those pranks that amaze the public and disgrace our already degraded age. Our scion, some half a year ago, dressed in spats like a foreigner, and shivering in an unlined, skimpy little coat, returned to Russia from Switzerland, where he had been under treatment for idiocy (*sic!*). It must be confessed that fortune smiled upon him after all, so that—to say nothing of the interesting malady for which he was undergoing treatment in Switzerland (well, can there be a treatment for idiocy, just imagine?!!)—he may serve as an illustration of the truth of the Russian proverb that good fortune falls to a certain class of persons! Judge for yourselves: left still a baby at his father's death—they say he was a lieutenant, who died while on trial for a sudden disappearance at cards of all the company's money, or possibly for an excessive use of the rod on some subordinate (you remember the old days, don't you, gentlemen!)—our baron was taken out of charity to be brought up by a very rich Russian squire. This Russian squire—let's call him P., if you will—the owner in the old golden days of four thousand bonded souls (bonded souls! Do you understand, gentlemen, such an expression? I don't. One must consult with a learned dictionary: 'It's a new tale, but hard to believe!'[40]), was apparently one of those do-nothings and parasites who spend their idle lives abroad, in summer at the waters, and in winter at the Parisian Château-de-Fleurs, where, in their time, they have left immeasurable sums. One may say with certainty that at least one third of the tribute

39. Lat., out of the depths. This phrase begins the Catholic prayer for the dead.
40. A quote from Griboedov's *Woe from Wit*.

paid by the entire former serf estate was received by the proprietor of the Parisian Château-de-Fleurs (he must have been a fortunate man!). Be that as it may, the carefree P. brought up the noble orphan like a prince, engaged tutors and governesses for him (no doubt pretty ones) whom, by the way, he brought himself from Paris. But the last scion of the noble house was an idiot. The governesses from the Château-de-Fleurs were of no use, and up to his twentieth year our ward could not even be taught to speak any language, including Russian. Though the latter, of course, is excusable. At last, a fancy entered P.'s Russian, feudal head that the idiot might be taught sense in Switzerland—a logical fancy, incidentally: a parasite and *propriéteur* might naturally suppose that even brains might be had on the market for money, especially in Switzerland. Five years were spent in Switzerland under the care of some celebrated professor, and thousands were spent on it: the idiot, it stands to reason, did not become sensible, but, they say, he did begin, after all, to resemble a human being, a poor excuse for one, no doubt. Suddenly P. dies. Of course, there is no will of any kind. His affairs are as usual in disorder, there is a crowd of greedy heirs, and they care not a whit for the last scions of noble families who are treated out of charity in Switzerland for congenital idiocy. The scion, though an idiot, still made an effort to pull one over on his professor, and, they say, succeeded in being treated gratis for two years, concealing from him the death of his benefactor. But the professor was quite a charlatan himself; alarmed, finally, at the cashlessness and still more at the appetite of this twenty-five-year-old parasite, he dressed him up in his old spats, made him a present of his worn-out cloak and, out of charity, sent him third-class *nach Russland*[41]—to get him out of Switzerland and off his back. Fortune seemed to have turned its back on our hero. But not a bit of it, sir: Fortuna, who kills off whole provinces with famine, showers all her gifts on the little aristocrat, like the cloud in Krilov's fable that passed in haste over the parched fields to empty itself into the ocean. Almost at the very moment of his arrival from Switzerland in Petersburg, a relation of his mother's (who had, of course, been of a merchant's family) dies in Moscow, a childless old bachelor, a merchant, a bearded old *Raskolnik*,[42] and leaves a good

41. Ger., to Russia.

42. A schismatic—from *raskol,* "schism" (see note 21, page 225); the beard also marks him as devout, traditionalist, and not in government service (see note 27 in Part I, page 97).

round, uncontested inheritance of several million in hard cash—and (if it had only been for you and me, readers!) it was all for our scion, it was all for our baron, who had been treated for idiocy in Switzerland! Well, it was a very different tune then. Our baron in spats, who made a play for a notorious beauty of easy virtue, was suddenly surrounded by a whole crowd of friends and acquaintances, even some relations turned up, and, above all, whole crowds of honorable maidens, hungering and thirsting for lawful matrimony, and what could be better: aristocrat, millionaire, idiot—all the qualifications at once, you couldn't find such a husband if you searched for him with a lantern, or had him made to order! . . ."

"That . . . that passes my comprehension!" exclaimed Ivan Fyodorovich, roused to the last pitch of indignation.

"Leave off, Kolya!" exclaimed the prince in a supplicating voice. Cries were uttered on all sides.

"Read it! Read it, whatever happens!" Lizaveta Prokofyevna rapped out, evidently making a desperate effort to restrain herself. "Prince! If you stop him reading, we shall quarrel!"

There was no help for it. Kolya, heated, flushed, in trepidation, continued reading in an agitated voice.

"But in the meantime, while our freshly baked millionaire was floating, so to speak, in the empyrean, an entirely extraneous circumstance occurred. One fine morning, a visitor calls on him, with a composed and stern face, with courteous but dignified and just speech, dressed modestly and like a gentleman, and with an evidently progressive cast of mind, and he explains, in brief, the reason of his visit: he is a well-known lawyer; he has been entrusted with a matter by a young man and is appearing on his behalf. This young man is neither more nor less than the son of the deceased P., though he bears a different name. The licentious P.—having in his youth seduced a virtuous, poor young girl, a house-serf, but educated in the European manner (whereby the seignorial rights of the bygone feudal state were, naturally, involved) and remarking the inevitable but approaching consequence of his liaison—married her off posthaste to a man of honorable character who was engaged in commerce, and even in the service, and had long been in love with the girl. At first he helped the newlyweds; but soon assistance from him was refused, owing to the honorable character of the husband. Some time passed and, little by little, P. completely forgot both the girl and the son she had borne him, and afterward, as we know, died without making any provision. Meanwhile his son, who was born in lawful wedlock, but grew up under a different name, and was completely adopted by the honorable character of his mother's husband, who had, nonetheless, in the course of time, also died, was thrown entirely on his own resources, with a sickly, suffering, bedridden mother in one of the remote provinces of Russia; for his part, he obtained money in the capital by his honorable daily labor, by giving lessons to merchants, and in that way supported himself, first at school, and afterward while attending courses of profitable lectures with a view to his future advancement. But how much can you get from a Russian merchant for lessons at a few coppers an hour, and with a sickly, bedridden mother to keep, who, at last, even by her death in the remote province provided him with almost no relief at all. Now the question arises: how, by all rights, should our scion have reasoned? You, reader, doubtless think that he said thus to himself: 'I have all my life enjoyed all the gifts of P.; tens of thousands went to Switzerland for my education, governesses and treatment for idiocy; and here I am now with millions, while the noble character of P.'s son, who is not at all to blame for the misdemeanors of his frivolous and forgetful father, is wasting away giving lessons. All that has been spent on me ought, by right, to have been spent on him. These vast sums that have been spent on me are, in essence, not mine. It was only the blind mistake of fortune; they ought to have come to the son of P. They ought to have been used for his benefit, and not for mine—the fruits of a fantastic whim of the frivolous and forgetful P. If I were entirely noble, considerate, and just, I would have to give up to his son half of my fortune; but as I am first of all a prudent person, and know only too well that this is no juridical matter, I am not going to give him half my millions. But, at any rate, it would be too base and shameless on my part (the scion forgot that it would not be prudent either) if I don't now return those tens of thousands that were spent by P. on my idiocy to his son. That would be nothing but the dictates of conscience and justice! For what would have become of me if P. had not brought me up and had looked after his son instead of me?'

"But no, gentlemen! Our scions do not reason like this. For all the picture painted of the young man by the lawyer, who had undertaken his cause solely from friendship and almost against his will, almost by force, no matter how he put before him the obligations of honor, generosity, justice, and even of simple prudence, the Swiss charge remained unbending, and what do you think? All that would have been nothing, but what was really unpardonable and not to be excused by any illness, however interesting: this millionaire, who had only just barely cast off the spats of his professor, could not even get the fact that this honorable character of a young man, who was wearing himself out giving lessons, was not asking for charity or for assistance, but for his right and his due, even if it were not in the legal sense, and did not ask for it even, but it was only his friends interceding on his behalf. With a majestic air and intoxicated by this opportunity he had been given to use his millions to crush people with impunity, our scion pulls out a fifty-ruble note and sends it to the honorable young man by way of an insulting handout. You don't believe it, gentlemen? You are outraged, you are pained, you are bursting with cries of indignation; but he did this, all the same! It stands to reason the money was returned to him at once, so to speak, flung back in his face. What else is left to resolve the matter! It is not a juridical matter, there is nothing left but publicity! We convey this incident to the public, vouching for its authenticity. It is said that one of our best-known humorists let slip a marvelous epigram on the subject that deserves to take a place not only in provincial sketches of our mores, but even in the capital:

> Dear little Lev for five long years,
> Wrapped warm in Schneider's cloak,
> Lived like a child and often played
> Some simple foolish joke.
> Then home he came in gaiters tight,
> And found himself an heir,
> And gaily he the students robbed,
> The idiot millionaire!"[43]

When Kolya had finished reading, he handed the paper hurriedly to the prince and, without saying a word, rushed into a corner, buried himself tightly in it and hid his face in his hands. He felt insufferably

43. This epigram is a parody of one written about Dostoevsky by the famous satirist Saltykov-Shchedrin. One of the latter's well-known works was *Provincial Sketches* (1856–57).

ashamed, and his boyish impressionability, not yet accustomed to such smut, was outraged beyond all measure. It seemed to him that something extraordinary had happened, which had shattered everything all at once, and that he was almost the cause of it, if only by the very fact of having read this aloud.

But everyone, it seemed, felt something of the same sort.

The girls felt very awkward and ashamed. Lizaveta Prokofyevna struggled to contain violent anger, and was also, perhaps, bitterly repenting that she had meddled in the business; now she was silent. The prince was experiencing the same thing that often happens in such cases with overly shy people: he was so much ashamed for the conduct of others, he felt such shame for his visitors, that for the first moment he was afraid to look at them. Ptitsyn, Varya, Ganya, even Lebedev—everyone seemed to have a rather embarrassed air. Strangest of all was that Ippolit and "the son of Pavlishchev" also seemed amazed by something; Lebedev's nephew, too, was evidently displeased. Only the boxer sat there quite serene, twisting his mustache, with a dignified air and his eyes cast down somewhat, not from embarrassment but, on the contrary, it seemed, as if from noble-minded modesty and all-too-evident triumph. It was clear by all signs that he liked the article enormously.

"What a devilish outrage," General Epanchin muttered in an undertone, "as though fifty footmen had met together and composed it."

"But ah-allow me to ask you, my good sir, how dare you make such insulting suppositions?" declared Ippolit, and trembled all over.

"This, this, this for an honorable man . . . You must admit yourself, General, that if it's an honorable man, it's insulting!" muttered the boxer, who also seemed roused all of a sudden, twisting his mustache and twitching his shoulders and body.

"In the first place, I am not 'your good sir,' and in the second place, I have no intention of giving you any explanation," Ivan Fyodorovich, who had grown terribly heated, answered harshly; he got up from his seat and without saying a word stepped away to the entrance of the terrace and stood on the top step with his back to the party—in violent indignation at his wife, who did not even now think fit to move from the spot.

"Gentlemen, gentlemen, allow me, at last, gentlemen, to speak," the prince exclaimed in anguish and agitation, "and be so good, let us talk so that we may understand one another. I say nothing about the article, gentlemen, let it alone; only, gentlemen, it's all untrue, what is printed in the article: I say so, because you know that yourselves; it's shameful, in fact. So that I should be positively amazed if it was one of you who has written it."

"I knew nothing about the article till this moment," Ippolit announced. "I don't approve of the article."

"Though I knew it was written . . . I too wouldn't have advised its being published, because it's premature," added Lebedev's nephew.

"I knew, but I have the right . . . I . . ." muttered "the son of Pavlishchev."

"What! You made all that up yourself?" asked the prince, looking with curiosity at Burdovsky. "But it's impossible!"

"We may, all the same, refuse to recognize your right to ask such questions!" Lebedev's nephew put in.

"I only wondered that Mr. Burdovsky managed . . . But . . . I meant to say, since you have given publicity to this matter, why were you so offended earlier when I talked about this same matter before my friends?"

"At last!" muttered Lizaveta Prokofyevna indignantly.

"And, Prince, you are pleased even to forget," Lebedev said, unable to restrain himself, suddenly slipping between the chairs, almost in a fever, "you are pleased to forget, indeed, that it was only your good will, and the incomparable goodness of your heart, to receive them and hear them out, and that they have no right to demand anything like this, especially as you have already entrusted the matter to Gavrila Ardalionovich, and that, too, you did through your excessive kindness; and that now, most illustrious prince, remaining in the midst of your chosen friends, you cannot sacrifice such a company to these gentlemen, no sir, and you might, so to speak, turn all these gentlemen out at once into the street, yes sir, so that I, as master of the house, would with the greatest pleasure, indeed sir . . ."

"Perfectly just!" General Ivolgin thundered suddenly from the depths of the room.

"Enough, Lebedev, enough, enough . . ." the prince would have begun, but his words were lost in a perfect explosion of indignation.

"No, excuse me, Prince, excuse me, but now that is not enough!"

Lebedev's nephew practically out-shouted everyone. "Now we must put the case on a firm and clear footing, for it is evidently not understood. Some legal quibbles have gotten mixed up in it, and on account of these quibbles, they threaten to turn us into the street! But can it really be, Prince, that you take us for such fools that we don't understand ourselves the extent to which our business is not a legal matter, and that if the case is analyzed from a legal point of view, we have no right to demand from you a single ruble according to the law? But we thoroughly grasp that, though there is no legal right here, there is a human, natural right, the right of common sense and the voice of conscience, and though that claim may not be written in any rotten human code, yet a noble-minded and honest man, in other words, a man of common sense, is bound to remain noble-minded and honest even in those points that are not written in the codes. That's why we've entered here without fearing that we'll be turned out into the street (as you've threatened just now) just for the fact that we don't *beg* but *demand,* and for the impropriety of our visit at such a late hour (though we didn't come at a late hour, and you yourself made us wait in the servants' hall); that's just why, I say, we came fearing nothing, because we assumed you to be, namely, a man of common sense, that is, of honor and conscience. Yes, it's true, we came in not humbly, not as beggars or supplicants of yours, but with our heads erect, like free men, and not a bit with a petition, but with a free and proud demand (do you hear, not with a petition, but a demand, mark these words!). We put the question to you directly and with dignity: do you admit yourself to be right or wrong in Burdovsky's case? Do you admit that you were benefited and even, perhaps, saved from death by Pavlishchev? If you admit it (and it's evident), do you intend, or do you think it just, having received millions yourself in turn, to compensate Pavlishchev's son in his need, even though he does bear the name of Burdovsky? Yes or no? If yes, that is, in other words, if you have what you call in your language honor and conscience, and what we more exactly designate with the term common sense, then satisfy us, and that'll be the end of it. Satisfy us without entreaties or gratitude on our part, don't expect them of us, for you are not doing it for us, but for justice. If you are, however, unwilling to satisfy us, that is, answer *no,* we go away at once and the case is over; and as for you, we tell you to your face before all your witnesses that you are a man of coarse intelligence and low development; that for the future you dare not call yourself a man of honor and conscience, and have no right to do so, that you are trying to buy that right too cheap. I've finished. I have put the question. Turn us into the street now, if you dare. You can do it, you have the power. But remember all the same that we demand, we do not beg. We demand, we do not beg!"

Lebedev's nephew stopped, much excited.

"We demand, we demand, we demand, we don't beg!" Burdovsky began to prattle and turned red as a crab.

After the words uttered by Lebedev's nephew, a general movement ensued, and indeed there arose a murmur, though everyone in the party was evidently anxious to avoid meddling in the affair, except perhaps Lebedev, who seemed in a perfect fever. (It was a queer thing: Lebedev, though evidently on the prince's side, now seemed to feel a certain pleasure of family pride after his nephew's speech; in any case, he looked at the whole company with a certain particular air of satisfaction.)

"In my opinion," the prince began rather quietly, "in my opinion, Mr. Doktorenko, in all that you have said just now, you are half perfectly right, even, I agree, in the far greater half, and I should agree with you entirely if you hadn't left something out of your speech. Just what, namely, you've left out here, it is not in my power to express to you exactly, I am not capable, but to make your speech quite just, of course, something is lacking. But we had better turn to the case, gentlemen; tell me, what made you publish that article? Why, there isn't a word in it that isn't slander; so that to my thinking, gentlemen, you've done a base deed."

"But if you please! . . ."

"My good sir!"

"This . . . this . . . this . . ." was heard at the same time from the excited visitors.

"As for the article," Ippolit took up shrilly, "as for that article, I have told you already that I and the rest don't approve of it! It was written by him here" (he pointed to the boxer, who was sitting beside him); "it's written disgracefully, I agree, it's written illiterately, and in the jargon used by retired army men like him. He is stupid, and, besides that, is a mercenary fellow, I agree; I tell him so to his face every day, but yet in half of it he was within his rights: publicity is the legal right of all, and therefore of Burdovsky, too. As for his absurdities, let him answer for that himself. And with regard to the fact that earlier I protested in the name of all against the presence of your friends, I consider it necessary to inform you, good sirs, that I protested simply to assert our rights, but in reality, we positively prefer that there should be witnesses, and earlier, before we had even come in here, we all four agreed on that. Whoever your witnesses might be, even if they were your friends, since they cannot dispute Burdovsky's right (because it's obviously mathematical), then it is even better that these witnesses are your friends; it will make the truth even more obvious."

"That's true, we agreed about that," Lebedev's nephew confirmed.

"Then why was there such a fuss and outcry before, at the outset, if that's just how you wanted it?" asked the prince in surprise.

"And as for the article, Prince," stuck in the boxer, terribly anxious to put in his word and becoming agreeably aroused (it might be suspected that he was visibly and strongly affected by the presence of the ladies), "as for the article, I confess that I am really the author of it, though my sickly friend, whom I am accustomed to excuse on account of his affliction, has just criticized it. But I wrote and I published it in the journal of a true friend, in the form of a letter. Only the verses are really not mine and really come from the pen of a well-known satirist. I only read it through to Mr. Burdovsky, and not all of it, and at once obtained his consent to publish it, but you must admit that I could have published it without his consent. Publicity is a general right, an honorable and beneficial one. I hope, Prince, that you yourself are progressive enough not to deny that . . ."

"I am not going to deny anything, but you must admit that your article . . ."

"Is harsh, you want to say? But, you know, it's for the public good, so to speak, you must admit, and finally, can one really allow such a provoking incident to go by? So much the worse for the guilty, but the public good goes before everything. As regards certain inaccuracies, hyperbole, so to speak, you must admit, too, that what matters most is the initiative, what matters most is the object and intention; what matters is the beneficial example; we can go into the individual cases afterward; and, finally, there is the turn of phrase, there is, so to speak, the humoristic challenge, and, finally—everyone writes like that, you must admit yourself! Ha-ha!"

"But that is an entirely false path! I assure you, gentlemen," the prince exclaimed. "You published the article on the supposition that nothing would induce me to agree to satisfy Mr. Burdovsky and, it would seem, in order to frighten me for it and revenge yourself somehow. But how do you know: perhaps I might have decided to satisfy Burdovsky. I declare straight out, before everyone, that I will satisfy ..."

"Well, finally, a wise and noble-minded word from a wise and most noble-minded man!" announced the boxer.

"Oh, Lord!" broke from Lizaveta Prokofyevna.

"This is insufferable!" muttered the general.

"But allow me, gentlemen, allow me, I will set out the case," pleaded the prince. "Some five weeks ago, in Z., the agent and representative of yours, Mr. Burdovsky, Chebarov, came to see me. Your description of him in your article was really much too flattering, Mr. Keller," the prince turned to the boxer, laughing suddenly, "but I did not like him at all. I only understood from the first moment that the whole heart of the matter resides in this Chebarov, and that perhaps he had indeed directed you, Mr. Burdovsky, taking advantage of your simplicity, to begin this whole business, if we speak candidly."

"You've no right to ... I'm ... not simple ... this ..." Burdovsky began to murmur in agitation.

"You've no sort of right to make such suppositions," Lebedev's nephew intervened sententiously.

"This is insulting in the highest degree!" squealed Ippolit. "The supposition is insulting, false, and irrelevant."

"My fault, gentlemen, my fault," the prince hurriedly apologized, "please excuse me; it's because I thought, wouldn't it be better for us to be perfectly candid with one another; but it's for you to decide, as you please! I told Chebarov that, as I was not in Petersburg, I would at once authorize a friend to take charge of the case, and would let you, Mr. Burdovsky, know about it. I tell you plainly, gentlemen, that the case struck me as the biggest swindle, just because Chebarov was mixed up in it ... Oh, don't take offense, gentlemen! For goodness' sake, don't take offense!" the prince cried in alarm, again seeing signs of offended perturbation in Burdovsky and of agitation and protest in his friends. "It can have no reference to you personally if I say that I considered this case a swindle! Why, I didn't know any one of you personally then, I didn't even know your names; I only judged by

Chebarov; I say it at all because . . . if only you knew how horribly I've been taken in since I came into my inheritance!"

"Prince, you are terribly naïve," Lebedev's nephew observed mockingly.

"Besides, you are a prince and a millionaire! For all that you may, perhaps, really have a kind and rather simple heart, all the same, you can't, of course, escape the general law," Ippolit declared.

"Possibly, gentlemen, very possibly," the prince hurried on, "though I don't understand what general law you are speaking of; but I'll go on, only don't take offense for nothing; I haven't the faintest desire to insult you. And really, gentlemen, one can't say one word sincerely without your being offended at once! But in the first place, it was a great shock to me to hear that there was a 'son of Pavlishchev,' and that he was in such a terrible situation, as Chebarov explained to me. Pavlishchev was my benefactor and my father's friend. (Ach, why did you write such falsehoods about my father, Mr. Keller, in your article! There never was any squandering of the company's money, nor ill treatment of subordinates—of that I am absolutely convinced, and how could you lift your hand to write such a calumny?) And as for what you've written about Pavlishchev, that is just completely past all endurance: you call that noble man lascivious and frivolous and do it so boldly and positively, as though you were really speaking the truth, and meanwhile, he was one of the most virtuous men in the world! He was even a remarkably learned man; he used to correspond with numbers of distinguished men of science, and he spent a great deal of money for the advancement of science. As for his heart and his good deeds, oh, of course, you write quite justly that I was almost an idiot at that time and could understand nothing (though I could talk Russian, all the same, and could understand it), but I am, after all, capable of assessing everything that I can recollect now, you know . . ."

"Excuse me," Ippolit squeaked, "isn't this too sentimental? We are not children. You meant to come straight to the point; it's after nine, remember that."

"If you will, if you will, gentlemen," the prince agreed at once. "After my first mistrustfulness, I decided that I might be mistaken and that Pavlishchev might really have had a son. But I was very much amazed that this son should so readily, that is, I mean to say, so publicly, give away the secret of his birth and, above all, disgrace his mother. For even at that time Chebarov threatened me with publicity . . ."

"What absurdity!" cried Lebedev's nephew.

"You've no right . . . you've no right!" cried Burdovsky.

"The son is not responsible for the dissolute conduct of his father and the mother is not to blame," Ippolit shrieked hotly.

"All the more reason for sparing her, I should have thought," the prince ventured timidly.

"You are not simply naïve, Prince, you go beyond that, perhaps," Lebedev's nephew sneered maliciously.

"And what right had you! . . ." Ippolit squeaked in a most unnatural voice.

"None whatever, none whatever!" the prince hurriedly interrupted. "You are right there, I admit it, but it was unwitting, and I said to myself at once that my personal feelings should not have any influence on the matter, for if I consider myself bound to satisfy Mr. Burdovsky's demands for the sake of my feeling for Pavlishchev, then I must satisfy them in any case whatever, that is, whether I respected or did not respect Mr. Burdovsky. I only began about this, gentlemen, because, all the same, it seemed unnatural to me for a son to reveal his mother's secret so publicly . . . In a word, it was chiefly on that ground that I was convinced that Chebarov must be a scoundrel and had egged Mr. Burdovsky on to such a swindle by deceit."

"But this is intolerable!" broke from his visitors, some of whom even leapt up from their seats.

"Gentlemen! Why, it was just because of that I decided that poor Mr. Burdovsky must be a simple, defenseless person, easily imposed upon by swindlers, and therefore I was all the more bound to help him as the 'son of Pavlishchev'—first, by opposing Mr. Chebarov, second, by my loyalty and friendship, in order to guide him, and third, I decided to give him ten thousand rubles, that is, everything that by my reckoning Pavlishchev could have spent upon me."

"What! Only ten thousand!" shouted Ippolit.

"Well, Prince, you are not at all good in arithmetic or else you are too good at it, though you do pretend to be a simpleton," cried Lebedev's nephew.

"I won't agree to ten thousand," said Burdovsky.

"Antip! Agree to it!" the boxer prompted him in a clear and rapid whisper, bending from behind over the back of Ippolit's chair. "Agree to it, and afterward we shall see!"

"Li-isten, Mr. Myshkin," shrieked Ippolit, "understand that we are not fools, not vulgar fools, as we are probably thought to be by all your guests, and by these ladies who sneer at us so indignantly, and especially by that grand gentleman"—he pointed to Yevgeny Pavlovich— "whom I, naturally, do not have the honor of knowing, though I fancy I have heard something about him . . ."

"Allow me, allow me, gentlemen, you misunderstand me again!" the prince addressed them in agitation. "In the first place you, Mr. Keller, in your article have described my fortune very inaccurately: I didn't inherit millions at all; I've only perhaps an eighth or a tenth part of what you suppose me to have; in the second place, there weren't any tens of thousands spent on me in Switzerland: Schneider was paid six hundred rubles a year, and that was only in the first three years; Pavlishchev never went to Paris to find pretty governesses, that's a calumny again. In my opinion far less than ten thousand was spent on me altogether, but I propose to give ten thousand, and you'll admit yourselves that, in repaying what's due him, I could never offer Mr. Burdovsky more, even if I were awfully fond of him, and I could not do so from a feeling of delicacy alone, precisely because I was giving back what's due him, and not sending him alms. I don't know, gentlemen, how you can fail to understand that! But still I did mean, afterward, to compensate for all this by my friendship, by taking an active part in the fate of the unfortunate Mr. Burdovsky, who has evidently been deceived, for, without deceit, he could not have himself agreed, could he, to anything so low as, for instance, publishing those things today about his mother in Mr. Keller's article . . . But gentlemen, really, why are you beside yourselves again? Why, we shall completely misunderstand each other! Why, it's turned out to be as I thought! I've become convinced with my own eyes now that my surmise was correct." The prince tried heatedly to persuade them, anxious to pacify their excitement, and not noticing that he was only increasing it.

"How? Convinced of what?" They fell upon him almost in a fury.

"Why, mercy, in the first place, I've had time to make out Mr. Burdovsky myself perfectly well, I see now myself what he is . . . He is an innocent man, but taken in by everyone! A defenseless man . . . and therefore I ought to spare him, and in the second place, Gavrila

Ardalionovich—to whom the case was entrusted and from whom I heard nothing for a long time, because I was traveling, and afterward was for three days ill in Petersburg—now suddenly, only an hour ago, at our first interview, tells me that he's seen through all of Chebarov's plans, that he has proof, and that Chebarov is just what I supposed him to be. I know, gentlemen, that many people consider me an idiot, and Chebarov, owing to my reputation for giving away money freely, thought that he could easily deceive me, and he reckoned precisely on my feelings for Pavlishchev. But the chief point is—but hear me out, gentlemen, do hear me out!—the chief point is that it appears now that Mr. Burdovsky is not Pavlishchev's son at all! Gavrila Ardalionovich has informed me of this, and assures me that he has obtained positive proof of it. Well, what will you make of that; why, it's scarcely to be believed after all that you've wrought! And listen: there is positive proof! I don't believe it yet, don't believe it myself, I assure you; I still doubt it, because Gavrila Ardalionovich has not had time to give me all the details yet, but that Chebarov is a scoundrel, there can be no doubt at all now! He has taken in poor Mr. Burdovsky and all of you gentlemen, who have so nobly come to support your friend (for he obviously needs support, why, I understand that, of course!), he has taken all of you in, and has embroiled you all in a fraudulent business, for you know it really is, in essence, a fraud and a swindle!"

"How, now, swindling!... How, now, not the 'son of Pavlishchev'?... How is it possible!..." Exclamations were heard on all sides. All Burdovsky's company were in inexpressible perturbation.

"Yes, of course, it's swindling! For if Mr. Burdovsky now turns out to be not the 'son of Pavlishchev,' then in that case, Mr. Burdovsky's claim is a fraud pure and simple (that is, of course, if he knew the truth!); but that's just the point, that he has been deceived, that's just why I insist that he is vindicated; that's just why I say that he deserves to be pitied for his simplicity, and can't be left without support; if it were not so, he would turn out to be a swindler in this business, too. But I am convinced myself that he doesn't understand anything! I was in that state myself, too, before I went to Switzerland; I also used to murmur disconnected words—you want to express yourself and can't... I understand that; I can sympathize very well because I am almost the same, I may be allowed to speak of it! And, finally, all the same I—although there is no 'son of Pavlishchev' now, and it all turns out to be humbug—I haven't changed my mind and am ready to give back ten thousand, in Pavlishchev's memory. Why, before Mr. Burdovsky came on the scene, you know, I meant to devote those ten thousand to founding a school in Pavlishchev's memory, but it makes no difference now whether it's for a school or for Mr. Burdovsky, for though Mr. Burdovsky is not the 'son of Pavlishchev,' he is almost as good as a 'son of Pavlishchev': because he himself has been so wickedly deceived; he himself genuinely believed that he was Pavlishchev's son! So hear Gavrila Ardalionovich out, friends, let us make an end of this, don't be angry, don't be agitated, sit down! Gavrila Ardalionovich will explain everything to us directly, and I confess I am extremely eager to hear all the details myself. He says he has even been to Pskov to see your mother, Mr. Burdovsky, who hasn't died at all, as they've made you say in the article . . . Sit down, gentlemen, sit down!"

The prince sat down and succeeded in making Burdovsky's company, who had leapt up from their seats, sit back down again. For the last ten or twenty minutes he had been talking heatedly, loudly, with impatient haste, carried away and trying to talk above the rest, to shout them down, and in the end, of course, he couldn't help bitterly regretting afterward certain words and assumptions that had escaped him now. If they had not gotten him so worked up and made him almost beside himself—he would not have allowed himself so baldly and hurriedly to utter aloud certain of his conjectures and unnecessarily candid statements. But he had no sooner sat down in his place than a burning remorse pierced his heart till it ached. Besides the fact that he had "insulted" Burdovsky by so publicly assuming that he had suffered from the same disease for which he himself had been treated in Switzerland—besides that fact, the offer of ten thousand, in the place of the school, had been made to his thinking coarsely and carelessly, like a charity, and precisely in that it had been spoken out loud before people. "I ought to have waited it out and offered it to him tomorrow, in private," the prince thought at once, "and now, perhaps, there will be no setting it right! Yes, I am an idiot, a real idiot!" he decided in a fit of shame and extreme distress.

Meanwhile, Gavrila Ardalionovich, who had hitherto kept to the side and maintained a persistent silence, came forward at the prince's invitation, stood beside him and began calmly and clearly giving an account of the case that had been entrusted to him by the prince. All talk was instantly silenced. Everyone listened with extreme curiosity, especially Burdovsky's party.

I X

"You certainly will not deny," Gavrila Ardalionovich began, directly addressing Burdovsky, who was listening to him with all his might, staring at him wide-eyed with wonder and, evidently, in a state of violent perturbation, "you will not attempt, and will certainly not wish seriously to deny, that you were born exactly two years after your worthy mother was legally married to Collegial Secretary Burdovsky, your father. The date of your birth can be easily proved as a fact, so that the distortion of this fact—too insulting to you and your mother—in Mr. Keller's article must be ascribed simply to the playfulness of the imagination of Mr. Keller, who supposed by this to make your right more apparent, and so promote your interest by it. Mr. Keller says that he read the article to you beforehand, though not the whole of it . . . there can be no doubt that he did not read so far as that passage . . ."

"No, I didn't, actually," the boxer interrupted, "but all the facts were given me by a competent person, and I . . ."

"Excuse me, Mr. Keller," Gavrila Ardalionovich stopped him, "allow me to speak. I assure you, we will come to your article in its turn, and then you can make your explanation, but now we had better take things in their proper order. Quite by chance, with the help of my sister, Varvara Ardalionovna Ptitsyn, I obtained from her intimate friend, Vera Alexeevna Zubkov, a landed widow, a certain letter of the late Mr. Pavlishchev, written to her from him from abroad, twenty-four years ago. Making Madame Zubkov's acquaintance, I applied, at her suggestion, to the retired Colonel Timofei Fyodorovich Vyazovkin, a distant relation who was in his day a great friend of Mr. Pavlishchev. From him, I succeeded in getting two more of Nikolai Andreevich's letters, also written from abroad. From these three letters, from the dates and facts mentioned in them, it can be mathematically proved, beyond all possibility of dispute or even doubt, that Nikolai Andreevich had at the time gone abroad (where he remained three years in a row), precisely a year and a half before you were born, Mr. Burdovsky. Your mother, as you know, has never been out of Russia . . . For the present I will not read these letters. It's late now; I simply announce the fact, in any case. But if you care to make an appointment to see me, Mr. Burdovsky, why, even tomorrow morning if you like, and bring your witnesses (in whatever numbers you please) and experts to examine the handwriting, I have no doubt that you cannot but be convinced of the obvious truth of the facts I have laid out. If this is so, then the whole case, of course, collapses and is over of itself."

Again general commotion and intense agitation followed. Burdovsky himself suddenly got up from his chair.

"If it's so, then I've been deceived, deceived, and not by Chebarov, but long, long ago; I don't want any experts, I don't want an appointment, I believe you, I withdraw my claim . . . I won't agree to the ten thousand . . . Good-bye."

He took up his cap and pushed away his chair to go out.

"If you can, Mr. Burdovsky," Gavrila Ardalionovich stopped him softly and sweetly, "stay, if only for another five minutes. Some other extremely important facts have come to light in this case; for you at any rate they are rather interesting. In my view, you must not fail to become acquainted with them, and perhaps it will be pleasanter for you if the case can be completely cleared up . . ."

Burdovsky sat down without speaking, bowing his head somewhat, as if deeply lost in thought. Lebedev's nephew, who had started to get up to accompany him out, sat down too; though he had not lost his head or his courage, still, he seemed greatly perplexed. Ippolit was scowling, dejected and apparently very much astonished. At that moment, moreover, he fell into such a violent coughing fit that he stained his handkerchief with blood. The boxer was almost in dismay.

"Ech, Antip!" he cried bitterly. "You see, I told you back then . . . the day before yesterday, that perhaps you really weren't Pavlishchev's son!"

There was a sound of smothered laughter; two or three laughed louder than the rest.

"The fact you stated just now, Mr. Keller," Gavrila Ardalionovich took up, "is rather valuable. Nevertheless, I have a perfect right to assert, on the most precise evidence, that though Mr. Burdovsky of course knew very well the period of his birth, he was in complete ignorance of the circumstance of Mr. Pavlishchev's residence abroad, where Mr. Pavlishchev spent the greater part of his life, returning to Russia only for brief periods. Besides, the fact of his going away at that time is rather too unremarkable in itself as to be remembered more than twenty years later, even by those who knew Pavlishchev well, to say nothing of Mr. Burdovsky, who was not born at the time. It has turned out, of course, not to be impossible to establish the fact; but I must own that the facts I've collected came to me quite by chance, and might well not have come into my hands; so that these facts were really almost impossible for Mr. Burdovsky, or even Chebarov, to obtain, even if it had occurred to them to inquire. But, you know, it may well not have occurred to them . . ."

"Allow me, Mr. Ivolgin," Ippolit suddenly cut him off irritably, "what's all this rigmarole (excuse me) for? The case has been cleared up, we agree to accept the main fact, why go on making a tedious and offensive fuss about it? You want, perhaps, to brag of the cleverness of your investigations, to display before us and the prince what a fine detective and sleuth you are? Or can it be you intend to undertake to excuse and justify Mr. Burdovsky by the fact that he got mixed up in this business through ignorance? But that's impudence, my good sir! Burdovsky has no need of your justifications and your excuses, let me tell you! It's painful for him, it's trying enough for him as it is now, he is in an awkward position, you should have surmised that, understood that . . ."

"Enough, Mr. Terentyev, enough," Gavrila Ardalionovich succeeded in interrupting. "Calm down, don't excite yourself; you are not at all well, it seems? I feel for you. In that case, if you like, I've finished, or rather I am obliged to state briefly only those facts that, I am convinced, it would not be a bad thing to know in full detail," he added, noticing a general movement suggestive of impatience. "I only want to state, with proof, for the information of all who had an interest in the matter, that your mother, Mr. Burdovsky, enjoyed the kind and considerate attentions of Mr. Pavlishchev solely because she was the sister of the serf-girl with whom Nikolai Andreevich Pavlishchev was in love in his early youth, and so much so that he would certainly have married her if she had not died suddenly. I have proof that this absolutely accurate and true familial fact is very little known, and even quite forgotten. Further, I could explain how your mother, while still a child of ten, was taken in by Pavlishchev to be brought up by him as though she had been a relation, that she had a considerable dowry set apart for her, and that all these solicitudes gave rise to extremely disquieting rumors among Pavlishchev's numerous relations: it was even thought that he was going to marry his ward, but in the end, she was married according to her own inclination (and that I can prove in a most certain way) to a surveying clerk, a Mr. Burdovsky, in her twentieth year. I have collected some most certain facts to prove that your father, Mr. Burdovsky, who had absolutely no head for business, gave up his post on receiving your mother's dowry of fifteen thousand rubles, entered upon commercial speculations, was deceived, lost his capital, could not bear his misfortune, took to drink, became ill in consequence, and finally died prematurely, eight years after marrying your mother. Then, according to your mother's own testimony, she was left utterly destitute, and would have come to grief entirely without the constant and generous assistance of Pavlishchev, who granted her a subsidy of up to six hundred rubles a year. There is innumerable testimony, too, that he was extremely fond of you as a child. From this testimony and, again, from the assertions of your mother, it appears that he was fond of you chiefly because, in your early youth, you looked like a tongue-tied cripple, like a wretched, miserable child (and as I have concluded from well-authenticated evidence, Pavlishchev had all his life a kind of especially tender inclination for everything afflicted and unfairly treated by nature, particularly in children—a fact, to my thinking, of great importance in our case). Finally, I can boast of the most precise research about that fact of prime importance—how this extreme attachment for you on the part of Pavlishchev (by whose efforts you were admitted to the gymnasium and taught under special supervision), finally, little by little, engendered in Pavlishchev's relations and the members of his household the idea that you were his son, and that your father was only a cuckolded husband. But the main thing is that this idea only grew into an absolute and general conviction in the latter years of Pavlishchev's life, when all his relations were alarmed about his will, and when the original facts were forgotten and inquiries impossible. No doubt that idea came to your ears too, Mr. Burdovsky, and took complete possession of you. Your mother, whose acquaintance I've had the honor of making personally, knew of these rumors, but even to this day she does not know (I concealed it from her too) that you, her son, had come under the spell of this rumor. I found your much respected mother, Mr. Burdovsky, in Pskov, in ill health and in a state of the most dire poverty, into which she had fallen upon Pavlishchev's death. She informed me with tears of gratitude that it was only through you and your help that she was still in this world; she expects a great deal of you in the future, and believes fervently in your future success . . ."

"This is really insufferable!" Lebedev's nephew suddenly proclaimed loudly and impatiently. "What's the object of this whole *roman*?"[44]

"It's disgusting, it's unseemly!" Ippolit stirred violently. But Burdovsky noticed nothing and did not even stir.

"What's the object of it? What's it for?" Gavrila Ardalionovich wondered slyly, maliciously preparing to present his conclusion. "Why, in the first place, Mr. Burdovsky is perhaps now fully convinced that Mr. Pavlishchev loved him from generosity and not as his son. This fact alone it was essential that Mr. Burdovsky should know, since he upheld Mr. Keller and approved of him earlier, after his article was read. I say this because I consider you an honorable man, Mr. Burdovsky. In the second place, it appears that there was not the least intention of robbery or swindling here, not even on the part of Chebarov; that's an important point for me too, because the prince, speaking warmly just now, mentioned that I shared his opinion of the dishonesty and fraudulence in this unfortunate case. On the contrary, there was absolute faith in it on all sides, and though Chebarov may really be a great rogue, in this case he appears as nothing more than a pettifogger and a mercenary. He hoped to make big money on it as a lawyer, and his calculation was not only acute and masterly, it was a sure thing: it was based on the readiness with which the prince gives away his money and his grateful respect for the late Pavlishchev; it was based, finally (and most important of all), on the prince's well-known chivalrous views as to the obligations of honor and conscience. As for Mr. Burdovsky personally, one may even say that, thanks to certain of his convictions, he was so worked upon by Chebarov and the company around him that he took up the case not from self-interest, but almost entirely as a service to truth, progress and humanity. Now, after the facts I have relayed, it must be clear to everyone that Mr. Burdovsky is an innocent man, in spite of all appearances, and the prince can now, more readily and zealously than before, offer him both his friendly as-

44. Fr., novel.

sistance and that active aid to which he referred just now when he spoke of schools and of Pavlishchev."

"Stay, Gavrila Ardalionovich, stay!" cried the prince in genuine dismay, but it was already too late.

"I have said, I have told you three times already," cried Burdovsky irritably, "that I don't want the money, I won't take it . . . What for . . . I don't want to . . . I'm getting out of here!"

And he nearly ran from the terrace. But Lebedev's nephew seized him by the arm and whispered something to him. The latter quickly turned back, and pulling a big unsealed envelope out of his pocket, threw it on a table near the prince.

"Here is the money! . . . How dare you! . . . how dare you! . . . The money!"

"Two hundred and fifty rubles that you dared to send him through Chebarov in the form of charity!" Doktorenko explained.

"It says fifty in the article!" cried Kolya.

"I am at fault," said the prince, going up to Burdovsky. "I'm very much at fault before you, Burdovsky, but I didn't send it to you as charity, believe me. And I am at fault now . . . I was at fault before." (The prince was much distressed, he looked tired and weak, and his words were disconnected.) "I talked of swindling . . . but I didn't mean you, I was mistaken. I said that you . . . were the same as me—afflicted. But you are not like me, you . . . give lessons, you support your mother. I said that you cast shame on your mother's name, but you love her; she says so herself . . . I didn't know . . . Gavrila Ardalionovich had not told me everything before . . . I am at fault. I dared to offer you ten thousand, but I am at fault, I ought to have done it differently, and now . . . it can't be done because you despise me . . ."

"But this is a madhouse!" cried Lizaveta Prokofyevna.

"Of course, a house of madmen!" Aglaia could not refrain from saying, sharply, but her words were lost in the general uproar; everyone was speaking loudly now, everyone was in discussion, some were arguing, some laughing. Ivan Fyodorovich Epanchin was indignant in the extreme and, with an air of wounded dignity, waited for Lizaveta Prokofyevna. Lebedev's nephew put in a final word:

"Yes, Prince, one must do you justice, you do know how to make use of your . . . well, illness (to express it more politely); you've managed to offer your friendship and money in such a clever way that now it's impossible for an honorable man to take it under any circumstances. That's either a bit too innocent or a bit too clever ... but you know best which."

"Excuse me, gentlemen!" exclaimed Gavrila Ardalionovich, who had meantime opened the envelope, "There aren't two hundred and fifty rubles here at all, but only a hundred. I say it, Prince, so that there should be no perplexity."

"Let it be, let it be!" cried the prince, waving his hands at Gavrila Ardalionovich.

"No, don't 'let it be,'" Lebedev's nephew caught it up at once. "Your 'let it be' is insulting to us, Prince. We don't hide ourselves, we declare it openly: yes, there are only a hundred rubles there, and not the whole two hundred and fifty, but isn't it just the same ..."

"N-no, it's not just the same," Gavrila Ardalionovich managed to stick in, with an air of naïve perplexity.

"Don't interrupt me; we are not such fools as you think, Mr. Advocate," cried Lebedev's nephew with spiteful vexation. "Of course, a hundred rubles is not two hundred and fifty, and it's not just the same, but the principle is what matters; the initiative is what matters here, and that a hundred and fifty rubles are missing is only a detail. What matters is that Burdovsky does not accept your charity, your excellency, that he throws it in your face, and in that sense it makes no difference whether it's a hundred or two hundred and fifty. Burdovsky hasn't accepted the ten thousand: you've seen that; he wouldn't have brought back the hundred rubles either if he had been dishonest! That hundred and fifty rubles has gone to Chebarov for his journey to see the prince. Go ahead, laugh at our awkwardness, at our inexperience in conducting business; you've already tried your very utmost to make us ridiculous as it is; but don't dare to say we are dishonest. We'll all chip in together, sir, to pay back that hundred and fifty rubles to the prince; we'll pay it back if it's a ruble at a time, and we'll pay it back with interest. Burdovsky is poor, Burdovsky hasn't millions, and after his journey, Chebarov presented his bill. We hoped to win ... Who would not have done the same in his place?"

"What do you mean, who?" exclaimed Prince Shch.

"I shall go out of my mind here!" cried Lizaveta Prokofyevna.

"It reminds me," laughed Yevgeny Pavlovich, who had long been standing there watching, "of the celebrated defense made recently by a lawyer who, bringing forward as an excuse the poverty of his client—who had murdered six people at once in order to rob them—suddenly concluded with something along these lines: 'It was natural,' said he, 'that in my client's poverty, the idea of murdering those six people should have occurred to him; and to whom indeed would it not have occurred in his place?' Something of that sort, only very amusing."[45]

"Enough!" Lizaveta Prokofyevna pronounced suddenly, almost shaking with wrath. "It's time to cut short this rubbish! . . ." She was in the most terrible excitement; she flung back her head menacingly and, with an air of haughty, fierce and impatient defiance, she scanned the whole party with her flashing eyes, scarcely able at the moment to distinguish between friends and foes. It was that pitch of long-suppressed but at last irrepressible wrath when the leading impulse becomes immediate conflict, the urgent need to pounce upon someone posthaste. Those who knew Lizaveta Prokofyevna felt at once that something unusual had happened to her. Ivan Fyodorovich told Prince Shch. the very next day that "it happens to her sometimes, but to such an extent as yesterday is rare, even for her; it happens to her once in three years or so, but not oftener. Not oftener!" he added emphatically.

"Enough, Ivan Fyodorovich! Let me alone!" cried Lizaveta Prokofyevna. "Why are you offering me your arm now? You couldn't manage to take me away before; you are the husband, you are the head of the family; you ought to have taken me, fool that I was, by the ear and led me out if I had not obeyed you and gone out. You might think of your daughters, anyhow! But now we can find the way without you! I've had shame enough to last me a year . . . Wait a bit, I must still thank the prince! . . . Thank you for the treat, Prince! And I went and made myself comfortable to listen to the young people . . . What baseness, what baseness! It's chaos, a disgrace, you couldn't dream it up! Why, can there be many like them? . . . Be quiet, Aglaia! Be quiet, Alexandra! It's not your business! . . . Don't fuss around me, Yevgeny Pavlovich, you bother me! . . . So you are asking their forgiveness, my dear?" she went on, addressing the prince. " 'I'm at fault,' says he, 'for daring to offer

---

45. Something along these lines was argued by Gorsky's defense attorney in the Zhemarin case.

you a fortune'... And what are you pleased to be laughing at, you little braggart!?" she pounced suddenly on Lebedev's nephew. "'We refuse the fortune,' says he, 'we demand, we don't ask!' As though he didn't know that this idiot will trail off again tomorrow to offer them his friendship and his money! You'll go, won't you? Will you go or not?"

"I'll go," said the prince in a soft and humble voice.

"You hear! Well, that's just what you are reckoning on," she turned again to Doktorenko. "Why, the money is as good as in your pocket, and so you blow your horn and try to raise some dust... No, my good man, you can find other fools, I see right through you.... I see your whole game!"

"Lizaveta Prokofyevna!" cried the prince.

"Come away, Lizaveta Prokofyevna, it's more than time we went, and let us take the prince with us," Prince Shch. said, smiling as calmly as he could.

The girls stood on one side, almost alarmed, the general was positively alarmed; everyone present was amazed. Some of those standing farther away smirked on the sly and exchanged whispers; Lebedev's face expressed perfect rapture.

"There's disgrace and chaos to be found everywhere, madam," said Lebedev's nephew significantly, though he was a good deal puzzled.

"But not like that! Not like that, my man, not like yours here!" Lizaveta Prokofyevna retorted with spiteful pleasure, as if in hysterics. "But will you let me alone!" she cried to those who tried to persuade her. "Well, since you yourself, Yevgeny Pavlovich, have just proclaimed that even a defense attorney in court declared that nothing is more natural than to butcher six people out of poverty, why, then, the end of all things has really come; I never heard of such a thing. It's all become clear to me now! And this stuttering fellow, why, wouldn't he murder anyone?" (She pointed to Burdovsky, who was gazing at her in extreme bewilderment.) "I am ready to bet that he will murder someone! Maybe he won't take your money, your ten thousand, maybe he won't take it for conscience's sake, but he'll come at night and murder you and take the money from your cash box. He'll take it for conscience's sake! That's not dishonorable by his reckoning! It's just 'a burst of noble desperation,' it's a 'protest,' or the devil knows what... Phooey! Everything's gone topsy-turvy, everything is upside down. A girl grows up at home, and suddenly in the middle of the street she jumps into a cab: 'Mamma, I was married the other day to some Karlych or Ivanych, good-bye.'[46] And is it the right thing to behave like that, do you think? Is it natural, is it deserving of respect? Is it the woman question? This silly boy"—she pointed to Kolya—"even he was arguing the other day that that's what the 'woman question' means. And let the mother be a fool, but all the same, you must behave like a human being to her! . . . Why did you come in before with your heads up in the air? 'Make way, we are coming! Give us every right and don't you dare breathe a word before us. Pay us every sort of respect, such as no one's heard of, and we shall treat you worse than the lowest lackey!' They search for truth, they stand on their rights, and yet they've slandered him in their article like heathens. 'We demand, we don't ask, and you'll get no gratitude from us, because you are acting for the satisfaction of your own conscience!' What a queer sort of morality: Why, if he'll get no gratitude from you, the prince may tell you in answer that he feels no sort of gratitude to Pavlishchev, because Pavlishchev too did good for the satisfaction of his own conscience. But you know it's just his gratitude to Pavlishchev you've been reckoning on: why, it wasn't you he borrowed money from, it isn't you he owes, so what are you reckoning on, if not his gratitude? So how can you repudiate it yourself? Madmen! They regard society as savage and inhuman because it cries shame on the seduced girl. But if you think society inhuman, you must think that the girl suffers at the hands of that society. And if she suffers, how is it you expose her to society yourself in the newspapers and demand that she must not suffer? Madmen! Vainglorious creatures! They don't believe in God, they don't believe in Christ! Why, you are so eaten up with vanity and pride that you'll end by devouring one another, that's what I prophesy. Isn't that topsyturviness, isn't that chaos, isn't it a disgrace? And after that, this shameful creature must needs go and beg their pardon, too! Are there many more like you? What are you laughing at: at my disgracing myself with you? Why, I've disgraced myself already, there's no help for it now! . . . Don't you go grinning, you filthy lout!" she pounced upon Ippolit. "He is almost at his last gasp, yet he is corrupting others! You've corrupted this silly boy"—she pointed to Kolya again—"he does nothing but rave

46. This is a reference to an incident in Chernishevsky's famous novel *What Is to Be Done?* [C.G.]

about you, you teach him atheism, you don't believe in God, and you are not too old for a whipping yourself, good sir! Fie upon you! . . . So you'll go to them tomorrow, Prince Lev Nikolaevich?" she asked the prince again, almost breathless.

"I will."

"Then I don't want to know you after this!" She turned quickly to go out, but suddenly turned back again. "And you'll go to this atheist too?" She pointed to Ippolit. "But why are you smirking at me!" she cried in an unnatural scream, and suddenly pounced toward Ippolit, unable to endure his caustic grin.

"Lizaveta Prokofyevna! Lizaveta Prokofyevna! Lizaveta Prokofyevna!" was heard on all sides at once.

"*Maman,* this is shameful," Aglaia cried loudly.

"Don't worry, Aglaia Ivanovna," calmly answered Ippolit, whom Lizaveta Prokofyevna, having dashed up to him, had seized upon and for some inexplicable reason was holding tightly by the arm; she stood before him, and practically pierced him with her enraged gaze. "Don't worry, your *maman* will see that you can't pounce upon a dying man . . . I am ready to explain why I laughed . . . I shall be very glad of being permitted . . ."

Here he fell into a terrible coughing fit and could not control the cough for a full minute.

"Why, he is dying, and still keeps holding forth!" cried Lizaveta Prokofyevna, letting go of his arm and looking almost with horror at the blood he wiped from his lips. "You are not fit for talking! You simply ought to go and lie down . . ."

"So I shall," Ippolit answered quietly, hoarsely, almost in a whisper. "As soon as I get home today, I'll lie down at once . . . In another fortnight, as I know, I shall die . . . B——n[47] himself told me so a week ago . . . So that if you allow me, I should like to say two words to you in parting."

"Why, have you lost your mind? Nonsense! You want nursing, it's not the time to talk! Go along, go along, go lie down!" Lizaveta Prokofyevna cried in horror.

"If I lie down, I shan't get up again till I die." Ippolit smiled. "Yesterday, I was already feeling like lying down so as not to get up till I die,

---

47. Dostoevsky was treated by a prominent physician named Botkin.

but I decided to put it off till the day after tomorrow, while my legs can still carry me ... so as to come here with them today ... only I am awfully tired ..."

"But sit down, sit down, why are you standing! Here's a chair." Lizaveta Prokofyevna reared up and pulled up a chair for him herself.

"Thank you," Ippolit went on softly, "and you sit down opposite, here, and we shall talk ... We must have a talk, Lizaveta Prokofyevna, I insist on it now ..." He smiled at her again. "Think, today is the last time I shall be out in the air and with people, and in a fortnight, I shall certainly be underground. So that this will be like a farewell to men and to nature. Though I am not very sentimental, yet would you believe it, I am very glad that all this has happened here at Pavlovsk: at least one can see the trees in leaf, anyway."

"But what sort of time is this for a talk?" Lizaveta Prokofyevna was growing more and more alarmed. "You are in a perfect fever. You were screeching and squeaking before, and now you can scarcely breathe, you are gasping!"

"I shall have a rest now. Why do you want to refuse my last wish? ... Do you know, I have been dreaming a long time of getting together with you somehow, Lizaveta Prokofyevna? I have heard a great deal about you ... from Kolya; he is almost the only one who hasn't given me up ... You are an original woman, an eccentric woman, I've seen that for myself now ... Do you know that I was rather fond of you even."

"Good heavens, and I was positively on the point of striking him!"

"Aglaia Ivanovna held you back; I am not mistaken, am I? This is your daughter, Aglaia Ivanovna, isn't it? She is so beautiful that, earlier, I guessed who she was at first sight, though I'd never seen her. Let me at least look at a beautiful woman for the last time in my life." Ippolit smiled a sort of awkward, crooked smile. "Here, and the prince is here too, and your husband, and the whole party. Why do you refuse my last wish?"

"A chair!" cried Lizaveta Prokofyevna, but she seized one herself and sat down opposite Ippolit. "Kolya," she commanded, "you will go with him at once, see him home, and tomorrow I'll certainly go myself ..."

"If you allow me, I would ask the prince for a cup of tea ... I am very tired. Do you know, Lizaveta Prokofyevna, I believe you meant to take the prince back to tea with you; why don't you stay here instead, let us spend time together, and the prince will surely give us all tea. Excuse my arranging it all . . . But I know you, you are good-natured, the prince is good-natured too . . . We are all ridiculously good-natured people."

The prince began to bustle. Lebedev flew headlong out of the room, Vera ran after him.

"That's true," the generaless decided abruptly. "Talk, only quietly, don't get carried away. You've softened my heart . . . Prince! You don't deserve that I should drink tea with you, but so be it, I'll stay, though I apologize to no one! To no one! Rubbish! . . . Still, if I've abused you, Prince, then forgive me—if you like, that is. But I am not keeping anyone," she turned with an expression of extraordinary wrath to her husband and daughters, as though they had done her some terrible wrong. "I can find my way home alone . . ."

But they didn't let her finish. They all approached and drew up around her readily. The prince at once began pressing everyone to stay to tea and apologized for not having thought of it before. Even the general was so amiable as to murmur something reassuring, and asked Lizaveta Prokofyevna solicitously if it was not, perhaps, too cool for her on the terrace. He almost came to the point of asking Ippolit how long he had been at the university, but he didn't ask him. Yevgeny Pavlovich and Prince Shch. became suddenly extremely amiable and merry; the faces of Adelaida and Alexandra even expressed, intermingled with continuing amazement, a certain pleasure; in a word, all were visibly delighted that the crisis with Lizaveta Prokofyevna had passed. Only Aglaia still frowned and sat down in silence off to the side. All the rest of the party remained, too; no one wanted to go away, not even General Ivolgin, to whom, however, Lebedev whispered something in passing, probably not quite pleasant, for the general at once effaced himself into a corner. The prince approached Burdovsky and his friends with invitations, too, leaving out no one. They muttered with a constrained air that they would wait for Ippolit, and at once withdrew to the furthest corner of the terrace, where they sat down all in a row again. Probably the tea had been got ready for Lebedev himself long before, for it appeared at once. It struck eleven.

X

Ippolit moistened his lips with the cup of tea handed to him by Vera Lebedev, put down the cup on the little table, and suddenly, as if disconcerted, looked about him almost in embarrassment.

"Look, Lizaveta Prokofyevna, these cups," he began with a sort of strange haste, "these china cups—and I think they are excellent china—always stand in Lebedev's sideboard under glass, locked up; they are never brought out . . . as is the custom; they are part of his wife's dowry . . . It's their custom . . . And here he's brought them out for us—in your honor of course, he is so pleased to see you . . ."

He wanted to add something more, but could not think of anything.

"He's become flustered after all, just as I expected!" Yevgeny Pavlovich whispered suddenly in the prince's ear. "It's dangerous, isn't it? It's a sure sign that now, out of spite, he'll pull something so eccentric that even Lizaveta Prokofyevna won't sit still for it, perhaps."

The prince looked at him inquiringly.

"You are not afraid of eccentricity?" added Yevgeny Pavlovich. "I am not either, you know; I should even like it; actually, all I'm after is that our dear Lizaveta Prokofyevna should be punished, and today, without fail, this very minute; I don't want to go without that. You are feverish, I think."

"Later, don't interrupt. Yes, I am unwell," the prince answered absently and even impatiently. He had caught his own name. Ippolit was speaking of him.

"You don't believe it?" Ippolit laughed hysterically. "That's as it should be, but the prince will believe it at once and not be a bit surprised."

"Do you hear, Prince," Lizaveta Prokofyevna turned to him, "do you hear?"

All around them, there was laughter. Lebedev kept officiously putting himself forward and fussed about Lizaveta Prokofyevna.

"He says that this affected buffoon, here, your landlord . . . helped this gentleman there to correct his article, the one they read earlier at your expense."

The prince looked at Lebedev in surprise.

"Why don't you speak?" Lizaveta Prokofyevna even stamped her foot.

"Well, now," muttered the prince, continuing to examine Lebedev, "I can already see that he did."

"Is it true?" Lizaveta Prokofyevna turned quickly to Lebedev.

"It's the honest truth, your excellency!" answered Lebedev firmly, without hesitation, laying his hand on his heart.

"He seems to be proud of it!" She nearly jumped from her chair.

"I am base, base!" muttered Lebedev, beginning to beat his breast and bowing his head lower and lower.

"What is it to me that you are base! He thinks he'll say he's 'base' and wiggle out of it! And aren't you ashamed, Prince, to have to do with such contemptible little people, I ask you once again? I shall never forgive you!"

"The prince will forgive me!" said Lebedev with conviction and tenderness.

"Simply from noble-mindedness," Keller said in a loud ringing voice, suddenly darting up to them and addressing Lizaveta Prokofyevna directly, "simply from good feeling, madam, and to avoid giving away a friend who is compromised, I concealed that about the corrections earlier, despite the fact that he did suggest kicking us out on the street, as you have heard yourself. To establish the truth, I confess that I really did apply to him, for six rubles, but not at all in the matter of the style, but namely, as a competent person, for the obtainment of the facts, which were for the most part unknown to me. Regarding the spats, regarding the appetite at the Swiss professor's, regarding the fifty rubles instead of two hundred and fifty, in a word, that whole arrangement, all that belongs to him, for six rubles, but he did not correct the style."

"I must observe," Lebedev interrupted him with feverish impatience and in a creeping sort of voice, amidst increasingly widespread laughter, "that I only corrected the first half of the article, but as we didn't agree in the middle and quarreled over one idea, I didn't correct the second half, gentlemen, so that everything that is ungrammatical there (for it is ungrammatical!), all that shouldn't be ascribed to me, gentlemen . . ."

"That's what he is worried about!" cried Lizaveta Prokofyevna.

"Allow me to ask you," said Yevgeny Pavlovich, addressing Keller, "when did you correct the article?"

"Yesterday morning," reported Keller, "we had a meeting, promising on our honor to keep the secret on both sides."

"This was while he was crawling before you protesting his devotion! A nice set of people, indeed! I don't want your Pushkin, and don't let your daughter come and see me!"

Lizaveta Prokofyevna was on the point of getting up, but suddenly turned irritably to Ippolit, who was laughing.

"Well, my sweet, you've decided to make me the laughingstock here, have you?"

"Heaven forbid," Ippolit smiled wryly, "but what amazes me most of all is your extraordinary eccentricity, Lizaveta Prokofyevna; I confess I brought up Lebedev on purpose; I knew the effect it would have on you and on you alone, for the prince really will forgive, and has probably forgiven already . . . He may have even found an excuse for him in his own mind; that's so, Prince, isn't it true?"

He was gasping for breath; his strange excitement grew at every word.

"Well? . . ." Lizaveta Prokofyevna uttered wrathfully, wondering at his tone. "Well?"

"I've heard a great deal about you, in that same vein . . . with great pleasure . . . I've learned to respect you extremely," Ippolit went on.

He said one thing, but in such a way as if by those very words he meant to say something entirely different. He spoke with a shade of mockery and at the same time was incommensurately agitated, looked about him mistrustfully, was obviously muddled, and lost his train of thought at every word, so that all this, together with his consumptive appearance and strange, glittering, and almost frenzied eyes, could not help but continue to attract attention to him.

"I should have been surprised, not knowing the world at all, of course (I confess that), at the fact that you not only remained yourself in the society of our present company, which was not fit for you, but even left these . . . young ladies to listen to a scandalous business, though they have read it all in novels already. Though I don't know, perhaps . . . because I am muddled, but in any case, who, other than you, could have stayed . . . at the request of a boy (well, yes, a boy, I confess it again) to spend the evening with him and to take . . . part in everything and . . . considering . . . you would be ashamed the next day . . . (I admit, anyway, I am not expressing myself properly). I commend all this exceedingly and respect it deeply, though one can see if only by the very face of his excellency, your husband, how unpleasant this all is for him . . . He-he!" he giggled, completely at a loss, and suddenly had such a fit of coughing that he could not go on for two minutes.

"Now he's choked!" Lizaveta Prokofyevna pronounced coldly and sharply, scanning him with stern curiosity. "Well, my sweet boy, we've had enough of you. It's time to go!"

"Allow me too, good sir, for my part, to tell you," Ivan Fyodorovich suddenly spoke up irritably, losing the last bit of patience, "that my wife is here visiting Prince Lev Nikolaevich, our mutual friend and neighbor, and that in any case it's not for you, young man, to judge Lizaveta Prokofyevna's actions, nor to comment aloud and to my person about what is written on my face. No, sir. And if my wife has remained here," he went on, growing more and more irritated almost at every word, "it's rather from amazement, sir, and from a modern curiosity, comprehensible to everyone, to see strange young people. I remained myself, as I sometimes stop in the street when I see something at which one can look as . . . as . . . as . . ."

"As a curiosity," Yevgeny Pavlovich prompted.

"Excellent and true." His excellency, somewhat at a loss for a comparison, was delighted. "Precisely as a curiosity. But in any case, what is most amazing of all and even most grievous of all to me, if one can say so grammatically, is that you, young man, are not even able to understand that Lizaveta Prokofyevna has stayed with you now because you are ill—if you really are dying—so to speak, from compassion, because of your piteous words, sir, and that no kind of slur can in any case attach to her name, character and consequence . . . Lizaveta Prokofyevna!" concluded the general, grown red-faced. "If you want to go, let us take leave of our kind prince and . . ."

"Thank you for the lesson, General," Ippolit interrupted earnestly and unexpectedly, looking thoughtfully at him.

"Let's go, *maman*. How much longer is this to go on! . . ." Aglaia pronounced impatiently and wrathfully, getting up from her chair.

"Two minutes more, dear Ivan Fyodorovich, if you allow it." Lizaveta Prokofyevna turned with dignity to her husband. "I believe he is in a fever and simply delirious; I am convinced of it by his eyes; he can't be left like this. Lev Nikolaevich! Could he stay the night with you, so as not to drag him to Petersburg tonight? *Cher prince*,[48] are you bored?" she suddenly, for some reason, turned to Prince Shch. "Come here, Alexandra; tidy up your hair, my dear."

She tidied her hair, which had no need of tidying, and kissed her; that was all she had called her for.

"I considered you capable of development . . ." Ippolit spoke up again, coming out of his reverie. "Yes! This was what I meant to say," he said, delighted, as though having suddenly remembered something. "Burdovsky here genuinely wants to protect his mother, doesn't he? And it turns out that he has disgraced her. The prince here wants to help Burdovsky, in the purity of his heart, offers him his tender friendship and a fortune, and is perhaps the only one of us who does not feel an aversion to him, and here they stand facing one another like genuine enemies . . . Ha, ha, ha! You all hate Burdovsky because, to your thinking, he treats his mother in an unseemly and ungraceful manner; isn't that so? Isn't it? Isn't it? Why, you are all awfully fond of seemliness and the gracefulness of form, they are all you put stock in, isn't it true? (I've suspected a long time they are all!) Well, you should know, then, that very likely not one of you has loved his mother like Burdovsky! You, Prince, I know, have sent money on the sly, with Ganechka, to Burdovsky's mother, and I'll bet (he, he, he!—he laughed hysterically), I'll bet that now Burdovsky will in turn accuse you of indelicacy of form and disrespect to his mother, upon my word, that's how it is, ha, ha, ha!"

At this point he choked again and coughed.

"Well, is that all? That's all now; you've said everything? Well, now go to bed; you have a fever," Lizaveta Prokofyevna interrupted impatiently, not taking her anxious gaze off him. "Oh, Lord! But he goes on speaking still!"

"I think you are laughing. Why do you keep laughing at me? I notice that you keep laughing at me!" he turned uneasily and irritably, all of a sudden, to Yevgeny Pavlovich; the latter was, in fact, laughing.

"I only wanted to ask you, Mr. . . . . Ippolit . . . excuse me, I've forgotten your family name."

48. Fr., dear prince.

"Mr. Terentyev," said the prince.

"Yes, Terentyev, thank you, Prince, it was said earlier, but it escaped me . . . I wanted to ask you, Mr. Terentyev, is it true what I've heard, that you are of the opinion that you have only to talk to the common folk out of the window for a quarter of an hour and they'll agree with you and follow you at once?"

"It's quite possible that I have said so . . ." answered Ippolit, seeming to recall something. "Most certainly I have!" he added suddenly, growing animated again and giving Yevgeny Pavlovich a firm look. "What of it?"

"Absolutely nothing; I was only inquiring, for the sake of completeness."

Yevgeny Pavlovich fell silent, but Ippolit still looked at him in impatient expectation.

"Well, have you finished, then?" Lizaveta Prokofyevna turned to Yevgeny Pavlovich. "Make haste and finish, dear man, it's time he turned in. Or don't you know how?" (She was in a state of terrible vexation.)

"Well, perhaps, I am rather not averse to adding," Yevgeny Pavlovich went on, smiling, "that everything I've heard from your companions, Mr. Terentyev, and everything you've set forth just now, and with such unmistakable talent, comes down, in my opinion, to the theory of the triumph of right before everything and despite everything, and even to the exclusion of everything else, and perhaps even before finding out what that right consists in. Perhaps I am mistaken?"

"Of course you are mistaken; I don't even understand you . . . further?"

There was a murmur in the corner, too. Lebedev's nephew muttered something in an undertone.

"Why, scarcely anything further," Yevgeny Pavlovich went on. "I only meant to observe that from there, the matter might spring directly to the right of might, that is, to the right of the individual fist and of personal caprice, as indeed has often turned out in the history of the world. Why, Proudhon[49] arrived at the right of might. In the American War, many of the foremost liberals declared themselves on the side of the plantation owners in the sense that Negroes are Ne-

49. Pierre-Joseph Proudhon (1809–65), radical French social theorist considered to be one of the founders of anarchism. His books were translated into Russian and were a topic of controversial debate. His death once again thrust the debate into the public eye.

groes, lower than the white race, and therefore that right of might was on the side of the white men . . ."

"Well?"

"So then, it would seem, you don't deny that might is right?"

"Further?"

"I must say you are logical; I only wanted to observe that from the right of might to the right of tigers and crocodiles, and even to Danilov and Gorsky, is not far."

"I don't know; further?"

Ippolit was scarcely listening to Yevgeny Pavlovich, and if he did ask him "well?" and "further?" then it seemed to be due more to an old habit he had formed in conversation, rather than from attention or curiosity.

"Why, nothing further . . . that's all."

"I am not angry with you, though," Ippolit suddenly concluded, completely unexpectedly, and, hardly entirely conscious of his act, he held out his hand, even smiling. Yevgeny Pavlovich was surprised at first, but with a most serious air touched the hand that was extended to him, just as if accepting forgiveness.

"I cannot fail to add," he said in the same ambiguously deferential tone, "my gratitude to you for the attention with which you have allowed me to speak, for, from my numerous observations, our liberals are never capable of letting anyone else have a conviction of his own without at once meeting their opponent with abuse or even something worse . . ."

"That's perfectly right," observed General Ivan Fyodorovich, and, folding his hands behind his back, he retreated with a most bored air to the steps of the terrace, where he yawned with vexation.

"Well, that's enough from you, my friend," Lizaveta Prokofyevna announced suddenly to Yevgeny Pavlovich. "I am tired of you . . ."

"It's time!" Ippolit suddenly rose, preoccupied and almost in alarm, gazing about him in confusion. "I've kept you; I wanted to tell you everything . . . I thought that this was it . . . the last time . . . It was fancy . . ."

It was evident that he revived by fits and starts, would emerge suddenly, for a few moments, out of nearly complete delirium, would suddenly remember and talk with complete consciousness, for the most part in disconnected phrases that had, perhaps, been long ago thought out and learned by heart in the drawn-out, tedious hours of his illness, in his bed, in sleepless solitude.

"Well, good-bye!" he suddenly uttered abruptly. "Do you think it's easy for me to say to you: good-bye? Ha, ha!" he smirked vexedly himself at his *awkward* question, and, suddenly, as if furious at continually failing to say what he wanted to say, he said loudly and irritably: "Your excellency! I have the honor of inviting you to my funeral, if only you think me worthy of such an honor, and . . . all of you, ladies and gentlemen, in the wake of the general!"

He laughed again; but it was already the laugh of a madman. Lizaveta Prokofyevna moved toward him in alarm and seized him by the arm. He looked at her intently with the same laugh, but it no longer continued, as if it had stopped short and become frozen on his face.

"Do you know that I came here to see the trees? These here . . ."— he pointed to the trees in the park—"that's not ridiculous, is it? There is nothing ridiculous in it?" he asked Lizaveta Prokofyevna seriously and suddenly sank into thought; then, a moment later, raised his head and began inquisitively looking about in the crowd. He was looking for Yevgeny Pavlovich, who was standing not very far at all, on the right, in the same place as before, but he had already forgotten and searched all around. "Ah, you've not gone away!" he found him at last. "You kept laughing before at my wanting to talk out of the window for a quarter of an hour . . . But do you know that I am not eighteen? I've lain so much on that pillow and looked so much out of that window and thought so much . . . about everyone . . . that . . . A dead man has no age, you know. I thought that last week when I woke up in the night . . . But do you know what you are afraid of more than anything? You are afraid of our sincerity more than anything, though you do despise us! I thought that too, lying on my pillow, that night . . . You think I meant to laugh at you before, Lizaveta Prokofyevna? No, I was not laughing at you, I only wanted to praise you . . . Kolya told me the prince called you a child . . . That's good. . . . But what was it now . . . I was going to say something more . . ."

He hid his face in his hands and fell into thought.

"Oh, that was it: when you were taking your leave before I suddenly thought: here are these people, and they'll never be there again, never! And the trees too—there will be nothing but a brick wall, the red one, of Meyer's house . . . opposite my window . . . Well, tell them about all that . . . Try and tell them; here's a beauty . . . Why, you are dead, you know; introduce yourself as a dead man; tell them that 'a dead man may say anything' . . . and that the Princess Marya Alexeevna won't rail at it,[50] ha, ha! . . . You don't laugh? . . ." He scanned them all mistrustfully. "But you know, a great many ideas have come into my head on the pillow . . . Do you know, I became persuaded that nature is very mocking . . . You said before that I am an atheist, but do you know this nature . . . Why are you laughing again? You are horribly cruel!" he pronounced suddenly with mournful indignation, surveying everyone. "I have not corrupted Kolya," he concluded in quite a different tone, earnest and convinced, as if he had suddenly also remembered something.

"Nobody, nobody is laughing at you here; calm down!" Lizaveta Prokofyevna was almost in agony. "A new doctor shall come tomorrow; the other one was mistaken; but do sit down, you can hardly stand on your legs! You are delirious . . . Ach, what are we to do with him now!" she fussed, making him sit down in an armchair. A tear gleamed on her cheek.

Ippolit stopped, almost amazed, raised his hand, stretched it out timidly, and touched the tear. He smiled some kind of childlike smile.

"I . . . you," he began joyfully, "you don't know how I . . . He has always talked to me with such delight about you, this one here, Kolya . . . and I like his delight. I've never corrupted him! He is the only friend I leave behind . . . I should like to have left everyone friends, everyone . . . but there were none, there were none . . . I wanted to be a man of action, I had the right. . . . Oh, how much I wanted! I don't want anything now, don't want to want anything, I made this promise to myself not to want anything; let them, let them seek the truth without me! Yes, nature is mocking. Why," he suddenly took up with heat, "why does she create the best creatures only to laugh at them afterward? Didn't she make it so that the sole creature who was recognized on earth as perfection . . . didn't she make it so that, showing him to men, it was him she preordained to say the very thing for which so much blood has been shed that if it had been shed at once, men must have been drowned in it for sure! O, it's a good thing that I am dying! Perhaps I

---

50. A reference to the closing words of Famusov's final monologue in *Woe from Wit:* "Oh! dear Lord! What will the Princess Marya Alexeevna say!"

too should have uttered some horrible lie, nature would have led me to it! I have not corrupted anyone ... I wanted to live for the happiness of all men, for the discovery and proclamation of the truth ... I gazed out of the window on Meyer's wall and thought to speak for a quarter of an hour and convince everyone, everyone, but for once in my life I've come together with ... you, if not with the people! and what has come of it, then? Nothing! What has come of it is that you despise me! So, it would seem I am not needed, it would seem I am a fool, it would seem it's time for me to go! And I haven't succeeded in leaving any memory behind! Not a sound, not a trace, not one deed, I haven't disseminated a single conviction! ... Don't laugh at the foolish fellow! Forget! Forget it all ... forget it, please; don't be so cruel! Do you know that if this consumption hadn't turned up, I should have killed myself."

He wanted to say a great deal more, it seemed, but did not finish, threw himself into the chair, covered his face with his hands, and began to cry like a little child.

"Well, what would you have us do with him now?" exclaimed Lizaveta Prokofyevna, darted to him, seized his head, and pressed it ever so firmly to her bosom. He sobbed convulsively. "There, there, there! Come, don't cry. Come, that's enough. You are a good boy. God will forgive you because of your ignorance! Come, that's enough; be brave ... Besides, you'll feel ashamed ..."

"Back there," said Ippolit, making an effort to raise his head, "I've a brother and sisters, little children, poor, innocent.... *She* will corrupt them! You are a saint, you ... are a child yourself—save them! Tear them away from that ... she ... a disgrace ... Oh, help them, help them, God will repay you a hundredfold, for God's sake, for Christ's sake!"

"Well, tell me, Ivan Fyodorovich, at last, what is to be done now!" Lizaveta Prokofyevna cried irritably. "Be so good as to break your majestic silence! If you don't decide it yourself, you may as well know that I shall stay the night here myself; you've tyrannized over me enough with your despotism!"

Lizaveta Prokofyevna questioned with vigor and wrath, and awaited an immediate reply. But in such cases, for the most part, those present, even if there are many of them, answer with silence, with passive curiosity, unwilling to take anything upon themselves, and only express their opinions long afterward. Among those present on this occasion there were some who were ready to sit there till morning if need be without uttering a word; for instance, Varvara Ardalionovna, who had been sitting the entire evening off to the side and listening the whole time with an extraordinary interest, having, perhaps, her own reasons for it.

"My opinion, my dear," the general spoke out, "is that what is needed now is rather more, so to speak, a nurse than our agitation, and perhaps a trustworthy, sober person for the night. In any case, the prince must be asked, and . . . the invalid must have rest at once. And tomorrow, we can show interest in him again."

"It's twelve o'clock now, we are going. Is he coming with us or staying with you?" Doktorenko turned irritably and angrily to the prince.

"If you like, you can stay at his side too," said the prince; "there'll be room."

"Your excellency!" Mr. Keller dashed up to General Epanchin unexpectedly and ecstatically. "If a satisfactory man is wanted for the night, I am ready to make a sacrifice for a friend . . . He is such a soul! I've long considered him a great man, your excellency! My education has been defective, of course, but his criticisms—they are pearls, pearls, your excellency! . . ."

The general turned away with despair.

"I shall be very glad if he will stay, of course; it's difficult for him to travel," the prince was proclaiming in response to Lizaveta Prokofyevna's irritable questions.

"But are you asleep? If you don't want him, my friend, I'll have him moved to my place! My goodness, why, he can hardly stand upright himself! Why, are you ill, then?"

Earlier, Lizaveta Prokofyevna, not finding the prince at death's door, had in fact greatly exaggerated the satisfactoriness of his state of health, judging by external appearances, but his recent illness, the painful recollections accompanying it, the fatigue from this evening's fuss, the incident with the "son of Pavlishchev," and the incident now with Ippolit—all that had indeed worked up his morbid sensibility into an almost feverish state. But, aside from that, there was now another anxiety, even a fear, in his eyes; he looked apprehensively at Ippolit, as though expecting something more from him.

Suddenly, Ippolit got up, horribly pale and with a look of terrible shame approaching despair on his distorted face. It was expressed chiefly in his eyes, which glanced hatefully and fearfully at the company, and in the dismayed, twisted, and abject sneer on his quivering lips. He dropped his eyes at once and shambled over—staggering and continuing to smile in that same way—to Burdovsky and Doktorenko, who were standing at the terrace steps; he was going away with them.

"Well, that's just what I was afraid of!" cried the prince; "that was bound to happen!"

Ippolit turned quickly to him with the most frenzied anger, and every feature in his face, down to the smallest one, seemed to be quivering and speaking.

"Ah, you were afraid of that, were you? 'That was bound to happen,' in your view? Then you should know, if I hate anyone here," he squealed hoarsely, with a shriek, with spittle spraying from his mouth, "(I hate all of you, all of you!) but you, you, Jesuitical, treacly little soul, idiot, philanthropic millionaire, you more than everyone and everything in the world! I understood and hated you long ago, when first I heard of you; I hated you with all the hatred of my soul ... This has all been your contriving! It was you that drove me to the point of breaking down! You drove a dying man to shame, you, you, you are to blame for my base faintheartedness! I would kill you if I were going to remain alive! I don't want your benevolence, I won't take anything from anyone, do you hear, not from anyone, not anything! I was in delirium, and don't you dare to triumph! ... I curse every one of you, once and for all!"

Here he choked completely.

"He is ashamed of his tears!" Lebedev whispered to Lizaveta Prokofyevna. "'That was bound to happen!' Bravo, Prince! He saw right through him ..."

But Lizaveta Prokofyevna did not deign to glance at him. She stood, holding herself proudly erect, with her head thrown back, surveying "these miserable little people" with contemptuous curiosity. When Ippolit had finished, the general started to shrug his shoulders; she looked him over wrathfully from head to toe, as though asking for an account of himself in his movement, and at once turned to the prince.

"Thank you, Prince, our eccentric family friend, for the agreeable evening you have given us all. I suppose your heart is now rejoicing that you've managed to hook us into your fooleries, too ... Enough, dear family friend, thank you for letting us finally have a good look at yourself, at least."

She began indignantly setting straight her mantle, waiting for "those people" to get off. At that moment, a hackney cab drove up for "those people"; Doktorenko had sent Lebedev's son, the schoolboy, to fetch it a quarter of an hour before. Immediately after his wife, General Epanchin managed to put in his word too.

"Yes, indeed, Prince, I should never have expected it . . . after everything, after all our friendly relations . . . and then Lizaveta Prokofyevna . . ."

"How can you! How can you!" exclaimed Adelaida. She walked up quickly to the prince and gave him her hand.

The prince smiled at her with a bewildered expression. Suddenly a hot, rapid whisper seemed to scorch his ear.

"If you don't throw these nasty people over at once, I shall hate you all my life, all my life!" Aglaia whispered; she seemed in a sort of frenzy, but she turned away before he had time to look at her. In any case, there was by now nothing and no one for him to throw over: they had in the meantime succeeded somehow in getting the sick Ippolit into the hackney, and the cab had driven away.

"Well, will this go on much longer, Ivan Fyodorovich? What is your opinion? How long am I to be tormented by these spiteful boys?"

"Well, my dear, I . . . I am ready, of course, and . . . the prince . . ."

Ivan Fyodorovich held out his hand to the prince all the same, but he did not have time to shake it and ran after Lizaveta Prokofyevna, who was descending the terrace steps with sound and fury. Adelaida, her betrothed, and Alexandra took leave of the prince with genuine tenderness. Yevgeny Pavlovich did the same, and he alone was in good spirits.

"It happened as I thought it would! Only it's a pity that you, poor fellow, have suffered here, too," he whispered, with a most charming smile.

Aglaia went away without taking leave.

But the adventures of that evening were not yet over; Lizaveta Prokofyevna still had to endure one rather unexpected encounter.

She had not yet had time to descend the terrace steps to the road (which ran along the edge of the park) when a splendid carriage, drawn by two white horses, came dashing past the prince's dacha. In the carriage sat two magnificent ladies. But, having gone no more than ten paces past the house, the carriage suddenly pulled up; one of the ladies turned around quickly, as though she had suddenly caught sight of some indispensable acquaintance.

"Yevgeny Pavlovich! *Q'est-ce-que tu?*"[51] suddenly cried a beautiful ringing voice, which made the prince and perhaps someone else, too, start. "Well, how glad I am that I've found you at last! I sent a messenger to you in town; two of them! They've been looking for you all day!"

Yevgeny Pavlovich stood on the terrace steps as though thunderstruck. Lizaveta Prokofyevna too stood still, but not in horror and petrification like Yevgeny Pavlovich: she looked at the audacious person as proudly and with the same cold contempt as she had five minutes before at "those miserable little people," and at once turned her steady gaze on Yevgeny Pavlovich.

"I have news!" the ringing voice continued. "Don't worry about Kupfer's promissory notes; Rogozhin has bought them up for thirty; I persuaded him. You can be easy for another three months at least. And as for Biskup and all those lowlifes, we'll certainly deal with them, through connections! Well, there you have it, then, everything's all right. Keep up your spirits. Till tomorrow!"

The carriage set off and quickly disappeared.

"She's out of her mind!" exclaimed Yevgeny Pavlovich at last, flushing with indignation and looking around him in bewilderment. "I haven't any idea what she was talking about! What promissory notes? Who is she?"

Lizaveta Prokofyevna went on looking at him for another two seconds; at last she set off quickly and abruptly toward her dacha, and all the rest followed her. One minute later Yevgeny Pavlovich came back to the prince on the terrace, extremely agitated.

"Prince, tell the truth; you don't know what this means?"

"I don't know anything," answered the prince, who was himself in a state of extreme and painful tension.

"No?"

"No."

51. Fr. "Is that you?" In the original, Nastasya Filippovna actually speaks Russian, not French. However, since it is absolutely crucial to the story that she uses the familiar *ty* form, I thought it appropriate to allow at least those English-speaking readers with a rudimentary knowledge of French to feel the full brunt of this glaring familiarity (see note 19, page 222).

"And I don't know." Yevgeny Pavlovich laughed suddenly. "I swear I've had nothing to do with these promissory notes, you may believe my word of honor! . . . But what's the matter? Are you going to faint?"

"Oh, no, no, I assure you, no. . . ."

X I

It was only on the third day that the Epanchins were entirely placated. Though the prince blamed himself for a great deal, as usual, and genuinely expected some punishment, all the same, he had at first the fullest inward conviction that Lizaveta Prokofyevna could not be seriously angry with him, and was really more angry with herself. And so such a long period of animosity had by the third day left him at a most gloomy impasse. He was left there by other circumstances, too, but by one of them primarily. All those three days, it grew progressively in the prince's suspicious mind (and of late the prince had blamed himself for two extremes: for his extraordinarily "senseless and bothersome" readiness to trust people and at the same time for his "gloomy, base" suspiciousness). In short, by the end of the third day, the incident with the eccentric lady who had spoken with Yevgeny Pavlovich from her carriage had taken on alarming and enigmatic proportions in his mind. The essence of the riddle, apart from other aspects of the affair, lay for the prince in the mortifying question: was he the one to blame for this new "monstrosity," or was it only . . . But he did not finish saying who else. As for the letters "N.F.B.," in his view, that was nothing but an innocent piece of mischief, the most childish mischief, indeed, so that one would have been ashamed to give it any thought at all, and in one respect it would have even been almost dishonorable.

However, on the very first day after the disgraceful "party," for the unseemly incidents of which he was such a chief "cause," the prince had the pleasure, in the morning, to receive Prince Shch. and Adelaida: "They had stopped by *principally* to inquire after his health." They had stopped by together, on a walk. Adelaida had just noticed in the park a tree, a wonderful spreading old tree with long twisted branches, with a big crack and hollow in it, all covered with young green leaves; she intended, most certainly, without fail, to paint it! So that she scarcely spoke of anything else for the whole half-hour of her visit. Prince Shch. was as usual cordial and amiable, asked the prince about the past, recalled the circumstances of their first acquaintance, so that hardly anything was said of the events of yesterday. At last, Adelaida could not stand it and, chuckling, admitted that they had come incognito; but her confession ended there, though from that "incognito" it could already be surmised that he was in special disfavor with her parents, that is to say, most important, with Lizaveta Prokofyevna. But neither Adelaida nor Prince Shch. uttered a single word about her or Aglaia, or even Ivan Fyodorovich, during their visit. Going away to continue their walk again, they did not invite the prince to go with them. And as for an invitation to the house, there was not so much as a hint; one very suggestive phrase may have even escaped Adelaida on that account: speaking of one of her watercolors, she suddenly expressed a great desire to show it. "How can we do that soon? Wait! I'll either send it to you today by Kolya, if he stops in, or I'll bring it by myself again tomorrow, when the prince and I go for a walk," she ended her perplexity at last, glad that she had managed to resolve this difficulty so cleverly and conveniently for everyone.

At last, having almost taken leave, Prince Shch. seemed suddenly to recollect.

"Ah, yes," he asked, "do you, perhaps, dear Lev Nikolaevich, know who that person was who shouted to Yevgeny Pavlych yesterday from the carriage?"

"It was Nastasya Filippovna," said the prince. "Haven't you found out yet that it was she? But I don't know who was with her."

"I know; I've heard!" Prince Shch. caught him up. "But what did that shout mean? It is, I must own, such a mystery to me . . . to me and to others."

Prince Shch. spoke with extreme and evident perplexity.

"She spoke of some promissory notes of Yevgeny Pavlovich's," the prince answered very simply, "which had come from some moneylender into Rogozhin's hand, at her request, and said Rogozhin will wait Yevgeny Pavlovich's convenience."

"I heard, I heard it, my dear prince; but you know that couldn't be so! There could not even be a question of any promissory notes with Yevgeny Pavlovich! With such a fortune . . . True, it has happened with him, out of carelessness, in the past, and I have even helped him out . . . But with his fortune, to give promissory notes to a moneylender and be worried about them—impossible. And he cannot possibly say *ty* and be on such friendly terms with Nastasya Filippovna—that's where the chief mystery lies. He swears he can't comprehend any of it, and I believe him completely. But the fact is, dear prince, that I want to ask you: do you know anything? That is, has no rumor, by some marvel, reached you, at least?"

"No, I don't know anything, and I assure you I was not involved in this in the least."

"Ach! How strange you've become, Prince! I simply don't recognize you today. As though I could suppose you to be involved in an affair of that kind! . . . Well, but you are out of sorts today."

He embraced and kissed him.

"What do you mean; involved in an affair of what 'kind'? I don't see any business of any 'kind.' "

"There is no doubt that person wished somehow and in some way to disturb Yevgeny Pavlovich by attributing to him in the eyes of the witnesses qualities that he does not and cannot have," Prince Shch. answered rather dryly.

Prince Lev Nikolaevich was confused, but, nonetheless, he continued to gaze steadily and inquiringly at the prince; but the latter fell silent.

"But isn't it simply promissory notes? Isn't it literally as she said yesterday?" the prince muttered at last in a sort of impatience.

"But I tell you—judge for yourself—what can there be in common between Yevgeny Pavlovich and . . . her, and Rogozhin to boot? I repeat, the fortune is immense, I know it for a fact; and there's another fortune, which he expects from his uncle. It's simply that Nastasya Filippovna . . ."

Prince Shch. suddenly fell silent again, evidently because he did not care to go on speaking of Nastasya Filippovna to the prince.

"So then, he knows her, in any case?" the prince asked suddenly after a minute's silence.

"That was so, I believe; he's a frivolous fellow! But, anyway, if it was so, it was long ago, in the past—that is, two or three years back. He used to be acquainted with Totsky, too, you know. But now, there could really be nothing of the sort; they could never have been on terms of intimate address! You know yourself that she hasn't been here either;

she hasn't been anywhere. Many people don't even know yet that she has turned up again. I have noticed the carriage for the last three days, not more."

"A splendid carriage!" said Adelaida.

"Yes, the carriage was splendid."

They took leave, however, with the most friendly, one might say the most brotherly, feelings toward Prince Lev Nikolaevich.

But for our hero, this visit contained something positively vital. Perhaps he had indeed suspected a good deal himself, ever since the previous evening (and possibly even earlier), but till their visit he had not brought himself to justify his apprehensions completely. But now it had become clear: Prince Shch., of course, put a mistaken interpretation on the incident, but still he kept circling around the truth; he had, after all, understood that there was an *intrigue* in it. ("Perhaps, though, he understands it quite correctly," thought the prince, "but only does not want to speak out, and so puts a false interpretation on it on purpose.") What was clearer than anything was that they (and Prince Shch. in particular) had come to see him just now in the hope of getting some sort of clarification; if that were so, then they plainly looked on him as being involved in the intrigue. Besides, if this were so and really were of consequence, then, it would seem, *she* must have some dreadful object. What object, then? Horrible! "And how's one to stop *her*? There is no possibility of stopping *her* when she is determined on her object!" That the prince knew by experience. "She is mad! She is mad!"

But far, far too many other unresolved circumstances had come together that morning, and all at the same time, and all requiring to be resolved at once, so that the prince was very sad. He was diverted a little by Vera Lebedev, who came to see him with Lyubochka and, laughing, told him a long story. She was followed by her sister, with her mouth open, and after them by the schoolboy, Lebedev's son, who informed him that the "star that is called Wormwood" in the Apocalypse, that fell upon the fountains of waters, was, by his father's interpretation, the network of railways spread over Europe. The prince did not believe that Lebedev interpreted it in this way, and it was decided that he himself should be asked at the first convenient opportunity. From Vera Lebedev, the prince learned that Keller had taken up his quarters with them the previous day and, by all appearances, they would not be rid of him for a long time, for he had found company in their house and had made friends with General Ivolgin; he declared, however, that he was remaining with them solely to complete his education. On the whole the prince began to like Lebedev's children more and more every day. Kolya had not been there all day: he had set off to Petersburg early in the morning. (Lebedev, too, had gone away as soon as it was light to see after some little business of his own.) But the prince impatiently expected a visit from Gavrila Ardalionovich, who was to come to see him without fail that day.

He came about six o'clock in the afternoon, just after dinner. At the first glance at him, the thought struck the prince that this gentleman, at any rate, must unmistakeably know all the dirty details—why, how could he fail to, with people like Varvara Ardalionovna and her husband to help him? But the prince's relations with Ganya were somewhat peculiar. The prince had, for instance, entrusted him with the management of Burdovsky's affair, and particularly asked him to look after it; but in spite of this confidence he put in him, and in spite of something else that had happened earlier, certain points always remained between them about which it was, as it were, mutually agreed not to speak. The prince fancied sometimes that Ganya would perhaps for his part have liked the fullest and most friendly candor; now, for instance, as soon as Ganya entered, the prince immediately fancied that Ganya was fully persuaded that, at this very moment, the time had come to break down the ice between them on all points. (Gavrila Ardalionovich was in haste, however; his sister was awaiting him at the Lebedevs'; they were both in a hurry on account of some business.)

But if Ganya really was expecting a whole series of impatient questions, impulsive confidences, friendly outpourings, he was, of course, much mistaken. During the entire twenty minutes of his visit, the prince was even positively pensive, almost absentminded. The expected questions, or better said, the one chief question Ganya was expecting, were not even a possibility. Then Ganya too decided to speak with great reserve. He talked incessantly for the whole twenty minutes, laughed, kept up the lightest, most charming and rapid chatter, but did not touch on the chief point.

Ganya told him, among other things, that Nastasya Filippovna had only been some four days here in Pavlovsk and was already attracting general attention. She is staying somewhere on some street called Matrossky, in a small, clumsy-looking little house, with Darya Alexeevna, but her carriage is almost the finest in Pavlovsk. A perfect crowd of suitors, old and young, had gathered about her already; the carriage is sometimes escorted by riders on horseback. Nastasya Filippovna was, as she always had been, very discriminating, and picks and chooses whom she receives. But all the same, a perfect regiment had formed around her; there were people to stand up for her, in case of need. One formally engaged young man who was summering there had already quarreled on her account with his betrothed; and one old general had all but cursed his son. She often takes out driving with her a charming girl, only just sixteen, a distant relative of Darya Alexeevna's; this girl sings well—so that in the evenings, their little house attracted attention. Nastasya Filippovna, however, conducts herself with extreme propriety, dresses simply but with extraordinarily good taste, and all the ladies "envy her taste, her beauty, and her carriage."

"The eccentric incident yesterday," Ganya let slip, "was, of course, premeditated, and, of course, must not be counted. To find any fault with her in something, one would have to seek it out on purpose, or smear her with slander, which, however, won't be long in coming," Ganya concluded, expecting that the prince would certainly ask at that point why he called yesterday's incident "premeditated." And why won't it be long in coming? But the prince did not ask this.

On the subject of Yevgeny Pavlovich, Ganya once again opened up on his own, without any particular inquiries, which was very strange, for he had stuck him into the conversation without any pretext. In Gavrila Ardalionovich's opinion, Yevgeny Pavlovich had not known Nastasya Filippovna, and even now he scarcely knew her, and only because he had been introduced to her by someone four days ago while taking a walk, and had most likely not been at her house, if even once, with all the others. As for the promissory notes, it might have happened, too (this, Ganya even knew for certain); Yevgeny Pavlovich's fortune was, of course, a large one, but "some business connected with his estate really was rather in a muddle." At this interesting point Ganya suddenly broke off. On the subject of Nastasya Filippovna's stunt of the previous evening he did not say a single word, aside from what he had said in passing above. At last, Varvara Ardalionovna came in looking for Ganya, stayed a minute, announced (also without being asked) that Yevgeny Pavlovich was spending that day, and perhaps the next as well, in Petersburg, that her husband (Ivan Petrovich Ptitsyn) was also in Petersburg and virtually on Yevgeny Pavlovich's business, too; that something had really happened there. As she was going, she added that Lizaveta Prokofyevna was in a fiendish temper today, but, what was most odd, that Aglaia had quarreled with her whole family, not only her father and mother, but even with her two sisters, and "that it was not at all good." After giving him, as it were in passing, this last piece of news (of extreme significance to the prince), the brother and sister departed. Of the business with the "son of Pavlishchev" Ganechka had not mentioned a word, possibly from false modesty, possibly to "spare the prince's feelings," but the prince nonetheless thanked him once more for his diligence in bringing the affair to a close.

The prince was very glad to be left alone at last; he walked off the terrace, crossed the road, and went into the park; he wanted to think over and decide upon one step. But this "step" was not one of those that can be thought over, but one of those which one precisely does not think over, but rather simply makes up one's mind to undertake: he suddenly had a terrible longing to leave all this here and to go away, back where he had come from, somewhere quite far, to some remote region, to go away at once without even saying good-bye to anyone. He had a foreboding that if he remained here even a few days longer he would certainly be drawn into this world irrevocably, and that this very world would then be his lot from then on. But he did not consider it even for ten minutes, and decided at once that it would be "impossible" to run away, that it would be almost faintheartedness, that there were such problems before him that he did not even have the right now not to resolve them, or at the very least to do his utmost to resolve them. Absorbed in such thoughts, he returned home, and his walk had hardly lasted a quarter of an hour. He was utterly unhappy at that moment.

Lebedev was still away from home, so that toward evening Keller succeeded in bursting in on the prince, not drunk, but with outpourings and confessions. He openly declared that he had come to tell the prince the whole story of his life, and that it was just for that purpose that he had remained in Pavlovsk. There was not the faintest possibility of throwing him out: nothing would have induced him to go.

Keller made ready to speak at very great length and very incoherently, but suddenly, almost at the first word, he skipped to the conclusion and announced that he had so completely lost "every trace of morality" (solely through lack of faith in the Almighty) that he had even become a thief. "Can you imagine that!"

"Listen, Keller, if I were in your place, I wouldn't confess that without special need," the prince began. "But perhaps you're saying things against yourself on purpose?"

"To you, to you alone, and solely to promote my own development! To no one else; I shall die and bear my secret to the grave! But, Prince, if you knew, if only you knew how hard it is to get money in our time! Where is one to get it, allow me to ask you? There's only one answer: 'Bring gold or diamonds, and we'll loan you something on them,' that is to say, just exactly what I haven't got, can you imagine that? Finally, I lost my temper, stood there a bit. 'And will you give a loan for emeralds?' I say; 'Yes, for emeralds too,' he says. 'Well, that's great,' I say, put on my hat and walk out; 'the devil take you, you're a bunch of scoundrels! By Jove!' "

"But had you emeralds then?"

"What emeralds could I have! Oh, Prince, what a sweet and innocent, even, one may say, pastoral view of life you have!"

The prince began, at last, to feel not exactly pity, but, as it were, something like pangs of conscience. The thought even occurred to him: "Might not something be made of this man by someone's good influence?" His own influence he considered for various reasons quite unsuitable—not out of self-deprecation, but due to a certain peculiar way of looking at things. Little by little, they fell into conversation, so much so that they were loath to part. Keller confessed with extraordinary readiness to such actions that it was impossible to imagine how it was possible to tell about such actions. Beginning each new story, he assured the prince positively that he repented and was inwardly "full of tears" but, in the meantime, told the tale as though he were proud of his deed, and, at the same time, sometimes so absurdly that he and the prince roared with laughter at last like madmen.

"The main thing is that there is a sort of childlike trustfulness and extraordinary truthfulness in you," said the prince at last. "Do you know that by that alone you make up for a very great deal?"

"Generous, generous, chivalrously generous!" Keller assented, much touched. "But you know, Prince, it is all in dreams and, so to say, in bravado; it never comes to anything in action! And why is it so? I can't understand it."

"Don't despair. Now, one can say positively that you have given me all the dirty details about you; at the very least, I fancy that it's impossible to add anything more to what you've told me, isn't that so?"

"Impossible?" Keller exclaimed, with something like regret. "Oh, Prince, how completely *à la Suisse*,[52] if I may say so, you still interpret human nature!"

"Is it really possible to add any more?" the prince brought out, with timid wonder. "But what did you expect from me, Keller, please tell me, and why have you come to me with your confession?"

"From you? What did I expect? In the first place, it's just a pleasure to see your simplicity; it's a pleasure to sit and talk to you; at the very least, I know there is a most virtuous person before me, and, secondly ... secondly ..."

He grew sheepish.

"Perhaps you wanted to borrow money?" the prince prompted very gravely and simply, even somewhat timidly, as it were.

Keller positively started; he glanced quickly with his former wonder straight into the prince's eyes, and pounded his fist down hard on the table.

"Well, there you are, that's just how you put a fellow completely off his stroke! Why, mercy, Prince: here's such simple-heartedness, such innocence, as was never heard of in the Golden Age, and suddenly, at the same time, you pierce right through a fellow like an arrow with such psychological depth of observation. But allow me, Prince, this requires explanation, for I ... I'm simply bowled over! Of course, ultimately, my object was to borrow money; but you asked me about money as if you saw nothing reprehensible in that, as though it were just as it should be."

"Yes ... from you it is just as it should be."

"And you're not indignant?"

"No ... at what?"

52. Fr., in the Swiss manner.

"Listen, Prince, I've remained here since yesterday first of all out of a particular respect for the French archbishop Bourdaloue[53] (we were uncorking bottles in Lebedev's room till three in the morning), and secondly, and chiefly (and I'll swear on all the crosses in the world that I'm speaking the honest truth!), I stayed because I wanted, having made you my full, heartfelt confession, so to speak, to foster my own development by it; it was with that same idea that I fell asleep, bathed in tears, toward four o'clock. Would you believe a most honorable man, now—at the very moment that I was falling asleep, genuinely filled with inward and, so to say, outward tears (for I was, finally, weeping, I remember it!), a hellish thought occurred to me: 'Well, what of it, couldn't I, when all's said and done, borrow money from him after my confession?' In this way, I prepared my confession, so to speak, like some kind of 'finezerf[54] with tear sauce,' for the purpose of paving the way with those same tears, so that you might be softened and fork out one hundred and fifty rubles. Is that not base, in your view?"

"But, most likely, that's not true; one thing simply came together with another. Two thoughts came together; that often happens. Constantly, with me. However, I think it's not a good thing, and, you know, Keller, I reproach myself most of all for it. You might have been telling me about myself just now. I've sometimes even happened to think," the prince continued very earnestly, genuinely and profoundly interested, "that all people are like that, so that I was even beginning to excuse myself, for it is awfully difficult to struggle against these *double* thoughts; I've been through it. God knows how they arise and come into one's mind. But here you've called it simply baseness! Now I'll start fearing these thoughts again too. In any case, I am not your judge. But still, as I see it, one can't call it simply baseness; what do you think? You were scheming to get money out of me through the tears, but you swear yourself that your confession had another objective as well, a noble one, and not just mercenary; as for the money—why, you want it for carousing, don't you? And after such a confession, of course, that's

53. Louis Bourdaloue was the favorite preacher at the court of Louis XIV. A selection of his sermons on human failings was published in Russian in the 1820s. Keller's remark about staying out of respect for Bourdaloue plays on the phonetic similarity of Bourdaloue and Bordeaux (i.e., the wine), as well as the Russian word *burda,* which means "hogwash."

54. In an attempt to make up a fancy, French-sounding dish, Keller distorts the words *fines herbes,* a common mixture of aromatic herbs used in many French dishes.

faintheartedness. But how are you to leave off carousing all in a minute? Why, that's impossible. What's to be done, then? It had better be left to your own conscience, don't you think?"

The prince looked at Keller with great interest. The problem of double ideas had evidently occupied his mind for some time.

"Well, why do they call you an idiot after that, I don't understand!" cried Keller.

The prince flushed a little.

"The preacher, Bourdaloue, he would not have spared a man, not he, but you've spared a man and judged me humanely! To punish myself now and to show that I am touched, I don't want a hundred and fifty rubles, give me only twenty-five, and it's enough! That's all that I need, for two weeks, at least. I won't come for money before the two weeks are out. I'd wanted to treat Agashka, but she's not worth it. Oh, dear Prince, God bless you!"

Finally, Lebedev—who had just returned—came in and, noticing the twenty-five-ruble note in Keller's hand, frowned. But Keller, finding himself in possession of the money, was already hurrying away and promptly made himself scarce. Lebedev at once began to speak ill of him.

"You're unjust, he really was genuinely repentant," the prince observed at last.

"Well, but what does his repentance amount to? It's just like I was yesterday: 'I'm abject, I'm abject,' but it's only words, you know, yes sir!"

"So that was only words with you? And I was beginning to think ..."

"Well, to you, only to you, I will proclaim the truth, because you see through a man: words and deeds and lies and truth—it's all mixed up in me and perfectly sincere. Truth and deeds consist in my genuine repentance, whether you believe it or not, but I swear it, and words and lies consist in the hellish (and always present) thought, how might one get the better of a man even here, too, how to gain something by the tears of repentance. By God, it's so! I wouldn't tell another man—he'd laugh or spit; but you, Prince, you would judge humanely."

"Well, now, that's exactly what he told me just now," cried the prince, "and you both seem to be proud of it! You positively surprise me, only he's more sincere than you are, and you've turned it into a regular trade. Now, now, that's enough, don't furrow your brow, Lebedev, and don't lay your hands on your heart. Haven't you something to say to me? You don't come in for nothing ..."

Lebedev simpered and hunched over.

"I've been waiting for you all day to put a question to you; for once in your life, answer the truth straight off: had you anything at all to do with that carriage yesterday or not?"

Lebedev simpered again, began tittering, rubbing his hands, and finally even had a sneezing fit, but he could not bring himself to speak.

"I see you had."

"But indirectly, only indirectly! I'm telling you God's honest truth! The only part I had in it was letting a certain personage know in good time that I had such a company in my house and that certain persons were present."

"I know that you sent your son *there*, he told me so himself earlier, but what sort of intrigue is this?" the prince cried impatiently.

"It's not my intrigue, not mine," Lebedev protested, waving the thought away, "there are others, others in it, and it's rather more a fantasy, so to speak, than an intrigue."

"But what's it all about? Explain it, for Christ's sake! Can you not understand that it concerns me directly? Why, it's blackening Yevgeny Pavlovich's character, you know."

"Prince! Most illustrious prince!" Lebedev began to hunch over again. "You won't allow me to tell the whole truth, you know; I've started in with the truth before, you know; not once; you wouldn't allow me to go on ..."

The prince paused and thought a little.

"Very well, tell the truth," he said dejectedly, evidently after a severe struggle.

"Aglaia Ivanovna ..." Lebedev promptly began.

"Be silent, be silent!" the prince cried furiously, flushing all over with indignation, and perhaps with shame too. "It's impossible, it's all nonsense! You've invented all that yourself, or some madmen like you. And let me never hear of it from you again!"

Late in the evening, after ten o'clock, Kolya arrived with a whole bushel of news. His news was of two kinds: of Petersburg and of Pavlovsk. He hastily related the chief items from Petersburg (mainly about Ippolit and the scene of the previous day), meaning to return to them later, and passed quickly to Pavlovsk. He had returned from

Petersburg three hours before and, without stopping in at the prince's, had gone straight to the Epanchins'. "There's an awful to-do there!" Of course, the carriage was in the foreground, but no doubt something else had happened here—something he and the prince knew nothing about. "I didn't spy, of course, and didn't care to question anyone; anyway, they received me well, so well that I did not even expect it; but of you not a word, Prince!" But most important and intriguing of all was that Aglaia had been quarreling with her people about Ganya. In what details the business consisted, he did not know—only that it was over Ganya (can you imagine that!), and they were quarreling terribly, so it must be something important. The general had arrived home late, had arrived frowning, had arrived with Yevgeny Pavlovich, who met with an excellent reception, and Yevgeny Pavlovich himself had been wonderfully gay and charming. The most serious piece of news was that Lizaveta Prokofyevna had, without any fuss, sent for Varvara Ardalionovna, who was sitting with the young ladies, and had once and for all turned her out of the house, in the most very polite manner, however—"I heard it from Varya herself." But when Varya came out of Madame Epanchin's and said good-bye to the young ladies, the latter did not even know that she had been forbidden the house forever, and that she was taking leave of them for the last time.

"But Varvara Ardalionovna was here at seven o'clock," the prince said, astonished.

"She was turned out going on eight o'clock, or at eight. I am very sorry for Varya, sorry for Ganya . . . no doubt they always have some intrigues going; they can't get on without it. I never could make out what they were hatching, and I don't want to find out. But I assure you, my dear, kind prince, that Ganya has a heart. He's a lost soul in many respects, of course, but in many respects he has such qualities that are worth the finding if you look, and I shall never forgive myself for not having understood him before . . . I don't know whether to go on now, after the story with Varya. It's true, from the very first I put myself on quite an independent and autonomous footing, but all the same I must think it over."

"You need not be too sorry for your brother," the prince observed. "If it has come to that, Gavrila Ardalionovich must be dangerous in Lizaveta Prokofyevna's eyes, and that must mean that certain hopes of his have been encouraged."

"How, what hopes?" Kolya cried in amazement. "Surely you don't think that Aglaia ... That's impossible!"

The prince kept silent.

"You're an awful skeptic, Prince," Kolya added some two minutes later. "I have noticed that for some time now you've become a great skeptic; you're beginning to believe nothing and presume everything ... But I did use the word 'skeptic' correctly in this case?"

"I believe you did, though I really don't know for certain myself."

"But I repudiate the word 'skeptic' myself, for I've found another explanation," Kolya cried suddenly. "You're not a skeptic, but you're jealous! You're fiendishly jealous of Ganya over a certain proud young lady!"

Saying this, Kolya jumped up and began to roar with laughter, as he had perhaps never laughed before. Seeing that the prince blushed all over, Kolya laughed more than ever; he was terribly taken with the idea that the prince was jealous over Aglaia, but he fell silent at once on observing that the latter was genuinely distressed. After that, they talked earnestly and anxiously for another hour or hour and a half.

Next day the prince spent the whole morning in Petersburg on urgent business. It was past four o'clock in the afternoon when, on the way back to Pavlovsk, he ran into General Epanchin at the railway station. The latter seized him hurriedly by the arm, looked about him as though in alarm, and dragged the prince after him into a first-class compartment that they might travel together. He was burning with desire to discuss something important.

"To begin with, dear prince, don't be angry with me, and if there's been anything on my side—forget it. I should have come to see you myself yesterday, but I didn't know how Lizaveta Prokofyevna would take ... And at my house ... it's simply hell, an inscrutable sphinx has settled in, and I wander about understanding nothing. As for you, to my thinking you're less to blame than any of us, though, of course, a great deal has happened through you. You see, Prince, being a philanthropist is pleasant, but not too much. You've tasted the fruits of it already, perhaps ... I like kindheartedness, of course, and respect Lizaveta Prokofyevna, but ..."

The general continued for a long time in this vein, but his words were astonishingly incoherent. It was evident that he was extremely shaken and disconcerted by something utterly beyond his comprehension.

"I have no doubt that you had nothing to do with it," he spoke out at last more clearly, "but I beg you as a friend not to visit us for some time, till the wind's changed. As for Yevgeny Pavlovich," he cried with extraordinary warmth, "it's all senseless slander—the most slanderous of slanders! It's a plot, it's an intrigue, an attempt to destroy everything and to make us quarrel. You see, Prince, I'll tell you for your ears alone: there hasn't been a single word said between Yevgeny Pavlovich and us yet, do you understand? We're not bound by anything—but that word may be said, and even very soon, perhaps! So it must be to do damage! But why, what for—I don't understand it! She's a marvelous woman, an eccentric woman, I'm so afraid of her I can hardly sleep. And what a carriage, white horses, why that's *chic*, you know, why, that's exactly what the French call *'chic'*! Who's provided it for her? By God, I did wrong, the day before yesterday my thoughts fell on Yevgeny Pavlovich. But it turns out that it's entirely out of the question, and if it's out of the question, then why does she want to upset things here? There you have it, there's the riddle! To keep Yevgeny Pavlovich for herself? But I tell you again, and upon this cross, that he doesn't know her, and that those promissory notes were an invention! And with what insolence she shouted *ty* to him across the street! It's purely a plot! It's clear that we must dismiss it with contempt and treat Yevgeny Pavlovich with redoubled respect. That's just what I've said to Lizaveta Prokofyevna. Now I'll tell you my most intimate thoughts: I'm utterly convinced that she's doing this to revenge herself on me personally for what happened before, d'you remember, though I hadn't wronged her in any way. I blush at the very thought of it. And there you have it, now she's turned up again; I thought she'd disappeared for good. Where's this Rogozhin hiding? Tell me that, if you please. I thought she'd become Madame Rogozhin long ago."

In a word, the man had completely lost his bearings. For almost the entire hour of the journey, he alone talked, asked questions, answered them himself, pressed the prince's hand, and did at any rate convince the prince that he did not dream of suspecting him of anything. This was important to the prince. He finished up with a story about Yevgeny Pavlovich's uncle, who was the head of some office in Petersburg—"in a highly visible position, seventy years old, a *viveur*,[55] a gourmand, and altogether an old gentleman with habits ... Ha, ha! I know he'd heard of Nastasya Filippovna, and even pursued her. I went to see him earlier; he wasn't receiving, not feeling well, but wealthy, wealthy, a man of consequence, and ... God grant he should flourish many years, but all the same it will all fall to Yevgeny Pavlovich ... Yes, yes ... but I'm afraid, after all! I don't understand what of, but I'm afraid ... It's as though there's something darting about in the air, like a bat, some trouble is hovering, and I'm afraid, afraid! ..."

And, at last, only on the third day, as we've already written above, the formal reconciliation of the Epanchins with Prince Lev Nikolaevich took place.

XII

It was seven o'clock in the evening; the prince was getting ready to go to the park. All of a sudden Lizaveta Prokofyevna came alone onto his terrace.

"*First of all,* don't even dare imagine," she began, "that I've come to beg your pardon. Nonsense! You're to blame all around."

The prince kept silent.

"Are you to blame or not?"

"Just as much as you. However, neither you nor I, neither of us is intentionally to blame for anything. I did think myself to blame the day before yesterday, but now I've come to the conclusion that it's not so."

"So that's what you say! Very well; listen and sit down, for I don't intend to stand."

They both sat down.

"*Second of all:* not one word about malicious urchins! I'll sit and talk to you for ten minutes; I've come to make an inquiry (and you thought God knows what, didn't you?), and if you drop a single word about insolent urchins, I shall get up and go away and break with you completely."

"Very well," answered the prince.

"Allow me to ask you: did you see fit some two or two and a half months ago, about Easter, to send Aglaia a letter?"

---

55. Fr. (from *vivre*, to live), someone who lives it up.

"I d-did write."

"With what object? What was in the letter? Show me the letter!"

Lizaveta Prokofyevna's eyes glowed, she was almost quivering with impatience.

"I haven't got the letter." The prince was surprised and horribly dismayed. "If it still exists, and is still in one piece, Aglaia Ivanovna has it."

"None of your sneaky tricks! What did you write about?"

"I'm not being sneaky, and I'm not afraid of anything. I don't see any reason why I shouldn't write . . ."

"Silence! You shall speak afterward. What was in the letter? Why are you blushing?"

The prince thought a little.

"I don't know what's in your mind, Lizaveta Prokofyevna. I only see that you really don't like this letter. You must admit that I could have refused to answer such a question; but to show you that I'm not uneasy about the letter and don't regret having written it, and am not blushing in the least on account of it (the prince blushed at least twice as red), I'll recite that letter to you, for I believe I remember it by heart."

Saying this, the prince recited the letter almost word for word as he had written it.

"What a string of nonsense! What can be the meaning of such twaddle, according to you?" Lizaveta Prokofyevna asked sharply, after listening to the letter with extraordinary attention.

"I don't quite know myself; I know that my feeling was sincere. At that time I had moments of intense life and extraordinary hopes."

"What hopes?"

"It's hard to explain, but not the hopes you're thinking of now, perhaps. Hopes . . . well, in one word, hopes for the future and joy that perhaps I was not a stranger, not a foreigner, *there*. I took suddenly a great liking to my fatherland. One sunny morning I took up a pen and wrote a letter to her; why to her—I don't know. Sometimes one longs for a friend at one's side, you know; and I suppose I was longing for a friend . . ." the prince added after a pause.

"Are you in love, then?"

"N-no. I . . . I wrote to her as to a sister; I signed myself her brother, too."

"Hm! On purpose; I understand."

"It's very distressing for me to answer these questions, Lizaveta Prokofyevna."

"I know it's distressing, but it doesn't matter to me in the least whether it's distressing. Listen, tell me the truth as you would before God: are you telling me lies or not?"

"I'm not."

"Do you speak truthfully that you are not in love?"

"I think quite truthfully."

"Well, you're a one, 'you think'! Did the urchin give it her?"

"I asked Nikolai Ardalionovich . . ."

"The urchin! The urchin!" Lizaveta Prokofyevna interrupted vehemently. "I know nothing about any Nikolai Ardalionovich! The urchin!"

"Nikolai Ardalionovich . . ."

"The urchin, I tell you!"

"No, not the urchin, but Nikolai Ardalionovich," the prince answered at last, firmly though rather softly.

"Oh, very well, my little dove, very well! I shall keep that against you."

For a minute she overcame her emotion and was calm.

"And what's the meaning of the 'poor knight'?"

"I don't know at all; it was done without me; some joke."

"Pleasant to find out about it all of a sudden! Only, could she really have been interested in you? Why, she has called you an ugly little freak and an idiot herself."

"You need not have told me that," the prince observed reproachfully, almost in a whisper.

"Don't be angry. The girl's willful, mad, spoiled—if she cares for anyone she'll be sure to rail at him aloud and mock him to his face; I was just like that. Only please don't be triumphant, my dear fellow, she's not yours; I don't even want to believe that, and it never will be! I speak that you may take measures now. Listen, swear you're not married to *that woman*."

"Lizaveta Prokofyevna, what are you saying? Mercy me!" The prince almost jumped up in amazement.

"But you nearly married her, didn't you?"

"I nearly married her," the prince whispered, and he bowed his head.

"Well, are you in love with *her*, then, if that's so? Have you come here on *her* account now—for *that woman's* sake?"

"I have not come to get married," answered the prince.

"Is there anything in the world you hold sacred?"

"Yes."

"Swear that it was not to get married to *that woman*."

"I'll swear by anything you like!"

"I believe you; kiss me. At last I can breathe freely; but let me tell you: Aglaia doesn't love you, take measures, and she won't marry you while I'm alive; do you hear?"

"I hear."

The prince blushed so much that he could not look at Lizaveta Prokofyevna directly.

"Carve that on your forehead. I've been awaiting you like Providence (you weren't worth it!). I've been bathing my pillow with my tears at night—not on your account, my dear, don't worry, I have my own, different grief, everlasting and always the same. But here's why I've been awaiting you with such impatience: I still believe that God Himself has sent you to me as a friend and brother. I have no one else, except old lady Belokonsky, and she's flown away, and to boot, she's grown stupid as a sheep from old age. Now answer me simply, yes or no: do you know why *she* shouted from her carriage the day before yesterday?"

"On my word of honor, I had nothing to do with it and know nothing about it!"

"That's enough; I believe you. Now I have other ideas about that, too, but only yesterday morning I put the whole blame of it on Yevgeny Pavlovich. The whole of the day before yesterday and yesterday morning. Now, of course, I can't help agreeing with them: it's more than evident that he's been mocked here, like a fool, on some account, for some reason, with some object (that in itself is suspicious! and it doesn't look well!)—but Aglaia won't marry him, I can tell you that! He may be a nice man, but that's how it's to be. I had doubts before, too, but now I've made up my mind for certain: 'Lay me in my coffin and bury me in the earth first, and then you can give away your daughter'; that's what I said straight out to Ivan Fyodorovich today. You see that I trust you. D'you see?"

"I see and understand."

Lizaveta Prokofyevna looked penetratingly at the prince; perhaps she keenly desired to find out what impression this news about Yevgeny Pavlovich made upon him.

"Do you know nothing about Gavrila Ivolgin?"

"You mean ... I know a great deal."

"Did you or did you not know that he was in correspondence with Aglaia?"

"I didn't know at all." The prince was surprised and even gave a start. "What! You say Gavrila Ardalionovich is in correspondence with Aglaia Ivanovna? It can't be!"

"Very recently. His sister has been paving the way for him here all the winter, working like a rat."

"I don't believe it," the prince repeated firmly, after some reflection and agitation. "If it had been so I should certainly have known it."

"I daresay he'd have come of himself and made a tearful confession on your bosom! Ach, you're a simpleton, a simpleton! Everyone deceives you like a ... like a ... And aren't you ashamed to put your trust in him? Surely you must see that he's duped you left and right?"

"I know very well he deceives me sometimes," the prince brought out reluctantly in a low voice, "and he knows that I know it . . ." he added and broke off.

"Knows it and goes on trusting him! As if the rest weren't enough! But then again, it's just what one would expect of you. And what am I surprised about? Good Lord! Was there ever such a man! Phooey! And do you know that this Ganjka or this Varjka has put her into correspondence with Nastasya Filippovna?"

"Whom?!" exclaimed the prince.

"Aglaia."

"I don't believe it! It's impossible! With what object?"

He leapt up from his chair.

"I don't believe it either, though there is evidence. The girl is willful, the girl is fanciful, the girl is mad! The girl is spiteful, spiteful, spiteful! I will declare it for a thousand years, she's spiteful! They are all like that now, even that wet hen, Alexandra, but this one's gotten completely out of hand. But I don't believe it either! Perhaps because

I don't want to believe it," she added, as though to herself. "Why haven't you been to see us?" She turned again suddenly to the prince. "Why haven't you been to see us for the last three days?" she cried impatiently once more.

The prince began telling her his reasons, but she interrupted him again.

"They all look upon you as a fool and deceive you! You went to town yesterday; I'll bet you've been on your knees, begging that scoundrel to accept the ten thousand!"

"Not at all, and I never considered it. I haven't even seen him, and besides, he's not a scoundrel. I've had a letter from him."

"Show me the letter!"

The prince took a note out of his portfolio and handed it to Lizaveta Prokofyevna. The note ran:

Dear Sir,—I have, of course, not the faintest right in other people's eyes to have any pride. In people's opinion I'm too insignificant for that. But that's in other people's eyes and not in yours. I have been too much persuaded, my dear sir, that you are perhaps better than others. I don't agree with Doktorenko, and part from him in this conviction. I shall never take a farthing from you, but you have helped my mother, and for that I am bound to be grateful to you, even though it be weakness. In any case, I look upon you differently and considered it necessary to inform you. And thereafter I suppose there can be no more communication of any sort between us. —ANTIP BURDOVSKY.

P.S. The sum that was missing from the two hundred rubles will be repaid you faithfully in course of time.

"What stuff and nonsense!" Lizaveta Prokofyevna decided, flinging back the note. "It wasn't even worth reading. What are you grinning at?"

"You must admit that you were pleased to read it, too."

"What! This vanity-ridden gibberish! Why, don't you see they've all gone out of their minds with pride and vanity?"

"Yes, but yet he's owned himself wrong after all, has broken with Doktorenko, and the vainer he is, the more it must have cost his vanity. Oh, what a little child you are, Lizaveta Prokofyevna!"

"Are you so bent on getting a slap in the face from me?"

"No, not at all. But because you're glad of the note and conceal it. Why are you ashamed of your feelings? You're like that in everything, you know."

"Don't you dare set foot in my house now," Lizaveta Prokofyevna jumped up, turning pale with anger. "Let there never be so much as sign of you in my house from now on!"

"And in another three days you'll come yourself and invite me . . . Come, aren't you ashamed? These are your best feelings; why are you ashamed of them? You only torment yourself, you know."

"I'll never invite you if I die for it! I'll forget your name! I've forgotten it!!"

She rushed away from the prince.

"I've already been forbidden to come as it is!" the prince called after her.

"Wha-at? Who's forbidden you?"

She turned in a flash, as though pricked with a needle. The prince hesitated to answer; he sensed that he had unintentionally, but grievously, let something slip.

"Who forbade you?" Lizaveta Prokofyevna cried in a frenzy.

"Aglaia Ivanovna forbids . . ."

"When? But spe-eak already!!!"

"Earlier this morning, she sent word that I must never dare come and see you again."

Lizaveta Prokofyevna stood as though petrified, but she was deliberating.

"What did she send? Whom did she send? By the urchin? A verbal message?" she exclaimed suddenly again.

"I had a note," said the prince.

"Where? Give it here! At once!"

The prince thought a minute, yet he pulled out of his waistcoat pocket an untidy scrap of paper on which was written:

Prince Lev Nikolaevich!—If, after all that's happened, you propose to astonish me by a visit to our dacha, you won't, rest assured, find me among those pleased to see you.

Aglaia Epanchin.

Lizaveta Prokofyevna reflected for a minute; then she rushed at the prince, seized him by the hand, and dragged him after her.

"Come along! At once! It must be at once, this minute!" she cried in a fit of extraordinary excitement and impatience.

"But you're exposing me to . . ."

"To what? You innocent simpleton! It's as if you're not even a man! Well, now I shall see it all for myself, with my own eyes . . ."

"But you might let me grab my hat, at least . . ."

"Here's your horrid little hat! Come along! Couldn't even choose the cut of his clothes with taste! . . . She did this . . . She did this after the recent . . . It was in a fever," muttered Lizaveta Prokofyevna, dragging the prince after her and not releasing his hand for one minute. "I stood up for you earlier, said aloud you were a fool not to come . . . But for that, she wouldn't have written such a senseless note! An improper note! Improper for a noble-minded, well-brought-up, clever, clever girl! . . . Hm!" She went on, "but of course, she was vexed herself that you didn't come, only she didn't consider that you can't write like that to an idiot, because he'd take it literally, just as it turned out. Why are you eavesdropping?" she cried, realizing she had said too much. "She wants a motley fool like you, it's long since she's seen one, that's why she's asking for you! And I'm glad, glad, that she'll make you grist for her mockery mill now! It's just what you deserve. And she's good at it, too, oh, how good she is! . . ."

PART THREE

I

Someone is always complaining that we have no practical people in Russia; that there are plenty of politicians, for instance; plenty of generals, too; managers of all sorts, as many as you need, any number can be found at a moment's notice—but there are no practical men. At least, everyone is complaining that there aren't. There are not even decent attendants, they say, on some of the railway lines; it's not even possible, they say, to set up a barely tolerable administration in any steamship company. In one place, we hear, on some newly opened railway line some cars have collided or fallen through a bridge; in another place, they write, a train nearly spent the winter in a snowdrift: they set out for a few hours, and spent five days stuck in the snow. In yet another place, they tell the tale, hundreds of tons of goods lie rotting in one place for two or three months at a time waiting to be dispatched. And, in yet another place again, they say (though it is hard to believe) that some administrator, that is some superintendent, was hounded by some merchant's agent about the dispatch of his goods, and instead of speedy discharge administered to him a blow to the teeth and, what's more, explained his administrative action on the grounds that he "lost his cool." It seems there are so many government offices that it staggers one to think of them; everyone has been in the service, everyone is in the service, everyone intends to be in the service—so that one wonders how, out of such material, some kind of decent steamship company administration can't be culled.

This question is often met by a very simple answer—so simple, in fact, that the explanation seems hardly credible. It's true, we are told, everyone has been or is in civil service in Russia, and this has been going on for two hundred years now following the best German model, from great-grandfather to great-grandson—but people in the civil service are precisely the most impractical of people, and it has gotten to the point that abstraction and lack of practical knowledge were only recently regarded, even among the civil servants themselves, as almost the highest virtue and recommendation. However, we should not have brought up civil servants; we wanted, namely, to talk about practical men. There's no doubt here that diffidence and complete lack of personal initiative have always been considered the chief and best characteristic of a practical man—are even so regarded still. But why blame only ourselves—if this opinion is regarded as an accusation? Lack of originality has always and everywhere, all the world over, from time immemorial, been considered to be a quality, and the best recommendation, of an active, businesslike and practical man, and at least ninety-nine percent of mankind (and that's at the very least) have always held that opinion, and perhaps only one percent, if that, always looked and now look at it differently.

Inventors and geniuses at the beginning of their careers (and very frequently at the end of them also) have almost always been considered by society to be no better than fools—this is the most hackneyed observation, familiar to everyone. If, for instance, over the course of decades, everybody had been stashing their money on deposit and had stashed away billions at four percent, then, naturally, when the bank had ceased to exist and everyone was left to their own initiative, the greater part of those millions would infallibly be lost in wild speculation and in the hands of swindlers—and indeed, this would even be called for by the dictates of propriety and decorum. Yes, decorum; if a decorous diffidence and proper lack of originality have to this day constituted for us, by general consensus, the integral characteristics of a practical and well-bred man, a sudden transformation would be far too ill-bred and almost indecent. What tender and devoted mother, for instance, wouldn't be dismayed and sick with fear if her son or daughter strayed from the track a bit. "No, better let him be happy and live in comfort without originality" is what every mother thinks as she rocks her baby to sleep. And our nursemaids, when rocking children to sleep, have from time immemorial sung and chanted: "He shall dress in gold, the pet—wear a general's epaulette!" Thus even with our nurses the rank of general has been considered the pinnacle of Russian happiness, and, it would seem, has been the most popular national ideal of peaceful and contented bliss. And indeed, after passing an examination without distinction and serving thirty-five years—who in our country could fail to become at last a general and to have accumulated a certain sum on deposit? In this way, the Russian man at last attained, almost without the slightest effort, the appellation of a practical man of business. Essentially, the only person among us who can fail to become a general is an original man, in other words, a restless one. Possibly there is some confusion here; but, speaking generally, it seems to be true, and our society has been perfectly just in designating its ideal of a practical man. All the same, we have said much that is superfluous; we had wanted, namely, to say a few words of explanation about our friends the Epanchins. These people, or at any rate the more reflective members of the family, suffered continually from a familial characteristic that was almost common to them all, the very opposite of the virtues we were just discussing above. Though they did not understand the fact entirely (for it is difficult to understand), still they sometimes suspected that everything in their family somehow did not go like it did in all the others. In all the others everything went smoothly, with them it was a bumpy ride; everyone else glided along as if on rails—and they were constantly going off the track. Other people were constantly and decorously growing timid, but they did not. Lizaveta Prokofyevna, it's true, was, even overly, given to being alarmed; but, all the same, this was not the decorous, worldly timidity for which they longed. But perhaps it was only Lizaveta Prokofyevna who was worried about it; the girls were still young—though they were a very penetrating and ironical set—and the general, though he did penetrate (not without some strain, however), never said anything more than "hm!" in difficult situations and put all his trust in Lizaveta Prokofyevna. So, it would seem, the responsibility rested on her. And it was not, for instance, that this family was distinguished by some kind of particular initiative or kept going off the track by a conscious inclination toward originality, which would have been quite entirely improper. Oh no! There was, in reality, nothing of the sort, that is, there was no consciously set goal, but yet, when all was said and done, it turned out that the Epanchin family, though highly respectable, was still not quite what every respectable family generally ought to be. Of late Lizaveta Prokofyevna had begun to find only herself and her "unfortunate" character to blame for everything—which increased her suffering. She was constantly reproaching herself with being "a foolish, ill-mannered little kook" and suffered from suspicion, continually lost her bearings, could see no way out of the most ordinary contingencies, and constantly magnified every misfortune.

At the beginning of our narrative we mentioned that the Epanchins enjoyed universal and genuine respect. Even General Ivan Fyodorovich, although a man of obscure origin, was received everywhere without question and with respect. He did, in fact, deserve respect—in the first place, as a wealthy and "not insignificant" man, and in the second place, as an entirely decent fellow, though somewhat limited. But a certain dullness of mind seems an almost necessary quality, if not for every man of action, then at least for everyone seriously engaged in making money. Finally, General Epanchin had good manners, was modest, knew how to hold his tongue and at the same time not let anyone step on his toes, and not simply by dint of being a general, but as an honest and honorable man. But most important of all was the fact that he was a man with powerful patronage. As for his wife, she was, as was explained above, of good birth, though birth is not too greatly considered among us, if the necessary connections do not also go along with it. But, in the end, she wound up having the connections, too; she was respected and, in the end, loved by such persons that, in their wake, everyone naturally had to respect and receive her. There could be no doubt that the familial torments she suffered were groundless, had insignificant causes and were exaggerated to the point of absurdity; but if you have a wart on your nose or on your forehead, you do always fancy that no one has anything else to do in the world than stare at your wart, make fun of it, and despise you for it, even though you have discovered America. There could be no doubt, either, that Lizaveta Prokofyevna was, in fact, considered in society to be a "little kook"; but at the same time, she was indisputably respected; but Lizaveta Prokofyevna came at last not to believe she was respected— wherein the whole trouble lay. Looking at her daughters, she was tormented by the suspicion that she was continually doing something to harm their prospects, that her manner was laughable, improper and insufferable—for which, of course, she continually blamed those same daughters and Ivan Fyodorovich and quarreled with them for days on end, while at the same time loving them to the point of distraction and almost to the point of passion.

Most of all, she was tormented by the suspicion that her daughters were becoming just as "kooky" as she was, and that girls like them were not to be found in society, nor ought to be. "They are growing into nihilists, and nothing but!"—she told herself continually. For the last year, and especially of late, this melancholy thought had grown more and more fixed in her mind. "To begin with, why don't they get married?"—she kept asking herself continually. "To torment their mother—they consider that the aim of their existence, and, of course, that's how it is because of all these new ideas, it's all the cursed woman question! Didn't Aglaia take it into her head some half a year ago to cut off her magnificent hair? (Heavens, even I hadn't hair like that in my day!) Why, she even had the scissors in her hand; why, I only just talked her out of it by begging on my knees! ... Well, let's say that one did it out of spite, to torment her mother, for the girl is spiteful, self-willed, spoiled, and above all spiteful, spiteful, spiteful! But didn't that fat Alexandra mean to follow suit and cut off her mane too, and not from spite, not from caprice, but in all sincerity, like a fool, because Aglaia persuaded her that without hair she would sleep easier and her head wouldn't ache? And the numbers and numbers and numbers—these five years now—of suitors they have had! And, truly, there happened to be good men, even first-rate men, among them! What are they waiting for, then? Why don't they accept them? Simply to spite their mother—there's no other reason for it! None whatever! None whatever!"

At last the sun seemed to be dawning even for her maternal heart; at least one daughter, at least Adelaida, would, finally, be settled. "There's one off our hands, at least," Lizaveta Prokofyevna would say when she had occasion to express herself aloud (in her thoughts, she expressed herself with incomparably more tenderness). And how well, and how properly, the whole business had come off; even in society, it was talked of with respect. He was a well-known man, a prince, with a fortune, and a good man, and, on top of it all, her heart had inclined toward him; what, it would seem, could be better? But she had always been less anxious about Adelaida than about the other daughters, though her artistic proclivities sometimes disconcerted Lizaveta Prokofyevna's ever-apprehensive heart. "For all that, she is of a cheerful disposition and has plenty of good sense, too—so she'll always land on her feet, that girl," she ultimately consoled herself. She was more alarmed for Aglaia than for any of them. But by the by, as regards the eldest, Alexandra, Lizaveta Prokofyevna did not even know herself what to think: whether to be alarmed or not. Sometimes she fancied the girl was "utterly hopeless"; twenty-five years old, so, it would seem, she'll remain a spinster. And "with her looks! ..." Lizaveta Prokofyevna positively shed tears for her at night, while during those same nights Alexandra herself lay sleeping tranquilly. "But what sort of thing is she—a nihilist or simply a fool?" That she was not a fool—of that, actually, even Lizaveta Prokofyevna had no doubt: she had the greatest respect for Alexandra Ivanovna's judgment and was fond of consulting her. But that she was "a wet hen"—there was not a single doubt of that: "so calm that there's no making her out! Though 'wet hens' are not calm, either—phooey! I am quite muddled over them!" Lizaveta Prokofyevna had some sort of inexplicable, compassionate fondness for Alexandra—more, in fact, than for Aglaia, whom she idolized. But the bilious outbursts (in which her maternal solicitude and fondness chiefly showed itself), the taunts and such names as "wet hen," only amused Alexandra. At times, it would get to the point that the most trivial matters angered Lizaveta Prokofyevna terribly and drove her beside herself. Alexandra Ivanovna, for instance, was fond of sleeping quite late and had a great many dreams; but her dreams were always marked by an extraordinary vapidness and innocence—fitting for a child of seven; well, and there you have it, even this very innocence of the dreams began for some reason to irritate *maman*. Once Alexandra saw nine hens in a dream, and it had been the cause of a formal quarrel between her and her mother—why? it would be difficult to explain. Once, and only once, she managed to see something in a dream that seemed to be original—she saw a monk, all alone, in some dark room that she kept on being afraid to enter. The dream was at once reported with triumph to Lizaveta Prokofyevna by the two sisters, roaring with laughter; but *maman* was angry again, and called them all three a set of fools. "Hm! she is as calm as a fool but a regular wet hen; there's no getting a rise out of her; and yet she is sad, she looks quite sad sometimes! What is she grieving over? What is it?" Sometimes she put that question to Ivan Fyodorovich, too—hysterically, as was her wont, threateningly, in the expectation of an immediate reply. Ivan Fyodorovich would hem and haw, frown, shrug his shoulders, and declare, at last, throwing up his arms:

"She needs a husband!"

"Only, God grant her, not one like you, Ivan Fyodorich," Lizaveta Prokofyevna would explode like a bomb at last, "not one like you in his thoughts and judgments, Ivan Fyodorich; not such a churlish churl like you, Ivan Fyodorich . . ."

Ivan Fyodorovich would promptly make his escape, and Lizaveta Prokofyevna would calm down after her "explosion." The same evening, of course, she would invariably be particularly attentive, gentle, affectionate and deferential to "her churlish churl," Ivan Fyodorovich, to her kind, dear and adored Ivan Fyodorovich, for she had loved him and was even in love with her Ivan Fyodorovich all her life—a fact of which Ivan Fyodorovich himself was well aware, and infinitely respected his Lizaveta Prokofyevna for.

But her chief and constant torment was Aglaia.

"She is exactly, exactly like me, the very picture of me in every respect," Lizaveta Prokofyevna used to say to herself. "Self-willed, horrid little imp! Nihilist, kook, mad and spiteful, spiteful, spiteful! Oh, Lord, how unhappy she will be!"

But, as we have said already, the sun had risen and had softened and brightened everything for a moment. There was almost a whole month in the life of Lizaveta Prokofyevna in which she had virtually a complete respite from all her anxieties. On account of Adelaida's approaching marriage, people in society began to talk about Aglaia too, and Aglaia's bearing had been so splendid, so poised, so clever, so winning; somewhat proud, but that suited her so well! How affectionate, how gracious she had been to her mother all that month! ("True, that Yevgeny Pavlovich must be examined very, very closely, he's a nut that must be cracked, but Aglaia doesn't seem to favor him much more than the rest!") Anyway, she had suddenly become such a delightful girl— and how good-looking she was, Lord, how good-looking, better and better from day to day! And then . . .

And then this wretched little prince, this miserable little idiot, had hardly made his appearance and everything was in a turmoil again, everything in the house was topsy-turvy!

But what had happened, though?

Nothing would have happened to other people, certainly. But what distinguished Lizaveta Prokofyevna was precisely that in the combinations and concatenations of the most ordinary things she always managed to see, through her ever-present anxiety, something that alarmed her, at times to the point of illness, and instilled an inexplicable fear born of suspicion, and for that reason hardest of all to bear. What must she have felt, then, when suddenly now, through her tangle of absurd and groundless anxieties, a glimpse of something actually came through that really seemed important indeed, something that really seemed indeed to call for anxiety, hesitation and suspicion!

"And how did they dare, how did they dare write me that accursed anonymous letter about that *creature*, that she is in communication with Aglaia?" Lizaveta Prokofyevna was thinking all the way home, as she drew the prince along, and at home, when she had made him sit down at the round table near which the whole family was assembled. "How did they dare even to think of such a thing? Why, I should die of shame if I believed a syllable of it, or showed Aglaia that letter! Such mockery of us, of the Epanchins! And all of it, all of it is due to Ivan Fyodorich; it's all due to you, Ivan Fyodorich! Ah, why didn't we spend the summer at Yelagin Island? I said we ought to have gone to Yelagin! It may be Varjka who wrote the letter, I know, or, perhaps . . . Ivan Fyodorich is to blame for everything, for everything! It was at his expense that *creature* pulled her prank, as a souvenir of their former relations, to make him look a fool, just as she laughed at him as a fool before and led him by the nose when he used to bring her pearls . . . But when all is said and done, we are embroiled in it after all, your daughters are embroiled in it after all, Ivan Fyodorich, young girls, young ladies, young ladies moving in the best society, marriageable girls; they were there, they were standing there, they heard it all, and they're embroiled in the scene with those urchins too; you may congratulate yourself, they were there too and heard it! I won't forgive, I won't forgive, I'll never forgive this wretched little prince, I'll never forgive! And why has Aglaia been hysterical for the last three days, why is she practically at odds with her sisters, even with Alexandra, whose hands she always kissed as though she were her mother—that's how much she respected her? Why has she been such a riddle to everyone these last three days? What has Gavrila Ivolgin to do with it? Why had she set out to praise Ivolgin today, and yesterday too, and then burst out crying? Why is that cursed 'poor knight' mentioned in that anonymous letter, when she never even showed the prince's letter to her sisters? And why . . . what, what induced me to run to him like a cat in a fit and to drag him here with me! Lord, I must have been out of my mind, what have I done! To talk to a young man about my daughter's secrets, and then . . . and then, about secrets that almost concern him! Lord, it's a good thing he's an idiot and . . . and . . . a friend of the family! But is it possible Aglaia is fascinated by such a little freak! Heavens, what am

I babbling! Phooey! We are a set of originals ... They ought to put us all in a glass case—me especially—and exhibit us at ten kopecks a head. I shall never forgive you this, Ivan Fyodorich, never! And why doesn't she needle him now? She declared she'd needle him and here she isn't needling him! There she is, there, gazing at him, all eyes; she doesn't speak, doesn't go away, stands there, yet she commanded him herself not to come ... He sits there all pale. And that confounded, confounded chatterbox, Yevgeny Pavlovich, keeps the whole conversation to himself! Just look at him spout on!—doesn't let one get a word in edgewise. I could have found out everything now, if I could only turn the conversation to it ..."

The prince really did sit, almost pale, at the round table, and, it seemed, he was at one and the same time in a state of extraordinary fright and, at moments, in a rapture, incomprehensible to himself, that gripped his soul. Oh, how he was afraid to glance in that direction, toward that corner from which two dark, familiar eyes were intently watching him, and at the same time how he was dazed with delight that he was sitting among them again, that he would hear her familiar voice—after what she had written to him! Heavens, what will she say now! He himself had not uttered one word yet, and he listened with strained attention to the "spouting" Yevgeny Pavlovich, who had rarely been in such a happy and excited state of mind as now, on this evening. The prince listened to him and for a long time understood hardly a word. Except for Ivan Fyodorovich, who had not yet returned from Petersburg, everyone was in attendance. Prince Shch. was there, too. They seemed to be meaning in a little time, before tea, to go and listen to the music. The present conversation had evidently arisen before the prince arrived. Soon, Kolya—who had turned up from somewhere—suddenly slipped onto the terrace. "So he is received here as before," the prince thought to himself.

The Epanchins' dacha was a luxurious dacha, built in the style of a Swiss chalet, gracefully adorned on all sides by flowers and foliage. It was surrounded on all sides by a small but lovely flower garden. Everyone sat on the terrace as at the prince's; only the terrace was rather more spacious and more fashionably appointed.

The subject of the conversation, it seemed, did not gladden the hearts of many of the party; the conversation, as one might have surmised, had arisen out of a heated argument, and, naturally, everyone would have liked to change the subject, but Yevgeny Pavlovich seemed to persist all the more obstinately, and paid no attention to the impression it made; the prince's arrival seemed to rouse him all the more. Lizaveta Prokofyevna frowned, though she did not quite understand everything. Aglaia, who was sitting off to the side, almost in a corner, did not leave, remained listening and maintained an obstinate silence.

"Allow me," Yevgeny Pavlovich was protesting warmly. "I say nothing against liberalism. Liberalism is not a sin; it is an essential, integral component of the whole, which would fall apart without it or die away; liberalism has just as much right to exist as the most proper conservatism; but I am attacking Russian liberalism, and I repeat again I attack it just for the reason that the Russian liberal is not a *Russian* liberal, but is an un-Russian liberal. Show me a Russian liberal and I'll kiss him in front of you all."

"That is, if he cares to kiss you," said Alexandra, who was in a state of extraordinary excitement. Even her cheeks were redder than usual.

"Well, look at that," thought Lizaveta Prokofyevna to herself, "here she does nothing but sleep and eat, and you can't rouse her, and then suddenly, once a year, she rears up and begins talking in such a way that one can only throw one's arms up at her."

The prince noticed in passing that Alexandra Ivanovna seemed very much to dislike that Yevgeny Pavlovich spoke too lightheartedly; he was talking about a serious subject, and seemed to be heated up about it, but at the same time seemed to be joking.

"I was maintaining just now, just before you came in, Prince," Yevgeny Pavlovich went on, "that in our country, liberals have so far come only from two classes of society—from the former squirearchy (now abolished)[1] and from the seminarian class. And since both estates have finally turned into perfect castes, into something perfectly distinct from the nation, and more and more so from generation to gen-

---

1. Though the Russian word *pomeshchik*—the proprietor of an estate—is generally translated simply as "landowner," I think the imagery it conjures in the Russian mind is more closely approximated by the English country squire, direct descendant of the feudal lord of the manor. The "souls" who lived and worked on the land were the squire's chattel; he owned their labor and had full authority over their affairs. In 1861, not long before this novel was written, the institution of serfdom was abolished by Tsar Alexandr II. This significantly changed the nature of the Russian landowning class and its relationship to the peasants who worked the land.

eration, therefore, it turns out, everything they have done and are doing is also perfectly nonnational ..."

"What? So it turns out, everything that has been done is not Russian?" protested Prince Shch.

"Not national; though it's Russian, it's not national. The liberals among us are not Russian, and the conservatives are not Russian either, any of them ... And you may be sure that the nation acknowledges nothing of what has been done by country squires and seminarians, either now or later ..."

"Well, that's a good one! How can you maintain such a paradox, that is, if you're in earnest? I can't let such outbursts about the Russian squire stand; you are a Russian squire yourself," Prince Shch. objected warmly.

"But I didn't speak of the Russian squire in the sense in which you are taking it. It's a venerable estate, if only because I belong to it; especially now that it has ceased to exist ..."

"Can you mean to say there has been nothing national in literature either?" Alexandra Ivanovna interrupted.

"I am not an authority on literature, but even Russian literature is in my opinion not Russian at all, except perhaps Lomonosov, Pushkin and Gogol."

"First of all, that's no small accomplishment; and second of all, one came from peasant stock and the other two were squires," said Adelaida, laughing.

"Quite so, but don't be triumphant. Since, of all Russian writers, these three are the only ones that have so far managed to say, respectively, something of their *own*, belonging to themselves and not borrowed from anyone, these three have by this very fact become national. Any one of the Russian people who says or writes or does anything of his own—something inalienably his *own* and not borrowed—inevitably becomes national, even if he were to speak Russian badly. For me, that is an axiom. But we did not start out talking of literature, we began talking of Socialists, and the conversation developed through them; well, then, I maintain that we haven't one single Russian Socialist; there are none and there never have been, for all our Socialists also come from the squirearchy or the seminary. All our arrant and professed Socialists, both here and abroad, are nothing more than liberals from the landed gentry of the serf-owning days. Why are you laughing? Show me their books, show me their teachings, their memoirs, and, though I am no literary critic, I can write you the most convincing literary criticism, in which I'll show you as clear as day that every page of their books, pamphlets, and memoirs has been written first of all by the Russian squire of the old school. Their anger, their indignation, their wit—all country-squireish (even pre-Famusovish![2]); their raptures, their tears are perhaps real, genuine tears, but—they are country-squireish! Country-squireish or seminarian . . . You are laughing again, and you are laughing too, Prince? You don't agree either, then?"

Indeed, everyone was laughing, and the prince chuckled too.

"I can't say offhand yet whether I agree or not," the prince brought out, suddenly leaving off smiling and starting with the air of a schoolboy caught red-handed, "but I assure you I am listening to you with the greatest pleasure . . ."

He was almost breathless as he said this, and cold sweat came out on his forehead. These were the first words he had uttered since he had been sitting there. He tried to look around at the company but had not the courage; Yevgeny Pavlovich caught his movement and smiled.

"I will tell you a fact, gentlemen," he went on in the same tone as before, that is, with extraordinary enthusiasm and warmth, but at the same time he was virtually laughing, possibly even at his very own words—"a fact the observation and discovery of which I have the honor of ascribing to myself and to myself alone; at least, nothing has been said or written about it. This fact expresses the whole essence of Russian liberalism of the sort of which I am speaking. In the first place, what is liberalism, speaking generally, but an attack (whether judicious or mistaken is another question) on the established order of things? That's so, isn't it? Well, my fact consists in this—that Russian liberalism is not an attack on the existing order of things, but is an attack on the very essence of our things, on the things themselves, not merely on the order; not on the Russian ways, but on Russia itself. My liberal goes so far as to deny even Russia itself, that is, he hates and beats his own mother. Every miserable and unhappy Russian fact ex-

---

2. From Famusov, a character in Griboedov's *Woe from Wit* (1831). [C.G.]

cites his laughter, if not practically delight. He hates the national customs, Russian history, everything. If there is any excuse for him, it is
perhaps only that he doesn't understand what he is doing and takes his
hatred of Russia for liberalism of the most fruitful kind (oh, you often
meet among us liberals who are applauded by the rest and who are, in
essence, perhaps the most absurd, the most stupid and dangerous of
Conservatives, and they don't know it themselves!). Not even that long
ago, some of our liberals nearly took this hatred of Russia for a sincere
love of the fatherland and boasted that they could discern better than
other people wherein that love should consist; but now they have become more candid and have become ashamed of the very term 'love
of the fatherland'; they have even dismissed and banished the very
conception of it as trivial and pernicious. This is a fact; I vouch for it
and . . . and the truth must be told sooner or later fully, simply and
openly. But at the same time, this is such a fact as has not existed or occurred anywhere at any time since the world began, not among any
single people, and therefore this fact is incidental and may pass, I
admit. There cannot be such a liberal anywhere else who would hate
his very fatherland. How can we explain it among us? Why, by the
same thing as before—that the Russian liberal is, as yet, not a Russian
liberal; by nothing else, to my mind."

"I take all that you have said as a joke, Yevgeny Pavlovich," Prince
Shch. countered earnestly.

"I haven't seen every liberal and don't venture to judge," said
Alexandra Ivanovna, "but I've heard out your idea with indignation:
you've taken an individual case and made it into a general rule, and so
you've been slanderous."

"An individual case? A-ha! The word's been uttered," Yevgeny
Pavlovich took up. "Prince, what do you think, is it an individual case
or not?"

"I, too, must say that I have seen very little and have been very little . . . with liberals," said the prince, "but it seems to me that you may
be partly right and that the sort of Russian liberalism of which you are
speaking really is in part disposed to hate Russia itself, not only the
order of things in it. Of course, this is only partly true . . . Of course, it
cannot possibly be just to say of everyone . . ."

He broke off in confusion. In spite of all his agitation, he was greatly interested in the conversation. The prince had one distinctive trait that consisted in the extraordinary naïveté of the attention with which he always listened to anything that interested him, and of the answers he gave when anyone turned to him with questions. His face, and even his attitude, somehow reflected that naïveté, that good faith, suspecting neither mockery nor humor. But though Yevgeny Pavlovich had for a long time past always addressed him not otherwise than with a certain shade of mockery, now, on hearing his answer, he looked very gravely at him, as though he had not expected such an answer from him.

"So . . . how strange it is of you, though!" he said. "And in all honesty, did you answer me in earnest, Prince?"

"Why, didn't you ask me in earnest?" countered the prince in surprise.

Everyone laughed.

"Believe him," said Adelaida. "Yevgeny Pavlych always makes fun of everyone! If you only knew the things he sometimes talks about with perfect seriousness!"

"In my view, this is a tedious conversation and it would be better not to begin it at all," Alexandra observed abruptly. "We wanted to go for a walk . . ."

"And let us go! It's an exquisite evening," cried Yevgeny Pavlovich. "But to show you that this time I was speaking perfectly seriously, and, most important, to prove it to the prince (you have interested me extremely, Prince, and I swear to you I am not quite yet such a shallow person as I must certainly—though I really am a shallow person!), and . . . if you'll allow me, ladies and gentlemen, I will ask the prince one last question, out of personal curiosity, and we'll conclude with it. This question occurred to me, as if by design, two hours ago (you see, Prince, I sometimes ponder serious things too); I resolved it, but let us see what the prince will say. We spoke just now about an 'individual case.' This little phrase is very significant with us, one often hears it. Recently everyone was speaking and writing of that dreadful murder of six persons by that . . . young man and of the strange speech made by the counsel for the defense, in which it was said that, considering the impoverished state of the criminal, it *naturally* must have occurred to him to murder these six people. Those are not precisely the words used, but the sense, I think, is that or comes close to it. In my personal opinion, the lawyer, in voicing such a strange thought, was perfectly convinced that he was speaking the most liberal, the most humane and progressive thing that could possibly be uttered in our day. Well, how would it be in your view? This corruption of ideas and convictions, this possibility of such a distorted and extraordinary perspective on the business—is it an individual case or a general one?"

Everyone burst out laughing.

"Individual; of course, individual," laughed Alexandra and Adelaida.

"And let me remind you again, Yevgeny Pavlych," added Prince Shch., "that your joke has already worn terribly thin."

"What do you think, Prince?" Yevgeny Pavlovich went on, not listening, having caught Lev Nikolaevich's earnest and interested gaze fixed upon him. "How does it seem to you: is it an individual case or a general one? I'll own it was for you that I came up with the question."

"No, not individual," the prince said gently but firmly.

"Mercy, Lev Nikolaevich," exclaimed Prince Shch. with some vexation, "don't you see that he is trying to trap you? He is decidedly in fun and has proposed to make you, and no other, grist for his mill."

"I thought Yevgeny Pavlovich was in earnest," said the prince, blushing and dropping his eyes.

"My dear prince," Prince Shch. went on, "but remember what we were talking about once, three months ago; we were talking precisely of the fact that you said that, in our newly established law courts, one could already point to so many remarkable and talented defenders! And how many highly remarkable verdicts had been handed down by the juries! How pleased you yourself were about it, and how pleased I was at the time seeing your pleasure . . . We said that we could be proud . . . And this inept defense, this strange argument is, of course, an incidental exception, the one among thousands."

The prince thought a moment, but with an air of perfect conviction, though speaking softly and even, it seemed, timidly, he answered:

"I only meant to say that the perversion of ideas and conceptions (as Yevgeny Pavlovich expressed it) is very often to be met with, is far more the general than the exceptional case, unfortunately. And so much so that if this perversion were not such a general case, then, perhaps, there would not be such impossible crimes as these, either . . ."

"Impossible crimes? But I assure you that just such crimes, and perhaps still more awful ones, have happened before, have always happened, and not only among us but everywhere, and, in my opinion, will happen again and again for a very long time. The difference is that, before, we had much less publicity, while now people have begun to talk of them out loud, and even to write of them, and that is why it seems as though these criminals have just come on the scene. That's where your mistake lies, an extremely naive mistake, Prince, I assure you." Prince Shch. smiled mockingly.

"I know myself that there were very many crimes and just as awful ones in the past; just recently I was in the prisons and succeeded in making the acquaintance of some criminals and convicts. There are even more terrible criminals than that one, ones who have killed up to ten people without feeling any remorse whatever. But at the same time, here's what I noticed: that the most hardened and unrepentant murderer knows all the same that he is a *criminal*, that is, he considers in his conscience that he has acted wrongly, though without any remorse. And every one of them is like that; while those of whom Yevgeny Pavlovich was speaking refuse even to consider themselves as criminals and think to themselves that they had the right and . . . that they have even acted well—it almost comes to that. Therein, to my mind, consists the terrible difference. And observe, they are all young, that is, they are precisely of the age in which one may most easily and defenselessly fall under the influence of perverted ideas."

Prince Shch. was no longer laughing and listened to the prince with bewilderment. Alexandra Ivanovna, who had long been wanting to make some remark, kept silent, as though some particular thought had checked her. And Yevgeny Pavlovich looked at the prince in definite surprise, and this time without a tinge of mockery.

"But why are you so surprised at him, my good sir?" Lizaveta Prokofyevna unexpectedly broke in. "Why, did you think he was more stupid than you and could not reason in your manner?"

"No, no, it wasn't that," said Yevgeny Pavlovich. "Only, how is it, Prince (excuse the question), if you see and observe this so clearly, how is it that you (excuse me again) . . . in that strange case . . . the other day, you know . . . of Burdovsky, I think . . . how is it that you did not notice the same perversion of ideas and moral convictions? Why, it's exactly the same. I fancied at the time that you didn't see it at all."

"But let me tell you, my dear man," said Lizaveta Prokofyevna, growing heated, "we all noticed it, and we sit here and show off before him, and meanwhile, he got a letter today from one of them, from the very chief one, the pimply one, remember, Alexandra? He begs his pardon in the letter, though after his own fashion, of course, and says he has broken with that companion who egged him on at the time— remember, Alexandra?—and that he puts more faith now in the prince. Well, but we haven't had such a letter yet, though we know how to turn up our noses at him."

"And Ippolit has just moved in with us at our dacha, too!" cried Kolya.

"What? Is he there already?" said the prince, growing alarmed.

"You had just gone out with Lizaveta Prokofyevna—and he arrived. I brought him!"

"Well, I'll bet anything," Lizaveta Prokofyevna practically boiled over all of a sudden, quite forgetting that she had just been praising the prince, "I'll bet that he went last night to see him in his garret and begged his pardon on his knees, so that that venomous viper might deign to move here. Did you go yesterday? You've confessed it yourself. Is it so or not? Did you go on your knees or not?"

"He didn't do anything of the kind," cried Kolya, "quite the contrary. Ippolit seized the prince's hand yesterday and kissed it twice, I saw it myself, and that was the end of the whole interview, except that the prince told him simply that he would feel better at the dacha, and he instantly agreed to come as soon as he felt better."

"There's no need, Kolya . . ." murmured the prince, getting up and grabbing for his hat. "Why are you talking about this? I . . ."

"Where are you going?" said Lizaveta Prokofyevna, stopping him.

"Don't trouble, Prince," Kolya went on, all fired up. "Don't go and disturb him; he's fallen asleep after the journey; he is very glad; and you know, Prince, I think it will be much better if you don't meet today; put it off till tomorrow, even, or else he'll get embarrassed again. Earlier this morning he was saying that he hadn't felt so strong and well for the last six months; he's even coughing three times less."

The prince noticed that Aglaia suddenly left her place and came to the table. He dared not look at her, but he felt with his whole being that she was looking at him at that moment and was perhaps looking at him wrathfully, that there must certainly be indignation in her black eyes and that her face was flushed.

"But it seems to me, Nikolai Ardalionovich, that you made a mistake in bringing him here, if it's that same consumptive boy who started crying then and invited us to his funeral," observed Yevgeny Pavlovich. "He talked so eloquently then of the wall of the neighboring house that he will certainly grow nostalgic for that wall; you may be sure of that."

"That's the truth; he will quarrel, break with you and go away—and that's the whole story for you!"

And Lizaveta Prokofyevna drew her sewing-basket to her with an air of dignity, forgetting that everyone was rising to go for a walk.

"I recollect that he bragged a lot of that wall," Yevgeny Pavlovich took up again. "Without that wall, he will not be able to die eloquently, and he wants so much to die eloquently."

"What of it?" muttered the prince. "If you won't forgive him, he'll die without you ... Now he has come here for the sake of the trees ..."

"Oh, for my part I forgive him everything; you can tell him so."

"That's not the way to take it," the prince answered softly and, as it were, reluctantly, continuing to look at one spot on the floor and not raising his eyes. "You must agree to receive his forgiveness too."

"How do I come in? What wrong have I done him?"

"If you don't understand, then . . . But you do understand; he wanted ... to bless you all then and to receive your blessing, that was all ..."

"Dear prince," Prince Shch. hastened to interpose somewhat apprehensively, exchanging glances with some of the others, "paradise on earth is not easily gained; but you still reckon on paradise somewhat; paradise—is a difficult matter, Prince, much more difficult than it seems to your good heart. We had better stop this, or else we may all become embarrassed again, and then ..."

"Let's go and hear the music," said Lizaveta Prokofyevna sharply, getting up from her place angrily.

Everyone rose after her.

I I

The prince suddenly went up to Yevgeny Pavlovich.

"Yevgeny Pavlych," he said with strange fervor, seizing him by the hand, "rest assured that I consider you as the best and most honorable of men in spite of everything; rest assured of that ..."

Yevgeny Pavlovich positively drew back a step with surprise. For a moment he was struggling with an irresistible desire to laugh; but looking closer he saw that the prince seemed not himself, or at least was in some kind of peculiar state of mind.

"I wager, Prince," he cried, "that you meant to say something completely different, and perhaps not to me at all . . . But what's the matter with you? Are you feeling ill?"

"That may be, that may very well be, and it was very subtle of you to observe that perhaps it was not you I meant to approach!"

Saying this, he gave a sort of strange and even ridiculous smile, but, suddenly, as if growing heated, he cried:

"Don't remind me of my conduct three days ago! I've been very much ashamed for the last three days . . . I know that I was to blame . . ."

"But . . . but what have you done that's so dreadful?"

"I see that you are perhaps more ashamed of me than anyone, Yevgeny Pavlovich; you are blushing, that's the sign of a wonderful heart. I'm going away directly, you may be sure of that."

"What's the matter with him? Do his fits begin like this?" Lizaveta Prokofyevna turned to Kolya in alarm.

"Pay it no mind, Lizaveta Prokofyevna, I'm not having a fit, I'll go away directly. I know that I . . . that nature's dealt me an unfair hand. I was ill for twenty-four years, from my birth till I was twenty-four years old. You must take it now as from a sick man, too. I'm going directly, directly, rest assured. I'm not ashamed—for it would be strange to be ashamed of that, wouldn't it? But I'm out of place in society . . . I'm not speaking from vanity . . . In these three days, I've thought it over and decided that I must explain things sincerely and honorably to you at the first opportunity. There are certain ideas, very great ideas, of which I ought not to begin to speak, because I should be sure to make everyone laugh; Prince Shch. has reminded me of that very thing just now . . . I have no proper gestures, no sense of proportion; my words are incongruous, not befitting the subject, and that's a degradation for those ideas. And therefore I have no right . . . Besides, I am leery, I . . . I am convinced that in this house, no one would hurt my feelings and I am more loved here than I deserve, but I know (I know for certain, you see) that after twenty years of illness something must have invariably been left over after all, so that it's impossible not to laugh at me . . . sometimes . . . It's so, isn't it?"

He seemed to be awaiting an answer and a decision, looking about him. All were standing in painful perplexity at this unexpected, morbid and, in any case, causeless, it would seem, outburst. But this outburst gave rise to a strange episode.

"But why are you saying that here?" cried Aglaia suddenly. "Why do you say it to *them*? Them! Them!"

She seemed to be stirred to the highest pitch of indignation: her eyes threw sparks. The prince stood before her, dumb and speechless, and suddenly turned pale.

"There's not one person here who might be worth such words!" Aglaia burst out. "There's no one here, no one, who is worth your little finger, nor your mind, nor your heart! You are more honorable than any of them, nobler, better, kinder, cleverer than any of them! Some of them are not worthy to stoop to pick up the handkerchief you have just dropped . . . Why do you debase yourself and put yourself below everyone? Why do you distort everything in yourself, why have you no pride?"

"Lord! Who could have expected this?" cried Lizaveta Prokofyevna, throwing up her hands.

" 'The poor knight.' Hurrah!" cried Kolya in rapture.

"Be silent! . . . How dare they insult me here in your house!" Aglaia suddenly flew at her mother, now in that hysterical state when one overlooks all boundaries and heeds no obstacles. "Why do you all torture me, every one of you? Why have they been pestering me for the last three days on your account, Prince? Nothing will induce me to marry you! Know that I'll never do it, not for anything! Know that! And is it possible to marry an absurd creature such as you? Take a look at yourself in the looking glass, now, what you look like standing there! Why, why do they tease me and say I'm going to marry you? You ought to know that! You are in the plot with them too!"

"No one has ever teased you!" muttered Adelaida in alarm.

"No one has ever thought of such a thing, there was not a word said about it!" cried Alexandra Ivanovna.

"Who teased her? When did they tease her? Who can have said such a thing to her? Is she raving or not?" Lizaveta Prokofyevna addressed everyone, quivering with anger.

"Everyone was saying it, every last one, for the last three days! I will never, never marry him!"

As she cried this, Aglaia began to weep bitter tears, hid her face in her handkerchief, and fell into a chair.

"But he hasn't even prop ..."

"I didn't ask you, Aglaia Ivanovna," broke suddenly from the prince.

"Wha-a-at?" Lizaveta Prokofyevna suddenly drawled out in amazement, in indignation, in horror. "What's tha-a-at?"

She did not want to believe her ears.

"I meant to say ... I meant to say," faltered the prince, "I only wanted to explain to Aglaia Ivanovna ... to have the honor to explain to her that I had no intention at all ... to have the honor of asking her for her hand ... at any time ... I'm not to blame for anything here, upon my word, I'm not to blame, Aglaia Ivanovna! I've never wanted to, and it never entered my head, I never shall want to, you'll see that for yourself: rest assured! Some spiteful person has slandered me to you! Put your mind at ease!"

As he said this, he approached Aglaia. She removed the handkerchief with which she was covering her face, stole a hasty glance at him and his whole panic-stricken figure, took in the meaning of his words, and suddenly burst out in a fit of laughter right into his face—such gay and irrepressible laughter, such droll and mocking laughter that Adelaida could not contain herself—especially when she too looked at the prince—and rushed up to her sister, embraced her, and broke into the same irrepressible, schoolgirlish and merry laughter as the latter. Looking at them, the prince suddenly began to smile too, and with a joyful and happy expression began repeating:

"Well, thank God, thank God!"

At that point Alexandra too gave way and burst into laughter heartily. It seemed as though the laughter of the three would have no end.

"Ah, the mad things!" muttered Lizaveta Prokofyevna. "First they frighten one, and then ..."

But Prince Shch. was already laughing too, and Yevgeny Pavlovich laughed as well, Kolya howled with laughter ceaselessly, and the prince howled with laughter too, looking at them all.

"Let's go for a walk, let's go for a walk!" cried Adelaida. "All of us together, and the prince must go with us without fail; there's no need for you to go away, you dear man! What a dear man he is, Aglaia! Isn't that true, Mother? What's more, I must, I must kiss him and embrace him for . . . for his explanation to Aglaia just now. *Maman* dear, will you let me kiss him? Aglaia, let me kiss your prince!" cried the mischievous girl; and she actually skipped up to the prince and kissed him on the forehead. The latter seized her hands, squeezed them so tightly that Adelaida almost cried out, looked at her with infinite gladness, and suddenly quickly raised her hand to his lips and kissed it three times.

"Come along!" Aglaia called. "Prince, you shall escort me. May he, *maman*—the suitor who's refused me? You've refused me for all time, haven't you, Prince? But that's not the way, that's not the way to offer your arm to a lady, don't you know how to take a lady under the arm? Like that, come along, we'll go ahead of everyone; would you like us to go ahead of everyone, *tête-à-tête*?"[3]

She talked incessantly, still continuing to laugh by fits and starts.

"Thank God! Thank God!" repeated Lizaveta Prokofyevna, not knowing herself what she was rejoicing in.

"Extraordinarily queer people!" thought Prince Shch., perhaps for the hundredth time since he had known them, but . . . he liked these queer people. As for the prince, he did not, perhaps, like him overly much; Prince Shch. looked rather gloomy and apparently preoccupied as they all set off for their walk.

Yevgeny Pavlovich, it seemed, was in the liveliest humor, all the way to the station[4] he amused Adelaida and Alexandra, who laughed at his jokes with such extreme, particular readiness that he began to be a trifle suspicious that perhaps they were not listening to him at all. At this thought he suddenly, and without explaining the reason, broke out at last in a fit of extraordinary and perfectly genuine laughter (such was his nature!). The sisters—who were incidentally in the most festive mood—kept looking continually at Aglaia and the prince, who were walking ahead; it was evident that their little sister had posed them quite a riddle. Prince Shch. kept trying to engage Lizaveta Prokofyevna in conversation about extraneous things, perhaps to distract her mind, and had become horribly tiresome to her. She seemed completely dazed, answered at random, and sometimes not at all. But

3. Fr. (lit. head to head), together in private.
4. At Pavlovsk, there is a bandstand with seats for the audience close to the railway station, which adjoins the park. [C.G.]

Aglaia Ivanovna's riddles were not yet at an end that evening. The last of them fell to the lot of the prince alone. When they had got about a hundred paces from the dacha, Aglaia said in a rapid half-whisper to her obstinately silent cavalier:

"Look there, to the right."

The prince looked.

"Look more carefully. Do you see that bench, in the park, over there where those three big trees are . . . a green bench?"

The prince answered that he did.

"Do you like the spot? Sometimes, early in the morning, around seven o'clock, when everyone else is still asleep, I come and sit here alone."

The prince murmured that it was a lovely spot.

"And now, leave me, I don't want to walk arm-in-arm anymore. Or, better, walk arm-in-arm with me, but don't speak a word to me. I want to think by myself . . ."

This warning was in any case unnecessary: the prince certainly would not have uttered a single word the entire way even without the command. His heart began throbbing violently when he heard what she said about the bench. After a minute, he thought better of it and dismissed his absurd idea with shame.

As is well known and as everyone, at any rate, asserts, the public that gathers at the Pavlovsk station on weekdays is more "select" than on Sundays and holidays, when "all sorts of people" flock there from town. The attire is not festive but it is elegant. It is the custom to assemble for the music. The orchestra is perhaps really the best of our park bands; it plays new pieces. There is great decorum and propriety, despite a certain general family atmosphere and even intimacy. Acquaintances—all of the summer set—gather to see and be seen. Many do this with genuine pleasure and come for that purpose alone; but there are also those who go just for the music. Unpleasant scenes are extraordinarily rare, though they do occasionally occur even on weekdays, however. But that, to be sure, is inevitable.

This time, it was an exquisite evening, and there was quite a large audience. All the places around the orchestra, which was playing, were taken. Our party sat down on chairs somewhat off to the side, close to the left-most exit from the station. The crowd and the music revived Lizaveta Prokofyevna a little and diverted the young ladies; they had already exchanged glances with several of their acquaintances and nodded affably to some of them from a distance; they had had time to scrutinize the dresses, detect some eccentricities, discuss them, and smile mockingly. Yevgeny Pavlovich also bowed frequently to acquaintances. Aglaia and the prince, who were still together, had already attracted some attention. Soon, *maman* and the young ladies were approached by some of the young men of their acquaintance; two or three remained to talk to them; they were all friends of Yevgeny Pavlovich's. Among them was a young and very handsome officer, very good-humored, very talkative; he hastened to start a conversation with Aglaia and did his utmost to attract her attention. She was very gracious to him and extremely easily amused. Yevgeny Pavlovich asked the prince to let him introduce this friend; the prince hardly understood what was wanted of him, but the introduction took place, both bowed and shook hands. Yevgeny Pavlovich's friend asked a question, but the prince, apparently, did not answer or mumbled something so strangely to himself that the officer looked at him very intently, then glanced at Yevgeny Pavlovich, understood at once why the latter had contrived this introduction, smirked a little and turned to Aglaia again. Only Yevgeny Pavlovich noticed that Aglaia suddenly flushed at this.

The prince did not even observe the fact that other people were talking and exchanging niceties with Aglaia, was at moments even on the point of forgetting that he was sitting beside her. Sometimes he longed to get away somewhere, to vanish from here altogether, and he would have even liked some gloomy, deserted place, only that he might be alone with his thoughts and that no one might know where he was. Or at least to be at home, on the terrace, but so that no one else was there, not Lebedev nor the children; to throw himself on his sofa, bury his head in the pillow, and lie like that for a day and a night and another day. At moments he dreamed of the mountains, and especially one familiar spot in the mountains that he always liked to recollect, to which he had been fond of going when he still lived there, and from which he used to look down on the village, on the waterfall barely gleaming like a white thread below, on the white clouds and the old ruined castle. Oh, how he longed to be there now, and to think of one thing—O! of nothing else for his whole life—and it would last him for a thousand years! And let him, oh, let him be utterly forgotten here. Oh, that must be! It would have been better indeed if they had never known him at all, and all of this had only been a vision in a dream. But wasn't it just the same, dream and reality! Sometimes he would begin looking intently at Aglaia and would not take his eyes off her face for five minutes at a time; but the look in his eyes was far too strange: he seemed to be looking at her as at an object that was a mile away from him, or as at her portrait, and not her herself.

"Why are you looking at me like that, Prince?" she said suddenly, interrupting her merry talk and laughter with the group around her. "I am afraid of you; I keep feeling as though you meant to put out your hand and touch my face with your finger in order to feel it. Isn't it true, Yevgeny Pavlych, doesn't he look like that?"

The prince heard, apparently in surprise, that he was being spoken to, grasped it, although perhaps he did not quite understand, and did not answer, but seeing that she and all the rest were laughing, he suddenly opened his mouth and began to laugh too. The laughter grew louder all around; the officer, who must have been a person easily amused, simply shook with laughter. Aglaia suddenly whispered wrathfully to herself:

"Idiot!"

"Good heavens! Surely she can't be ... A man like that ... Is she utterly mad?" Lizaveta Prokofyevna muttered to herself through her teeth.

"It's a joke. It's the same joke as that time with the 'poor knight,'" Alexandra whispered firmly in her ear, "and nothing more! She's made him the butt of her jokes again, as is her wont. But the joke has gone too far; we must put a stop to it, *maman*! She was going through contortions like an actress earlier, scaring us out of pure mischief ..."

"It's a good thing she's pitched on such an idiot," her mother whispered back. Her daughter's remark had relieved her after all.

The prince, however, heard them call him an idiot and started, but not at being called an idiot. He forgot "the idiot" immediately. But in the crowd, not far from where he was sitting, somewhere off to the side—he could never have pointed out at what exact place and what point—he caught a glimpse of a face, a pale face, with curly black hair, with a familiar, a very familiar smile and gaze; he caught a glimpse of it and it vanished. It was very possible that he only imagined it; the only impression that remained with him of the entire vision was a wry smile, the eyes and the jaunty pale-green necktie worn by the barely glimpsed gentleman. Whether the figure had disappeared in the crowd or slipped into the station the prince could not have determined either.

But a minute later he suddenly began quickly and uneasily looking about him; this first apparition might be the harbinger and forerunner of a second. That would certainly have to be so. Could he have forgotten the possibility of an encounter when they set off for the station? Admittedly, when he entered the station, it seemed he had no idea that he was coming there—such a state was he in. If he had been able, or known how, to be more observant, then he might have already noticed some quarter of an hour before that from time to time Aglaia also cast her glance about uneasily and also seemed to be looking for something all around her. Now, when his uneasiness had become very marked, Aglaia's agitation and uneasiness also increased, and as soon as he looked around him, she at once looked about too. The resolution of their alarm followed quickly.

From the very same side entrance to the station near which the prince and the whole Epanchin party were situated, there suddenly emerged an entire crowd, some ten people at least. At the head of the crowd were three women; two of them incredibly good-looking, and there was nothing strange about the fact that they were followed by so many admirers. But both the admirers and the women—all of this was rather peculiar, something entirely unlike the rest of the audience gathered to listen to the music. They were at once noticed by almost everyone, but for the most part, people tried to look as though they had not seen them at all, and if anything, only some of the young set smiled at them, exchanging some words with one another in an undertone. Not to see them at all was impossible: they announced their presence quite clearly, talking loudly and laughing. One could surmise that many among them were drunk, too, though by all appearances, some of them wore fashionable and elegant clothes; yet right next to them were also persons of very strange appearance, in strange clothes, with strangely flushed faces; among them were a few military men; some were no longer the youngest, too; there were some who were affluently dressed in loose and elegantly tailored clothes, with rings and studs, and splendid pitch-black wigs and sideburns, with an especially stately though somewhat disdainful dignity in their faces, who would, however, have been shunned in society like the plague. Among our suburban gatherings, there are, of course, some that are distinguished for exceptional respectability and enjoy a particularly good reputation; but even the most cautious person cannot defend himself at every moment against a brick that falls from the neighboring house. Such a brick was now preparing to fall on the respectable public that had gathered to listen to the band.

In order to cross from the station to the bandstand, one must go down three steps. It was just at these very steps that the crowd stopped; they did not venture to go down, but one of the women stepped forward; only two of her entourage made so bold as to follow her. One was a middle-aged man with a rather modest appearance, who looked like a decent man in every respect, yet he had the forlorn appearance of an utter *bobyl*,[5] that is to say, one of those men who never know anybody and whom nobody ever knows. The other, who had not left his lady's side, was a complete ragamuffin of a most dubious appearance. Nobody else followed the eccentric lady; but going down the steps she did not even look back, as though she decidedly did not care whether they followed her or not. She laughed and talked loudly as before; she was dressed richly and with exceptional taste, but somewhat more luxuriously than was warranted. She set off past the orchestra toward the other side of the bandstand, where somebody's carriage was waiting for someone near the side of the road.

The prince had not seen *her* for more than three months now. All these days, since he had arrived in Petersburg, he had been intending to go and see her, but perhaps a secret presentiment had deterred him. At any rate, he could by no means gauge what impression meeting her would make upon him, though he sometimes tried, with dread, to imagine it. One thing was clear to him—that the meeting would be painful. Several times during those six months he had recalled the first sensation stirred in him by that woman's face, when he had only seen it in the portrait; but even in the impression made by the portrait, he remembered, there was already too much that was painful. That month in the provinces, when he had seen her almost every day, had had a terrible effect upon him, so much so that he sometimes tried to

5. An impoverished, landless bachelor peasant; also used in the figurative sense for a lonely person with no family.

drive away all recollection of this still-recent past. In the very face of this woman, there was for him always something torturous: talking with Rogozhin, the prince had interpreted this feeling as a feeling of infinite pity, and that was the truth—that face, even in the portrait, had roused in his heart a perfect agony of pity; the sensation of compassion and even of suffering over this creature had never left his heart, and did not leave it now. Oh, no, it was stronger than ever. But the prince remained dissatisfied with what he had said to Rogozhin; and only now, at this moment of her sudden appearance, did he understand, perhaps by means of direct sensation, what had been lacking in his words to Rogozhin. Words had been lacking that might have expressed horror; yes, horror! Now at this moment he felt it fully; he was certain, he was fully convinced, for particular reasons of his own, that this woman was mad. If, loving a woman more than anything in the world, or foretasting the possibility of such love, one were suddenly to see her in chains, behind iron bars, and beneath the rod of a prison warder—then such a sensation would be somewhat similar to what the prince felt at that moment.

"What's the matter with you?" Aglaia whispered quickly, looking around at him and naïvely tugging him by the arm.

He turned his head toward her, looked at her, glanced into her black eyes, which, at that moment, had a gleam he found incomprehensible, tried to grin at her, but suddenly, as though forgetting her at once, again turned his eyes away to the right and again began to follow his extraordinary vision. Nastasya Filippovna was at that moment passing right by the young ladies' chairs. Yevgeny Pavlovich went on telling Alexandra Ivanovna something that must have been very amusing and interesting, talking rapidly and animatedly. The prince remembered that Aglaia had suddenly uttered in a half-whisper: "What a . . ."

It was a vague and unfinished phrase; she instantly checked herself and added nothing more, but that was enough. Nastasya Filippovna, who was passing by as if she noticed no one in particular, suddenly turned in their direction and noticed Yevgeny Pavlovich, as though she had done so only just now.

"B-bah! Why, here he is!" she exclaimed, suddenly standing still. "First, he's nowhere to be found though you may send all the messengers in the world to look for him, and then there he sits, as if on cue, just where you would have never imagined . . . I thought you[6] were there . . . at your uncle's!"

Yevgeny Pavlovich flushed, looked furiously at Nastasya Filippovna, but hurriedly turned away from her again.

"What?! Don't you know? Only fancy, he doesn't know yet! He's shot himself! Earlier this morning, your uncle shot himself! I was told earlier, this morning, at two o'clock; and half the town knows it by now; three hundred and fifty thousand rubles of government money are missing, they say; and others say five hundred. And I always counted on his leaving you a fortune; he's burned through it all. He was a most dissipated old fellow . . . Well, good-bye, *bonne chance*![7] Aren't you really going there? So that's why you retired from the service in good time, you sly fellow! Oh, nonsense, you knew, you knew ahead of time: perhaps even yesterday . . ."

Though in her insolent harassment, in this advertising of an acquaintance and intimacy that did not exist, there was certainly an object, and of that there could be no doubt now—yet Yevgeny Pavlovich had intended at first simply to brush it off somehow and take no note of the offender no matter what. But Nastasya Filippovna's words hit him like a thunderbolt; hearing of his uncle's death, he blanched like a sheet and turned toward the news-bearer. At that moment Lizaveta Prokofyevna rose quickly from her seat, made everyone get up after her, and practically ran away from there. Only Prince Lev Nikolaevich stayed in his place for a moment, as if in indecision, and Yevgeny Pavlovich still remained standing, unable to collect himself. But the Epanchins were scarcely twenty paces away when a horrible scene broke out.

The officer and great friend of Yevgeny Pavlovich's who had been talking to Aglaia was highly indignant.

"One wants a whip, there's no other way of dealing with such a worthless creature!" he said almost loudly. (He had apparently been Yevgeny Pavlovich's confidant in the past.)

Nastasya Filippovna instantly turned to him. Her eyes flashed; she rushed up to a young man—a complete stranger to her standing two

6. Nastasya Filippovna is once again using the familiar *ty* form.

7. Fr., good luck.

paces away, holding a thin, plaited riding whip—snatched it out of his hand, and struck the offender with all her might across the face. All this happened in one moment . . . The officer, forgetting himself, flew at her; Nastasya Filippovna no longer had her entourage around her; the respectable middle-aged gentleman had already managed to disappear altogether, while the merrymaking gentleman stood to the side, laughing for all he was worth. In another minute, of course, the police would have appeared, but during that minute Nastasya Filippovna would have fared badly, if unexpected help had not been at hand; the prince, who was also standing two steps away, succeeded in seizing the officer by the arms from behind. Wresting his arm away, the officer shoved him violently in the chest; the prince was flung three paces back and fell on a chair. But Nastasya Filippovna already had two other champions come on the scene. Before the attacking officer stood the boxer, the author of the article already known to the reader and an active member of Rogozhin's former company.

"Keller! Retired lieutenant," he introduced himself forcibly. "If you care for some hand-to-hand, Captain, replacing the weaker sex, I'm at your service; I've gone through the whole course of English boxing. Don't push, Captain. I sympathize about the *bloody* insult, but I can't allow you to exercise the law of the fist with a woman in public. But if, like a decent, most honora-ablest person, you care for a different method, then—I'm sure you understand me, of course, Captain . . ."

But the captain had come to his senses and was no longer listening to him. At that instant Rogozhin appeared out of the crowd, quickly seized Nastasya Filippovna by the arm, and led her after him. For his part, Rogozhin seemed terribly shaken; he was white and trembling. As he led Nastasya Filippovna away, he still managed to laugh malignantly in the officer's face and, with an air of a gleeful tavern boy, brought out:

"Whew! Well, he caught it! His mug's all bloody! Whew!"

Coming to himself and completely realizing with whom he had to deal, the officer turned politely (though covering his face with his handkerchief) to the prince, who had already got up from the chair.

"Prince Myshkin, whose acquaintance I have had the pleasure of making?"

"She's mad! She's insane! I assure you!" responded the prince in a shaking voice, for some reason holding out his trembling hands to him.

"I, of course, cannot boast of so much information; but I had to know your name."

He nodded and walked away. The police hurried up exactly five seconds after the last of the persons concerned had disappeared. But anyway, the scene had not lasted more than two minutes. Some of the audience had got up from their chairs and gone away; others had simply moved from one place to another; while still others were delighted at the scene, and some were eagerly talking and inquiring about it. In a word, the business ended in the usual way. The band began playing again. The prince followed the Epanchins. If he had guessed, or had had time to look to the left when he was sitting in the chair after he had been pushed away, he might have seen, some twenty paces from him, Aglaia, who had stood still to watch the scandalous scene, not heeding the calls of her mother and sisters, who had already moved farther off. Prince Shch. had run up to her and at last persuaded her to come quickly away. Lizaveta Prokofyevna remembered that Aglaia had returned to them so excited that she could scarcely have heard their calling her. But within two minutes, when they had just entered the park, Aglaia said in her usual indifferent and capricious tone:

"I wanted to see how the farce would end."

III

The incident at the station had struck both mother and daughters almost with horror. In alarm and agitation, Lizaveta Prokofyevna had literally almost run with her daughters all the way home from the station. In her view and conception of things, too much had happened and been brought to light during the incident, so that in spite of all the confusion and alarm, certain ideas were already taking definite shape in her brain. But everyone realized that something peculiar had happened, and that perhaps, and fortunately too, some extraordinary secret was on the verge of being disclosed. In spite of all Prince Shch.'s former assurances and explanations, Yevgeny Pavlovich had been "brought out into the open," unmasked, exposed, "and publicly found out in his connection with that disgraceful creature." So thought the mother and even both her elder daughters. The net benefit of this conclusion was that the mysteries proliferated even more. Though the girls were secretly somewhat indignant at their mother's overly ex-

treme alarm and such conspicuous flight, yet they did not venture to
worry her with questions during the initial period of the confusion.
Moreover, it seemed to them for some reason that their sister, Aglaia
Ivanovna, perhaps knew more of the matter than their mother and all
of them put together. Prince Shch., too, looked black as night, and was
very pensive, too. Lizaveta Prokofyevna did not say a word to him all
the way home, but he did not even seem to notice it. Adelaida made
an attempt to ask him, "What uncle had been spoken of just now and
what had happened in Petersburg?" But, with an extremely sour face,
he muttered something very vague in reply about making some sort
of inquiries, and that all of it was, of course, sheer absurdity. "There is
no doubt of that!" answered Adelaida, and she asked nothing more.
Aglaia, though, became exceptionally quiet, and only observed on the
way that they were hurrying too fast. Once she turned around and
caught sight of the prince, who was hastening after them. Observing
his efforts to overtake them, she smiled sardonically and did not look
back at him again.

At last, when they had nearly reached their dacha, they encountered Ivan Fyodorovich, who had just arrived from Petersburg, walking
toward them. His first word was to ask after Yevgeny Pavlovich. But his
wife walked by him wrathfully, without answering or even looking at
him. From the faces of his daughters and Prince Shch. he guessed at
once there was a storm in the house. But even without this, there was
already an unusual uneasiness in his own expression. He took Prince
Shch. by the arm at once, stopped him at the entrance to the house,
and exchanged a few words with him almost in a whisper. From the
troubled air of both as they ascended to the terrace afterward and went
in to Lizaveta Prokofyevna it might be surmised that they had both
heard some extraordinary news. Little by little, they were all gathered
in Lizaveta Prokofyevna's room upstairs, and no one but the prince
was left at last on the terrace. He sat in the corner as though expecting
something, but actually, he didn't know why himself; it did not even
occur to him to go away, seeing the commotion in the house; it seemed
that he had forgotten the whole universe and was ready to go on sitting
for the next two years, wherever he might be put. From time to time,
echoes of anxious conversation reached him from above. He could not
have said himself how long he had been sitting there. It had grown late

and was quite dark. Suddenly, Aglaia came out onto the terrace; judging by appearances, she was calm, though rather pale. Seeing the prince, whom she had "obviously not expected" to find sitting there in the corner, Aglaia smiled, as if in bewilderment.

"What are you doing here?" she asked, going up to him.

The prince muttered something in confusion, and jumped up from his seat; but Aglaia at once sat down beside him, and he sat down again. Suddenly she examined him attentively, then looked as though aimlessly out the window, and then again at him. "Perhaps she wants to laugh," it occurred to the prince, "but no, she'd have laughed back then."

"Perhaps you'd like some tea. I'll order some," she said, after a silence.

"N-no. I don't know ..."

"Well, how can you not know about a thing like that! Oh, by the way, listen: if someone challenged you to a duel, what would you do? I wanted to ask you before."

"Why ... Who ... No one will challenge me to a duel."

"Well, and if they did? Would you be very much frightened?"

"I think I should be very ... much afraid."

"Seriously? Then you are a coward?"

"N-no; perhaps not. A coward is a man who's afraid and runs away; and if one's afraid and doesn't run away, one's not a coward." The prince smiled after a moment's thought.

"And you wouldn't run away?"

"Perhaps I shouldn't run away." He laughed at last at Aglaia's questions ...

"Though I'm a woman, nothing would make me run away," she observed, almost offended. "But you're laughing at me and putting on airs, as you usually do, to make yourself more interesting; tell me: they usually fire at twelve paces? Or sometimes even at ten? So then, it must mean being either killed or wounded?"

"They rarely hit their mark at duels, I imagine."

"What do you mean, rarely? Pushkin was killed."

"That may have been accidental."

"It wasn't at all an accident, it was a duel to the death and he was killed."

"The bullet struck him so low down that no doubt d'Anthès[8] aimed higher, at his head or at his chest; but no one aims for where it struck, so it's most likely that the bullet hit Pushkin by accident, having already missed its mark. People who understand told me so."

"But a soldier I talked to once told me that they were ordered by the regulations, at target practice, to aim at the midriff, that's their phrase, 'in the midriff.' So they're purposely ordered to fire not at the head or the chest, but in the midriff. I asked an officer afterward and he told me it was perfectly true."

"It's true because they fire from a long distance."

"But can you shoot?"

"I have never shot."

"Don't you even know how to load a pistol?"

"No. That is, I understand how it's done, but I've never done it myself."

"Well, that means you don't know how, for it wants practice! Now listen and remember: first, you must buy some good gunpowder, not damp (they say it must not be damp, but very dry), some very fine powder, you must ask for that sort, not what's used to fire cannon. The bullets, I'm told, people somehow cast themselves. Have you pistols?"

"No, and I don't want them," laughed the prince.

"Oh, what nonsense! You must buy one without fail: a good one, French or English, they say they're the best. Then take a thimbleful of powder, or two thimblefuls, perhaps, and sprinkle it in. Better put in plenty. Ram it in with felt (they say it must certainly be felt for some reason); you can get that somewhere, out of some mattress, or doors are sometimes lined with felt. Then, when you've poked the felt in, insert the bullet—do you hear, the bullet afterward, the powder first, or it won't shoot. Why are you laughing? I want you to shoot several times every day, and learn to hit a mark, you absolutely must. Will you do it?"

The prince laughed; Aglaia stamped her foot with vexation. The earnest air with which she carried on such a conversation somewhat surprised him. He rather felt that he ought to have found out something, to have asked about something—in any case, something more

---

8. George d'Anthès, an officer in the Imperial guards, shot Pushkin in a duel over the honor of the latter's wife. Pushkin died of the wound two days later.

serious than how to load a pistol. But everything had flown out of his head except the one fact that she was sitting before him, and that he was looking at her, and whatever she might have talked about, it would have almost been all the same to him at that moment.

Ivan Fyodorovich himself came downstairs to the terrace at last; he was going out somewhere with a sullen, preoccupied and resolute air.

"Ah, Lev Nikolaevich, it's you . . . Where are you going now?" he asked, despite the fact that the prince had no intention of moving from his seat. "Come along, I've a word to say to you."

"Good-bye," said Aglaia, and held out her hand to the prince.

It was rather dark on the terrace by now, the prince could not have made out her face quite clearly. A minute later, when he had left the dacha with the general, he suddenly flushed hotly and tightly squeezed his right hand.

It turned out that Ivan Fyodorovich had to go the same way; Ivan Fyodorovich, despite the late hour, was in a hurry to have a talk with someone about something. But meanwhile, he suddenly began talking to the prince, quickly, agitatedly, and somewhat incoherently, frequently mentioning Lizaveta Prokofyevna. If the prince could have been more attentive at that moment, he might perhaps have guessed that Ivan Fyodorovich wanted, by the by, to find out something from him, or better said, to ask him about something flat out, but somehow couldn't manage to touch upon the very chief point. To his shame, the prince was so distracted that at first he heard nothing at all, and when the general stopped before him with some excited question, he was forced to confess that he had not understood a word.

The general shrugged his shoulders.

"You've all become such queer people, on all sides," he began again. "I tell you that I am at a loss to understand the notions and alarms of Lizaveta Prokofyevna. She's in hysterics, cries and declares that we've been disgraced and shamed. Who? How? By whom? When and why? I confess I am to blame (I admit it), I'm very much to blame, but the persecution of this . . . troublesome woman (who's behaving badly into the bargain) can be restrained, ultimately, by the police, and I intend to see someone this very day and apprise them. Everything can be arranged quietly, gently, kindly even, through acquaintances and without a breath of scandal. I agree, too, that the future is fraught with unforeseen events, and that there's a great deal that's unexplained; there's an intrigue in it, too; but if they know nothing about it here, and again can make no explanation there; if I've heard nothing and you've heard nothing, this one's heard nothing, and the other one's heard nothing, then who, finally, has heard, I ask you? How is it to be explained, in your view, except that half the business is a mirage, nonexistent, something like, for instance, moonshine or other hallucinations."

"*She* is mad," muttered the prince, suddenly recalling with pain all that had recently passed.

"That's just what I said, if you're talking of that one. That idea had come to me too at times, and I slept peacefully. But now I see that what they think here is more correct, and I don't believe in madness. She's given to absurdities, I grant, but at the same time, she's subtle as well, and far from mad. Her stunt today about Kapiton Alexeich proves that too clearly. It's a fraudulent business on her side, that is, at the least, a Jesuitical business for objects of her own."

"What Kapiton Alexeich?"

"Ah, my God, Lev Nikolaevich, you're not listening to anything. Why, that's where I began, by telling you about Kapiton Alexeich; I was so stunned that I'm still trembling in every limb. That's what kept me so long in town today. Kapiton Alexeich Radomsky, Yevgeny Pavlovich's uncle . . ."

"Well!" cried the prince.

"Shot himself at daybreak this morning, at seven o'clock. A venerable old man, seventy, an Epicurean—and it's just exactly as she said—a sum of government money, a large sum!"

"Where could she have . . ."

"Heard of it? Ha-ha! Why, a whole regiment has formed around her from the moment she arrived here. You know what sort of people visit her now and seek 'the honor of her acquaintance.' Naturally, she might have heard something earlier from some visitor; for all Petersburg knows it by now, and half Pavlovsk here, or perhaps the whole of Pavlovsk. But what a subtle remark she made about the uniform, as it was repeated to me, that is, about the fact that Yevgeny Pavlovich managed to retire in the nick of time! What a fiendish hint! No, that doesn't smack of madness. I refuse to believe, of course, that Yevgeny Pavlovich could have known of the catastrophe beforehand, that is, that at

seven o'clock on a certain day, and so on. But he may have had a presentiment of it all. And I, and all of us, and Prince Shch., reckoned that
the other would leave him a fortune, too! It's frightful! Frightful! But
understand me, though, I don't charge Yevgeny Pavlovich with anything, and I hasten to make that clear to you, but still, it's suspicious, all
the same. Prince Shch. is tremendously struck by it. It's all fallen out so
strangely."

"But what is there suspicious about Yevgeny Pavlovich's conduct?"

"There's nothing! He's borne himself most honorably. And I wasn't
hinting at anything. His own estate, I believe, is untouched. Lizaveta
Prokofyevna, of course, won't even hear of it ... But above all—there's
all these domestic catastrophes, or rather all these squabbles, so that
one really doesn't know what to call it ... You're a friend of the family
in the real sense, Lev Nikolaevich, and just imagine, it turns out now,
though it's not certain, that Yevgeny Pavlovich apparently proposed to
Aglaia a month ago, and apparently received a formal refusal from
her."

"It can't be!" cried the prince warmly.

"Why, do you know anything about it? You see, my dear fellow,"
cried the general, startled and surprised, stopping short as though
rooted to the spot, "perhaps I may have chattered on to you more than
I should, or than was proper, but that's because you ... because you ...
one may say, you're that sort of man. Perhaps you know something
particular?"

"I know nothing ... about Yevgeny Pavlovich," muttered the prince.

"I don't either! As for me ... as for me, my boy, they definitively want
to see me dead and buried, and they won't consider that it's hard on a
man, and that I won't bear it. Just now, there was such a scene, it was
awful! I speak to you as though you were my son. Above all, Aglaia
seems to be laughing at her mother. The news about the fact that she'd
apparently refused Yevgeny Pavlovich and that they had had a rather
formal interview about a month ago was announced by her sisters, in
the form of a guess ... though a rather solid guess. But she's such a
willful and fantastical creature that it's beyond words! Every generous
impulse and every brilliant quality of mind and heart—she has all that
in her, perhaps, but at the same time caprice, mockery—in a word, a
devilish nature, and full of fancies besides. She laughed at her mother

to her face just now, at her sisters too, and at Prince Shch.; I say nothing of myself, of course, for she rarely does anything but laugh at me; but what of me, I love her, you know, I even love that she laughs—and, I believe, the little devil loves me specially for it, that is, more than all the rest, I believe. I'll bet anything she's made fun of you for something too. I found her in conversation with you just now after the recent storm upstairs; she was sitting with you as though nothing had happened."

The prince flushed terribly and squeezed his right hand, but said nothing.

"My dear, good Lev Nikolaevich!" the general said suddenly with warmth and feeling, "I . . . and even Lizaveta Prokofyevna herself (though she's begun to rail against you again, and me too, on your account, though I don't understand why), we do love you after all, we sincerely love you and respect you, in spite of everything, I mean of all appearances. But you'll admit yourself, my dear friend, you'll admit how mystifying and how vexing it is to hear when that cold-blooded little devil (for she stood before her mother with a look of profound contempt for all our questions, mine especially, for, devil take it, I was fool enough to take it into my head to make a show of sternness, seeing I'm the head of the family—well, and I was a fool), that cold-blooded little devil suddenly declares with a derisive laugh that that 'mad woman' (she put it this way, and it strikes me as queer that she's of a mind with you: 'How can you have failed to surmise it till now,' she says), that mad woman 'has taken it into her head at all costs to marry me to Prince Lev Nikolaevich, and for that purpose to get Yevgeny Pavlovich turned out of our house' . . . She simply said that; she gave no further explanation, she went on laughing to herself while we simply gaped at her, slammed the door and went out. They told me afterward of what passed between her and you this afternoon . . . and . . . and listen, dear prince, you're a very sensible man and not given to take offense, I've observed that about you, but . . . don't be angry: upon my word, she's laughing at you. Laughing like a child, and so don't be angry with her, but that's certainly so. Don't think anything of it—she's simply making a fool of you and all of us, out of idleness. Well, good-bye! You know our feelings? Our genuine feelings for you? They'll never change in any respect . . . but . . . now I must go this way, good-bye! I've not often been in such a tight hole (what's the expression?) as I am now ... A pretty summer holiday!"

Left alone at the crossroads, the prince looked around him, rapidly crossed the road, went close up to the lighted window of a dacha, unfolded the little piece of paper that he had held tightly in his right hand during the entire conversation with Ivan Fyodorovich, and by a faint beam of light, read:

Tomorrow morning at seven o'clock I will be on the green bench, in the park, and will wait for you. I have made up my mind to talk to you about an exceedingly important matter which concerns you directly.

P.S. I hope you will show no one this note. Though I'm ashamed to give you such a caution, but I have judged that you deserve it, and I write it—blushing with shame at your absurd character.

P.P.S. I mean the green bench I pointed out to you earlier. Shame on you! I am forced to write this, too.

The letter had been scribbled in haste and folded any which way, most likely just before Aglaia came out to the terrace. In indescribable agitation that was almost like fright, the prince held the paper clenched tightly in his right hand again, and hastily leapt away from the window, from the light, like a frightened thief; but in doing so he suddenly collided heavily with a gentleman who turned out to be standing just behind his back.

"I have been following you, Prince," said the gentleman.

"Is that you, Keller?" cried the prince in surprise.

"I was looking for you, Prince. I've been watching for you by the Epanchins'; couldn't go in, of course. I walked behind you while you walked with the general. I am at your service, Prince, you may dispose of Keller. I am ready to make sacrifices, even to die, if need be."

"But ... what for?"

"Well, no doubt, a challenge will follow. That Lieutenant Molovtsov ... I know him, that is, not personally ... He won't put up with insult. The likes of us, that is, Rogozhin and me, he is inclined to look upon as dirt, and perhaps deservedly, so you are the only one left to answer for it. You'll have to pay the piper, Prince. He's been inquiring about you, I hear, and no doubt a friend of his will call on you tomorrow or, perhaps, is already waiting for you now. If you do me the honor to choose me for your second, I'm ready to don the red cap[9] for you. That's why I've been looking for you, Prince."

"So, you're talking of a duel too!" The prince suddenly broke out laughing, to Keller's great surprise. He laughed heartily. Keller, who had really been on tenterhooks until he had satisfied himself by offering to be the prince's second, was almost offended at the sight of the prince's merry laughter.

"But after all, Prince, you seized him by the arms this afternoon. For a man of honor, and in public, that's hard to put up with."

"And he gave me a shove in the chest!" cried the prince, laughing. "There's nothing for us to fight about! I'll beg his pardon, that's all. But if we must fight, let us fight! Let him shoot, I should like it. Ha-ha! I know how to load a pistol now! Do you know, someone's just instructed me on how to load a pistol? Can you load a pistol, Keller? First you have to buy powder, pistol powder, not damp, and not as coarse as for cannon; then you have to put the powder in first, and get some felt somewhere from a door, and only then drop in the bullet, and not the bullet before the powder, or it won't go off. Do you hear, Keller: because it won't go off. Ha-ha! Isn't that a magnificent reason, friend Keller? Ach, Keller, do you know I will hug and kiss you right now! Ha-ha-ha! How was it that you turned up so suddenly before him earlier? Come and see me sometime soon and have some champagne. We'll all drink till we're drunk! Do you know I've twelve bottles of champagne at home in Lebedev's cellar? He sold them to me, on a 'chance opportunity,' the day before yesterday, the very day after I moved into his house, I bought them all! I'll get the whole company together! Are you going to sleep tonight?"

"As I do every night, Prince."

"Well, pleasant dreams, then! Ha-ha!"

The prince crossed the road and vanished into the park, leaving the somewhat puzzled Keller lost in thought. He had never yet seen the prince in such a strange mood, and could not have imagined it till now.

"Fever, perhaps, for he's a nervous man, and all this has had an effect; but, of course, he won't run scared. It's just that sort that don't run

9. Since dueling was illegal, Lieutenant Keller might well expect the "red cap"—i.e., demotion to common soldier—as punishment for his participation.

scared, by God!" Keller was thinking to himself. "Hm, champagne! An interesting bit of news, though! Twelve bottles, yes sir, a dozen; well, well, a decent provision. But I'll bet that Lebedev got that champagne as a pledge from someone. Hm! . . . He's rather nice, though, that prince; truly, I'm fond of such fellows; there's no point in losing time, though, and . . . if there's champagne, then the time is now . . ."

That the prince was almost in a fever was, of course, a fair assumption.

He wandered a long while about the dark park, and at last "found himself" walking along an alley. There was an impression left upon his consciousness that he had already walked back and forth down this alley—from the bench to a tall, conspicuous old tree, only about a hundred paces—some thirty or forty times. He could never have remembered, even had he wanted to, what he had been thinking all that time, at least an entire hour, in the park. He caught himself, however, thinking one thought that made him burst out laughing; though there was nothing to laugh about, he kept wanting to laugh. It occurred to him that the surmise about the duel might have arisen not only in Keller's mind, and that, therefore, the story about how to load a pistol may not have been incidental after all . . . "Bah!" He stopped suddenly, as another idea dawned upon him. "Earlier, she came down to the terrace, when I was sitting there in the corner, and was awfully surprised to find me there and—how she laughed . . . She started talking about tea; but she had that paper in her hands all the while, of course, so she must have certainly known that I was sitting on the terrace, so why then was she surprised? Ha-ha-ha!"

He snatched the letter from his pocket and kissed it, but at once stopped and pondered.

"How strange it is! How strange it is!" he said, a minute later, even with a certain sadness: in moments of intense joy he always grew sad, he himself did not know why. He surveyed his surroundings attentively and was surprised that he had come there. He was very tired, went to the bench and sat down on it. There was an extraordinary stillness all around. The music at the station had ceased. There was perhaps no one left in the park; of course, it must have been at least half past eleven. It was a still, warm, clear night—a Petersburg night in early June, but in the thick shady park, in the alley where he was sitting, it was almost entirely dark.

If anyone had told him at that moment that he had fallen in love, that he was passionately in love, he would have rejected the idea with surprise and perhaps with indignation. And if anyone had added that Aglaia's letter was a love letter, appointing a lovers' tryst, he would have burned for shame on that man's account, and would perhaps have challenged him to a duel. All this was perfectly sincere, and he never once doubted it, or admitted the slightest "double" thought of the possibility of this girl's love for him or even the possibility of his love for this girl. The possibility of love for him, "for such a man as he was," he would have considered a monstrous thing. He fancied that it was only mischief on her part, if there was really anything in it; but he was somehow far too indifferent toward that bit of mischief itself and found it far too much along the natural order of things; he himself was occupied and absorbed with something entirely different. He fully believed the words that had slipped earlier from the agitated general—that she was making fun of everyone, and of him, the prince, particularly. He did not feel in the least insulted at this; in his opinion, it was quite as it should be. To him the chief thing was that tomorrow he would see her again early in the morning, would sit beside her on the green bench, would hear about how to load a pistol, and would look at her. He needed nothing more. The question of what it was she meant to say to him, and what was this important matter that concerned him directly, also flashed once or twice through his mind. Moreover, he did not for a moment doubt the real existence of this "important matter" for which he was summoned, but he hardly thought of that important matter at all now, to the point of not even feeling the slightest inclination to think about it.

The crunch of slow footsteps on the sand of the alley made him raise his head. A man whose face was difficult to distinguish in the dark came up to the bench and sat down beside him. The prince quickly moved over to him, almost touching him, and discerned the pale face of Rogozhin.

"I knew you were wandering about here somewhere. I haven't been long in finding you," Rogozhin muttered through his teeth.

It was the first time they had come together since their meeting in the corridor of the inn. Stunned by Rogozhin's sudden appearance, the prince could not for some time collect his thoughts, and an agonizing sensation rose up again in his heart. Rogozhin evidently understood the effect he had produced; but though he faltered at first, talked with an air of some kind of studied ease, still it soon seemed to the prince that there was nothing studied about him, nor even any particular embarrassment: if there were any awkwardness in his gestures and speech at all, it was only on the surface; in his soul, this man could not change.

"How did . . . you find me here?" asked the prince, in order to say something.

"I heard it from Keller (I went to see you), 'He's gone into the park,' says he; well, thought I, that's just how it is."

"What is?" The prince anxiously picked up on the phrase he had let slip.

Rogozhin smirked but gave no explanation.

"I got your letter, Lev Nikolaich; It's all futile on your part . . . and why you bother! . . . But now I've come to you from *her:* she bade me bring you without fail; she is very anxious to say something to you. She asked for you today."

"I'll come tomorrow. I'm going home now; are you . . . coming to me?"

"What for? I've said all I have to say to you; good-bye."

"You really won't come?" the prince asked him gently.

"You're a queer fellow, Lev Nikolaich, one has to marvel at you."

Rogozhin smirked venomously.

"Why? Where does this bitterness of yours against me come from now?" the prince took up, sadly and with warmth. "Why, you know yourself now that everything you thought was untrue. But then, anyway, I did expect that this bitterness against me had still not subsided in you, and do you know why? Because you yourself made an attempt on my life, that's why your bitterness does not subside. I tell you I only remember that Parfyon Rogozhin with whom I fraternally exchanged crosses that day; I wrote that to you in last night's letter, so that you would put all that raving nonsense out of your mind and not even bring it up with me again. Why do you turn away from me? Why do you hide your hand from me? I tell you that everything that happened then, I consider simply as raving nonsense: I know the way you were that day inside and out, like I know myself. What you imagined did not exist and could not exist. Why should we have any bitterness?"

"What bitterness could you have!" Rogozhin laughed again in response to the prince's sudden and heated speech. He was indeed keeping away from him, having taken a couple of steps back and hidden his hands.

"It's not the thing for me to come and see you now at all, Lev Nikolaich," he added slowly and sententiously in conclusion.

"You hate me that much, then?"

"I don't like you, Lev Nikolaich, so why should I come and see you? Ah, Prince, you're like a child; you want a plaything—and you must have it at once, but you don't grasp the business. What you're saying now, it's all just exactly what you wrote in your letter, and do you suppose I don't believe you? I believe every word, and I know that you never have deceived me, and never will deceive me in the future; but I don't like you all the same. You wrote that you've forgotten everything and you only remember the brother Rogozhin with whom you exchanged crosses, and not that Rogozhin who raised his knife against you. But how do you know my feelings? (Rogozhin smirked again.) Why, perhaps I've never once repented of it since then, while you've already sent me your brotherly forgiveness. Perhaps I was already thinking of something else that evening, while that . . ."

"Wasn't even in your mind!" the prince caught up. "I should think so! I bet that you rushed straight to the train and then here to Pavlovsk, where the music was playing, and spied her out and followed her about in the crowd just as you did today. You don't surprise me with that! If you hadn't been in such a state at the time that you could think of nothing else, perhaps you wouldn't have raised the knife against me. I had already had a presentiment that time in the morning, looking at you; do you know what you were like then? When we exchanged crosses, that idea began to stir in me. And why did you take me to the old lady then? Did you think to stay your hand that way? But it cannot be that you thought it, rather, you only felt it just as I did . . . We were feeling just the same then, word for word. Had you not raised your hand against me then (which God averted), what should I have turned out to be before you now? Why, I would have still suspected you of it, our sin was the same, word for word. (But don't scowl! Well, and what are you laughing for?) You've 'not repented'! Why, even if you wanted to, you couldn't have repented of it, perhaps, because you don't like me into the bargain. And were I as innocent as an angel before you, you'd still detest me so long as you think she loves me and not you.

Well, that must be jealousy. But here's what I thought about this week, Parfyon, and I'll tell you: do you know that she may love you now more than anyone, and in such a way that the more she torments you, the more she loves you? She won't tell you so, but you must know how to see it. Why else, when all's said and done, is she going to marry you, anyway? Someday she will tell you so herself. Some women even want to be loved like that, and that's just her character! And your love and your character must impress her! Do you know that a woman is capable of torturing a man with her cruelty and mockery without feeling the faintest twinge of conscience, because she'll think to herself every time she looks at you: 'I'm tormenting him to death now, but I'll make up for it with my love, later . . .' "

Rogozhin broke out laughing when he had heard out the prince.

"But, I say, Prince, have you yourself fallen into the hands of one like that somehow? I've heard one thing or another about you, if it's true."

"What, what could you have heard?" The prince suddenly shuddered, and stopped in extreme confusion.

Rogozhin went on laughing. He had listened to the prince not without curiosity and perhaps not without some pleasure; the joyous and warm enthusiasm of the prince had greatly amazed and encouraged him.

"And I've not merely heard it; I see now myself that it's true," he added. "When have you ever talked like this before? Why, such talk sounds like it's coming from a different person. If I hadn't heard something of the sort about you, I shouldn't have come here: to the park, to boot, and at midnight."

"I don't understand you at all, Parfyon Semyonych."

"She'd explained to me about you a long time ago already, but now I've seen it for myself today as you sat listening to the music with that girl. She vowed to me, today and yesterday, she vowed that you were in love with Aglaia Epanchin like a puppy dog. That's nothing to me, Prince, and it's no business of mine: if you have left off loving her, she has still not left off loving you. You know, don't you, that she's set on marrying you to her, she's given her word, he-he! She says to me: 'Without that, I won't marry you; when they've gone to church, we'll go to church.' I can't understand what's going on here, and I never have understood: she either loves you beyond all measure, or . . . If she does love you, why does she want to marry you to someone else? She says, 'I want to see him happy,' so that must mean she loves you."

"I've told you and written to you that she's ... out of her mind," said the prince, who had listened to Rogozhin in anguish.

"The Lord knows! You may be mistaken, too ... By the way, she fixed the wedding day today, when I brought her home from the concert: in three weeks' time or perhaps sooner, she said, we will certainly go to the altar; she swore it, took down the icon, kissed it. The business rests with you now, it seems, Prince, he-he!"

"That's all raving nonsense! What you've said about me will never, never be! I'll come and see you both tomorrow ..."

"How can you call her mad?" observed Rogozhin. "How is it she seems sane to everyone else, and only out of her mind with you alone? How could she send letters there? If she were mad, they'd have noticed it in her letters!"

"What letters?" asked the prince in alarm.

"Why, she writes them to *her*, and that one reads them. Don't you know? Well, then, you'll find out; no doubt she'll show them to you herself."

"It's not to be believed!" cried the prince.

"Ach! Lev Nikolaevich, but it's clear you haven't gone very far down that path yet, as far as I can see; rather, you're only just beginning. Wait a bit: you'll keep your own detectives yet and be on the watch day and night too, and know of every step she takes, if only ..."

"Stop, and never speak of that again!" cried the prince. "Listen, Parfyon, just before you came, I was walking here and suddenly began laughing; what about—I don't know, but the only reason was that I remembered that tomorrow happens to be my birthday, as if by design. It's almost twelve o'clock. Come, let us meet the day! I've got some wine, let's drink some wine, wish for me what I don't know how to wish for myself, and you in particular must wish it, while I'll wish all happiness to you. Or else give back the cross! You didn't send the cross back to me next day, did you! You've got it on you, haven't you? Is it on you now?"

"It's on me," said Rogozhin.

"Well, then, come along. I don't want to greet my new life without you, for my new life has begun! You don't know, Parfyon, that my new life has begun today."

"I see for myself now, and know myself that it has begun; and I'll tell *her* so. You're not like yourself at all, Lev Nikolaevich!"

IV

With great surprise, the prince noticed, as he approached his dacha with Rogozhin, that his terrace was brightly lit up and that a noisy and numerous company was assembled there. The merry group roared with laughter and shouted; it seemed they were even arguing at the top of their voices; the first glance suggested that they were having a most hilarious time. And, indeed, when he mounted to the terrace he saw that they were all drinking, and drinking champagne, and apparently had been drinking for some time now, so that many of the revelers had managed to become very agreeably exhilarated. The guests were acquaintances of the prince, but it was strange that they should all have come together at once, as though by invitation, though the prince had invited no one, and had only recollected that it was his birthday just now, by chance.

"No doubt you told someone you'd put out the champagne, and so they've all come running," muttered Rogozhin, following the prince onto the terrace. "We know that score; you've only to whistle to them . . ." he added, almost with bitterness, doubtless recalling his own recent past.

They all greeted the prince with shouts and good wishes, and surrounded him. Some were very noisy, others much quieter, but hearing that it was his birthday, everyone hastened to congratulate him, and each waited his turn. The prince was curious about the presence of some persons, for instance, Burdovsky; but what was most surprising was that Yevgeny Pavlovich suddenly turned out to be among the company; the prince could scarcely believe his eyes, and was almost alarmed at seeing him.

In the meantime, Lebedev, flushed and almost ecstatic, ran up with explanations; he was pretty *ripe* already. From his babble it appeared that the party had come together quite naturally, and indeed by chance. First of all, toward the evening, Ippolit had arrived and, feeling much better, had expressed the desire to wait for the prince on the terrace. He had installed himself on the sofa; then Lebedev had gone down to join him and then all the household—that is, his daughters and General Ivolgin. Burdovsky arrived with Ippolit, having accompanied him. Ganya and Ptitsyn, it seems, stopped in not long ago, when they were passing by (their appearance coincided with the incident at the station); then Keller had turned up, announced it was the prince's birthday, and demanded champagne. Yevgeny Pavlovich had only stopped in half an hour ago. Kolya, too, had insisted for all he was worth on the champagne and on making a party of it. Lebedev had readily produced the wine.

"But my own! My own!" he murmured to the prince. "At my own expense, to celebrate your birthday and congratulate you; and there'll be some supper, some light refreshments, my daughter is seeing to that; but, Prince, if only you knew the subject they're discussing. Do you remember in *Hamlet*, 'To be or not to be'? A topical subject, yes sir, very topical! Questions and answers . . . And Mr. Terentyev is extremely . . . unwilling to go to bed! As for the champagne, he's only had a sip, just a sip, it won't hurt him . . . Come closer, Prince, you settle it! They've all been waiting for you, they've all been doing nothing but waiting for your happy wit . . ."

The prince noticed the sweet and kindly gaze of Vera Lebedev, who was also hurrying to make her way to get to him through the crowd. Passing over the rest, he held out his hand first to her: she flushed with pleasure, and wished him "a happy life *from that day forward*." Then she rushed full speed to the kitchen, where she was preparing some light supper; but even before the prince had arrived—whenever she could tear herself for a minute from her work—she would appear on the terrace and listen, all ears, to the heated arguments, which did not cease among the tipsy guests, concerning things that were entirely abstract and mysterious to her. Her younger sister, with her mouth gaping, was asleep in the next room on top of a chest, but the boy, Lebedev's son, was standing by Kolya and Ippolit, and the look on his exhilarated face showed that he was ready to stand there, enraptured and listening, for another ten hours at a stretch.

"I have been waiting particularly to see you, and I'm very glad that you've come in such a happy mood," said Ippolit, when the prince went up to shake his hand, immediately after Vera's.

"How do you know I'm in a happy mood?"

"One can see it from your face. Greet the gentlemen and hurry back to sit down with us here. I've been waiting particularly to see you," he added, significantly stressing the fact that he had been waiting. At the prince's admonition—was it not bad for him to be sitting up so late?— he replied that he indeed wondered at himself, how it was that he was on the point of dying three days ago, and yet he had never felt better in his life than that evening.

Burdovsky jumped up and muttered that he "had only brought Ippolit," and that he was glad, too; that he had "written nonsense" in his letter, but now was "simply glad ..." Without finishing his sentence, he firmly grasped the prince's hand and sat down on a chair.

Last of all the prince went up to Yevgeny Pavlovich. The latter at once took him under the arm.

"I have a couple of words to say to you," he whispered in an undertone, "and about an extremely important circumstance; let us step aside for a moment."

"A couple of words," whispered another voice in the prince's other ear; and another hand took him under the arm on the other side. With surprise, the prince observed a terribly unkempt, flushed, winking and laughing figure, in which he instantly recognized Ferdyshchenko, who had turned up from goodness knows where.

"Do you remember Ferdyshchenko?" asked the latter.

"Where have you come from?" cried the prince.

"He repents!" cried Keller, running up. "He was hiding, he didn't want to come out to you, he was hiding in the corner there, he repents, Prince, he feels himself to blame."

"But what for? What for?"

"It was I who met him, Prince, I met him just now and brought him along; he is a rare one among my friends. But he repents."

"Delighted, gentlemen; go and sit down there with the rest. I'll come directly," said the prince, getting away at last and hurrying to Yevgeny Pavlovich.

"It's very entertaining here," observed the latter. "And I've been waiting for you this half hour with pleasure. Look here, dear Lev Nikolaevich, I've settled everything with Kurmyshev and I've come to set your mind at rest; you have no need to be uneasy, he is taking the thing very, very sensibly, especially as, to my thinking, it was more his fault."

"With what Kurmyshev?"

"Why, the one whose arms you seized earlier . . . He was so enraged that he meant to send to you for an explanation tomorrow."

"You don't mean it! What nonsense!"

"Of course it is nonsense, and could only end in nonsense; but such people in our part of the world . . ."

"You've come about something else, too, perhaps, Yevgeny Pavlovich?"

"Oh, of course, about something else, too," laughed the other. "At first light tomorrow, dear prince, I'm setting off, on account of that unhappy business (about my uncle, you know), to Petersburg; would you believe it: it's all true, and everyone knows it already except me. I have been so overwhelmed by it that I haven't had a chance to go *there* (to the Epanchins'); and won't go there tomorrow either for I shall be in Petersburg, do you understand? I may not be here for three days, perhaps—in short, my affairs are starting to falter. Though the affair is not immeasurably important, yet I decided that I must speak with you most candidly about something, and without delay—that is, before I go. I'll sit and wait now, if you like, till your party has broken up; besides, I've nowhere else to go: I'm so agitated that I couldn't go to bed. Finally, though it's unconscionable and unseemly to pursue a man like this, I'll tell you straight out: I have come to seek your friendship, my dear prince; you're a man without equal—that is, you don't tell a lie at every turn, and perhaps not at all, and I want a friend and adviser in a certain matter; for there's not a doubt I'm one of the unlucky now . . ."

He laughed again.

"The trouble is this," the prince pondered for a moment, "you want to wait till they've broken up, but God knows when that will be. Wouldn't it be better for us to go down to the park now? They'll wait for me, of course; I'll excuse myself."

"No, no, I have my own reasons for not letting them suspect us of having a pressing conversation with a special object; there are people here who are very curious about our relations with one another—don't you know that, Prince? And it will be much better if they see that our dealings are, anyway, of the most friendly and not simply pressing sort—do you understand? They'll break up in another two hours; I'll take up twenty minutes of your time, well—half an hour . . ."

"By all means, you are very welcome; I am delighted to see you even without explanations; and thank you for your kind words about our friendly relations. Pardon me for having been distracted today; you should know, I somehow can't be attentive just now."

"I see, I see," muttered Yevgeny Pavlovich, with a faint smirk. He was very easily amused this evening.

"What do you see?" said the prince, startled.

"But you don't suspect, dear prince," Yevgeny Pavlovich continued to smirk, not answering his direct question, "you don't suspect that I've simply come to pull one over on you, and, by the by, to get something out of you, eh?"

"That you have come to get something out of me I have no doubt," the prince laughed too, at last, "and perhaps you have planned to deceive me a little too. But what of it? I am not afraid of you; besides, it's somehow all the same to me now, would you believe it? And . . . and . . . and as I am convinced above all that you're a splendid fellow, we shall perhaps actually end by becoming friends. I like you very much, Yevgeny Pavlovich, you . . . are, in my opinion, a very decent man!"

"Well, in any case, it's most pleasant to have any dealings with you, whatever they may be," concluded Yevgeny Pavlovich. "Come, I'll drink a glass to your health; I'm awfully glad I've come to bother you. Ah!" he stopped suddenly, "that Mr. Ippolit has come to live with you, hasn't he?"

"Yes."

"He isn't going to die directly, I think, is he?"

"Why do you ask?"

"Oh, nothing; I've spent the half-hour with him here . . ."

Ippolit had been waiting this entire time for the prince and constantly kept glancing over at him and Yevgeny Pavlovich while they were talking off to the side. He became feverishly animated when they came up to the table. He was uneasy and agitated; sweat stood out on his forehead. In his glittering eyes could be seen a sort of vague impatience, aside from some kind of wandering, constant uneasiness; his gaze strayed aimlessly from object to object, from one face to another. Though he had up till now taken a leading part in the noisy general conversation, his liveliness was simply feverishness; in fact, he was not attentive to the conversation itself; his arguments were incoherent, sarcastic, and carelessly paradoxical; he would break off in the middle and drop whatever he himself had begun with fervent enthusiasm. The prince learned with surprise and regret that that evening he had been allowed without protest to drink two full glasses of champagne, and that the drained glass that stood before him was already the third. But he learned this only later; at the moment he was not very observant.

"Do you know I'm awfully glad that your birthday is today, of all days!" cried Ippolit.

"Why?"

"You'll see; hurry and sit down; in the first place, because your whole . . . crowd has gathered here. I'd reckoned there'd be a crowd; for the first time in my life I've been right in my reckoning! It's a pity I didn't know about your birthday, or else I'd have come with a present . . . Ha-ha! But perhaps I have come with a present! Is it long till daylight?"

"It's not two hours now till daybreak," observed Ptitsyn, looking at his watch.

"What need of daybreak, when one can read out in the yard without it?" remarked someone.

"Because I need to see a tiny sliver of the sun. Can we drink to the health of the sun, Prince? What do you think?"

Ippolit asked the question sharply, addressing the whole company unceremoniously, as though he were giving orders, but he was apparently unconscious of doing so himself.

"Let's drink to it if you like; only you ought to calm down, Ippolit, how about it?"

"You're always going on about sleep; you might be my nurse, Prince! As soon as the sun shows itself and 'resounds' in the sky (who was it wrote the verse, 'The sun resounded in the sky'?[10] It's nonsensical, but it's good!) then we'll go to bed. Lebedev! The sun's the spring of life, isn't it? What's the meaning of 'springs of life' in the Apocalypse? Have you heard of the 'star that is called Wormwood,' Prince?"

"I've heard that Lebedev identified this 'star that is called Wormwood' with the network of railways spread over Europe."

---

10. The line is an inexact citation from Goethe's *Faust.*

"No, sir, excuse me, sir, that won't do, sir!" cried Lebedev, leaping up and waving his arms, as though he were trying to stop the general laughter that followed. "Excuse me! With these gentlemen . . . all these gentlemen," he turned suddenly to the prince, "why, I tell you on certain points, it's simply this, sir . . ." and without ceremony, he rapped the table twice, which increased the general mirth.

Though Lebedev was in his usual "evening" condition, he was on this occasion far too excited and irritated by the preceding long, "learned" discussion, and on such occasions he treated his opponents with unbounded and extremely candid contempt.

"That's not right, no sir! Half an hour ago, Prince, we made a compact not to interrupt; not to laugh while one was speaking; to allow him to express himself freely, and only then let the atheists contradict him, if they like; we chose the general as president, that's how it was, sir. For else you might trip up anyone like that in a lofty idea, sir, a profound idea, sir . . ."

"But speak, speak: nobody's tripping you up!" cried voices.

"Talk, but don't get carried away."

"What is this 'star that is called Wormwood'?" someone inquired.

"I haven't the slightest idea!" answered General Ivolgin, taking his former seat as president with an important air.

"I'm wonderfully fond of all these arguments and disputations, Prince—learned ones, of course," Keller muttered in the meantime, fidgeting on his chair with absolute delight and impatience. "Learned and political," he turned suddenly and unexpectedly to Yevgeny Pavlovich, who was sitting almost next to him. "Do you know, I'm awfully fond of reading in the papers about the English Parliament, that is, not in the sense of what they discuss (I'm not a politician, you know), but in the sense of the way they discuss things amongst themselves, and behave like politicians, so to speak: 'the noble viscount sitting opposite,' 'the noble earl who shares my view,' 'my honorable opponent who has amazed Europe by his proposal'—that is to say, all those little expressions, all this parliamentarianism of a free people—that's what's so fascinating to people like us. I'm enchanted, Prince. I've always been an artist at the bottom of my soul; I swear to you, Yevgeny Pavlovich."

"Why, then," Ganya was growing heated in another corner, "it would follow on your account that railways are damned, that they are the ruin of mankind, that they are a pestilence that has fallen upon the earth to pollute the 'springs of life'?"

Gavrila Ardalionovich was in a particularly excited mood that evening, and in a gay, almost triumphant mood, so the prince fancied. He was joking with Lebedev, of course, turning up the flame, but he soon got hot himself.

"Not railways, no sir!" objected Lebedev, who was at one and the same time losing his temper and feeling incomparable delight. "The railways alone won't pollute the 'springs of life,' but all of it as a whole is damned, yes sir; the whole tendency of the last few centuries in its general entirety, scientific and practical, is perhaps really damned, yes indeed, sir."

"Certainly damned, or only perhaps? That's important in this case, you know," queried Yevgeny Pavlovich.

"Damned, damned, most certainly damned!" Lebedev maintained with zeal.

"Don't rush, Lebedev, you're much kinder in the mornings," remarked Ptitsyn with a smile.

"But in the evenings, more candid! In the evenings, more heartfelt and candid!" Lebedev turned to him fervently. "More open-hearted and definite, more honest and honorable; and although I am exposing my weak side to you, I don't care a whit, no sir; I challenge you all now, all you atheists: with what will you save the world, and wherein have you found a normal path for it—you men of science, of industry, of cooperation, of wage labor and all the rest of it? With what? With credit? What's credit? Where will credit lead you?"

"Ach! Why, that's some curiosity you've got there!" observed Yevgeny Pavlovich.

"Well, and my opinion is that anyone who isn't interested in such questions is a fashionable *chenapan*,[11] yes sir."

"But at least it leads to general solidarity and a balance of interests," observed Ptitsyn.

"That's all! That's all! Without acknowledging any moral basis except the satisfaction of individual egoism and material necessity? Universal peace, universal happiness—from necessity! Do I understand you right, my dear sir, may I venture to ask?"

11. Fr., scoundrel.

"But the universal necessity is to live, eat and drink, while the complete and ultimately scientific conviction that these necessities are not satisfied without general cooperation and solidarity of interests is, it would seem, a sufficiently powerful idea to serve as a basis and 'spring of life' for future ages of humanity," observed Ganya, who had by now become heated in earnest.

"The necessity of eating and drinking, that is merely the instinct of self-preservation . . ."

"But isn't the mere instinct of self-preservation enough in itself? Why, the instinct of self-preservation is the normal law of humanity . . ."

"Who told you that?" cried Yevgeny Pavlovich suddenly. "It's a law, that's true; but it's no more normal than the law of destruction, or even self-destruction. Can the whole normal law of mankind lie in self-preservation?"

"A-ha!" cried Ippolit, turning quickly to Yevgeny Pavlovich and scrutinizing him with wild curiosity; but seeing that he was laughing, he started to laugh himself, nudged Kolya who was standing beside him, and asked him again what time it was, even took hold of Kolya's silver watch himself and looked eagerly at the hands. Then, as though forgetting everything, he stretched out on the sofa, threw his arms behind his head, and began staring at the ceiling; half a minute later, he sat at the table again, drawing himself up and listening attentively to the babble of Lebedev, who had grown heated to the utmost degree.

"An insidious and irreverent idea, an idea that drives it home!" Lebedev greedily caught up Yevgeny Pavlovich's paradox; "an idea expressed with the object of inciting opponents to battle—but a true idea! For you, a worldly scoffer and cavalier[12] (though not without abilities!), do not know yourself the extent to which your idea is a profound idea, that is, a true idea! Yes, sir. The law of self-destruction and the law of self-preservation are equally strong in humanity! The devil has equal dominion over humanity till the limit of time, which is yet unknown to us. You laugh? You don't believe in the devil? Disbelief in the devil is a French idea, it is a frivolous idea. Do you know who the devil is? Do you know his name? And without even knowing his name,

12. Here, a member of a cavalry rather than a gallant (Russian has two different words— *kavalerist* and *kavaler*—for these two meanings, so there is no double entendre).

you laugh at the form of him, following Voltaire's example, at his hoofs, at his tail, at his horns, which you yourselves have invented; for the evil spirit is a mighty and menacing spirit, and he has not the hoofs and horns you've invented for him. But he's not the point now . . ."

"How do you know that he's not the point now?" cried Ippolit suddenly, and burst out laughing as though in a fit.

"A clever and insinuating thought!" Lebedev approved. "But, again, that's not the point. Our question is whether the 'springs of life' have not grown weaker with the increase of . . ."

"Railways?" cried Kolya.

"Not railway communication, young but impetuous youth, but all that tendency of which railways may serve, so to speak, as the pictorial, artistic expression. They make haste and thunder, they thump and hurry, for the happiness of humanity, they say! 'Mankind has grown too noisy and industrial; there is little spiritual peace,' one secluded thinker has complained. 'So be it; but the rumble of the wagons that bring bread to starving humanity is better, maybe, than spiritual peace,' another thinker, who is always traveling everywhere, replies to the former triumphantly, and walks away from him with glory. But, vile Lebedev that I am, I don't believe in the wagons that bring bread to humanity! For the wagons that bring bread to all humanity, without any moral basis for the deed, may coldly exclude a considerable part of humanity from enjoying what is brought, which has happened in the past . . ."

"Is it the wagons that can coldly exclude?" someone took up.

"Which has happened in the past," asserted Lebedev, not dignifying the question with his attention. "We've already had Malthus, the friend of humanity. But the friend of humanity with shaky moral foundations is the devourer of humanity, to say nothing of his vanity; for wound the vanity of any one of these numerous friends of humanity, and he's ready at once to set fire to the four corners of the world out of petty revenge—incidentally, just like all the rest of us, to be fair; just like myself, vilest of all, for I might well be the first to bring the firewood and run away myself. But that's not the point again!"

"Well, what is it, finally?"

"You're getting tiresome!"

"The point lies in the following, in a story from centuries past; for I absolutely must tell you a story from centuries past. In our times, and in our fatherland, which I trust you love as much as I do, gentlemen, for, on my part, I am ready to shed the last drop of my blood for..."

"Go on! Go on!"

"In our fatherland, just as in Europe, general, widespread and terrible famines visit humanity, as far as they can be reckoned, and as far as I can remember, not oftener now than once in a quarter of a century, in other words, every twenty-five years. I won't dispute the exact number, but they are comparatively rather rare."

"Compared with what?"

"With the twelfth century, or the adjoining centuries on the one and the other side. For then, as is written and asserted by authors, widespread famines visited the human population once every two years, or at least every three years, so that with such a state of affairs men even took recourse to anthropophagy, though they kept it secret. One of these cannibals, approaching old age, announced of his own accord, without being compelled at all, that in the course of his long and wretched life he had killed and eaten, by himself and in dead secret, sixty monks and a few layman infants, a matter of six, but not more, that is to say, extraordinarily few compared with the number of ecclesiastics he had consumed. As regards layman adults, it turned out that he had never approached them with that object."

"That can't be!" cried the president himself, the general, virtually in a hurt tone. "I often reason and dispute with him, gentlemen, and always about ideas of this kind; but most often he puts forth such absurdities that it makes your ears ache, without a shred of credibility!"

"General! Remember the siege of Kars, and as for you, gentlemen, you should know that my story is the naked truth. For myself, I will only note that almost every reality, even though it has its unalterable laws, is almost always incredible and improbable. Indeed, the more real it is, the more improbable it often seems."

"But is it possible to eat sixty monks?" They laughed all around.

"And if he didn't eat them all at once, which is evident, but, perhaps, in the course of fifteen or twenty years, which is then perfectly comprehensible and natural..."

"And natural?"

"And natural!" Lebedev snapped with pedantic persistence. "And aside from everything else, a Catholic monk is, from his very nature, easily led and inquisitive, and it would be too easy to lure him into the forest, or to some hidden place, and there to deal with him as aforesaid. But I don't dispute that the number of persons devoured turned out to be excessive, even to the point of intemperance."

"It may be true, gentlemen," observed the prince suddenly.

Till then he had listened in silence to the disputants and had taken no part in the conversation; he had often laughed heartily in the wake of the general outbursts of laughter. It was evident that he was awfully glad that they were so gay and so noisy; even that they were drinking so much. He might perhaps not have uttered a word the whole evening, but suddenly he somehow took it into his head to speak. And he spoke with extraordinary earnestness, so that everyone turned to him at once with curiosity.

"What I mean, gentlemen, is that such famines used to be frequent then. I have heard of that, though I don't know history well. But, it seems, that's how it must have been. When I found myself in the Swiss mountains, I was greatly amazed at the ruins of the old feudal castles, built on the mountain slopes, on precipitous cliffs, and with at least half a verst of vertical drop (which means several versts of mountain path). You know what a castle is: it's a perfect mountain of stones. A terrible, impossible labor! And, of course, they were all built by those poor people, the vassals. Besides which, they had to pay all sorts of taxes and support the priesthood. How could they have sustained themselves and tilled the land? They must have been few in number at that time, they died off terribly from famine, and there may have been literally nothing to eat. I've sometimes wondered, indeed: how is it that the people didn't become extinct altogether then and that something didn't happen to them; how did they manage to survive and endure? No doubt Lebedev is right that there were cannibals, and perhaps many of them; only I don't understand why he threw in the monks, in particular, and what he means by that?"

"Probably because in the twelfth century it was only the monks who were fit to eat, because only the monks were fat," observed Gavrila Ardalionovich.

"A most magnificent and true idea!" cried Lebedev, "seeing he didn't even touch laymen—not one layman to sixty members of the clergy, and that's a frightful thought, an historical thought, a statistical thought, finally, and it is just such facts that give rise to history in the hands of a competent person; for it may be derived with arithmetical exactitude that the clergy lived at least sixty times as happily and comfortably as all the rest of mankind at that period. And perhaps they were at least sixty times as fat as the rest of mankind ..."

"An exaggeration! An exaggeration, Lebedev!" They roared with laughter all around.

"I agree that it's a historical thought; but what are you leading up to?" the prince continued to inquire. (He spoke with such gravity and such a lack of any jest or mockery of Lebedev, at whom all the rest were laughing, that his tone, amidst the general tone of the company, could not help sounding comic; only a little more and they would have begun to snicker at him too, but he did not notice it.)

"Don't you see, Prince, that he's a madman?" Yevgeny Pavlovich bent over to him. "I was told here just now that he's mad on being a lawyer and making lawyers' speeches, and wants to sit for an examination. I expect a glorious parody."

"I am leading up to a tremendous ratiocination," Lebedev was roaring meanwhile. "But let us first of all analyze the psychological and legal position of the criminal. We see that the criminal, or so to speak, my client, in spite of all the impossibility of finding any other comestible, several times in the course of his curious career, discovers a desire to repent and thrusts the clergy from him. We see this clearly from the facts: it will be remembered that he did, after all, consume five or six infants—a number relatively insignificant, yet remarkable in another respect. It is evident that, tormented by terrible pangs of conscience (for my client is a religious man and conscientious, as I shall prove) and to minimize his sin as far as possible, by way of experiment, he six times exchanged the nourishment of the cloister for the nourishment of the world. That it was by way of experiment is beyond doubt again; for had it been simply for the sake of gastronomic variety, the number six would be too insignificant: why only six counts, and not thirty? (I've taken half and half.) But if it were only an experiment, arising simply from despair at the fear of sacrilege and of offending the church, then the number six becomes all too intelligible; for six attempts to appease the pangs of conscience are more than enough, as the attempts could not, after all, be successful. And in the first place, in my opinion, an infant is too small, that is, not large, so that in the time in question it would have needed a number three, five times as large of layman infants as clergy, so that the sin, though lessened on the one side, would when all is said and done be greater on the other, not in quality, but in quantity. Reasoning thus, gentlemen, I am of course descending into the heart of a criminal of the twelfth century. As for me, a man of the nineteenth century, I would have, perhaps, reasoned differently, of which I beg to inform you, so you need not grin at me, gentlemen, and it's quite entirely unseemly for you, of all people, General. In the second place, an infant, in my personal opinion, is not nutritious, and perhaps even too sweet and mawkish, so that without satisfying the need, it would leave only the pangs of conscience. Now for the conclusion, the finale, gentlemen, in which lies the solution of one of the greatest questions of that age and of ours! The criminal ends by going and informing against himself to the clergy and gives himself up into the hands of the authorities. Now I ask you, what tortures awaited him in that age, what wheels, stakes, and fires? Who was it made him go and inform against himself? Why not simply stop at the number sixty and keep the secret till his dying breath? Why not simply relinquish the monastic order and live in penitence as a hermit? Why not, indeed, enter a monastery himself? And here is the solution! There must have been something stronger than stake and fire, or even twenty-year-old habit! There must have been an idea stronger than any misery, famine, torture, plague, leprosy and all that hell, which mankind could not have endured without that idea, which bound men together, guided their hearts and fructified the springs of life! Well, then, show me anything like such a force in our age of vices and railways . . . that is, one should say our age of steamers and railways, but I say: our age of vices and railways, because I am drunk, but I am just![13] Show me an idea binding mankind together today with even half the power it had in those centuries. And dare to tell me, finally, that the springs of life have not been weakened and muddied beneath this 'star,' beneath this network in which men are enmeshed. And don't try to frighten me with your well-being, your wealth, the rarity of famine, and the rapidity of the means of communication! There is more wealth, but there is less strength; the idea binding mankind is gone; everything's gone soft, everything has gone to rot and everyone has

13. There is an untranslatable play on words here. The word for steamship is *parakhod* and the word Lebedev uses instead to describe the age is *porok* (failing); thus, his substitution of the phrase *"vek porokov i zheleznykh dorog"* for the usual *"vek parakhodov i zheleznykh dorog"* could almost be taken for a drunken slip of the tongue.

gone to rot . . . We have all, all, all gone to rot! . . . But that's enough, and that's not the point now; the point is, honored prince, whether we shouldn't see to getting the supper that's been prepared for your guests."

Lebedev, who had nearly roused some of the listeners to the point of genuine indignation (it must be noted that the bottles did not cease to be uncorked the entire time), had, by unexpectedly concluding his oration with a reference to supper, reconciled all his opponents to him at once. He called such a conclusion "a clever, lawyerly windup of the thing." Merry laughter rang out again, the guests grew animated; everyone got up from the table to stretch their limbs and take a turn on the terrace. Only Keller remained displeased with Lebedev's speech, and was much excited.

"He attacks enlightenment and upholds the fanaticism of the twelfth century, he puts on airs, and there's not even a trace of any heartfelt innocence: and how did he himself come by this house, allow me to ask?" he said aloud, appealing to each and all.

"I used to know a real interpreter of the Apocalypse," the general was saying in another corner to another group of listeners, among them Ptitsyn, whom he had buttonholed—"the late Grigory Semyonovich Burmistrov: he used to burn through your soul, so to speak. First, he'd put on his spectacles, and open a big old book in a black leather binding, well, and he'd a gray beard besides and two medals for works of charity. He used to begin sternly and severely, generals would bow down before him, and ladies fell into swoons, well—and this one here concludes with supper! It's beyond anything!"

Ptitsyn listened to the general, smiled, and seemed to want to reach for his hat, but apparently could not make up his mind on it, or was continually forgetting his intention. Ganya, even before they had gotten up from the table, had suddenly left off drinking and pushed away his glass; something dark passed over his face. When they rose from the table, he went up to Rogozhin and sat down beside him. One might have supposed that they were on the friendliest terms. Rogozhin, who, at first, had also been several times on the point of slipping away quietly, now sat motionless with his head bowed, as though he had also forgotten that he wanted to leave. He had not drunk a drop of wine all evening, and was very pensive; only from time to time he raised his eyes and surveyed each and every one. Now, it might have been supposed that he was expecting something here, something of great importance to him, and had made up his mind not to leave before this time.

The prince had drunk no more than two or three glasses, and was only lighthearted. Rising from the table, he caught the eye of Yevgeny Pavlovich, recalled the impending explanation they were to have, and smiled amicably. Yevgeny Pavlovich nodded to him and suddenly indicated Ippolit, whom he was intently watching at the moment. Ippolit was asleep, having stretched out on the sofa.

"Tell me, Prince, why has this wretched boy forced himself upon you?" he said suddenly, with such undisguised vexation and even malice that the prince was surprised. "I'll bet he's got some mischief in his mind!"

"I have noticed," said the prince, "I have fancied, at any rate, that you are very much interested in him today, Yevgeny Pavlovich; is that true?"

"And you might add: considering my own circumstances, I've enough to think about myself, so that I'm surprised at myself that I haven't been able to tear myself away from that detestable physiognomy all the evening."

"He has a handsome face . . ."

"Look, look!" cried Yevgeny Pavlovich, pulling the prince by the arm. "Look! . . ."

The prince surveyed Yevgeny Pavlovich with wonder again.

V

Ippolit, who had suddenly fallen asleep on the sofa toward the end of Lebedev's dissertation, now just as suddenly woke up, as though some-one had poked him in the ribs, started, sat up, looked around him, and turned pale; he seemed to gaze about him in some kind of alarm; but there was almost a look of horror on his face when he remembered everything and collected his thoughts.

"What, are they going? Is it over? Is it all over? Has the sun risen?" he kept asking in agitation, clutching the prince's hand. "What's the time? For God's sake: the time? I've overslept. Have I been asleep long?" he added, with an almost desperate air, as though he had slept through something on which his whole fate, at the very least, depended.

"You've been asleep seven or eight minutes," answered Yevgeny Pavlovich.

Ippolit looked greedily at him and collected his thoughts for some moments.

"Ah . . . that's all! Then, it must be, I . . ."

And he took a breath, deeply and greedily, as though casting off some exceptional weight. He realized at last that nothing was "over," that it was not yet daybreak, that the guests had got up from the table only on account of supper, and that the only thing that was over was Lebedev's chatter. He smiled and a consumptive flush, in the form of two bright spots, flared up on his cheeks.

"And you've actually been counting the minutes while I slept, Yevgeny Pavlych," he commented, mockingly. "You couldn't tear yourself away from me all the evening, I've seen that . . . Ah, Rogozhin! I saw him just now in a dream," he whispered to the prince, frowning, and nodding toward Rogozhin, who was sitting at the table. "Ah, yes!" he jumped to another subject. "Where's the orator, where's Lebedev? Lebedev is finished, it would seem? What was he talking about? Is it true, Prince, that you said once that the world would be saved by 'beauty'? Gentlemen!" he shouted loudly to everyone. "The prince asserts that the world will be saved by beauty! But I assert that the reason he has such playful ideas is that he is in love now. Gentlemen, the prince is in love; earlier, as soon as he came in, I became convinced of it. Don't blush, Prince, it makes me sorry for you. What sort of beauty will save the world? Kolya told me . . . Are you a zealous Christian? Kolya says that you call yourself a Christian."

The prince examined him attentively and did not answer him.

"You don't answer me? Perhaps you think I'm very fond of you?" Ippolit added suddenly, practically snapping.

"No, I don't think so. I know you don't like me."

"What! Even after what happened yesterday? Was I sincere with you yesterday?"

"I knew yesterday, too, that you didn't like me."

"You mean because I envy you, envy you? You always thought that and think so now, but . . . but why do I speak of that to you? I want to drink some more champagne; pour me some, Keller."

"You can't drink any more, Ippolit, I won't let you . . ."

And the prince moved away the glass.

"Right you are . . ." he agreed immediately, reflecting, as it were. "Maybe they'll say . . . But what the devil do I care what they say? Isn't that the truth, isn't that the truth? Let 'em say so afterward, eh, Prince? What does it matter to any of us what happens *afterward*! . . . But then, I'm not quite awake yet. What an awful dream I had, I've only just remembered it . . . I don't wish you such dreams, Prince, though perhaps I really don't like you. However, if you don't like a man, why wish him harm, isn't that the truth? How is it I keep asking questions, I'm the one who keeps asking questions! Give me your hand; I'll press it warmly, like this . . . You held out your hand to me, though! So you must know that I shall shake it sincerely? . . . Perhaps I won't drink any more. What time is it? But you needn't tell me, I know what time it is. The time has come! Now is the very moment. What, are they laying supper over in that corner? So this table must be free, then? Excellent! Gentlemen, I . . . but these gentlemen are not even listening . . . I intend to read an article, Prince; supper, of course, is more interesting, but . . ."

And suddenly, entirely unexpectedly, he pulled out of his breast-pocket a large, office-sized envelope, sealed with a large red seal. He laid it on the table before him.

This unexpected action produced quite an effect on the company, which was not quite ripe for it, or, better said, they were more than *ripe*, but not for this. Yevgeny Pavlovich positively jumped in his chair; Ganya quickly moved closer to the table; Rogozhin as well, but with a sort of peevish vexation, as though he understood what was going on. Lebedev, who happened to be close by, came up with inquisitive little eyes and stared at the envelope, trying to guess what was going on.

"What have you there?" the prince asked uneasily.

"At the first peep of sunshine I shall go to bed, Prince, I've said so; on my honor: you shall see!" cried Ippolit. "But . . . but . . . do you really think that I'm not capable of unsealing that envelope?" he added, scanning everyone around him with his eyes with a sort of challenge, and apparently addressing all of them indiscriminately. The prince noticed that he was trembling all over.

"None of us is thinking such a thing," the prince answered for everyone. "And why should you suppose someone should have such a thought, and what . . . what a strange idea you've had to read to us? What have you there, Ippolit?"

"What is it? What's happened to him now?" they were asking all around.

Everyone came up, some of them still eating; the envelope with the red seal drew them all like a magnet.

"I wrote it myself, yesterday, directly after I'd given you my word I would come to live with you, Prince. I was writing it all day yesterday, and all night, and finished it this morning; in the night, toward morning, I had a dream . . ."

"Wouldn't it be better tomorrow?" the prince interrupted timidly.

"Tomorrow 'there will be no more time'!" Ippolit laughed hysterically. "However, don't worry, I'll read it in forty minutes, or, well—an hour . . . And see how interested they all are; they've all come up, they're all staring at my seal, but, you know, if I hadn't sealed the article up in an envelope, there wouldn't have been any effect! Ha-ha! You see what mystery does! Shall I break the seal or not, gentlemen?" he shouted, laughing his strange laugh, and staring at them with glittering eyes. "A secret! A secret! And do you remember, Prince, who proclaimed that 'there will be no more time'? It was proclaimed by the great and mighty angel in the Apocalypse."

"Better not read it!" Yevgeny Pavlovich cried suddenly, but with a look of uneasiness so unexpected in him that it struck many persons as strange.

"Don't read it!" cried the prince too, laying his hand on the envelope.

"It's no time for reading; it's supper now," observed someone.

"An article? What, a magazine article?" inquired another.

"Dull, perhaps," added a third.

"But what is all this?" inquired the rest. But the prince's timid gesture seemed to have intimidated Ippolit himself.

"So . . . I'm not to read it?" he whispered to him, almost apprehensively, with a wry smile on his blue lips. "Not to read it?" he muttered, scanning his whole audience with his gaze, all their eyes and faces, and, as it were, grasping at all of them again with the same aggressive effusiveness. "Are you . . . afraid?" He turned again to the prince.

"What of?" asked the latter, his face changing more and more.

"Has anyone got a *dvugrivennyi*, twenty kopecks?" Ippolit suddenly leapt up from his chair as though he had been yanked. "Or any little coin?"

"Here you are." Lebedev gave it to him at once; the idea flashed through his head that the ailing Ippolit had gone out of his mind.

"Vera Lukyanovna!" Ippolit hurriedly invited her. "Take it, throw it on the table—heads or tails? Heads—I read it!"

Vera looked in alarm at the coin, at Ippolit, and then at her father, and awkwardly, somehow, throwing back her head as if in the conviction that she herself ought not to look at the coin, she tossed it on the table. It came up heads.

"I read it!" whispered Ippolit, as though crushed by the judgment of fate; he could not have turned more pale if he had heard his death sentence. "But," he started suddenly, after half a minute's silence, "what is this? Can I really have cast my lot just now?" With the same importunate frankness he scrutinized the whole circle. "But, you know, that's an amazing psychological feature!" he cried suddenly, addressing the prince in genuine astonishment. "It's . . . it's an unfathomable feature, Prince," he asserted, reviving, and seeming to recover himself. "You must make a note of this, Prince, remember it, for I believe you are collecting material relating to capital punishment . . . I've been told so, ha-ha! Oh, my God, what senseless absurdity!" He sat down on the sofa, put his elbows on the table, and clutched at his head. "Why, it's positively shameful! . . . But what the devil do I care if it is shameful!" He raised his head almost at once. "Gentlemen, gentlemen! I will break the seal of my envelope!" he proclaimed, with sudden determination. "I . . . I don't compel you to listen, though!"

With hands trembling with excitement he unsealed the envelope, took out several sheets of notepaper covered with small handwriting, put them before him and began to arrange them.

"What is it? What's going on here? What's he going to read?" some people muttered gloomily; others were silent. But everyone sat down and stared inquisitively. Perhaps they really did expect something unusual. Vera caught hold of her father's chair, and was almost crying with fright; Kolya was almost in the same state of fright as well. Lebedev, who had already sat down, suddenly rose, grabbed the candles and moved them nearer to Ippolit so there would be more light for reading.

"Gentlemen, this . . . you'll see directly what it is," Ippolit added for some reason, and he suddenly began reading: " 'My essential explanation!' Motto: *Après moi le déluge.*'¹⁴ . . . Phooey! damn it!" he cried out, as though he had been scalded. "Can I seriously have written such a stupid motto? . . . Listen, gentlemen! . . . I assure you that all this, when all is said and done, is perhaps the most terrible nonsense! It's only some thoughts of mine . . . If you think there's . . . anything mysterious about it or . . . anything prohibited . . . in a word . . ."

"If you'd only read it without a preface!" interrupted Ganya.

"It's affectation!" someone added.

"There's too much talk," put in Rogozhin, who had been silent the entire time.

Ippolit suddenly looked at him, and when their eyes met, Rogozhin gave a bitter and bilious grin, and slowly pronounced some strange words:

"That's not the way to work this thing, lad, that's not the way . . ."

No one, of course, knew what Rogozhin meant, but his words made a rather strange impression on everyone; everyone seemed to catch a passing glimpse of a common idea. On Ippolit these words made a terrible impression; he trembled so much that the prince started to put out his arm to support him, and would certainly have cried out if his voice had not evidently failed him. For a whole minute he could not speak a word, and stared at Rogozhin, breathing painfully. At last, gasping for breath, with an immense effort he articulated:

"So it was you . . . you . . . It was you?"

"What was I? What about me?" answered Rogozhin, bewildered, but Ippolit, flushing red and almost with a fury that had suddenly seized him, shouted sharply and violently:

"*You* were in my room last week at night, past one o'clock, on the day I had been to see you in the morning, *you*!! Confess, was it you?"

"Last week, at night? Have you gone clean out of your senses, lad?"

The "lad" was silent again for a minute, putting his forefinger to his forehead, and seeming to reflect; but there was a gleam of something sly, even triumphant, in his pale smile that was still distorted by fear.

"It was you!" he repeated at last, almost in a whisper, but with intense conviction. "*You* came to me and sat silently in my room, on the

14. Fr., after me—the deluge, a play on the phrase *après nous le déluge*, attributed to Mme de Pompadour (1721–64), the mistress of Louis XV.

chair by the window, for a whole hour; more; in the first two hours after midnight; then, afterward, when it was going on three, you got up and walked out . . . It was you, you! Why did you frighten me? Why did you come to torment me? I don't understand it, but it was you."

And there was a sudden flash of boundless hatred in his eyes, despite the shivers from his fright, which had still not subsided.

"You shall know all about it directly, gentlemen . . . I . . . I . . . listen . . ."

Once more, and with terrible haste, he clutched at his sheets of paper; they had spread out and fallen apart and he endeavored to put them together; they shook in his shaking hands; it was a long time before he could get himself arranged.[15]

The reading began at last. At the beginning, for the first five minutes, the author of the unexpected *article* still gasped for breath, and read jerkily and incoherently; but then his voice grew stronger and began to express fully the sense of what he was reading. Only at times he was interrupted by a rather violent fit of coughing; before he was halfway through the article, he was very hoarse; his extreme animation, which had taken a greater and greater hold of him the more he read, reached the ultimate pitch at last, as did the painful impression on his audience. Here is the whole "article":

My Essential Explanation.
Après moi le déluge!

"The prince came to see me yesterday morning; among other things, he persuaded me to move to his dacha. I knew that he would certainly insist upon this, and felt sure that he would blurt straight out that at the dacha it would be 'easier to die among people and trees,' as he expresses it. But today he did not say *'die,'* but said 'it will be easier to live,' which comes to much the same thing, however, in my position. I asked him what he meant by his everlasting 'trees,' and why he keeps pestering me with those 'trees'—and learned from him to my surprise that I had myself apparently said on that evening that I'd come to Pavlovsk to look at the trees for the last time. When I told him I should

15. The following line was deleted in the 1874 edition: *"He's gone mad, or delirious,"* muttered Rogozhin barely audibly.

die just the same, whether under the trees or looking out of my window at brick walls, and that there was no need to make such a fuss about a fortnight, he agreed at once; but the greenery and fresh air will be sure, in his opinion, to effect a physical change in me, and my excitement and *my dreams* will alter and perhaps be mitigated. I told him again, laughing, that he spoke like a materialist. He answered with his smile that he had always been a materialist. As he never tells a lie, those words do mean something. He has a nice smile; I have examined him more carefully now. I don't know whether I like him or not now; I haven't time now to bother about it. My five-month-long hatred of him, I must observe, has begun to abate entirely this last month. Who knows, maybe I came to Pavlovsk chiefly to see him. But . . . why did I leave my room then? A man condemned to death ought not to leave his corner; and if I had not now taken my final decision, but had decided, on the contrary, to wait till the last minute, then, of course, nothing would have induced me to leave my room and I should not have accepted his invitation to move in with him in order 'to die' in Pavlovsk.

"I must make haste and finish this 'explanation' before tomorrow, without fail. So that means I shan't have time to read it over and correct it; I shall read it over tomorrow, when I'm going to read it to the prince and two or three witnesses, whom I mean to find there. Since there will not be one word of falsehood in it, and nothing but the truth, the ultimate and solemn truth, I am already curious beforehand to know what impression it will make on myself at the hour and minute when I shall read it over. However, I should not have written the words: 'ultimate and solemn truth'; it's not worthwhile telling lies for a fortnight, as it is, for it's not worthwhile living a fortnight; that's the best possible proof that I shall write nothing but the truth. (NB—Not to forget the thought: am I not perhaps mad at this minute, or rather these minutes? I was told positively that in the last stage consumptives sometimes go out of their minds for a time. Must verify this tomorrow at the reading from the impression made on my audience. The question must be settled absolutely without fail; or else I may not undertake a thing.)

"I believe I have just written something awfully stupid; but as I said, I've no time to correct it; besides, I've promised myself on purpose not to correct one line of this manuscript, even if I notice that I contradict myself every five lines. What I want to determine during the reading tomorrow is precisely whether the logical flow of my thought is correct; whether I notice my mistakes, and therefore whether all I have thought over in this room for the last six months is true, or nothing but delirious raving.

"If I had had to leave my rooms only two months ago, as I do now, and say good-bye to Meyer's wall, I'm certain I should have been sad. But now I feel nothing, and meanwhile, tomorrow I am leaving my room and the wall *forever*! So, it would seem, my conviction—that for the sake of a fortnight, it is no longer worthwhile to regret anything or to give in to any feelings—has mastered my whole nature, and can dictate to my emotions. But is it true? Is it true that my nature is completely vanquished now? If somebody began torturing me now, I should certainly begin to scream, and I shouldn't say that it was not worthwhile screaming and feeling pain because I only had a fortnight more to live.

"But is it true that I have only a fortnight left to live, not more? I told a lie that day at Pavlovsk: B——n told me nothing, and never laid eyes on me; but a week ago they brought a student called Kislorodov[16] to see me; by his convictions, he is a materialist, an atheist, and a nihilist, that's just why I sent for him, particularly. I needed a man to tell me the naked truth at last, without any tender feeling or ceremony. And so he did, and not only readily and without ceremony, but with obvious satisfaction (which was going too far to my thinking). He blurted out to me directly that I had about a month left; perhaps a little more, if my circumstances were favorable, but perhaps I might die much sooner, too. In his opinion, I might die suddenly, even, for instance, tomorrow: such actualities have happened, and no more than two days ago a young lady in Kolumna, in consumption and in a condition similar to mine, was just about to go to the market to buy provisions, when she suddenly felt ill, lay down on the sofa, gave a sigh and died. All this Kislorodov told me, even with a certain flaunting of his insensitivity and carelessness, as though he were doing me an honor by it, that is, as though showing in this way that he takes me, too, for the same sort of all-repudiating, superior creature as himself, for whom

16. *Kislorod* is the Russian word for "oxygen."

dying, clearly, is a trifling matter. When all's said and done, it's an established fact after all; a month and no more! I am absolutely certain he's not mistaken.

"I wondered very much how the prince guessed that I had 'bad dreams'; he used those very words, that in Pavlovsk, 'my excitement and *dreams*' would change. And why dreams? He's either a medical man, or really does have an exceptional mind and is able to surmise very many things. (But that he is, after all is said and done, an 'idiot' there can be no doubt.) Just before he came in, I had, as though by design, a pretty dream (though, as a matter of fact, I have hundreds of dreams like that now). I fell asleep—I think about an hour before he came in—and dreamt that I was in a room (but not my own). The room was larger and loftier than mine, better furnished, and lighter; there was a wardrobe, a chest of drawers, a sofa, and my bed, big and wide and covered with a green silk quilted blanket. But in this room I noticed an awful animal, a sort of monster. It was like a scorpion, yet was not a scorpion, but rather more disgusting and much more awful, and it seemed to be so precisely because there was nothing like it in nature, and because it had come *expressly* to me, and because there seemed to be some secret contained in that very fact. I examined it very carefully: it was brown and covered with shell, a crawling reptile, seven inches long, two fingers thick at the head, and tapering down to the tail, so that the very tip of the tail was only about a sixth of an inch thick. Almost two inches from the head, sprouting from the body at an angle of forty-five degrees, were two paws, one on each side, nearly four inches long, so that the whole animal, if looked at from above, appeared in the shape of a trident. I couldn't make out the head but I saw two whiskers, not long, and also brown, looking like two strong needles. There were two whiskers of the same sort at the end of the tail, and at the end of each of the paws, making eight whiskers in all. The animal was running about the room very quickly, supporting itself on its paws and tail, and, when it ran, the body and the paws wriggled like little snakes, with extraordinary swiftness in spite of its shell, and that was very disgusting to look at. I was terribly afraid it would sting me; I had been told it was poisonous, but what caused me anguish most of all was who had sent it into my room, what had they meant to do to me, and what was the secret of it? It hid under the chest of drawers, under the cupboard, crawled into corners. I sat on a chair and drew my legs up under me. It quickly ran diagonally right across the room and vanished somewhere near my chair. I looked about in terror, but as I sat with my legs drawn up I hoped that it would not crawl up in the chair. Suddenly I heard behind me, almost at my head, a sort of crackling rustle; I looked around and saw that the reptile was crawling up the wall, and was already on a level with my head and actually touching my hair with its tail, which was twirling and writhing with extraordinary rapidity. I sprang up, and the creature vanished. I was afraid to lie down on the bed for fear it should creep under the pillow. My mother came into the room with some girlfriend of hers. They began trying to catch the reptile, but were calmer than I was, and were not even afraid of it. But they didn't understand anything. Suddenly the reptile crawled out again; this time, it crawled very placidly, and as if with some special design, writhing slowly, which was more revolting than ever, crawling once again diagonally across the room toward the door. Here, my mother opened the door and called Norma, our dog—a huge, shaggy black Newfoundland; she died five years ago. She rushed into the room and stopped short over the reptile as if rooted to the spot. The reptile stopped too, but still writhed and snapped at the ground with the ends of its paws and tail. Animals cannot feel mystical terror, unless I'm mistaken; but at that moment it seemed to me that there was something very extraordinary in Norma's terror, as though there were something almost mystical in it too, and that she, therefore, also had some presentiment, as I did, that there was something ominous and some kind of mystery in the animal. She moved back slowly before the reptile, which crept slowly and cautiously toward her; it seemed to be meaning to dart at her and sting her. But in spite of her fear, Norma looked very fierce, though she was trembling all over. All at once she slowly bared her terrible teeth and opened her huge red jaws, crouched, prepared for a spring, made up her mind, and suddenly seized the creature with her teeth. The reptile must have lunged violently to slip away, so that Norma caught it once more as it was escaping, and twice over got it full in her jaws, seeming to gobble it up as it ran. Its shell cracked between her teeth; the tail and paws of the animal, hanging out of the mouth, moved with terrible speed. All at once Norma gave a piteous squeal: the reptile had managed to sting her tongue after all. Whining and howling she opened her mouth from the pain, and I saw that the chewed-up reptile was still wriggling across her mouth, emitting from its half-crushed body, onto the dog's tongue, a quantity of white fluid such as the fluid that comes out of a squashed black roach . . . Then I woke up and the prince came in.

"Gentlemen," said Ippolit, suddenly breaking off from his reading, and seeming almost ashamed, "I haven't read this over, but I believe I have really written a great deal that's superfluous. That dream . . ."

"Indeed," Ganya hastened to put in.

"There's too much that's personal in it, I agree, that is, about myself, in particular . . ."

As he said this, Ippolit had a weary and exhausted air, and wiped the sweat off his forehead with his handkerchief.

"Yes, sir, you're too much interested in yourself," hissed Lebedev.

"I don't force anyone, let me say again, gentlemen; if anyone doesn't want to hear, he can go away."

"He turns them out . . . of another man's house," Rogozhin grumbled, hardly audibly.

"And how if we all suddenly get up and go away?" unexpectedly said Ferdyshchenko, who had till then not dared to say a word aloud.

Ippolit dropped his eyes suddenly and clutched his manuscript; but at the same second he raised his head again, and with flashing eyes and two patches of red on his cheeks, he said, looking fixedly at Ferdyshchenko:

"You don't like me at all!"

There was laughter; however, most of the party did not laugh. Ippolit flushed horribly.

"Ippolit," said the prince, "fold up your manuscript and give it to me, and go to bed here, in my room. We'll talk before you go to sleep, and tomorrow; but on condition that you never open these pages again. Would you like that?"

"Why, is this possible?" Ippolit looked at him in positive amazement. "Gentlemen!" he cried, growing feverishly animated again. "This is a stupid episode, in which I haven't known how to conduct myself. I won't interrupt the reading again. Whoever wants to listen—let him listen . . ."

He took a hurried gulp of water from the glass, hurriedly put his elbows on the table to shield himself from their eyes, and stubbornly resumed his reading. His shame, incidentally, soon wore off . . .

"The idea" (he went on) "that it's not worthwhile to live a few weeks began to take hold of me in earnest, I think, a month ago, when I still had four weeks to live; but it took complete hold of me only three days ago, when I came back from that evening at Pavlovsk. The first moment that I was fully, directly seized by that thought occurred on the prince's terrace, at the very instant when I was meaning to make a last trial of life, when I wanted to see people and trees (granted I said that myself), when I got excited, insisted on the rights of Burdovsky, 'my neighbor,' and dreamed that they would all suddenly fling wide their arms, and clasp me in their embrace, and beg my forgiveness for something, and I theirs; in short, I behaved like a witless fool. And it was at that time that the 'ultimate conviction' sprang up in me. I wonder now how I could have lived for six whole months without that 'conviction'! I knew for a fact that I had consumption and it was incurable. I didn't deceive myself and understood the case clearly. But the more clearly I understood it, the more feverishly I longed to live; I clutched at life and wanted to live no matter what. I admit, I might well have resented then the dark and impassive lot that had ordained to crush me like a fly, and, of course, with no reason; but why didn't I stop at pure resentment? Why did I actually *begin* living, knowing that I could no longer begin? Why did I try, knowing that trying was futile? And in the meantime, I could not even read books, and gave up reading: what use is it to read, what use to learn anything for six months? That thought had driven me to fling aside a book more than once.

"Yes, that wall of Meyer's could tell a story! I have written a great deal on it. There isn't a spot on that filthy wall which I haven't studied. Cursed wall! And yet it's dearer to me than all the trees of Pavlovsk, that is, it would be dearer than all, if it were not all the same to me now.

"I recollect now with what greedy interest I began, at that time, watching *their* life: I had had no such interest in the past. I used to wait with impatience and curses for Kolya sometimes, when I was so ill that I could not leave my room myself. I pried into every little detail, and was so interested in every rumor that I believe I became a regular gossip. I couldn't understand, for instance, how these people, who had so much life, could not manage to become rich (and, indeed, I don't understand it now). I knew one poor fellow, who, I was told afterward, died of hunger, and I remember that it made me furious: if it had been possible to bring the poor devil back to life, I believe I'd have had him executed. I was sometimes better for weeks at a time and able to go out to the street; but the street began, at last, to arouse such rancor in me that I purposely sat indoors for days together, though I could have gone out like everyone else. I couldn't endure these scurrying, bustling, eternally preoccupied, dreary and agitated people, who flitted to and fro about me on the pavement. What was it for, their everlasting gloom, uneasiness and bustle; their everlasting sullen spite (for they are spiteful, spiteful, spiteful). Whose fault is it that they are miserable and don't know how to live, though they've sixty years of life in front of them? Why did Zarnitsyn allow himself to die of hunger when he had sixty years in front of him? And each one points to his rags, his toil-worn hands, rails, and cries savagely: 'We toil like cattle, we labor, we are hungry as dogs, and poor! Others don't toil, and don't labor, and they are rich!' (The eternal wail!) And beside them, running and bustling from morning to night, is some miserable sniveler, 'noble-born,' like Ivan Fomich Surikov—he lives in our house, right above us—always out at the elbows, with his buttons dropping off, running errands for all sorts of people, at someone's behest, and from morning till night at that. And if you should talk to him: he's 'poor, destitute and wretched, his wife died, he had nothing to buy medicine with, and in the winter they froze his baby to death; his elder daughter has gone to be a kept woman . . .'—always whimpering, always wailing! Oh, I've never felt the least, the least pity for these fools, not then and not now—I say so with pride! Why isn't he a Rothschild? Whose fault is it that he hasn't millions, like Rothschild, that he hasn't a mountain of golden imperials[17] and napoleons, such a mountain, just such a heaping mountain, as they make under the tents in carnival week? If he's alive, then he has everything in his power! Whose fault is it he doesn't understand that?

"Oh, now I don't care, now I've no time to be angry, but then, then, I repeat, I literally gnawed my pillow at night and tore my quilt with rage. Oh, how I used to dream then, how I longed, how I purposely longed, to be suddenly turned out into the street, eighteen years old, barely clothed, barely covered, to be abandoned and left utterly alone, without lodging, without work, without a crust of bread, without rela-

---

17. A gold coin minted in Russia.

tions, without a single acquaintance in a great city, hungry, beaten (so much the better!) but healthy—and then I would show them . . .

"What would I show?

"Oh, no doubt you suppose I don't know how I've humiliated myself as it is by my 'Explanation'! Well, who wouldn't consider me a sniveler who knows nothing of life, forgetting that I'm no longer eighteen, forgetting that to live as I have lived for these six months means as much as living to gray old age! But let them laugh and say that this is all fairy tales. It's true, I have told myself fairy tales. I have filled whole nights in succession with them, I remember them all now.

"But should I really tell them all again now—now when the time for fairy tales is over, even for me? And to whom, then? Why, I amused myself with them back then, when I saw clearly that I was forbidden even to learn Greek grammar, as I had once thought of doing: 'I shall die before I get to the syntax,' I thought at the first page, and threw the book under the table. It's lying there still; I've forbidden Matryona to pick it up.

"Let anyone into whose hands my 'Explanation' falls, and who has the patience to read it through, look upon me as a madman, or even a schoolboy, or, more likely still, as a man condemned to death, who, naturally, begins to fancy that everyone aside from him does not hold life dear enough, is apt to waste it too cheaply, use it too lazily, too shamelessly, and therefore every single last one of them is unworthy of it! And what then? Well, I proclaim that my reader is mistaken, and that my conviction is entirely independent of my death sentence. Ask them, just ask them what they all, down to the last one of them, understand by happiness. Oh, you may be sure that Columbus was happy not when he had discovered America, but when he was discovering it; you may be sure that the highest moment of his happiness was, perhaps, exactly three days before the discovery of the New World, when the mutinous crew, in despair, nearly turned the ship around, back to Europe! The New World's not what matters, though it were to fall off the face of the earth. Columbus died almost without seeing it; and, essentially, not knowing what he had discovered. It's life that matters, nothing but life—the processes of its discovery, everlasting and perpetual, and not at all the discovery itself, at all! But what's the use of talking! I suspect that all I'm saying now is so like the usual commonplaces that I shall certainly be taken for a lower-form schoolboy presenting his composition on 'the sunrise,' or they'll say that perhaps I did want to express something but, for all my desire, did not know how . . . to 'develop' it. But I'll add though that in every brilliant and new human thought, or even simply in every serious human thought that springs up in someone's mind, something always remains that can never be communicated to others, even if you were to fill whole volumes with writing and explicated your idea for thirty-five years on end; something will always remain that won't want to emerge from your skull, and will remain with you forever; and with it you will die, without communicating to anyone, perhaps, the most important aspect of your idea. But if I too have failed to convey all that has been tormenting me for the last six months, it will, at least, be understood that, having attained my present 'ultimate conviction,' I have perhaps paid too dearly for it; this is what I felt necessary, for certain objects of my own, to put forward in my 'Explanation.'

"However, I will continue."

VI

"I don't want to tell a lie; reality had caught me on its hook, too, in the course of these six months, and sometimes so carried me away that I would forget my death sentence, or rather did not care to think of it, and even took care of some business. Speaking of which, about my surroundings then. When eight months ago I became very ill I broke off all my ties and left all my former comrades. As I had always been a glum sort of person, my comrades easily forgot me; of course, they'd have forgotten me even apart from that circumstance. My surroundings at home—that is, in my 'family'—were solitary too. Five months ago, I shut myself up inside once and for all and cut myself off completely from the rooms of the family. They always obeyed me, and no one dared to come in to me, except at a fixed time to tidy my room and bring me my dinner. My mother trembled before my commands and did not even dare to whimper in my presence when I made up my mind sometimes to let her come to me. She was continually beating the children on my behalf so they would not make noise and disturb me; I'll own I often complained of their shouting; they must be fond of me by now! I think I tormented 'faithful Kolya,' as I called him, pretty thoroughly too. Toward the end, he tormented me too: all that was natural, for people are made to torment one another. But I noticed that he put up with my irritability as though he had promised himself beforehand not to be hard on an invalid. Naturally that irritated me; but I believe he had taken it into his head to imitate the prince in 'Christian meekness,' which was rather funny. The boy is young and ardent, and of course imitates everything; but it has seemed to me occasionally that it was high time for him to live by his own wit. I'm very fond of him. I tormented Surikov too, who lives above us and runs around on someone's errands from morning till night; I was continually proving to him that he was to blame for his own poverty, so that he was scared at last and gave up coming to see me. He's 'a very meek man, the meekest of beings.' (NB: They say meekness is a tremendous power; I must ask the prince about that, it's his own expression.) But in March, when I went upstairs to see how they had 'frozen'—as he himself put it—the baby and accidentally smirked at the corpse of this infant, for I had begun to explain to Surikov again that it was 'his own fault,' the sniveler's lips suddenly began to quiver, and seizing my shoulder with one hand, he pointed to the door with the other, and softly, that is, almost in a whisper, said to me: 'Go, sir!' I left, and I liked it very much, liked it at the time, even at the very minute when he showed me out; but for long afterward his words produced a painful impression on me when I remembered them: a sort of contemptuous pity for him, which I didn't want to feel at all. Even at the moment of such an insult (I do feel that I insulted him, you know, though I didn't mean to), even at such a moment this man could not get angry! His lips jerked then not at all from anger, I swear: he seized my arm and uttered his magnificent 'Go, sir!' absolutely without anger. There was dignity, a good deal of it, indeed, not at all becoming to his face, in fact (so that, to tell the truth, there was much that was comical about it, too), but there was no anger. Perhaps he simply began to despise me all of a sudden. Since then, when I have met him two or three times on the stairs, he began suddenly taking off his hat to me, which he never used to do before, but did not stop as he used to, running by instead in confusion. If he did despise me it was in his own fashion: he 'despised me *meekly*.' But perhaps he simply took off his hat to me out of apprehension, as the son of a creditor, for he was constantly in debt to my mother and isn't at all capable of digging himself out from under his debts. And that, in fact, is most probable of all. I meant to have it out with him, and I know for certain he would have begged my pardon within ten minutes; but I judged that it was better to let him alone.

"Just at that time—that is, about the time that Surikov 'froze his baby,' about the middle of March—I suddenly felt much better for some reason, and it lasted for a fortnight. I began going out, most often at dusk. I loved the March evenings when it began freezing and the gas was lighted; I sometimes walked a long way. Once, on Shestilavochnaya Street,[18] I was passed in the dark by some 'noble-born' person, I did not get a good look at him; he was carrying something wrapped in paper and wore some sort of cropped and hideous little overcoat, too light for the time of year. Just as he reached the street lamp ten paces ahead of me, I noticed that something fell out of his pocket. I made haste to pick it up, and was only just in the nick of time, for someone in a long caftan sprang forward, but seeing the thing in my hand did not quarrel over it, stole a quick glance at what was in my hand and slipped by. The thing was a large, old-fashioned billfold, stuffed full; but for some reason I guessed at first glance that it might contain anything at all, only not money. The passerby who had lost it was already walking forty paces ahead of me, and was soon lost to sight in the crowd. I ran and began shouting to him, but as I had nothing to shout but 'hey!' he did not turn around. Suddenly he darted to the left, into the gateway of a house. When I ran into the gateway, under which it was very dark, there was no one there anymore. It was a house of immense size—one of those monsters built by speculators for tenement flats; some of these houses sometimes contain up to a hundred units. When I ran in at the gate, I fancied I saw a man walking in the farthest right-hand corner of the huge yard, though in the darkness I could scarcely distinguish him. Running to the corner, I saw an entrance to the stairs; the staircase was narrow, extremely dirty and not lit at all; but I could hear that, above, a man was still running up the stairs, and I started up the staircase reckoning that while the door was being opened to him somewhere, I would overtake him. And so it turned out. The flights of stairs were extremely short; they seemed endless in number, so that I was fearfully out of breath; a door was opened and shut again on the fifth story; I surmised that when I was still three flights below. While I ran up, while I was getting my breath on the landing, while I was looking

18. Literally, "six market stalls"—a street known for its cheap little shops.

for the bell, several minutes passed. The door was opened at last by a peasant woman who was blowing up a samovar in a tiny kitchen; she heard my questions in silence, not understanding a word I said, of course, and in silence opened the door into the next room, which was also tiny and fearfully low-pitched, wretchedly furnished with the barest essentials, with an immense, wide bed under curtains, on which lay 'Terentyich' (as the woman called him), who, I fancied, was drunk. There was a candle-end burning in an iron candlestick on the table, and there was a half-*shtoff*[19] beside it, nearly emptied. Terentyich grunted something to me from the bed and waved toward the next door, while the woman went away, so there was nothing for me to do but to open that door. I did so and walked into the next room.

"This room was even smaller and more cramped than the last, so that I did not even know which way to turn; the narrow single bed in the corner took up a great deal of the space; the rest of the furniture consisted simply of three plain chairs, heaped up with rags of all sorts, and the plainest kitchen table in front of a little old sofa covered with oilcloth, so that there was scarcely room to pass between the table and the bed. On the table burned a tallow candle in an iron candlestick just like in the previous room, and on the bed a tiny baby was wailing, perhaps not more than three weeks old, to judge from the cries; it was being 'changed,' that is, having a fresh diaper put on it, by a pale and sickly-looking woman, apparently young, in complete déshabillé, and perhaps only just beginning to get up after the confinement; but the child did not settle down and went on crying in anticipation of the emaciated breast. On the sofa, another child was sleeping, a girl about three, covered, it seemed, with a man's dress coat. At the table stood a gentleman in a very tattered jacket (he had already taken off the overcoat and it was lying on the bed), unwrapping a blue paper parcel that contained about two pounds of wheat bread and two little sausages. On the table, besides, was a teapot with tea in it, and some bits of black bread were strewn about. A partly opened trunk and two bundles of rags poked out from under the bed.

"In a word, there was horrible disorder. It struck me at the first glance that both of them, the gentleman and the lady, were decent people who had been reduced by poverty to that degrading condition

19. A *shtoff* is an old-Russian measure for a vodka bottle, equal to about a quart.

in which disorder overpowers at last any effort to contend with it, and even drives people to a bitter impulse to find in this very disorder, which increases daily, a sort of bitter and, as it were, vindictive sensation of pleasure.

"When I went in, this gentleman, who had also only entered just before me and was unwrapping his provisions, was discussing something rapidly and heatedly with his wife; though the latter had not finished her diapering, she had already begun to whimper; the news must have been bad as usual. The face of this gentleman, who looked to be about twenty-eight, was swarthy and lean, framed by black sideburns, with a cleanly shaved, shiny chin, and struck me as rather refined and even agreeable; it was morose, with a morose look in the eyes, but with a sort of morbid shade of pride, much too easily inflamed. Upon my entrance, there occurred a strange scene.

"There are people who derive extraordinary enjoyment from their irritable tendency to take offense, especially when it attains its ultimate pitch (which always happens very quickly); at that moment I believe it is even more pleasant for them to be offended than not offended. These irritable people are always horribly fretted by remorse afterward, if they have sense, of course, and are capable of realizing that they had grown ten times as heated as was warranted. The gentleman stared at me for some time in amazement, and his wife in alarm, as though there were something terribly bizarre in anyone's coming to see them; but all at once he flew at me almost with fury; I had not yet had time to mumble two words, but he—especially seeing that I was decently dressed—must have considered himself fearfully insulted at my daring to peep into his corner so unceremoniously, and to see the hideous surroundings of which he was so ashamed. Of course, he was glad of an opportunity to at least have someone on whom to vent his rage at all his misfortunes. For a minute, I even thought he would attack me; he turned pale, just like a woman in hysterics, and alarmed his wife dreadfully.

" 'How dare you come in like this? Get out!' he shouted, trembling, and scarcely able to pronounce the words. But suddenly he saw his billfold in my hands.

" 'I believe you dropped this,' I said as calmly and dryly as I could. (That was as it should be, in fact.)

"The other stood before me in a perfect state of alarm, and for some time seemed unable to understand a thing; then he grabbed at his side pocket, opened his mouth in horror, and clapped his hand to his forehead.

" 'Good God! Where did you find it? How?'

"I explained in the briefest words, and, if possible, still more dryly, how I'd picked up the billfold, how I'd run after him, calling, and how at last, on a guess and almost feeling my way, I had run after him up the stairs.

" 'Oh, God!' he cried, turning to his wife. 'Here are all our papers, here are the last of my instruments—everything. . . . Oh, merciful sir, do you know what you've done for me? I should have been lost!'

"Meanwhile I had taken hold of the door handle to go out without answering; but I was out of breath myself, and suddenly my excitement brought on such a violent fit of coughing that I could scarcely stand. I saw how the gentleman rushed from side to side to find an empty chair, how he had finally snatched the rags off one, flung them onto the floor, and hurriedly set the chair for me, helping me carefully to sit down. But my cough went on without stopping for three minutes more. When I recovered he was already sitting beside me on another chair, from which he must have also flung the rags onto the floor, and was examining me intently.

" 'You seem to be . . . suffering,' he said, in the tone in which doctors usually open proceedings with a patient. 'I am a . . . medical man myself' (he didn't say 'doctor'), and as he said it, he pointed with his hand to the room for some reason, as though protesting against his current situation. 'I see that you . . .'

" 'I'm in consumption,' I said as curtly as possible and got up.

"He jumped up too at once.

" 'Perhaps you are exaggerating and . . . if you take measures . . .'

"He was very discombobulated and still seemed unable to pull himself together; the billfold was sticking out of his left hand.

" 'Oh, don't trouble yourself,' I interrupted again, taking hold of the door handle. 'B——n examined me last week, and my business is settled.' (I stuck B. in again.) 'Excuse me . . .'

"I would have wanted to open the door again and leave my chagrined and grateful doctor, who was crushed with shame, but the cursed cough seized me once more. Then my doctor insisted that I should sit down again and rest; he turned to his wife, and the latter, without moving from her place, uttered a few grateful and cordial words—whereby she was very chagrined, so that a red flush even suffused her thin, pale, yellow cheeks. I remained, but with such an air that made it apparent every moment that I was horribly afraid of discomfiting them (which was as it should be). My doctor's remorse had worn him down at last, I saw that.

" 'If I . . .' he began, constantly breaking off and jumping from thought to thought. 'I am so grateful to you, and I behaved so badly to you . . . I . . . You see . . .' again he indicated the room, 'at the present moment I am placed in such a position . . .'

" 'Oh,' said I, 'there's no need to see; it's the usual thing; I expect you've lost your post, and have come up here to explain yourself, and try to get another post.'

" 'How did you . . . know?' he asked in surprise.

" 'It's obvious from the first glance,' I said, scoffing involuntarily. 'Lots of people come here from the provinces full of hope and run about and live like this.'

"He suddenly began speaking with warmth and with quivering lips; he began complaining, began telling his story, and I must own he engrossed me; I stayed nearly an hour with him. He told me his story, a very common one, incidentally. He had been a provincial doctor, had a government post, but some intrigues were got up against him, in which they had even embroiled his wife. His pride was touched; he lost his temper; there occurred a change in the provincial government that was in his enemies' favor; they undermined him, made complaints against him; he lost his post, and had used his last remaining means to come to Petersburg to make his explanation. Here, of course, for a long time, he could get no hearing; then he got a hearing; then he was answered by a refusal; then he was deluded with promises; then he was answered with severity; then he was directed to write something by way of explanation; then they refused to accept what he had written, and ordered him to file a petition—in short, he had been running around for five months now, and had gone through all his funds: his wife's last rags were in pawn, and now there was a new baby, and, and . . . 'today a final refusal of my petition, and I've hardly any bread—nothing—my wife just gave birth . . . I . . . I . . .'

"He jumped up from his chair and turned away. His wife was crying in the corner, the baby began squealing again. I took out my notebook and began making notes in it. When I had finished and stood up, he was standing before me, looking at me with timid curiosity.

" 'I have put down your name,' I said, 'well, and all the rest of it: the place where you served, the name of the governor, the days of the month. I have a comrade, an old schoolfellow, called Bakhmutov, and his uncle, Pyotr Matveich Bakhmutov, is an Active State Counselor[20] and serves as director . . .'

" 'Pyotr Matveich Bakhmutov!' exclaimed my doctor, almost trembling. 'Why, he's the one on whom it nearly all depends!'

"Indeed, everything about my doctor's story and its denouement, which I chanced to assist in bringing about, came together and smoothed itself out as though by design, just exactly as in a novel. I told these poor people that they must try not to build any hopes on me, that I was a poor schoolboy myself (I intentionally exaggerated my humbleness; I finished my studies long ago and am not a schoolboy) and that there was no need for them to know my name, but that I'd go at once to Vassilevsky Island to my schoolfellow Bakhmutov; and as I know for a fact that his uncle, the Active State Counselor, a bachelor without children, positively worships his nephew and loves him passionately, seeing in him the last branch of his family, 'my comrade may perhaps be able to do something for you, and for me, with his uncle, of course . . .'

" 'If only they would allow me an explanation with his excellency! If only they would vouchsafe me the honor of explaining it in my own words!' he exclaimed, shivering as though he were in a fever, and with glittering eyes. That was what he said, 'vouchsafe.' Repeating once more that the business would certainly be a bust and it would all turn out to be nonsense, I added that if I didn't come to see them next morning, it would mean that the matter was over and they had nothing to expect. They showed me out with bows; they were almost beside themselves. I shall never forget the expression on their faces. I took a cab and at once set off for Vassilevsky Island.

"At school I had been for years on bad terms with this Bakhmutov. He was considered an aristocrat among us, or I at least used to call him one: he dressed wonderfully, drove his own horses, did not blow his own horn a bit, was always a first-rate comrade, was always exceptionally good-humored and sometimes even very witty, though he was not at all bright, despite the fact that he was always first in the class; I, on the other hand, was never first in anything. All his schoolfellows liked him, except me. Several times in those several years, he had approached me; but each time I had turned sullenly and irritably away from him. Now I had not seen him for a year; he was at the university. When toward nine o'clock I went in to him (with great ceremony: I was announced), he met me at first with amazement, and far from affably, but he soon brightened up and, looking at me, suddenly burst out laughing.

" 'What possessed you to come and see me, Terentyev?' he cried with his invariable good-natured ease, which was sometimes impudent but never offensive, which I liked so much in him and for which I hated him so much. 'But how's this?' he exclaimed with dismay. 'You are very ill!'

"My cough racked me again. I dropped into a chair and could scarcely get my breath.

" 'Don't trouble, I'm in consumption,' I said. 'I've come to you with a request.'

"He sat down with surprise, and I at once related to him the whole story of the doctor, and explained that he himself, having an exceptional influence over his uncle, might, perhaps, be able to do something.

" 'I'll do it, I'll certainly do it, and I'll attack my uncle tomorrow; and indeed I'm glad, and you've told it all so well ... But, after all, what put it into your head, Terentyev, to come to me?'

" 'So much depends upon your uncle in this case, and, moreover, we were always enemies, Bakhmutov, and as you're an honorable man, I though you wouldn't refuse an enemy,' I added with irony.

" 'As Napoleon appealed to England!' he cried, bursting out with laughter. 'I'll do it! I'll do it! I'll go at once if it's possible!' he added hastily, seeing that I was gravely and sternly getting up from my chair.

"And indeed, most unexpectedly, we could not have worked out this affair any better. Within a month and a half our doctor was again given a post, in another province, had received his traveling expenses, and even a subsidy. I suspect that Bakhmutov, who had taken to visiting them pretty often (I therefore purposely ceased to visit them and received the doctor coolly when he stopped in to see me)—Bakhmutov, as I suspect, had even induced the doctor to accept a loan from him. I saw Bakhmutov about twice in the course of those six weeks, and we got together for the third time when we were seeing the doctor off. Bakhmutov hosted the send-off at his own house, in the form of a dinner with champagne, at which the doctor's wife too was present; she, however, left very soon to go to her child. It was at the beginning of May, the evening was fine, the huge ball of the sun was sinking into the bay. Bakhmutov saw me home; we went by the Nikolaevsky Bridge; we were both a little drunk. Bakhmutov spoke of his delight at the successful conclusion of the business, thanked me for something, explained how pleased he felt now after a good deed, declared that the credit of it all was mine, and that people were wrong in preaching and maintaining, as many do now, that individual benevolence is meaningless. I had a great longing to speak too.

" 'Anyone who infringes upon individual charity,' I began, 'infringes upon human nature and despises his personal dignity. But the organization of "public charity" and the question of individual freedom are two distinct questions, and not mutually exclusive. Individual benevolence will always remain, because it's an individual impulse, the living impulse of one personality to exert a direct influence upon another. There was an old fellow at Moscow, a "General," that is, an Active State Counselor,[21] with a German name; he spent his whole life making the rounds of the prisons seeing prisoners; every party of exiles to Siberia knew beforehand that the "old General" would visit them on the Sparrow Hills. He carried out his business with the greatest earnestness and piety; he would turn up, walk through the rows of prisoners, who surrounded him, stop before each, questioning each as to his needs, almost never admonished anyone, called them all "dear fellows." He used to give them money, send them the most necessary articles—leg-wrappers, undergarments, linen—and sometimes brought them devotional books, which he bestowed on every literate man among them in the full conviction that they would read them on the way, and that the literate would read them to the illiterate. He rarely asked a prisoner about his crime; he simply listened if the criminal began speaking of it himself. All the criminals were on an equal footing with him,

---

21. The civilian rank of Active State Counselor is equal in grade to the army rank of major general.

he made no distinction between them. He talked to them as though they were brothers, but they came in the end to look on him as a father. If he saw a woman exile with a baby in her arms, he would go up, fondle the child, and snap his fingers to make it laugh. He did this for many years, up until his death; it got to the point that he was known all over Russia and all over Siberia—that is, by all the criminals. A man who had been in Siberia told me that he had been witness himself to how the most hardened criminals remembered the general, and meanwhile, the latter could rarely give more than twenty farthings per fellow on his visits. It's true, it's not as if they spoke of him with any great warmth or some particular earnestness. Some one or another of these "unhappy" creatures, who had murdered a dozen people and slaughtered six children solely for his own pleasure (they say there are such men), would suddenly, apropos of nothing, and perhaps only once in all of twenty years, heave a sigh and say: "What about that old general, is he still alive, I wonder?" And perhaps he even chuckles as he says it—and that's all. But how can you tell what seed may have been sown forever in his soul by that old general, whom he hasn't forgotten for twenty years? How can you tell, Bakhmutov, what significance such an affiliation of one personality with another may have on the destiny of the affiliated personalities? ... Why, there's a whole lifetime here, you know, an infinite multitude of ramifications hidden from us. The best chess player, the sharpest of them, can only reckon out a few moves ahead; a French player who could reckon out ten moves ahead was written about as a marvel. And how many moves are there here, how much that is unknown to us? In scattering your seed, scattering your "charity," your good deeds in one form or another, you are giving away part of your personality, and taking into yourself part of another; you become mutually affiliated, one with the other; a little more attention and you will already be rewarded with the knowledge, with the most unexpected discoveries. You will come at last to look upon your work as a science; it will lay hold of all your life, and may fill up your whole life. On the other hand, all your thoughts, all the seeds scattered by you, perhaps forgotten by you, will take on form and grow; whoever has received them from you will hand them on to another. And how can you tell what part you may have in the future determination of the destinies of mankind? If this knowledge and a whole lifetime of this work should raise you at last to such heights that you shall be capable of sowing some mighty seed, of bequeathing the world some mighty thought, then . . .' and so on. I talked a great deal then.

" 'And to think with all this that you, of all people, are condemned to death!' cried Bakhmutov, with a warm note of reproach against someone in his voice.

"At that moment we were standing on the bridge, leaning our elbows on the rail, and looking into the Neva.

" 'And do you know what's just occurred to me?' I said, bending even lower over the rail.

" 'Not to throw yourself into the water!' cried Bakhmutov, almost in alarm. Perhaps he read my thought in my face.

" 'No; for the time being, only the following reflection: here I have two or three months left to live, perhaps four; but, for instance, when I've only two months left, if I'm terribly anxious to do a good deed that requires a great deal of work, running about and bother, like the business with our doctor, then in that case I would have to refuse this business on account of the insufficient time left to me and seek some other "good work" on a smaller scale, which would be within my *means* (if I am still so taken with doing good deeds). You must own that's an amusing idea!'

"Poor Bakhmutov was much distressed on my account; he accompanied me to my very door, and was so tactful that he did not even once attempt to console me and kept silent almost the whole time. Taking leave of me, he pressed my hand warmly and asked permission to come and see me. I answered him that if he came to me in the function of 'consoler' (for, even if he kept silent, he would still come as a consoler, I explained that to him), then by that very fact he would have to remind me of death more than ever. He shrugged his shoulders, but agreed with me; we parted fairly civilly, which I had not even expected.

"But that evening and that night was sown the first seed of my 'ultimate conviction.' I clutched eagerly at this *new* idea and eagerly analyzed it in all its branches, in all its aspects (I didn't sleep all night), and the more deeply I went into it, the more I absorbed it, the more frightened I became. An awful terror came over me at last and did not leave me in the days following this. Sometimes, thinking of that continual terror of mine, I quickly grew cold with another dread: from that dread I could not but conclude that my 'ultimate conviction' had become too gravely deep-seated in me, and must certainly lead to its logical conclusion. But I had not resolve enough for that conclusion. Three weeks later it was all over and the resolve came to me, but through a very strange circumstance.

"Here in my 'Explanation' I note down all these numbers and dates. Of course it will make no difference to me, but *now* (and perhaps only for this moment) I should like those who will judge my action to be able to see clearly what long chain of logical reasoning led to my 'ultimate conviction.' I have just written above that the final resolve, which I had lacked for carrying out my 'ultimate conviction,' came about in me, it seems, not from logical reasoning, but from some sort of strange impetus, from one strange circumstance, perhaps not at all related to the course of events. Ten days ago, Rogozhin came to see me about an affair of his own, which there is no need to go into here. I had never seen Rogozhin before, but I had heard a great deal about him. I gave him all the necessary information and he soon went away, and as he had simply come for the information, the whole business between us might have ended there. But he interested me too much, and all that day I was possessed by strange ideas, so that I made up my mind to go to him next day, to return his visit. Rogozhin was evidently not pleased to see me, and even dropped a 'delicate' hint that it was no good for us to continue the acquaintance; but all the same, I spent a very interesting hour, and probably he did the same. There was such a contrast between us, which could not have failed to manifest itself to both of us, to myself especially: I was a man whose days were already numbered, while he was living the fullest, the most vivid life in the present moment, without a care about 'ultimate' deductions, numbers, or anything whatever that did not relate to what ... what ... what he was mad upon, if you will; Mr. Rogozhin must forgive me that expression, if only as a poor hand at literature who doesn't know how to express his thought. In spite of all his unfriendliness, I thought he was a man of intelligence and capable of understanding much, though he had few outside interests. I gave him no hint of my 'ultimate conviction,' but for some reason I fancied that he guessed it as he listened to me. He kept silent; he is awfully closemouthed. As I took leave I hinted to him that, in spite of all the difference and the contrast between us—*les extremités se touchent*[22] (I explained that in Russian for him), so that per-

---

22. Fr., the extremes meet—the phrase comes from Blaise Pascal (1623–62).

haps he was by no means as far from my 'ultimate conviction' as he seemed. To that he responded with a very grim and sour grimace, got up, found my cap for me himself, pretending as though I were going away of my own accord, and without more ado led me out of his gloomy house, on the pretense that he was seeing me out from politeness. His house made quite an impression on me; it's like a graveyard, and I believe he likes it, which is, however, very natural: such a full, vivid life as he leads is too full in itself to need a setting.

"That visit to Rogozhin exhausted me very much. Aside from that, I had felt unwell since that morning; toward the evening I grew very weak and lay down on my bed, and from time to time I felt a tremendous fever and was even delirious for some moments. Kolya stayed with me till eleven o'clock. I remember everything he talked of, however, and everything we talked about. But when at moments my eyes would close, I kept seeing Ivan Fomich, who seemed to be receiving millions of money. He kept not knowing what to do with it, racked his brains about it, trembled with fear that it would be stolen, and at last seemed to decide to bury it in the earth. Finally, I advised him, instead of digging such a mountain of gold into the earth for nothing, to have the whole heap melted down into a gold coffin for the 'frozen' baby and to have the baby dug up for the purpose. This mockery of mine seemed to be accepted by Surikov with tears of gratitude, and he set out to execute the plan at once. I seem to have spat in disgust and left him. Kolya assured me, when I was quite myself again, that I had not slept at all, and that I had been talking to him all that time about Surikov. At moments I was in extraordinary misery and perturbation, so that Kolya was uneasy when he left me. When I got up myself to lock the door after him, I suddenly recalled a painting I had seen earlier at Rogozhin's, in one of the dreariest rooms of his house, over the door. He showed it to me himself in passing; I believe I stood before it for five minutes. There was nothing good about it from an artistic point of view: but it produced some kind of strange uneasiness in me.

"The picture represented Christ, who had only just been taken from the cross. I believe painters are usually given to painting Christ both on the cross and taken from the cross, still with the shade of extraordinary beauty on his face; they strive to preserve that beauty in him even in the midst of the most terrible agonies. But in Rogozhin's picture there's not even a mention of beauty; it is in every detail the corpse of a man who has endured infinite agonies before the crucifixion, wounds, tortures, beatings from the guards, beatings from the crowd when He carried the cross on His back and fell beneath the cross, and, finally, the agony on the cross, lasting for six hours (upon my reckoning, at least). It's true it's the face of a man *only just* taken from the cross—that is to say, still retaining in itself much that is warm and alive; nothing has had time to grow rigid yet, so that there is even a look of suffering that shows through on the face of the dead man, as though he were still feeling it (that has been very well caught by the artist); yet the face has not been spared in the least; it is simply nature, and such must truly be the corpse of a man, whoever he might be, after such suffering. I know that the Christian Church laid it down, even in the first centuries, that Christ suffered not figuratively but actually, and that His body, therefore, must have been fully and completely subject to the laws of nature on the cross. In the painting this face is fearfully crushed by blows, swollen, covered with fearful, swollen and bloodstained bruises, the eyes are open, the pupils have rolled to the side: the great wide-open whites of the eyes glitter with a sort of deathly, glassy reflection. But, strangely, when one looks at this corpse of a tortured man, a peculiar and curious question arises: if just such a corpse (and it must have been just like that) was seen by all His disciples, His chief future apostles, was seen by the women who followed Him and stood by the cross, by all who believed in Him and adored Him, how could they have believed, looking at such a corpse, that this martyr would be resurrected? The notion involuntarily comes of itself that if death is so awful and the laws of nature so mighty, how can they be overcome? How can they be overcome when they were not vanquished now even by the one who had vanquished nature in His lifetime, whom it had obeyed, who exclaimed, 'Maiden, arise!' and the maiden arose—'Lazarus, come forth!' and the dead man came forth? Looking at such a picture, nature appears to one in the shape of an immense, implacable and dumb beast, or to speak correctly, much more correctly, though it is strange—in the form of a huge machine of the most modern construction which, deaf and insensible, has senselessly clutched, crushed and swallowed up a great priceless Being, such a Being that by itself was worth all nature and its laws, the whole earth, which was created perhaps solely for the sake of the advent of that Being! This painting seems indeed to express this very conception of a dark, insolent, senselessly eternal power to which everything is subjected, and to convey it to you involuntarily. These people surrounding the dead man, not one of whom is in the picture, must have felt the most terrible sorrow and consternation on that evening, which had crushed in one blow all their hopes, and almost their beliefs. They must have dispersed in the most awful terror, though each one took away with him a mighty thought that could never be driven out of him. And if the teacher himself could have seen his image on the eve of the crucifixion, would He himself have ascended the cross in that way, and died in that way, as He did? That question involuntarily appears before one too, as one looks at the painting.

"All this appeared before my mind too, in snatches, perhaps indeed between bouts of delirium, sometimes taking definite shape, for fully an hour and a half before Kolya went away. Can anything that has no shape appear in a shape? But I seemed to fancy at times that I saw, in some strange and impossible form, that infinite power, that deaf, dark, mute creature. I remember that someone seemed to lead me by the hand, holding a candle, to show me some huge and loathsome tarantula and begin to assure me that this was that same dark, deaf and almighty creature, and laughed at my indignation. In my room, before the icon, they always light a little lamp for the night—it is a dim and feeble light, yet one can make out everything, and under the lamp, you can even read. I think it must have been shortly after midnight; I had not slept at all and lay with wide-open eyes; suddenly the door to my room opened and Rogozhin walked in.

"He walked in, shut the door, looked at me in silence, and went quietly to the corner, toward the chair that stands almost right under the lamp. I was very much surprised and looked at him in expectation; Rogozhin put his elbows on the little table and began to stare at me in silence. So passed two or three minutes, and I remember his silence greatly offended and vexed me. Why didn't he want to talk? The fact that he had come so late at night did strike me as strange, of course, but I remember that I was not so tremendously amazed by that in particular. Rather on the contrary: for though I had not expressed my thought clearly to him in the morning, I know he understood it; and this thought was of such a nature that, on account of it, one might well have come to talk once more, even at a very late hour. That's just what I thought—that he had come for that. In the morning we had parted with some hostility, and I remember that he looked at me once or twice very mockingly. I saw that very same mockery in his look now, and it was that which offended me. That it was actually Rogozhin himself and not an apparition, not a hallucination, I at first did not doubt in the slightest. The thought did not even occur to me.

"Meanwhile, he went on sitting there and staring at me with the same mocking look. I turned angrily on my bed, also leaned with my elbow on the pillow, and resolved on purpose to be silent too, even if we had to sit like that the entire time. For some reason, I wanted without fail that he should begin first. I think twenty minutes must have passed in that way. Suddenly the idea occurred to me: what if it's not Rogozhin, but only an apparition?

"Neither during my illness nor any time before had I ever once seen a single apparition; but it always seemed to me, when I was still a boy, and even now too, that is, quite lately, that if I should ever see an apparition even once I should die on the spot at once, despite the fact I don't believe in any apparitions. But when the idea struck me that it was not Rogozhin but only an apparition, I remember I wasn't in the least frightened. Not only that, it actually made me angry. What was also strange was that the resolution of the question—was it an apparition or Rogozhin himself—somehow did not interest or worry me as it would seem it should; it seems to me that I was thinking of something else at the time. I was much more interested, for instance, in the question of why Rogozhin, who had been in his dressing gown and slippers earlier, was now wearing a dress coat, a white waistcoat and a white tie. The thought struck me too: if it is an apparition and I'm not afraid of it, why not get up, go to him and see for myself? Perhaps, after all, I didn't dare and was afraid. But I'd no sooner thought that I was afraid than an icy shiver ran down my entire body; I felt a cold chill in my spine and my knees trembled. At that very instant, as though guessing that I was afraid, Rogozhin moved away the hand on which he was leaning, drew himself up and began to open his mouth, as though he were getting ready to laugh; he stared straight at me. I was seized with such fury that I decidedly longed to fall upon him, but as I had vowed not to be the first to speak, I remained in bed, especially as I was still not sure whether it was Rogozhin or not.

"I don't remember for certain how long this lasted; neither can I remember for certain whether I didn't lose consciousness from time to time. Only at last Rogozhin got up, looked me over as deliberately and intently as before, upon coming in, but had stopped grinning, and softly, almost on tiptoe, went to the door, opened it, closed it and went out. I did not get out of bed; I don't remember how long I continued to lie there with my eyes open, thinking; goodness knows what I thought about; I don't remember either how I lost consciousness. But I woke next morning at ten o'clock when they knocked at my door. I have arranged that, if I don't open the door myself before ten o'clock and don't call for tea to be brought to me, Matryona should knock on my door herself. When I opened the door to her, the thought occurred to me at once: how could he have come in when the door was locked? I made inquiries, and convinced myself that the real Rogozhin could not have come in, as all our doors are locked at night.

"Well, and this peculiar incident, which I have described so minutely, was the cause of my becoming completely 'resolved.' Therefore, it would seem, the final decision was brought about not by logic, not by a logical conviction, but by repulsion. I could not go on living a life that was taking such strange, humiliating forms. That apparition degraded me. I am not able to submit to a dark power that takes the shape of a tarantula. And it was only when, at dusk, I at last felt within me the final moment of complete resolve that I felt better. But that was only the first moment; for the second moment I had to go to Pavlovsk, but I have explained that sufficiently already."

VII

"I had a little pocket-pistol; I got it when I was quite a child, at that absurd age when one suddenly begins to like stories about duels or about attacks by robbers, or about how I, too, might be challenged to a duel and how nobly I would face the pistol-shot. A month ago I examined it and got it ready. In the box where it lay I found two bullets, and in the powder horn there was powder enough for three charges. The pistol is a piece of junk, it doesn't aim straight, and wouldn't kill further than fifteen paces; but, of course, it would blow one's skull off, if one put it right to the temple.

"I mean to die at Pavlovsk, when the sun rises, and to go into the park, so as not to upset anyone at the dacha. My 'Explanation' will explain the matter sufficiently to the police. Lovers of psychology, and anyone else who needs to, are welcome to conclude from it anything they wish. But I would not want this manuscript to be made public, however. I beg the prince to keep one copy for himself, and give another to Aglaia Ivanovna Epanchin. Such is my will. I bequeath my skeleton to the Medical Academy, for the good of science.

"I do not recognize the authority of any judges over me, and know that I am now beyond the power of any court. Not long ago I was much amused by this supposition: what if the fancy suddenly took me to kill someone, why, even ten people at once, or to do something awful, something considered the most awful crime in the world—in what a predicament would the court be placed before me, with my two or three weeks left to live, and with the abolishment of corporal punishment and torture. I should die comfortably in their hospital, warm and snug, with an attentive doctor, and perhaps much more snug and comfortable than at home. I don't understand why the same idea doesn't strike people in my position, if only as a joke. But perhaps it does, however: there are plenty of merry people to be found, even among us.

"But though I do not recognize the authority of any court over me, I know I shall be judged when I have already become a deaf and mute defendant. I don't want to go away without leaving some word in response—a free response, not a compelled one, and not to justify myself—oh no! I have no one's forgiveness to ask, and nothing to ask forgiveness for—it's simply because I want to.

"First of all, there's a strange thought here: by what right, with what motive could anyone presume to dispute my right to dispose of these two-three weeks of my term? Whose business is it to judge? What is it to anyone that I should not only be condemned but should conscientiously endure the full term of my sentence? Can it really matter to anyone? For the sake of morality? I quite understand that if, in the bloom of health and strength, I were to take my life, which might be 'of use to my neighbor,' etc., morality might reproach me, along the lines of the old routine, for disposing of my life without asking leave, or for whatever else, as it knows best. But now, now that the term of my sentence has been pronounced? What moral obligation demands not only your life, but the last gasp with which you give up your last atom of life, listening to the consolations of the prince, who, in his Christian arguments, is sure to arrive at the happy thought that, in essence, it is even for the best that you should die. (Christians like him always do arrive at that idea: it's their hobbyhorse.) And what do they want with their ridiculous 'trees of Pavlovsk'? To sweeten the last hours of my life? Don't they understand that the more I forget myself, the more I give myself up to this last semblance of life and love with which they are trying to screen from me my Meyer's wall and all that is so candidly and simply written on it, the more unhappy they shall make me? What use to me is your nature, your Pavlovsk park, your sunrises and sunsets, your blue sky and your contented faces, when this whole feast, which has no end, began by the fact that it considered me alone to be superfluous. What is there for me in this beauty when, every minute, every second, I am obliged and forced to recognize that even the tiny little fly, which is buzzing beside me now in a ray of sunshine, even it has its share in the feast and the chorus, knows its place, loves it and is happy, and I alone am an outcast, and only my cowardice has made me not want to understand it till now! Oh, but I know how the prince and all of them would have liked to bring me to such a point that, instead of these 'insidious and spiteful' speeches, I should sing, out of sheer virtue and for the triumph of morality, the celebrated and classic verse of Millevoix.

> Ah, puissent voir longtemps votre beauté sacrée
> Tant d'amis sourds à mes adieux!
> Qu'ils meurent pleins de jours, que leur mort soit pleurée,
> Qu'un ami leur ferme les yeux![23]

"But believe me, believe me, simple-hearted souls, that in those virtuous lines, in that academic benediction of the world in French verse, there lodges so much concealed bile, so much irreconcilable malice, reveling in rhyme, that even the poet himself, perhaps, has fallen into a trap and taken that malice for tears of tenderness, and died in that faith; peace be to his ashes! Know, then, there is a limit of ignominy in the consciousness of one's own insignificance and impotence beyond which a man can no longer go, and beyond which he begins to feel im-

---

23. These lines are, in fact, part of a poem by Gilbert. [C.G.]

> Oh, let them see your sacred beauty
> All these friends deaf to my goodbyes!
> That they might die aged, that at their deaths there are tears aplenty,
> That a friend might close their eyes!

mense delight in his very degradation . . . Oh, of course humility is a great force in that sense, I admit that—though not in the sense in which religion accepts humility as a force.

"Religion! I admit eternal life, and perhaps I always have admitted it. Let consciousness be kindled by the will of a higher power, let it have looked around upon the world and said: 'I am!' and let it suddenly be ordained by that power to be annihilated, because, for one purpose or another—and indeed, without explaining what for—it is necessary; let it be, I admit it all, but again the eternal question: what need is there of my humility? Can't I simply be devoured without being expected to praise what devours me? Will someone up there really be aggrieved that I don't want to wait another fortnight? I don't believe it; and it's much more likely to suppose simply that my insignificant life, the life of an atom, was needed here to complete some universal harmony of the whole, for some sort of plus and minus, for some sort of contrast, and so on, and so on, just as there is a daily need to sacrifice the life of millions of creatures, without whose death the rest of the world could not go on (though that's not a very generous idea in itself, I must observe). But so be it! I agree that otherwise, that is without the continual devouring of one another, it would have been impossible to arrange the world; I am even ready to allow that I don't understand anything in this arrangement; but this I do know for certain: that if I have once been allowed the cognition that 'I am,' then what does it matter to me that there are mistakes in the arrangement of the world, and that it couldn't go on otherwise? Who will condemn me after that, and on what charge? Say what you like, it's all impossible and unjust.

"And yet, in spite of all my desire to do it, I could never conceive of there being no future life, no Providence. It's most likely that it all exists, but that we don't understand anything about the future life or its laws. But if this is so difficult and even impossible to understand, can I really be held responsible for not being able to comprehend the inconceivable? It's true, they say, and the prince, of course, is with them, that it's just here that submission is needed, that one must submit without reasoning, simply from virtue, and that I shall certainly be rewarded in the next world for my meekness. We degrade Providence too much, ascribing to it our ideas, in vexation at being unable to understand it. But, again, if it's impossible to understand it, I repeat it's hard to have to answer for what it is not given to man to understand.

And if it is so, how shall they judge me for being unable to understand the real will and laws of Providence? No, we'd better leave religion to one side.

"And I've said enough, indeed. When I reach these lines, the sun will no doubt be rising and 'resounding in the sky,' and a vast immeasurable power will pour out upon all that dwells on the sunny side. Well, let it! I shall die looking straight at the source of power and life, and I shall not want this life! If I'd had the power not to be born, I would certainly not have accepted existence upon conditions that are such a mockery. But I still have the power to die, though the days I give back are numbered. It's no great power, and it's no great mutiny.

"My last explanation: I am dying not at all because I haven't the strength to bear these three weeks; oh, I should have the strength, and, if I cared to, I should be consoled enough just by the recognition of the wrong done me; but I'm not a French poet, and I do not care for such consolation. Finally, there's temptation too: nature has so limited my activity by its three weeks' sentence that perhaps suicide is the only action I still have time to begin and end by my own will. And, perhaps, I want to take advantage of the last opportunity of *action*. A protest is sometimes no small action . . ."

The "Explanation" was over; Ippolit had stopped at last . . .

There is, in extreme cases, such a stage of ultimate cynical frankness when a nervous man, exasperated and beside himself, shrinks from nothing, and is ready for any scandal, even glad of it; he flies at people with a vague but firm determination to fling himself from a belfry a minute later, and so resolve any misunderstandings, if any should arise. One symptom of this condition is usually the approaching exhaustion of physical powers. The extraordinary, almost unnatural tension that had braced Ippolit till that moment had reached that ultimate stage. Left to himself, this eighteen-year-old boy, wasted by illness, seemed as weak as a trembling leaf torn from a tree; but the moment he had swept his gaze over his audience—for the first time in the course of the last hour—the most haughty, most disdainful and resentful repugnance was at once apparent in his eyes and his smile. He made haste with his challenge. But his listeners too were completely indignant. They were getting up from the table with noise and vexation. Weariness, wine, nervous strain increased the disorderliness and, as it were, filthiness of the impression, if one may put it that way.

Suddenly Ippolit leapt up quickly from his chair, as though he'd been torn from his place.

"The sun has risen!" he cried, seeing the gleaming tops of the trees and pointing them out to the prince just like a marvel. "It has risen!"

"Why, did you think it wasn't going to rise?" observed Ferdyshchenko.

"It will be baking hot again all day," muttered Ganya with careless annoyance, holding his hat in his hands, stretching and yawning. "Well, and what if there's a month of this drought! . . . Are we going or not, Ptitsyn?"

Ippolit listened with an astonishment that approached stupefaction; suddenly, he turned fearfully pale and began trembling all over.

"You're putting on your indifference very awkwardly to insult me," he said, staring Ganya straight in the face. "You're a cur!"

"Well, that's beyond anything, to let it all hang out like that!" roared Ferdyshchenko. "What phenomenal feebleness!"

"He's simply a fool," said Ganya.

Ippolit pulled himself together a little.

"I understand, gentlemen," he began, trembling as before, and stumbling at every word, "that I may deserve your personal vindictiveness, and . . . I'm sorry I've distressed you with these ravings (he pointed to the manuscript), or, actually, I'm sorry that I haven't distressed you at all . . ." (he smiled foolishly). "Have I distressed you, Yevgeny Pavlovich?" He suddenly leapt over to him with the question. "Did I distress you or not? Speak out!"

"It was rather drawn out, but in any case . . ."

"Speak out! Don't tell lies for once in your life!" Ippolit trembled and commanded.

"Oh, it's absolutely nothing to me! Do me a favor, I beg of you, and leave me alone," Yevgeny Pavlovich turned away disdainfully.

"Good-night, Prince," said Ptitsyn, going up to the prince.

"But he's going to shoot himself directly, what are you doing? Look at him!" cried Vera, and flew to Ippolit in great alarm, and even clutched at his arms. "Why, he said he would shoot himself at sunrise! What are you doing!"

"He won't shoot himself!" several voices, among them Ganya's, muttered with malicious pleasure.

"Gentlemen, take care!" cried Kolya, also catching Ippolit's arm. "Only look at him! Prince, Prince, what are you thinking of?"

Vera, Kolya, Keller, and Burdovsky crowded around Ippolit; all four seized him with their hands.

"He has the right, the right!..." Burdovsky muttered, though he too seemed somehow entirely befuddled.

"Excuse me, Prince, what arrangements do you propose to make?" said Lebedev, going up to the prince; he was drunk and enraged to the point of insolence.

"What arrangements?"

"No, sir; excuse me, sir; I'm the master of the house, sir, and I don't wish to be lacking in respect to you ... Granting that you are master here too, still, in my own house, I don't wish that such things ... such things, sir."

"He won't shoot himself; the wretched boy is playing about!" General Ivolgin cried unexpectedly, with indignation and aplomb.

"Bravo, General!" Ferdyshchenko took up.

"I know he won't shoot himself, General, honored general, but all the same ... seeing I'm master of the house."

"Listen, Mr. Terentyev," said Ptitsyn suddenly, having taken leave of the prince and holding out his hand to Ippolit, "I believe you speak in your notebook of your skeleton and bequeath it to the Academy? You mean it's your own skeleton, that is, your bones you mean, that you bequeath?"

"Yes, my bones ..."

"Good, good. For there might be a mistake: I've been told there already was such a case."

"Why are you teasing him?" cried the prince suddenly.

"You've brought him to tears," added Ferdyshchenko.

But Ippolit was not crying at all. He would have moved from his place, but the four surrounding him seized his arms at once. There was a sound of laughter.

"That's what he was leading up to, that they should hold his hands; that's what he read his notebook for," observed Rogozhin. "Good-bye, Prince. Ech, we've been sitting too long—my bones ache."

"If you really did mean to shoot yourself, Terentyev," laughed Yevgeny Pavlovich—"if I were you, after such compliments, I should make a point of not shooting myself in your place, to tease them."

"They're awfully eager to see me shoot myself!" Ippolit flew at him.

He spoke as though he were pouncing upon someone.

"They're vexed that they won't see it."

"So you too think that they won't see it?"

"I'm not egging you on; quite the contrary; I think it's very likely you will shoot yourself. The main thing is not to lose your temper . . ." drawled Yevgeny Pavlovich, patronizingly stretching out his words.

"I only see now that I made a terrible mistake in reading them this notebook!" said Ippolit, looking at Yevgeny Pavlovich with such a suddenly trusting air, as though asking a friend for friendly advice.

"It's an absurd position, but . . . truly, I don't know what to advise you," answered Yevgeny Pavlovich, smiling.

Ippolit looked him straight in the face sternly, without turning away, and kept silent. It might have been supposed that for moments at a time, he forgot himself entirely.

"No sir, excuse me, sir, why, what a way of doing things, sir," uttered Lebedev. " 'I'll shoot myself in the park,' says he, 'so as not to bother anyone!' That's his notion, that he won't bother anyone if he goes down the steps three paces into the garden."

"Gentlemen . . ." began the prince.

"No sir, allow me, sir, honored prince," Lebedev seized upon him with fury, "as you can see for yourself that it's not a joke and as half your guests at least are of the same opinion, and are convinced that now, after the words that have been spoken here, he must certainly shoot himself out of honor, I, as master of the house, sir, and in front of witnesses, declare that I call upon you to assist me!"

"What should be done, Lebedev? I am ready to assist you."

"Here's what, sir: in the first place he must immediately give up the pistol he boasted about before us all with all its accoutrements. If he gives it up, I consent to allow him to stay the night in this house, on consideration of his invalid state, on the condition, of course, that it shall be under supervision on my part. But tomorrow let him certainly go wherever he will; excuse me, Prince! If he won't give up his weapon, I shall at once, without delay, take him by the arms, I on one side, the general on the other, and send at once to inform the police, and then the affair can be left for the police to examine, yes, sir. Mr. Ferdyshchenko, as a friend, will go; yes, sir."

There was an uproar; Lebedev grew heated and went beyond all bounds; Ferdyshchenko prepared to go for the police; Ganya insisted frantically that no one was going to shoot himself. Yevgeny Pavlovich kept silent.

"Prince, have you ever jumped from a belfry?" Ippolit whispered to him, suddenly.

"N-no," the prince answered naïvely.

"Did you really imagine that I did not foresee all this hatred!" Ippolit whispered again, flashing his eyes and looking at the prince, as though he really expected an answer from him. "Enough!" he cried suddenly to the whole party. "I am to blame . . . more than anyone! Lebedev, here's the key" (he took out a wallet and from it a steel ring with three or four little keys). "Here, this one, the last but one . . . Kolya will show you . . . Kolya! Where is Kolya?" he cried, looking at Kolya and not seeing him. "Yes . . . he'll show you; he packed my bag with me yesterday. Take him, Kolya; in the prince's study, under the table . . . my bag . . . with this key, at the bottom, in a little box . . . my pistol and powder horn. He packed it himself before, Mr. Lebedev; he'll show you; but on condition that tomorrow, early, when I leave for Petersburg, you'll give the pistol back to me. Do you hear? I do it for the prince, not for you."

"Well, that's better!" Lebedev snatched at the key and, smirking malignantly, he ran into the next room.

Kolya stopped and seemed to want to remark something, but Lebedev dragged him after him.

Ippolit looked at the laughing guests. The prince noticed that his teeth were chattering, as though he were in a terrible chill.

"What wretches they all are!" Ippolit whispered again to the prince in a frenzy. Whenever he spoke to the prince, he kept bending over and whispering.

"Leave them; you're very weak . . ."

"In a minute, in a minute . . . I'll go in a minute."

Suddenly he embraced the prince.

"You find, perhaps, that I am mad?" He looked at him, laughing strangely.

"No, but you . . ."

"In a minute, in a minute, be quiet; don't say anything, stand still . . . I want to look you in the eyes . . . Stand like that, and I shall look. I say good-bye to Man."

He stood and looked fixedly and silently at the prince for ten seconds, very pale, his temples soaked with sweat, and somehow strangely grasping at the prince with his hand, as though afraid to let him go.

"Ippolit, Ippolit, what is the matter with you?" cried the prince.

"In a minute . . . Enough . . . I'm going to lie down. I'll drink one sip to greet the sun . . . I want to, I want to . . . Let me be!"

He quickly seized a glass from the table, sprang up from his seat, and in one instant reached the terrace steps. The prince was about to run after him, but it happened, as though by design, that at that very moment Yevgeny Pavlovich held out his hand to say good-bye to him. A second went by, and suddenly there was a general outcry on the terrace. Then followed a minute of extreme consternation.

Here is what happened.

Coming right up to the terrace steps, Ippolit had stopped, holding the glass in his left hand and plunging his right hand into the right-hand pocket of his coat. Keller afterward maintained that Ippolit had kept that hand in his right-hand pocket before, while he was still talking to the prince and clutching with his left hand at his shoulder and his collar, and that this very same right hand in his pocket, Keller maintained, had, apparently, engendered the first suspicion in him. However that may have been, some uneasiness compelled him to run after Ippolit. But he was too late. He saw only how something shone suddenly in Ippolit's right hand, and at the same second a little pocket pistol appeared right against his temple. Keller rushed to seize his hand, but, at that second, Ippolit pressed the trigger. There was the sound of the sharp, dry click of the trigger, but no shot followed. When Keller seized Ippolit, the latter fell into his arms, as if unconscious, perhaps really imagining that he was already killed. The pistol was already in Keller's hand. They held Ippolit up, brought him a chair, sat him down, and everyone crowded around, everyone was shouting, everyone was asking questions. Everyone had heard the click of the trigger and saw the man alive without even a scratch. Ippolit himself sat, not understanding what was going on, and surveyed everyone around him with his insensible gaze. Lebedev and Kolya ran in at that instant.

"Was it a misfire?" they asked all around.

"Perhaps it was not loaded?" others surmised.

"It was loaded!" Keller pronounced, examining the pistol. "But . . ."

"Was it really a misfire?"

"There was no cap in it at all," Keller announced.

It is hard to even describe the piteous scene that followed. The initial and universal alarm quickly began to be succeeded by laughter; some of the party positively roared, and seemed to find a malicious pleasure in it. Ippolit sobbed as though in hysterics, wrung his hands, rushed up to everyone, even to Ferdyshchenko, whom he clutched with both hands, swearing that he had forgotten, "forgotten quite accidentally and not on purpose," to put in the cap; that "the caps were all here, in his waistcoat pocket, some ten of them" (he showed them to everyone about him); that he hadn't put them in before for fear of its going off by accident in his pocket; that he had counted on always having time to put a cap in when it was necessary and he had suddenly forgotten it. He rushed up to the prince, to Yevgeny Pavlovich, besought Keller to give him back the pistol, that he would prove it to them all at once, that "his honor, his honor" . . . that he was now "dishonored forever! . . ."

In the end, he actually fell unconscious. He was carried into the prince's study and Lebedev, completely sobered, sent at once for a doctor, while he himself, together with his daughter, his son, Burdovsky and the general, remained by the invalid's bedside. When Ippolit had been carried out unconscious, Keller stood in the middle of the room and, decidedly inspired, proclaimed for all to hear, setting apart and hammering out every word:

"Gentlemen, if any one of you ever once, in my presence, expresses any doubt out loud that the cap was forgotten intentionally, and maintains that the unhappy young man was only acting out a farce, he will have to deal with me."

But no one answered him. The guests were at last dispersing, in a crowd and in haste. Ptitsyn, Ganya and Rogozhin set off together.

The prince was much surprised that Yevgeny Pavlovich had changed his mind and was going away without explaining himself.

"But you wanted to speak to me when the others had gone, didn't you?" he asked him.

"Just so," said Yevgeny Pavlovich, suddenly sitting down on a chair and making the prince sit beside him. "But now I have changed my mind for a time. I confess that I am somewhat disconcerted, and so are you. My thoughts have become muddled; besides, what I want to discuss with you is too important a matter for me and for you too. You see, Prince, for once in my life, I want to do an absolutely honorable deed, that is, something absolutely without any ulterior motive; and, well, I think, at this moment, I'm not quite capable of an absolutely honorable deed, and you too perhaps . . . And so . . . well, we'll discuss it later. And perhaps the matter will gain in clarity for me and for you if we wait another three days, which I shall spend now in Petersburg."

Here he got up from his chair again, so that it was strange he should have sat down at all. The prince fancied, too, that Yevgeny Pavlovich was displeased and irritated, that his gaze was hostile, that there was a completely different look in his eyes than earlier.

"By the way, are you going to the sufferer now?"

"Yes . . . I'm afraid," said the prince.

"Don't be afraid; he'll certainly live another six weeks, and he may even get well here. But better yet, do throw him out tomorrow, won't you."

"Perhaps I really forced his hand by . . . not saying anything; he may have thought I doubted that he would shoot himself? What do you think, Yevgeny Pavlych?"

"Not at all. It's too good-natured of you to keep on being concerned. I've heard tell of such things, but I've never in real life seen a man shoot himself on purpose so that he might be praised, or from spite because he was not praised for it. And, most important, I wouldn't have believed in such an open exhibition of feebleness! But do throw him out tomorrow all the same."

"Do you think he'll shoot himself again?"

"No, he won't do it now. But be on your guard with these home-grown Lasseners[24] of ours! I repeat, crime is the all-too-common refuge of these mediocre, impatient and greedy nonentities."

"Is that a Lassener, then?"

"The essence is the same, though the *emplois*[25] are different, perhaps.

24. The Frenchman Pierre François Lassener was a notoriously cruel murderer who manifested great pride in his crimes. He was executed in Paris in 1836, and his "Notes" and "Conversations" were subsequently published. In 1861 they were translated into Russian by a member of Petrashevsky's circle and appeared with a foreword by Dostoevsky.

25. Fr., theatrical term for stock character types.

You'll see whether this gentleman isn't capable of doing away with ten souls just for the sake of a mere 'joke,' as he read us himself just now in his 'Explanation.' Those words of his won't let me sleep now."

"You are too anxious, perhaps."

"You're amazing, Prince; you don't believe he's capable of killing ten people *now*?"

"I'm afraid to answer you; it's all very strange; but . . ."

"Well, as you like, as you like!" Yevgeny Pavlovich concluded irritably. "Besides, you're such a valiant person; just don't wind up becoming one of the ten yourself."

"It's most likely that he won't kill anyone," said the prince, looking pensively at Yevgeny Pavlovich.

The latter laughed maliciously.

"Good-bye, it's time! But did you notice that he bequeathed a copy of his confession to Aglaia Ivanovna?"

"Yes, I did, and . . . I'm thinking about it."

"That's right, in case of the ten souls." Yevgeny Pavlovich laughed again and went out.

An hour later, when it was already past three o'clock, the prince went down into the park. He had tried to sleep at home, but could not, due to the violent throbbing of his heart. In the house, however, everything had been ordered and quieted as far as possible; the invalid had fallen asleep, and the doctor arrived and declared that there was no special danger. Lebedev, Kolya and Burdovsky lay down in the invalid's room, so as to take turns in watching him; and so, there was nothing to fear.

But the prince's uneasiness grew from moment to moment. He wandered in the park, looking absently about him, and stopped in surprise when he reached the open space before the station, and saw the row of empty benches, and the music-stands for the orchestra. This place astounded him and for some reason struck him as horribly repugnant. He turned back, and taking precisely the path along which he had walked to the station the day before with the Epanchins, he reached the green bench that had been fixed as the trysting place, sat down on it, and suddenly laughed out loud, which at once threw him into a state of exceeding indignation. His dejection persisted; he longed to go away somewhere . . . he knew not where. Above him, in the tree, a bird was singing, and he began looking for it among the leaves; all at once the bird flitted from the tree, and at the same instant, for some reason, he recalled the "little fly" in the "hot ray of sunshine," of which Ippolit had written that "it knew its place and took part in the general chorus, but he alone was an outcast." The phrase had struck him at the time; and he recalled it now. One long-forgotten memory stirred within him and suddenly rose up clearly before him.

It was in Switzerland, during the first year of his treatment, in the early part of it, in fact. At the time, he was still completely like an idiot, he could not even speak well, and sometimes could not understand what was wanted of him. He once went up into the mountains, on a bright, sunny day, and walked a long time with one thought that was torturous but refused to formulate itself. Before him was the brilliant sky, below, the lake, and all around the horizon, bright and boundless, which had no end. He gazed a long time and agonized. He remembered now how he had stretched out his arms to that bright, infinite blueness, and cried. What tortured him was that he was an utter stranger to all this. What was this feast, what was this grand, everlasting festival to which there was no end, and which he could never manage to get in on. Every morning the same bright sun rises, every morning there is a rainbow at the waterfall; every evening the very highest snowy mountain, there, in the distance, at the edge of the sky, glows, with a purple flame; every "little bitty fly that buzzes about him in the hot ray of sunshine has its part in the chorus: knows its place, loves it and is happy"; every blade of grass grows and is happy! And everything has its path, and everything knows its path, and with a song goes forth, and with a song returns; only he knows nothing, and understands nothing, neither men nor sounds; he is a stranger to everything and an outcast. Oh, of course he could not have said it then in those words and expressed his question; he suffered insensibly and dumbly; but now it seemed to him that he had said all this at the time, those very words, and that the bit about the "fly" Ippolit had taken from him himself, from his words and tears at the time. He felt sure of it, and for some reason the thought set his heart beating . . .

He dozed off on the seat, but his agitation still persisted even in his sleep. Just as he was falling asleep he remembered that Ippolit was to kill ten people, and chuckled at the absurdity of the notion. All around him was exquisite, clear stillness, only broken by the rustle of the leaves which seemed to make it even more silent and solitary all around. He had many dreams, and all disquieting ones, which continually made him start uneasily. At last a woman came to him; he knew her, knew her to the point of torment; he could have named her anywhere and pointed her out—but strangely—her face now did not seem to be at all the same face that he had always known, and he felt an agonizing reluctance to acknowledge her as that woman. There was such remorse and horror in this face that it seemed this was a terrible criminal, and she had just committed some awful crime. A tear quivered on her pale cheek; she beckoned to him with her hand and put her finger to her lips, as though to warn him to follow her quietly. His heart froze; not for anything, not for anything in the world did he want to acknowledge her as a criminal; but he sensed that something awful was about to happen, to his whole entire life. She seemed anxious to show him something not far off, in the park. He got up to follow her, and suddenly he heard beside him someone's bright, fresh laugh; someone's hand appeared in his; he seized this hand, pressed it tight and woke up. Standing before him and laughing loudly was Aglaia.

VIII

She was laughing, but she was indignant, too.

"Asleep! You were asleep!" she cried with disdainful surprise.

"It's you!" muttered the prince, not yet entirely awake, and recognizing her with surprise. "Ah, yes! The rendezvous . . . I've been asleep here."

"So I see."

"Did no one wake me but you? Has no one been here but you? I thought there was . . . another woman here . . ."

"Another woman was here?"

At last he came to himself entirely.

"It was only a dream," he said pensively. "Strange, that at such a moment, such a dream . . . Sit down."

He took her by the hand and seated her on the bench; he sat beside her himself and sank into thought. Aglaia did not begin the conversation, but only scrutinized her companion intently. He glanced at her too, though sometimes in such a way as though he did not see her before him at all. She began to flush.

"Ah, yes!" the prince started. "Ippolit shot himself!"

"When? In your rooms?" she asked, but without great surprise. "Why, he was still alive only yesterday evening, I think? How could you have been sleeping here after all that?" she cried, becoming suddenly animated.

"But he's not dead, you know; the pistol did not go off."

At Aglaia's insistence, the prince was obliged at once to recount, and even in great detail, the whole story of the previous evening. She continually urged him on in his story, but kept interrupting him herself with incessant questions, and almost always irrelevant ones. Among other things, she listened with great interest to what Yevgeny Pavlovich had said, and even asked about it again several times.

"Well, that's enough! We must make haste," she ended, after hearing everything out. "We've only an hour to be here, till eight o'clock, for at eight I must be at home without fail, so that they won't find out I've been sitting here, and I've come out with an object; I have a great deal to inform you of. Only you've gotten me completely muddled now. About Ippolit, I think that his pistol was supposed to not go off that way, that suits him more. But you're sure that he really meant to shoot himself, and that there was no deception about it?"

"There was no deception."

"That's more likely, indeed. And that's just what he wrote, that you were to bring me his confession? Why didn't you bring it, then?"

"Why, he's not dead. I'll ask him for it."

"Bring it without fail, and there's no need to ask. He'll certainly be very pleased, for perhaps it was with that aim that he shot at himself, so that I would read his confession afterward. Please, I beg you not to laugh at my words, Lev Nikolaevich, because it may very well be so."

"I'm not laughing, for I'm convinced myself that it might very well be so, in part."

"Convinced? Can you really think so, too?" Aglaia was suddenly extremely surprised.

She asked questions rapidly, spoke quickly, but sometimes seemed to flounder, and often did not finish her sentences; she was continually in haste to warn him about something; altogether she was in extraordinary agitation, and, though her gaze was very bold and had some kind of challenge in it, she was perhaps a little scared too. She was wearing a very plain, everyday dress, which suited her extremely well. She started often, blushed, and sat on the edge of the seat. The prince's affirmation that Ippolit had shot himself so that she would read his confession surprised her very much.

"Of course," the prince explained, "he wanted us all to praise him, not just you ..."

"How praise him?"

"That is, it's ... How shall I tell you? ... It's very difficult to say. Only he certainly wanted everyone to gather around him and tell him that they loved him very much and respected him, and for everyone to really plead with him to remain among the living. It may very well be that he had you in his mind more than anyone, because he mentioned you at such a moment ... though, perhaps, he didn't know himself that he had you in mind."

"That I don't understand at all; that he had it in mind and didn't know he had it in mind. But then again, I think I do understand: do you know that thirty times I, myself, even when I was still a thirteen-year-old girl, dreamed of poisoning myself, and writing it all in a letter to my parents; and I, too, thought how I would lie in my coffin, and they would all weep over me, and blame themselves for having been so cruel to me ... Why are you smiling again?" she added quickly, furrowing her brow. "And what do you think about when you dream by yourself? Perhaps you fancy yourself a field marshal, and dream you've vanquished Napoleon?"

"Well, now, upon my word, I do think of that, especially when I'm dropping off to sleep," laughed the prince. "Only it's always the Austrians I vanquish, not Napoleon."

"I have no wish to joke with you at all, Lev Nikolaevich. I'll see Ippolit myself; I beg you to apprise him. And as for you, I find it's all very wicked on your part, for it's very churlish to look upon it in that way and to judge a man's soul as you judge Ippolit. You have no tenderness: nothing but truth, and so—it's unjust."

The prince pondered.

"It seems to me you're unjust to me," he said. "Why, I find nothing wicked in the fact that he thought that way, because all people are inclined to think like that; besides, perhaps he didn't think at all, but only wanted it ... He longed for the last time to come together with people, to earn their respect and love; why, those are very good feelings, you know, only it somehow all came out wrong; it's his illness, and something else, too! Besides, for some people, everything always comes out well, while with others, it all looks like God knows what . . ."

"You added that about yourself, I suppose?" observed Aglaia.

"Yes, about myself," answered the prince, not conscious of any malice in the question.

"Only, all the same, I would never have fallen asleep in your place; so it must be that wherever you pitch, you fall asleep on the spot; it's not at all nice on your part."

"But I haven't slept all night, and afterward I went walking; I've been where the music was."

"What music?"

"Where the band was playing, yesterday; and then I came here, sat down, thought and thought, and fell asleep."

"Oh, so that's how it was! That changes things in your favor . . . But why did you go where the music was?"

"I don't know; just like that . . ."

"All right, all right, later; you keep interrupting me; and what does it matter to me that you went where the music was? What woman was it you were dreaming about?"

"It was . . . about . . . you've seen her . . ."

"I understand, I quite understand. She's very much in your . . . How did you dream of her? What was she doing? But then again, I don't care to know anything about it," she suddenly snapped out with vexation. "Don't interrupt me . . ."

She waited a little, as though summoning up her courage or trying to dispel her vexation.

"Here's the whole heart of the matter, what I asked you to come for: I want to make you a proposition that you should be my friend. Why are you staring at me all of a sudden?" she asked almost wrathfully.

The prince certainly was peering at her very intently at that moment, observing that she had again begun to blush terribly. In such cases, the more she blushed, the more angry, it seemed, she became with herself, which manifested itself clearly in her flashing eyes; normally, a minute later she would already transfer her anger to the person she was talking to, whether he were to blame or not, and would begin quarreling with him. Conscious and keenly aware of being unsociable and easily embarrassed, she normally did not enter into conversation very much, and was more taciturn than her sisters, sometimes too taciturn, indeed. And when, particularly in such ticklish cases, it was absolutely necessary to speak, she would begin the conversation with an extraordinary haughtiness and as if with some kind of challenge. She always sensed beforehand when she was beginning or about to begin to blush.

"Perhaps you don't care to accept my proposition?" She looked haughtily at the prince.

"Oh, yes, I should like to; only it was quite unnecessary . . . that is, I should never have thought it necessary to make such a proposition," said the prince, growing discomfited.

"What did you think, then? What do you suppose I would have asked you to come here for? What's in your mind? But perhaps you consider me a little fool, as they all do at home?"

"I didn't know that they considered you a fool. I . . . I don't."

"You don't? Very clever on your part. Particularly cleverly expressed."

"I think you may be quite clever at times," the prince went on. "You said something very clever before. You said of my uncertainty about Ippolit: 'There's nothing but truth in it, and so it's unjust.' I shall remember that and think it over."

Aglaia suddenly crimsoned with pleasure. All these changes took place in her in an exceedingly open manner and with extraordinary rapidity. The prince, too, was delighted, and even laughed with pleasure, watching her.

"Listen, then," she began again. "I've been waiting for you for a long time, so as to tell you all about it, waiting ever since you wrote me that letter from there, and even before then . . . You heard half of it from me yesterday already: I consider you the most honest and truthful of men, more honest and truthful than anyone; and if they do say about you that your mind . . . that is, that you're sometimes afflicted in your mind, it's unjust; I've decided so and argued it, because, though you really are afflicted in your mind (you won't be angry at that, of course; I'm speaking from a higher point of view), yet the mind that matters is better in you than in any of them, it's even such a mind as they have never dreamed of, for there are two sorts of mind: the one that matters, and the one that doesn't matter. Is that so? That is so, isn't it?"

"Perhaps it is," the prince barely brought out. His heart was trembling and throbbing terribly.

"I just knew that you would understand," she went on with gravity. "Prince Shch. and Yevgeny Pavlovich don't understand anything about these two minds, not Alexandra either, but, imagine, *maman* understood."

"You're very like Lizaveta Prokofyevna."

"How so? Really?" Aglaia was surprised.

"Upon my word, it's true."

"I thank you," she said, after a moment's thought. "I am very glad that I'm like *maman*. You must have a great respect for her, then?" she added, quite unconscious of the naïveté of the question.

"Very great, very great, and I'm glad you've understood it so directly."

"And I'm glad, because I've noticed how people sometimes ... laugh at her. But listen to the main thing: I pondered a long time, and at last picked you. I don't want them to laugh at me at home; I don't want them to look on me as a little fool; I don't want them to tease me ... I realized it all at once, and refused Yevgeny Pavlovich point-blank, because I don't want to be continually being married off! I want ... I want ... well, I want to run away from home, and I've chosen you to help me."

"Run away from home!" cried the prince.

"Yes, yes, yes! Run away from home," she cried suddenly, flaring up with extraordinary anger. "I don't want, I don't want them to eternally make me blush there. I don't want to blush before them, or before Prince Shch. or before Yevgeny Pavlovich, or before anyone, and therefore I've chosen you. With you, I want to say everything, everything, even about the most important thing, whenever I want to; and for your part, you must not hide anything from me either. I want, with one person at least, to speak of everything, as I can to myself. They suddenly began saying that I was waiting for you, and that I loved you. That began even before you came, though I didn't show them the letter; and now they're all talking about it. I want to be bold, and not to be afraid of anything. I don't want to go to their balls, I want to be of use. I've been wanting to get away for a long time. For twenty years I've been bottled up at home, and they keep trying to marry me off. I'd already thought of running away when I was fourteen, though I was a fool. Now I've worked it all out, and was waiting for you to ask you all about foreign countries. I have never seen a Gothic cathedral, I want to go to Rome, I want to visit all the cabinets of learned societies, I want to study in Paris; I was preparing myself and studying all last year, and read a great many books; I have read all the forbidden books. Alexandra and Adelaida read any books, they're allowed to; but I am not allowed all of them; they supervise me. I don't want to quarrel with my sisters, but I informed my mother and father long ago that I want to make a complete change in my social position. I propose to go into education, and I was counting on you because you said you were fond of children. Couldn't we go into education together, not at once perhaps, but in the future? We should be doing good together; I don't want to be a general's daughter . . . Tell me, are you a very learned person?"

"Oh, not at all."

"That's a pity, and I thought . . . How was it I thought so? You'll be my guide all the same because I have chosen you."

"That's absurd, Aglaia Ivanovna."

"I want to run away from home—I want to!" she cried, and again her eyes flashed. "If you won't consent, I shall marry Gavrila Ardalionovich. I don't want to be considered a despicable woman at home, and be accused of goodness knows what."

"Are you in your right mind!" The prince nearly leapt up from his seat. "What are you accused of? Who accuses you?"

"Everyone at home, Mother, my sisters, Father, Prince Shch., even your despicable Kolya! If they don't say so straight out, they think so. I told them all so to their faces, Mother and Father too. *Maman* was ill for a whole day; and next day Alexandra and Papa told me that I didn't understand what nonsense I was talking and what words I was speaking. And I retorted straight out that I understood everything, all the words; that I wasn't little anymore; that I read two novels of Paul de Kock[26] two years ago on purpose, so as to find out everything. *Maman* almost fainted when she heard me."

A strange idea suddenly occurred to the prince. He looked intently at Aglaia and smiled.

---

26. Charles-Paul de Kock (1794–1871), a popular Parisian author of rather candid and risqué novels of Parisian life.

He could scarcely believe that the very same haughty young lady who had once so proudly and disdainfully read him Gavrila Arda- lionovich's letter was actually sitting before him. He could not con- ceive how in such a disdainful, stern beauty there could turn out to be such a child, a child who perhaps did not *even now* understand *all the words*.

"Have you always lived at home, Aglaia Ivanovna?" he asked. "I mean to say, did you never go to school or study at some institute?"

"I've never been anywhere; I've always sat at home, as though I were corked up in a bottle, and I'm to be married straight out of the bottle; why are you chuckling again? I notice that you, too, seem to be laugh- ing at me, and taking their part," she added, frowning menacingly. "Don't make me angry. I don't know what's happening to me as it is . . . I'm certain you came here fully persuaded that I am in love with you, and had asked you to a rendezvous," she snapped out irritably.

"Indeed, I was afraid of that yesterday," the prince blurted out with simplicity (he was very disconcerted). "But I am convinced today that you . . ."

"What?" cried Aglaia, and her lower lip suddenly quivered. "You were afraid that I . . . You dared to imagine that I . . . Good heavens! You suspected perhaps that I invited you here to ensnare you, so that they might catch us here afterward and compel you to marry me . . ."

"Aglaia Ivanovna! Aren't you ashamed? How could such a nasty idea arise in your pure, innocent heart? I'd bet anything that you don't be- lieve a word of it yourself . . . and you don't know what you're saying!"

Aglaia sat, looking doggedly at the ground, as though frightened herself of what she had said.

"I'm not ashamed at all," she muttered. "How do you know that my heart is so innocent? How dare you send me a love letter, then?"

"A love letter? My letter—a love letter! That letter was most re- spectful; that letter was the outpouring of my heart at the most dif- ficult moment of my life! I thought of you then as of some light . . . I . . ."

"Oh, all right, all right," she interrupted suddenly, but now in a completely different tone, rather, with absolute remorse and almost in a fright; she even bent toward him, still trying to avoid looking di- rectly at him, and seemed on the point of touching his shoulder, to beg him more persuasively not to be angry. "All right," she added, terribly shamefaced. "I feel I used a very stupid expression. I said that just . . . to test you. Take it as though it were never said. And if I offended you, then forgive me. Don't look straight at me, please, turn away. You said that was a very nasty idea; I said it on purpose to prick you. Sometimes I'm afraid myself of what I would like to say, then all at once I go and say it. You said just now that you wrote that letter at the most difficult moment of your life . . . I know what moment it was," she said softly, looking at the ground again.

"Oh, if you could know everything!"

"I do know everything!" she cried, with renewed excitement. "You were living then, for a whole month, in the same rooms with that despicable woman with whom you ran away . . ."

She did not turn red this time, but paled as she uttered the words, and suddenly she stood up from her seat as though forgetting herself, but, coming to herself, at once sat back down; her lip continued to quiver for a long time. The silence lasted a minute. The prince was greatly taken aback by the suddenness of her outburst, and did not know to what he should ascribe it.

"I don't love you at all," she said suddenly, as though rapping out the phrase.

The prince made no answer; again they were silent for a minute.

"I love Gavrila Ardalionovich . . ." she uttered hurriedly, but scarcely audibly, bending her head still lower.

"That's not true," uttered the prince, also in a near-whisper.

"So then I'm lying? It's true; I gave him my word the day before yesterday, on this very bench."

The prince was frightened, and pondered a minute.

"That's not true," he repeated decisively. "You've invented all that."

"How wonderfully polite. You should know, he's reformed; he loves me more than his life. He burned his hand before my eyes just to prove that he loved me more than his life."

"Burned his hand?"

"Yes, his hand. You may believe it or not—it's all the same to me."

The prince fell silent again. There was no trace of jesting in Aglaia's words; she was angry.

"Well, now, did he bring a candle with him here, if this is where it happened? Otherwise, I can't imagine . . ."

"Yes . . . a candle. What is there unlikely about it?"

"A whole one or in a candlestick?"

"Oh, well . . . no . . . half a candle . . . a candle-end . . . a whole one. It doesn't matter. Let me alone! . . . He brought matches, too, if you like. He lighted the candle, for a whole half an hour kept his finger over the candle. Is there anything impossible in that?"

"I saw him yesterday; his fingers were unhurt."

Aglaia suddenly gushed with laughter, entirely like a child.

"Do you know why I lied just now?" She suddenly turned to the prince with the most childlike confidence, and the laugh still quivering on her lips. "Because, when you are lying, if you skillfully put in something not quite ordinary, something eccentric, well, you know, something that happens only very rarely or not at all, the lie becomes much more credible. I've noticed that. Only it didn't come out well with me because I wasn't able . . ."

Suddenly she frowned again, as though recollecting herself.

"When," she turned to the prince, looking seriously and even mournfully at him, "when I read to you that time about the 'poor knight,' though I did mean to . . . praise you for one thing, yet at the same time I wanted to put you to shame for your behavior, and to show you that I knew everything . . ."

"You are very unjust to me . . . to that unhappy woman of whom you spoke so horribly just now, Aglaia."

"It's because I know everything, everything, that's why I spoke like that! I know that six months ago, in the presence of everyone, you offered her your hand. Don't interrupt me, you see, I speak without commentary. After that she ran away with Rogozhin; then you lived with her in some country place or in the town, and she left you for someone else" (Aglaia blushed terribly). "Then she went back again to Rogozhin who loves her like . . . like a madman. Then you, a very clever person, too . . . galloped after her here, as soon as you heard she had gone back to Petersburg. Yesterday evening you rushed to defend her, and just now you were dreaming about her . . . You see that I know everything; why, it was for her sake, for her sake you came here, wasn't it?"

"Yes, for her sake," the prince answered softly, sadly and pensively lowering his head and not suspecting with what flashing eyes Aglaia glared at him. "For her sake, only to find out . . . I don't believe in her being happy with Rogozhin, though . . . In a word, I don't know what I could do for her here, or how I could help her, but I came."

He shuddered and looked at Aglaia; the latter was listening to him with a look of hatred.

"If you came, not knowing why, then you must love her very much indeed," she brought out at last.

"No," answered the prince, "no, I don't love her. Oh, if you only knew with what horror I recall the time I spent with her!"

A shudder even ran down his body at those words.

"Tell me all," said Aglaia.

"There is nothing in it you might not hear about. Why it is I wanted to tell you in particular, and only you, all about it, I don't know. Perhaps because I really did love you very much. That unhappy woman is firmly convinced that she is the most fallen, the most sinful creature in the whole world. Oh, don't cry shame on her, don't throw stones at her. She has tortured herself too much with the consciousness of her undeserved shame! And how is she to blame, my God!? Oh, she cries out every minute in a frenzy that she doesn't admit any blame on her part, that she was the victim of others, the victim of a debaucher and a villain; but whatever she may say to you, you must know that she's the first not to believe it and that she believes with her whole conscience, on the contrary, that she is . . . herself to blame. When I tried to dispel this gloom, she approached such torments that my heart will never heal as long as I remember that awful time. It's as though my heart had been pierced once and for all. She ran away from me; do you know what for? Precisely to prove to me alone that she was base. But the most awful thing is that perhaps she didn't even know herself that she only wanted to prove that to me, but ran away because she had an irresistible inner craving to do something shameful, so as to say to herself at once: 'There, you've done something shameful again, so you must be a base creature!' Oh, perhaps you won't understand this, Aglaia! Do you know that in that continual consciousness of shame there is perhaps a sort of awful, unnatural delight for her, just like a sort of revenge on someone. Sometimes I did bring her to the point of seeing light around her once more, as it were; but she would become indignant again at once, and even came to the point of accusing me bitterly of setting myself up above her (when I had not even a thought of such a thing) and announced to me flat out, at last, in response to a proposal of marriage, that she didn't want condescending sympathy or help from anyone, nor to be brought up to anyone's level. You saw her yesterday; can you really think she's happy with that set, that they are fitting company for her? You don't know how well-educated she is, and what she can understand! She even surprised me sometimes!"

"Did you preach her such . . . sermons then, too?"

"Oh, no," the prince went on pensively, not observing the tone of the question. "I was almost always silent. I often wanted to speak, but I really didn't know what to say. You know, in some cases, it is better not to speak at all. Oh, I loved her; oh, I loved her very much, but afterward . . . afterward . . . afterward she guessed it all."

"What did she guess?"

"That I only pitied her, but that I . . . didn't love her anymore."

"How do you know? Perhaps she really fell in love with that . . . country squire she went away with?"

"No, I know all about it; she was only laughing at him."

"And did she never laugh at you?"

"N-no. She used to laugh in anger; oh, back then she would reproach me horribly, in a fury—and she was wretched herself! But . . . afterward . . . Oh, don't remind me, don't remind me of that!"

He hid his face in his hands.

"And do you know that she writes letters to me almost every day?"

"So then it is true!" cried the prince in alarm. "I heard so, but I still didn't want to believe it."

"From whom did you hear it?" Aglaia started in dismay.

"Rogozhin told me yesterday, though not quite clearly."

"Yesterday? Yesterday morning? What time yesterday? Before the music or after?"

"After; in the evening, past eleven."

"Ah, well, if it was Rogozhin . . . But do you know what she writes to me in these letters?"

"I shouldn't be surprised at anything; she's insane."

"Here are the letters." (Aglaia pulled three letters in three envelopes out of her pocket and threw them down before the prince.) "For a whole week now, she's been beseeching, urging and cajoling me to get me to marry you. She . . . yes, well, she's clever, though she's mad, and you're right in saying she's much cleverer than I am . . . She writes that she's in love with me, that every day she seeks the opportunity to see me, even from a distance. She writes that you love me, that she knows it, that she noticed it long ago, and that you used to talk to her about me then. She wants to see you happy; she's certain that only I can constitute your happiness . . . She writes so wildly . . . so strangely . . . I haven't shown her letters to anyone; I was waiting for you. Do you know what this means? Can you not surmise anything?"

"It's madness; proof of her insanity," the prince brought out, and his lips began to tremble.

"You're not crying now, are you?"

"No, Aglaia, no, I'm not crying." The prince looked at her.

"What am I to do about it? What do you advise me? I simply can't go on getting these letters!"

"Oh, leave her alone, I entreat you!" cried the prince. "What business can you have in this gloom? I shall make every effort to prevent her writing to you again."

"If that's so, then you're a man without a heart!" cried Aglaia. "Can you really not see that she's not in love with me, but with you, it's you alone she loves! Can you really have managed to notice everything in her, but did not notice that? Do you know what it is, what these letters mean? It's jealousy; it's more than jealousy! She . . . do you suppose she'd really marry Rogozhin, as she writes here in her letters? She'll kill herself the very next day, as soon as we are married!"

The prince started; his heart stood still. But he gazed in amazement at Aglaia; it was strange to him to admit that the child had long since been a woman.

"God knows, Aglaia, that to give her back her peace of mind and make her happy, I would give up my life; but . . . I can't love her anymore, and she knows it!"

"Then sacrifice yourself—it does suit you so! Why, you're such a great altruist! And don't say 'Aglaia'[27] to me . . . You said simply 'Aglaia' to me earlier, too . . . You must resurrect her, it's your duty; you must go away with her again so as to appease and calm her heart. Why, you love her, you know!"

"I can't sacrifice myself like that, though I did want to at one time . . . and perhaps I want to even now. But I know *for certain* that she'll come to ruin with me, and so I leave her. I was to have seen her today at seven o'clock; but perhaps I won't go now. In her pride she will

27. Much like the familiar *ty* form, the use of the first name without the patronymic (i.e., just "Aglaia" rather than "Aglaia Ivanovna") signals great intimacy unless addressed to a child.

never forgive me for my love—and we shall both come to ruin! It's unnatural, but everything here is unnatural. You say she loves me, but is this love? Can there really be such love after what I have already endured? No, it's something else, not love!"

"How pale you've grown!" Aglaia was suddenly alarmed.

"It's nothing; I've not had much sleep; I'm exhausted ... We really did talk about you then, Aglaia ..."

"So that's true? You actually *could talk to her about me* and ... and how could you have fallen in love with me when you had only seen me once?"

"I don't know how. In my darkness then I dreamed ... I had an illusion perhaps of a new dawn. I don't know how I thought of you at the first. It was the truth I wrote you then, that I didn't know. All that was only a dream, from the horror then ... Afterward I began to work; I wouldn't have come here for three years ..."

"So then you must have come for her sake?"

And something trembled in Aglaia's voice.

"Yes, for her sake."

Two minutes of gloomy silence followed on both sides. Aglaia got up from the seat.

"If you say," she began in an unsteady voice, "if you yourself believe that this ... woman of yours ... is insane, then of what concern are her insane fantasies to me ... I beg you, Lev Nikolaevich, to take these three letters and fling them back to her from me! And if," Aglaia cried suddenly, "and if she dares write me a single line again, tell her I shall complain to my father and they'll have her put in a house of correction ..."

The prince jumped up, and gazed in alarm at Aglaia's sudden fury; a mist seemed to fall before his eyes.

"You can't feel like that ... It's not true!" he muttered.

"It's the truth! It's the truth!" screamed Aglaia, almost beside herself.

"What's the truth? What truth?" a frightened voice called out beside them.

Before them stood Lizaveta Prokofyevna.

"It's the truth that I'm going to marry Gavrila Ardalionovich! That I love Gavrila Ardalionovich, and that I'm going to run away from home with him tomorrow!" Aglaia flew out at her. "Do you hear? Is your curiosity satisfied? Is that enough for you?"

And she ran home.

"No, my friend, don't you go away, now," Lizaveta Prokofyevna stopped the prince. "You'll be so good as to give me an explanation . . . What sort of torment is this; I've been awake all night as it is."

The prince followed her.

IX

Upon entering her house, Lizaveta Prokofyevna stopped in the very first room; she could get no further and sank onto the couch perfectly limp, forgetting even to ask the prince to sit down. It was a rather large room, with a round table in the middle of it, with a fireplace, with quantities of flowers on stands by the windows, and with another glass door leading into the garden in the back wall. Adelaida and Alexandra came in at once, looking inquiringly and with perplexity at the prince and at their mother.

At their dacha, the girls usually got up about nine o'clock; only Aglaia, in the last two or three days, had gotten in the habit of getting up somewhat earlier and going for a walk in the garden, though not at seven o'clock, but rather at eight or even later. Lizaveta Prokofyevna, who really hadn't slept all night due to her various worries, got up about eight o'clock expressly with the purpose of meeting Aglaia in the garden, reckoning on her being up already; but she did not find her either in the garden or in her bedroom. Here she grew thoroughly alarmed at last and woke her daughters. From the maidservant, they learned that Aglaia Ivanovna had already gone out into the park before seven o'clock. The girls scoffed at their whimsical sister's new whim, and observed to their mother that Aglaia might very likely be angry if she went to the park to look for her, and that she was probably sitting now with a book on the green bench of which she had been talking the day before yesterday, and on account of which she had almost quarreled with Prince Shch. because he had found nothing special in the location of this bench. Coming upon the rendezvous, and hearing her daughter's strange words, Lizaveta Prokofyevna was greatly alarmed, for many reasons; but, having now brought the prince home with her, she grew apprehensive about having started the business: "After all, why couldn't Aglaia have met the prince in the park and talked to him, even, finally, if it was a meeting arranged between them beforehand?"

"Don't imagine, Prince, my good friend," she finally braced herself to say, "that I dragged you here to cross-examine you ... After yesterday evening, my dear, I might well not have been anxious to see you for some time ..."

She seemed to falter a bit.

"But all the same you would very much like to find out how Aglaia Ivanovna and I came to meet this morning?" the prince concluded with perfect serenity.

"Well, I did want to!" Lizaveta Prokofyevna flared up at once. "I won't shy away from speaking plainly. For I've not offended anyone, and I had no wish to offend anyone ..."

"Why, pardon, it's natural to want to know, without any offense; you are her mother. Aglaia Ivanovna and I met this morning at the green bench, at seven o'clock, in consequence of her invitation of yesterday. She let me know by a note yesterday evening that she had to see me and speak to me of an important matter. We met and talked for a whole hour of matters that personally concern only Aglaia Ivanovna. That's all."

"Of course that's all, my good sir, and without a shadow of doubt, that's all," Lizaveta Prokofyevna pronounced with dignity.

"Capital, Prince!" said Aglaia, suddenly entering the room. "I thank you with all my heart for considering me incapable of lowering myself here to the point of telling lies. Is that enough for you, *maman,* or do you intend to cross-examine him further?"

"You know that I have never yet had to blush for anything before you ... though you would perhaps be glad of it," Lizaveta Prokofyevna replied pompously. "Good-bye, Prince; forgive me for having troubled you. And I hope you will remain convinced of my unchanged respect for you."

The prince at once bowed to both sides, and silently withdrew. Alexandra and Adelaida chuckled and whispered together about something. Their mother looked sternly at them.

"*Maman,*" laughed Adelaida, "it was only that the prince bowed so marvelously; at times he's just a clumsy sack, but here, suddenly, he was just like ... like Yevgeny Pavlych."

"Tact and dignity are taught by the heart and not the dancing-master," Lizaveta Prokofyevna concluded sententiously, and went upstairs to her rooms without even looking at Aglaia.

When the prince returned home about nine o'clock he found Vera Lukyanovna and the maid on the terrace. They were cleaning up and sweeping together after the disorder of the previous evening.

"Thank goodness we've had time to finish before you came!" said Vera joyfully.

"Good morning; my head is spinning a bit; I didn't sleep well; I should like a nap."

"Here, on the terrace, as you did yesterday? Good. I'll tell them all not to wake you. Father's gone off somewhere."

The maid went out; Vera was about to follow her, but she returned and went anxiously up to the prince.

"Prince, have pity on that . . . unhappy fellow; don't turn him out today."

"I won't on any account; it's as he pleases."

"He won't do anything now, and . . . don't be severe with him."

"Certainly not, why should I?"

"And . . . don't laugh at him, that's the main thing."

"Oh, not at all!"

"I'm silly to speak of it to a man like you," said Vera, flushing. "But though you're tired," she laughed, half turning to go away, "still, your eyes look so fine at this moment . . . happy."

"Happy, really?" the prince asked eagerly, and he laughed, delighted.

But Vera, who was as simple-hearted and unceremonious as a boy, grew suddenly sheepish, turned even redder and, still laughing, hurriedly left the room.

"What a . . . fine girl," thought the prince to himself, and immediately forgot her. He went to the corner of the terrace where there was a sofa with a little table before it, sat down, hid his face in his hands and sat so for some ten minutes. All at once, with haste and agitation, he put his hand into his side pocket and took out three letters.

But again the door opened and in came Kolya. The prince was positively glad that he was obliged to replace the letters in his pocket and put off the moment.

"Well, what an adventure!" said Kolya, sitting down on the sofa and coming straight to the point, like all people of his sort. "How do you view Ippolit now? Without respect?"

"Why, then . . . but, Kolya, I'm tired . . . Besides, it's too sad to begin about that again . . . How is he, though?"

"He's asleep and will sleep another two hours. I understand; you haven't slept at home; you were walking in the park . . . It was the excitement, of course . . . and no wonder!"

"How do you know that I have been walking in the park and haven't slept at home?"

"Vera said so just now. She tried to persuade me not to come in, but I couldn't resist it, for a minute. I've been keeping watch for the last two hours by his bedside; now Kostya Lebedev is taking his turn. Burdovsky has gone off. Then lie down, Prince: good-night . . . well, rather day! Only, do you know, I'm amazed!"

"Of course . . . all this . . ."

"No, Prince, no; I'm amazed at his confession. Especially the part in which he spoke of Providence and the future life. There's a gi-gan-tic thought in it!"

The prince looked affectionately at Kolya, who had of course come precisely to talk posthaste about the gigantic thought.

"But the main thing, the main thing was not simply in the thought, but in the whole setting! If it had been written by Voltaire, Rousseau, Proudhon, I should have read it and taken note, but I should not have been amazed to such a degree. But a man who knows for certain that he has only ten minutes left, and talks like that—why, that's proud. Why, that's the highest autonomy of personal dignity; why, it means flaunting defiance straight out . . . No, it's gigantic strength of will! And after that to assert that he left the cap out on purpose—it's base, unnatural! But you know, he deceived us yesterday; he was sly: I never packed his bag with him at all, and I never saw the pistol; he packed everything up himself, so that he threw me off entirely all of a sudden. Vera says that you're keeping him here; I swear there'll be no danger, especially as we are all constantly at his side."

"And which of you was there in the night?"

"Myself, Kostya Lebedev, Burdovsky. Keller was there a little while, but then he went off to Lebedev's part to sleep, because there we had nothing to lie down on. Ferdyshchenko, too, slept at Lebedev's. He went off at seven. The general is always at Lebedev's—he went off too . . . Lebedev will come to see you presently, perhaps; he's been looking for you, I don't know why; he asked for you twice. Shall I let him in or not, as you want to sleep? I'm going to sleep, too. Oh, by the way, I should like to tell you one thing; the general surprised me earlier: Burdovsky woke me shortly after six to go on watch, almost at six, in fact; I came out for a minute and suddenly met the general, still so drunk that he didn't recognize me: he stood before me like a post; he fairly flew at me when he came to himself. 'How's the invalid?' he says, 'I came to ask after the invalid. . . .' I reported . . . well—this and that. 'That's all very well,' he says, 'but what I really came out for, what I got up for, was to warn you; I have reasons for supposing that one can't say everything before Mr. Ferdyshchenko and . . . one must exercise restraint.' Do you understand, Prince?"

"Really? But then again . . . it doesn't matter to us."

"Yes, doesn't matter, without a doubt, we're not masons! So that I even wondered at the general's coming on purpose to wake me on that account."

"Ferdyshchenko has left, you say?"

"At seven o'clock, he came in to see me on the way: I was keeping watch! He said he was going to finish off the night with Vilkin—there's a drunken fellow here called Vilkin. Well, I'm off! And here's Lukyan Timofeich . . . The prince is sleepy, Lukyan Timofeich; hitch it in reverse!"

"Only for a moment, much honored prince, on a certain matter of great consequence in my view," Lebedev, coming in, pronounced in a strained and somehow charged undertone and bowed with consequence. He had only just returned and had not even had time to stop by his own rooms, so that he still held his hat in his hands. His face was preoccupied and had a peculiar, unusual shade of personal dignity. The prince asked him to sit down.

"You've inquired for me twice already? You are still anxious perhaps on account of what happened yesterday?"

"On account of that boy yesterday, you suppose, Prince? Oh, no, sir; yesterday my ideas were in disorder . . . but today I don't propose to countercarry your propositions in anything whatever."

"Counter—? What did you say?"

"I said 'countercarry'; a French word, like many other words that have entered the body of the Russian language; but I don't particularly stand behind it."

"What's the matter with you this morning, Lebedev? You're so dignified and formal, and you speak as though you were spelling it out," chuckled the prince.

"Nikolai Ardalionovich!" Lebedev addressed Kolya in an almost emotional tone—"having to acquaint the prince with a matter affecting, in particular . . ."

"Yes, yes, of course, of course, none of my business! Good-bye, Prince!" Kolya retired at once.

"I like the child for his astuteness," pronounced Lebedev, looking after him, "a quick boy, but invasive. I've suffered an extraordinary misfortune, respected prince, last night or this morning at daybreak . . . I still hesitate to determine the precise hour."

"What is it?"

"The loss of four hundred rubles from my side pocket, much honored prince; there's a birthday for you!" added Lebedev with a sour smirk.

"You've lost four hundred rubles? That's a pity."

"And particularly for a poor man living honorably by his own labor."

"Of course, of course. How did it happen?"

"The consequence of wine, sir. I have come to you as my Providence, much honored prince. I received a sum of four hundred rubles in silver from a debtor yesterday, at five o'clock in the afternoon, and I came back here by train. I had my wallet in my pocket. When I changed my uniform for my house-coat, I put the money in the jacket, having in mind to keep it with me, and counting on handing them over that very evening on a certain request . . . I was expecting an agent."

"Speaking of which, Lukyan Timofeich, is it true you put an advertisement in the papers that you would lend money on gold or silver articles?"

"Through an agent; my own name does not appear, nor my address. Having paltry capital, and in view of the addition to my family, you will admit yourself that a fair rate of interest . . ."

"Quite so, quite so; I only ask for information; forgive my interrupting."

"The agent did not turn up. Meantime the unfortunate boy was brought here; I was already in an over-elevated condition, after dinner; these visitors came, we drank . . . tea, and . . . and I grew merry to my ruin. When Keller came in late and announced your fête day and the order for champagne, since I have a heart, dear and much-honored prince (which you have probably remarked already, for I have deserved it), since I have a heart, I will not say sensitive, but grateful—of which I am proud—I had the notion to add to the pageantry of the coming festivity and, in expectation of congratulating you personally, the notion of going to change my shabby old house-coat for the uniform I had taken off on my return—which indeed I did, as you, Prince, probably observed, seeing me in my uniform the whole evening. Changing my attire, I forgot the wallet in the coat . . . So true it is that when God will chastise a man, He first of all deprives him of his reason. And only this morning, at half past seven, on waking up, I jumped up like a madman, and snatched first thing at my coat—the pocket was empty! The wallet had vanished without a trace!"

"Ach, that is unpleasant!"

"Unpleasant indeed; and with true tact you have at once found the proper expression," Lebedev added, not without guile.

"But how, then . . ." the prince said uneasily, pondering. "Why, it's serious, you know."

"Serious indeed. Again, Prince, you have found the word to describe . . ."

"Ach, enough, Lukyan Timofeich. What is there to find? The import does not lie in words . . . Do you think you could have dropped it out of your pocket in a drunken state?"

"I might have. Anything may happen in a drunken state, as you so sincerely express it, much honored prince! But I beg you to consider, sir: if I had dropped the wallet from my pocket when I changed my coat, the dropped article ought to have been lying right there on floor. Where is that article, then, sir?"

"Could you have put it away somewhere in a drawer, in a table?"

"I've searched through everything, rummaged everywhere, and moreover, I hadn't hidden it anywhere and hadn't opened any drawer, as I distinctly remember."

"Have you looked in your cupboard?"

"First thing, sir, and even several times today . . . And how could I have put it in the cupboard, truly honored prince?"

"I must own, Lebedev, this distresses me. Then someone must have found it on the floor?"

"Or picked it out of my pocket! Two alternatives, sir."

"This distresses me very much, for who, namely . . . That's the question!"

"Not a doubt of it, that's the main question; how wonderfully precisely you find the words and notions and define the position, most illustrious prince."

"Ach, Lukyan Timofeich, give over scoffing, this . . ."

"Scoffing!" cried Lebedev, throwing up his hands.

"Well, well, well, all right, I'm not angry, you know. It's quite another matter . . . I'm afraid for people. Whom do you suspect?"

"A most difficult and . . . complicated question! The maidservant I can't suspect; she was sitting in the kitchen. Nor my own children either . . ."

"I should think not!"

"So it must be some one of the guests, sir."

"But is that possible?"

"Utterly, and in the highest degree impossible, but so it must certainly be. I'm prepared to admit, however, I'm convinced, indeed, that if a theft occurred, it was not committed in the evening when we were all together, but in the night or even in the morning by someone who passed the night here."

"Ach, my God!"

"Burdovsky and Nikolai Ardalionovich I naturally exclude; and they didn't even come into my room, sir."

"I should think so! Even if they had come in! Who spent the night in your rooms?"

"Counting me, there were four of us in two adjoining rooms: the general, Keller, Mr. Ferdyshchenko, and I. So it must have been one of us four, sir!"

"Of the three, that is. But which?"

"I counted myself for the sake of fairness and correctness; but you will admit, Prince that I could hardly have robbed myself, though there have been such cases in the world . . ."

"Ach, Lebedev, how tiresome this is!" cried the prince impatiently. "Come to the point. Why are you dragging it out?"

"So, then, that leaves three, sir, and first of all, Mr. Keller, an inconstant man, a drunken man, and in certain cases a liberal, that is, as regards the pocket, sir, but in all other respects with tendencies that are, so to speak, rather more chivalrous than liberal. He went to sleep here in the sick man's room at first, and only in the night came to us, on the pretext that the bare floor was hard to sleep on."

"You suspect him?"

"I did suspect him, sir. When, shortly after seven o'clock, I jumped up like a madman and struck myself on the forehead with my hand, I at once woke the general, who was sleeping the sleep of the innocent. Taking into consideration the strange disappearance of Ferdyshchenko, which of itself had aroused our suspicions, we both resolved at once to search Keller, who was lying there like ... like ... almost like a doornail, sir. We searched him thoroughly: he hadn't a farthing in his pockets, and we couldn't even find one pocket without a hole in it. He'd a blue check cotton handkerchief in a disgusting condition, sir. Then there was a love letter from some parlormaid, with demands for money and threats, and some shreds of the feuilleton with which you're familiar, sir. The general decided that he was innocent. To complete our investigation we woke the man himself—barely just managed to shove him awake; he could hardly understand what was the matter; he opened his mouth with a drunken air; the expression on his face was absurd and innocent, foolish even—it was not he, sir!"

"Well, I am so glad!" the prince sighed joyfully. "I did fear for him!"

"You feared? Then you must have had some grounds for it?" Lebedev narrowed his eyes.

"Oh, no, I meant nothing," faltered the prince. "I was very stupid to say I feared for him. Do me the favor, Lebedev, don't repeat it to anyone ..."

"Prince, Prince! Your words are in my heart ... at the bottom of my heart! It is a tomb, sir! ..." uttered Lebedev ecstatically, pressing his hat to his heart.

"Good, good! ... Then it must have been Ferdyshchenko? That is, I mean to say, you suspect Ferdyshchenko?"

"Who else?" Lebedev pronounced, looking intently at the prince.

"Well, yes, it stands to reason . . . Who else is there . . . But, I mean, after all, what evidence is there?"

"There is evidence, sir. First, his disappearance at seven o'clock, or before seven in the morning."

"I know; Kolya told me that he went in to him and said that he was going to finish off the night with . . . I forget with whom . . . some friend of his."

"Vilkin, sir. So Nikolai Ardalionovich must have told you already, then?"

"He told me nothing about the theft."

"He doesn't know, for I've kept it secret for the time being. And so he went to Vilkin's; and, seemingly, what is there so queer in a drunken man's going to see another man, as drunken as himself, even if it were before daybreak, and without any reason—eh, sir? But here a clue is discovered: going out, he leaves the address . . . Now, follow me, Prince, here's a question: why did he leave an address? . . . Why does he purposely go to Nikolai Ardalionovich, making a detour, sir, to inform him that 'I'm going to finish up the night at Vilkin's'? And who would be interested in the fact that he was leaving, or, indeed, that he was going to Vilkin in particular? Why announce it? No, here we have the cunning, sir, the cunning of a thief! It's as much as to say: 'You see, I purposely don't cover up my traces, so how can I be a thief after that? Would a thief announce where he was going?' It's an excess of anxiety to avert suspicion, and to efface, so to say, his footprints in the sand . . . Do you understand me, honored prince?"

"I understand, I understand quite well, but you know that's not enough."

"A second clue, sir: the track turns out to be a false one, and the address given was not exact. An hour later, that is, at eight o'clock, I was already knocking at Vilkin's; he lives here in Fifth Street, sir, and I know him too, sir. There turned out to be no sign of Ferdyshchenko, though I did get out of the maidservant, who was stone deaf, sir, that an hour before, someone really had knocked, and been pretty vigorous, too, so that he even broke the bell. But the maidservant wouldn't open the door, not wishing to wake Mr. Vilkin, and perhaps not anxious to get up herself. It does happen, sir."

"And is that all your evidence? It's not enough."

"Prince, but who is there to suspect, sir? Judge for yourself," Lebedev concluded entreatingly, and there was a glimmer of something sly in his grin.

"You ought to search your rooms once more and in the drawers!" the prince pronounced anxiously, after some pondering.

"I have searched them, sir!" Lebedev sighed even more entreatingly.

"Hm!... And what, oh, what did you want to change that coat for?" cried the prince, thumping the table in vexation.

"That's a question from an old-fashioned comedy, sir. But, most kind prince! You take my misfortune too much to heart! I don't deserve it. That is, I alone don't deserve it; but you are anxious for the criminal, too... for that wretched Mr. Ferdyshchenko?"

"Well, yes, yes, you certainly have worried me," the prince cut him off absently and with displeasure. "Now then, what do you intend to do... if you are so convinced it is Ferdyshchenko?"

"Prince, honored prince, who else could it be, sir?" said Lebedev, wriggling with the increasing urgency of his entreaty. "You see, the lack of any other on whom to fix, and, so to say, the complete impossibility of suspecting anybody but Mr. Ferdyshchenko—why, that is, so to speak, another piece of evidence against Mr. Ferdyshchenko, already the third piece of evidence. For, I ask again, who else could it be? Why, you wouldn't have me suspect Mr. Burdovsky, would you, he-he-he!"

"Well, there you are, what nonsense!"

"Nor the general, then, he-he-he!"

"How outlandish!" the prince said, almost angrily, turning impatiently in his seat.

"I should think it's outlandish! He-he-he! And didn't the man amuse me, too, I mean the general, sir! I went with him before, while the track was hot, to Vilkin's, sir... And you must note that the general was even more astounded than I was when, first thing after finding out my loss, I woke him up—he even changed in his face, turned red and pale, and at last flew into such violent and righteous indignation as I would never have expected, indeed, to such a degree, sir. He is a most honorable man! He tells lies incessantly, from weakness, but he's a man of the loftiest sentiments, a man, too, of little shrewdness, who inspires the fullest confidence by his naïveté. I have told you already, honored prince, that I've not just a weakness, but indeed a love for him, sir. Sud-

denly, he stops in the middle of the street, throws open his coat, bares
his chest: 'Search me!' he says. 'You searched Keller, why don't you
search me? Justice demands it!' And his arms and legs were trembling,
he even turned all pale; he looked so threatening. I laughed and said,
'Listen, General, if anyone else had said such a thing about you, I'd
have taken my head off at once with my own hands, would have put it
on a big platter, and would have served it myself on the platter to anyone who doubted you: do you see this head? I would say, well, I'll answer for him with this very head of mine, and not only with this head,
but I'd go through fire for him. That's how I'm ready to vouch for you,'
said I. Then he threw himself into my arms, still in the middle of the
street, sir, shed a tear, trembling, and clasped me so tight to his breast
that I barely gasped for breath: 'You're the only friend left to me in my
misfortunes!' said he. He's an emotional man, sir! Then, of course,
apropos of the incident, he told me an anecdote on the spot, of how he
had once, in his youth, been suspected of stealing five hundred thousand rubles, but that next day he had thrown himself into the flames of
a burning house, and had dragged out of the fire the count who had
suspected him, and Nina Alexandrovna, who was a girl at the time.
The count embraced him, and that is how his marriage with Nina
Alexandrovna came about, and the very next day, in the ruins of the
fire, they found a box with the missing money in it; it was an iron box
of English make, with a secret lock, and it had somehow fallen under
the floor so that no one noticed it, and it was only found due to the fire.
A complete lie, sir. But when he spoke of Nina Alexandrovna, he positively blubbered. A most honorable person, Nina Alexandrovna, though
she is angry with me."

"You are not acquainted with her?"

"As near as not, sir, but I should like to be, with all my heart, if only
to justify myself to her. Nina Alexandrovna has a grievance against me,
claiming that I lead her spouse astray into drunkenness. But not only
do I not lead him astray, more like than not, I restrain him; it may be I
entice him away from more pernicious society. Besides, he's my friend,
sir, and I confess it to you, I won't desert him now, no, sir, that is to say,
sir, it's like this: where he goes, there I go, for you can only manage him
through his sensibility. Nowadays, he doesn't even visit his captainess,
though he secretly longs for her, and even sometimes moans for her,
especially every morning, when he gets up and puts on his boots; I

don't know why it's at that time in particular. He's no money, sir, that's the trouble, and without money, there's no going to see that woman, no, sir. Hasn't he asked you for money, honored prince?"

"No, he hasn't."

"He's ashamed to. He did mean to; he owned to me, indeed, that he meant to trouble you, but he's bashful, sir, seeing as you obliged him not long ago, and besides he supposes that you won't give it to him. He confessed this to me as his friend."

"And you don't give him money?"

"Prince! Honored prince! For that man I'd give not only money but, so to say, my life ... No, then again, I don't want to exaggerate—not my life, but if it were, so to speak, fever, some kind of abscess, or even a cough, then, upon my word, I'd be ready to bear it for him, if only there's a very great need; for I consider him a great, though fallen, man! Yes, sir, there you have it, not only money, sir!"

"Then you must give him money?"

"N-no, sir; money I have not given him, sir, and he knows himself that I won't give it to him, no, sir; but that's solely with a view to his moderation and reformation. Now he is insisting on coming to Petersburg with me; you see, I'm going to Petersburg, sir, to catch Mr. Ferdyshchenko while the trail is still hot, for I know for certain that he is there by now, sir. My general is practically aboil, sir; but I suspect that he'll give me the slip in Petersburg to visit his captainess. I'm letting him go on purpose, I must own, as we've already agreed, upon arrival, to go in different directions so as to catch Mr. Ferdyshchenko more easily. And so I shall let him go, and then, all of a sudden, like snow on the head, come upon him at the captainess's—just to put him to shame, as a family man, and as a man, speaking generally."

"Only don't make a disturbance, Lebedev, for goodness' sake, don't make a disturbance," the prince said in an undertone and in great agitation.

"Oh, no, sir, simply just to put him to shame and to see what sort of a face he makes—for one can judge a great deal from the face, honored prince, especially with a man like that! Ah, Prince! Great as my own trouble is now, I cannot help thinking of him and the reformation of his morals. I have a great favor to ask of you, Prince, and I must confess it was expressly for that I have come to you, yes, sir: you are already acquainted with their house, you have even lived with them, sir;

so if you would decide to assist me in this, most beneficent prince, entirely for the sake of the general alone and for his happiness ..."

Lebedev positively clasped his hands, as though in supplication.

"What's that? Assist you how? Rest assured, I am extremely anxious to understand you fully, Lebedev."

"It was entirely with that conviction I have come to you! We could act through Nina Alexandrovna; observing and, so to speak, watching over his excellency continually in the bosom of his own family. I'm not acquainted, unfortunately ... moreover, there's Nikolai Ardalionovich, who adores you, so to speak, with every fiber of his youthful heart, perhaps he could help ..."

"N-no ... to bring Nina Alexandrovna into this business ... Heaven forbid! Nor Kolya either ... But perhaps I still fail to understand you, Lebedev."

"Why, there's nothing to understand!" Lebedev actually sprang up from his chair. "Sympathy, only sympathy, and tenderness—that's all the medicine our sick man requires. You, Prince, will allow me to consider him a sick man?"

"Indeed, this shows your delicacy and intelligence."

"I shall explain it to you with an example, taken, for the sake of clarity, from experience. You see the kind of man he is, sir: his only weakness now is for that captainess, before whom he mayn't appear without money and at whose house I am determined to discover him today, for his own good, sir; but supposing it were not only the captainess, supposing he had committed an actual crime, or anyway, a most dishonorable deed (though of course he's entirely incapable of it), even then, I tell you, you could achieve everything with him simply by generous tenderness, so to speak, for he is the most sensitive of men, yes, sir! Believe me, he wouldn't hold out for five days; he'd spill it all himself; he would weep and confess everything—and especially if one went to work cleverly, and in an honorable style, by means of his family's vigilant watch, and yours, over all his comings and goings, so to speak ... Oh, most noble-hearted prince!" Lebedev leapt up in a sort of exaltation. "Why, I'm not asserting positively that he ... I am ready at this very moment to shed my last drop of blood for him, so to speak, though you'll agree that his intemperance and drunkenness and the captainess, and all that taken together, may lead him to anything."

"In such a cause I am naturally always ready to assist," said the prince, getting up. "Only I confess, Lebedev, I am dreadfully uneasy; tell me, do you still . . . in a word, you say yourself that you suspect Mr. Ferdyshchenko."

"Why, who else? Who else, true-hearted prince?" Again Lebedev clasped his hands in exhortation, with a solicitous smile.

The prince frowned and rose from his place.

"Look here, Lukyan Timofeich, a mistake here would be a dreadful thing. This Ferdyshchenko . . . I should not like to speak ill of him . . . but this Ferdyshchenko . . . that is, who knows, perhaps it is he! . . . I mean to say that perhaps he really is more capable of it than . . . anyone else."

Lebedev opened his eyes and pricked up his ears.

"You see," said the prince, becoming muddled and frowning more and more, as he paced up and down the room, trying not to look at Lebedev—"I was given to understand . . . I was told about Mr. Ferdyshchenko that he was, apparently, aside from everything, a man before whom one must keep oneself in check and not say anything . . . unnecessary—you understand? I say this because perhaps he really might be more capable of it than anyone else . . . so as not to make a mistake, that's the main thing—do you understand?"

"And who told you that about Mr. Ferdyshchenko?" Lebedev fairly pounced.

"Oh, it was whispered to me; but then again, I don't believe it myself . . . I'm awfully vexed to be obliged to tell you. . . . I assure you I don't believe it myself . . . It's some nonsense . . . Phooey! How stupid I've been!"

"You see, Prince," Lebedev was positively quivering all over, "this is important. This is exceedingly important now—that is, not on account of Mr. Ferdyshchenko, but on account of the way this information reached you" (saying this Lebedev ran backward and forward after the prince, trying to keep step with him). "Here's what I've to tell you, too, Prince: earlier, the general—when I was going with him to this Vilkin's, and after he had already told me about the fire—was boiling over, of course, with anger, and suddenly began insinuating the same thing to me about Mr. Ferdyshchenko, but so incoherently and clumsily that I couldn't help posing him some questions, in consequence of which I was fully convinced that all this information was solely an inspiration of his excellency's . . . arising alone from the generosity, so to speak, of his own heart. For he lies solely because he can't restrain his sentimentality. Now, kindly consider this, sir: if he told a lie, and I'm sure he did, how could you have heard of it? Don't you see, Prince, it was the inspiration of the moment with him—so, then, who could have told you? That's important, sir, that is very important, and . . . so to say . . ."

"Kolya told me just now, and he was told earlier by his father, whom he met at six o'clock—between six and seven—in the foyer, when he came out for something."

And the prince told the whole story in detail.

"Ah, well, there you are, sir, that's what's called a clue, sir!" Lebedev laughed noiselessly, rubbing his hands. "It's just as I thought, sir! That means that his excellency intentionally interrupted his sleep of the innocent, going on six o'clock, expressly to go and wake his beloved son and inform him of the extraordinary danger of associating with Mr. Ferdyshchenko! What a dangerous man Mr. Ferdyshchenko must be, and what parental solicitude on the part of his excellency, he-he-he!"

"Listen, Lebedev," the prince was utterly chagrined, "listen, go about it quietly! Don't make an uproar! I beg you, Lebedev, I entreat you . . . In that case I swear I'll assist you, but on condition that nobody should know; nobody should know!"

"Rest assured, most noble-hearted, most sincere and generous prince," cried Lebedev in perfect exaltation—"rest assured that all this will be buried in my most honorable heart! I'd give every drop of my blood . . . Most illustrious prince, I'm a base creature in soul and spirit, but ask any base creature, any villain even: whom would he rather have to deal with, a villain like himself, or a noble-hearted man like you, most true-hearted prince? He'll answer that it's with the noble-hearted man, and that's the triumph of virtue! Good-bye, honored prince! Treading softly . . . treading softly, and . . . together, sir."

X

The prince understood at last why he turned cold every time he touched those three letters, and why he had put off the moment to read them until the evening. When, in the morning, he had sunk into a heavy sleep on his couch without having brought himself to open any one of those three envelopes, he had another painful dream, and again the same "criminal woman" came to him. Again she looked at him with tears sparkling on her long eyelashes, again beckoned him to follow her, and again he woke up, as he had done before, recalling her face with anguish. He wanted to go to *her* at once, but could not; at last, almost in despair, he unfolded the letters and began reading them.

These letters, too, resembled a dream. Sometimes one dreams strange, impossible and unnatural dreams; on awakening you remember them clearly and are amazed at a strange fact: you remember first of all that your reason did not desert you throughout your dream; you recollect even that you acted extremely cunningly and logically throughout this entire long, long time, while you were surrounded by murderers who were contriving to outwit you, hid their intentions, treated you amicably while they already had a weapon at the ready and were only waiting for some signal; you remember how cleverly you deceived them at last, hiding from them; then you figured out that they knew your deception inside and out and were only pretending not to know where you were hidden; but you were sly and deceived them again; all this you remember clearly. But how was it that, at the same time, your reason could reconcile itself to such obvious absurdities and impossibilities with which, by the way, your dream was filled to overflowing? One of your murderers, before your very eyes, turned into a woman, and the woman into a little, sly, loathsome dwarf—and you accepted it all at once as an accomplished fact, almost without the slightest bewilderment, at the very time when, on the other hand, your reason was exerting itself to the utmost and demonstrated extraordinary power, cunning, sagacity, and logic? And why, too, on waking from the dream and fully returning to reality, do you feel almost every time, and sometimes with extraordinary intensity, that you have left something unexplained behind with the dream? You chuckle at the absurdities of your dream, and feel at the same time that enclosed within the mesh of these absurdities is some thought, but a thought that is real, something belonging to your actual life, something that exists and has always existed in your heart; it's as though you were told by your dream something new and prophetic, something that you were awaiting; your impression is vivid, it may be joyful or agonizing, but in what it consists, and what was said to you—all this you cannot understand or recall.

It was almost like this, after reading these letters. But even before he had unfolded them, the prince felt that the very fact of the existence and the possibility of them was like a nightmare. How could *she* have brought herself to write to *her,* he asked himself as he wandered about in the evening alone (at times not knowing himself where he was going). How could she write of *that,* how could such a mad fantasy have arisen in her mind? But that fantasy had by now taken shape, and the most amazing thing of all for him was that, as he read those letters, he himself almost believed in the possibility and the justification of that fantasy. Yes, of course, it was a dream, a nightmare and a madness; but there was also something in it that was tormentingly real and agonizingly true, which justified the dream and the nightmare and the madness. For several hours together he seemed to be as if in the delirious grip of what he had read, continually recalling fragments of it, brooding over them, pondering them. Sometimes he was even inclined to tell himself that he had anticipated and presaged all this earlier; it even seemed to him as though he had read it all before, some long, long time ago, and that everything that he had mourned about since, everything that had tormented him and which he feared—all this was contained in these letters, which he had already read long ago.

"When you open this letter"—so the first epistle began—"you will look first of all at the signature. The signature will tell you everything, and explain everything, so there's no need for me to justify myself to you and there's nothing to explain. If I were even the slightest bit your equal, you might have been offended at such impertinence; but who am I, and who are you? We are two such opposite extremes, and compared to you I am so beyond the pale, that I simply cannot insult you in any way, even if I wanted to."

In another place she further wrote:

"Don't consider my words the sick ecstasy of a sick mind, but you are for me perfection! I have seen you, I see you every day. And I don't judge you, you know; I did not arrive at the conviction that you're perfection through reason; I simply believed it. But in one thing I have sinned before you: I love you. But perfection must not be loved; perfection may only be looked upon as perfection, is that not so? Yet I am in love with you. Though love makes people equal, yet don't be uneasy, I do not equate myself with you even in my most secret thoughts. I wrote you, 'don't be uneasy'; can you possibly be uneasy? . . . If it were possible, I would kiss your footprints. Oh, I don't put myself on a level with you . . . Look at my signature, quick, look at my signature!"

"I notice, however," she wrote in another letter, "that I join you with him, and I have never once asked whether you love him. He fell in love with you having seen you only once. He thought of you as of 'light'; those are his own words, I heard them from him. But even without words I understood that you were light for him. I've lived a whole month beside him, and understood then that you love him too; to me, you and he are one.

"What does this mean?" she goes on writing. "Yesterday I passed by you and you seemed to blush? It can't be so, I only fancied it. If you were brought to the filthiest den and shown vice in its nakedness, you should not blush; you cannot possibly be indignant over an insult. You can hate everyone base and low, but not for your own sake, rather for the sake of others, for the ones whom they insult. But you—no one can insult. Do you know I think you even ought to love me? For me, you are just what you are for him: a bright spirit; an angel cannot hate, cannot help loving. Can one love everyone, all men, all one's neighbors? I have often asked myself that question. Of course not, and it's even unnatural. In abstract love for humanity one almost always loves no one but oneself. But that's impossible for us, while you are a different matter: how could you not love anyone, when you cannot compare yourself with anyone, and when you are above every insult, above every personal indignation. You alone can love without egoism, you alone can love not for yourself, but for the sake of the one you love. Oh, how bitter it would be for me to find out that you feel shame or anger on account of me! That would be your ruin: you would sink to my level at once.

"Yesterday, after meeting you I went home and invented a picture. Artists always paint Christ following the narratives of the Gospels; I would paint Him differently: I would represent Him alone—His disciples did sometimes leave Him alone, after all. I would leave with Him only a little child. The child would be playing beside Him, perhaps be telling Him something in his childish language; Christ has been listening, but now He has sunk into thought; His hand has unconsciously, absently remained on the child's fair little head. He is looking into the distance, at the horizon; thought, great as the whole world, dwells in His gaze; His face is sorrowful. The child has fallen silent, leans with his elbow on Christ's knees, propping up his cheek on his little hand, raises his little head and, sunk in thought, the way little children sometimes sink into thought, looks intently at Him. The sun is setting . . .That is my picture! You are innocent, and in your innocence lies all your perfection. Oh, only remember that! What do you care about my passion for you? You are now altogether mine, I shall be all my life beside you . . . I shall soon die."

Finally, in the very last letter stood the words:

"For God's sake, think nothing of me; and don't think that I am abasing myself by writing to you like this, or that I belong to the sort of creatures who enjoy abasing themselves, even if from pride. No, I have my consolation; but it is difficult for me to explain it to you. It would be difficult for me to say it clearly even to myself, though it torments me. But I know that I cannot abase myself, even from a fit of pride. And as for self-abasement from purity of heart, I am incapable of it. And so I do not abase myself at all.

"Why do I so want to bring you together—for your sake, or for my own? For my own sake, of course; all my remedies lie in it, I have said so to myself long ago . . . I have heard that your sister Adelaida said of my portrait then that with such beauty one might turn the world upside down. But I have renounced the world; does it amuse you to hear that from me, meeting me decked in lace and diamonds, in the company of drunkards and scoundrels? Pay no mind to that, I have almost ceased to exist and I know it; God knows what lives within me in my stead. I read that every day in two terrible eyes that are always gazing at me, even when they are not before me. Those eyes are *silent* now (they are always silent), but I know their secret. His house is gloomy and dreary, and there is a secret in it. I'm sure that he has, hidden in a drawer, a razor, wrapped in silk like that murderer in Moscow; he too lived in the same house with his mother, and also wrapped a razor in silk to cut a throat with. All the time I was in their house, I kept fancying that somewhere under the floorboards there might be a dead man hidden there by his father perhaps, wrapped in oilcloth, just like that Moscow one, and surrounded in the same way with jars of Zhdanov's fluid;[28] I could even show you the corner. He is always silent: but I know he loves me so much that he can't help hating me. Your marriage and ours are to take place together: he and I have fixed on that. I have no secrets from him. I could kill him from terror . . . But he will kill me first . . . He laughed just now and said I was raving; he knows I am writing to you."

And there was much, much more of the same kind of raving in those letters. One of them, the second, was on two large-format sheets of notepaper, covered in small writing.

At last the prince came out of the dark park, where he had been wandering aimlessly for a long time, as he had the previous night. The clear, transparent night seemed to him lighter than usual; "Can it still be so early?" he thought. (He had forgotten to take his watch.) He fancied he heard music somewhere in the distance; "It must be at the station," he thought again, "of course, they've not gone there today." Perceiving this, he saw that he was standing right by their dacha; he had known, indeed, that he was invariably bound to find himself here at last, and with a beating heart he stepped onto the terrace. No one met him, the terrace was empty. He waited, and opened the door into the room. "They never shut that door," the thought flickered through his mind, but the room was empty too. It was almost dark in it. He stood still in the middle of the room in perplexity. Suddenly the door opened and Alexandra Ivanovna came in, with a candle in her hand. On seeing the prince she was surprised and stopped short before him, as though in inquiry. Obviously she was simply crossing the room from one door to the other, with no idea of finding anyone there.

"How do you come here?" she asked at last.

"I . . . came in . . ."

"*Maman* is not quite well, nor Aglaia either. Adelaida is going to bed, I'm going too. We've been at home by ourselves all the evening. Papa and the prince are in Petersburg."

"I've come . . . I've come to you . . . now . . ."

"Do you know what time it is?"

"N-no . . ."

28. A disinfecting fluid. This is another reference to the Mazurin case, which Nastasya Filippovna had already mentioned on the night of her birthday (see note 47 in Part I, page 174). Mazurin hid the body of his victim in the basement of his house, covering it with oilcloth and placing four containers of Zdanov's fluid near the corpse to mask the stench.

"Half past twelve. We always go to bed by one."

"Oh! I thought that . . . it was half past nine."

"No matter!" She laughed. "And why didn't you come before? Perhaps you were even expected."

"I . . . thought . . ." he murmured, going out.

"Good-bye! Tomorrow I shall amuse everyone."

He went homeward by the road that encircled the park. His heart was beating, his thoughts were in a jumble, and everything around him seemed to resemble a dream. And suddenly, just as before, when he had woken up both times at one and the same apparition, the same apparition rose before him again. The same woman came out of the park and stood before him, as though she had been waiting for him there. He started, and stood still; she seized his hand and pressed it tight. "No, this is no apparition!"

And there, at last, she stood before him, face to face, for the first time since their parting; she was saying something to him, but he looked at her in silence; his heart was filled to overflowing and began to ache with anguish. Oh, he could never afterward forget that meeting with her and always recalled it with the same anguish. She sank on her knees before him, right there in the street, like a demented woman; he stepped back in horror, while she tried to catch his hand to kiss it, and just as in his dream before, the tears glistened now on her long eyelashes.

"Stand up! Stand up!" he said in a frightened whisper, raising her. "Stand up, at once!"

"Are you happy? Happy?" she asked. "Only say one word to me, are you happy now? Today, this minute? Have you been with her? What did she say?"

She did not get up; she did not heed him; she questioned him hurriedly, and hurried to speak, as though she were being pursued.

"I'm going tomorrow as you've commanded. I won't . . . It's the last time I shall see you, you know, the last time! Now it's absolutely the last time!"

"Calm yourself, stand up!" he brought out in despair.

She peered greedily into his face, clutching at his hands.

"Farewell!" she said at last, got up and went quickly away from him, almost running. The prince saw that Rogozhin had suddenly appeared beside her, caught her under the arm, and was leading her away.

"Wait a minute, Prince," cried Rogozhin, "I'll return for a time in five minutes."

Five minutes later he did, in fact, arrive; the prince was waiting for him at the same place.

"I've put her in the carriage," he said. "It's been waiting there at the corner since ten o'clock. She knew you'd spend the whole evening at that young lady's. The thing you wrote to me before, I have conveyed in every detail. She won't write to that other one again, she's promised; and she'll go away from here tomorrow as you wish. She wanted to see you for the last time, though you refused her; and we've been waiting for you here, on that bench there, to catch you as you came back."

"Did she take you with her of her own accord?"

"Why not?" grinned Rogozhin. "I saw what I knew before. You've read the letters, I suppose?"

"Is it true you've really read them?" asked the prince, astonished by that idea.

"Rather! She showed me each letter herself. About the razor, too, do you remember, he-he!"

"She's mad!" cried the prince, wringing his hands.

"Who knows about that, perhaps not," Rogozhin said, softly, as though to himself.

The prince did not answer.

"Well, good-bye," said Rogozhin. "I'm going away tomorrow, too, you know: don't remember evil against me! And I say, brother," he added, turning quickly, "why didn't you tell her anything in answer? 'Are you happy or not?'"

"No, no, no!" cried the prince with boundless grief.

"As if you could have said 'yes'!" laughed Rogozhin maliciously, and went off without looking back.

PART FOUR

I

About a week had passed since the meeting of the two persons of our story on the green bench. One bright morning about half past ten, Varvara Ardalionovna Ptitsyn, having gone out to visit some friends, returned home plunged in dejected reflection.

There are people about whom it is difficult to say something that might present them completely and entirely in their most typical and characteristic aspect; these are the people who are usually called "ordinary," "the majority," and who do actually make up the vast majority of any society. In their tales and novels, authors for the most part attempt to take types in society and represent them vividly and artistically— types extremely rarely met with in actual life in their entirety, though they are nevertheless almost more real than real life itself. Podkolyosin[1] as a type is perhaps exaggerated, but not at all unheard of. What numbers of clever people after being introduced by Gogol to Podkolyosin at once began to discover that tens and hundreds of their good friends and acquaintances were terribly like Podkolyosin! They knew even before reading Gogol that their friends were like that, like Podkolyosin, only they did not know that this was what they were called, in particular. In real life, bridegrooms awfully rarely jump out of windows just before their wedding, for, to say nothing of all the rest, it is not even convenient; nonetheless, how many bridegrooms, even intelligent and worthy persons, on the eve of their wedding day have been ready to acknowledge at the bottom of their hearts that they were Podkolyosins. Not all husbands, too, exclaim at every turn: *"Tu l'a voulu, Georges Dandin!"*[2] But, Lord, how many millions and billions of times has that cry been uttered from the heart by husbands all the world over after the honeymoon, and—who knows?—even perhaps the day after the wedding.

And so, without going into more serious explanations, we will say

1. The protagonist of Gogol's comedy *The Wedding*. The name is a compound made up of the words "under" and "wheel," i.e., "one who has gotten under the wheels."

2. Fr., "You wished it, Georges Dandin"; from Molière's comedy *Georges Dandin*.

only that in actual life the typicalness of personalities is watered down, as it were, and all these Georges Dandins and Podkolyosins exist in reality, scurry and run about before our eyes every day, but only in a diluted form, as it were. Stipulating, finally, for the sake of complete veracity, that Georges Dandin, whole and entire as Molière created him, may also be met with in real life, though rarely, we will conclude our reflections, which are beginning to resemble newspaper criticism. Nonetheless, the question remains: what is a novelist to do with commonplace people, absolutely "ordinary," and how can he put them before his readers so as to make them at all interesting? To pass over them in the narrative altogether simply may not be done, for commonplace people are, at every moment and by majority, the essential link in the chain of human affairs; passing over them, then, would necessarily ruin the verisimilitude. To fill novels with nothing but types, or even simply, for the sake of interest, with strange and incredible characters, would be unrealistic, and, perhaps, even uninteresting. To our thinking, a writer ought to try to seek out interesting and instructive features even among commonplaces. And when, for instance, the very essence of some commonplace characters lies precisely in their perpetual and invariable commonplaceness, or, better still, when in spite of the extraordinary efforts of these characters to escape, at all costs, out of the rut of ordinariness and routine, they end, nonetheless, by remaining invariably and forever nothing but routine, then such characters indeed acquire a certain typicalness of their own—such as a commonplaceness that wouldn't, for anything in the world, want to remain that which it is, and longs, at all costs, to become original and independent, without having the slightest means of attaining independence.

To this class of "ordinary" or "commonplace" people belong certain persons in our tale, who have hitherto (I realize that) been insufficiently explained to the reader. Such, namely, were Varvara Ardalionovna Ptitsyn, her husband, Mr. Ptitsyn, and Gavrila Ardalionovich, her brother.

There is, indeed, nothing more vexing than to be, for instance, wealthy, of good family, decent-looking, not badly educated, fairly intelligent, even good-natured, and at the same time, to have no talents, no peculiarities, not even a single quirk, not one idea of one's own, to be decidedly "like everyone else." You have wealth, but it's not that of a Rothschild; your family is honorable, but has never distinguished it-self in any way; your appearance is seemly, but expresses very little; you have a decent education, but have no idea what use to make of it; you have brains, but *no ideas of your own;* you have a heart, but no magnanimity; and so on and so forth, in every respect. There is an ex-traordinary multitude of such people in the world, far more, indeed, than it appears; they may, like all other people, be divided into two major classes: some of limited intelligence, the others "much cleverer." The first are happier. There is, for instance, nothing easier for a limited "ordinary" person than to imagine himself as an exceptional and origi-nal person and to revel in that without the slightest hesitation. Some of our young ladies have only to crop their hair, put on blue spectacles and dub themselves nihilists, to become immediately convinced that they have at once acquired "convictions" of their own. Some men have only to feel the faintest stirring in their hearts of some human and kindly sentiment to become immediately convinced that no one feels as they do, and they are the vanguard of social development. Some have only to accept some idea on someone's word, or to read a stray page of something without beginning or end, to believe at once that these were their "own personal ideas" and were conceived in their own brain. The impudence of naïveté, if one may so express it, approaches the astonishing in such cases; all this is incredible, but one encounters it every moment. This impudence of naïveté, this unhesitating confi-dence of the stupid man in himself and his talents, is superbly de-picted by Gogol in the wonderful character of Lieutenant Pirogov.[3] Pirogov does not even doubt that he is a genius, superior indeed to any genius; he is so positive of this that he never even poses a single ques-tion to himself about it; but then again, indeed, questions don't exist for him at all. The great writer was compelled in the end to give him a whipping to satisfy the outraged moral feelings of his reader, but, seeing that the great man simply shook himself and—to fortify him-self after the ordeal—consumed a layered pie, he flung up his hands in amazement and left his readers at that. I always regretted that Gogol took his great Pirogov from so humble a rank; for Pirogov was so self-satisfied that nothing could be easier for him than to imagine

3. The protagonist of the story "Nevsky Prospect"; the name comes from the word *pirog*, a very common sweet or savory pie.

himself—commensurately with the epaulettes growing thicker and more twisted on his shoulders with the years and with promotion "up the line"—as, for example, an extraordinary military leader; or rather, not imagine it, but, indeed, simply have no doubt of it: how not a military leader, if they've promoted him to general? And how many such later bring about a terrible fiasco on the field of battle! And how many Pirogovs there have been among our literary men, scholars, and propagandists! I say "have been," but of course we have them still ...

One major figure of our narrative, Gavrila Ardalionovich Ivolgin, belonged to the other class; he belonged to the class of the "much cleverer" people, though he was completely infected from head to foot with the desire for originality. But that class, as we observed above, is far more unhappy than the first. For it's just the rub that the *clever* "ordinary" man, even if he occasionally (or even all his life) fancies himself a man of genius and great originality, nonetheless preserves in his heart the worm of doubt, which drives the clever man, sometimes, to end by utter despair; and if he does submit, it is only after being completely poisoned by vanity that has been driven inward. But, in any case, we have taken an extreme example: in the vast majority of this *clever* class of people, things don't happen so tragically at all; perhaps, in their declining years, their liver is apt to be affected, more or less, that's all. But all the same, before reconciling and submitting themselves, such men sometimes make mischief for an exceedingly long time, starting from their youth until the age at which they submit, and all from the desire of originality. Indeed, one meets with some strange cases: from a desire to be original, an honest man sometimes resolves to do something base; it is even known to happen that one of these unfortunates is not only honest but good, is the guardian angel of his family, maintaining and feeding by his labor not only his own kindred, but even outsiders, and what do you think?—he can find no peace his whole entire life! For him, it is not at all a soothing or consoling thought that he has so well fulfilled his human obligations; on the contrary, this very fact actually irritates him: "This is what I've wasted all my life on," he says; "this is what has fettered me, hand and foot; this is what has hindered me from discovering gunpowder! Had it not been for this, I should certainly have discovered either gunpowder or America—and certainly I don't know what else, but I would have discovered it without fail!" What is most characteristic of these gentle

men is, indeed, that they can never find out for certain what it is precisely that they are so anxious to discover and what precisely they are
on the point of discovering their entire lives: gunpowder or America?
But their sufferings, their longings for what was to be discovered,
would have sufficed for a Columbus or a Galileo.

Gavrila Ardalionovich was starting out precisely in that vein; but he
was only just starting out; he had many years of mischief-making before him. A profound and continual consciousness of his own lack of
talent, and, at the same time, the overwhelming desire to prove to himself that he was a man of great independence, had deeply wounded his
heart almost from the time he was a boy. He was a young man with envious and violent desires, who seemed to have been positively born
with overwrought nerves. The violence of his desires he took for their
strength. Given his passionate desire to distinguish himself, he was
sometimes ready to make the most imprudent leap; but as soon as the
time for the imprudent leap would come, our hero would always turn
out to be far too sensible to venture it. This devastated him. Perhaps he
would have, given the right opportunity, indeed resolved to undertake
some extremely base thing, if only he could achieve any of his dreams;
but, as if by design, whenever it came time to cross the line, he always
turned out to be too honest for any extremely base thing. (To trivially
base things, on the other hand, he was always ready to agree.) He
looked with loathing and hatred on the downfall and poverty of his
family. He treated even his mother haughtily and contemptuously,
though he understood perfectly well himself that, for the time being,
his mother's reputation and character constituted the pivotal point on
which his own career rested as well. Upon entering Epanchin's service,
he said to himself at once: "Since I must be mean, let me be thoroughly
mean, if only I can win"—and was scarcely ever thoroughly mean.
And why did he even imagine that he would necessarily need to be
mean? Of Aglaia he was simply frightened at the time, but he did not
abandon the business with her, but dragged it out on the off chance,
though he never seriously believed that she would stoop to him. Afterward, at the time of his adventure with Nastasya Filippovna, he suddenly imagined that the means of attaining *everything* lay in money.
"If I must be mean, then I'll be really mean," he repeated to himself
every day, then, with satisfaction, but also with a certain dismay; "if
one must be mean, then let us go to the very top"—he urged himself

continually—"the run-of-the-mill grow timid in such cases, but we shall not grow timid!" Having lost Aglaia and crushed by circumstances, he completely lost heart, and actually brought the prince the money flung him by a mad woman, to whom it had also been brought by a madman. A thousand times afterward he regretted having returned that money, though he was continually priding himself upon it. He did actually cry for three days while the prince remained in Petersburg back then, but in those three days he grew to hate the prince for looking upon him too compassionately, when it was a fact that he had given back such a sum of money, and "not just anyone could have resolved to do it." But the noble-minded confession to himself that all his misery was nothing but continually crushed vanity tormented him horribly. Only long afterward did he discern, and become convinced of, the extent to which matters might have turned out seriously for him with such a strange and innocent creature as Aglaia. Remorse gnawed at him; he threw up his post and sank into despondency and dejection. He lived in Ptitsyn's house and at the latter's expense, together with his father and mother, and despised Ptitsyn openly, although at the same time he followed his advice and had the good sense almost always to ask it of him. Gavrila Ardalionovich was angry, for instance, at the fact that Ptitsyn did not propose to become a Rothschild and did not set that goal for himself. "If you go in for usury, do it thoroughly—squeeze people, coin money out of them, show willpower, be a king among the Jews!" Ptitsyn was unassuming and quiet; he only smiled; but once, indeed, he thought it necessary to have a talk with Ganya seriously, and he even carried out the task with a certain degree of dignity. He had proved to Ganya that he was doing nothing dishonest and that he had no right to call him a dirty *zhid;* that if money had such a price, it was not his fault; that he was acting honestly and honorably, and that in reality he was only an intermediary in "these affairs," and that finally, thanks to his fastidiousness in business, he was already favorably known to the most first-rate people and his business was increasing. "I shall never be Rothschild, and it's not necessary," he added laughing; "but I shall have a house in Liteinaya, perhaps two even, and there I shall stop." "And who knows, perhaps even three!" he thought to himself, but he never uttered this aloud and concealed the dream. Nature loves such people and is kind to them: she will surely reward Ptitsyn not with three but with four houses, and precisely because he already knew from childhood on that he would never become a Rothschild. But beyond four houses nothing will induce nature to go, and there things will end with Ptitsyn.

Gavrila Ardalionovich's sister was quite a different person. She too possessed strong desires, but they were rather persistent than impulsive. She had plenty of common sense when it came down to the wire, and it did not abandon her before it came down to the wire, either. It is true that she also was one of the "ordinary" people who dream of originality; yet she managed very soon to recognize that she had not a drop of any particular originality, and did not take it too much to heart, perhaps—who knows?—from a peculiar sort of pride. She took her first practical step with extraordinary resolve, getting married to Mr. Ptitsyn; but in getting married she did not at all say to herself: "If I must be mean, I will be mean so long as I gain my end," as Gavrila Ardalionovich would certainly not have failed to express it at such a moment (and virtually expressed it aloud in her very presence, when he gave his approval of her decision as elder brother). Quite the contrary, in fact: Varvara Ardalionovna married after having thoroughly assured herself that her future husband was an unassuming, pleasant, almost educated man, who could never be induced to commit any great meanness. As for minor acts of meanness, Varvara Ardalionovna did not worry about such trifles; and where, indeed, are trifles like that not to be found? It's no good looking for an ideal, after all! She knew, besides, that by marrying she would provide a refuge for her mother, her father and her brothers. Seeing her brother in his misfortune, she wanted to help him, in spite of all their previous familial misunderstandings. Ptitsyn would sometimes spur Ganya on, in a friendly way, of course, to take a post. "There you are despising generals and the institution of generals," he would say to him sometimes in jest; "but mind, 'they' will all finish by being generals in their turn; if you live long enough you will see." "But where do they get that I despise generals and the institution of generals?" Ganya thought sarcastically to himself. In order to help her brother, Varvara Ardalionovna resolved to enlarge her circle of operations: she managed to insinuate herself at the Epanchins', wherein she was much assisted by childhood memories: she and Ganya had both played with the Epanchins as children. We may observe here that if Varvara Ardalionovna had visited the Epanchins in pursuit of some fantastic dream, she would have, by this very fact, been excluded at once from that class of people into which she had placed herself; but what she was pursuing was not a dream; there was a rather well-founded calculation here on her side: it was founded on the character of this family. And as for Aglaia's character, she studied it tirelessly. The task she set before herself was to bring those two, Aglaia and her brother, around to each other again. Possibly she actually did attain this object to some extent; possibly she made blunders, counting perhaps too much on her brother, for instance, and expecting from him what he could never and not under any circumstances have given. In any case, she proceeded at the Epanchins' in a rather artful manner: for weeks together she made no mention of her brother; she was always extremely truthful and sincere, carried herself simply but with dignity. And as for the depths of her conscience, she was not afraid to look into them and did not reproach herself for anything in the least. It was this that gave her power. There was only one thing she sometimes noticed in herself, that she too, perhaps, was spiteful; that in her, too, was a great deal of amour-propre and possibly even almost devastated vanity; she noticed it particularly at certain moments, almost every time she went away from the Epanchins'.

And now, too, she was on her way back from them, and, as we have said already, she was plunged in dejected reflection. There was a shade of something bitterly mocking in this dejection. At Pavlovsk, Ptitsyn occupied a roomy but not very attractive-looking wooden house in a dusty street, which would within a short period become completely his own property; so that he was already beginning, in his turn, to sell it to someone else. Ascending to the porch, Varvara Ardalionovna heard an extraordinary noise from the top of the house and distinguished the shouting voices of her father and brother. Coming in to the drawing room and seeing Ganya running to and fro across the room, pale with fury and almost tearing out his hair, she frowned and sank with a weary air on the sofa without taking off her hat. Knowing full well that if she kept silent a minute and did not ask her brother why he was running like that, then he would certainly be angry, Varya hastened, at last, to pronounce, in the form of a question:

"The usual story?"

"The usual story indeed!" cried Ganya. "The usual story! No! The devil only knows what is happening here now, and not at all the usual! The old man is on the point of raving ... Mother is bawling. Upon my word, Varya, I'll turn him out, say what you like, or ... or I'll go away myself," he added, probably recollecting that it was not possible to turn people out of someone else's house.

"You must show some leniency," murmured Varya.

"Leniency for what? For whom?" cried Ganya, firing up. "For his loathsome habits? No, you may say what you like, that's impossible! Impossible, impossible, impossible! And what a way to behave: he is in the wrong, and it makes him all the more impertinent. 'I won't use the gate, take down the fence!' ... Why are you sitting there like that? Your face looks all drained."

"My face looks like any face," Varya answered with displeasure.

Ganya looked at her more intently.

"You were there?" he asked suddenly.

"Yes, there."

"Stay, shouting again! What a disgrace, and at such a time too!"

"What sort of time? It's no such special time."

Ganya surveyed his sister even more intently.

"Have you found something out?" he asked.

"Nothing unexpected, anyway. I found out that it's all true. My husband was more right than either of us; it's turned out just as he predicted from the beginning. Where is he?"

"Not at home. What's turned out?"

"The prince is formally betrothed to her. The thing is settled. The elder girls told me. Aglaia consents; they have even left off concealing it. (There's always been so much mystery there till now, you know.) Adelaida's wedding will be put off again, to have the two weddings all at once, on one day—how romantic! It resembles poetry. Why don't you compose a poem for the occasion of the betrothal, instead of running about the room to no purpose. Belokonsky will be there this evening; she's come just at the right time; there are to be guests. He is to be presented to Belokonsky, though he is acquainted with her already; I believe they'll be announcing it publicly. They are only anxious that he not drop or break something when he walks into the drawing room in front of the guests, or else plop down himself; it's quite in his line."

Ganya listened very attentively, but to his sister's surprise this news, which was astonishing for him, did not at all, it seemed, produce such an astonishing effect.

"Well, that was clear," he said after a moment's thought. "So it's the end!" he added, with a strange smirk, glancing slyly into his sister's face and continuing to walk up and down the room, but much more quietly.

"It's a good thing you take it like a philosopher; I am glad, really," said Varya.

"Yes, it's a load off one's shoulders; off yours, anyway."

"I think I've served you sincerely, without any deliberation or badgering; I didn't ask you what sort of happiness you wanted to seek with Aglaia."

"Why, was I . . . seeking happiness from Aglaia?"

"Oh, please don't indulge in philosophizing! Of course you were. Of course, and that's it for us: we've been left the fools. I confess to you, I could never take this business quite seriously; I only took it up 'on the off chance,' reckoning on her funny character, and, mainly, to please you; it was ten to one that it would be a bust. I don't myself know to this day what it was you were trying to achieve."

"Now you and your husband will go prodding me to get a job; you'll give me lectures on perseverance and strength of will, and not despising small profits, and all the rest of it. I know it by heart." Ganya burst out laughing.

"There's something new on his mind," Varya thought to herself.

"So what's going on there—are the parents glad, then?" Ganya asked suddenly.

"N-no, it seems. However, you can judge for yourself; Ivan Fyodorovich is pleased; the mother is anxious; she's always viewed him with dislike as a suitor before; we know that."

"I don't mean that; he's an impossible suitor, unthinkable, that's evident. I'm asking about the present situation, what's it like there now? Has she given her formal consent?"

"She hasn't so far said no, that's all; but it couldn't be otherwise with her. You know how insanely shy and bashful she still is: as a child, she would climb into a cupboard and sit there for two or three hours, simply to avoid coming out to visitors; though she has grown such a maypole, she is just the same now. You know, for some reason, I think there's really something serious there, even on her side. They say she laughs at the prince with all her might, from morning till night, so as to hide her feelings; but she must manage to say something on the sly to him every day, for he looks as though he were walking in the clouds, beaming ... He is fearfully funny, they say. I heard it from them. I fancied too that they laughed at me to my face, the elder ones, I mean."

Ganya at last began to frown; perhaps Varya kept going deeper into the subject on purpose to get at his real view. But there was a shout again upstairs.

"I'll turn him out!" Ganya fairly roared, as though glad to vent his annoyance.

"And then he will go disgracing us again everywhere, as he did yesterday."

"What—what do you mean, yesterday? What is it; what was yesterday? Why, did he ..." Ganya seemed dreadfully alarmed all of a sudden.

"Oh, my Lord, didn't you know?" Varya pulled herself up.

"What ... Surely it isn't true that he has been there?" cried Ganya, flushing crimson with shame and rage. "Lord, but you've come from there! Have you found something out? Has the old man been there? Has he, or not?"

And Ganya rushed to the door; Varya flew to him and clutched him with both hands.

"What are you doing? Well, where are you going?" she said. "If you let him out now, he will do more harm than ever; he will do the rounds! ..."

"What damage did he do there? What did he say?"

"Well, they couldn't tell me themselves, they hadn't understood it; he only frightened them all. He went to see Ivan Fyodorovich—the latter was out; he demanded to see Lizaveta Prokofyevna. First he asked her about a post—wanted to get a job, and then he began complaining of us, of me, of my husband, of you especially ... He talked a lot of stuff."

"You couldn't find out what?" Ganya quivered as if in hysterics.

"Well, how, then! He scarcely knew what he was saying himself; and perhaps they did not tell me everything."

Ganya clutched at his head and ran to the window; Varya sat down at the other window.

"Aglaia is an absurd creature," she observed suddenly. "She stopped me and said, 'Please give your parents my personal, particular respects. I shall certainly have an opportunity of seeing your father one of these days.' And she said that so seriously; it was awfully queer ..."

"Not in derision? Not in derision?"

"That's just it, it wasn't; that is what was so queer."

"Does she know about the old man, or not, what do you think?"

"There is no doubt in my mind that they don't know in the family; but you've given me an idea: Aglaia perhaps does know. She alone knows, for her sisters were surprised too when she sent her greeting to Father so seriously. And why to him particularly? If she does know, the prince must have told her."

"It's not difficult to guess who told her! A thief! That's just what was needed. A thief in our family, 'the head of the house'!"

"That's nonsense!" cried Varya, completely losing her temper. "A drunken prank, that's all. And who made it up? Lebedev, the prince . . . they are a nice lot themselves; they haven't got a heap of wits between them. I give it about as much credence as my little finger."

"The old man is a thief and a drunkard," Ganya went on bitterly, "I'm a beggar, my sister's husband is a moneylender—there was certainly something for Aglaia to set her sights on! A lovely state of things and no mistake!"

"That sister's husband, the moneylender, is . . ."

"Keeping me, you mean? Don't stand on ceremony, please."

"Why are you so cross?" said Varya, thinking better of it. "You don't understand anything, just like a schoolboy. You think all this might injure you in Aglaia's eyes? You don't know her nature; she'd refuse the most eligible suitor and run off delighted with some student to starve in a garret—that's her dream! You've never been able to understand how interesting you would have become in her eyes if you had been able to bear our surroundings with pride and fortitude. The prince has hooked her, in the first place, because he wasn't even fishing for her; and secondly, because he is looked upon by everyone as an idiot. The very fact that she'll churn things up in her family on his account— that's what's such a pleasure to her now. Ah, you don't understand!"

"Well, we shall see whether I understand or not," Ganya muttered enigmatically. "Still, I shouldn't like her to know about the old man. I thought the prince would restrain himself and not tell her. He kept Lebedev in check; and he didn't even want to speak out to me about everything when I persisted . . ."

"So you see yourself that it must all be out apart from him. And what does it matter to you now? What are you hoping for? And even if you had any hope left, it would only make you look like a martyr in her eyes."

"Well, even she would turn tail before a scandal, in spite of all her romantic notions. Everything up to a certain point, and everyone draws the line somewhere. You are all alike."

"Aglaia would turn tail?" Varya fired up, looking contemptuously at her brother. "But what a mean little soul you've got! You are all a worthless lot. She may be absurd and a little kook, but she is a thousand times more noble-minded than any of us."

"Well, never mind, never mind, don't be cross," Ganya murmured again smugly.

"I am sorry for Mother, that's all," Varya went on. "I am so afraid this scandal about father may reach her ears. Ach! I'm afraid!"

"No doubt it has reached her," observed Ganya.

Varya had risen to go upstairs to Nina Alexandrovna, but she stopped and looked attentively at her brother.

"And who could have told her?"

"Ippolit, most likely. I expect he considered it the greatest pleasure to report it to Mother as soon as he moved here."

"But how does he know? Tell me that, pray. The prince and Lebedev resolved to tell nobody; even Kolya knows nothing."

"Ippolit? He found it out for himself. You can't imagine what a sly beast he is; what a gossip he is; what a nose he has for sniffing out anything bad, any sort of scandal. Well, believe it or not, but I am convinced he has succeeded in getting a hold on Aglaia! And if he hasn't, he will. Rogozhin has begun to have relations with him too. How can the prince not notice it! And how eager he is to stick it to me now! He considers me his personal enemy, I saw through that long ago—why and with what object, since he is dying, I can't make out! But I'll pull one over on him; you'll see, I'll stick it to him, not he to me!"

"What made you, then, entice him here, if you hate him so? And is he worth sticking it to?"

"But it was you who advised me to entice him here."

"I thought he would be of use; but do you know that he has fallen in love with Aglaia himself, now, and has been writing to her? They plied me with questions about him . . . He may even have written to Lizaveta Prokofyevna."

"He is not dangerous in that sense!" said Ganya with a spiteful laugh. "But surely you didn't get something right. It's very possible he is in love, for he is a boy. But . . . he wouldn't write anonymous letters to the old lady. He is such a spiteful, insignificant, self-satisfied mediocrity! . . . I am convinced, I know for certain, that he represented me to her as a scheming adventurer; that's what he began with. I must own that, like a fool, I talked to him freely at first; I thought that, simply to revenge himself on the prince, he'd work in my interests; he's such a sly beast! Oh, I have seen through him now completely. And about that theft, he heard it from his own mother, from the captainess. If the old man did bring himself to it, it was for the captainess's sake. All of a sudden, apropos of nothing, he tells me that 'the general' had promised his mother four hundred rubles; and it was absolutely apropos of nothing, without the least ceremony. Then I understood it all. And he peered right into my eyes with a sort of glee; he's told Mother too, most likely, for the mere pleasure of breaking her heart. And why on earth doesn't he die, pray, tell me? Why, he promised to die in three weeks, and here he is getting fatter! He is coughing less; he said himself last night that he hadn't brought up blood for two days."

"Turn him out."

"I don't hate him, I despise him!" Ganya pronounced proudly. "Well, yes, yes, I do hate him then, I do!" he shouted suddenly with extraordinary fury, "and I'll tell him so to his face, even if he lies dying on his pillow! If you'd read his confession—good Lord, what naïveté of insolence! He is a regular Lieutenant Pirogov, a Nozdryov[4] in a tragedy, and, above all—a puppy! Oh, how I should have enjoyed thrashing him then, simply to surprise him. Now he's revenging himself on everyone because back then he didn't manage to . . . But what's that? There noise there again! What can it be, really? I won't put up with it any longer. Ptitsyn!" he cried to his brother-in-law, who was coming into the room. "What's the meaning of this? What are we coming to, at last? This is . . . this is . . ."

But the noise was quickly coming nearer, the door was suddenly flung open, and old Ivolgin, wrathful, crimson in the face, shaken, and beside himself, attacked Ptitsyn too. The old man was followed by Nina Alexandrovna, Kolya and, last of all, Ippolit.

4. A character in Gogol's novel *Dead Souls*.

I I

It was five days since Ippolit had moved to Ptitsyn's house. This had happened naturally, somehow, without any particular words passing, and with no break of any sort, between him and the prince; far from quarreling, they appeared to part as friends. Gavrila Ardalionovich, who had been so antagonistic to Ippolit on that evening, came to see him himself—although it was three days after the incident—probably guided by some sudden idea. Rogozhin, for some reason, took to visiting the invalid too. It seemed to the prince at first that it would indeed be better for the "poor boy" if he were to move out of his house. But at the time of his move Ippolit had stated that he was going to stay with Ptitsyn, "who was so kind as to give him a corner," and, as though by design, never once stated that he was going to stay with Ganya, though it was Ganya who had insisted on his being received into the house. Ganya noticed it at the time, and it rankled in his heart.

He was right when he told his sister that the invalid was better. Indeed, Ippolit was somewhat better than before, which was evident at the first glance. He came into the room unhurriedly, after everyone else, with a sardonic and malignant smile. Nina Alexandrovna came in very much frightened. (She was greatly changed during the last six months, had grown thinner; having married her daughter off and moved in to live with her, she had almost given up outwardly interfering in her children's affairs.) Kolya was worried and seemed puzzled; there was a great deal he did not understand in the "general's madness," as he put it, being, of course, unaware of the chief reasons of this latest commotion in the house. But it was clear to him that his father was carrying on so much, all the time and everywhere, and had suddenly changed so much that it was as if he had become a completely different person from before. It made him uneasy, too, that the old man had, for the last three days, entirely given up drinking. He knew that his father had fallen out and even quarreled with Lebedev and the prince. Kolya had just returned home with a half-*shtoff* of vodka, which he had obtained at his own expense.

"Really, Mother," he had assured Nina Alexandrovna while still upstairs, "really, it's better to let him drink. It's three days since he touched a drop; he must be feeling wretched. It's really better; I used to take it to him in the debtor's prison, too . . ."

The general flung the door wide open and stood on the threshold, seeming to quiver with indignation.

"My dear sir!" he shouted to Ptitsyn in a thundering voice. "If you have really decided to sacrifice to a milksop and an atheist a venerable old man, your father, that is, at least, the father of your wife, who has served his sovereign, I shall cease to set my foot in your house from this hour. Choose, sir, choose at once: it's either me or that . . . screw! Yes, a screw! I said it without thinking, but he is a screw! for he bores into my soul with a screw, and with no respect whatsoever . . . with a screw!"

"D'you mean a corkscrew,[5] perhaps?" Ippolit put in.

"No, not a corkscrew! For I stand before you a general, not a bottle. I have decorations, the rewards of distinction . . . and you've got nothing but a fig. It's either he or I! Make up your mind sir, at once, at once!" he shouted frantically again to Ptitsyn. Here, Kolya set a chair for him and he sank onto it exhausted.

"You really had better . . . have a nap," muttered Ptitsyn, overwhelmed.

"And he threatens, to boot!" Ganya said to his sister in an undertone.

"Have a nap!" shouted the general. "I am not drunk, dear sir, and you insult me. I see," he went on, getting up again, "I see that everything is against me here, everything and everybody. Enough! I am going . . . But you may be sure, dear sir, you may be sure . . ."

They did not allow him to finish and made him sit down again; began begging him to be calm. Ganya retired into a corner in a fury. Nina Alexandrovna was trembling and weeping.

"But what have I done to him? What's he complaining of?" cried Ippolit, baring his teeth.

"And haven't you done anything?" Nina Alexandrovna observed suddenly. "It's particularly shameful, for you of all people, and . . . inhuman to torment an old man . . . and in your place, too."

---

5. Unlike the English, the Russian word for corkscrew, *shtopor,* has no resemblance of any sort to the word for "screw," *vint.* Neither does the word *vint* carry any of the colloquial or vulgar connotations of the English "screw" (i.e., it is not used to connote swindling or copulating).

"To begin with, what sort of place, madam! I respect you very much, you personally, but . . ."

"He's a screw!" bawled the general. "He bores into my heart and soul! He wants me to believe in atheism! Let me tell you, you milksop, that before you were even born I was already showered with honors. And you're only an envious worm, torn in two with coughing . . . and dying of spite and lack of faith . . . And why did Gavrila bring you here? They're all against me, from strangers down to my own son."

"Oh, leave off, what a tragedy you've made of it!" cried Ganya. "If you didn't put us to shame all over the town, it would be better."

"What, I put you to shame, milksop! You? I can only do you credit, and not discredit you!"

He leapt up, and they could no longer restrain him; but Gavrila Ardalionovich had evidently reached the end of his tether too.

"You talk about honor!" he shouted angrily.

"What did you say?" thundered the general, turning pale and taking a step toward him.

"That I need only open my mouth to . . ." Ganya howled suddenly, and broke off. They stood facing one another, shocked beyond measure, especially Ganya.

"Ganya, what are you doing!" cried Nina Alexandrovna, rushing to restrain her son.

"Such rubbish, on everyone's part," Varya snapped out in indignation. "That's enough, Mother." She took hold of her.

"It's only for Mother's sake I spare him," Ganya brought out with a tragic air.

"Speak!" roared the general in a perfect frenzy. "Speak on pain of your father's curse! . . . Speak!"

"As though I were frightened of your curse! And whose fault is it that you've been like a madman for the last eight days? Eight days, you see I know the dates . . . Mind you don't drive me too far. I'll tell everything . . . What did you go dragging yourself off to the Epanchins' for yesterday? And you call yourself an old man, gray-haired, the father of a family! A fine specimen!"

"Shut up, Ganjka!" shouted Kolya. "Shut up, you fool!"

"But how have I, how have I insulted him?" Ippolit persisted, but still seemingly in the same jeering tone. "Why does he call me a screw, you heard him? He came pestering me himself; he came just now, talking of some Captain Yeropegov. I don't desire your company at all, General; I've always avoided it before, as you know yourself. What business of mine is Captain Yeropegov, you will admit yourself. I didn't come here for the sake of Captain Yeropegov. I simply expressed aloud to him my opinion that this Captain Yeropegov may possibly never have existed. And then he raised the devil."

"Without a doubt, he never existed!" Ganya rapped out.

But the general stood looking as though stupefied, and gazed blankly about him. His son's words had shocked him by their extraordinary openness. In the first instant he could not even find words. And at last, only when Ippolit burst out laughing at Ganya's response and cried out: "There, did you hear, your own son, too, says there was no such person as Captain Yeropegov," the old man mumbled, thrown completely off his stride:

"Kapiton Yeropegov, and not Captain . . . Kapiton . . . the retired Lieutenant-Colonel Yeropegov . . . Kapiton."

"And there was never a Kapiton, either!" cried Ganya, thoroughly exasperated.

"Wh-why . . . why wasn't there?" muttered the general, and the color rushed to his face.

"But that's enough now!" Ptitsyn and Varya tried to subdue them.

"Hold your tongue, Ganjka!" Kolya shouted again.

But this interceding seemed to rouse the general to himself, too.

"How can you say there wasn't? Why didn't he exist?" he flew out menacingly at his son.

"Just because there wasn't. There wasn't and that's all, and there couldn't be! So there. Leave me alone, I tell you."

"And this is my son . . . my own son, whom I . . . Oh, heavens! . . . No such person as Yeropegov, Yeroshka Yeropegov!"

"Well there you are, first he's Yeroshka, then Kapitoshka!" Ippolit stuck in.

"Kapitoshka, sir, Kapitoshka, not Yeroshka! Kapiton, Captain Alexeevich, I mean, Kapiton . . . Lieutenant-Colonel . . . retired . . . he was married to Marya . . . to Marya Petrovna Su . . . Su . . . a friend and comrade . . . Sutogov . . . from the time of the cadets. For his sake I shed . . . I shielded . . . he was killed. No such person as Kapitoshka Yeropegov! No such person!"

The general shouted in a passion, but in such a way that one might think that the heart of the matter was about one thing, while the shouting was about quite another. Truth be told, at another time he would have put up with something far more insulting than the news of Kapiton Yeropegov's absolute nonexistence; he would have shouted, made a fuss, been beside himself, but yet, when all was said and done, he would have retired upstairs to bed. But now, such is the extraordinary strangeness of the human heart, it happened that precisely such an insult as the doubt about Yeropegov was fated to fill his cup to overflowing. The old man turned crimson, raised his arms and shouted:

"Enough! My curse! . . . Out of this house! Nikolai, bring me my bag . . . I am going . . . away from here!"

He went out in haste and extreme wrath. Nina Alexandrovna, Kolya and Ptitsyn rushed after him.

"Well, what have you done now!" Varya said to her brother. "He'll be off there again, perhaps. The disgrace of it, the disgrace!"

"He shouldn't steal," cried Ganya, almost choking with rage; suddenly his eyes met Ippolit's; Ganya practically shook. "As for you, sir," he shouted, "you ought to remember that you're in another person's house, after all, and . . . enjoying his hospitality, and not to irritate an old man who has obviously gone out of his mind . . ."

A shudder seemed to go through Ippolit too, but he instantly controlled himself.

"I don't quite agree with you that your papa has gone out of his mind," he answered calmly, "on the contrary, it seems to me that he has even acquired more sense of late, upon my word; you don't believe it? He has become so cautious, suspicious, keeps prying into everything, weighs every word . . . Why, he began talking to me about that Kapitoshka with an object, you know: only fancy, he wanted to lead me on to . . ."

"Aie, what the devil do I care what he wanted to lead you on to! I beg you not to try your shifty tricks and dodges on me, sir!" shrieked Ganya. "If you, too, know the real cause why the old man is in such a state (you've been spying here so much these five days that you certainly know) you ought not to have irritated . . . the unhappy man, and tormented my mother by exaggerating the matter; for it's all nonsense, simply a drunken story, nothing more, proved by nothing, and I give it as much credence as my little finger ... But you must sting and spy because you ... you are ..."

"A screw!" smirked Ippolit.

"Because you are scum, worrying people for half an hour, thinking to frighten them by shooting yourself with your unloaded pistol, with which you made such a shamefully cowardly display, you feckless suicide, you walking ... puddle of bile. I gave you hospitality, you've grown fat, you've left off coughing, and you repay it ..."

"Allow me, two words only, sir; I am in Varvara Ardalionovna's house, not yours; you have not given me any hospitality, and I believe, indeed, that you yourself are enjoying the hospitality of Mr. Ptitsyn. Four days ago I asked my mother to find an apartment for me in Pavlovsk and to move here herself because I do, in fact, feel better here, though I have not grown fat at all and am still coughing. Mother informed me yesterday evening that the apartment was ready, and I hasten to inform you on my side that, thanking your mother and sister, I will move to my own lodgings this very day, which I had already decided last night. Excuse me, I interrupted you; I believe you wanted to say a great deal more."

"Oh, if that's so ..." quivered Ganya.

"And if that's so, then allow me to sit down," added Ippolit, seating himself with perfect composure in the chair where the general had been sitting. "After all, I am ill, you know; well, now I'm ready to listen to you, especially as this is our last conversation, and perhaps indeed our last meeting."

Ganya suddenly felt ashamed.

"You may be sure I won't stoop to settling accounts with you," said he, "and if you ..."

"You need not be so lofty," interrupted Ippolit, "for my part, on the very first day of my coming here, I vowed I would not deny myself the pleasure of laying it all on the line for you, and in the most candid manner, when we came to part. I intend to carry this out now, but after you, of course."

"I beg you to leave this room."

"You'd better speak, you'll regret not having spoken out, you know."

"Stop it, Ippolit, it's all so terribly shameful; do me the favor and stop it!" said Varya.

"Only to oblige a lady," laughed Ippolit, getting up. "If you please, Varvara Ardalionovna, for you I am ready to cut it short, but only to cut it short, for some explanation between myself and your dear brother has become absolutely essential, and not for anything would I resolve to go away leaving a misunderstanding."

"In plain words, you're a scandalmonger," screamed Ganya, "and so you can't resolve to go away without a scandal."

"There, you see," Ippolit observed coolly, "you've lost your restraint already. Truly, you will regret not speaking out. Once more I cede the floor to you. I shall wait."

Gavrila Ardalionovich kept silent and looked at him contemptuously.

"You won't speak. You mean to keep up your part—please yourself. On my side, I will be as brief as possible. Two or three times today I have heard the reproach about hospitality; that's unfair. By inviting me to stay with you, you tried to catch me in your trap yourself; you reckoned I would want to take revenge on the prince. You heard, besides, that Aglaia Ivanovna had shown interest in me and read my confession. Reckoning for some reason that I would simply give myself entirely over to your interests, you hoped that you might get help from me. I won't explain more in detail! And from your side, I demand neither admission nor confirmation; it's enough that I leave you to your conscience, and that now we thoroughly understand each other."

"But goodness knows what you make out of the most ordinary things!" cried Varya.

"I told you: he's a scandalmonger and a nasty boy," said Ganya.

"Allow me, Varvara Ardalionovna, I'll go on. The prince, of course, I can neither like nor respect; but he is certainly a kind man, though ... rather ridiculous. But I've certainly no reason to hate him; I didn't let on to your brother when he was egging me on against the prince; I was precisely counting on having a laugh at him at our parting. I knew that your brother would spill it all to me and make the greatest possible blunder. And so it has turned out ... I am ready to spare him now, but only out of respect for you, Varvara Ardalionovna. But having made clear to you that it is not so easy to hook me on the line, I'll also make it clear why I was so anxious to make your brother look a fool. You must know that I did it out of hatred, I confess it openly. When I die (for I will die after all, even if I have grown fatter as you assert), when I die, I feel I shall go to paradise with my heart incomparably more at ease if I succeed in making a fool of at least one representative of that innumerable class of people who have persecuted me all my life, whom I have hated all my life, and of which your excellent brother serves as such a vivid illustration. I hate you, Gavrila Ardalionovich, simply because of that—this will perhaps seem amazing to you—*simply because* you are the type and the embodiment, the personification and pinnacle of the most insolent and self-satisfied, the most vulgar and loathsome commonplaceness! You are a pompous commonplace, a cocksure commonplace of Olympian serenity; you are the most routine of all routines! Not the smallest idea of your own is fated to be conceived, neither in your mind nor in your heart—ever. But you are infinitely envious; you are firmly convinced that you are the greatest genius; but yet doubt does visit you sometimes at black moments, and you grow spiteful and envious. Oh, there are still black spots on your horizon; they will pass when you become entirely stupid, and that's not too far off; but still, a long and checkered path lies before you, I don't say it's a cheerful one and I'm glad of it. In the first place, I foretell that you will not attain a certain person known to us . . ."

"Oh, this is unbearable!" cried Varya. "Will you leave off, you horrid, spiteful creature?"

Ganya turned white, quivered and kept silent. Ippolit stopped, looked intently and with relish at him, turned his eyes to Varya, smirked, bowed, and went out, without adding another word.

Gavrila Ardalionovich might with justice have complained of his fate and his misfortune. For some time Varya did not venture to speak to him, she did not even glance at him as he paced to and fro before her with long strides; at last he walked away to the window and stood with his back to her. Varya thought of the Russian proverb: "A stick has two ends."[6] A noise began again overhead.

"Are you going?" Ganya turned to her suddenly, hearing that she got up from her seat. "Wait a bit; take a look at this."

He went up and threw on the chair before her a little piece of paper folded into the shape of a tiny note.

---

6. I.e., there's no telling whether something will come out well or badly.

"Good heavens!" cried Varya, throwing up her hands.

There were just seven lines in the note:

Gavrila Ardalionovich! As I am convinced that you are well-disposed toward me, I venture to ask your advice in one matter of great importance to me. I should like to meet you tomorrow, at exactly seven o'clock in the morning, at the green bench. It's not far from our dacha. Varvara Ardalionovna, who must accompany you *without fail*, knows the place very well.

A.E.

"Well, go and reckon with her after that!" Varvara Ardalionovna flung up her hands.

Little as Ganya was inclined to swagger at that moment, he could not help showing his triumph, especially after Ippolit's humiliating predictions. A self-satisfied smile openly lit up his face, and Varya, too, beamed all over with delight.

"And that on the very day when her betrothal is to be announced! Well, go and reckon with her after that!"

"What do you think, what does she mean to speak about tomorrow?" asked Ganya.

"That doesn't matter, the main thing is that she wants to see you for the first time after six months. Now listen to me, Ganya: whatever happens there, whatever turn it takes, keep in mind that it's *important*! Don't swagger again, don't make another blunder, but don't be fainthearted either, mind that! Could she have not caught on to why I've been trudging off there for the last six months? And fancy: she didn't say a word to me today, she made no sign. I went in to see them on the sly, you know. The old woman did not know I was there, or maybe she'd have turned me out. I took a risk to go there for your sake, to find out at all costs . . ."

Again there was shouting and uproar overhead; several persons were coming downstairs.

"This mustn't be allowed now on any account!" cried Varya in haste and alarm. "There must not be a shadow of scandal now! Go, ask his forgiveness!"

But the head of the family was already in the street. Kolya was dragging his bag after him. Nina Alexandrovna was standing on the steps and crying; she would have run after him, but Ptitsyn held her back.

"You only egg him on all the more with that," he said to her. "He has nowhere to go, in half an hour they'll bring him back again, I've spoken to Kolya already; let him play the fool."

"Why these heroics? Where can you go?" Ganya shouted from the window. "You've nowhere to go!"

"Come back, Father!" cried Varya. "The neighbors will hear."

The general stopped, turned around, stretched out his hand, and exclaimed:

"My curse on this house!"

"He must take that theatrical tone!" muttered Ganya, closing the window with a bang.

The neighbors certainly were listening. Varya ran out of the room.

When Varya had gone out, Ganya took the note from the table, kissed it, clicked his tongue and kicked up his heels.

III

At any other time, the hubbub with the general would never have come to anything. Instances of sudden whims in that same vein had happened to him before, too, though rather rarely; for, generally speaking, he was a very docile man, with almost kindly tendencies. A hundred times perhaps he had struggled against the disorder that had gained mastery over him of late years. He used suddenly to remember that he was "the head of the family," would make it up with his wife and shed genuine tears. He respected Nina Alexandrovna to the point of adoring her for having forgiven him so much in silence, and for loving him, even in his grotesque and humiliating state. But his noble-hearted struggle with disorder did not usually last long; the general, too, was an overly "impulsive" man, though in his own peculiar fashion; he normally could not stand the penitent and futile life he led in his family and ended in revolt; he flew into a paroxysm of excitement, for which perhaps he was inwardly reproaching himself at the very moment, though he could not restrain himself: he quarreled, began talking pompously and rhetorically, demanded to be treated with immeasurable and impossible respect and finally would disappear from the house, sometimes even for a long time. For the last two years, he knew of his family's affairs only generally and from hearsay; he had given up going into them in more detail, feeling not the slightest impulse to do so.

But this time, there was something extraordinary in the "hubbub with the general": everyone seemed to be aware of something, and everyone seemed afraid to speak of it. The general had "formally" presented himself to his family, that is to Nina Alexandrovna, only three days before, but not humble and penitent as on all previous "reappearances," but on the contrary—with extraordinary irritability. He was loquacious, restless, eagerly started conversations with everyone he came across, virtually hurling himself at a person, as it were, but always about such varied and unexpected subjects that it was impossible to get to the bottom of what it was, per se, that worried him so much now. At moments he was cheerful, but more often he was sunk in thought, not knowing himself, however, about what in particular; he would suddenly begin to tell some story—about the Epanchins, about the prince and Lebedev—and then he would suddenly break off and cease speaking altogether, and only responded to further questions with a vacant smile, and actually, without even being aware that he was being questioned or that he was smiling. He had spent the previous night moaning and groaning and had exhausted Nina Alexandrovna, who had for some reason been up all night warming up hot compresses for him; toward morning, he had suddenly fallen asleep, slept four hours and woke up with a most violent and disorderly attack of hypochondria, which ended, indeed, in the quarrel with Ippolit and the "curse on this house." They noticed, too, that for those three days he was continually overcome by the most violently vainglorious ambition and, as a consequence of it, by an extraordinary readiness to take offense. Kolya insisted, assuring his mother, that this was all due to a craving for drink, and perhaps for Lebedev, with whom the general had become extraordinarily friendly of late. But three days before he had suddenly quarreled with Lebedev, and had parted from him in a terrible fury; there had even been some sort of a scene with the prince. Kolya begged the prince for an explanation, and began at last to suspect that he too, apparently, did not want to tell him something or other. If there had been, as Ganya supposed with complete likelihood, some special conversation between Ippolit and Nina Alexandrovna, it was strange that this spiteful gentleman, whom Ganya had so openly called a scandalmonger, had not found pleasure in apprising Kolya in much the same way. It is very possible that he was not such a malicious and nasty "puppy" as Ganya had sketched him out to be in speaking to his sister, but was malicious in some different way; and it's unlikely that he related some observation of his to Nina Alexandrovna simply in order "to break her heart." Don't let us forget that the causes of human actions are usually immeasurably more complex and varied than we always subsequently explain them, and are rarely distinctly defined. It's best sometimes for the storyteller to confine himself to a simple narration of the events. And that's how we shall proceed in the further explication of the present catastrophe with the general; for, struggle as we might, we find ourselves faced with the absolute necessity of giving this secondary personage in our narrative somewhat more space and attention than we have hitherto proposed.

These events had succeeded one another in the following order.

When, after his trip to Petersburg to look for Ferdyshchenko, Lebedev returned on the very same day, together with the general, he told the prince nothing in particular. If the prince had not been at the time too preoccupied and busy with other impressions of great importance to him, he might soon have noticed that during the two following days, too, Lebedev not only did not present him with any clarification but indeed, on the contrary, seemed, for some reason, to be trying to avoid meeting him. Taking note of this at last, the prince was surprised that during those two days, upon his chance encounters with Lebedev, he could not recollect him in any but the most radiant spirits, and almost always in company with the general. The two friends were never apart for a moment. The prince sometimes heard loud and rapid talk and merry, laughing dispute, which carried to him from above; once, very late at night, there was even a sudden and unexpected burst of a martial and bacchanalian song that carried down to him, and he recognized at once the husky bass of the general. But the song did not come off and ceased suddenly before the end. Then, for about another hour, there went on an extremely animated and, from all signs, drunken conversation. It might be surmised that the merrymaking friends upstairs were embracing and that one of them finally began to weep. Then, suddenly, there ensued a violent quarrel, which also ceased suddenly soon after. All this time Kolya was in some sort of particularly preoccupied frame of mind. The prince was for the most part not at home, and returned to his rooms very late sometimes; he was always told that Kolya had been looking for him all day, and asking for him. But when they met, Kolya could tell him nothing special except that he was decidedly "dissatisfied" with the general and his present conduct: "They tramp about and get drunk in a tavern close by, embrace one another and bicker in the street; they egg each other on and can't be parted." When the prince observed to him that it had been just the same almost every day before, Kolya positively did not know what to say in reply and how to explain wherein, precisely, his present uneasiness consisted.

The morning after the bacchic song and quarrel, when the prince was leaving the house about eleven o'clock, the general suddenly appeared before him, extremely excited by something, almost overwhelmed.

"I've long been seeking the honor and opportunity of seeing you, honored Lev Nikolaevich, very long," he muttered, squeezing the prince's hand very tightly, almost painfully. "A very, very long time."

The prince asked him to sit down.

"No, I won't sit down. Besides, I'm keeping you, I'll come another time. I believe I may take the opportunity of congratulating you on . . . the fulfillment . . . of your heart's desire."

"What heart's desire?"

The prince was disconcerted. Like many people in his position, he fancied that absolutely nobody saw, guessed or understood anything.

"Rest easy, rest easy! I will not upset your most delicate feelings. I have experienced it myself and I know what it is when another man pokes . . . so to speak, his nose . . . as the saying goes . . . crashes in where he isn't wanted. I experience that every morning. I have come about another matter, an important one. A very important matter, Prince."

The prince once more asked him to be seated and sat down himself.

"If only for one second . . . I have come to ask advice. I, of course, lead a life without any practical aims, but as I respect myself and . . . the practical nature in which the Russian man is so deficient, generally speaking . . . I wish to place myself and my wife and my children in a position . . . In a word, Prince, I seek advice."

The prince warmly applauded his intention.

"Well, that's all rubbish," the general quickly interrupted, "that's not what I want to say, but something else, something important. And namely, I have resolved to explain to you, Lev Nikolaevich, as a man in the sincerity of whose welcome and the nobility of whose feelings I have complete confidence, as . . . as . . . You are not surprised at my words, Prince?"

The prince observed his visitor if not with particular surprise then with extreme attention and curiosity. The old man was rather pale, his lips quivered slightly at times, his hands seemed unable to find a resting place. He remained seated only for a few minutes, and had already twice managed to get up from his chair for some reason and suddenly sit down again, obviously not paying the slightest attention to his maneuvers. There were books lying on the table; he took up one and, still talking, glanced at the opened page, shut it again at once and, laid it back on the table, snatched up another book, which he did not open, and instead held it the whole rest of the time in his right hand, waving it continually in the air.

"Enough!" he shouted suddenly. "I see that I have been greatly disturbing you."

"Why, not in the least, pray, be so good, on the contrary, I'm listening carefully and anxious to make out . . ."

"Prince! I am anxious to place myself in a respectable position . . . I am anxious to respect myself and . . . my rights."

"A man with such desires is deserving of every respect on that ground alone."

The prince brought out his copybook phrase in the firm conviction that it would produce an excellent effect. He guessed somehow instinctively that with some hollow but agreeable phrase of this sort, uttered at the right moment, one might at once conquer and appease the soul of such a man, and especially in such a position, as the general. In any case, it was necessary to send such a visitor away with a lighter heart, and that was the problem.

The phrase flattered, touched and greatly pleased: the general suddenly melted, instantly changed his tone, and launched into a long, ecstatic explanation. But however the prince may have strained, however intently he listened, he could make literally nothing of it. The general talked for ten minutes, heatedly, rapidly, as though he could not manage to express his crowding thoughts quickly enough; tears even shone in his eyes toward the end, but all the same, it was nothing but phrases without beginning or end, unexpected words and unexpected ideas, bursting out rapidly and unexpectedly and stumbling over one another.

"Enough! You have understood me, and I am at ease," he concluded, suddenly getting up. "A heart such as yours cannot fail to understand a suffering man. Prince, you are honorable as an ideal! What are other men beside you? But you are young and I bless you. When all is said and done, I came to ask you to appoint an hour for an important conversation with me, and therein lies my chief hope. I seek only friendship and heart, Prince; I have never been able to come to grips with the demands of my heart."

"But why not now? I am ready to listen . . ."

"No, Prince, no!" the general interrupted hotly. "Not now! Now is a vain dream! It is too, too important, too important! The hour of that conversation will be an hour of irrevocable destiny. That will be *my* hour, and I should not wish it to be possible for us to be interrupted at such a sacred moment by the first chance comer, the first impudent fellow, and such an impudent fellow is not rare." He bent down suddenly to the prince, with a strange, mysterious and almost frightened whisper. "Such an impudent fellow as is not worthy of the heel . . . of your shoe, beloved prince! Oh, I don't say: of my shoe. Note particularly that I make no mention of my own shoe; for I have too much self-respect to say that straight out; but you alone are able to understand that by repudiating my heel in such a case I demonstrate perhaps the utmost pride of dignity. Except you, no one else will understand it, *he* least of all. *He* understands nothing, Prince; he is utterly, utterly incapable of understanding! One must have a heart to understand!"

Toward the end, the prince was almost alarmed and made an appointment with the general for the same hour next day. The latter went out with a confident air, extremely comforted, and almost put at ease. In the evening, between six and seven, the prince sent to ask Lebedev to come to him for a minute.

Lebedev made his appearance with extraordinary alacrity, "esteemed it an honor," as he began at once on entering; there seemed to be not even the shadow of a hint that he'd been practically in hiding for the last three days, and was obviously trying to avoid meeting the prince. He sat down on the edge of the chair, with smiles and grimaces, with laughing and watchful little eyes, rubbing his hands and assuming an air of the most naive expectation of hearing something along the lines of some major communication, long expected and guessed by everyone. The prince chafed again: it was becoming clear to him that everyone had suddenly begun to expect something of him, that everyone looked at him as though wanting to congratulate him on something, with hints, smiles, and winks. Keller had run in for a minute two or three times already, also with an air of wanting to congratulate him; each time he began vaguely and delightedly, did not finish anything, and quickly made himself scarce again. (He had taken to drinking particularly heavily somewhere of late, and was making a sensation in some billiard room.) Even Kolya, in spite of his sadness, had also attempted, once or twice, to take up some vague subject with the prince.

The prince asked Lebedev directly and somewhat irritably what he thought of the general's present state, and why the latter seemed so anxious. In a few words he told him of the scene that morning.

"Everyone has his own anxieties, Prince . . . and . . . especially in our strange and anxious age, sir, so it is, sir," Lebedev answered with a certain dryness, and relapsed into offended silence, with the air of a man deeply deceived in his expectations.

"What philosophy!" chuckled the prince.

"Philosophy would be useful, sir, very useful in our age in its practical application, but it's despised, sir, that's how it is, sir. For my part, honored prince, though I have been honored by your confidence in me on a certain point you know of, sir, yet only to a certain degree, and no further than circumstances relating to one point in particular . . . that I understand, and I don't in the least complain."

"Lebedev, you seem to be angry about something?"

"Not at all, not in the least, honored and resplendent prince, not in the least!" Lebedev cried ecstatically, laying his hand upon his heart. "On the contrary, I precisely realized at once that, neither by my position in the world, nor by the qualities of my mind or my heart, not the amount of my fortune, nor my former behavior, nor my knowledge—in no way do I deserve the confidence with which you honor me, so far above my hopes, and that if I can serve you, it is only as a slave and hireling, and not otherwise . . . I am not angry, but I am sad, sir."

"Come, come, Lukyan Timofeich!"

"Not otherwise! So it is in the present case! Meeting you and attending to you with my heart and my thoughts, I said to myself: 'I am unworthy of friendly confidences, but as the landlord of your house perhaps I may receive at the fitting time, before the anticipated event, so to speak, an indication, or at least some notice, in view of certain changes expected in the future ...' "

As he uttered this, Lebedev positively fastened his sharp little eyes on the prince, who was looking at him in astonishment; he was still in hopes of satisfying his curiosity.

"I absolutely don't understand a word!" cried the prince, almost with anger, "and ... you're an awful intrigant!" He suddenly broke into a most genuine laugh.

Instantly, Lebedev laughed too, and his beaming face showed clearly that his hopes were confirmed, and even redoubled.

"And do you know what I'll tell you, Lukyan Timofeich? Only don't be angry with me, but I wonder at your naïveté, and not only yours! You are expecting something of me with such naïveté now, at this very moment, that I feel positively ashamed and conscience-stricken at having nothing to satisfy you with; but I swear that I have absolutely nothing. Can you fancy that?"

The prince laughed again.

Lebedev put on a dignified air. It was true that he was sometimes too naïve and persistently intrusive in his curiosity; but at the same time he was a rather cunning and wily man, and in some cases even too insidiously silent; the prince had almost made an enemy of him by continually putting him off. But the prince put him off not because he despised him, but because the subject of his curiosity was a delicate one. The prince had only a few days before looked on some of his own dreams as a crime, while Lukyan Timofeich took the prince's rebuffs simply as proof of an aversion and mistrust to himself personally, would withdraw with a rankled heart and feel jealous not only of Kolya and Keller, but even of his own daughter, Vera Lukyanovna. Even at that very moment, perhaps, he could have told, and genuinely wanted to tell, the prince a piece of news of the greatest interest to the prince, but he fell silent gloomily and did not tell him.

"How, in particular, can I be of use to you, honored prince, since, after all, you did ... call me just now," he said at last after some silence.

"Why, in particular, it was about the general," the prince, who had been musing for a moment too, answered hurriedly, "and ... in regard to that theft of yours that you told me about ..."

"In regard to what, sir?"

"Well, really, as though you don't understand me now! Oh, good Lord, Lukyan Timofeich, you're always acting a part! The money, the money, the four hundred rubles you lost that day in your wallet, and about which you came to tell me in the morning, as you were setting off for Petersburg—do you understand at last?"

"Ah, you're talking about that four hundred rubles?" drawled Lebedev, as though he had only just figured it out. "I thank you, Prince, for your sincere interest; it's too flattering to me, but . . . I've found it, sir, and some time since."

"Found it! Ah, thank God!"

"That exclamation is most generous on your part, for four hundred rubles is truly no insignificant matter for a poor man who lives by his hard work, with a large family of motherless children . . ."

"But I didn't mean that! Of course, I am also glad that you found the money," the prince corrected himself quickly, "but . . . how did you find it?"

"Very simply, sir. I found it under the chair on which my coat had been hung, so that, evidently, the wallet had slipped out of the pocket onto the floor!"

"How, under a chair? It's impossible! Why, you told me yourself you had searched thoroughly in every corner; how did you overlook it in this most important place, then?"

"That's just the thing, I did look, sir! I remember only too, too well how I looked, sir! I crawled on all fours, felt the place with my hands, moving back the chair and not trusting my own eyes: and I saw there was nothing there, for the place was as smooth and empty as the palm of my hand, sir, and yet I went on feeling for it. Such weakness, sir, will happen again and again to a man when he is very anxious to find anything . . . in the face of significant and tragic losses, sir: he sees there's nothing there, the place is empty, and yet he peeps into it a dozen times anyway."

"Yes, I grant you that; only, how is this, all the same? . . . I still don't understand," muttered the prince, befuddled. "Before, you said it wasn't there, and you had looked in that place, and then it suddenly turned up!"

"And then it suddenly turned up, sir."

The prince looked strangely at Lebedev.

"And the general?" he asked suddenly.

"How do you mean, sir, the general, sir? . . ." Lebedev was a loss again.

"Oh, good Lord! I'm asking you what the general said when you found the wallet under the chair? Why, you did look for it together, didn't you?"

"We did look together before, sir. But this time, I confess, I held my tongue, sir, and preferred not to inform him that the wallet had been found by me, alone."

"But . . . why, then? . . . And was the money all there?"

"I opened the wallet; the money was all there, down to the last ruble, sir."

"You might have come to tell me, at least," the prince observed thoughtfully.

"I was afraid to disturb you personally, Prince, in view of your personal and perhaps, so to speak, extraordinary experiences; and besides, I myself made as though I had found nothing. I opened the wallet and examined it, then I shut it and put it back under the chair."

"But what for?"

"Oh, n-nothing; out of further curiosity, sir," Lebedev suddenly giggled, rubbing his hands.

"Then it is still lying there now, since the day before yesterday?"

"Oh, no, sir; it only lay there for a day and a night. You see, it was partly that I wanted the general to find it, sir. For, after all, since I had found it, then why should the general, too, not notice the object, which caught the eye, so to speak, poking out from under the chair. I lifted that chair several times and moved it so that the wallet was completely in view, but the general simply didn't notice it, and so it went on for twenty-four hours. He is, evidently, rather absentminded now, and there's no making him out; he talks, tells stories, chuckles, roars with laughter, and then suddenly becomes terribly angry with me, I don't know why, sir. At last, as we were going out of the room, I left the door open on purpose; he did hesitate, would have said something, most likely he was alarmed about the wallet with such a sum of money in it, but grew terribly angry and said nothing, so it is, sir; before we had gone two steps in the street, he left me and walked away in the other direction. We only met in the evening in the tavern."

"But, finally, you did, after all, take the wallet from under the chair?"

"No, sir; it vanished from under the chair that same night, sir."

"Then where is it now?"

"Oh, here, sir." Lebedev laughed suddenly, rising from the chair to his full height and looking amiably at the prince. "It suddenly turned up here, in the flap of my coat. Here, have a look yourself, if you please, feel about."

Indeed, in the left flap of the coat, right in the front, in plain view, a whole pouch had virtually been formed and it was clear at once to the touch that there was a leather wallet there that had fallen in from a torn pocket.

"I took it out and looked, sir, it's all there. I dropped it in again, and so I've been walking about since yesterday morning, carrying it about in the flap, and it even knocks against my legs."

"And you take no notice of it?"

"And I take no notice of it, sir, he-he! And would you believe it, most honored prince, though the subject is not worthy of such particular attention on your part, my pockets were always as whole as they could be, and here, suddenly, in one night, a hole like that! I began to look at it more curiously; it's as though someone had cut it with a penknife; almost incredible, isn't it, sir?"

"And . . . the general?"

"Fumed all day; both yesterday and today; fearfully displeased, sir; first he's overjoyed and downright bacchic, so that he even fawns, then he's sentimental even to tears, and then he suddenly grows angry, and so much so that I'd become scared, indeed, sir, upon my word, sir; after all, Prince, I'm not a military man, no sir. We were sitting yesterday in the tavern, and the flap of my coat stood right out to view as though by chance, a perfect mountain; he looked askance at it, fumed. He hasn't looked me straight in the face for a long time now, sir, unless perhaps he's very drunk or sentimental; but yesterday he looked at me once or twice in such a way that it simply sent a chill down my spine. Anyway, tomorrow, I mean to find the wallet, but I shall have another night out with him before tomorrow yet."

"Why are you tormenting him so?" cried the prince.

"I'm not tormenting him, Prince, I'm not tormenting him," Lebedev took up with warmth. "I sincerely love him, sir, and . . . respect him, yes, sir; and now, believe it or not, he's become dearer to me than ever, yes, sir. I have come to appreciate him even more, sir!"

Lebedev said all this so earnestly and sincerely that the prince was positively indignant.

"You love him and you torment him like this! Pray, but alone by the fact that he placed the lost object so clearly in your view, under the chair and in your coat, just by that alone, he plainly shows you that he doesn't want to play at deception with you, but simple-heartedly asks your forgiveness. Do you hear? He's asking your forgiveness! So it must be he's relying on the delicacy of your feelings, so it must be he believes in your friendship for him. And yet you reduce such a man . . . a most honest man . . . to such humiliation!"

"Most honest, Prince, most honest!" Lebedev took up, with a gleam in his eyes. "And only you, most noble prince, you particularly, are capable of saying such a just word! For that, I am devoted to you and ready to worship you, sir, though I am rotten to the core with vices of all sorts! That settles it! I will find the wallet now, at once, and not tomorrow; here, I take it out before your eyes, sir; here it is; and here's the money, untouched; here, take it, most noble prince, take it and keep it till tomorrow. Tomorrow or next day I'll take it, sir; and, do you know, Prince, it's evident that it must have been lying somewhere in my garden, hidden under some stone, the first night it was lost, sir; what do you think?"

"Mind, you don't tell him directly to his face that you've found the wallet. Let him quite simply see that there's nothing in the flap of your coat anymore, and he'll understand."

"You think so, sir? Wouldn't it be better to tell him I have found it, sir, and to pretend I had not guessed about it till now?"

"N-no," the prince pondered, "n-no; it's too late now; that's more risky; truly, you'd better not speak of it! And be kind to him, but . . . don't pretend too much, and . . . and . . . you know . . ."

"I know, Prince, I know. That is, I know that I shan't do it properly, perhaps; for one needs to have a heart like yours to do it. Besides, he's irritable and prone to it himself, he has begun to treat me now too haughtily sometimes; one minute he is whimpering and embracing me, and then he'll suddenly begin to demean me, and sneer at me contemptuously; well, and then I just go and stick the flap out at him on purpose, he-he! Good-bye, Prince; for it's clear I'm keeping you and interrupting you in your most interesting feelings, so to speak . . ."

"But for goodness' sake, the same secrecy as before!"

"Treading softly, sir, treading softly!"

But, though the matter was settled, still the prince remained concerned, almost more than ever. He awaited with impatience his meeting with the general next day.

I V

The hour fixed was shortly after eleven, but the prince was quite unexpectedly late. On his return home he found the general waiting. From the first glance, he noticed that the latter was displeased, and, perhaps, precisely with the fact that he had had to wait. Apologizing, the prince made haste to sit down, but he felt strangely timid, as though his guest were made of porcelain and he were continually afraid of breaking him. He had never felt timid with the general before; it had never entered his head to feel timid. The prince soon perceived that he was a completely different person from what he had been yesterday: instead of discomfiture and distraction, some sort of extraordinary reserve was evident; it might be surmised that this was a man who had irrevocably resolved to do something. His composure was, however, more apparent than real. But in any case the visitor displayed a gentlemanly ease of manner, though with reserved dignity; at first, he even treated the prince as if with a certain air of condescension— precisely the way that some proud people who have been unfairly insulted will sometimes behave with gentlemanly ease. He spoke affably, though not without a certain aggrieved intonation.

"Your book, which I borrowed from you the other day," he nodded significantly at a book he had brought, which was lying on the table. "I thank you."

"Oh, yes; have you read that article, General? How did you like it? It's interesting, isn't it?" The prince was delighted at the chance of quickly starting the conversation off on the most extraneous possible subject.

"Interesting, perhaps, but crude and of course absurd. Probably also a lie at every turn."

The general spoke with aplomb, and even drew out his words a little.

"Ah, it's such a simple-hearted account; the account of an old soldier who was an eyewitness to the arrival of the French in Moscow;

some things in it are charming. Besides, any eyewitness memoir is precious, whoever the eyewitness may be. Don't you think?"

"I would not have printed it in the editor's place; as for the memoirs of eyewitnesses in general, people are more ready to believe a crude but amusing liar than a man of worth who has seen service. I know some memoirs about the year 1812 that . . . I've made a decision, Prince, I am leaving this house—the house of Mr. Lebedev."

The general looked significantly at the prince.

"You have your own rooms at Pavlovsk at . . . at your daughter's . . ." said the prince, not knowing what to say. He remembered that the general had, after all, come to ask his advice about an urgent matter, on which his fate depended.

"At my wife's; in other words, at home and in my daughter's house."

"I beg your pardon, I . . ."

"I am leaving Lebedev's house because, dear prince, because I have broken with that man; I broke with him yesterday evening and regret I did not do so before. I insist on respect, Prince, and I wish to receive it even from those persons upon whom I bestow, so to speak, my heart. Prince, I often bestow my heart, and I am almost always deceived. That man was not worthy of my gift."

"There's a great deal of haphazardness in him," the prince observed guardedly, "and some traits . . . but in the midst of it all one can perceive a heart, a sly and sometimes amusing intelligence."

The nicety of the expressions and the respectful tone evidently flattered the general, though he still glanced at the prince sometimes with sudden mistrustfulness. But the prince's tone was so natural and sincere that it was impossible to doubt him.

"That he has good qualities," the general took up, "I was the first to declare, when I almost bestowed my friendship on that individual. I have no need of his house and his hospitality, having a family of my own. I do not justify my failings; I am intemperate; I have drunk wine with him, and now perhaps I am weeping for it. But it was not for the sake of the drink alone (excuse, Prince, the coarseness of candor in an irritated man), it was not for the sake of the drink alone I became friendly with him, was it? What allured me was just, as you say, his qualities. But everything only up to a certain point, even his qualities; and if he suddenly has the impudence to declare to one's face that in 1812, when he was still a little child, he lost his left leg, and buried it in the Vagankovsky cemetery in Moscow, he is going beyond the limit, evidencing disrespect and showing impertinence..."

"Perhaps it was only a joke to raise a laugh."

"I understand, sir. An innocent lie to raise a laugh, however crude, does not wound a human heart. One man will tell a lie, if you like, simply from friendship, to give pleasure to his companion; but if a trace of disrespect comes through, if, perhaps, precisely by such disrespect one means to show that one is weary of the association, there's nothing left for a man of honor but to turn away and break off the association, putting the offender in his proper place."

The general positively flushed as he spoke.

"But Lebedev could not even have been in Moscow in 1812; he's too young for that; it's absurd."

"That's the first thing; but let us suppose he could have been born then; but how can he declare to one's face that the French chasseur aimed a cannon at him and shot off his leg, just like that, for fun; that he picked the leg up and carried it home, and afterward buried it in the Vagankovsky cemetery; and he says that he put a monument over it with an inscription on one side: 'Here lies the leg of Collegiate Secretary Lebedev,' and on the other: 'Rest in peace, beloved ashes, till the dawn of a happy resurrection,' and, finally, that he has a service read over it every year (which is nothing short of blasphemy) and goes to Moscow every year for the occasion. To prove it, he invites me to go to Moscow to show me the tomb, and even the very same French cannon (which was captured) in the Kremlin; he assures me it's the eleventh from the gate, a French falconet of an old-fashioned design."

"And besides, both his legs are after all uninjured and in plain view!" laughed the prince. "I assure you it was a harmless jest; don't be angry."

"But allow me to have my own interpretation, too, sir; as for the legs in plain view—that, let us grant, is not altogether improbable; he asserts the leg is from Chernosvitov..."[7]

"Oh, yes, they say you can dance with a leg from Chernosvitov."

"I'm perfectly aware of that, sir; when Chernosvitov invented his leg, the first thing he did was run and show it to me. But Chernosvitov's leg was invented incomparably later... What's more, he asserts that

---

7. R. A. Chernosvitov was another member of the Petrashevsky circle whose death sentence was commuted. His book on the construction of artificial legs appeared in Petersburg in 1855.

even his late wife never knew, all the years they were married, that he, her husband, had a wooden leg. When I observed to him how absurd it all was, he said to me: 'If you served as a page of Napoleon's in 1812, you might let me bury my leg in Vagankovsky."

"Why, were you actually . . ." the prince began, and broke off embarrassed.

The general[8] looked at the prince with distinct condescension and virtually with mockery.

"Go on, Prince," he drawled with peculiar suavity. "Go on. I can make allowances, tell all: confess that you are amused at the very thought of seeing before you a man in his present degradation and . . . uselessness, and to hear at the same time that this man was personally a witness of . . . great events. Hasn't *he* already had a chance to . . . gossip to you?"

"No: I've heard nothing from Lebedev—if it's Lebedev you are talking about . . ."

"Hm! . . . I had supposed the contrary. In fact, the whole conversation between us yesterday came about on account of that . . . strange article in the *Archives*. I remarked on its absurdity, and since I had myself been an eyewitness . . . You are smiling, Prince, you are looking at my face?"

"N-no. I . . ."

"I am youngish-looking," the general stretched out the words, "but I am somewhat older in years than I in fact appear. In 1812 I was in my tenth or eleventh year. I don't quite know my own age exactly. In my service list my age is given as less; I've had the weakness to subtract from my age myself in the course of my life, you know."

"I assure you, General, that I don't find it at all strange that you should have been in Moscow in 1812, and . . . of course you could describe . . . like everyone else who was there. One of our autobiographers begins his book just with the fact that in 1812, as a suckling babe in Moscow, he was fed with bread by the French soldiers."[9]

"There, you see," the general condescendingly approved, "what

---

8. The following phrase was deleted in the 1874 version: *seemed a bit embarrassed too, but at the same instant.*

9. The "autobiographer" is Alexandr Herzen (1812–70), the leading socialist thinker of this period, who left Russia in 1847 to escape persecution but continued to greatly influence Russian revolutionary thought from abroad through his writings.

happened to me was of course out of the ordinary, but there is nothing incredible in it. Truth very often seems impossible. A page! It sounds strange, of course. But the adventure of a ten-year-old boy may perhaps be explained precisely by his age. It wouldn't have happened to a boy of fifteen, that's certain; for at fifteen, I should not, on the day of Napoleon's entry into Moscow, have run out of the wooden house in Old Bassmann Street from my mother, who had not left the town in time and was trembling with fear. At fifteen I too should have been afraid, but at ten, I feared nothing and I forced my way through the crowd to the very steps of the palace just when Napoleon was dismounting from his horse."

"Without a doubt, you have made an excellent observation that at ten years old one might not be afraid . . ." the prince acquiesced, growing timid and tormented by the thought that he was about to blush.

"Without a doubt, and it all happened so simply and naturally, as it can only happen in reality; were a novelist to set to work on this affair, he would weave in all sorts of fables and improbabilities."

"Oh, that's so!" cried the prince. "I was struck by the same idea, and quite lately even. I know a genuine case of murder over a watch—it's already in the newspapers now. Let some author invent that—pundits of the national way of life and critics would have cried out at once that it was improbable; but when you read it in the newspapers as a fact, you feel that it is just through such facts that you learn Russian reality. That's an excellent observation of yours, General!" the prince concluded warmly, awfully glad that he could evade the obvious color in his face.

"Isn't that the truth? Isn't that the truth?" cried the general, his eyes sparkling with pleasure. "A boy, a child who does not understand the danger, makes his way through the crowd to see the dazzle, the uniforms, the suite and, at last, the great man about whom he has heard such a lot of noise. For at that time, for several years in a row, people had done nothing but make a lot of noise about him. The world was full of that name; I took it in with my milk, so to speak. Napoleon, walking past just two paces away, chanced to catch my eyes. I looked like a little nobleman, they dressed me well. There was no one like me in the crowd, you'll admit . . ."

"No doubt it must have struck him and have shown him that not everyone had left, and that some noblemen had remained with their children."

"Just so, just so! He wanted to attract the boyars! When he cast his eagle gaze upon me, my eyes must have flashed in response. *'Voilà un garçon bien éveillé! Qui est ton père?'*[10] I answered him at once, almost breathless with excitement: 'A general who died in the fields for his country.' *'Le fils d'un boyard et d'un brave par-dessus le marché! J'aime les boyards. M'aimes tu, petit?'*[11] To this rapid question I answered as rapidly: 'A Russian heart can discern a great man even in the enemy of his country!' That is, actually, I don't remember whether I literally used those words ... I was a child ... but that was certainly the meaning! Napoleon was struck, he thought a moment and said to his suite: 'I like the pride of that child! But if all Russians think like that child, then ...' He did not finish, but walked into the palace. I at once mingled with the suite and ran after him. They already made way for me in the suite and looked upon me as a favorite. But all that was but a flash ... I only remember that, entering the first room, the emperor stopped suddenly before the portrait of the Empress Catherine, looked at it a long time thoughtfully, and at last pronounced: 'That was a great woman!' and passed by. Two days later everyone already knew me in the palace and the Kremlin and called me *'le petit boyard.'*[12] I only went home to sleep. At home they nearly went out of their minds. Another two days later, Napoleon's page-in-waiting, Baron de Basencour, died, exhausted by the campaign.[13] Napoleon remembered me; they took me, brought me without explaining the matter, tried on me the uniform of the deceased, a boy of twelve, and when they had brought me in the uniform to the emperor and he had nodded his head at me, they announced to me that I had been found worthy of favor, and appointed a page-in-waiting to his majesty. I was glad; I had, in fact, long felt a fervent attraction for him ... and besides, you will admit, a brilliant uniform, which means a great deal to a child ... I went about in a dark green dress coat, with long narrow tails; gold buttons, red edgings worked on the sleeves with gold, and a high, erect, open collar, worked in gold,

---

10. Fr., Here's a sharp lad! Who is your father?

11. Fr., The son of a boyar [old Russian nobility] and a brave one into the bargain! I love the boyars. Do you love me, little one?

12. Fr., the little boyard.

13. Basencour was, in fact, a general under Napoleon and did not die until 1830.

and embroidery on the tails; tight white chamois leather breeches, a white silk waistcoat, silk stockings, shoes with buckles ... and when the emperor rode out on his horse, if I was one of the suite, I wore high top boots. Although the situation was far from brilliant, and there was already a foreboding of the huge calamities, etiquette was kept up as far as possible, and indeed all the more punctiliously, the greater the foreboding of these calamities."

"Yes, of course ..." muttered the prince with an almost bewildered air. "Your memoirs would be ... extremely interesting."

The general, of course, had been recounting the story he had already told Lebedev the day before, and so he recounted it smoothly; but at this point he again stole a mistrustful glance at the prince.

"My memoirs," he pronounced with redoubled dignity—"write my memoirs? That has not tempted me, Prince! If you will, my memoirs are already written, but ... they are lying in my desk. Let them—when my eyes are covered over with earth—let them be published then and, no doubt, translated into foreign languages, not for the sake of their literary value, no, but from the importance of the tremendous facts of which I have been eyewitness, though as a child; the more for that, indeed: as a child I gained entry into the most intimate, so to speak, bedroom of the 'Great Man'! I heard at night the groans of that 'Titan in agony,' he could not feel ashamed to groan and weep before a child, though I understood even then that the cause of his distress was the silence of the Emperor Alexander."

"To be sure, he did write letters ... with overtures of peace ..." the prince assented timidly.

"Actually, we don't know precisely with what overtures he wrote, but he wrote every day, every hour, and letter after letter! He was fearfully agitated! One night, when we were alone, I flew to him weeping (oh, I loved him!): 'Beg, beg forgiveness of the Emperor Alexander!' I cried to him. That is, I ought to have used the expression: 'Make peace with the Emperor Alexander,' but like a child I naïvely expressed all I felt. 'Oh my child!' he replied—he was pacing up and down the room—'Oh, my child!' He did not seem to notice at that time that I was only ten, and liked to talk to me, indeed. 'Oh, my child, I am ready to kiss the feet of the Emperor Alexander, but on the other hand the king of Prussia, but on the other hand the Austrian emperor ... Oh, for them my hatred is everlasting, and ... ultimately ... You understand nothing of politics!' He seemed suddenly to remember to whom he was speaking and fell silent, but there were still gleams of fire in his eyes long after. Well, say I described all these facts—and I was the eyewitness of the greatest facts—say I publish them now, and all these critics, all these literary vanities, all the envy, the partisanship . . . no, sir, your humble servant!"

"As for the partisanship, you've made a fair observation, of course, and I agree with you," the prince replied quietly after a moment's silence. "Very recently, I was just reading Charasse's book about the Waterloo campaign.[14] It is evidently a serious book, and experts say that it is written with extraordinary knowledge. But on every page one detects glee at the humiliation of Napoleon; and if it had been possible to dispute even every last sign of Napoleon's talent in the other campaigns too, Charasse, it seems, would have been extremely glad of it; and that's not right in such a serious work, because that is the spirit of partisanship. Were you very busy then in the service of . . . the emperor?"

The general was delighted. The earnestness and simplicity of the prince's question dissipated the last traces of his mistrustfulness.

"Charasse! Oh, I was indignant myself! I wrote to him at once at the time, but . . . actually, I don't remember now . . . You ask if I was very busy in Napoleon's service? Oh, no! I was called a page-in-waiting, but even at the time I did not take it seriously. Besides, Napoleon soon lost all hope of winning over the Russians, and no doubt he would have forgotten me, whom he had adopted from policy, if he had not . . . if he had not become personally fond of me; I say that boldly now. As for me, my heart was drawn to him. My duties were not demanding: I had sometimes to appear in the palace and to . . . accompany the emperor on horseback when he rode out, that was all. I rode a horse fairly well. He used to drive out before dinner. Davoust, I, and a Mameluke, Roustan,[15] were generally in his suite . . ."

"Constant,"[16] the prince blurted out suddenly for some reason.

"N-no, Constant was not there then; he had gone with a letter . . . to

14. Jean Baptiste Adolphe Charasse, *Histoire de la campagne de 1815. Waterloo* (1858).

15. Davoust was Napoleon's minister of war and Roustan his favorite bodyguard; a Mameluke is a descendant of a military class that ruled Egypt and Syria from the thirteenth to the sixteenth centuries.

16. Napoleon's personal valet.

the Empress Josephine; but in his place were two orderlies and some Polish uhlans[17] . . . and there you had the whole suite, except for the generals, obviously, and the marshals, whom Napoleon took with him to survey the environs, the position of the troops, to consult . . . The one who was oftenest in attendance was Davoust, as I remember now: a huge, stout, cold-blooded man, in spectacles, with a strange look in his eyes. He was consulted more often than anyone by the emperor. He valued his thoughts. I remember they were in consultation for several days; Davoust would come morning and evening. Often, they even argued; at last Napoleon seemed to be brought to agree. They were alone in the study, I was the third, scarcely observed by them. Suddenly Napoleon's eye chanced to fall upon me, a strange thought gleamed in his eye. 'Child,' said he to me suddenly, 'what do you think: if I adopt the Orthodox faith, and set free your slaves, will the Russians stand behind me or not?' 'Never!' I cried indignantly. Napoleon was astonished. 'In the eyes of that child, which are shining with patriotism,' said he, 'I have read the verdict of the whole Russian people. Enough, Davoust! That's all a fantasy! Explain your other project.' "

"Yes, but that project, too, was a powerful idea!" said the prince, evidently growing interested. "So you ascribe that project to Davoust?"

"At any rate, they consulted together. No doubt, the idea was Napoleon's, the idea of an eagle, but the other project was also an idea . . . That was the famous *'conseil du lion,'* as Napoleon himself called that advice of Davoust's. It consisted in this: to shut themselves up in the Kremlin with all the troops, build barracks, dig themselves in with fortifications, place cannons, kill as many horses as possible and salt their flesh, procure by purchase or pillage as much bread as possible, and to spend the winter there till spring; and in the spring to fight their way through the Russians. This project greatly fascinated Napoleon. We used to ride around the Kremlin walls every day; he would show where to demolish, where to construct, here lunettes, there ravelins, or a row of blockhouses—the eye, the speed, the sally! Everything was settled at last; Davoust pestered him for a final decision. Once more they were alone, and I made up the third. Again Napoleon paced the room with folded arms. I could not take my eyes off his face, my heart throbbed. 'I am going,' said Davoust. 'Where?' asked Napoleon. 'To salt

17. Lancers in a light cavalry unit.

the horses,' said Davoust. Napoleon shuddered, fate hung in the balance. 'Child,' said he to me, suddenly, 'what do you think of our intention?' Obviously, he asked me the way that a man of the greatest intelligence will sometimes, at the last moment, resort to heads or tails. I turned to Davoust instead of Napoleon and spoke as though by inspiration: 'You'd better beat it fast, General, homeward-bound!' The project was demolished. Davoust shrugged his shoulders and, going out, said in a whisper: *'Bah, il devient superstitieux!'*[18] And the next day the retreat was ordered."

"All that is extremely interesting," the prince brought out in an awfully quiet voice, "if all that was so ... that is, I mean to say ..." he hastened to correct himself.

"Oh, Prince!" cried the general, so carried away by his own story that perhaps he could not have stopped short even before the most flagrant indiscretion. "You say, 'all that was so!' But there was more, I assure you, far more! These are only paltry political facts. But I repeat I was the witness of the tears and groans of that great man at night; and that no one saw but I! Toward the end, it's true, he ceased to weep, there were no more tears, he only moaned at times; but his face was veiled more and more, as it were, with darkness. As though eternity had already cast its dark wing about him. Sometimes at night we spent whole hours alone together, in silence—the Mameluke Roustan would be snoring in the next room; that fellow slept fearfully soundly. 'But he is devoted to me and to the dynasty,' Napoleon used to say about him. Once I was dreadfully grieved, and suddenly he noticed tears in my eyes; he looked at me with tenderness: 'You feel for me!' he cried. 'You, a child, and perhaps another child will feel for me—my son, *le roi de Rome;*[19] all the rest, all, all hate me, and my brothers would be the first to betray me in misfortune!' I began to sob and flew to him; here he couldn't bear it; we embraced, and our tears flowed together. 'Do, do write a letter to the Empress Josephine!' I sobbed to him. Napoleon started, pondered, and said to me: 'You remind me of the one other heart that loves me; I thank you, my friend!' He sat down on the spot, and wrote that letter to the Empress Josephine that was taken by Constant next day."[20]

18. Fr., Bah, he's becoming superstitious!
19. Fr., the king of Rome.
20. Napoleon had divorced Josephine in 1809.

"You did splendidly," said the prince. "In the midst of his evil thoughts you led him to good feelings."

"Just so, Prince, and how splendidly you put it! How like your own good heart!" cried the general rapturously, and, strange to say, genuine tears were gleaming in his eyes. "Yes, Prince, yes, that was a magnificent spectacle! And do you know I very nearly went after him to Paris, and would certainly have shared with him his 'sultry prison isle,'[21] but alas!—our fates were parted! We went separate ways: he to the 'sultry prison isle,' where, perhaps, if only once, in a moment of terrible grief, he may have recalled the tears of the poor boy who embraced him and forgave him Moscow. As for me, I was sent to the cadets' corps, where I found nothing but drill, the coarseness of comrades, and . . . alas! Everything turned to dust and ashes! 'I don't want to take you away from your mother, and do not take you with me,' he said to me on the day of the retreat, 'but I should like to do something for you.' He had already mounted his horse. 'Write something as a souvenir for me in my sister's album,' said I, timidly, for he was very troubled and gloomy. He turned, asked for a pen, took the album. 'How old is your sister?' he asked me, already holding the pen. 'Three years old,' I answered. '*Petite fille alors!*'[22] And he wrote in the album.

> *Ne mentez jamais!*
> *Napoléon, votre ami sincère.*[23]

Such advice and in such a moment, you'll agree, Prince!"

"Yes, that was remarkable."

"That page, in a gold frame under glass, hung all her life in my sister's drawing room, in the most conspicuous place, until her very death—she died in childbirth; where it is now—I don't know . . . but . . . ah, my God! It's two o'clock already! How I have kept you, Prince! It's unpardonable!"

The general got up from his chair.

"Oh, on the contrary," mumbled the prince. "You have so entertained me, and . . . finally . . . it's so interesting; I am so grateful to you!"

"Prince!" said the general, squeezing his hand again till it hurt and

21. A line from Pushkin's poem "Napoleon" (1826).
22. Fr., a little girl, then!
23. Fr., Never lie! Napoleon, your sincere friend.

looking at him intently with sparkling eyes, as though he had suddenly come to himself and was virtually dumbfounded by some startling thought. "Prince! You are so kind, so good-hearted, that I'm sometimes positively sorry for you. I am touched when I look at you. Oh, God bless you! May a new life begin for you, blossoming . . . with love. Mine is over! Oh, forgive me, forgive me!"

He went out quickly, covering his face with his hands. The prince could not doubt the genuineness of his emotion. He understood as well that the old man had gone away enraptured at his success; yet he had a foreboding that he was one of that class of liars who—though they lie till they begin to lust after the pleasure and forget themselves entirely—still, even at the very acme of their intoxication they secretly suspect, after all, that they are not believed, and that they cannot be believed. In his present position the old man might come to himself, be incommensurately overcome with shame, start to suspect the prince of a boundless compassion for him and feel insulted. "Haven't I made it worse by leading him on to such exhilaration?" the prince worried, and suddenly he could not restrain himself and laughed violently for ten minutes. He was nearly beginning to reproach himself for his laughter, but at once realized that he had nothing to reproach himself with, since he pitied the general infinitely.

His forebodings turned out to be true. That very evening he received a strange note, brief but resolute. The general informed him that he was parting from him forever as well, that he respected him, and was grateful to him, but that even from him he could not accept "proofs of compassion that were derogatory to the dignity of a man who was unhappy enough without that." When the prince heard that the old man had taken refuge with Nina Alexandrovna, he felt almost at ease about him. But we have seen already that the general had caused some sort of trouble at Lizaveta Prokofyevna's too. Here we cannot go into the details, but we will mention briefly that the upshot of the interview consisted in the general's scaring Lizaveta Prokofyevna and, by his bitter insinuations against Ganya, rousing her to indignation. He was led out in disgrace. That was why he had spent such a night and such a morning, become completely unhinged and had run out into the street almost in a state of frenzy.

Kolya had not yet fully grasped the state of affairs and even hoped to bring him around by severity.

"Well, where are we trudging off to now, d'you suppose, General?" he said. "You don't want to go to the prince's, you've quarreled with Lebedev, you've no money, and I never have any: well, and here we are right in the soup, in the middle of the street."

"It's more pleasant to sit over the soup than in the soup," muttered the general. "With that . . . pun I aroused great delight . . . in the officers' mess . . . in 'forty-four . . . in eighteen . . . forty-four, yes! . . . I don't remember . . . oh, don't remind me, don't remind me! 'Where is my youth, where is my freshness!' as exclaimed . . . who exclaimed it, Kolya?"

"That's from Gogol, Father, in 'Dead Souls,'" answered Kolya, and stole a timid glance at his father.

"Dead Souls! Oh, yes, dead! When you bury me, write on the tombstone: 'Here lies a dead soul!'

Disgrace pursues me!

Who said that, Kolya?"

"I don't know, Father."

"There was no such person as Yeropegov! Yeroshka Yeropegov! . . ." he cried in a frenzy, stopping short in the street. "And that was my son, my own son! Yeropegov, a man who for eleven months took the place to me of a brother, for whom I fought a duel . . . Prince Vygoretsky, our captain, said to him over a bottle: 'Tell me something, Grisha, where did you get your Anna?'[24] 'On the battlefield of my country, that's where I got it!' I shouted: 'Bravo, Grisha!' Well, and that's where it came to a duel, and afterward, he was married . . . to Marya Petrovna Su . . . Sutugin, and was killed in the field . . . A bullet glanced off the cross on my breast and hit him straight in the brow. 'I shall never forget!' he cried, and fell on the spot. I . . . I've served with honor, Kolya; I've served nobly, but disgrace—'disgrace pursues me!' You and Nina will come to my little grave . . . 'Poor Nina!' I used to call her that, Kolya, long ago in our early days, and how she loved . . . Nina, Nina! What have I made of your lot in life! What can you love me for, long-suffering soul! Your mother has the soul of an angel, Kolya, do you hear, of an angel!"

24. The Order of St. Anne, an imperial medal of honor.

"I know that, dear father. Dear father, be a dove, let's go back home to Mother! She was running after us! Well, why are you standing still? As though you don't understand . . . Well, and why are you crying?"

Kolya was crying himself and kissing his father's hands.

"You're kissing my hands, mine!"

"Yes, yours, yours. Well, what is there to wonder at? Come, what are you bawling for in the middle of the street? And you call yourself a general, an army man; come, let's go!"

"God bless you, dear boy, for having been respectful to a disgraceful . . . yes! a disgraceful old man, your father . . . May you, too, have such a boy . . . *le roi de Rome* . . . Oh, 'a curse, a curse on this house!' "

"But, really now, what on earth is going on here?" Kolya suddenly boiled over. "What has happened? Why won't you go home now? Why, have you gone out of your mind?"

"I'll explain, I'll explain to you . . . I'll tell you everything; don't shout, people will hear . . . *le roi de Rome* . . . Oh, I'm sick, I'm sad!

Nanny, where is thy tomb![25]

Who was it that cried that, Kolya?"

"I don't know, I don't know who cried it! Let's go home, at once, at once! I'll give Ganjka a hiding if necessary . . . but where are you off to again?"

But the general was pulling him to the stoop of a house close by.

"Where are you going? That's someone else's stoop!"

The general sat down on the stoop, and went on pulling Kolya to him by his hand.

"Bend down, bend down!" he muttered. "I'll tell you everything . . . disgrace . . . bend down . . . your ear, your ear; I'll tell you in your ear . . ."

"But what's the matter with you!" Kolya grew terribly alarmed, nonetheless offering him his ear.

"*Le roi de Rome* . . ." whispered the general, seeming to tremble all over as well.

"What? . . . But why do you keep harping on *le roi de Rome*? . . . What?"

"I . . . I . . ." whispered the general again, clinging more and more

25. The line is from "Humor," an unfinished poem by N. P. Ogarev (1813–77).

tightly to "his boy's" shoulder. "I . . . want . . . I'll tell . . . you everything, Marya . . . Marya . . . Petrovna Su-su-su . . ."

Kolya tore himself away, seized the general by the shoulders himself, and looked at him like a madman. The old man flushed crimson, his lips turned blue, faint spasms were still running over his face. Suddenly he bent forward and began slowly sinking into Kolya's arms.

"A stroke!" the boy shouted out loud to the entire street, surmising, at last, what was the matter.

V

Truth be told, Varvara Ardalionovna had in her conversation with her brother somewhat exaggerated the exactness of her information concerning the prince's engagement to Aglaia Epanchin. Perhaps, like a sharp-sighted woman, she had foreseen what was bound to come to pass in the immediate future; perhaps, disappointed on account of the dream that had gone up in smoke (in which, truth be told, she had never really believed herself), she was, being human, unable to deny herself the gratification of pouring even more vitriol into her brother's heart by exaggerating the calamity, even though she loved him sincerely and compassionately. But in any case, she could not have received such exact information from her friends the Epanchins; there were only hints, half-uttered words, silences, riddles. And perhaps Aglaia's sisters had even let something slip with design, so that they might themselves find out something from Varvara Ardalionovna; it may have been, finally, that they, too, did not want to deny themselves the feminine pleasure of teasing a friend a little, though a childhood one: after all, they could not in so long a time have failed to get at least a glimpse of her designs.

On the other hand, the prince, too, though he was perfectly right in assuring Lebedev that he had nothing to relate to him, and that absolutely nothing special had happened to him, may, perhaps, have also been mistaken. In fact, something apparently very strange was happening to all of them: nothing had happened, and yet, at the same time, it was as if a great deal had happened. And it was this last that Varvara Ardalionovna had indeed guessed with her unfailing feminine instinct.

How did it come about, however, that at the Epanchins', everyone at once was given to one and the same corresponding thought concerning the fact that something vital had happened to Aglaia, and that her fate was being decided—this is very difficult to relate in proper order. But as soon as this idea had flashed at once in all their minds, they all at once insisted that they had seen through everything long ago and had foreseen everything quite clearly; that everything had already been clear since the "poor knight," and even before, only, at that time, they were still unwilling to believe in anything so absurd. So the sisters declared; and of course, Lizaveta Prokofyevna had foreseen and known everything long before anyone, and her "heart had been aching" for quite some time now; but—whether long ago or not—now, the thought of the prince suddenly went far too much against her grain, namely, because it made her completely lose her bearings. Here was a question that required an immediate resolution; but not only was it impossible to resolve, but poor Lizaveta Prokofyevna could not even pose the question to herself with complete clarity, however much she struggled. It was a difficult matter: "Was the prince good or no good? Was all this good or no good? If it were no good (which was without a doubt), then in what way, namely, was it no good? And if, perhaps, it were good (which was also possible), in what way, again, was it good?" The head of the family himself, Ivan Fyodorovich, was of course first of all surprised, but then suddenly made the confession that "By Jove, he too had fancied something of the sort all this time, for a while there'd be nothing, and then suddenly he would seem to fancy it!" He fell silent at once under at the threatening gaze of his wife, but he fell silent in the morning, while in the evening, alone with his wife and compelled to speak again, he suddenly and, as it were, with a particular boldness, expressed some unexpected opinions: "I say, what does it amount to after all?" . . . (Silence.) "Of course, all this is very strange, if it really is true, and he didn't dispute it, but . . ." (Silence again.) "But, on the other hand, if one looked at the thing straight on, why the prince was a most splendid fellow, upon my word, and . . . and, and— well, finally, the name, you know, our family name, all that would have the air, so to say, of keeping up the family name which had fallen low in the eyes of the world, that is, looking at it from that point of view, that is, because . . . of course, the world; the world was the world; but still the prince was not without fortune, if it was only a middling one;

he had ... and ... and ... and" (prolonged silence and utter collapse). Hearing her husband, Lizaveta Prokofyevna exploded beyond all bounds.

In her opinion all that had happened was "unpardonable and even criminal folly, a fantastic vision, stupid and monstrous!" First of all, there was already the fact that "this miserable little prince was a sickly idiot, and in the second place, he is a fool, neither knows anything of the world nor has a place in it: to whom could you present him, where would you put him? He's some kind of inadmissible democrat; he hadn't even got the merest rank ... and ... and ... what would Princess Belokonsky say? And was this, was this the sort of husband we had imagined and planned for Aglaia?" The last argument, of course, was the chief one. The mother's heart shuddered at this reflection, awash in blood and tears, though at the same time something stirred within this heart, suddenly saying to her: "And how is the prince not like what you wanted?" Well, and it was those very protestations of her own heart that were more troublesome to Lizaveta Prokofyevna than anything.

Aglaia's sisters were for some reason pleased at the thought of the prince; it didn't even strike them as very strange; in a word, they might at any moment have wound up entirely on his side. But they both resolved to keep quiet. It had been noted once and for all in the family that, in any odd general and disputed point concerning the family, the more obstinate and insistent Lizaveta Prokofyevna's objections and repudiations sometimes grew to be, the more might it serve as a sign for everyone that she was, perhaps, already in agreement with that point. But for Alexandra Ivanovna, however, it was not possible to be perfectly silent. Having long ago acknowledged her as her adviser, her mother was now calling for her every minute and demanding her opinions, and above all her recollections; that is, "How did all this come to pass? Why did nobody see it? Why did no one say anything at the time? What was the meaning of that horrid 'poor knight'? Why was she alone, Lizaveta Prokofyevna, condemned to worry about everyone, to notice and foresee everything, while all the others did nothing but count the crows," and so on, and so on. Alexandra Ivanovna was on her guard at first, and remarked only that she found rather correct her father's notion about how in the eyes of the world the choice of Prince Myshkin as the husband of one of the Epanchins might seem very satisfactory. Little by little, becoming more heated, she even added that the prince was by no means "a little fool," and never had been, and as for his consequence—why, God only knew what a decent man's consequence would depend upon in a few years' time among us in Russia: whether on the formerly required successes in the service, or on something else. To all this her mamma promptly retorted that Alexandra was "a freethinker, and this was all their hateful 'woman question.'" Then, half an hour later she set off for town, and from there to Kamenny Island, to find Princess Belokonsky, who happened, as if by design, to be in Petersburg at the time, though she was soon going away. Belokonsky was Aglaia's godmother.

"Old lady" Belokonsky listened to all of Lizaveta Prokofyevna's feverish and desperate confessions, and was not in the least moved by the tears of the bewildered mother; she even looked at her mockingly. She was a terrible despot; she could not bear parity in her friendships, not even in the very oldest ones, and she looked on Lizaveta Prokofyevna decidedly as her protégée, just like thirty-five years before, and she never could reconcile herself to the abruptness and independence of her character. She observed, among other things, that "they had all apparently, as was always their wont, gotten much too far ahead of themselves, and were making a mountain out of a molehill; that hard as she might listen, she was not convinced that anything serious had really happened with them; and wouldn't it be better to wait until something would come of it; that the prince, in her opinion, was a decent young man, though sickly, strange and much too inconsequential. The worst thing was that he was openly keeping a mistress." Lizaveta Prokofyevna understood quite well that Belokonsky was somewhat cross at the failure of Yevgeny Pavlovich, who had come with her recommendation. She returned home to Pavlovsk in a state of even greater irritation than when she had set out, and everyone got theirs at once, chiefly, for the fact that "they'd all gone crazy," that things were decidedly not done like that by anyone else, only by them; "Why were they in such a hurry? What has come of it? Hard as I might look, I simply can't conclude anything has really come of it! Wait till something comes of it! Ivan Fyodorovich might fancy all sorts of things, but should one really make mountains out of molehills?"

The upshot of it, so it would seem, was that one should calm down, look on with cool composure, and wait. But alas! the calm did not last even ten minutes. The first blow to cool composure was struck by the news of what had happened during the absence of *maman* at Kamenny Island. (Lizaveta Prokofyevna's visit had taken place on the very next day after the prince had paid a visit at midnight instead of at nine o'clock.) In reply to their mother's impatient inquiries, the sisters answered in great detail; to begin with that "absolutely nothing, it seems, had happened in her absence," that the prince had come, that Aglaia had not come down to him for a long time, quite half an hour, then came down, and as soon as she came down, at once proposed to the prince that they play chess; that the prince knew not a single move of chess, and Aglaia had beaten him at once; she became very merry and shamed the prince dreadfully for his incompetence, laughed at him dreadfully, so that the prince became pitiful to look at. Then she proposed a card game, "fools."[26] But that had come out quite the other way: at playing fools, the prince turned out to have such prowess, like . . . like a professor; he played masterfully; Aglaia had even cheated and switched cards, and had stolen tricks from under his very nose, and still he had made a fool of her every time; five times running. Aglaia flew into a terrible rage, quite forgot herself, in fact; she said such biting and insolent things to the prince that he was no longer laughing, and turned quite pale when she told him at last that "she wouldn't set foot in the room as long as he were there, and that it was positively unconscionable of him to come to them, especially at night, past twelve o'clock, *after all that had happened.*" Then she slammed the door and went out. The prince walked out as though from a funeral, in spite of all their efforts to console him. All of a sudden, a quarter of an hour after the prince had gone, Aglaia had run downstairs to the terrace in such haste that she had not dried her eyes—and her eyes were still wet with tears. She ran down because Kolya had come and had brought a hedgehog. They had all begun looking at the hedgehog; at their questions, Kolya explained that the hedgehog was not his, but that he was out for a walk with a friend, another schoolboy, Kostya Lebedev, who had stayed in the street and was too shy to come in, because he was carrying a hatchet; that they had just bought the hedgehog and the hatchet from a peasant they had met. The peasant was offering the

26. An extremely simple game: One player leads a card, the other must beat it or else take it up into his own hand. The player with cards still left in his hand at the end of the game is the "fool."

hedgehog up for sale and took fifty kopecks for it; as for the hatchet, they had talked him into selling it themselves, because it seemed opportune, and it was a very good hatchet. All of a sudden Aglaia had begun pestering Kolya terribly to sell her the hedgehog at once; she was quite beside herself and even called Kolya "dear." For a long time, Kolya would not consent, but at last he couldn't bear it and summoned Kostya Lebedev, who did in fact come in with a hatchet and grew rather abashed. But then it had suddenly turned out that the hedgehog was not theirs at all, but belonged to some third boy, Petrov, who had given the two of them money to buy Schlosser's *History*[27] for him from some fourth boy, which the latter, being in want of money, was selling cheap; that they had been going to buy Schlosser's *History,* but hadn't been able to resist and bought the hedgehog, so that it followed that the hedgehog and the hatchet belonged to the third boy, to whom they were now carrying them instead of Schlosser's *History.* But Aglaia pestered them so much that at last they made up their minds and sold her the hedgehog. As soon as Aglaia had obtained the hedgehog, she put him down at once, with Kolya's help, in a wicker basket, covered it with a table-napkin, and began asking Kolya to go straightaway, with no dallying, and bring the hedgehog to the prince from her, begging him to accept it as a sign of her "profound respect." Kolya agreed, delighted, and gave his word to deliver it, but began immediately pestering her: "What was meant by the hedgehog and by making him such a present?" Aglaia had answered that it was not his business. He answered that he was convinced there was some allegory in it. Aglaia became angry and snapped that he was nothing but a "silly boy." Kolya at once retorted that if it were not for the fact that he respected her sex and, what was more, his own convictions, he would have shown her on the spot that he knew how to answer such insults. It had ended, however, in Kolya's going off delightedly, after all, to deliver the hedgehog, and Kostya Lebedev had run after him. Aglaia could not resist and, seeing that Kolya was swinging the basket too much, shouted to him from the terrace: "Please, Kolya, don't drop it, pet!" just as though she had not been quarreling with him just before; Kolya had stopped, and he, too, as though he had not been quarreling, had shouted with the ut-

---

27. The *World History* of the German historian F. C. Schlosser appeared in Russian translation between 1861 and 1869.

most readiness: "No, I won't drop him, Aglaia Ivanovna. Be entirely at ease!" and had run on again at breakneck speed. After that Aglaia had broken out in an awfully hearty laugh and ran up to her own room exceedingly pleased, and had been in high spirits the rest of the day.

Such a piece of news completely confounded Lizaveta Prokofyevna. What was there in it, one might ask? But such, evidently, was the mood that had come over her. Her apprehension was aroused to an extreme degree, above all—the hedgehog; what did the hedgehog mean? What compact underlay it? What was understood by it? What sort of sign was this? What sort of telegram? Moreover, poor Ivan Fyodorovich, who happened to be present during the inquisition, completely spoiled the whole business by his reply. In his opinion, there was no telegram of any kind, and the hedgehog "was simply a hedgehog and nothing more—at most it meant to be friends, forget all insults, and make up; in a word it was all mischief, but harmless and excusable."

We may note in parenthesis that he had guessed completely right. The prince, returning home from Aglaia's after being ridiculed and banished by her, sat for half an hour in the blackest despair, when Kolya suddenly appeared with the hedgehog. The sky cleared at once; the prince was as if risen again from the dead, questioned Kolya, hung on his every word, repeated his questions ten times over, laughed like a child, and continually shook hands with the two laughing boys who gazed at him so frankly. The upshot of it, it would seem, was that Aglaia forgave him, and that he could go and see her again that very evening, and that was for him not only the chief thing but actually everything.

"What children we still are, Kolya! And ... and ... how nice it is that we are such children!" he cried at last, joyfully.

"The simple fact is she's in love with you, Prince, and that's all there is to it!" Kolya answered authoritatively and compellingly.

The prince flushed, but this time he did not say a word, and Kolya simply laughed and clapped his hands. A minute later the prince started laughing too, and afterward, until the very evening, he kept looking at his watch every five minutes to see how much time had passed and how much was left till evening.

But the mood got the upper hand: in the end, Lizaveta Prokofyevna could not resist, and gave in to the hysteria of the moment. In spite of all the protests of her husband and daughters, she immediately sent for Aglaia in order to put the ultimate question to her and to receive from her the most clear and ultimate answer: "To make an end of it once and for all, and get it off our backs, so as never to refer to it again!" "Otherwise," she announced, "I shan't survive till evening!" And only then they all realized to what an absurd pass they had brought things. They could get nothing out of Aglaia except feigned amazement, indignation, laughter and jeers at the prince and at all who questioned her. Lizaveta Prokofyevna took to her bed and only came out to tea, when the prince was expected. She awaited the prince with trepidation, and when he arrived, she almost went into hysterics.

And the prince, for his part, came in timidly, feeling his way, as it were, smiling strangely, peering into everyone's eyes, as if posing everyone a question, for Aglaia was not in the room again, of which he was instantly afraid. That evening, there was no one else present, only the members of the family. Prince Shch. was still in Petersburg, on account of the affair of Yevgeny Pavlovich's uncle. "If only he could have been here and said something, anyway," Lizaveta Prokofyevna grieved over his absence. Ivan Fyodorovich sat with an extremely perturbed mien; the sisters were serious and, as though by design, silent. Lizaveta Prokofyevna did not know how to begin the conversation. At last she suddenly energetically abused the railway, and looked at the prince with resolute challenge.

Alas! Aglaia did not come down, and the prince was lost. Barely muttering and completely befuddled, he began to express the opinion that fixing the railway would be exceedingly useful, but Adelaida suddenly laughed and he squelched himself again. At that very instant Aglaia came in, calmly and with dignity, ceremoniously made the prince a bow, and solemnly took the most conspicuous place at the round table. She looked inquiringly at the prince. Everyone understood that the resolution of all misunderstandings had come.

"Did you get my hedgehog?" Aglaia asked firmly and almost angrily.

"I did," answered the prince, blushing and with his heart in his mouth.

"Then explain at once what you think about it. That's essential for the peace of mind of *maman* and our whole family."

"Listen, Aglaia . . ." the general suddenly began to fret.

"This goes beyond all bounds!" Lizaveta Prokofyevna was suddenly alarmed about something.

"There aren't any bounds to speak of here, *maman*," her daughter answered sternly and at once. "I sent the prince a hedgehog today and I want to know his opinion. Well, Prince?"

"What opinion do you mean, Aglaia Ivanovna?"

"About the hedgehog."

"That is . . . I think, Aglaia Ivanovna, you want to know how I took . . . the hedgehog . . . or, better said, how I regarded this . . . sending . . . of the hedgehog . . . that is . . . in such a case, I suppose that . . . in a word . . ."

He gasped and fell silent.

"Well, you've not said much." Aglaia waited some five seconds. "Very well, I agree to drop the hedgehog; but I am very glad that I can put an end, at last, to all these accumulated misunderstandings. Allow me, at last, to find out from you yourself, and in person: are you courting me or not?"

"Good heavens!" broke from Lizaveta Prokofyevna.

The prince shuddered and fell back; Ivan Fyodorovich froze; the sisters furrowed their brows.

"Don't lie, Prince, tell the truth. I am persecuted with strange inquisitions on your account; do these inquisitions have any sort of foundation? Come!"

"I have not been courting you, Aglaia Ivanovna," said the prince, suddenly reviving. "But . . . you know yourself how I love you and believe in you . . . even now . . ."

"I asked you: do you ask for my hand, or not?"

"I do," the prince answered with his heart in his mouth.

A general and violent stir ensued.

"All this is not right, dear friend," uttered Ivan Fyodorovich, violently agitated. "This . . . this is almost impossible, if it's so, Glasha[28] . . . Your pardon, Prince, your pardon, my dear fellow! . . . Lizaveta Prokofyevna!" He turned to his wife for assistance. "It would be well . . . to go into it . . ."

"I refuse, I refuse!" Lizaveta Prokofyevna waved her hands.

28. A very tender diminutive of Aglaia.

"But allow me to speak, too, *maman:* why, I myself do count for something in such a business: the extreme moment of my fate is being decided" (this was precisely how Aglaia expressed it) "and I want to find out for myself, and aside from that, I'm glad that it's before everyone . . . Allow me to ask you, Prince, if you 'cherish such intentions,' how, namely, do you propose to secure my happiness?"

"I really don't know, Aglaia Ivanovna, how to answer you; in this case . . . in this case, what is there to answer? And besides . . . is it necessary?"

"You seem to be embarrassed and out of breath; take a rest and marshal your strength; drink a glass of water; however, they'll give you tea directly."

"I love you, Aglaia Ivanovna. I love you very much; I love no one but you and . . . don't jest, I implore you . . . I love you very much."

"But this is an important matter, though; we are not children and one must look at it practically . . . Do endeavor now to explain what your fortune is?"

"Come, come, come, Aglaia! What's with you! This is not right, not right . . ." Ivan Fyodorovich muttered in dismay.

"Disgraceful!" Lizaveta Prokofyevna whispered loudly.

"She's out of her mind!" Alexandra whispered just as loudly.

"My fortune . . . that is, money?" said the prince, surprised.

"Precisely."

"I have . . . I have now one hundred and thirty-five thousand," the prince muttered, reddening.

"Is that all?" said Aglaia aloud, in open wonder, without the faintest blush. "Then again, it doesn't matter; especially with economy . . . Do you intend to enter the service?"

"I was thinking of taking an examination to become a private tutor . . ."

"Very appropriate; of course, that will increase our income. Are you proposing to be a *kammerjunker?*"

"A *kammerjunker?* I never imagined such a thing, but . . ."

But at this point the two sisters could not contain themselves and burst in peals of laughter. Adelaida had long noticed in the twitching features of Aglaia's face symptoms of imminent and irrepressible laughter, which she was, for the time, controlling with all her might. Aglaia would have looked menacingly at her laughing sisters, but she could not bear it a second herself, and went off in a fit of the most mad, almost hysterical laughter; at last she leapt up and ran out of the room.

"I knew it was all a joke and nothing else!" cried Adelaida. "From the very beginning, from the hedgehog."

"No, this I will not allow; I will not!" Lizaveta Prokofyevna suddenly boiled over with anger and set off hastily after Aglaia. The sisters at once ran out after her too. Left behind in the room were the prince and the head of the family.

"This is, this is . . . Could you have imagined anything like it, Lev Nikolaich?" General Epanchin cried abruptly, evidently not comprehending himself what he wanted to say. "No, seriously, seriously speaking?"

"I see that Aglaia Ivanovna was laughing at me," replied the prince sadly.

"Wait a bit, dear chap; I'll go and you wait a bit . . . because . . . You at least, Lev Nikolaich, you at least, explain to me: how did all this happen, and what does it all mean, in all, so to speak, its entirety? You must admit, dear chap—I'm her father; after all, I'm her father and so I don't understand anything; so you, at least, explain it to me!"

"I love Aglaia Ivanovna; she knows that, and . . . I think she has known it a long time."

The general shrugged his shoulders.

"Strange, strange! . . . And do you love her very much?"

"Very much."

"It's all so strange, so strange to me. That is, such a surprise and blow that . . . You see, dear fellow, it's not the fortune (though I did expect you had rather more), but . . . my daughter's happiness . . . finally . . . Are you in a position to secure, so to speak, this . . . happiness? And . . . and . . . what is it: a joke or the real thing on her side? That is, not on your side, but on hers?"

Alexandra's voice was heard at the door: Papa was wanted.

"Wait a bit, dear chap, wait a bit! Wait a bit and think it over, and I'll be back directly . . ." he uttered hurriedly, and almost in alarm rushed out to heed Alexandra's call.

He found his wife and daughter in each other's arms, bathing each other with tears. They were tears of joy, tenderness and reconciliation. Aglaia was kissing her mother's hands, cheeks and lips; both were hugging each other with great warmth.

"Well, there you are, look at her, Ivan Fyodorovich, there you have the whole of her, now!" said Lizaveta Prokofyevna.

Aglaia turned her happy, tearstained little face from her mother's bosom, looked at her father, laughed loudly, jumped up to him, embraced him tightly, and kissed him several times. Then she flung herself on her mother again and hid her face completely in her bosom so that no one could see it, and began crying again at once. Lizaveta Prokofyevna covered her with the end of her shawl.

"Well, what, now, what are you doing with us, you cruel girl—that's what I want to know after this," she said, but joyfully, as though she could breathe more easily now.

"Cruel! Yes, cruel!" Aglaia chimed in suddenly. "Rotten! Spoiled! Tell Papa that. Ah yes, why, he's here. Papa, you're here? Do you hear?" She laughed through her tears.

"My dear, my idol!" The general kissed her hand, beaming all over with happiness. (Aglaia did not take her hand away.) "So, it would seem, then, you love this . . . young man?"

"No-no-no! I can't stand . . . your young man, I can't stand him!" Aglaia suddenly boiled over and raised her head. "And if you ever dare again, Papa . . . I'm serious; do you hear? I'm serious!"

And she was serious indeed; she flushed all over and her eyes gleamed. Her father faltered and grew alarmed, but Lizaveta Prokofyevna gave him a sign behind Aglaia's back, and he took it to mean: "Don't ask questions."

"If it is so, my angel, then it's as you like, you know, it's your decision, he's waiting there alone; shouldn't we hint to him, delicately, that he should go away?"

Ivan Fyodorovich, in his turn, winked at his wife.

"No, no, that would be superfluous; especially if you do it 'delicately': you go in to him yourself; I'll come in afterward, directly. I want to beg that . . . young man's pardon, because I hurt his feelings."

"And very much so," Ivan Fyodorovich confirmed seriously.

"Well, then . . . you all had better stay here, and I'll go in first alone, you shall come directly after me, the very second after; that would be better."

She had already reached the door but suddenly turned back.

"I shall laugh! I shall die laughing!" she declared sorrowfully.

But at the same second she turned and ran in to the prince.

"Well, what's the meaning of this? What do you think?" Ivan Fyodorovich uttered hastily.

"I am afraid to even say aloud," Lizaveta Prokofyevna answered as hastily. "But, in my view, it's clear."

"And in my view, it's clear. Clear as day. She loves him."

"Not only loves; she's in love with him!" echoed Alexandra. "But only with whom, when you think of it?"

"God bless her if such is her fate!" Lizaveta Prokofyevna crossed herself devoutly.

"Then it's fate," the general agreed, "and there's no escaping fate!"

And they all went into the drawing room where a surprise awaited them again.

Aglaia not only did not burst out in laughter on going up to the prince, as she had feared, but even said to him almost timidly:

"Forgive a stupid, rotten, spoiled girl" (she took him by the hand) "and rest assured that we all respect you immensely. And if I dared to turn into ridicule your splendid . . . kind simplicity, forgive me as you'd forgive a child for being naughty; forgive me for persisting in an absurdity, which could not, of course, have the slightest consequence . . ."

The last words Aglaia uttered with particular emphasis.

Father, mother and sisters all hastened into the drawing room in time to see and hear all this, and all were struck by the words "absurdity which cannot have the slightest consequence," and still more so by the earnest air with which Aglaia spoke of that absurdity. Everyone exchanged glances questioningly; but the prince, it seemed, did not understand these words and was at the very summit of happiness.

"Why do you talk like that?" he muttered. "Why do you . . . ask . . . forgiveness . . ."

He even would have said that he wasn't worthy of being asked for forgiveness. Who knows, perhaps he did notice the meaning of the words about the "absurdity which cannot, of course, have the slightest consequence," but, being such a strange man, perhaps, he was even relieved at those words. Indisputably, it was for him already the very pinnacle of bliss simply that he could come and see Aglaia again without hindrance, that he was allowed to talk to her, sit with her, walk with her, and, who knows, perhaps he would have been content with that alone for the rest of his life! (It was just this contentment, it seems, that

Lizaveta Prokofyevna secretly dreaded; she guessed it; she dreaded many things in secret that she could not have put into words herself.)

It's difficult to imagine the degree to which the prince regained his spirits and courage that evening. He was so merry that one grew merry just looking at him—as Aglaia's sisters expressed it afterward. He grew talkative, and that had not happened to him again since that very morning when, six months ago, he had first made the acquaintance of the Epanchins; upon his return to Petersburg he was noticeably and intentionally taciturn, and had very recently, in front of everyone, let slip to Prince Shch. that he must restrain himself and be silent, for he had no right to degrade an idea by expressing it himself. He was almost the only one who talked that evening, he told of many things; he answered questions clearly, with pleasure and in detail. But, in fact, there was not even a glimmer of anything resembling polite conversation in his words. It was all such serious, at times even complicated thoughts. The prince even expounded some of his own views, his own secret observations, so that it would have been positively funny, if it had not been so "well expressed," as all his listeners agreed later on. Although the general did like serious subjects of conversation, still, both he and Lizaveta Prokofyevna considered in private that it was far too academic, so that by the end of the evening they actually felt sad. However, toward the end, the prince went so far as to tell some very amusing anecdotes, which he was the first to laugh at himself, so that the others laughed more at his joyful laugh than at the anecdotes themselves. As for Aglaia, she hardly spoke all evening; but on the other hand, she listened to Lev Nikolaevich with rapt attention, and, rather, not so much listened to him, but looked at him.

"How she gazes at him without taking her eyes off him; she hangs on his every little word; how she catches it, how she catches it!" Lizaveta Prokofyevna would say afterward to her husband. "But tell her that she loves him and you'll have the walls about your ears!"

"What can one do—it's fate!" The general shrugged his shoulders, and long afterward kept repeating the phrase, of which he had grown fond. We will add that, as a practical man, he too was extremely displeased by a great deal in the present state of things, above all—the lack of clarity in the business; but he, too, resolved for the time being to keep quiet, and face up . . . to Lizaveta Prokofyevna.

The happy mood of the family did not last long. The very next day Aglaia again quarreled with the prince, and that is how things went on continually in all the ensuing days. For hours together she would jeer at the prince and particularly turn him into a laughingstock. It is true they would sometimes sit for an hour or two together in the garden of the house, in the arbor, but it was observed that, at such times, the prince almost always read aloud the newspaper or some book to Aglaia.

"Do you know," Aglaia once said to him, interrupting the newspaper, "I have noticed that you are dreadfully uneducated; you don't know anything thoroughly if one asks you for information: not who exactly it was, nor in what year, nor according to what treaty. You're rather pitiful."

"I told you that I have not much learning," answered the prince.

"What have you if you haven't that? How can I respect you after that? Read on; but then again, don't; leave off reading."

And again, that evening, there was a glimpse of something mystifying on her part. Prince Shch. came back. Aglaia was very kind to him, she made many inquiries about Yevgeny Pavlovich. (Prince Lev Nikolaevich had not been in yet.) Suddenly, Prince Shch. somehow permitted himself an allusion to "another imminent transformation in the family," to a few words that had escaped Lizaveta Prokofyevna to the effect that they might have to put off Adelaida's wedding again in order that the two weddings might take place together. It was impossible to even picture how Aglaia flared up at "all these stupid suppositions"; and, among other things, the words burst from her that she had "no intention as yet of taking the place of anybody's mistress."

These words astonished everybody, but above all her parents. In a secret consultation with her husband, Lizaveta Prokofyevna insisted that he must have it out with the prince once and for all on the question of Nastasya Filippovna.

Ivan Fyodorovich swore that all this was only "an outburst," and occurred due to Aglaia's "proneness to embarrassment"; that if Prince Shch. had not referred to the wedding there would not have been this outburst, for Aglaia knew herself, knew on good authority, that it was all the slander of ill-natured people, and that Nastasya Filippovna was going to marry Rogozhin; that the prince had nothing to do with it, let alone a liaison with her; and never had had, if one's to speak the whole honest truth.

Meanwhile the prince was unabashed by anything, all the same, and went on being blissful. Oh, of course, he too sometimes noticed something, as it were, gloomy and impatient in Aglaia's eyes; but he had more faith in something different, and the gloom vanished of itself. Having once come to have faith, he was no longer capable of wavering in anything. Perhaps he was too much at his ease; so, at least, it seemed to Ippolit, who chanced to meet him once in the park.

"Well, didn't I tell you the truth when I said that time that you were in love?" he began, going up to the prince himself and stopping him. The latter gave him his hand and congratulated him on "looking well." The invalid seemed to be encouraged himself, as consumptives are wont to be.

He had come up to the prince with the express intention of saying something caustic about his happy air, but lost the train of thought at once and began to talk about himself. He began complaining, and complained of many things, and at length, and rather incoherently.

"You wouldn't believe," he concluded, "to what extent they are all irritable there, petty, egoistic, vain, commonplace; would you believe that they only took me on condition of my dying as quickly as possible, and now they're all in a fury that I am not dying but, on the contrary, better. It's a farce! I bet you don't believe me!"

The prince had no inclination to object.

"I sometimes even think of moving back to you again," Ippolit added carelessly. "So, then, you don't consider them capable of taking a man in on condition of his dying as quickly as possible?"

"I thought they invited you with something else in mind."

"Oho! Why, you are, after all, by no means so simple as you are reputed to be! Now is not the time, or I'd reveal something to you about that Ganechka and his hopes. You are being undermined, Prince, mercilessly undermined, and . . . it's indeed pitiful that you're so calm. But, alas!—you could not do otherwise!"

"There's a thing to pity me for!" laughed the prince. "Why, then, in your opinion, I would be happier if I were more uneasy?"

"Better be unhappy but in the *know*, than be happy and live . . . like a fool. You don't believe at all, it seems, that you have a rival, and . . . from that quarter?"

"Your words about rivalry are rather cynical, Ippolit; I am sorry I have not the right to answer you. As for Gavrila Ardalionovich, you must admit yourself, how can he remain calm after everything that he has lost—if you know anything at all about his affairs, that is? It seems to me better to look at it from that point of view. There's time for him to change; he has many more years to live before him, and life is rich ... but then again ... then again ..." The prince suddenly lost his train of thought. "As for undermining, I don't even comprehend what you are talking about; we'd best drop this conversation, Ippolit."

"We'll drop it for the time; besides, of course, it would be impossible for you not to be noble on your side. Yes, Prince, you'd have to poke with your own finger in order not to believe it again, ha, ha! And do you despise me very much now, what do you think?"

"What for? Because you have suffered and are still suffering more than we?"

"No, but because I am unworthy of my suffering."

"Anyone who is able to suffer more, it would seem, must be worthy of more suffering. Aglaia Ivanovna, when she read your confession, wanted to see you, but ..."

"She's putting it off ... she mustn't. I understand, I understand ..." Ippolit interrupted, as though trying to turn the conversation in another direction as quickly as possible. "By the way, they say that you read all that rigmarole aloud to her yourself; it was written and ... done ... in genuine delirium. And I don't understand how anyone can be so—I won't say cruel (it would be humiliating for me), but so childishly vain and vengeful, as to reproach me with this confession and to use it against me as a weapon! Don't worry, I'm not saying it on your account ..."

"But I am sorry that you repudiate that notebook, Ippolit; it is sincere, and, you know, even the most absurd aspects of it, and there are many" (Ippolit scowled dreadfully), "are redeemed by the suffering, because to confess them was also suffering and ... perhaps great bravery. The idea that moved you certainly had a noble foundation, however it may seem. I see that more clearly as time goes on, I swear to you. I don't judge you, I say it to speak my mind, and I'm sorry that I was silent at the time ..."

Ippolit flushed hotly. The thought flashed through his mind that the prince was pretending, and setting a trap for him; but, peering closely into his face, he could not help believing in his sincerity; his face brightened.

"Yet I must die all the same!" he said, almost adding, "a man like me!" "And only fancy how your Ganechka plagues me; he has trumped up, by way of objection, that perhaps, of the people who heard my notebook at the time, three of four will likely die before me! How's that for you! He supposes that's a comfort to me, ha-ha! In the first place, they haven't died yet; and even if these people did die off, what sort of comfort is there in that to me, you will admit! He judges on his own example; however, he's gone even further; he simply abuses me now, says that a decent man in such a case would die in silence and that it was nothing but egoism on my part! How's that for you! No, what egoism it is on his part! What refinement, or, better said, at the same time, what oxlike coarseness of their egoism, which they can't see in themselves, however! . . . Have you ever read, Prince, of the death of Stepan Glebov in the eighteenth century? I happened to read about it yesterday . . ."

"What Stepan Glebov?"[29]

"He was impaled in the time of Peter."

"Oh dear, yes, I know! He spent fifteen hours on the stake, in the frost, in a fur coat, and died with extraordinary grandeur; of course, I've read about it . . . What of it?"

"Well, doesn't God grant such deaths to men—but not to us! You think, perhaps, I'm not capable of dying like that, like Glebov?"

"Oh, not at all," the prince said, confused. "I only meant to say that you . . . that is, not that you would not resemble Glebov, but . . . that you . . . that you would be more likely then to be . . ."

"I'll guess: like Osterman,[30] and not Glebov—that's what you meant to say?"

"What Osterman?" wondered the prince.

---

29. Glebov became the lover of Peter the Great's ex-wife Eudoxia during her exile to a convent, where he was the captain of her guards. Accused of being involved in a conspiracy to secure the throne for Eudoxia's son Alexis, Glebov was sentenced to die a painful death. He was tortured for three days and then impaled. According to legend, Peter himself offered to relieve his pain by killing him at once if he confessed to treason, but Glebov spat in his face.

30. A key member of the Russian Foreign Office under Peter the Great, Osterman became vice chancellor after Peter's death. He maintained political influence for nearly twenty years while a number of Peter's heirs struggled for the throne. When political intrigue finally brought his enemies to power, he was sentenced to death, but the sentence was commuted to exile in Siberia, where he died an unremarkable death six years later.

"Osterman, the diplomat Osterman, Peter's Osterman," muttered Ippolit, suddenly somewhat disconcerted. A certain perplexity followed.

"Oh, n-n-no! I wanted to say something else," the prince suddenly drawled, after some silence. "You would never, I think ... never have been an Osterman ..."

Ippolit frowned.

"Then again, the reason I maintain that, you know," the prince took up suddenly, obviously anxious to set things right, "is because the men of those days (I swear I've always been struck by it) were virtually entirely not the same people that we are now; it wasn't the same tribe as now,[31] in our age, truly, it's virtually a different breed ... In those days they were men of one idea, as it were, but now we are more nervous, more developed, more sensitive, somehow of two or three ideas at once ... Modern man is broader-minded—and I swear this very thing prevents his being so all-of-a-piece as they were in those days. I ... I simply said it with that idea, and not ..."

"I understand; to make up for the naïveté with which you disagreed with me, you're now doing your level best to console me, ha, ha! You're a perfect child, Prince. I notice, though, that you keep handling me like ... like a china cup ... It's all right, it's all right, I'm not angry. In any case, our conversation turned out to be awfully funny; you're sometimes a perfect child, Prince. Let me tell you, though, that I should like perhaps to be something better than Osterman; it would not be worthwhile to rise from the dead for the sake of Osterman ... But anyway, I see I ought to die as soon as possible, or else I, myself, shall ... Leave me. Good-bye! Well, all right then, come, tell me yourself, come, what is your view: what would be the best way for me to die? ... So that it would turn out with the most possible ... virtue, that is? Come, tell me!"

"Pass by us and forgive us our happiness!" said the prince in a low voice.

"Ha, ha, ha! Just as I thought! I certainly expected something in that vein! Though you are ... though you are ... Well, well! Eloquent people! Good-bye! Good-bye!"

---

31. A paraphrase of some well-known lines from Lermontov's poem "Borodino" (1837).

VI

What Varvara Ardalionovna had told her brother about the evening gathering at the Epanchins' dacha, at which Princess Belokonsky was expected, was also absolutely true; the guests were expected that same day, in the evening; but once again, she had expressed herself somewhat more strongly than was warranted. It had, indeed, all been arranged with too much hurry, and even with a certain, and quite unnecessary, excitement—namely, because in that family "everything was done quite like nowhere else." It could all be explained by the impatience of Lizaveta Prokofyevna, who "did not wish to have any more doubts," and by the feverish tremors of both parental hearts on account of the happiness of their favorite daughter. Moreover, Belokonsky really was going away soon; and as her patronage did, in fact, have great significance in society, and as they hoped she would be well disposed to the prince, the parents reckoned that "society" would accept Aglaia's betrothed straight from the hands of the omnipotent "old lady," and that therefore if there were to be anything strange about it, under such patronage it would seem much less strange. And that was indeed the heart of the matter, that the parents were quite unable to decide for themselves: "Was there—and precisely to what extent was there—anything strange in this whole matter? Or was there nothing strange at all?" The candid and friendly opinion of influential and competent persons would be of use just at the present moment when, thanks to Aglaia, nothing had been finally settled. In any case, sooner or later the prince would have to be introduced into society, of which he had not the faintest idea. In short, they were determined to "show" him. The party was, however, projected in the simplest terms; only "friends of the family" were expected, and the smallest possible number of them. Aside from Princess Belokonsky, they expected one other lady, the wife of a very important gentleman and dignitary. Of the young people, they were counting virtually exclusively on Yevgeny Pavlovich; he was to come escorting Princess Belokonsky.

The prince heard that Belokonsky would be there almost three days before the party; but of the party as such he learned only the previous day. Of course, he noticed the busy air of the members of the family, and—from certain insinuating and anxious attempts to broach the subject to him—he even ascertained that they were afraid of the impression he might make. But the Epanchins, every last one of them, had somehow formed the impression that, in his simplicity, he was incapable of guessing on his own that they were so uneasy on his account. And so, looking at him, everyone was inwardly desolate. Actually, he did in fact attach almost no significance to the approaching event; he was occupied with something entirely different: Aglaia was becoming every hour more gloomy and capricious—that was killing him. When he found out that they were expecting Yevgeny Pavlovich, he was greatly delighted, and said that he had long been wishing to see him. For some reason no one liked these words; Aglaia went out of the room in vexation, and only late in the evening, after eleven o'clock, when the prince was already going away, she seized an opportunity to say a few words to him alone, seeing him out.

"I should like you not to come to see us all day tomorrow, but to come in the evening when these . . . guests are all gathered. You know that there are to be guests?"

She spoke impatiently and with intensified severity; for the first time, she brought up the subject of this "party." To her, too, the idea of these visitors was almost insufferable; everyone noticed it. Perhaps she was even terribly eager to quarrel with her parents about it, but pride and embarrassment kept her from speaking. The prince understood at once that she also was afraid on his account (and did not want to admit that she was afraid), and he too felt suddenly alarmed.

"Yes, I've been invited," he answered.

She was evidently in difficulties over the continuation.

"Can one speak to you about anything serious? Just once in your life?" She suddenly grew extremely angry, not knowing why, and not able to control herself.

"You can, and I am listening; I'm very glad," muttered the prince.

Aglaia paused again for a minute, and began with evident repugnance:

"I didn't want to argue with them about it; in certain cases, you can't make them see reason. Some of *maman*'s principles have always been revolting to me. I say nothing about Papa; it's no use expecting anything from him. *Maman* is a noble-minded woman, of course; if you dared to propose anything base to her, you'd see. Well, but before this . . . nasty rubbish—she bows down! I don't mean just Belokonsky: she's a nasty little old woman, and nasty in character, but clever and knows how to keep them all in the palm of her hand—one can say that for her, anyway. Oh, the baseness of it! And it's absurd: we've always been people of the middle class, as middle-class as could possibly be; so why force ourselves into that aristocratic circle? And my sisters are on the same tack; it's Prince Shch. that's got them all muddled. Why are you pleased that Yevgeny Pavlovich will be there?"

"Listen, Aglaia," said the prince. "It seems to me that you are very much afraid that I'll blow it tomorrow . . . in this company."

"Me, afraid? On your account?" Aglaia flushed all over. "Why should I be afraid on your account, even if you . . . even if you do utterly disgrace yourself. What is it to me? And how can you use such words? What does that mean, 'blow it'? It's a nasty phrase, vulgar!"

"It's . . . a schoolboy phrase."

"Well, yes, a schoolboy phrase! A nasty phrase! You are determined, it seems, to use words like that all the evening tomorrow. Do look up some more such words at home in your dictionary: you'll make a sensation! It's a pity that you seem to know how to come into the room well. Where did you learn it? Will you be able to take a cup of tea and drink it properly, when everyone's looking at you on purpose?"

"I think I will."

"That's a pity; or I should have had a good laugh. Well, at least, break the Chinese vase in the drawing room! It's valuable. Please do break it; it was a present; Mother would go out of her mind and would cry before everyone—that's how much she values it. Make some gesture as you always do, knock it over and break it. Sit near it on purpose."

"On the contrary, I'll try to sit as far from it as I can: thank you for warning me."

"So, then, you are afraid you will make gestures. I'll bet anything you'll start expounding about some 'subject,' about something serious, academic and lofty. That will be . . . proper!"

"I think that would be stupid . . . if it's not apropos."

"Listen, once and for all," Aglaia lost her patience at last. "If you start talking about anything like capital punishment, or the economic position of Russia, or of how 'beauty will save the world' . . . of course I should be delighted and laugh at it . . . but I warn you in advance:

never show yourself before me again! Do you hear? I'm in earnest! This time I'm in earnest!"

She really did speak her threat *in earnest*, so much so that something exceptional could even be heard in her words and seen in her eyes, which the prince had never noticed before, and which, of course, did not resemble a joke.

"Well, now you've made it so that I shall certainly start 'expounding' and even ... perhaps ... break the vase, too. I wasn't afraid of anything before, and now I'm afraid of everything. I shall certainly blow it."

"Then hold your tongue. Sit quiet and hold your tongue."

"I shan't be able to; I'm sure I shall start talking out of fear and shall break the vase out of fear. Perhaps I shall fall down on the slippery floor, or something of that sort will turn out, for that has happened to me before; I shall dream about it all night tonight; why did you start talking about it!"

Aglaia looked gloomily at him.

"I know what: I'd better not come at all tomorrow! I'll report myself ill, and that will be the end of it!" he decided at last.

Aglaia stamped her foot and turned positively white with anger.

"Good Lord! Did anyone ever see anything like it? He's not coming, when it was all on his account that ... my God! What a treat to have to do with such ... a senseless person like you!"

"Well, I'll come, I'll come!" the prince broke in hastily. "And I give you my word of honor that I'll sit the whole evening without saying a word. I'll manage it."

"You'll do well to manage. You said just now you'd 'report yourself ill.' Where, indeed, do you pick up such expressions? What possesses you to talk to me in such language? Are you trying to tease me?"

"I beg your pardon; that's a schoolboy expression too. I won't use it. I quite understand that you are ... anxious ... on my account (but don't be angry, then!), and I'm awfully glad of it. You won't believe how frightened I am now—and how glad I am of your words. But I swear to you, all this fear is nothing but trifles and nonsense. Upon my word, Aglaia! But the joy will remain. I really love it that you're such a child, such a kind good child! Oh, how splendid you can be, Aglaia!"

Aglaia would have flown into a rage, of course, and was already on the point of it, but suddenly some kind of unexpected feeling took possession of her entire soul in one instant.

"And you won't reproach me for my rude words just now . . . some day . . . afterward?" she asked suddenly.

"How can you? How can you? And why are you flaring up again? And now you're looking gloomy again! You've taken to looking too gloomy sometimes now, Aglaia, as you never used to look. I know why that is . . ."

"Be silent, be silent!"

"No, it's better to say it. I've been wanting to say it a long time; I've said it already, but . . . it was too little, for you didn't believe me. There is, after all, a creature who stands between us . . ."

"Silence, silence, silence, silence!" Aglaia interrupted suddenly, gripping his hand tightly and looking at him almost in terror. At that moment her name was called; almost relieved, she left him at once and ran away.

The prince was in a fever all night. Strangely, he had been feverish for several nights running. This time, half in delirium, the thought occurred to him: what if, tomorrow, in front of everyone, he should have a fit? He had had fits in public, after all. He turned cold at the thought; all night he imagined himself in some wondrous and incredible company, among some queer people. The worst of it was that he started "expounding"; he knew he ought not to talk, but he went on talking all the time; he was trying to persuade them of something. Yevgeny Pavlovich and Ippolit were also of the party, and seemed extremely friendly.

He woke up after eight o'clock with a headache, with confusion in his mind and with strange impressions. For some reason, he felt an intense desire to see Rogozhin; to see him and to say a great deal to him—what about, exactly, he did not know himself; then he fully made up his mind to go for some reason and see Ippolit. There was something vaguely muddled in his heart, so much so that the impression left by the adventures that befell him this morning, though it was extremely strong, was still somehow incomplete. One of these adventures consisted in a visit from Lebedev.

Lebedev made his appearance rather early, soon after nine, and was almost completely drunk. Although the prince had not been observant of late, still it had somehow struck his eye that ever since General Ivolgin had left them, these last three days now, Lebedev had begun behaving very badly. He seemed to have suddenly become extremely sullied and grimy, his cravat was off to one side, and the collar of his coat was torn. In his own rooms, he actually kept up a continual storm, and this was audible across the little courtyard; Vera had come in on one occasion in tears and told some story. On presenting himself that morning, he talked very strangely, beating himself on the breast and blaming himself for something...

"I have received ... I have received the retribution for my baseness and treachery ... I've received a slap in the face!" he concluded tragically at last.

"A slap in the face! From whom? ... And so early in the day?"

"So early?" Lebedev smiled sarcastically. "Time has nothing to do with it ... even for physical retribution ... but I've received a moral, not a physical, slap in the face!"

He suddenly sat down without ceremony and began to tell his story. The story was a very incoherent one; the prince frowned and wanted to leave, but suddenly some words astonished him. He was struck dumb with amazement ... Mr. Lebedev told of strange things.

It was, apparently, at first about some letter; Aglaia Ivanovna's name was mentioned. Then Lebedev began all at once bitterly reproaching the prince himself; it could be gathered that he was offended with the prince. At first, he said, the prince had honored him with his confidence in dealings with a certain "personage" (with Nastasya Filippovna); but afterward had broken with him completely and had cast him from himself with ignominy, and even to such an insulting pitch that, last time, supposedly, he had repelled with rudeness "an innocent question about the approaching changes in the house." With drunken tears, Lebedev confessed that "after that, he could endure no more, especially as he knew a great deal ... a very great deal ... from Rogozhin, and from Nastasya Filippovna, and from Nastasya Filippovna's friend, and from Varvara Ardalionovna ... herself, sir ... and from ... and from even Aglaia Ivanovna, would you believe it, sir, through Vera, sir, through my beloved daughter Vera, my only ... yes, sir ... but then again, not my only, for I've three. And who was it informed Lizaveta Prokofyevna by letter, and even in dead secret, sir, he-he! Who has been writing to her about all the connections and ... about the comings and goings of the 'personage' of Nastasya Filippovna? He-he-he! Who, who is this anonymous writer, allow me to ask?"

"Can it be you?" cried the prince.

"Just so," the drunkard replied with dignity, "and this very morning at half past eight, only half an hour—no, sir, three-quarters of an hour ago—I informed the most noble-hearted mother that I had one . . . significant . . . incident to communicate to her. I informed her by a note, through a girl at the back door, sir. She received it."

"You've just seen Lizaveta Prokofyevna?" asked the prince, hardly able to believe his ears.

"I saw her just now and received a slap in the face . . . a moral one. She gave me back the letter; in fact she flung it back unopened . . . and as for me, she threw me out head first . . . only morally speaking, not physically . . . but then again, almost physically, though it was almost physical too, not far off it!"

"What letter was it she flung at you unopened?"

"Why, didn't I . . . he-he-he! But I haven't told you yet! And I thought I'd already said . . . It was this little letter I'd received, to pass on, sir . . ."

"From whom? To whom?"

But some of Lebedev's "explanations" were extremely difficult to make out, or to understand anything in them. The prince, however, gathered as far as he could that the letter had been conveyed in the early morning, by the servant girl, to Vera Lebedev, to be delivered to the person to whom it was addressed . . . "just as before . . . just as before, to a certain personage, and from the same person, sir . . . (for I designate one of them a 'person,' sir, and the other only a 'personage,' for the purpose of degradation and differentiation; for there is a great distinction between an innocent and high-born young lady of a general's family . . . and a cocotte, sir) and so, the letter was from that 'person' beginning with the letter 'A' . . ."

"How can that be? To Nastasya Filippovna? Nonsense!" cried the prince.

"It's happened, it's happened, sir, and if not to her, then to Rogozhin, sir; it's all the same, to Rogozhin, sir . . . And there was even one to Mr. Terentyev, to be passed on, once, from the person beginning with 'A.'" Lebedev winked and smiled.

As he was continually mixing one thing up with another and forgetting what he had begun to speak about, the prince held his peace to let him speak out. But it was still extremely unclear: did the letters go through him, namely, or through Vera? Since he himself declared that "it was just the same whether the letters were for Rogozhin or for Nastasya Filippovna," that meant it was more likely that they did not go through him, if there actually had been letters. The circumstance by which this letter had come into his hands now remained decidedly unexplained; most likely, one would have to suppose that he had somehow sneaked it from Vera . . . stolen it on the sly and carried it for some object to Lizaveta Prokofyevna. That was what the prince gathered and understood at last.

"You've gone out of your mind!" he cried in extreme agitation.

"Not quite, honored prince," Lebedev replied, not without malice. "It's true, I meant to hand it to you, to put it into your own hands; to do you a service . . . but I reflected that it was better to be of use in that quarter and to reveal everything to the noble-hearted mother . . . as I had communicated with her before once by letter anonymously; and when I wrote to her before on a little note, preliminarily, asking for an audience at twenty minutes past eight, I signed myself again 'your secret correspondent.' I was admitted at once, without delay, even with the utmost haste, by the back door . . . to the noble-hearted mother."

"Well? . . ."

"And there, as you know already, sir, she nearly beat me, sir; that is, very nearly, sir, so that one might almost say she practically did beat me, sir. And as for the letter, she flung it at me. It's true she wanted to keep it for herself—I saw it, I noticed it—but she thought better of it and flung it: 'Since a fellow like you has been entrusted to deliver it, then go and deliver it!' . . . She was positively offended. If she wasn't ashamed to say so before me, she must have been offended. She's hot-tempered by nature!"

"Where is the letter now, then?"

"Why, I've got it still. Here it is, sir."

And he handed the prince Aglaia's note to Gavrila Ardalionovich, which the latter, two hours later that same morning, showed to his sister with such triumph.

"That letter can't remain with you."

"It's for you, for you! It's to you I am bringing it, sir," Lebedev took up with warmth. "Now I'm yours again, entirely yours, from head to heart, your servant, sir, after my momentary betrayal, sir! Punish the heart, spare the beard, as Thomas More said . . . in England and in Great Britain, sir. 'Mea culpa, mea culpa,' as the Roman Pappy says . . . that is, he's the Roman Pope, but I call him Roman Pappy."[32]

"This letter must be sent off at once," fussed the prince. "I'll deliver it."

"But wouldn't it be better, wouldn't it be better, most highly bred prince, wouldn't it be better . . . to do like so, sir!"

Lebedev made a strange, ingratiating grimace; he suddenly began to fidget terribly in his place, as though he had been suddenly pricked by a needle, and, winking slyly, was doing and demonstrating something with his hands.

"What is this?" the prince asked menacingly.

"Wouldn't it be better to open it beforehand, sir!" he whispered ingratiatingly and, as it were, confidentially.

The prince leapt up in such a fury that Lebedev would have taken to his heels; but having run to the door, he paused to see whether there would be mercy.

"Ech, Lebedev! Is it possible, is it possible to sink to such base indecency, as you have done?" cried the prince sorrowfully. Lebedev's face brightened.

"I'm abject, abject!" he approached at once, with tears, beating himself on the breast.

"You know this is abominable!"

"Abominable, precisely, sir! That's the word for it, sir!"

"And what a habit you have of such . . . queer behavior! Why you're . . . simply a spy! Why do you write anonymously and worry . . . such a noble and kind-hearted woman? And why, finally, has not Aglaia Ivanovna a right to write to whom she pleases? What, did you go to complain of it today, then? What did you hope to gain? What induced you to tell tales?"

"Simply out of agreeable curiosity and . . . out of the solicitude of a

32. I have attempted here to convey the irreverent flavor of some untranslatable and nonsensical wordplay. In the original, Lebedev takes the adjective "Roman" in "Roman Pope" and inflects it in the feminine, effectively turning the pope into a female entity. This works particularly well in Russian because the word for pope—*papa*—ends in an *a*, which is a common ending for many feminine nouns. *Papa* is also a common diminutive form of "father," which led me to the present solution.

generous soul, yes, sir!" muttered Lebedev. "Now I am all yours, all yours again! You may hang me!"

"Did you show up at Lizaveta Prokofyevna's in the condition you're in now?" the prince inquired with disgust.

"No, sir . . . I was fresher, sir . . . and even more decent; it was only after my humiliation that I reached . . . this state, sir."

"Well, all right, leave me."

However, this request had to be repeated several times before the visitor resolved, at last, to go. He had even opened the door completely when he returned again, walked on tiptoe to the middle of the room, and began anew to make signs with his hands, demonstrating how to open a letter; he did not venture to put his advice into words; then he went out, with a quiet and kindly smile.

All this had been exceptionally painful to hear. One chief and exceptional fact stood out from everything: that Aglaia was in great agitation, in great uncertainty, in great torment for some reason ("from jealousy," the prince whispered to himself). It turned out, too, that she was being worried by ill-intentioned people, and it was very strange that she placed so much confidence in them. Of course, that inexperienced but hot and proud little head was hatching some special schemes, perhaps ruinous, and . . . and beyond everything. The prince was greatly alarmed, and in his perturbation did not know what to decide upon. There was something that had, without fail, to be forestalled, he sensed that. He looked once more at the address on the sealed letter; oh, there was no doubt and no uneasiness there for him, for he had faith; something else made him uneasy about that letter: he did not trust Gavrila Ardalionovich. And yet, he was on the point of deciding to give him the letter himself, personally, and he even left the house with that object, but he changed his mind on the way. Almost at Ptitsyn's door, as if by design, Kolya chanced to turn up, and the prince charged him to put the letter into his brother's hands as though it had come straight from Aglaia Ivanovna. Kolya asked no questions and delivered it, so that Ganya did not even imagine that the letter had seen so many stops along the way. Returning home, the prince asked Vera Lukyanovna to come to him, told her what was necessary, and set her mind at rest, for she was still hunting for the letter and crying. She was horrified when she learned that her father had carried off the letter. (The prince found out from her afterward that she had more than once served Rogozhin and Aglaia Ivanovna in secret; it had never even occurred to her that there could be anything detrimental to the prince in it.)

And the prince was at last so upset that when, two hours later, a messenger from Kolya ran in with the news of his father's illness, for the first minute he could hardly grasp what was the matter. But it was this event that restored him, because it greatly distracted his attention. He stayed at Nina Alexandrovna's (where the sick man, of course, had been carried) almost right up to the evening. He was scarcely of any use, but there are people whom one is, for some reason, glad to have about one in times of grief. Kolya was terribly shocked and cried hysterically, but, all the same, was continually being sent on errands: he ran for a doctor and hunted up three; ran to the chemist's and to the barber's. They succeeded in resuscitating the general, but did not bring him to himself; the doctors opined that "the patient was in any case in danger." Varya and Nina Alexandrovna never left the sick man's side; Ganya was disconcerted and shaken, but did not want to go upstairs, and was even afraid to see the sick man; he wrung his hands, and in an incoherent and disconnected conversation with the prince he managed to say that it was "such a calamity, and, as if by design, at such a moment!" The prince fancied he understood just precisely what moment the other had been talking about. The prince was not in time to find Ippolit at Ptitsyn's. Toward evening, Lebedev, who after the morning's "explanation" had slept all day without waking, ran in. Now he was almost sober and shed real tears over the sick man, as though he had been his own brother. He blamed himself aloud without explaining the matter, however, and pestered Nina Alexandrovna, assuring her every moment that it was "he, he was the cause of it; he and no one else . . . simply from agreeable curiosity," and that the "departed" (as he for some reason persisted in calling the still-living general) was positively a "man of genius!" He insisted with particular seriousness on his genius, as though it might be of extraordinary use at that moment. Seeing his genuine tears, Nina Alexandrovna said to him at last without a note of reproach, and almost with kindness: "Well, God bless you! Come, don't cry. Come, God will forgive you!" Lebedev was so much struck by these words and their tone that he was unwilling to leave Nina Alexandrovna's side all the evening (and all the following days, until the general's death, almost from morning till night, he spent all his time in their house). Twice in the course of the day, a messenger came to Nina Alexandrovna from Lizaveta Prokofyevna to inquire after the sick man's health. And when, at nine o'clock in the evening, the prince made his appearance in the Epanchins' drawing room, which was already full of guests, Lizaveta Prokofyevna at once began questioning him, with sympathy and in great detail, about the sick man and replied with dignity to Belokonsky's question: "Who is this sick man, and who is Nina Alexandrovna?" The prince was much pleased at this. He himself, explaining the situation to Lizaveta Prokofyevna, spoke "splendidly," as Aglaia's sisters put it afterward: "modestly, quietly, without unnecessary words, without gestures, with dignity; he made a splendid entrance; was superbly dressed," and far from "falling down on the slippery floor," as they had feared the day before, he had evidently even made a pleasing impression on everyone.

For his part, sitting down and looking around, he noticed at once that this whole company did not in the least resemble the bogies of yesterday with whom Aglaia had tried to frighten him, nor the nightmare figures he had seen in last night's dreams. For the first time in his life he saw a tiny corner of what is called by the dreadful name "society." For some time past now, as a consequence of certain particular intentions, considerations and inclinations of his, he yearned to penetrate into that enchanted circle, and so he was deeply interested by his first impression. This first impression of his was positively charming. It somehow seemed to him at once and all of a sudden that these people were, as it were, born to be together; that there was no "party" at the Epanchins' that evening and no guests, that these were all "their people," and that he himself seemed to have long been their devoted friend and shared their thoughts, and was now returning to them after a brief separation. The charm of elegant manners, simplicity and apparent guilelessness was almost magical. It could never have even entered his head that all this guilelessness and generosity, wit and lofty personal dignity was perhaps only an exquisite artistic veneer. The majority of the guests, indeed, in spite of the prepossessing exterior, was made up of rather empty-headed people, who were, however, themselves unaware—in their self-satisfied complacency—that much that was good in them was mere veneer, for which they were not to blame, at that, for it had come to them unconsciously and by inheritance. The prince had no desire to suspect this under the spell of his charming first impression. He saw, for instance, that this old man, this important dignitary, who might have been his grandfather, actually interrupted his talk in order to hear him out—such a young and inexperienced man—and not only heard him out, but evidently valued his opinion, was so affectionate with him, so genuinely kindhearted, and yet they were strangers, meeting for the first time. Perhaps it was the refinement of this courtesy that produced the greatest effect on the prince's eager impressionability. Perhaps he was already, ahead of time, far too predisposed, even induced, to have a happy impression.

And in the meantime, all these people—though of course they were "friends of the family" and of one another—were, nonetheless, by no means such great friends either of the family or of one another as the prince took them to be as soon as he had met them and was introduced to them. There were people here who would never on any account have recognized the Epanchins as their equals in any respect. There were even people here who absolutely hated one another; old lady Belokonsky had all her life "despised" the wife of the "old dignitary," while the latter in turn was far from being fond of Lizaveta Prokofyevna. This "dignitary," her husband, who for some reason had been a patron of the Epanchins from their youth and was presiding over the gathering, was a personage of such vast consequence in the eyes of Ivan Fyodorovich that the latter was incapable of any sensation except reverence and awe in his presence, and he would have truly despised himself if he had only for one minute considered himself as the other's equal, and the other as anything less than the Olympian Jove. There were people here who had not met one another for some years, and felt nothing toward one another but indifference if not revulsion, yet they met each other now as though they had seen one another only yesterday in the most friendly and pleasant company. However, the gathering was not a large one. Besides Belokonsky and the "old dignitary," who really was a person of consequence, and his wife, there was in the first place one very solid military general, a baron or count with a German name—a man of extraordinary taciturnity, with a reputation for a marvelous acquaintance with government affairs, and almost with a reputation for learning—one of those Olympian administrators who know everything, "except perhaps Russia itself," a man who makes one pronouncement every five years that is "remarkable in its profoundness" but, then again, is of the sort that inevitably become proverbial and are known even in the most select circle; one of those governing officials who usually, after an extremely protracted (even strangely so) term of service, die possessed of great rank, in splendid posts and with large fortunes, though without any great exploits and, indeed, with a certain hostility to exploits. This general was Ivan Fyodorovich's immediate superior in the service, and one whom the latter, in the zeal of his grateful heart and through a peculiar form of vanity, also regarded as his patron, but who by no means considered himself Ivan Fyodorovich's patron, looked upon him with absolute indifference and, though he gladly availed himself of his numerous services, would have replaced him with another official at once, if this had been called for by any consideration, not even a particularly noble one. There was too an elderly and important gentleman who was supposed to be a relation of Lizaveta Prokofyevna's, though this was quite untrue—a man of good rank and position, a man of birth and fortune, stout and in very good health, a great talker, and with the reputation, even, of a discontented man (though, indeed, only in the most acceptable sense of the word), even a splenetic man (though even this was agreeable in him), with the pretensions of the English aristocracy and with English tastes (as regards, for example, bloody roast beef, harness, footmen, and so on). He was a great friend of the other "dignitary," amused him, and, moreover, Lizaveta Prokofyevna for some reason cherished the strange idea that this elderly gentleman (a somewhat frivolous person with a certain weakness for the female sex) might suddenly take it into his head to make Alexandra happy with the offer of his hand. Below this top and most solid layer of the assembly came the layer of the younger guests, though these too shone with rather elegant qualities. To this group belonged, aside from Prince Shch. and Yevgeny Pavlovich, the well-known and enchanting Prince N., formerly a seducer and conqueror of female hearts all over Europe, now a man of five-and-forty, still of handsome appearance, a wonderful storyteller, a man of fortune—though, in fact, somewhat dissipated— who lived the majority of the time abroad, out of habit. Finally, there were people here who even seemed to make up a third special layer, who did not belong in their own right to the "inner sanctum" of society, but whom, like the Epanchins, one may sometimes encounter, for some reason, in that inner "sanctum." Out of a certain sense of tact that they had adopted as a principle, the Epanchins liked, on the rare occasions they gave parties, to mix the highest society with people from a rather lower layer, with select representatives of the "middling sort of people." The Epanchins were indeed praised for doing so, and it was said of them that they understood their position and were people of tact, and the Epanchins were proud of such an opinion of them. One of the representatives of this middling sort of person was that evening a certain engineer, a colonel, a serious man, a very intimate friend of Prince Shch., by whom he had, in fact, been introduced to the Epanchins—a man, however, who was taciturn in society and wore on the large index finger of his right hand a large and conspicuous ring, in all probability a present. There was, finally, even one literary man, of German origin, but a Russian poet, and, on top of that, perfectly presentable, so that he could be introduced into good society without apprehension. He was of comely, though for some reason somewhat repulsive, appearance, some eight-and-thirty years old, dressed irreproachably, belonged to a highly bourgeois but highly respectable German family; he was adroit in taking advantage of every opportunity, gaining the patronage of persons in high places and retaining their favor. Once, he had translated from the German some important work of some important German poet, was adroit in dedicating his translations in verse, adroit in boasting of his friendship with a celebrated but deceased Russian poet (there's a whole strata of writers who are exceedingly fond of counting themselves, in print, among the friends of great but deceased writers), and he had been quite recently brought to the Epanchins by the wife of the "old dignitary." This lady was reputed to be a patron of literary and learned men, and, indeed, had even actually procured one or two writers a pension through the intervention of highly placed personages with whom she had influence. And she did have influence, in her own way. She was a lady of five-and-forty (and therefore a very young wife for so aged a man as her husband), a former beauty who still, like many ladies at forty-five, had a mania for dressing far too luxuriously; she was of slight intelligence and rather dubious knowledge of literature. But the patronage of literary men was the same sort of mania with her as was luxurious dress. Many compositions and translations had been dedicated to her; two or three writers had, with her permission, printed letters they had written to her on subjects of the greatest importance... And all this society the prince took for truest coin, for pure gold without alloy. And incidentally, all these people were too, as though by design, in the happiest frame of mind that evening, and rather well pleased with themselves. Every last one of them knew that they were doing the Epanchins a great honor by their visit. But, alas, the prince did not even suspect such subtleties. He did not suspect, for instance, that, while the Epanchins were contemplating so important a step as deciding the fate of their daughter, they would not have dared to omit exhibiting him, Prince Lev Nikolaevich, to the old dignitary who was the acknowledged patron of the family. Though the old dignitary for his part would have borne with perfect equanimity the news of the most awful calamity having befallen the Epanchins, he would certainly have been offended if the Epanchins had betrothed their daughter without his advice and, so to speak, without his leave. Prince N., that charming, indisputably witty man of such lofty sincerity, was firmly persuaded that he was something like a sun that had risen that night over the Epanchins' drawing room. He regarded them as infinitely beneath him, and it was just this open-hearted and generous thought that engendered in him his wonderfully charming ease and friendliness toward those same Epanchins. He knew very well that this evening he would certainly have to tell some story to delight the company, and even prepared for it with a certain exhilaration. Prince Lev Nikolaevich, hearing this story later, felt that he had never heard anything like such brilliant humor and such marvelous gaiety and naïveté, almost touching on the lips of such a Don Juan as Prince N. And in the meantime, if he had only known how old and hackneyed that story was, how it was known by heart, and had become threadbare and tedious in every drawing room, and only at the innocent Epanchins' passed again for a novelty, for an impromptu, genuine and brilliant reminiscence of a brilliant and splendid man! Even the little German poet, in fact, although he behaved with great modesty and politeness—but even he practically considered himself to be doing an honor to the house by his visit. But the prince did not notice the other side, did not notice any undercurrent. This was a misfortune that Aglaia had not foreseen. She was looking particularly attractive that evening. All three young ladies were dressed up, though not very luxuriously, and even had their hair styled in some particular way. Aglaia was sitting with Yevgeny Pavlovich, and was talking and joking with him with exceptional friendliness. Yevgeny Pavlovich seemed to be conducting himself somewhat more seriously than at other times, also perhaps from respect to the dignitaries. He was already well known in society, however; he was quite at home there, though he was so young. He arrived at the Epanchins' that evening with crepe on his hat, and Belokonsky praised him for this crepe: some other fashionable nephew, under such circumstances, would have, perhaps, not put on crepe for such an uncle. Lizaveta Prokofyevna too was pleased at it, though she seemed on the whole far too preoccupied. The prince noticed that Aglaia looked at him intently once or twice, and he fancied she was satisfied with him. By degrees, he began to feel terribly happy. His recent "fantastical" ideas and apprehensions (after his conversation with Lebedev) seemed to him now, when he suddenly, but frequently, recalled them, an inconceivable, incredible, even ridiculous dream! (And as it was, his chief, though unconscious, impulse and desire earlier and all day long had been to do something somehow to make him disbelieve that dream!) He spoke little and only in answer to questions, and finally fell silent altogether, sitting still and listening, but quite obviously engulfed by delight. By degrees, something like an inspiration was developing in him too, ready to ignite at the first opportunity . . . He began talking, indeed, by chance, also in answer to questions, and apparently quite without any special design.

VII

While he was delightedly absorbed in watching Aglaia, who was talking merrily to Prince N. and Yevgeny Pavlovich, suddenly the elderly Anglomaniac gentleman, who was entertaining the "dignitary" in another corner and with animation telling him about something, uttered the name of Nikolai Andreevich Pavlishchev. The prince turned quickly in their direction and began to listen.

The subject was the current order of things, and some sort of disorderly affairs on estates in the ———— Province. There must have been something amusing in the Anglomaniac's account, for the old man began laughing at last at the bilious fervency of the speaker. He was recounting, drawing out his words somehow smoothly and peevishly, with soft emphasis on the vowels, why he had been forced, and precisely by the current order of things, to sell a splendid estate of his in the ———— Province and for half its value, too, though he was in no particular need of money, and at the same time to keep an estate that had gone to ruin, was encumbered, and a subject of litigation, and even to pay more for it. "To avoid another lawsuit with the Pavlishchev estate, too, I ran away from them. Another inheritance or two of that kind and I shall be ruined. Though I should have come in for three thousand hectares of excellent land, however."

"Why, of course . . . Ivan Petrovich is a relation of the late Nikolai Andreevich Pavlishchev, you know . . . You had looked for relations, I believe," Ivan Fyodorovich, who suddenly happened to be near and noticed the prince's extraordinary attention to the conversation, said to the prince in an undertone. He had till then been entertaining the general, his superior, but had for some time been noticing Lev Nikolaevich's exclusive isolation, and was becoming uneasy; he wanted to bring him into the conversation to a certain extent and in that way show him and recommend him to the "great personages" for a second time.

"Lev Nikolaevich was left a ward of Nikolai Andreevich Pavlishchev on the death of his parents," he put in, meeting Ivan Petrovich's eye.

"De-lighted to hear it," observed the latter. "And I remember it well, indeed. When Ivan Fyodorovich introduced us earlier, I knew you at once, and from your face, too. You've changed very little, truly, though I only saw you as a child, you were ten or eleven. There is something about your features that jogs the memory . . ."

"You saw me when I was a child?" the prince asked, with extraordinary surprise.

"Oh, it was very long ago," Ivan Petrovich went on. "At Zlatoverhovo, where you were living at the time with my cousins. In the old days, I used to go pretty often to Zlatoverhovo—don't you remember me? It's ve-ery likely that you don't remember . . . You were then . . . you had some sort of illness then, so much so that I even wondered at you on one occasion . . ."

"I don't remember anything!" the prince asserted with warmth.

There were a few more words of explanation, extremely calm on the part of Ivan Petrovich, and amazingly agitated on the part of the prince, and it came out that the two ladies, elderly spinsters, kinswomen of the late Pavlishchev, who had lived on his estate, Zlatoverhovo, and to whose care the prince had been entrusted, were, in their turn, cousins of Ivan Petrovich's. Ivan Petrovich, like everyone else, was also able to explain almost nothing about the reasons that induced Pavlishchev to take so much trouble over the little prince, his charge. "It hadn't, in fact, occurred to me to be curious about that," but yet, it turned out that he had an excellent memory, for he even recollected how severe the elder cousin, Marfa Nikitishna, had been with the little ward, "so that once I even upbraided her on your account over her system of education; for the rod, and nothing but the rod with a sick child—why, that's . . . you'll admit . . ." and how tender, on the other hand, the younger sister, Natalya Nikitishna, had been to the poor child . . . "They have both," he explained further, "been living in ———— Province now (only I don't know whether they're alive now), where Pavlishchev left them a rather substantial little property. I believe Marfa Nikitishna wanted to go into a convent; but, then again, I don't claim to know; I may have heard that of someone else . . . Yes, I heard that the other day, about a doctor's wife."

The prince listened to this with eyes shining with delight and emotion. With extraordinary warmth he declared that he, for his part, would never forgive himself that, in these six months of his trip to the inner provinces, he had not taken the opportunity to seek out and visit the ladies who had brought him up. He had "been meaning to set off every day, but had been continually distracted by circumstances . . . but that now he promised himself . . . without fail . . . even though it were to ———— Province . . . So you know Natalya Nikitishna? What a splendid, what a saintly soul! But Marfa Nikitishna, too . . . forgive me . . . but I think you are mistaken in Marfa Nikitishna! She was severe, but . . . how could she help losing patience . . . with such an idiot as I was then (hee-hee!). Why, I was a complete idiot back then, you wouldn't believe it (ha-ha!). Though . . . though you saw me then, and . . . how is it that I don't remember you, tell me that, please? So you . . . Oh, my God, are you really a relation of Nikolai Andreevich Pavlishchev?"

"I as-sure you I am." Ivan Petrovich smiled, scrutinizing the prince.

"Oh, but I didn't say that because I . . . doubted it . . . and, ultimately, could one really doubt that (he-he!) . . . in the slightest? . . . That is to say, even in the slightest! (He-he!) But I only meant that the late Nikolai Andreevich Pavlishchev was such a splendid man! A most noble-hearted man, I assure you!"

The prince was not exactly breathless, but "choking with good-heartedness," as Adelaida expressed it next morning in a conversation with her betrothed, Prince Shch.

"Oh, my goodness!" Ivan Petrovich laughed. "Why shouldn't I be a relation of a noble-hearted man, even?"

"Oh, my goodness!" cried the prince, overcome with confusion and growing more and more hurried and animated. "I . . . I've said something stupid again, but . . . that's bound to happen because I . . . I . . . I . . . but, actually, that's out of place again! And of what consequence am I, pray tell, beside such interests . . . beside such vast interests! And in comparison to such a noble-hearted man! For you know, upon my word, he really was a noble-hearted man, isn't that true? Isn't that true?"

The prince was positively trembling all over. Why he was suddenly so agitated, why he was in such an emotional state of ecstasy, completely apropos of nothing and, it seems, out of all proportion with the subject of conversation, it was difficult to decide. He was in just such a frame of mind, and in that moment, he almost seemed to feel the warmest and most tender gratitude to someone for something—perhaps even to Ivan Petrovich, if not to practically all the guests as a whole. He had simply grown far too "slaphappy." Ivan Petrovich began at last peering at him more intently; the "dignitary" examined him very intently too. Belokonsky fixed her wrathful gaze on the prince and tightened her lips. Prince N., Yevgeny Pavlovich, Prince Shch., the young ladies—everyone broke off their conversation and listened. It seemed that Aglaia was frightened, and Lizaveta Prokofyevna's heart simply failed her. They, too, the mother and daughters, had behaved strangely: they themselves had supposed and decided that it would be better for the prince to sit still and be silent the whole evening; but as soon as they saw him in the corner, in complete solitude, perfectly satisfied with his lot, they were at once dreadfully perturbed. Alexandra had been on the point of going to him and cautiously, across the entire room, joining their company, that is Prince N.'s company, near Belokonsky. And now that the prince had begun talking of his own accord they were even more perturbed.

"That he was a most excellent man, there you are right," Ivan Petrovich pronounced imposingly, and no longer smiling. "Yes, yes . . . he was a wonderful man! Wonderful and worthy," he added, after a pause.

"Worthy, one may say, of all respect," he added even more imposingly, after a third pause. "And . . . and it is very agreeable to see on your part . . ."

"Wasn't it the same Pavlishchev with whom transpired some . . . queer story . . . with the abbé . . . the abbé . . . I've forgotten which abbé . . . only everybody was talking about it at one time," the "dignitary" pronounced, as though recollecting something.

"With the Abbé Goureau, a Jesuit," Ivan Petrovich prompted. "Yes, sir, there you have our most excellent and worthy people, sir! Because he was after all a man of good birth and fortune, a *kammerherr*,[33] and if he had . . . remained in the service . . . And there you are, he suddenly throws up the service to convert to Catholicism and become a Jesuit, and almost openly, with a sort of enthusiasm. Truly, he died at a suitable moment . . . yes; everybody said so. . . ."

The prince was beside himself.

"Pavlishchev . . . Pavlishchev, converted to Catholicism? Impossible!" he cried in horror.

"Well, now, 'impossible!' " Ivan Petrovich said in a stately mumble. "That's saying a good deal, and you must admit yourself, my dear prince . . . However, you have such a high opinion of the deceased . . . indeed, he was a most good-natured man, and it is to that, in the main, that I attribute the success of that rascal Goureau. But ask me, ask me, what a fuss and bother I had afterward over that affair . . . and precisely with that very same Goureau! Only fancy," he turned suddenly to the old man, "they even wanted to put in a claim under the will, and I was even forced to have recourse to the most, that is, to vigorous measures . . . to bring them to their senses . . . for they're masters at that kind of thing. Am-a-zing people! But thank goodness it all happened in Moscow. I went straight to the Count, and we soon . . . brought them to their senses . . ."

"You wouldn't believe how you've grieved and astonished me!" exclaimed the prince again.

"I am sorry; but, essentially, all this was, strictly speaking, but a trifle and would have ended in trifles, as always; I'm convinced of it. Last summer," he turned again to the old man, "Countess K., they say, also

33. Ger., "gentleman of the chamber"—a chamberlain; originally a high-level office at the royal palace that later came to be given as an honorary title, it was awarded only to members of the aristocracy who had a civil service grade of at least IV.

went into some Catholic convent abroad; our people never can hold out if once they give in to those . . . rogues . . . especially abroad."

"It all comes from our . . . weariness, I think," the old dignitary mumbled authoritatively. "And their manner of proselytizing is . . . elegant and their own . . . and they know how to scare people. They gave me a good scare, too, I assure you, in Vienna in 1832: only I wouldn't give in and ran away from them, ha-ha! Truly, I ran away from them . . ."

"I heard, my dear chap, that back then you flung up your post and ran away from Vienna to Paris with the beauty Countess Levitzky and not from the Jesuits," Belokonsky put in suddenly.

"Well, you see, it was from a Jesuit; it turns out after all that it was from a Jesuit!" the old dignitary took up, laughing at the agreeable recollection. "You seem to be very religious, which one rarely meets with nowadays in a young man," he turned kindly to Prince Lev Nikolaevich, who was listening to the tale open-mouthed and still stunned; the old man evidently wanted to study the prince more closely; for some reason he had begun to interest him greatly.

"Pavlishchev was a clearheaded man and a Christian, a genuine Christian," the prince brought out suddenly. "How could he have accepted a faith . . . that's unchristian? . . . Catholicism is as good as an unchristian faith!" he added suddenly, looking before him with flashing eyes, as though scanning the whole company together.

"Come, that's too much!" muttered the old man and looked with surprise at Ivan Fyodorovich.

"How do you mean, Catholicism is an unchristian faith," Ivan Petrovich turned round in his chair. "What sort is it then?"

"An unchristian faith, in the first place!" the prince began again, in extreme agitation and with excessive brusqueness. "That's in the first place, and in the second place, Roman Catholicism is even worse than atheism itself, that's my opinion! Yes, that's my opinion! Atheism only preaches nothing, but Catholicism goes further: it preaches a distorted Christ, a Christ calumniated and defamed by themselves, the opposite of Christ! It preaches the Antichrist, I swear to you, I assure you! This is the conviction I have long held, and it has tormented me, myself . . . Roman Catholicism believes that without universal governmental power, the church will not endure on earth, and cries: '*Non possumus!*[34] In my view, Roman Catholicism is not even a faith, but simply the continuation of the Western Roman Empire, and everything in it is subordinated to that idea, beginning with the faith. The pope seized the earth, and earthly throne, and grasped the sword; and everything has gone on in the same way since, only they have added to the sword lying, guile, deceit, fanaticism, superstition, villainy; they have trifled with the most holy, truthful, sincere, fervent feelings of the people; they have bartered it all, all for money, for base earthly power. And is that not the teaching of Antichrist?! How could atheism fail to come from them? Atheism has sprung from them, from Roman Catholicism itself! Atheism originated, first of all, with them themselves: can they have believed themselves? It has been strengthened by aversion to them; it is begotten by their lying and their spiritual impotence! Atheism! Among us it is only the exceptional classes who don't believe, those who, as Yevgeny Pavlovich splendidly put it the other day, have lost their roots; but over there, in Europe, a terrible mass of the people themselves are beginning to lose their faith—previously, from darkness and lying, and now from fanaticism, from hatred of the church and Christianity!"

The prince paused to catch his breath. He had been speaking terribly fast. He was pale and breathless. Everyone was exchanging glances; but at last the old dignitary frankly burst out laughing. Prince N. drew out his lorgnette and, with his gaze fixed upon him, examined the prince. The little German poet crept out of his corner and moved nearer to the table, smiling a most malicious smile.

"You are ex-ag-ge-rating very much," Ivan Petrovich drawled with an air of being bored, and even rather ashamed of something. "In that Church, there are also representatives who are worthy of all respect and vir-tu-ous . . ."

"I never said anything about individual representatives of the Church. I was speaking of Roman Catholicism in its essence. I am speaking of Rome. Why, can a Church disappear altogether? I never said that!"

"I agree. But all that's well known and—unnecessary, indeed, and . . . belongs to theology . . ."

---

34. Lat., *we cannot*; a phrase traditionally used in papal missives to indicate a refusal to comply with demands made by a secular head of state.

"Oh no, oh no! Not only to theology, I assure you, that's not so! It concerns us much more closely than you think. That's our whole mistake, that we can't see yet that this business is not exclusively theological! Why, Socialism too is born of Catholicism and the essence of Catholicism! Like its brother, atheism, it also came out of despair, in opposition to Catholicism in the moral sense, to take the place of the lost moral power of religion, to quench the spiritual thirst of parched mankind, and to save it not by Christ but also by force! That, too, is freedom through force, that, too, is unification by sword and blood. 'Don't dare to believe in God, don't dare to have property, don't dare to have individuality, *fraternité ou la mort*,[35] two million heads!' By their works ye shall know them—so it is said! And don't imagine that all this is so innocent and harmless for us. Oh, we need resistance, and posthaste, posthaste! Our Christ, whom we have kept and they have never known, must shine forth in resistance to the West! It is not slavishly swallowing the Jesuit line, but rather carrying our Russian civilization to them that we must stand before them now, and let it not be said among us that their proselytizing is elegant, as someone said just now..."

"But allow me, allow me!" Ivan Petrovich grew dreadfully concerned, looking about him and positively beginning to lose heart. "All your ideas, of course, are very praiseworthy and full of patriotism, but all this is exaggerated in the extreme, and...it would even be better to leave it..."

"No, it's not exaggerated, but rather more understated; indeed, understated, because I am not capable of expressing myself, but..."

"But al-low me!"

The prince ceased speaking. He sat, pulling himself upright in his chair, and gazed with a fiery look at Ivan Petrovich.

"I fancy the incident with your benefactor has shocked you far too much now," the old man observed kindly and without losing his composure. "You have grown over-ardent...perhaps from solitude. If you were to live more among people—and I should hope you would be welcome in society as a remarkable young man—then, of course, you would calm your lively spirits and see that it is all much simpler...and

35. Fr., fraternity or death (from the French Revolutionary slogan, "liberty, equality and fraternity").

besides such exceptional cases . . . occur, in my view, in part out of our over-satiation, and in part out of . . . boredom."

"Just so, just so!" exclaimed the prince. "A splendid idea! It's precisely 'out of boredom, out of our boredom,' not from over-satiation, but on the contrary, from thirst . . . not from over-satiation, you're mistaken in that! Not simply from thirst, but from inflammation, from burning thirst! And . . . and don't think that it's to such a slight extent that one can simply laugh at it; excuse me, one must know how to read the writing on the wall! Our Russian brothers, no sooner do they reach the shore and verify that it's the shore, are so delighted at it that they at once go to the limit; why is that? Here you are surprised at Pavlishchev, you ascribed it all to his madness or kindheartedness, but that's not right! And it is not only we alone who are amazed at our Russian fervor in such cases, but all of Europe: if one among us turns Catholic, he is sure to become a Jesuit, and one of the most underground; if he becomes an atheist, he's sure to start demanding the extirpation of belief in God by force, that is, by the sword! Why is this, why such frenzy all at once? Can it be you don't know? Because he has found the fatherland that he has missed here, and rejoices; he has found the shore, he has found land, and rushes to kiss it! For, you know, Russian atheists and Russian Jesuits are not simply the outcome of vanity alone, of rotten, vain feelings, but also of spiritual pain, of spiritual thirst, of a longing for the loftiest matters, for a firm shore, for a fatherland in which they have ceased to believe, because they have never even known it! Why, it's easier for a Russian to become an atheist than for anyone else in the world! And our people do not merely become atheists, but they invariably come to *believe* in atheism, as in a new religion, without noticing that they are putting faith in naught. So great is our thirst! 'He who has no ground beneath his feet has no god either.' That's not my own expression. It's the expression of a merchant, an Old Believer, whom I met when I was traveling. Truth be told, he didn't put it that way; he said: 'He who renounces his native soil renounces his god as well.' Why, if one only thinks that among us, the most educated people take to flagellantism . . . But then again, how is flagellantism in that case worse than nihilism, Jesuitism, or atheism? It may even be rather more profound! But that's what their longing can come to! Reveal to the thirsting and feverish companions of Columbus the shores of the 'New World,' reveal to the Russian man the Russian

'World,' let him find this gold, this treasure hidden from him in the earth! Show him the renewal and resurrection of all mankind in the future, perhaps alone through Russian thought, through the Russian God and Christ, and you shall see what a mighty and honest, wise and gentle giant will rise up before the eyes of the astounded world, astounded and dismayed, because they expect nothing of us but the sword, the sword and violence, because they cannot imagine us, judging by their own example, free of barbarism. And this has been so till now, and it is all the more so as time goes on! And ..."

But at this point an event took place, and the orator's speech was cut short in the most unexpected manner.

This whole wild tirade, this whole flood of passionate and agitated words and enraptured ideas, jostling one another, as it were, in a kind of flurry and tumbling one over the other, all of this portended something ominous, something peculiar in the mood of the young man who had boiled over so suddenly, and evidently apropos of nothing. Of those present in the drawing room, everyone who knew the prince wondered apprehensively (and some with shame) at this outburst, which was so out of keeping with his habitual and even diffident restraint, with his rare and peculiar tact in certain cases, and with his instinctive sense of the highest propriety. They could not understand what it was due to: certainly the news about Pavlishchev could not have been the cause. In the ladies' corner, they gazed at him as at a madman, and Belokonsky confessed afterward that "another minute more and she was on the verge of fleeing." The "old gentlemen" nearly lost their bearings in their first amazement; the department chief gazed out sternly and with displeasure from his chair. The engineer colonel sat in absolute immobility. The little German turned positively pale, but still smiled his artificial smile, stealing glances at the rest to see how they would respond. But actually, all this and the "whole scandal" might have been resolved in the most ordinary and natural way, perhaps even a minute later; Ivan Fyodorovich, who was extremely astonished but had grasped the situation sooner than the rest, had already made several attempts to stop the prince; not having achieved success, he was now making his way toward him, with a firm and resolute aim. One more minute and, had it really been necessary, he would have perhaps resolved to lead the prince amicably out of the room on the pretext of his being ill, which would, perhaps, have in fact been the truth, and which Ivan Fyodorovich very much believed himself . . . But the matter took a different turn.

At the beginning, when the prince first entered the drawing room, he seated himself as far as possible from the Chinese vase with which Aglaia had so frightened him. Is it possible to believe that after Aglaia's words of the day before he was seized by some sort of indelible conviction, some astonishing and impossible presentiment that he would be sure to break this vase on the very next day, however much he kept away from it, however much he tried to avoid disaster? But so it was. In the course of the evening other strong but radiant impressions began to flow into his soul; we have spoken of that already. He forgot his presentiment. When he heard about Pavlishchev and Ivan Fyodorovich brought him up and presented him to Ivan Petrovich once more, he moved to a seat nearer to the table and wound up right in the armchair next to the huge, beautiful Chinese vase, which stood on a pedestal almost near his elbow, a little behind him.

At his last words he suddenly rose from his seat, incautiously waved his arm, somehow twitched his shoulder and . . . a shout was heard all around! The vase tottered, as though wavering in indecision at first whether to fall upon the head of one of the old gentlemen, but suddenly inclined in the opposite direction, toward the little German, who had barely managed to leap aside in alarm, and crashed to the ground. Thunder, shouting, precious shards spilling over the carpet, alarm, astonishment—oh, what was happening to the prince is difficult, and virtually unnecessary, to portray! But we cannot omit to mention one odd sensation, which struck him precisely at that very moment and suddenly stood out clearly from the mass of other vague and strange sensations: not the shame, not the scandal, not the fear, not the suddenness of it struck him most, but the fulfillment of the prophecy! He would not have been able to explain even to himself what was so arresting about that thought; he only felt that he was struck to the core, and he stood in a terror that was almost mystical. Another instant and everything seemed to open out before him; instead of horror there was light and joy, ecstasy; his breath began to fail him, and . . . but the moment passed. Thank God, it was not that! He caught his breath and looked about him.

He seemed for a long time unable to understand the commotion that was churning all around him, or, rather, he understood it perfectly and saw everything, but stood as though he were a man apart who had no share in anything and who, like an invisible figure in a fairy tale, had crept into the room and was watching people with whom he is not involved but finds interesting. He saw how they cleaned up the shards, heard rapid conversations, saw Aglaia, pale and looking at him strangely, very strangely: there was absolutely no hatred in her eyes, no anger at all; she was looking at him with such a frightened, but such an amiable, expression, while her eyes flashed so at everyone else . . . His heart suddenly began to ache with a sweet pain. At last he saw with a strange amazement that they had all sat down again and were even laughing, as though nothing had happened! In another minute the laughter grew louder: they were now laughing just looking at him, at his dumb stupefaction; but they were laughing amicably and merrily; many of them addressed him and spoke so affectionately, Lizaveta Prokofyevna most of all: she was speaking with laughter and saying something very, very kind. Suddenly, he felt that Ivan Fyodorovich was patting him amicably on the shoulder; Ivan Petrovich was laughing too; but the old gentleman was even better, more charming and more amiable; he took the prince by the hand and, slightly squeezing it, and slightly patting it with the palm of the other hand, urged him to come to his senses, just as though he were talking to a little frightened boy, which pleased the prince awfully, and finally made him sit down right beside him. The prince peered with delight into his face, and was still unable to speak for some reason, his breath failed him; he liked the old man's face so much.

"What," he muttered at last, "you really forgive me? And . . . you, too, Lizaveta Prokofyevna?"

The laughter grew louder; tears came into the prince's eyes—he could hardly believe his senses and was enchanted.

"It was a fine vase, to be sure. I can remember it here for the last fifteen years, yes . . . fifteen . . ." Ivan Petrovich began to utter.

"Well, here's a terrible disaster! Even a man must come to an end, and all this to-do about a clay pot!" said Lizaveta Prokofyevna loudly. "Surely, you weren't really so alarmed, Lev Nikolaevich?" she added, indeed, with some apprehension. "That's enough, my pet, that's enough; you're scaring me in earnest."

"And you forgive me for *everything*? For *everything*, besides the vase?" The prince was on the verge of suddenly rising from his seat, but the old man at once drew him down again by the arm. He did not want to let him go.

"*C'est très curieux et c'est très sérieux!*"[36] he whispered across the table to Ivan Petrovich, speaking, however, rather loudly; the prince may have heard it.

"So I've not insulted anyone? You won't believe how happy I am at the notion; but that was bound to be so! Could I possibly insult anyone here? I should be insulting you again, if I could think such a thing."

"Calm yourself, my friend, this is all exaggerated. And there's nothing at all for you to be so thankful about; that's an excellent feeling, but exaggerated."

"I'm not thanking you, I am only . . . admiring you, I'm happy looking at you; perhaps I'm talking foolishly, but—I have to speak, I have to explain . . . if only from self-respect."

Everything in him was spasmodic, confused, feverish; it is quite likely that the words he uttered were often not those he wanted to speak. He seemed to be asking with his gaze whether he might speak. His gaze fell upon Belokonsky.

"It's all right, dear fellow, go on, go on, only don't run out of breath," she observed. "You began in such a breathless hurry before, and you see what you've come to; but don't be afraid to speak; these ladies and gentlemen have seen even queerer folk than you, you won't astonish them, and Lord knows you're not so outlandish, either; you've only broken a vase and given us all a fright."

The prince listened to her, smiling.

"Why, was it you," he suddenly turned to the old gentleman, "why, was it you who saved a student called Podkumov and an official called Shvabrin[37] from exile three months ago?"

The old man positively flushed somewhat, and muttered that he must calm himself.

"And wasn't it about you I heard," he turned at once to Ivan Petrovich, "in the ——— Province that when your peasants, who were already freed and had given you a lot of trouble, were burned out of house and home you gave them timber to rebuild for nothing?"

"Well, that's an ex-ag-ge-ra-tion," muttered Ivan Petrovich, though

36. Fr., this is very curious and very serious.
37. The name is taken from Pushkin's *The Captain's Daughter*. In the novel, Alexei Ivanovich Shvabrin was sent into exile for dueling.

taking on a pleasantly dignified air; but this time he was absolutely right that it was "an exaggeration": it was only an incorrect rumor that had reached the prince.

"And did not you, Princess," he suddenly turned to Belokonsky with a radiant smile, "did not you receive me six months ago in Moscow like your own son, upon Lizaveta Prokofyevna's letter; and, indeed, just as if I were your own son, you gave me one piece of advice that I shall never forget. Remember?"

"Well, why are you climbing the walls?" uttered Belokonsky with vexation. "You're a good-natured fellow but ridiculous: let someone give you a halfpenny and you thank him just as though he had saved your life. You think it praiseworthy, but it's disgusting."

She was on the verge of losing her temper entirely, but suddenly burst out laughing, and this time her laughter was good-natured. Lizaveta Prokofyevna's face brightened too; and Ivan Fyodorovich beamed as well.

"I said that Lev Nikolaevich was a man . . . a man . . . in a word, if only he wouldn't be in such a breathless hurry, as the princess observed . . ." the general murmured in delighted rapture, repeating Belokonsky's words, which had struck him.

Only Aglaia was somehow mournful; but her face was still aflame, perhaps with indignation.

"He truly is very charming," the old man muttered again to Ivan Petrovich.

"I entered here with anguish in my heart," the prince went on, with some sort of increasing perturbation, speaking more and more quickly, more and more queerly and eagerly. "I . . . I was afraid of you, afraid of myself too. Of myself most of all. Coming back here to Petersburg, I promised myself without fail to see our foremost people, the elders of our society, the people of ancient lineage, to whom I belong myself, among whom I am myself one of the foremost by birth. And now I'm sitting with princes like myself, isn't that so? I wanted to get to know you, and it was necessary; very, very necessary! . . . I've always heard too much that was bad about you, more than what was good—about your pettiness and the exclusiveness of your interests, about your backwardness, about your shallow education, about your ridiculous habits—oh, why, there is so much said and written about you! I came here today with curiosity, with perturbation: I needed to see for myself and make up my own mind whether this whole upper crust of Russian society really is good for nothing, has outlived its time, is drained of its ancient life, and is only fit to die, but still persists in a petty, jealous strife with men . . . of the future, getting in their way and not noticing that it is dying itself. I did not entirely believe in this view before either, because there never has been an actual upper class amongst us, except perhaps at the court, by uniform or . . . by accident, and now it has entirely disappeared. That's so, isn't it?"

"No, that's not so at all." Ivan Petrovich laughed caustically.

"Well, now he's striking up again!" Belokonsky could not restrain herself from uttering.

"*Laissez le dire*,[38] he's trembling all over," the old man warned again in an undertone.

The prince was decidedly beside himself.

"Well, and what, then? I saw elegant people, simple-hearted and intelligent; I saw an old man who is kind and attentive to a boy like me; I see people who are capable of understanding and forgiving, Russian and kindhearted people, almost as kind and warmhearted as I met there, almost no worse. You can judge what a delightful surprise it is! Oh, do let me put it all into words! I had heard so often and fully believed myself that in society everything was manners, everything was antiquated form, and the essence of things had run dry; but I see now for myself that that cannot be so among us; it may be so somewhere else, but just not here among us. Can you all be Jesuits and frauds? I heard Prince N. tell you a story earlier: isn't that simple-hearted, inspired humor; isn't that genuine frankness? Can such words come from the lips of a man . . . who is dead; whose heart and talent have run dry? Could the dead have treated me as you have treated me? Isn't that material . . . for the future, for hope? Can such people lag behind and fail to understand?"

"I beg you again, calm yourself, my dear boy; we'll talk about all this another time and I shall be delighted . . ." grinned the "dignitary."

Ivan Petrovich squawked and turned around in his chair; Ivan Fyodorovich stirred; the department chief began talking to the dignitary's wife, no longer paying the slightest attention to the prince; but the dignitary's wife frequently listened and glanced at him.

38. Fr., let him speak.

"No, it's better for me to speak, you know!" the prince continued with another feverish burst, addressing the old man particularly trustingly somehow and even confidentially. "Aglaia Ivanovna forbade me yesterday to speak and even named the subjects that I must not speak about; she knows I am ridiculous in them! I'm twenty-seven, but I know that I'm like a child. I have no right to express my thought, I've said that long ago; it's only in Moscow, with Rogozhin, that I talked openly . . . He and I read Pushkin together, we read all of it. He knew nothing of him, not even the name Pushkin . . . I'm always compromising the thought and the *main idea* with my ridiculous manner. I have no command of gesture. My command of gesture is always antithetical, and that causes laughter and debases the idea. I've no sense of proportion either, and that's the main thing; that's absolutely the main thing, in fact . . . I know it's better for me to sit still and keep quiet. When I stand firm and keep quiet, I even seem very sensible, and what's more, I think things over. But now it's better for me to talk. I started talking because you look at me so wonderfully; you have such a wonderful face! I promised Aglaia Ivanovna yesterday that I'd be silent all evening!"

"*Vraiment?*"[39] The old man smiled.

"But at moments I think that I am not right to think so: why, sincerity is worth the price of gesture, isn't it? Isn't it?"

"Sometimes."

"I want to explain everything, everything, everything! Oh, yes! You think I'm a utopian? An ideologue? Oh, no, upon my word, my ideas are really all so simple . . . You don't believe it? You smile? Let me tell you that I'm contemptible sometimes, for I lose my faith; earlier, on my way here, I was thinking: 'Well, and how shall I talk to them? With what words must one begin in order for them to understand even anything at all?' How frightened I was, but I was more frightened for you, terribly, terribly! And in the meantime, how could I have been afraid? Wasn't it shameful to be afraid? What does it matter that for one man in the vanguard there is such a host of backward and nasty ones? That's just what I'm so happy about, that I'm convinced now that there is no such host, but that it's all living material! And there's no reason to be disconcerted by the fact that we're absurd, isn't that true? Why, you

39. Fr., Indeed?

know it really is true that we're absurd, frivolous, have bad habits, are bored, don't know how to look at things, don't know how to comprehend; why, we're all like that, all of us, you, and I, and they! And see here, you are not offended, after all, at my telling you to your faces that you're absurd, are you? And if that's so, aren't you material? Do you know, to my thinking it's a good thing sometimes to be absurd, even better in fact: it makes it easier to forgive one another, easier to reconcile; one can't understand everything at once, after all, one can't begin straight off with perfection! In order to attain perfection one must first fail to understand a great deal! And if we understand things too quickly, perhaps we shan't understand them well. And I say that to you— you, who have already been able to understand, and ... fail to understand, so much. I'm not afraid for you now; why, you are not angry that a boy like me is saying such things to you, are you? Of course not! Oh, you will know how to forget and to forgive those who have offended you and those who have done nothing to offend you; for, you know, it's most difficult of all to forgive those who have done nothing to offend us, and precisely because they *did not* offend, and so, then, our complaint is groundless: that's what I expected of the loftiest people, that's what I was in a hurry to say to them, coming here, and did not know how to say ... You are laughing, Ivan Petrovich? You think that I was afraid for *the others*, that I'm *their* champion, a democrat, an advocate of equality?" He laughed hysterically (he had been continually laughing with brief and ecstatic bursts of laughter). "I'm afraid for you, for all of you, and for all of us together. Why, I am a prince of ancient lineage myself and I am sitting with princes. I speak to save us all, that our class may not vanish in vain, in darkness, having guessed nothing, abusing everything, and having gambled everything away. Why disappear and make way for others when we might remain elders and in the vanguard? If we are in the vanguard then we shall be elders too. Let us be servants in order to be elders."

He began struggling to get up from his chair, but the old man constantly held him back, looking at him with growing uneasiness, however.

"Listen! I know it's not good to talk: it's better simply to set an example, better simply to begin ... I have already begun ... and—and can one really, in fact, be unhappy? Oh, what is my grief, what is my sorrow, if I am capable of being happy? Do you know, I don't understand how one can walk past a tree and not be happy that one sees it? Talk to a man and not be happy that one loves him! Oh, it's only that I'm not able to express it ... but how many such beautiful things there are at every step, that even the most hopeless man finds to be beautiful? Look at a child, look at God's sunrise, look at the dear grass, how it grows! Look at the eyes that gaze at you and love you ..."

He had for some time been standing as he talked. The old man looked at him in alarm. Lizaveta Prokofyevna exclaimed, "Ah, my God!," having surmised it before everyone else, and threw up her hands in dismay. Aglaia quickly ran up to him, in time to catch him in her arms, and with horror, with a face distorted with pain, heard the wild scream of the "spirit that racked and prostrated"[40] the unhappy man. The sick man lay on the carpet. Someone hastened to put a pillow under his head.

No one expected this. A quarter of an hour later, Prince N., Yevgeny Pavlovich, and the old man attempted to revive the party, but within another half an hour everyone had dispersed. Many words of sympathy were expressed, many regrets, a few opinions. Ivan Petrovich expressed, among other things, that "the young man was a Slavophile or something of that sort, but that, on the other hand, there was nothing very dangerous about that." The old man expressed nothing. Although it's true that later, on the next day and the day after, everyone grew rather cross; Ivan Petrovich was even offended, but not very much so. The department chief was for some time rather cold to Ivan Fyodorovich. The "patron" of the family, the dignitary, for his part, also mumbled something to the father of the family by way of admonishment, whereby he expressed in flattering terms that he was very, very much interested in Aglaia's fate. He really was a rather goodhearted man; but one reason for his curiosity regarding the prince in the course of that evening was also the old story of the prince and Nastasya Filippovna; he had heard something about that story and had been very much interested by it, and would have even liked indeed to inquire about it.

Belokonsky, as she was leaving the party, said to Lizaveta Prokofyevna:

---

40. A reference to an episode from the New Testament in which Jesus heals a young man possessed by an evil spirit who throws him into convulsions (Mark 9:17–29; Luke 9:39–43).

"Well, he's both good and bad; and if you care to know my opinion, rather more bad. You can see for yourself what a man he is, a sick man!"

Lizaveta Prokofyevna decided privately, once and for all, that he was an "impossible" suitor, and that night she vowed to herself that "as long as she was living, the prince would not be the husband of Aglaia." She got up with that in the morning. But in the course of the morning, going on one o'clock, over breakfast, she was drawn into a surprising self-contradiction.

In reply to one of her sisters'—incidentally, extremely cautious—questions, Aglaia suddenly replied coldly, but haughtily, virtually snapping:

"I've never given him a promise of any sort, I've never in my life considered him my betrothed. He is of as much concern to me as any other person."

Lizaveta Prokofyevna suddenly flared up.

"That I should never have expected of you," she pronounced with chagrin. "As a suitor he's impossible, I know, and thank God that it's agreed; but I didn't expect such words from you, of all people! I thought there'd be something different from you. I would turn away all those people from yesterday and keep him, that's the kind of man he is! . . ."

At that point she stopped short, frightened herself at what she said. But if only she had known how unjust she was to her daughter at that moment! Everything was settled in Aglaia's mind; she too was waiting for the hour that was to decide everything, and every hint, every incautious touch rent a deep wound in her heart.

VIII

For the prince, too, that morning began under the influence of painful forebodings; they might be explained by his invalid state, but his sadness was too indefinite, and that was more distressing than anything to him. True, there were vivid, painful, mortifying facts before him, but his sadness went beyond everything he recollected and reflected upon; he understood that he could not calm himself alone. Little by little there took root in him an expectation that something special and definitive would happen to him that very day. His fit of the previous evening had been a slight one; besides a splenetic weariness, a certain heaviness in his head and pain in his limbs, he felt no other disturbances. His head was working rather clearly, though his soul was ailing. He got up rather late, and at once distinctly recalled the previous evening; he remembered, too, though not quite clearly, how he had been escorted home half an hour after the fit. He learned that a messenger had already come from the Epanchins to ask after his health. At half past eleven another one showed up; this pleased him. Vera Lebedev was among the first to visit him and wait upon him. The first minute she saw him, she suddenly burst out crying, but when the prince at once reassured her she began laughing. He was somehow suddenly struck by this girl's deep compassion for him; he seized her hand and kissed it. Vera flushed.

"Ah, what are you doing, what are you doing!" she cried in dismay, hastily drawing her hand away.

She went away soon in some kind of strange confusion. She had time though to tell him, among other things, that her father had run off today, with the first light, to see the "departed," as he called the general, to find out whether he had died in the night, and it was reported, so they said, that he was certain to die soon. Going on twelve o'clock, Lebedev himself put in an appearance at home and before the prince, but, in fact, merely "for a minute to inquire after his precious health," and so on, but also to have a look in the "cubby." He did nothing but sigh and groan and the prince soon dismissed him, but the latter still tried to question him about yesterday's fit, though it was evident he already knew about it in detail. After him Kolya ran in, also for a minute; he really was in a hurry, and was in a great and woeful agitation. He began by directly and insistently asking the prince for an explanation of all that they had been concealing from him, interjecting that he had learned almost everything the day before. He was greatly and profoundly shaken.

With all the possible sympathy that he was capable of, the prince told him the whole affair, reproducing the facts with complete accuracy, and the poor boy was thunderstruck. He could not utter a word and began to cry in silence. The prince felt that this was one of those impressions that remain forever and constitute a breaking point in the life of a young man for all time. He hastened to give him his view of the case, adding that in his opinion, perhaps, the death of the old man was occurring chiefly due to the horror remaining in his heart after his misdeed, and that not everyone was capable of that. Kolya's eyes flashed as he listened to the prince.

"They're a worthless lot—Ganjka and Varya and Ptitsyn! I'm not going to quarrel with them, but we go down different paths from this moment on! Ah, Prince, I've had so many new feelings since yesterday! It's a lesson for me! I consider Mother entirely on my hands now, too; though she's provided for at Varya's, but all that's not the thing . . ."

He jumped up, remembering that he was expected, hurriedly asked after the prince's health and, listening to the answer, suddenly added in haste:

"Isn't there something else? I heard yesterday . . . (but then again, I've no right), but if, at any time and for anything, you ever need a devoted servant, here he is before you. It seems as though we're both of us not quite happy, isn't that so? But . . . I'm not prying, I'm not prying . . ."

He went away, and the prince sank into still deeper reflection: everyone was prophesying misfortune, everyone had already drawn conclusions, everyone looked at him as though they knew something and something he did not know; Lebedev interrogates, Kolya hints at it directly, while Vera weeps. At last, he waved his arm dismissively in vexation. "Damned morbid suspiciousness," he thought. His face brightened when, after one o'clock, he saw the Epanchins, who came to visit him "for a moment." The latter really did come only for a moment. Rising from the breakfast table, Lizaveta Prokofyevna announced that they were all going for a walk at once, and all together. The declaration was made in the form of a command, abruptly, dryly, and with no explanations. They all went out, that is, *maman,* the girls and Prince Shch. Lizaveta Prokofyevna set off at once in a direction exactly opposite to that which they took every day. Everyone understood what was the matter and everyone kept silent for fear of irritating *maman;* for her part, as though hiding from reproaches and objections, she walked in front of everyone without looking back. At last Adelaida observed that there was no need to race like that on a walk, and there was no catching up with *maman.*

"Now then," Lizaveta Prokofyevna turned around suddenly, "we're just passing his door. Whatever Aglaia may think, and whatever may happen afterward, he is not a stranger to us, and on top of that, now he's in trouble and ill; I, at least, shall stop in to see. Whoever cares to join me should come, and whoever doesn't—walk on by; the way is open."

They all went in, of course. The prince, as was proper, hastened once more to beg forgiveness for yesterday's vase and . . . the scene.

"Oh, that's no matter," answered Lizaveta Prokofyevna. "I'm not sorry about the vase, I'm sorry for you. So, then, now you're aware yourself that there was a scene: that's what 'the morning after' means; but that's no matter, either, for everyone sees now that one mustn't expect anything of you. Well, good-bye, though; if you feel strong enough, go for a little walk, and sleep again—that's my advice. And if you fancy, come visit as before; rest assured, once and for all, that whatever happens, you'll still remain our family friend: mine, at least. I can, at least, answer for myself . . ."

Everyone answered the challenge and confirmed *maman*'s sentiments. They went out, but in this simple-hearted haste to say something kind and encouraging there lay hidden a great deal that was cruel, of which Lizaveta Prokofyevna had not even become aware. In the invitation to come "as before" and in the words "mine at least"— there again sounded some portentous note. The prince began to think of Aglaia; true, she had smiled wonderfully at him upon entering and upon taking leave, but she had not said a word, even when everyone was offering their assurances of friendship, though she had looked intently at him once or twice. Her face was paler than usual, as though she had slept badly that night. The prince resolved to visit them without fail that very evening, "as before," and he glanced feverishly at his watch. Vera came in exactly three minutes after the Epanchins had gone.

"Lev Nikolaevich, Aglaia Ivanovna just conveyed a word to me in secret, for you," she said.

The prince positively trembled.

"A note?"

"No, sir, verbally; she had hardly time for that, even. She begs you very earnestly not to absent yourself from the grounds the entire day today, not even for a minute, right up till seven o'clock this evening, or till nine o'clock, I couldn't quite hear."

"But . . . what for? What does it mean?"

"I know nothing of that; only she bade me most firmly to convey it."

"That's what she actually said: 'most firmly'?"

"No, sir, she didn't say it directly: she barely managed to turn away and utter it; luckily, I ran up to her myself. But it was evident from her face when she was charging me whether it was most firm or not. She gave me such a look that my heart stopped beating . . ."

A few more inquiries, and the prince, though he learned nothing more, instead became all the more agitated. Left alone, he lay down on the sofa and began to think again. "Perhaps there'll be someone there till nine o'clock and she's afraid for me again, that I might pull some stunt in front of guests," he came up with at last, and again began waiting impatiently for evening and looking at his watch. But the solution ensued long before the evening, and also in the form of a new visitor—a solution in the form of a new and agonizing riddle: exactly half an hour after the Epanchins' visit, Ippolit came in to him, so tired and exhausted that, having entered without uttering a word, he literally fell, as if senseless, into an easy chair, and was instantly engulfed by an insufferable cough. He coughed till the blood came. His eyes glittered and red spots flushed his cheeks. The prince murmured something to him, but the latter did not answer, and for a long time afterward, without answering, only waved his hand dismissively that he should not be disturbed yet. At last he came to himself.

"I'm going!" he pronounced at last with an effort in a husky voice.

"Would you like me to escort you," said the prince, rising from his seat, and suddenly faltered, recollecting the recent injunction against leaving the grounds.

Ippolit laughed.

"I'm not going away from you," he went on, continually gasping and coughing, "on the contrary, I found it necessary to come to you, and on business . . . but for which I would not have disturbed you. I'm going *over there*, and this time, it seems, in earnest. It's all up! I don't say so for sympathy, believe me . . . I lay down today already, at ten o'clock, so as not to get up again till *the time* came, but you see I changed my mind and got up once more to come to you . . . so it would seem I had to."

"It grieves me to look at you; you'd better have sent for me instead of making the effort yourself."

"Well, that's enough. You've expressed your regret, then, and that's enough to satisfy the requirements of worldly politeness . . . But I forgot: how is your health, then?"

"I'm well. Yesterday I was ... not quite ..."

"I heard, I heard. The Chinese vase had a bad time of it; it's a pity I wasn't there! I've come on business. In the first place, I've had the pleasure today of seeing Gavrila Ardalionovich at a rendezvous with Aglaia Ivanovna by the green bench. I marveled at the degree to which it is possible for a man to look stupid. I remarked upon it to Aglaia Ivanovna herself, when Gavrila Ardalionovich had gone ... You seem not to be surprised at anything, Prince," he added, looking mistrustfully at the prince's calm face. "To be surprised at nothing, they say, is a sign of great intelligence; to my mind, it might equally well be a sign of great stupidity ... I'm not implying anything about you, however, excuse me ... I am very unfortunate in my expressions today."

"I already knew yesterday that Gavrila Ardalionovich ... ," the prince faltered, evidently disconcerted, though Ippolit was vexed at his not being surprised.

"You knew! Well, that's news! But then again, perhaps you shouldn't tell me about it ... You weren't a witness of the interview today, I suppose?"

"You saw that I was not there, since you were there yourself."

"Well, you may have been sitting behind a bush somewhere. But then, in any case, I'm glad, for your sake, of course, for I was beginning to think that Gavrila Ardalionovich—was the favorite!"

"I beg you not to speak of this to me, Ippolit, and in such terms."

"Especially since you know everything already."

"You are mistaken, I know almost nothing, and Aglaia Ivanovna knows for a fact that I know nothing. And even of this rendezvous, I knew absolutely nothing ... You say there was a rendezvous? Very well then, let's drop it ..."

"But how's this—one minute you know, the next you don't? You say, 'Very well and let's drop it'? Oh, no, don't you be so trustful! Especially if you don't know anything. And you are trustful because you don't know anything. And do you know what those two characters, the brother and sister, are reckoning on? Do you perhaps suspect that? ... Very well, very well, I'll drop it ..." he added, noticing the prince's impatient gesture. "But I've come about my own affairs and I want to ... explain about it. Damn it all, it's impossible to die without explanations; it's awful how much I explain myself. Do you care to hear?"

"Speak; I'm listening."

"But I'll change my mind again, though: I'll begin with Ganechka, after all. Can you imagine that I had an appointment to come to the green bench today too? But then, I don't want to tell a lie: I insisted on the rendezvous myself, I cajoled, I promised to reveal a secret. I don't know whether I came too early (I think I really did come too early), but I had no sooner taken my place, beside Aglaia Ivanovna, when I saw Gavrila Ardalionovich and Varvara Ardalionovna coming along, arm in arm, as though they were out for a walk. I fancy they were both very much amazed at meeting me; they were expecting something else, and were even disconcerted. Aglaia Ivanovna flushed and, believe it or not, was even a bit flustered, whether because I was there or simply at the sight of Gavrila Ardalionovich, for he is far too handsome, you know, anyway she flushed, and ended the business in one second, very absurdly: she got up, answered Gavrila Ardalionovich's bow, and Varvara Ardalionovna's ingratiating smile, and suddenly snapped: 'I've only come to express in person my pleasure at your sincere and friendly feelings, and if I am in need of them, believe me . . .' Here she bowed farewell and they both went off—I don't know whether like fools or in triumph; Ganechka, of course, a fool; he couldn't make out a word, and turned red as a lobster (he has such an extraordinary facial expression sometimes!), but Varvara Ardalionovna, it seems, understood that they should make themselves scarce posthaste, and that this was more than enough from Aglaia Ivanovna, and she dragged her brother away. She's cleverer than him and I've no doubt she's triumphant now. And for my part, I came to talk to Aglaia Ivanovna in order to make arrangements about a meeting with Nastasya Filippovna."

"With Nastasya Filippovna!" exclaimed the prince.

"Aha! You are losing your cool indifference and beginning to be surprised, it seems? I'm very glad you want to resemble a human being. I'll comfort you for that. Here's what it means to do a service to young and high-minded ladies: I got a slap in the face from her today!"

"A m-moral one?" the prince asked involuntarily.

"Yes, not a physical one. It seems to me that no one could raise a hand against a creature like me, even a woman would not strike me now; even Ganechka wouldn't strike me! Though I did think at one point yesterday that he was going to fly at me . . . Bet you anything I know what you're thinking about now? You're thinking: 'Granted, he mustn't be beaten, but he might be smothered with a pillow or a wet rag in his sleep—in fact one ought to . . .' It's written on your face that you're thinking that at this very second."

"I've never thought of such a thing," the prince uttered with disgust.

"I don't know, I dreamt last night that I was smothered with a wet rag by . . . a man . . . well, I'll tell you who it was: just imagine— Rogozhin! What do you think? Could a man be smothered with a wet rag?"

"I don't know."

"I've heard it can be done. Very well, we'll drop it. Come, why am I a gossip? Why did she accuse me of being a gossip today? And take note, it was after she'd heard every last word and even questioned me, too . . . But that's what women are like! For her sake I've gotten into communication with Rogozhin, an interesting person; and it was in her interests I arranged a personal interview with Nastasya Filippovna for her. Could it be because I wounded her vanity by hinting that she was glad of Nastasya Filippovna's leftovers? But it was in her own interests that I tried to impress that upon her the whole time, I don't deny it; I wrote her two letters in that vein, and today for the third time, at our interview . . . That's just what I began with before, that it was humiliating on her part . . . And on top of that, the word 'leftovers' wasn't mine, but someone else's; at any rate, at Ganechka's, everybody was saying it; and she even confirmed it herself. So then why am I a slanderer to her? I see, I see; it's awfully amusing for you to look at me now, and I'll bet anything you're applying those stupid verses to me:

> And on the gloom of my declining hour
> Perchance the farewell smile of love may shine.[41]

Ha-ha-ha!" he suddenly gushed with hysterical laughter and was overcome with coughing. "Mark," he gasped through the cough, "what a fellow Ganechka is: he talks of 'leftovers' and what does he want to take advantage of now himself!"

For a long while the prince was silent; he was horror-struck.

"You spoke of an interview with Nastasya Filippovna?" he murmured at last.

41. From Pushkin's poem "Elegy" (1830).

"Eh, but are you honestly unaware that Aglaia Ivanovna is going to see Nastasya Filippovna today, for which purpose Nastasya Filippovna was bid to come, extra, through Rogozhin, from Petersburg, at Aglaia Ivanovna's invitation and by my efforts, and now finds herself, together with Rogozhin, not too far from you, in the same house as before, staying with that lady … Darya Alexeevna … a very dubious lady, a friend of hers, and to that very place, that dubious house, Aglaia Ivanovna is headed today to have an amicable chat with Nastasya Filippovna, and to resolve various problems. They want to work at arithmetic. Didn't you know it? Honor bright?"

"That's incredible!"

"Well, that's all right if it's incredible; but then again, how could you know? Though this is such a place, if a fly buzzes everyone knows of it! But I've warned you, anyhow, and you may be grateful to me. Well, till we meet again—in the next world probably. But another thing: though I have been a cad to you, because … well, why should I lose my due; kindly judge for yourself. For your advantage, perhaps? Why, I dedicated my 'Confession' to her (you didn't know that?). And how she received it too! He-he! But anyway I've not been a cad to her, I've done her no wrong; while she's put me to shame and let me down … But then again, I've done you no wrong either; if I did refer to those 'leftovers' and things of that sort there, still, now I'm telling you the day and the hour and the address of their meeting, and letting you in on the whole game … from resentment of course, not from generosity. Good-bye, I'm as garrulous as a stammerer or a consumptive; mind you take measures, and posthaste, if you're worthy of being called human. The meeting is this evening, that's a fact."

Ippolit went toward the door, but the prince called after him and the latter stopped in the doorway.

"So then, according to you, Aglaia Ivanovna is going herself today to Nastasya Filippovna?" asked the prince. Patches of red came out on his forehead and cheeks.

"I don't know the details, but that's probably so," answered Ippolit, half-turning to look back. "And anyway, it couldn't be otherwise. Nastasya Filippovna couldn't go to her, now, could she? And it wouldn't be at Ganechka's, either, would it; he's practically got a dead man in his house himself. And how about that general, now?"

"It can't be, if only for that reason alone," the prince put in. "How could she go out even if she wanted to? You don't know . . . the habits of that household: she couldn't get away from home alone to see Nastasya Filippovna; it's nonsense!"

"Look here, Prince: nobody jumps out of windows, but if there's a fire, then perhaps the grandest gentleman and the grandest lady are ready to jump out a window. When the need arises, there's no help for it, and our young lady will go to see Nastasya Filippovna. Why, don't they let them go anywhere, your young ladies?"

"No, I didn't mean that . . ."

"Well, if not that, then she's only to go down the steps, and walk straight ahead, and after that she needn't even go home again. There are cases when one may sometimes burn one's ships and not go home again: life does not consist only of lunches and dinners and Prince Shch.'s. I fancy you take Aglaia Ivanovna for some kind of proper young lady or boarding-school miss; I've said that to her already; it seemed that she agreed. Wait till seven or eight o'clock . . . In your place, I'd send someone to be on the watch there, to catch the very minute when she comes down the steps. Well, you might send Kolya even; he'll be delighted to play spy, believe me, for your sake, that is . . . for it's all relative . . . Ha-ha!"

Ippolit went out. The prince had no reason for asking anyone to spy, even if he had been capable of doing so. Aglaia's command that he should stay at home was now almost explained: possibly she meant to come and fetch him. Of course, it was possible that she specifically did not want him to turn up there, and so had ordered him to stay at home . . . That might be so, too. His head was spinning; the whole room was going round and round. He lay down on the sofa and closed his eyes.

In either case, the matter was definitive and final. No, the prince did not consider Aglaia a proper young lady or boarding-school miss; he felt now that he had been fearing something for a long time, and precisely something of that sort; but what did she want to see her for? A shiver ran over the prince's whole body; he was in a fever again.

No, he didn't consider her a child! He had been horrified by some of her looks of late, some of her words. At times he fancied that she was holding back too much, was too controlled, and he remembered that this alarmed him. True, he had been trying not to think about it all those days and banished oppressive thoughts, but what lay hidden in that soul? This question had tormented him for a long time, though he had faith in that soul. And now all this would be resolved and revealed that very day. An awful thought! And again—"that woman!" Why had he always fancied that this woman would turn up precisely at the last moment and tear asunder his entire fate like a rotten thread? That he had always fancied this, he was ready to swear now, though he was almost delirious. If he had tried to forget *her* of late, it was simply because he was afraid of her. Well, then: did he love that woman or hate her? He had not put that question to himself once that day; here his heart was clear: he knew whom he loved . . . He was not so much afraid of the meeting of the two, nor of the strangeness, nor of the unknown cause of that meeting, nor of its resolution, whatever that might be—he was afraid of Nastasya Filippovna herself. He remembered afterward, a few days later, that all through those feverish hours he kept picturing her eyes, her gaze, and hearing her words—strange sorts of words, though little remained of them in his memory after those feverish and gloomy hours. He scarcely remembered, for instance, that Vera had brought him his dinner and he ate it, and did not remember whether he slept after dinner or not. All he knew was that he only began to see things clearly that evening from the moment when Aglaia suddenly came in to him on the terrace and he jumped up from the sofa and went to the middle of the room to meet her: it was a quarter past seven. Aglaia was all by her lonesome, dressed simply, and as if hastily, in a light little burnous. Her face was pale as it had been earlier, and her eyes glittered with a bright and hard light; he had never seen such an expression in her eyes. She surveyed him attentively.

"You are quite ready," she observed quietly, and with apparent calm. "You are dressed and have your hat in your hand; so you've been forewarned, and I know by whom: Ippolit?"

"Yes, he told me . . ." muttered the prince, almost half-dead.

"Come along, then: you know that you must escort me without fail. You are strong enough to go out, I think?"

"I'm strong enough, but . . . can this be possible?"

He broke off in an instant and could bring out nothing more. This was his one attempt to restrain the mad girl, and after that he followed her like a slave. As murky as his thoughts were, he still understood that she would go *there* even without him, and that therefore he was bound to go with her in any case. He divined how strong her determination was; it was not for him to check this wild impulse. They walked in silence, scarcely uttering a word the whole way there. He only remarked that she knew the way well, and when he wanted to go around the long way by a side street, because the road was more deserted there, and suggested this to her, she heard him out, seeming to strain her attention, and answered abruptly: "It's all the same!" When they had almost reached Darya Alexeevna's house (a big, old wooden house) an opulently dressed lady came down the steps, and a young girl with her; they both got into a splendid carriage waiting by the steps, talking and laughing loudly, and did not even once glance at the approaching couple, just as if they had not noticed them. As soon as the carriage had driven off, the door instantly opened a second time, and Rogozhin, who had been waiting there, admitted the prince and Aglaia and locked the door behind them.

"There's no one in the whole house now, except us four," he observed aloud, and looked strangely at the prince.

In the very first room they went into, Nastasya Filippovna was waiting, also dressed very simply and all in black; she stood up to greet them, but did not smile or even give the prince her hand.

Her intense and uneasy gaze fixed impatiently upon Aglaia. They both sat down at a little distance from one another—Aglaia on a sofa in a corner of the room, Nastasya Filippovna at the window. The prince and Rogozhin did not sit down, and they were not invited to sit. The prince looked with bewilderment and as if with pain at Rogozhin, but the latter still smiled with the same smile. The silence lasted some moments more.

At last, an ominous look passed over Nastasya Filippovna's face; her gaze grew obstinate, hard and almost hateful, and it did not tear itself away from her visitor for a minute. Aglaia was evidently discomfited, but did not grow timid. As she walked in, she scarcely glanced at her rival and, for the time being, continued to sit with downcast eyes, as though musing. Once or twice, as though inadvertently, she cast her gaze over the room; revulsion was evident on her face, just as if she were afraid of being contaminated here. She mechanically arranged her dress, and even once uneasily changed her seat, moving toward the corner of the sofa. It was unlikely that she was even conscious herself of all her actions; but their unconsciousness reinforced their offensiveness all the more. At last she looked firmly and squarely into Nastasya Filippovna's eyes and clearly read at once all that was glittering in the spiteful gaze of her rival. Woman understood woman; Aglaia shuddered.

"You know, of course, why I asked you to come," she brought out at last, but in a very low voice, and pausing once or twice even in this brief little phrase.

"No, I know nothing," Nastasya Filippovna answered, dryly and abruptly.

Aglaia flushed. Perhaps it struck her suddenly as terribly strange and incredible that she should now be sitting here with "that woman" in "that woman's" house, and craved her answer. At the first sound of Nastasya Filippovna's voice a sort of shiver ran over her body. All this, of course, "that woman" saw quite clearly.

"You understand everything . . . but you pretend not to understand on purpose," said Aglaia almost in a whisper, looking sullenly at the floor.

"But why should I do that?" Nastasya Filippovna smirked ever so slightly.

"You want to take advantage of my position . . . of my being in your house," Aglaia went on, awkwardly and absurdly.

"You're to blame for your position, not I!" Nastasya Filippovna suddenly flared up. "You're not here at my invitation, but I at yours, and I don't know to this hour with what object."

Aglaia raised her head haughtily.

"Restrain your tongue; I've not come to fight you with that weapon of yours . . ."

"Ah! So then, it seems you've come to fight me after all! Would you believe it, though, I thought that you were . . . cleverer . . ."

They both looked at one another, no longer concealing their spite. One of these women was the very same one who had only so lately written such letters to the other. And now it all fell to pieces at their first meeting and from their first words. And what, then? In that moment, it seemed, not one of the four persons present in the room found it strange. The prince, who, only the day before, would not have believed it possible to see this even in a dream, now stood, looked and listened as though he had foreseen this long ago. The most fantastic dream suddenly turned into the most vivid and sharply defined reality.

One of these women so despised the other at that moment and so keenly desired to express this to her (possibly, she had indeed come simply to do so, as Rogozhin put it next day) that, as fanciful as the other was with her disordered intellect and sick soul, no preconceived idea she might have had ahead of time would have stood up, it seems, against the malignant, purely feminine contempt of her rival. The prince was certain that Nastasya Filippovna would not bring up the letters of her own accord; he could guess from her flashing eyes what those letters must be costing her now; but he would have given half his life for Aglaia not to bring them up now either.

But Aglaia seemed suddenly to pull herself together, and mastered herself all at once.

"You misunderstood," she said. "I have not come . . . to quarrel, though I don't like you. I . . . I came to you . . . to speak to you as one human being to another. When I sent for you, I had already decided what to speak to you about, and I won't depart from that decision now, though you should not understand me at all. That will be the worse for you and not for me. I wanted to answer what you have written to me, and to answer you in person, because I thought it more convenient. Hear my answer to all your letters, then: I felt sorry for Prince Lev Nikolaevich for the first time the very day when I first made his acquaintance, and when I found out afterward about everything that had transpired at your party. I felt sorry for him because he is such a simple-hearted man and in his simplicity believed that he might be happy . . . with a woman . . . of such character. What I was afraid of for him came to pass: you were incapable of loving him, you tortured him, you tortured him and abandoned him. You could not love him because you were too proud . . . no, not proud, I made a mistake, but because you are vain . . . not even that: you are narcissistic to the point . . . of madness, of which your letters to me serve as proof as well. You couldn't love a simple-hearted man like him, and maybe you even secretly despised him and laughed at him; you could love nothing but your shame and the continual thought that you've been brought to shame and done an injury. If your shame were less or entirely gone altogether, you would be more unhappy . . ." (Aglaia pronounced with relish these too hastily uttered but long-prepared and pondered words—already pondered over back when she did not even imagine the present meeting in her dreams; she watched with a malignant gaze for their effect on Nastasya Filippovna's face, distorted with agitation.) "You remember," she went on, "he wrote me a letter then; he says that you know about that letter and have even read it? From that letter I understood everything and understood it correctly; he confirmed it to me himself not long ago, that is, everything I'm telling you now, word for word, indeed. After the letter I began to wait. I guessed that you were sure to come here, because you can't exist without Petersburg after all: you are still too young and too good-looking for the provinces . . . Incidentally, those are not my words either," she added, turning terribly red, and from that moment the color did not leave her face any longer until the very end of her speech. "When I saw the prince again, I felt terribly pained and sorry on his account. Don't laugh; if you are going to laugh, you're not worthy of understanding this."

"You see that I'm not laughing," Nastasya Filippovna pronounced mournfully and sternly.

"Then again, it's all the same to me, laugh as much as you please. When I began to question him myself, he told me that he had ceased loving you long ago, that even the memory of you was a torture to him, but that he was sorry for you, and that when he thought of you, it was as though his heart was 'pierced forever.' I have to tell you, too, that I have never in my life met a single man like him in noble simplicity and boundless trustfulness. I surmised after his words that anyone who chose could deceive him, and whoever may deceive him, he would forgive anyone afterward, and it was for that very thing that I grew to love him . . ."

Aglaia paused for a moment as though amazed, as though hardly able to believe her own ears that she could have uttered such words; but at the same time an infinite pride shone in her eyes; it seemed that it made no difference to her now even if "that woman" did laugh at once at the avowal that had broken from her.

"I've told you everything, and now, no doubt, you understand what I want of you?"

"Perhaps I do understand; but tell me yourself," Nastasya Filippovna answered softly.

Anger ignited in Aglaia's face.

"I wanted to learn from you," she pronounced firmly and distinctly, "by what right you meddle in his feelings for me? By what right have you dared to send me letters? By what right do you continually declare to him and to me that you love him, after abandoning him of your own accord and running away from him so insultingly and with such ... disgrace?"

"I did not declare, either to him or to you, that I love him," Nastasya Filippovna articulated with effort, "and ... you are right, I ran away from him ..." she added, hardly audibly.

"How, never declared 'to him or to me'?" cried Aglaia. "And what about those letters of yours? Who asked you to arrange a match for us and try to persuade me to marry him? Wasn't that a declaration? Why do you force yourself upon us? I thought at first that you wanted, on the contrary, to instill in me an aversion for him by interfering with us, to make me give him up, and only afterward did I guess what it meant: you simply fancied that you were doing some highly heroic deed with all these affectations ... Well, could you have possibly loved him if you love your vanity so much? Why didn't you simply go away from here instead of writing me ridiculous letters? Why don't you now marry the noble-minded man who loves you so much and did you an honor by offering you his hand? It's all too clear why: if you marry Rogozhin, what injury will you have to complain of? You'll even have too much honor done you! Yevgeny Pavlovich said about you that you'd read too much poetry and 'were too educated for your ... position'; that you're a bluestocking and an idler; add to that your vanity, and there are all your reasons ..."

"And you're not an idler?"

Too hastily, too bluntly, things had come to such an unexpected point—unexpected because when Nastasya Filippovna set off for Pavlovsk, she still dreamt of something, though, of course, she anticipated rather more ill than good; but Aglaia was decidedly carried away by the impulse of the moment, as though she were falling down a precipice, and could not hold back before the terrible delectation of vengeance. It was positively strange for Nastasya Filippovna to see Aglaia like this; she looked at her and it seemed as though she could not believe her eyes, and was decidedly at a loss for the first moment. Whether she was a woman who had read too much poetry, as Yevgeny

Pavlovich had supposed, or simply mad, as the prince was convinced, in any case this woman—though she sometimes had such a cynical and impudent way of behaving—was really far more modest, soft and trustful than one might have concluded about her. True, there was much in her that was bookish, dreamy, self-involved and fantastical, but, for all that, strong and deep . . . The prince understood that; suffering was evident in his face. Aglaia noticed this and trembled with hatred.

"How dare you address me like that?" she uttered with unspeakable haughtiness, in reply to Nastasya Filippovna's comment.

"You must have misheard," said Nastasya Filippovna in surprise. "How have I addressed you?"

"If you wanted to be a respectable woman, why didn't you leave your seducer, Totsky, simply . . . without theatrical scenes?" Aglaia said suddenly, apropos of nothing.

"What do you know of my position that you dare to judge me?" Nastasya Filippovna shuddered, turning terribly pale.

"I know that you didn't go to work, but went off with a rich man, Rogozhin, to make yourself out to be a fallen angel. I don't wonder the fallen angel made Totsky want to shoot himself!"

"Leave it!" Nastasya Filippovna brought out with repulsion, and as though in anguish. "You've understood me about as well as . . . Darya Alexeevna's parlormaid, who took her betrothed to the magistrate's court the other day. She'd have understood better than you . . ."

"Very likely, a respectable girl who works for a living. Why do you look on a parlormaid with such contempt?"

"I don't look with contempt upon work, but upon you when you speak of work."

"If you'd wanted to be respectable, you'd have gone to be a washerwoman."

They both rose and gazed with pale faces at each other.

"Aglaia, stop! Why, it's unjust," cried the prince, like someone at a complete loss. Rogozhin was no longer smiling, but was listening with compressed lips and folded arms.

"There, look at her," Nastasya Filippovna was saying, trembling with anger, "look at this young lady! And I took her for an angel! Have you come to see me without a governess, Aglaia Ivanovna? . . . But

would you like . . . would you like me to tell you right now, straight out
and without any folderol, why you came to see me? You were scared,
and that's why you came."

"Scared of you?" asked Aglaia, beside herself with naïve and impudent amazement that this woman dared to speak to her like this.

"Of course, of me! You're afraid of me, if you resolved to come and
see me. Whomever you're afraid of—you don't despise. And to think
that I respected you, even up to this very moment! But do you know
why you are afraid of me and what your chief object is now? You
wanted to determine for yourself whether he loves me more than you
or not, for you're terribly jealous . . ."

"He has told me already that he hates you . . ." Aglaia barely murmured.

"Perhaps; perhaps I am not worthy of him either, only . . . only
you're lying, I think! He cannot hate me and he could not have said so!
But then, I am ready to forgive you . . . in consideration of the position
you're in . . . only I did think better of you; I thought that you were
smarter, and better looking even, upon my word! . . . Well, take your
treasure . . . Here he is, looking at you, unable to pull himself together;
take him for yourself, but on one condition: that you get out of here at
once! This very minute! . . ."

She dropped into an armchair and burst into tears. But suddenly
something new glittered in her eyes; she looked intently and fixedly at
Aglaia, and rose from her seat.

"But if you[42] want, right now, I'll . . . com-mand, do you hear? I've
only to com-mand him, and he'll throw you up at once and stay with
me forever, and marry me, and you'll go running home alone. You want
it, you want it?" she cried, like a mad creature, perhaps scarcely able
herself to believe that she could be saying such things.

Aglaia started to run in alarm to the door, but stopped in the doorway, as if riveted, and listened.

"Do you want me to cast Rogozhin away? You thought that I'd
even married Rogozhin already to please you? Well, here, right now, in
your presence I shall cry: 'Go away, Rogozhin!' and say to the prince,
'Do you remember what you promised?' Heavens! But why have I

<hr>

42. In addressing Aglaia here, Nastasya Filippovna suddenly switches from the polite to
the familiar mode of address. She continues to address Aglaia with the informal *ty* throughout the remainder of the scene.

humiliated myself so before them? Why, didn't you assure me yourself, Prince, that you would follow me whatever happened to me, and
would never abandon me; that you love me and forgive me everything
and re ... resp ... Yes, you said that too! And it was only to set you free
that I ran away from you then, but now I don't want to! Why has she
treated me like a loose woman? Am I a loose woman; ask Rogozhin,
he'll tell you! Now, when she has covered me with shame, and before
your eyes too, will you turn away from me also, and lead her away with
you, arm in arm? Well, a curse upon you then, for you were the only
one I trusted. Go away, Rogozhin, you're not wanted!" she shouted on,
almost out of her senses, wresting the words with effort from her
breast, with a distorted face and with parched lips, evidently not believing a bit of her spectacular tirade herself, but at the same time
wishing, if only for another second, to prolong the moment and deceive herself. The outburst was so violent that she might even have
died, or so at least it seemed to the prince. "Here he is, look!" she cried
to Aglaia at last, pointing to the prince. "If he doesn't come to me at
once, if he does not take me and abandon you, then take him for yourself, I yield, I have no need of him! ..."

Both she and Aglaia stood, as if in suspense, and both gazed like
demented creatures at the prince. But he, perhaps, did not even understand all the force of this challenge; indeed, we may say that for certain. He only saw before him the despairing, deranged face which, as
he had once said to Aglaia, had "pierced his heart forever." He could
bear no more and he turned, with entreaty and reproach, to Aglaia,
pointing to Nastasya Filippovna:

"But is this conceivable! Why, she is ... so unhappy!"

But that was all he managed to utter, dumbstruck under Aglaia's
terrifying gaze. That gaze expressed so much suffering and at the same
time such boundless hatred that he threw up his hands, cried out and
rushed toward her, but it was already too late! She could endure not
even an instant of his hesitation, hid her face in her hands, exclaimed,
"Oh, my God!" and rushed out of the room; Rogozhin followed her to
unbolt the street-door for her.

The prince ran too, but on the threshold he was seized by two arms.
The crushed, contorted face of Nastasya Filippovna was gazing fixedly
at him, and her blue lips moved, asking:

"Going after her? Going after her?"

She dropped senseless into his arms. He lifted her up, carried her into the room, laid her in an armchair, and stood over her in dumb expectation. There was a glass of water on the little table; Rogozhin, coming back, seized it up and sprinkled water in her face; she opened her eyes, and for a minute comprehended nothing; but suddenly, she looked around her, started, cried out, and rushed to the prince.

"Mine, mine!" she exclaimed. "Has the proud young lady gone? Ha-ha-ha!" she laughed in hysterics. "Ha-ha-ha! I gave him up to that young lady! And why? What for? I was mad! Mad! . . . Get away, Rogozhin, ha-ha-ha!"

Rogozhin looked at them intently, did not utter a word, took his hat and went out. Ten minutes later the prince was sitting by Nastasya Filippovna, with his eyes fastened upon her, stroking her head and cheeks with both hands, as though she were a little child. He burst out laughing at her bursts of laughter and was ready to cry at her tears. He said nothing, but listened intently to her broken, excited, and incoherent babble, likely understanding nothing, but smiling gently, and as soon as he fancied that she was beginning again to grieve or cry, to reproach him or complain, he would begin at once stroking her head again and tenderly passing his hands over her cheeks, soothing and comforting her like a child.

IX

A fortnight had passed since the events narrated in the last chapter, and the positions of our narrative's protagonists had changed so much that it is extremely difficult for us to attempt to continue without special explanations. And yet we feel that we must confine ourselves to the bare presentation of facts, as far as possible without special explanations, and for a rather simple reason: because we are ourselves, in many instances, at pains to explain what occurred. Such a preliminary declaration on our part must seem rather strange and obscure to the reader: how can you relate that of which you have neither a clear notion nor a personal opinion? To avoid putting ourselves in a still more false position, we had better try to explain ourselves using an example, and perhaps the kindly disposed reader will understand where, exactly, our difficulty lies—especially as this example will represent not a step away from but, on the contrary, a direct continuation of our narrative.

A fortnight later, that is, at the beginning of July, and in the course of that fortnight, the story of our hero, and particularly the last incident of that story, was transformed into a strange, rather amusing, almost incredible, and at the same time almost palpably convincing anecdote, which spread little by little through all the streets adjoining the dachas of Lebedev, Ptitsyn, Darya Alexeevna and the Epanchins, in short, almost all over the town, and even its outlying districts. Almost the whole society—the natives, the summer residents, the people who came to hear the band—everyone took to telling the very same story, in a thousand different variations, about how a prince, after causing a scandal in a well-known and honorable family and jilting a young girl of that family, who was already his betrothed, had been captivated by a well-known cocotte, had broken all his previous ties and, heedless of everything, heedless of threats, heedless of the general indignation of the public, was intending in a few days' time to marry a dishonored woman, right here in Pavlovsk, openly, publicly, with head held high and looking everyone straight in the eyes. The anecdote was becoming so richly adorned with scandalous details, so many well-known and distinguished persons were introduced into it, and so many fantastic and enigmatic shades of significance were given to it, while on the other hand it was presented with such incontestable and palpable facts, that the universal curiosity and gossip were, of course, very pardonable. The most subtle, artful, and at the same time plausible interpretation must be put to the credit of a few serious gossips belonging to that class of sensible people who are always, in every rank of society, in haste, first of all, to explain an event to others—in which they find their vocation, and often their consolation, too. According to their interpretation, a young man—who was of good family, a prince, almost wealthy, a fool, but a democrat who had gone mad for the contemporary nihilism discovered by Mr. Turgenev[43] and was scarcely able to speak Russian—had fallen in love with the daughter of General Epanchin, and had succeeded in being received by the family as her be-

---

43. Ivan Turgenev's influential novel *Fathers and Sons* (1862) describes the conflict between the emerging culture of young radical reformers and the older generation.

trothed. But like the French seminarist about whom a story had just appeared in print, who had allowed himself on purpose to be consecrated as a priest, had on purpose begged for this consecration himself, had performed all the rites, all the genuflections and kissings and vows, and so on, in order the very next day to inform his bishop publicly by letter that, not believing in God, he considered it dishonorable to deceive the people and be kept by them for nothing, and therefore was resigning the office he'd assumed the day before and sending his letter to be printed in the liberal papers—like this atheist, the prince had supposedly played false in his own way too. It was said that he had supposedly waited on purpose for the formal evening party given by the parents of his betrothed, at which he was presented to a great many distinguished personages, in order to declare his way of thinking aloud and before everyone, abuse the venerable old dignitaries, renounce his betrothed publicly and insultingly and, while struggling with the servants who were leading him out, break a magnificent Chinese vase. It was added, by way of attesting to contemporary mores, that the brainless young man really did love his betrothed, the general's daughter, but had renounced her simply on account of nihilism, and for the sake of the imminent scandal, so as not to deny himself the pleasure of getting married, in sight of all the world, to a fallen woman and thereby proving that in his conviction there were neither fallen nor virtuous women but only one kind of woman, a free woman; that he did not believe in the societal and antiquated division, but had faith only in the "woman question." That, finally, a fallen woman was in his eyes even somewhat superior to one who was not fallen. This explanation appeared extremely plausible and was accepted by the majority of the summer residents, especially as it seemed to be supported by quotidian facts. True, a great number of things still remained unclarified: it was said that the poor girl so adored her betrothed—as some would have it, her "seducer"—that she went running to him on the very next day after he left her and while he was sitting at his mistress's; others maintained, on the contrary, that she had been purposely lured by him to his mistress's simply out of nihilism, that is, for the sake of shaming and insulting her. However that may have been, the fascination of the incident grew greater every day, especially as there remained not the slightest doubt that the scandalous marriage was really to take place.

And there you have it; if we should be asked for clarification—not about any shades of nihilism in the incident but simply about the extent to which the appointed wedding satisfied the prince's actual desires, what those desires actually were at the present moment, how, exactly, the spiritual condition of our hero was to be defined at the present time, and so on and so forth in that vein, we would, we admit, find ourselves at great pains to answer. We know only one thing, that the wedding actually was arranged, and that the prince himself had authorized Lebedev, Keller and some acquaintance of Lebedev's, whom the latter had presented to the prince just for the occasion, to undertake all the bothersome details of the business, religious as well as secular; that they were bidden not to spare money; that the wedding was being hurried along and insisted upon by Nastasya Filippovna; that Keller, at his own ardent request, had been appointed the prince's *shaffer*,[44] and Nastasya Filippovna's—Burdovsky, who accepted the appointment with delight, and that the wedding day was arranged for the beginning of July. But besides these rather certain circumstances, some other facts are also known to us that throw us completely out of our reckoning, and namely because they contradict the preceding ones. We strongly suspect, for instance, that, having authorized Lebedev and the others to undertake all the details, the prince practically forgot the very same day that he had a master of ceremonies, and a *shaffer*, and a wedding; and that if he did make arrangements posthaste, handing over the details to others, it was simply so as not to think about it himself, and even, perhaps, to forget about it posthaste. Of what, then, was he himself thinking in that case, what did he want to remember, and for what did he strive? There is also no doubt that there was no sort of coercion applied to him here (from Nastasya Filippovna's quarter, for instance); that it was certainly, in fact, Nastasya Filippovna's wish to have the wedding quickly, and that it was she who had thought up the wedding, and not the prince at all; but the prince had agreed freely, even somewhat absently, and as though he had been asked for some quite ordinary thing. Such strange facts are before us in abundance, but they do not only fail to clarify things, but, in our view,

---

44. The Orthdox sacrament of marriage involves a crowning ritual in which the bride and groom are each accompanied to the altar by an attendant who holds a crown, or wedding wreath, over their heads during the ceremony. These attendants are called *shaffers*.

positively obscure any interpretation of the matter, however many of them one may present; but, nonetheless, let us present one more example.

So then, we know for a fact that during that fortnight the prince spent whole days and evenings with Nastasya Filippovna; that she took him with her for walks and to hear the band; that he drove out with her every day in her carriage; that he began to worry about her if only an hour passed without his seeing her (and so, by all signs, he loved her sincerely); that he listened to her with a soft and gentle smile, whatever she was telling him about, for hours together, saying scarcely anything himself. But we know too that in the course of those same days he had several times, indeed, many times, suddenly gone off to the Epanchins' without concealing the fact from Nastasya Filippovna, which had driven the latter almost to despair. We know that at the Epanchins', as long as they remained at Pavlovsk, he was not received and was consistently refused an interview with Aglaia Ivanovna; that he would go away without saying a word and the very next day go to them again as though he had completely forgotten about yesterday's refusal, and, of course, would be refused again. We know, too, that an hour after Aglaia Ivanovna had run away from Nastasya Filippovna, perhaps even less than an hour after, the prince was already at the Epanchins', confident, of course, of finding Aglaia there, and that his arrival had caused extraordinary discomfiture and alarm in the household because Aglaia had not yet returned home and it was only from him the Epanchins first learned that she had gone with him to Nastasya Filippovna's. It was said that Lizaveta Prokofyevna, her daughters and even Prince Shch. treated the prince in a very harsh and hostile manner on that occasion; and that they had there and then in the strongest terms renounced all friendship and acquaintance with him, especially when Varvara Ardalionovna had suddenly turned up to see Lizaveta Prokofyevna and announced that Aglaia had been in her house for the last hour in a terrible state, and seemed unwilling to return home. This last piece of news astonished Lizaveta Prokofyevna more than anything, and it was absolutely true: on coming away from Nastasya Filippovna's, Aglaia would indeed sooner have died than have her family see her now, and so she flew to Nina Alexandrovna's. And Varvara Ardalionovna found it essential, for her part, to inform Lizaveta Prokofyevna of all this without the slightest delay. Mother and daughters all rushed off at once to Nina Alexandrovna's, followed by the head of the family, Ivan Fyodorovich, who had just returned home; Prince Lev Nikolaevich trudged along after them, in spite of his banishment and the harsh words; but on Varvara Ardalionovna's orders, he was not allowed to see Aglaia there either. The end of the matter, by the by, was that when Aglaia saw her mother and sisters shedding tears over her and not reproaching her one bit, she threw herself into their arms and returned home with them at once. It was said, though the rumors were not entirely precise, that Gavrila Ardalionovich was particularly unlucky on that occasion, too; that, seizing the opportunity while Varvara Ardalionovna ran to see Lizaveta Prokofyevna, he—left alone with Aglaia—took it into his head to begin talking of his love; that, listening to him, Aglaia had, despite all her dejection and her tears, suddenly burst out laughing and had suddenly put a strange question to him: would he, to prove his love, burn his finger in the candle right then and there? Gavrila Ardalionovich was, so they said, dumbfounded by the question and was so much at a loss, expressing such extreme bewilderment in his face, that Aglaia roared with laughter at him as though she were in hysterics and ran away from him upstairs to Nina Alexandrovna, where her parents found her. This story reached the prince through Ippolit next day. No longer able to get out of bed, Ippolit sent for the prince on purpose to give him this bit of news. How the rumor had reached Ippolit is not known to us, but when the prince heard about the candle and the finger, he laughed so much that even Ippolit was surprised; then, suddenly, he began to tremble and burst into tears . . . Altogether, he was during those days in a state of great uneasiness and extraordinary perturbation, vague and tormenting. Ippolit asserted bluntly that he found him out of his mind; but it was still impossible to say this with certainty.

In presenting all these facts and declining to explain them, we have absolutely no desire to justify our hero in the eyes of the reader. What is more, we are quite prepared to share the indignation he excited even in his friends. Even Vera Lebedev was indignant with him for a time; even Kolya was indignant; even Keller was indignant, till he was chosen as *shaffer*, to say nothing of Lebedev himself, who even began intriguing against the prince, also from indignation, which was quite genuine indeed. But of that we will speak later. On the whole, we are completely and to the greatest extent in sympathy with some rather strong—and indeed profound in their psychology—words of Yevgeny Pavlovich's, which the latter conveyed to the prince directly and unceremoniously in friendly conversation, on the sixth or seventh day after the incident at Nastasya Filippovna's. We must observe, by the way, that not only the Epanchins themselves but everyone directly or indirectly connected with the Epanchin family had found it necessary to break off all relations with the prince. Prince Shch., for instance, even turned aside when he met the prince and did not return his bow. But Yevgeny Pavlovich was not afraid of compromising himself by visiting the prince, despite the fact that he had begun visiting the Epanchins every day again, and was even received by them with an unmistakable increase of cordiality. He came to see the prince the very day after all the Epanchins had left Pavlovsk. Coming in, he already knew of all the rumors that were circulating in society, indeed, had perhaps abetted them himself. The prince was terribly glad of him and at once began speaking of the Epanchins; such a simple and direct opening completely loosened up Yevgeny Pavlovich too, so that he, too, went straight to the point without beating about the bush.

The prince did not yet know that the Epanchins had left; he was shocked and turned pale; but a minute later he shook his head, chagrined and meditative, and acknowledged that "so it was bound to be"; then he asked quickly, "Where had they gone?"

Meanwhile Yevgeny Pavlovich observed him intently, and he marveled not a little at all this—that is, the rapidity of the questions, their simplicity, the chagrin and, at the same time, some sort of strange frankness, the agitation and excitement. However, he informed the prince of everything courteously and in detail; there was a great deal the latter still had not known, and this was the first emissary from that house. He confirmed that Aglaia had in fact been ill and had lain for nearly three days and nights together in a fever without sleeping; that now she was better and out of all danger, but in a nervous and hysterical state . . . "It's a good thing at least that there is perfect harmony in the house! They try not to hint at the past, even amongst themselves, and not only before Aglaia. The parents had already conferred between themselves about a trip abroad in the autumn, right after Adelaida's wedding; Aglaia had received in silence the preliminary allusions to this plan." He, Yevgeny Pavlovich, might very possibly be going abroad too. Even Prince Shch. might possibly go with Adelaida for a couple of months if business permitted. The general himself would remain. They had all moved now to Kolmino, their estate some twenty versts out of Petersburg, where they had a spacious manor house. Belokonsky had not left for Moscow, and it seemed even that she had remained on purpose. Lizaveta Prokofyevna had insisted emphatically that it was impossible to stay on in Pavlovsk after all that had happened; he, Yevgeny Pavlovich, had reported to her daily about the rumors that were circulating in the town. They did not find it possible to move to the dacha at Yelagin, either.

"And, well, in fact," added Yevgeny Pavlovich, "you'll admit yourself, could they have endured ... especially knowing everything that's going on with you here every hour, Prince, in your house, and after your daily calls *there* in spite of the refusals ..."

"Yes, yes, yes, you're right, I wanted to see Aglaia Ivanovna." The prince began to shake his head again.

"Ah, dear prince," cried Yevgeny Pavlovich with animation and sorrow. "How could you have allowed ... everything that happened then? Of course, of course, it was all so unexpected for you ... I agree that you could not help being at a loss and ... you could not have restrained the mad girl, after all, that was not in your power! But, you know, you ought to have understood how earnestly and strongly the girl ... felt for you. She did not care to share you with another woman and you ... and you could desert and shatter such a treasure!"

"Yes, yes, you're right; yes, I'm to blame," the prince began again with terrible dejection. "And do you know: why, it was she alone, only Aglaia alone, who looked at Nastasya Filippovna like that ... Why, no one else ever looked at her like that."

"But that's just what makes it all so outrageous, that there was nothing serious in it!" cried Yevgeny Pavlovich, completely carried away. "Forgive me, Prince, but ... I ... I've been thinking about it, Prince; I have thought it over a lot; I know everything that happened before, I know everything that happened six months ago, everything, and— there was nothing serious in it! It was nothing but an intellectual infatuation, a picture, a fantasy, smoke, and nothing but the frightened jealously of an utterly inexperienced girl could have taken it for anything serious! ..."

At this point, entirely without ceremony, Yevgeny Pavlovich gave full vent to his indignation. Clearly and reasonably and, we repeat, with extraordinary psychological insight, he unfolded before the prince the picture of all his past personal feeling toward Nastasya Filippovna. Yevgeny Pavlovich had always had a gift for language, and at this moment he rose to positive eloquence. "From the very first," he declared, "it began for you with a lie. What begins with a lie must end with a lie; that's a law of nature. I don't agree, and, in fact, I'm indignant when somebody—well, say, anyone at all—calls you an idiot; you're too clever for such a name; but you're so strange that you're not like other people—you must admit that yourself. I've decided that the foundation of everything that's happened consists, first of all, in your innate, so to speak, inexperience (mark that word, Prince, 'innate'), and then in your extraordinary simple-heartedness; and further in the phenomenal lack of feeling for proportion (which you have several times confessed yourself), and finally in the huge, inpouring mass of intellectual convictions, which you, with your extraordinary honesty, continue to this day to take for genuine, inherent, unmediated convictions! You must admit yourself, Prince, that from the start, something *symbolically democratic* (I put it that way for the sake of brevity) had entered into your feeling for Nastasya Filippovna, the fascination, so to speak, of the 'woman question' (to put it still more briefly). Why, I know all the details of the strange, scandalous scene that took place at Nastasya Filippovna's when Rogozhin brought his money. If you like, I will analyze you to yourself on my fingers, I will show you to yourself as in a looking glass, that is how perfectly I know what the matter was and why it turned out as it did! As a youth in Switzerland, you yearned for your native country, and were drawn to Russia as to an unknown land of promise; you had read a great many books about Russia, excellent books perhaps, but pernicious for you; you arrived in the first flush of eagerness for action, rushed to seize the action, so to speak! And there you have it, on that very day, a sad and heartening story is told to you of an injured woman, told to you, that is, a virginal knight—and about a woman! The very same day you see that woman; you are bewitched by her beauty, her fantastic, demonic beauty (I admit that she's a beauty of course). Add to that your nerves, add your epilepsy, add our nerve-shattering Petersburg thaw, add that whole day, in an unknown and to you almost fantastical town, a day of scenes and encounters, a day of unexpected acquaintances, a day of the most unexpected reality, a day of the three Epanchin beauties, Aglaia among them; add fatigue and the turmoil in your head; add the drawing room of Nastasya Filippovna, and the tone of that drawing room, and . . . what could you expect of yourself at such a moment, do you think?"

"Yes, yes; yes, yes," the prince shook his head, beginning to flush crimson. "Yes; why, that's almost exactly how it was; and do you know, I really had scarcely slept at all in the railway carriage the night before, and all the night before that, and was very much a wreck . . ."

"Well, yes, of course, what do you think I am driving at?" Yevgeny Pavlovich went on heatedly. "It's a clear matter that you, intoxicated with enthusiasm, so to speak, threw yourself at the opportunity of publicly proclaiming the generous idea that you, a prince by birth and a man of purity, did not regard a woman as dishonored who had been put to shame not through her own fault, but through the fault of a revolting debaucher from the higher circles of society. O, Lord, why, that's understandable! But that's not the point, dear prince, the point is whether there was truth, whether there was genuineness in your feeling, whether it was nature or only intellectual enthusiasm? What do you think: in the temple, the woman—just such a woman—was forgiven, but then she wasn't told that she'd done well, that she was deserving of all respect and honor, was she? Didn't common sense tell you, three months later, how the matter stood? But let's grant that she's innocent now—I won't insist on that for I don't want to—could all her adventures really justify such intolerable, fiendish pride on her part, such insolent, such rapacious egoism? Forgive me, Prince, I'm getting carried away, but . . ."

"Yes, all that may be so; maybe you're right . . ." the prince began muttering again, "she certainly is very much irritated, and you're right, of course, but . . ."

"Deserving of compassion? That's what you mean to say, my kindhearted prince? But for the sake of compassion and for the sake of her pleasure, could you really have put to shame another, a pure and highminded girl, humiliate her in *those* haughty, those hated eyes? Well, what will compassion come to next after that? Why, it's an exaggeration beyond belief! How can you, loving a girl, humiliate her like this before her very rival, jilt her for the sake of another, before the eyes of that same other, after you had yourself already made her an honorable offer . . . and you did make her an offer, after all; you put it to her before her parents and her sisters! Well, and are you an honorable man after that, allow me to ask you, Prince? And . . . and didn't you deceive that heavenly girl when you assured her that you loved her?"

"Yes, yes, you're right; ach, I feel that I am to blame!" the prince uttered, in indescribable dejection.

"Why, can that be enough?" cried Yevgeny Pavlovich in indignation. "Is it sufficient to cry out: 'Ach, I'm to blame!' You are to blame, but yet you persist! And where was your heart then, your 'Christian' heart! Why, you saw her face at that moment: well, was she suffering less than *the other*, that other one of *yours*, the one who broke you up? How could you have seen it and allowed it? How?"

"But . . . why, I didn't allow it," muttered the unhappy prince.

"How do you mean, you didn't allow it?"

"Upon my word, I didn't allow anything. I don't understand to this hour how it all came about . . . I—I ran after Aglaia Ivanovna at the time, but Nastasya Filippovna fell down in a faint; and afterward, they haven't let me see Aglaia Ivanovna since then."

"That doesn't matter! You ought to have run after Aglaia even if the other woman was in a faint!"

"Yes . . . yes, I ought to have . . . She would have died, you know! She would have killed herself, you don't know her, and . . . It doesn't matter, I would have told Aglaia Ivanovna everything afterward, and . . . You see, Yevgeny Pavlovich, I see that you don't know everything, I think. Tell me, why won't they let me see Aglaia Ivanovna? I would have explained everything to her. You see: they both talked of the wrong thing, altogether the wrong thing; that's why it turned out that way between them . . . There's no way I can explain it to you; but perhaps I could explain it to Aglaia . . . Oh, my God, my God! You speak of her face at that moment when she ran away . . . Oh, my God, I remember it! Let's go, let's go!" He suddenly dragged Yevgeny Pavlovich by the sleeve, hurriedly jumping up from his seat.

"Where?"

"Let's go to Aglaia Ivanovna, let's go at once! . . ."

"But she's not in Pavlovsk, I told you. And why go?"

"She will understand, she will understand!" the prince muttered, clasping his hands imploringly. "She will understand that all this is not at all *that*, but something entirely, entirely different!"

"How do you mean, entirely different? Why, you are going to be married, after all, aren't you? So it would seem you persist in it . . . Are you going to be married or not?"

"Well, yes . . . I am; yes, I am!"

"Then how is it not that?"

"Oh no, it's not that, not that! It doesn't matter that I'm going to marry her, that's nothing!"

"How do you mean it doesn't matter and it's nothing? Why, it's not a trifling matter, is it? You're marrying a woman you love to secure her happiness, and Aglaia Ivanovna sees that and knows it, so how can it not matter?"

"Happiness? Oh, no! I'm just simply marrying her; she wants me to; and what is there in my marrying her? I . . . oh, well, all that's no matter! Only she would certainly have died. I see now that this marriage to Rogozhin was madness! I understand everything now that I didn't understand before, and, you see: when they both stood there facing one another, I could not endure Nastasya Filippovna's face . . . You don't know, Yevgeny Pavlovich"—he dropped his voice mysteriously—"I've never said this to anyone, not even to Aglaia, but I cannot endure Nastasya Filippovna's face . . . It was true what you said before about that evening at Nastasya Filippovna's; but there was one other thing you left out because you don't know: I looked at *her face*! I already couldn't endure that morning, in her portrait . . . Now take Vera—Vera Lebedev—she has completely different eyes; I . . . I'm afraid of her face!" he added with extraordinary terror.

"You're afraid?"

"Yes; she's mad!" he whispered, turning pale.

"You know this for certain?" asked Yevgeny Pavlovich, with extreme interest.

"Yes, for certain; now I'm certain. Now, during these last days, I've become quite certain!"

"But what are you doing to yourself, Prince?" Yevgeny Pavlovich cried in alarm. "So it would seem you're marrying her from some kind of fear? There's no understanding it . . . Without even loving her, perhaps?"

"Oh, no. I love her with all my soul! Why, she's . . . a child! Now she's a child, quite a child! Oh, you don't know anything!"

"And at the same time you assured Aglaia Ivanovna of your love?"

"Oh, yes, yes!"

"How can that be? Then it would seem you want to love both of them?"

"Oh, yes, yes!"

"Mercy, Prince, think what you're saying, come to your senses!"

"Without Aglaia, I'm . . . I absolutely must see her! I . . . I shall soon die in my sleep; I thought I should have died last night in my sleep. Oh, if Aglaia only knew, if she only knew everything . . . that is, absolutely everything. For in this case one needs to know everything, that's the first order of the day! Why is it we never can know *everything* about another person when it's necessary, when that other is to blame! . . . But then, I don't know what I'm saying. I'm muddled. You've shocked me terribly . . . And does her face really look now as it did then, when she ran away? Oh, yes, I am to blame! It is most likely that I am to blame for everything! I don't yet know exactly what for, but I am to blame . . . There's something in all this I can't explain to you, Yevgeny Pavlovich, and I can't find the words, but . . . Aglaia Ivanovna will understand! Oh, I've always believed that she would understand."

"No, Prince, she won't understand! Aglaia Ivanovna loved you like a woman, like a human being, and not like . . . an abstract spirit. Do you know what, my poor prince: the most likely thing is that you've never loved either one of them!"

"I don't know . . . perhaps, perhaps; you're right in a great deal, Yevgeny Pavlovich. You are very clever, Yevgeny Pavlovich; ah, my head is beginning to ache again, let's go to her! For God's sake, for God's sake!"

"But I tell you she's not in Pavlovsk, she's in Kolmino."

"Let's go to Kolmino. Let's go at once!"

"That's im-pos-sible!" Yevgeny Pavlovich drawled out, getting up.

"Listen, I'll write a letter; take a letter there!"

"No, Prince, no! Spare me such a commission. I can't!"

They parted. Yevgeny Pavlovich went away with odd convictions: and in his view, too, the upshot of it was that the prince was not quite in his right mind. And what was the meaning of that *face* he feared and loved so much! And yet perhaps he really would die without Aglaia, so that Aglaia would perhaps never learn that he loved her to such a great extent! Ha-ha! And how can one love two at once? With two different sorts of love? That's interesting ... poor idiot! And what will become of him now?

X

But the prince did not die before his wedding, neither awake nor "in his sleep," as he had predicted to Yevgeny Pavlovich. Perhaps he really did not sleep well and had bad dreams; but by day, with people, he seemed kind and even contented, only very pensive at times, but that was when he was alone. The wedding was being hurried on; it was fixed for about a week after Yevgeny Pavlovich's visit. With such haste even the very best friends of the prince, if he'd had any, would have been bound to be disappointed in their efforts to "save" the poor crazy fellow. There were rumors that supposedly General Epanchin and his wife, Lizaveta Prokofyevna, were in part to blame for Yevgeny Pavlovich's visit. But if, in the infinite kindness of their hearts, they both might indeed have wished to save the pitiful lunatic from the abyss, they were, of course, bound to limit themselves just to this one feeble attempt; neither their position nor, perhaps, the inclination of their hearts (naturally enough) could be compatible with more serious efforts. We have mentioned already that even those around the prince in part rose up against him. Vera Lebedev, however, confined herself to shedding a few tears in solitude, and also to staying in her own room more and looking in upon the prince less than before. Kolya was burying his father at this time; the old man had died of a second stroke some eight days after the first. The prince greatly shared in the grief of the family, and for the first few days spent several hours daily with Nina Alexandrovna; he was at the funeral and at the church. Many people noticed that the crowd in the church greeted and ushered out the prince with involuntary whispers; it was the same thing in the streets and in the gardens: whenever he walked or drove by, there was talk, his name was mentioned, he was pointed out, and Nastasya Filippovna's name was heard. People looked for her at the funeral, too, but she was not at the funeral. Absent from the funeral as well was the captainess, whom Lebedev had managed to stop and discharge in time. The burial service made a strong and painful impression on the prince; while still at the church, he whispered to Lebedev in answer to some question of his that it was the first time he had been present at an Orthodox burial service, though he had a faint memory of a similar burial service at a village church in his childhood.

"Yes, indeed, sir, it's just as though it's not the same man lying there, in the coffin, I mean, sir, as we elected to be our president so recently—do you remember, sir?" Lebedev whispered to the prince. "Whom are you looking for, sir?"

"Oh, nothing, I fancied . . ."

"Not Rogozhin?"

"Why, is he here?"

"In the church, sir, indeed."

"So that's why I fancied I saw his eyes," the prince muttered in confusion. "But what . . . why is he here? Was he invited?"

"They never even gave it a thought, sir. Why, he's a complete stranger, sir, you know. There are all kinds of people here, yes sir, it's the public. But why are you so amazed? I often meet him now; I've met him some four times already this last week, here in Pavlovsk."

"I've never seen him once yet . . . since that time," muttered the prince.

As Nastasya Filippovna too had not once told him that she had met Rogozhin "since that time," the prince concluded now that Rogozhin was for some reason keeping out of sight on purpose. All that day he was deeply lost in thought, while Nastasya Filippovna was exceptionally merry all that day and that evening.

Kolya, who had already made up with the prince before his father's death, suggested that he should ask Keller and Burdovsky to act as *shaffer* (as the matter was vital and not to be put off). He vouched for Keller that the latter would behave properly and would perhaps even "be of use," while there was no need to even speak of Burdovsky, a quiet and retiring person. Nina Alexandrovna and Lebedev observed to the prince that if the marriage were a settled thing, then, at any rate, why in Pavlovsk, and in the height of the fashionable summer season to boot, why so publicly? Wouldn't it be better in Petersburg and even in the house? The prince saw only too clearly the drift of all these apprehensions; but he replied briefly and simply that such was Nastasya Filippovna's particular wish.

Next day Keller called on the prince, having been informed that he was to be a *shaffer*. Before coming in he paused in the doorway, and as soon as he saw the prince, he raised his right hand, straightening his index finger, and exclaimed as though swearing a vow:

"I won't drink!"

Then he went up to the prince, firmly pressed and shook both his hands, and announced that certainly, in the beginning, when he first heard of it, he was hostile and had proclaimed it at billiards, and for no other reason than that he had high hopes for the prince and had daily, with the impatience of a friend, awaited to see by his side none other than the Princess de Rohan, or at least de Chabot;[45] but now he saw for himself that the prince thinks at least twelve times as nobly as all of them "put together!" For he did not care for pomp or wealth, nor even veneration, but cared only for the truth! The inclinations of lofty persons were too well known, and the prince was too lofty in his education not be a lofty person, speaking generally! "But the filth and riffraff of the common sort judge differently; in the town, in the houses, in the assemblies, at the dachas, at the bandstand, in the taverns and over billiards, there was what all but talking and shouting of the coming event. I have heard that they were even talking of getting up a charivari[46] under the windows—and that, so to say, on the wedding night! If you should need, Prince, the pistol of an honest man, I am ready to exchange half a dozen gentlemanly shots before you rise in the morning from the nuptial bed." He advised, too, for fear of a great flood of eager souls upon coming out of the church, to have the fire-hose ready in the courtyard; but Lebedev reared in opposition: "The house," he said, "would be pulled to pieces in the case of the fire-hose, you know."

"That Lebedev is intriguing against you, Prince, he is, upon my word! They want to make you a ward of the state, can you imagine that, with everything, your free will and your money, that is with the two objects that distinguish everyone of use from a quadruped! I've heard it, I've heard it on good authority! It's nothing but God's honest truth!"

The prince recollected that he seemed to have heard something of the sort already himself, but of course he had paid no attention to it. Now, too, he merely laughed and forgot it again on the spot. Lebedev had indeed been at pains for some time; the schemes of this man always sprang up as if by inspiration, and in the excess of his ardor de-

45. Two of the most prominent French aristocratic families, with centuries of noble lineage.

46. A mock serenade involving boisterous noisemaking.

veloped complications, branching out in all directions and becoming far removed from his original starting point; and that was why there was little in his life he could succeed in. When he came afterward, almost on the wedding day, to repent before the prince (it was his invariable habit always to go to those against whom he had been intriguing and repent, and especially when he had not succeeded), he announced to him that he had been born a Talleyrand[47] and it was a mystery how he was left merely a Lebedev. Then he disclosed to him his entire game, which interested the prince in the extreme. Going by his own words, he had begun by seeking out the patronage of high-ranking personages on whose support he might reckon in case of need, and he had gone to General Ivan Fyodorovich. General Ivan Fyodorovich was bewildered, very much wished the "young man" well, but declared that, "for all his desire to save him, it was unseemly for him to act in the matter." Lizaveta Prokofyevna wanted neither sight nor sound of him; Yevgeny Pavlovich and Prince Shch. only waved him away. But he, Lebedev, did not lose heart, and consulted one shrewd lawyer, a venerable old man and a great friend of his, almost a benefactor; the latter had concluded that the matter was utterly possible, as long as there were competent witnesses as to his mental derangement and utter insanity, and in addition, and above all, the patronage of high-ranking personages. Lebedev was not discouraged here either, and had, on one occasion, even brought a doctor—also a venerable old man, a summer resident, with an Anna around his neck[48]—to see the prince, with the sole purpose of surveying, so to speak, the lay of the land, to make the prince's acquaintance and impart his conclusion about him, not officially, for the time being, but amicably, so to speak. The prince remembered this doctor's visit to him; he remembered that Lebedev had pestered him the evening before about his not being well and, when the prince decidedly refused the medical arts, suddenly made his appearance with a doctor on the pretext that they had both just come from Mr. Terentyev, who was very ill, and that the doctor

47. The prominent French diplomat Charles-Maurice de Talleyrand (1754–1838) managed to have a brilliant political career serving a succession of revolutionary, Napoleonic and restoration governments, and was known for his wiliness.

48. The Order of St. Anne was awarded in two different classes—one worn on a short ribbon pinned on the breast and the other on a long ribbon hung around the neck, with the latter representing the higher class of honor.

had something to tell the prince about the invalid. The prince praised Lebedev and received the doctor with exceptional courtesy. They began talking at once about the sick Ippolit; the doctor asked him to relate in more detail that evening's suicide scene, and the prince completely captivated him with his narration and explanation of the incident. They talked of Petersburg's climate, of the prince's own illness, of Switzerland, of Schneider. With his account of Schneider's system of treatment and his stories, the prince so interested the doctor that the latter stayed two hours; all the while, he smoked the prince's excellent cigars, while from Lebedev's quarter there appeared a delicious liqueur, which was brought by Vera, whereupon the doctor, who was married and a family man, launched into quite particular compliments before Vera, arousing her profound indignation. They parted friends. On leaving the prince, the doctor informed Lebedev that if everyone like that were to be made a ward, then whom would one have to make the guardians? In reply to the tragic account, on Lebedev's part, of the rapidly approaching event, the doctor slyly and insidiously shook his head and observed at last that, to say nothing of the fact that "there's all sorts a man might marry," "the enchanting personage"—as far as he had heard, at least—"possessed not only incomparable beauty, which in itself might well attract a man of means, but also capital, both from Totsky and Rogozhin, pearls and diamonds, shawls and furniture; and therefore the impending choice, far from being the expression of peculiar, so to speak, glaring foolishness on the part of the dear prince, was rather even a testimony to the cunning of a subtle, worldly mind and prudence, and, so it would seem, supported the contrary conclusion, and one entirely gratifying for the prince . . ." This idea astonished even Lebedev; and that's what he'd been left with, and now, he added to the prince, "now, you will see nothing from me but devotion and the shedding of my blood; that's just what I've come to you with."

These last days, the prince was diverted by Ippolit, too; he sent for him only too often. They lived not far off, in a little house; the little children, Ippolit's brother and sister, were glad of the dacha, if only because they could escape from the invalid into the garden; but the poor captainess was left entirely at his mercy and was completely his victim; the prince was obliged to separate and reconcile them every day, and the invalid continued to call him his "nurse," at the same time not daring, as it were, not to despise him for his role as peacemaker. He was in high dudgeon with Kolya because the latter scarcely visited him, having stayed at first beside his dying father and afterward with his widowed mother. Finally, he took the prince's approaching marriage to Nastasya Filippovna as the object of his mockery, and ended by offending the prince and finally making him beside himself with anger; the latter ceased coming to visit him. Two days later, in the morning, the captainess trudged in and begged the prince, in tears, to come to them or *that* fellow would put her in the grave. She added that he wanted to reveal a great secret. The prince went. Ippolit wanted to make up, started crying, and after his tears, of course, felt more spiteful than ever, but was afraid to show his spite. He was very ill, and it was evident by all signs that he would die very soon now. There was no secret of any sort, except for some urgent appeals—breathless, so to speak, with agitation (possibly shammed)—"to beware of Rogozhin." "This is a man who will never yield his ground; he's not our kind, Prince: if he wants a thing, he won't waver . . ." etc., etc. The prince began questioning him in more detail, tried to get at facts of some sort; but there were no facts of any sort, except for Ippolit's personal sentiments and impressions. To his extreme gratification, Ippolit ended by scaring the prince terribly at last. At first the prince was unwilling to answer certain particular questions of his, and only smiled at his advice "to flee, even abroad; there were Russian priests everywhere, and one could be married there, too." But at last, Ippolit ended with the following thought: "It's only for Aglaia Ivanovna I am afraid, you know; Rogozhin knows how you love her; love for love; you took Nastasya Filippovna away from him, he will kill Aglaia Ivanovna; though she's not yours now, but still you'd be grieved, wouldn't you?" He attained his object; when the prince left him he was practically out of his mind.

These warnings about Rogozhin came the day before the wedding. That very evening, for the last time before going to the altar, the prince saw Nastasya Filippovna as well; but Nastasya Filippovna was in no state to reassure him; indeed, on the contrary, she had been making his discomfiture more and more intense lately. Previously, that is to say a few days before, whenever she saw him she would make every effort to cheer him up and was dreadfully afraid of his sorrowful air; she even tried singing to him; but most often, she would tell him everything amusing she could think of. The prince almost always pretended to laugh heartily, and sometimes he really did laugh at the brilliant wit and radiant feeling with which she sometimes told stories when she was carried away, and she was carried away often. Seeing the prince's laughter, seeing the impression made on him, she would become delighted and begin to feel proud of herself. But now her melancholy and pensiveness grew almost with every hour. His views about Nastasya Filippovna were firmly established—else, it stands to reason, everything in her would have seemed enigmatic and incomprehensible to him now. But he sincerely believed that she came to life again. He had been quite truthful in telling Yevgeny Pavlovich that he loved her sincerely and completely, and his love for her did indeed contain an element of being drawn, as it were, to some pitiful and sickly child whom it was difficult, and even impossible, to leave to its own devices. He did not explain his feelings for her to anyone, and even disliked speaking of it when it was impossible to avoid the subject; and as for Nastasya Filippovna herself, they never discussed "feelings" when they sat together, just as though they had both made a promise of that kind to themselves. Anyone might have taken part in their ordinary, gay and lively conversation. Darya Alexeevna used to say afterward that in all this time she had done nothing but marvel and delight when she looked at them.

But that same view he had of Nastasya Filippovna's spiritual and mental state partly relieved him of many other perplexities as well. Now she was a completely different woman from the one he had known three months before. He no longer wondered now, for instance: why had she run away from marrying him then with tears, with curses and reproaches, yet now was insisting on the marriage herself, posthaste? "So it would seem she's no longer afraid, as she was back then, that by marrying him she'd bring misery upon him," thought the prince. Such a quickly emerging self-confidence, in his opinion, could not be natural in her. But, then again, this self-confidence could not have come about simply from her hatred for Aglaia, could it: Nastasya Filippovna was capable of feeling rather deeper than that. But it wasn't from dread of her fate with Rogozhin, was it? In a word, all these causes, together with the rest of it, could well have a part in it; but it was clearest of all to him that at play here was precisely what he had suspected long ago, and that the poor sick soul had been unable to endure it. Though all this did indeed relieve him, in its own way, of perplexities, it could give him neither peace of mind nor rest in all that time. At times he tried, as it were, not to think of anything. He really did, so it seemed, look on the marriage as though it were some insignificant formality; he valued his own future too cheaply. As for objections, conversations of the sort he had with Yevgeny Pavlovich, here he would have been decidedly unable to respond and felt himself absolutely incompetent, and for that reason stayed away from any conversation of that sort.

He noticed, however, that Nastasya Filippovna knew and understood only too well what Aglaia meant for him. She did not speak, but he saw her "face" at those times when she sometimes found him, at the beginning, preparing to go to the Epanchins'. When the Epanchins left, she grew positively radiant. However unobservant and unastute he may have been, still the thought began to worry him that Nastasya Filippovna decided to venture some scandal to force Aglaia out of Pavlovsk. The noise and clamor about the wedding in all the dachas was, of course, partly kept up by Nastasya Filippovna in order to irritate her rival. As it was difficult to meet the Epanchins, Nastasya Filippovna, seating the prince in her carriage on one occasion, arranged to drive with him right past the very windows of their dacha. This was a horrible surprise for the prince; he realized it, as was his wont, when it was no longer possible to set things right and when the carriage was already passing by the very windows. He said nothing, but afterward was ill for two days together; Nastasya Filippovna did not repeat the experiment. During the last few days before the wedding she began to grow deeply pensive; she always ended by overcoming her melancholy and becoming cheerful again, but somehow more quietly, not as noisily, not as happily cheerful as she had been before, only so lately. The prince redoubled his attention. It struck him as curious that she never spoke of Rogozhin to him. Only once, five days before the wedding, a message was suddenly sent him from Darya Alexeevna that he should come without delay, for Nastasya Filippovna was in a bad way. He found her in a condition approaching complete madness: she let out shouts, shuddered, cried out that Rogozhin was hidden in the garden, in their very house, that she had seen him just now, that he would kill her in the night . . . butcher her! She could not settle down all day. But that same evening, when the prince looked in on Ippolit for a moment, the captainess, who had only just returned from town, where she had been on some trifling affairs of her own, told him that Rogozhin had been to her apartment that day in Petersburg and had questioned her about Pavlovsk. Upon the prince's question as to when exactly Rogozhin had come, the captainess named almost the very same hour at which he had supposedly been seen that day by Nastasya Filippovna in her garden. The matter explained itself as a simple mirage; Nastasya Filippovna went to the captainess herself to make more detailed inquiries, and was extremely comforted.

On the day before the wedding the prince left Nastasya Filippovna in a state of great elation: the next day's finery arrived from the dressmaker's in Petersburg—the wedding dress, the headdress, and so on and so forth. The prince had not expected that she would be so much excited by the finery; he praised everything, and his praises made her even happier. But she let something slip: she had already heard that there was indignation in the town, and that some scamps or other were really getting up a charivari, with music, and practically with verses composed for the purpose, and all this was practically approved of by all the rest of the society. And so, precisely now, she wanted to hold up her head higher than ever before them, to outshine them all with the taste and richness of her attire—"Let them shout, let them whistle if they dare!" Her eyes flashed at the very thought of it. She had another secret fantasy, but she did not utter it aloud: she envisioned that Aglaia, or at any rate someone sent by her, would also be in the crowd incognito, in the church, would look on and see, and she was secretly preparing herself. She parted from the prince completely occupied by these ideas, around eleven o'clock in the evening; but before it had struck midnight they came running to the prince from Darya Alexeevna that he should "make haste to come, she's very bad." The prince found his bride shut up in her bedroom, in tears, in despair, in hysterics; for a long time she would hear nothing that was said to her through the closed door. At last she opened it, let in only the prince, shut the door, and fell on her knees before him. (So at least Darya Alexeevna, who managed to get a peep of something, reported afterward.)

"What am I doing! What am I doing! What am I doing to you, then!" she cried, embracing his feet convulsively.

The prince sat with her a whole hour; we do not know what they talked about. Darya Alexeevna said that they parted peaceably and happily after an hour. The prince sent once more that night to inquire, but Nastasya Filippovna had already fallen asleep. In the morning, even before she awoke, two more messengers were sent by the prince to Darya Alexeevna, and it was the third who was charged to report that "Nastasya Filippovna was now surrounded by a perfect swarm of dressmakers and hairdressers from Petersburg, that there was not a trace of yesterday; that she was occupied, as occupied as such a beauty might well be with her outfit before going to the altar; and that now, that very minute, there was a special conference in progress about which of the diamonds to wear and how to wear them." The prince was completely reassured.

The whole subsequent story about this wedding was told by people in the know as follows, and, it seems, accurately:

The marriage ceremony was fixed for eight o'clock in the evening; Nastasya Filippovna was ready by seven. As early as six o'clock, a crowd of gaping onlookers had gradually begun gathering around Lebedev's dacha, but particularly around Darya Alexeevna's house; from seven o'clock, the church began to fill up too. Vera Lebedev and Kolya were in most terrible alarm on the prince's account; however, they had a great deal to do in the house; they were arranging the reception and refreshments in the prince's rooms. However, they hardly expected much of a gathering after the marriage ceremony; aside from the necessary persons present at the ceremony, Lebedev had invited the Ptitsyns, Ganya, the doctor with the Anna around his neck, and Darya Alexeevna. When the prince asked Lebedev out of curiosity why he had gotten it into his head to invite the doctor, "almost a complete stranger," Lebedev replied self-importantly: "An order around his neck, a man who is respected, sir, for the sake of appearances, sir"—and made the prince laugh. Keller and Burdovsky, in tails and gloves, looked quite decent; only Keller still somewhat discomfited the prince and those who put their confidence in him by certain undisguised inclinations for combat, and cast very hostile looks at the gaping onlookers who were gathering around the house. At last, at half past seven, the prince set off for the church in a coach. We may observe, by the way, that he himself purposely did not wish to omit any of the usual customs and rituals; everything was done openly, publicly, and "as it should be." In the church, making his way somehow or other through the crowd, amongst continual whispers and exclamations, under the guidance of Keller, who cast menacing looks to right and left, the prince disappeared for a time behind the altar[49] while Keller went off to fetch the bride, where he found, at the steps to Darya Alexeevna's house, a crowd not only two or three times as dense as at the prince's but, perhaps, fully three times as presumptuous. As he mounted the steps, he heard such exclamations that he could not restrain himself and would have already turned around to the crowd with the intention of delivering an appropriate speech, but, luckily, he was checked by Burdovsky and by Darya Alexeevna herself, who had run out from the porch; they seized him and drew him indoors by force. Keller was irritated and in a hurry. Nastasya Filippovna got up, looked once more into the looking glass, observed with a "wry" smile, as Keller reported afterward, that she was "as pale as a corpse," bowed devoutly to the icon, and went out onto the steps. A hum of voices greeted her appearance. For the first moment, it's true, there were sounds of laughter, applause, practically whistling; but after a moment other voices were heard too:

"What a beauty!" they cried in the crowd.

"She's not the first and she's not the last!"

"The wedding veil hides everything, you fools!"

"Well, you try and find such a beauty now, hurrah!" cried those standing nearest.

"A princess! For a princess like that I'd sell my soul," cried some clerk. " 'One night at the price of a life!' " he quoted.[50]

Nastasya Filippovna did indeed come out white as a sheet; but her great black eyes glittered at the crowd like burning coals; and it was just this gaze that the crowd could not withstand; indignation turned into enthusiastic cries. The doors of the carriage were already open, Keller had already offered the bride his arm, when suddenly she uttered a cry and rushed from the steps straight into the crowd. All of her escorts froze in amazement, the crowd parted before her, and five or six paces from the steps suddenly appeared Rogozhin. It was his eyes Nastasya Filippovna had caught in the crowd. She ran to him like a mad creature and seized him by both hands.

"Save me! Take me away! Where you will, at once!"

49. In Russian churches, the altar is shut off by partition from the rest of the church. [C.G.]

50. From a poem about Cleopatra in Pushkin's story "Egyptian Nights" (1835).

Rogozhin caught her up almost in his arms and practically carried her to the carriage. Then in a flash he pulled a hundred-ruble note from his wallet and handed it to the driver.

"To the railway station, and if you catch the train, there's another hundred for you!"

And he leapt into the carriage after Nastasya Filippovna and shut the doors. The coachman did not hesitate for one moment and whipped the horses. Keller blamed it all afterward on happenstance: "Another second and I would have found my bearings, I wouldn't have allowed it!" he explained, recounting the adventure. He and Burdovsky would have grabbed another coach that happened to be there and rushed off in pursuit, but he reconsidered, already on the way, reflecting that "it was in any case too late! You can't bring her back by force!"

"And the prince won't wish it, either!" decided the stunned Burdovsky.

As for Rogozhin and Nastasya Filippovna, they galloped to the station in time. After they had gotten out of the carriage, Rogozhin—almost on the point of getting on the train—managed to stop a girl who was passing by in an old but decent dark little mantle and a silk kerchief thrown over her head.

"Would you like fifty rubles for your mantle?" He suddenly held out the money to the girl. While she was still lost in amazement and endeavoring to understand, he had already thrust the fifty-ruble note into her hand, pulled off the mantle and kerchief, and flung everything on the shoulders and head of Nastasya Filippovna. Her overly splendid outfit was eye-catching, would have attracted attention in the railway carriage, and it was only afterward that the girl understood why her old and worthless rags had been bought from her at so much profit to herself.

The hubbub about the adventure reached the church with astounding rapidity. As Keller was making his way to the prince, numbers of people who were complete strangers to him rushed up to question him. There was loud talking, shaking of heads and even laughter; no one left the church, everyone was waiting to see how the bridegroom would take the news. He turned pale, but took the news quietly, saying barely audibly: "I was afraid; but all the same, I did not think it would be this . . ." And then, after a brief silence, he added: "Then again . . . in her condition ... it's entirely in the natural order of things." Such a response even Keller described afterward as "unexampled philosophy." The prince came out of the church apparently calm and energetic; so at least many people noted and recounted afterward. It seemed that he was very anxious to get home and to be alone as soon as possible; but they did not let him. He was followed into his room by several of the invited guests, among them Ptitsyn, Gavrila Ardalionovich, and with them the doctor, who was not disposed to leave. Moreover, the whole house was literally besieged by an idle crowd. Even from the terrace, the prince could hear how Keller and Lebedev had entered into a violent dispute with some persons who were complete strangers, though they appeared to have some rank, and were bent on entering the terrace at any cost. The prince came up to the disputants, inquired what was the matter and, politely waving aside Lebedev and Keller, tactfully addressed a stout, gray-headed gentleman who was standing on the steps at the head of several other aspirants, and invited him to honor him with his visit. The gentleman was somewhat disconcerted, but went all the same; and after him came a second and a third. Out of the whole crowd seven or eight sightseers were found who went in after all, trying to do it in as offhand a manner as possible; but there did not turn out to be any more eager parties, and soon, in the crowd itself, they began to censure the upstarts. Those who had gone in were seated; a conversation sprang up; tea was being served—all this with exceptional decorum and modesty, to the considerable surprise of the arrivals. There were, of course, some attempts to enliven the conversation and turn it to the most "germane" theme; a few indiscreet questions were uttered, a few "daring" remarks were made. The prince answered everyone so simply and cordially, and at the same time with such dignity, with such trust in the decency of his guests, that the indiscreet questions died away of themselves. Little by little the conversation became almost serious. One gentleman, seizing the word, suddenly swore with extraordinary indignation that he would not sell his property, whatever happened: that on the contrary he would wait and wait it out and that "enterprise was better than money"; "there you are, my dear sir, therein consists my economic system, yes, sir, you might as well know." As he was addressing the prince, the latter warmly praised him, though Lebedev whispered in his ear that this gentleman had never had so much as a bedpost, nor any property of any kind. Almost an hour passed, the tea was finished, and after tea the visitors began, at last, to be ashamed to stay any longer. The doctor and the gray-haired gentleman took their leave of the prince with warmth; and they all took their leave with warmth and noise. Good wishes were expressed, and opinions along the lines that "it was no use grieving, and that maybe it was all for the best this way," and so on. There were, it's true, some attempts to ask for champagne, but the older guests checked the younger ones. When all were gone, Keller bent over to Lebedev and declared: "You and I would have made a row, gotten in a fight, disgraced ourselves, have dragged in the police; but look at him, he's acquired some new friends—and what friends; I know them!" Lebedev, who was a little "ripe," sighed, and articulated, "Thou hast hid these things from the wise and prudent, and hast revealed them unto babes; I said so about him before, but now I'll add that God has preserved the babe himself, has saved him from the abyss, He and all His saints!"

At last, about half past ten, they left the prince alone, he had a headache; Kolya, who had helped him change his wedding clothes for his house clothes, was the last to leave. They parted very warmly. Kolya did not enlarge upon the event, but promised to come early next day. He bore witness afterward that the prince had given him no warning at their last parting, and, so it would seem, was concealing his intentions even from him. Soon there was scarcely anyone left in the house: Burdovsky went to Ippolit's, Keller and Lebedev set off somewhere. Only Vera Lebedev remained for some time in the rooms, hurriedly restoring them from a festive to an ordinary state. As she went out, she looked in on the prince. He was sitting at the table, propped up on it with both elbows and his head hidden in his hands. She went softly up to him and touched him on the shoulder; the prince looked at her in bewilderment and seemed as if he were trying to recollect for nearly a minute; but recollecting and realizing everything, he suddenly became extremely agitated. However, it all culminated in an urgent and fervent request to Vera that next morning, with the first train, at seven o'clock, she should knock at his door. Vera promised; the prince began with warmth to beg her not to inform anyone of this; she promised that too, and at last, when she had already opened the door to go, the prince stopped her for the third time, took her hands, kissed them, then kissed her on her forehead, and with some sort of "extraordinary" air, brought out: "Till tomorrow!" So at least Vera related it afterward. She went away in great anxiety about him. She was somewhat heartened in the morning, when at seven o'clock she knocked at his door as agreed and informed him that the train for Petersburg would leave in a quarter of an hour; it seemed to her that he opened the door to her quite in good spirits, and even with a smile. He had hardly undressed in the night, though he had slept. In his opinion, he might be back that same day. It appeared therefore that he had found it possible and necessary to inform no one but her at that moment that he was going to town.

X I

An hour later he was already in Petersburg and soon after nine he was ringing at Rogozhin's door. He went in at the front entrance and for a long time no one opened for him. At last the door to old lady Rogozhin's apartment opened and an elderly, trim-looking serving-woman appeared.

"Parfyon Semyonovich is not at home," she announced from the door. "Whom do you want?"

"Parfyon Semyonovich."

"He is not at home, sir."

The serving-woman looked at the prince with wild curiosity.

"At least tell me, did he sleep at home last night? And . . . did he come back alone yesterday?"

The old woman went on looking at him but made no reply.

"Did he perhaps have with him, yesterday, here . . . in the evening . . . Nastasya Filippovna?"

"But allow me to ask who may you be pleased to be?"

"Prince Lev Nikolaevich Myshkin, we are very well acquainted."

"He is not at home, sir."

The woman dropped her eyes.

"And what about Nastasya Filippovna?"

"I know nothing about that, sir."

"Stay, stay! When is he coming back?"

"We don't know that either, sir."

The door was closed.

The prince determined to come back in an hour. Glancing into the yard he saw the porter.

"Is Parfyon Semyonovich at home?"

"Yes, sir."

"How is it I was told just now that he was not at home?"

"Did they tell you that at his place?"

"No, the servant at his mother's; I rang at Parfyon Semyonovich's, but no one opened."

"Perhaps he's gone out," the porter decided. "He won't announce himself, you know. And sometimes he takes the key away with him; the rooms stay locked up for three days at a time."

"Do you know for a fact that he was at home yesterday?"

"He was. Sometimes he'll go in at the front door and you won't see him."

"And was Nastasya Filippovna with him yesterday, perhaps?"

"That I don't know, sir. She don't please to come too often; you'd think it would be plain when she did."

The prince went out and for some time walked up and down the sidewalk lost in thought. The windows of the rooms occupied by Rogozhin were all shut; the windows of the part occupied by his mother were almost all open; it was a bright, hot day; the prince crossed the street to the sidewalk on the opposite side and stopped to look once more at the windows: they were not only shut, but white curtains were down almost everywhere.

He stood still a minute, and—strange—he suddenly fancied that the corner of one curtain was lifted and Rogozhin's face flashed in the window, flashed and vanished in the same moment. He waited a little longer and resolved to go back and ring again, but reconsidered and put it off for an hour. "And who knows, perhaps it was only my fancy . . ."

Most important, he was in haste now to get to Izmailovsky Polk, to the lodging Nastasya Filippovna had lately occupied. He knew that when, at his request, she had moved back from Pavlovsk three weeks before, she had settled in Izmailovsky Polk in the house of a good friend of hers, the widow of a teacher, an estimable lady with a family, who let a well-furnished apartment by which, indeed, she almost made her living. It was most likely that, when Nastasya Filippovna moved to

Pavlovsk again, she had kept her lodging; at the least, it was rather likely that she had spent the night at those lodgings, where Rogozhin, of course, would have brought her yesterday. The prince took a cab. On the way it occurred to him that he ought to have begun there, because it was unlikely she should have gone straight to Rogozhin's in the night. Here he remembered the porter's words that Nastasya Filippovna did not please to come often. If she did not come often as it is, what would have induced her to stay at Rogozhin's now? Heartening himself with these consoling thoughts, the prince arrived in Izmailovsky Polk at last more dead than alive.

To his utter amazement, at the widow's they had not only heard nothing of Nastasya Filippovna, either the day before or today, but they all ran out to stare at him, as at a wonder. The lady's numerous family—all girls, a year apart, starting from fifteen and going down to seven years old—scrambled out after their mother and surrounded him, gaping their mouths at him. They were followed by their lean, yellow-faced aunt in a black kerchief, and, last of all, the grandmother of the family appeared, a very aged old lady in spectacles. The teacher's widow earnestly begged him to go in and sit down, which the prince did. He guessed at once that they were fully informed about who he was and knew quite well that his wedding was to have taken place the day before, and that they were dying to ask about the wedding and about the marvelous fact that he was inquiring of them about the woman who should have been at that moment nowhere other than with him at Pavlovsk, but they were too tactful. In brief outlines he satisfied their curiosity about the wedding. Cries and exclamations of wonder and dismay followed, so that he was obliged to tell almost all the rest of story, in its main outline, of course. Finally, the council of the sage and agitated ladies determined that the first thing certainly was to knock at Rogozhin's till he got an answer and to find out positively from him about everything. If he were not at home (and that he must ascertain for certain), or if he were unwilling to say, then he should go to Semyonovsky Polk, to a certain lady, a German, who lived with her mother and was a friend of Nastasya Filippovna's: possibly Nastasya Filippovna, in her excitement and desire to conceal herself, might have passed the night with them. The prince got up completely crushed; they said afterward that he had "turned pale something terrible"; indeed, his legs were almost giving way under him. At last, through the terrible shrill patter of their voices, he made out that they were arranging to act with him and were asking for his address in town. He turned out not to have an address; they advised him to put up at some hotel. The prince reflected and gave the address of his previous hotel, the one where he had had a fit five weeks before. Then he set off again to Rogozhin's. This time, not only did they not open at Rogozhin's, but even the door to the old lady's apartment did not open. The prince went down to the porter and with some difficulty found him in the yard; the porter was busy with something and hardly answered him, hardly looked at him even, but nonetheless, he asserted positively that Parfyon Semyonovich "had gone out from early morning, had gone to Pavlovsk, and would not be home that day."

"I will wait; perhaps he will be back toward the evening?"

"Or maybe he won't be back for a week, who knows with him?"

"So then, he spent the night here today, in any case?"

"Spent the night, aye, that he did . . ."

All this was suspicious and shady. It was quite possible that the porter had received fresh instructions in the interim: he had been quite chatty before, but now he simply turned his back on him. But the prince resolved to come back once more, around two hours later, and even to keep watch near the house if necessary; but now there was still hope at the German lady's, and he galloped off to Semyonovsky Polk.

But at the German lady's they did not even understand him. From certain little words that were dropped, he was even able to surmise that, some two weeks back, the German beauty had quarreled with Nastasya Filippovna, so that she had heard nothing of her in all this time and let it be known now with all her might that she did not care to hear "though she had married all the princes in the world." The prince made haste to leave. The thought occurred to him, among other things, that perhaps she had gone to Moscow, as she had done before, and Rogozhin of course had gone after her or perhaps even with her. "If I could at least find some kind of trace!" He remembered, however, that he must stop at the inn, and he hurried to Liteinaya; there, he was at once given a room. The hall-man inquired as to whether he would like a bite to eat; in his distraction, he answered that he would, and, realizing too late, was terribly furious with himself that the meal delayed him by an extra half an hour; and only afterward did it occur to him that nothing kept him from leaving the meal that was served to him and not eating anything. A strange sensation possessed him in that dingy and stuffy corridor, a sensation that strove agonizingly to materialize into some kind of thought; but he was continually unable to surmise what that new niggling thought consisted in. He went out of the hotel at last, hardly knowing what he was doing; his head was spinning, but—where, after all, should he go? He rushed off to Rogozhin's again.

Rogozhin had not come back; no one opened at the ring; he rang at old lady Rogozhin's; they opened up and also announced that Parfyon Semyonovich was not at home and might not be there for three days. What disconcerted the prince was the fact that, as before, he was scrutinized with such wild curiosity. This time he could not find the porter at all. He crossed over to the opposite sidewalk as before, gazed up at the windows and walked up and down in the stifling heat for half an hour, possibly more; but this time nothing stirred; the windows did not open, the white curtains were motionless. He made up his mind for good that certainly he had only fancied it before, that even the windows, to all appearances, were so dingy and had not been cleaned for so long that it would have been difficult to make out, even if anyone had in fact peeped out through the glass. Relieved by this reflection he set off to the teacher's widow at Izmailovsky Polk again.

There they were already expecting him. The widow had already been to three or four places and had even stopped by Rogozhin's: there was not a peep to be heard. The prince listened in silence, went into the room, sat down on the sofa and began to stare at them all, as though he did not understand what they were talking about. Strange: he was at times extremely observant, and suddenly he would become absent-minded to an impossible degree. The whole family declared afterward that he was a "marvelously" strange person that day, so that "perhaps it all had become clear by then already." At last he got up and asked to be shown Nastasya Filippovna's rooms. These were two large, light, lofty rooms, very decently furnished, and they were not rented cheap. All those ladies related afterward that the prince had scrutinized every object in the room, had seen on the table an open book from the reading library, the French novel *Madame Bovary*, took note of it, turned down the corner of the page at which the book was open, asked permission to take it with him, and on the spot, not heeding the objection that it was a library book, put it in his pocket. He sat down at the open window, and seeing a card-table marked with chalk, asked who played. They told him that Nastasya Filippovna used to play every evening with Rogozhin at fools, preference, millers, whist, your own trumps—all sorts of games, and that they had only taken to playing cards lately, after she moved back from Pavlovsk to Petersburg, because Nastasya Filippovna was always complaining that she was bored, that Rogozhin sat whole evenings on end in silence and did not know how to talk about anything, and she would often cry; and suddenly the next evening Rogozhin had taken a pack of cards out of his pocket; here Nastasya Filippovna had laughed and they began to play. The prince asked, where were the cards they used to play with? But the cards were not forthcoming; the cards were always brought by Rogozhin himself in his pocket, every day a new pack, and were taken away with him again.

Those ladies advised him to go one more time to Rogozhin's and to knock one more time, more firmly, not at once but rather when it was already evening: "Perhaps something will turn up." The widow herself offered meanwhile to go before evening to Pavlovsk, to Darya Alexeevna's: perhaps they would know something there? They asked the prince to come again around ten o'clock in the evening, in any case, that they might make plans for next day. In spite of all the reassurances and encouragements, utter despair came over the prince's soul. In inexpressible dejection he went on foot to his hotel. Dusty, stifling, summertime Petersburg gripped him like a vise; he was jostled by grim or drunken people, peered aimlessly into faces, and perhaps walked much farther than was necessary; it was almost evening when he went into his room. He decided to rest a little and then to go to Rogozhin's again, as he had been advised, sat down on the sofa, leaned with both his elbows on the table and began to reflect.

God knows how for long and God knows of what he thought. There were many things he dreaded and he felt painfully, agonizingly, that he was in terrible dread. Vera Lebedev came into his head; then the thought struck him that Lebedev perhaps knew something in this affair, or, if he did not, might find out more quickly and easily than he could. Then he remembered Ippolit, and that Rogozhin used to go to see Ippolit. Then he remembered Rogozhin himself: recently at the funeral, then in the park, then—suddenly here in the corridor, when he hid that time in the corner and waited for him with a knife. He recalled his eyes now, as they peered then into the darkness. He shuddered: the recent niggling thought suddenly came into his head now. It consisted in part of this—that if Rogozhin were in Petersburg, even though he were hiding for a time, he would nonetheless certainly end by coming to him, the prince, with good or with evil intention, perhaps even as he had done then. In any case, if Rogozhin did feel the need to come for some reason, there would be nowhere else for him to go but here, to this same corridor. He did not know his address: so then he might very well think that the prince would stay at the same inn as before; at the least, he would try looking for him here . . . if he felt a great need. And who knows, perhaps he really would feel a great need?

That is what he thought, and this thought seemed to him for some reason entirely possible. On no account could he have explained to himself, if he began to probe his thought more deeply: "Why, for instance, should Rogozhin suddenly have such need of him, and why was it so absolutely out of the question that they should not finally come together?" But the thought was an oppressive one: "If he is doing well, he will not come," the prince went on thinking; "he is more likely to come if he is not doing well; but then, he is certain not to be doing well . . ."

Of course, if he held this conviction, logically he ought to have waited for Rogozhin at home, in his room; but he seemed unable to endure his new idea, jumped up, grabbed his hat and ran out. In the corridor, it was already almost entirely dark: "What if he suddenly comes out of that corner now and stops me by the stairs?" flashed through his mind, as he was approaching the familiar spot. But no one came out. He went down under the gate, went out into the sidewalk, wondered at the dense crowd of people who had poured out into the street with the sunset (as they always do in Petersburg when it's vacation time) and set off in the direction of Gorokhovaya. Fifty paces from the inn, at the first crossing, someone in the crowd suddenly touched his elbow, and in an undertone said right above his ear:

"Lev Nikolaevich, come along, my man, follow me, there's need of it."

It was Rogozhin.

Strange: the prince suddenly, in his joy, began to tell him, murmuring and almost failing to bring out the words, how he had awaited him just now in the corridor at the inn.

"I've been there," Rogozhin unexpectedly answered. "Let's go."

The prince wondered at the answer, but he wondered after at least two minutes had passed already, when he had taken it in. When he took in the answer, he was alarmed and began to look intently at Rogozhin. The latter was already walking almost half a step ahead, looking straight before him and not glancing at any one of the passersby, making way for everyone with mechanical care.

"Why didn't you ask for me at my room . . . if you were at the inn?" asked the prince suddenly.

Rogozhin stopped, looked at him, thought a little and, as though he did not understand the question at all, said:

"I say, Lev Nikolaevich, you go straight along here, right up to the house, you know? And I'll walk on the other side. And keep an eye out, so that we keep together . . ."

Saying this, he crossed the road, stepped onto the opposite sidewalk, looked to see whether the prince was coming and, seeing that he was standing still and staring at him popeyed, motioned him with his arm toward Gorokhovaya and walked on, turning every moment to glance at the prince and inviting him to follow. He was evidently encouraged, seeing that the prince had understood him and was not crossing over to him from the opposite sidewalk. It occurred to the prince that Rogozhin needed to look out for someone and not miss him on the way, and for that reason he had crossed to the opposite sidewalk. "Only why didn't he say whom to look out for?" In this manner, they walked some five hundred paces, and suddenly, for some reason, the prince began to tremble; Rogozhin did not cease to look back at him, though not so often; the prince could not stand it and beckoned to him. Rogozhin at once crossed the road to him.

"Is Nastasya Filippovna at your place, then?"

"She's at my place."

"And before, was that you looking at me from behind the curtain?"

"It was me . . ."

"But how is it you . . ."

But the prince did not know what more to ask or how to finish his

question; moreover, his heart was beating so violently that it was difficult to speak. Rogozhin kept silent too and gazed at him as before, that
is, as if lost in thought.

"Well, I am going," he said suddenly, preparing to cross the road
again, "and you keep on your way. Let us be apart on the street ... that's
better for us ... on different sides ... You'll see."

When at last they turned, from two separate sidewalks, onto Gorokhovaya and began to approach Rogozhin's house, the prince's legs
began to give way under him again, so that it was almost difficult to
walk. It was already about ten o'clock in the evening. As before, the
windows in the old lady's part of the house stood open, in Rogozhin's
shut, and in the twilight the white curtains drawn over them seemed
still more conspicuous. The prince approached the house from the opposite sidewalk, while Rogozhin stepped onto the stoop straight from
his sidewalk and waved his arm to him. The prince crossed over to the
stoop to join him.

"Even the porter doesn't know about me that I've come back home
now. I said earlier that I was going to Pavlovsk, and I left word at
Mother's too," he whispered, with a sly and almost pleased smile.
"We'll go in and no one will hear."

The key was already in his hand. As he went up the staircase, he
turned around and gestured warningly at the prince to go up more
quietly, quietly opened the door to his rooms, let the prince in, cautiously went in after him, shut the door behind him, and put the key in
his pocket.

"Let's go," he pronounced in a whisper.

He had already begun to speak in a whisper on the sidewalk on
Liteinaya. In spite of all his outward composure, he was inwardly in
some sort of profound agitation. When they went into the drawing
room, just before the study, he went to the window and mysteriously
beckoned to the prince.

"Well, now, as you were ringing at my door earlier, I guessed at once
here that it was none other than you; I went up to the door on tiptoe
and heard that you're talking with Pafnutyevna—and as for that one, I
told her at the first light of day: if you or anyone from you, or anyone
whatever, began knocking at my door, she wasn't to tell a word on any
account; and especially if you yourself came asking for me, and I in-

formed her of your name. And afterward, when you went out, the thought struck me: what if he's standing there now and looking out, or watching for whatnot from the street? I went up to this very window, drew aside the curtain, you know, had a look-see, and there you are, standing there looking straight at me ... That's how that business happened."

"But where's ... Nastasya Filippovna?" the prince brought out breathlessly.

"She's ... here," Rogozhin uttered slowly, as if biding his time a bit to answer.

"Where, then?"

Rogozhin raised his eyes at the prince and looked intently at him.

"Let's go."

He still talked in a whisper and unhurriedly, slowly and, as before, somehow with a strange pensiveness. Even when he was telling the story about the curtain, it was as if with his story he wanted to express something else, for all the effusiveness of the story.

They went into the study. There was some change in this room since the prince had been in it last: hung across the entire length of the room was a heavy green silk curtain, with two entries on either end, and it divided the study from the alcove where Rogozhin's bed was set up. The heavy curtain was down, and the entries drawn shut. But the room was very dark; the "white" summer nights of Petersburg were beginning to grow darker and, if it were not for the full moon, it would have been difficult to make out anything in Rogozhin's dark rooms with the window shades down. Though it was still possible to make out faces, if only very indistinctly. Rogozhin's face was pale as usual; his eyes watched the prince intently, with a strong gleam, but somehow without any motion.

"Maybe you should light a candle?" said the prince.

"No, no need," answered Rogozhin, and, taking the prince by the arm, pulled him down toward a chair; he himself sat opposite, moving his chair up so that he almost touched the prince with his knees. Between them, a little to the side, there happened to be a small round table. "Sit down, let's stay here awhile!" he said, as though persuading the prince to stay. They were silent for a minute. "I just knew that you'd stop at that same inn," he began, the way people sometimes start, when approaching an important conversation, with extraneous particulars not directly relevant to the matter at hand. "As soon as I got into the corridor I thought: you know, maybe he's sitting and waiting for me now, just as I am for him at this very moment? Have you been to the teacher's widow, then?"

"Yes," the prince was hardly able to articulate from the violent beating of his heart.

"I thought of that, too. There'll be talk, I thought . . . and then I thought again: I'll bring him here for the night, so that we may spend this night together . . ."

"Rogozhin! Where is Nastasya Filippovna?" the prince whispered suddenly, and stood up trembling in every limb. Rogozhin got up too.

"There," he whispered, motioning with his head toward the curtain.

"Asleep?" whispered the prince.

Again Rogozhin looked at him intently, as before.

"Well, then, let's go! . . . Only you . . . Well, never mind, let's go!"

He lifted up the curtain a bit, stood still and turned to the prince again.

"Come in!" he nodded at the curtain, inviting him to go on ahead. The prince went in.

"It's dark here," he said.

"There's enough to see!" muttered Rogozhin.

"I can scarcely see . . . a bed."

"Well, get closer, then," Rogozhin suggested softly.

The prince stepped closer, one step, then another, and stopped. He stood still and peered at it for a minute or two; neither of them uttered a word all the while they stood by the bedside; the prince's heart beat so violently that it seemed as though it were audible in the room, with the room's deathlike stillness. But his eyes had already grown acclimated, so that he could make out the whole bed; someone lay asleep on it, in a perfectly motionless sleep; not the faintest stir, not the faintest breath could be heard. The sleeper was covered over from head to foot with a white sheet, but the limbs were vaguely defined somehow; all that could be seen, from the elevation, was that a human figure was lying there, stretched out. All around, in disorder, on the bed, at the feet, beside the bed on chairs and even on the floor, discarded clothes had been flung about; a luxurious white silk dress, flowers, ribbons. On a little table by the headboard glittered some diamonds that had been taken off and flung down. At the foot, some lace had been crumpled into a heap, and on the white lace, peeping out from under the sheet, the tip of a naked foot was revealed; it appeared as if carved out of marble and was terribly still. The prince looked and felt that the more he looked, the more deathly still and quiet it became in the room. Suddenly, a fly that had awakened began to buzz, flew over the bed and settled by the headboard. The prince started.

"Let's go out." Rogozhin touched his arm.

They went out, sat down again on the same chairs, facing one another again. The prince trembled more and more violently, and never took his questioning eyes off Rogozhin's face.

"There, Lev Nikolaevich, I notice you're trembling," Rogozhin brought out at last, "almost like when you get your trouble, remember, there was that time in Moscow? Or like that time before a fit? I can't think what I should do with you now ..."

The prince listened, straining with every effort to understand and continuing to question with his eyes.

"Was it you?" he brought out at last, nodding his head at the curtain.

"It was ... I," whispered Rogozhin and cast down his eyes.

They were silent for five minutes.

"Because," Rogozhin suddenly began to go on, as though he had not broken off his speech at all, "because if your illness were to come now, and a fit, and screaming, perhaps someone from the street or from the yard might hear, and guess that people are spending the night in the apartment; they'll begin knocking and come in ... for they all think that I am not at home. I haven't even lighted a candle so they shouldn't guess from the street or the yard. For when I am away, I take the keys too, and in my absence they don't even come to tidy up, that's my arrangement. So, you see, in order that they not find out that we're spending the night ..."

"Hold on," said the prince. "I asked the porter and the old woman earlier whether Nastasya Filippovna hadn't spent the night here. So then they must know already."

"I know that you asked. I told Pafnutyevna that Nastasya Filippovna stopped by here yesterday evening and went away to Pavlovsk that same evening, and that she stayed only ten minutes at my place. And they don't know she stayed the night here—no one knows. Yesterday we came in the same way, completely on the quiet, like you and I did today. I was thinking to myself on the way that she wouldn't care to come in on the quiet—but not a bit of it! She whispered, she walked on tiptoe, drew her dress around her so it wouldn't rustle, carried it in her hands, shook her finger at me herself on the stairs—that was you she was afearin'. On the train she was quite like a madwoman, all from fear, and she herself wanted to come here to my place to spend the night; I was thinking at first to take her to the apartment at the teacher's widow's—but not a bit of it! 'He'll find me there as soon as day breaks,' she says, 'but you'll hide me and tomorrow, soon as day breaks—to Moscow,' and then she wanted to go somewhere to Orel. And as she went to bed she kept on saying we'd go to Orel . . ."

"Hold on; what do you think now, Parfyon, what do you want to do?"

"Well, I'm in doubt of you, you keep trembling. Tonight we'll spend the night here, together. There's no bed other than that one, but I figured it out like this—that we take the pillows off the two sofas, and right here, by the curtain, I'll make a bed beside it, for you and me, so that we're together. For if they come in, start looking around or searching, they'll see her at once and carry her away. They'll begin questioning me, I'll say it was me, and they'll take me away at once. So let her lie here now beside us, beside you and me . . ."

"Yes, yes!" the prince agreed warmly.

"So, no confessing and no letting them carry her away."

"N-not on any account!" the prince decided. "No-no-no!"

"That's what I decided, lad, not to give her up on any account to anyone! We'll spend the night quietly. I only left the house for a single hour today, in the morning, except for that I've been with her all the time. And then in the evening, I went to get you. Another thing I am afraid of is that it's so stifling hot and there may be a smell. Do you notice a smell or not?"

"Perhaps I do, I don't know. There certainly will be by the morning."

"I covered her with oilcloth, good American oilcloth, and the sheet over the oilcloth, and I put out four jars of Zhdanov's fluid uncorked, they're standing there now."

"That's just like that time . . . in Moscow?"

"Because, brother, the smell. And you see how she is lying . . . In the morning, when it's light, take a look. What's the matter, can't you stand up?" Rogozhin asked with apprehensive surprise, seeing that the prince was trembling so much that he could not get up.

"My legs won't move," muttered the prince, "it's from fear, I know ... When the fear is gone I shall get up ..."

"Hold on, then, meantime I'll make up our bed myself, and you'd better lie down ... and I'll lie down with you ... and we'll listen ... for, my lad, I don't know yet ... my lad, I still don't know everything now, and so I'm telling you ahead of time, so that you should know all about it ahead of time...."

Muttering these unintelligible words, Rogozhin began making up the beds. It was evident that, perhaps, he had figured out these beds in his head as early as that morning. The previous night he had lain on the sofa himself. But two couldn't lie side by side on the sofa, and he was most definitely set on making the beds side by side now, and that was why he now dragged, with much effort, the variously sized cushions off the two sofas, across the entire room, and right up to the curtain. The bed was arranged after a fashion; he went up to the prince, tenderly and excitedly took him by the arm, raised him and led him to the bed; but it turned out that the prince could walk by himself; so it would seem the "fear was passing"; and yet he still went on trembling.

"It's because, my man," Rogozhin suddenly began, having settled the prince down on the left cushion, the best one, and stretching out himself on the right side, without undressing, and clasping both hands behind his head, "it's hot presently, and it's well known, the smell ... I am afraid to open the windows; at my mother's, there are pots of flowers, heaps of flowers, and they have such a wonderful smell; I thought of bringing them over, but Pafnutyevna would have figured it out, for she is inquisitive."

"She is inquisitive," the prince assented.

"Perhaps we should buy some, surround her with nosegays and flowers? But I think it'll be a sad sight, my friend, all in flowers, I mean!"

"Listen ..." asked the prince, as if confused, as if he were searching for what, precisely, had to be asked and apparently forgetting it again at once, "listen, tell me: what did you do it with? A knife? The same one?"

"The same one . . ."

"Hold on though! I want to ask you something else, Parfyon . . . I'm going to ask you a great many things, about everything . . . but you had better tell me first, to begin with, so that I may know: did you want to kill her before my wedding, before the ceremony, on the church steps, with a knife? Did you want to or not?"

"I don't know whether I wanted to or not . . ." Rogozhin answered dryly, as if even somewhat surprised at the question and not comprehending it.

"Did you ever take the knife with you to Pavlovsk?"

"No, never. All I can tell you about the knife is this, Lev Nikolaevich," he added after a pause, "I took it out of a locked drawer this morning, for it all happened this morning, as it was going on four o'clock. It had been lying in a book all the time . . . And . . . and here's what else seemed queer to me: the whole knife seemed to go in by three . . . or even by four inches . . . just under the left breast . . . but there wasn't more than half a tablespoonful of blood flowed onto her chemise, there was not more . . ."

"That, that, that," the prince sat up suddenly in terrible agitation, "that I know, I've read about it . . . That's called internal bleeding . . . Sometimes there's not even a drop. That's when the stab goes straight to the heart . . ."

"Hold on, do you hear?" Rogozhin suddenly interrupted quickly and sat up in fear on the covers. "Do you hear?"

"No!" brought out the prince just as quickly and fearfully, looking at Rogozhin.

"Steps! Do you hear? In the drawing room . . ."

They both began listening.

"I hear," the prince whispered firmly.

"Footsteps?"

"Footsteps."

"Shall we shut the door or not?"

"Shut it . . ."

They shut the door and both lay down again. For a long time, they kept silent.

"Oh, yes!" the prince began suddenly in the same excited and hurried whisper, as though he had caught his thought again and was dreadfully afraid of losing it again; he even sat up on the bed. "Yes . . .

but I wanted . . . those cards! Cards . . . You played cards with her, they said?"

"Yes, I did," said Rogozhin, after a brief silence.

"But where are . . . the cards?"

"The cards are here," Rogozhin brought out after keeping silent some more, "here . . ."

He brought a used pack of cards wrapped up in paper out of his pocket and held them out to the prince. The latter took it, but with a sort of bewilderment. A new sad and hopeless sensation crushed his heart; he realized suddenly that at that moment, and for a long time past, he had been talking about something other than what he needed to talk about, and doing something other than what needed to be done, and that these cards, which he was holding in his hands and was so pleased about, would not help anything now. He stood up and threw up his hands. Rogozhin lay motionless and seemed not to hear and see his movement; but his eyes glittered brightly through the darkness and were wide open and motionless. The prince sat down on a chair and began looking at him with terror. Half an hour passed; suddenly Rogozhin cried out loudly and abruptly and roared with laughter, as though he had forgotten that they must speak in a whisper:

"That officer, that officer . . . Do you remember how she lashed that officer at the bandstand, remember, ha-ha-ha! And the cadet . . . the cadet . . . the cadet rushed up too . . ."

The prince jumped up from the chair in new alarm. When Rogozhin grew quiet (and he suddenly grew quiet), the prince bent softly over him, sat down beside him and, with his heart beating violently and his breath strained, began to scrutinize him. Rogozhin did not turn his head toward him and seemed indeed to have forgotten about him. The prince watched and waited; time was passing, it was beginning to get light. From time to time Rogozhin began, infrequently and all of a sudden, to mutter, loudly, harshly and incoherently; he began shouting and laughing, and then the prince stretched out his trembling hand to him and softly touched his head, his hair, stroking them and stroking his cheeks . . . there was nothing more he could do! He himself began trembling again, and again his legs seemed suddenly to fail him. Some kind of quite new sensation gnawed at his heart with infinite anguish. Meanwhile it had become quite light; at last he lay down on the pillow, as though in utter helplessness and despair, and pressed his face to the pale and motionless face of Rogozhin; tears flowed from his eyes onto Rogozhin's cheeks, but perhaps he no longer noticed his own tears then and no longer knew anything about them . . .

In any case, when after many hours the door was opened and people came in, they found the murderer completely unconscious and in a fever. The prince was sitting beside him motionless on the covers and hastened softly, each time the sick man erupted in screaming or raving, to pass his trembling hand over his hair and cheeks, as though caressing and soothing him. But he no longer understood anything of what they were asking him, and did not recognize the people who had come in and surrounded him. And if Schneider himself had come from Switzerland now to have a look at his former pupil and patient, he too, remembering the condition in which the prince had sometimes been during the first year of his treatment in Switzerland, would have flung up his hands in despair and would have said as he did then: "Idiot!"

XII

CONCLUSION

The teacher's widow, racing into Pavlovsk, went straight to Darya Alexeevna, who was upset by the events of the previous day, and telling her everything she knew threw her into panic once and for all. The two ladies decided at once to get into communication with Lebedev, who was also in agitation in his role as a friend of his lodger and in his role as the landlord of the apartment. Vera Lebedev reported everything she knew. On Lebedev's advice they decided to set off, all three of them, to Petersburg, for the swiftest possible prevention of what "might very well have happened." In this way, it came about that on the very next morning, at about eleven o'clock, Rogozhin's apartment was opened in the presence of the police, of Lebedev, of the ladies and of Rogozhin's brother, Semyon Semyonovich Rogozhin, who lodged in the annex. The success of the business was facilitated most of all by the evidence of the porter that the previous evening he had seen Parfyon Semyonovich with a guest going in by the front steps and as though on the quiet. After this evidence was given, they no longer hesitated to break down the doors, which had not been opened at the ringing of the bell.

Rogozhin suffered inflammation of the brain for two months, and when he recovered, there came the investigation and the trial. He gave direct, precise and fully satisfactory evidence on every point, in consequence of which the prince, from the very start, was kept out of court. Rogozhin was taciturn during his trial. He did not contradict his skilled and eloquent counsel, who proved clearly and logically that the crime committed was a consequence of the inflammation of the brain, which had already set in long before the crime in consequence of the accused's troubles. But he added nothing of his own in confirmation of this opinion and, as before, clearly and precisely confirmed and recollected the minutest circumstances of the transpired event. He was sentenced, in view of mitigating circumstances, to fifteen years hard labor in Siberia, and heard his sentence grimly, silently and "pensively." His entire huge fortune, except for a certain, rather small, relatively speaking, portion that he had squandered in the initial period of debauchery, passed to his brother, Semyon Semyonovich, to the great satisfaction of this latter. Old lady Rogozhin continues to live on in this world and seems from time to time to remember her beloved son, Parfyon, but vaguely: God has saved her mind and her heart from the awareness of the horror that has befallen her melancholy house.

Lebedev, Keller, Ganya, Ptitsyn and many other persons in our story go on living as before, have changed little, and there is practically nothing for us to report about them. Ippolit passed away in a state of terrible excitement and somewhat sooner than he had expected, some two weeks after the death of Nastasya Filippovna. Kolya was deeply struck by what had happened; he grew closer with his mother once and for all. Nina Alexandrovna fears for him that he is too thoughtful for his years; he may, perhaps, turn out to be a man of action. By the way, in part due to his efforts, the further fate of the prince was settled as well: long before, he had already distinguished, among all the other persons whom he had come to know of late, Yevgeny Pavlovich Radomsky; he was the first to go to him and tell him all the particulars of the transpired events that he knew and of the prince's present condition. He was not mistaken: Yevgeny Pavlovich took the most fervent interest in the fate of the unfortunate "idiot," and as a consequence of his efforts and care the prince once again wound up abroad, in the Swiss establishment of Schneider. Yevgeny Pavlovich himself—who has gone abroad, intends to live for a very long time in Europe, and openly declares himself an "absolutely superfluous man in Russia"— visits his sick friend at Schneider's pretty often, at least once every few months; but Schneider furrows his brow and shakes his head more and more; he hints at complete impairment of the intellectual capacities; he does not yet speak positively of incurability, but he allows himself the most melancholy hints. Yevgeny Pavlovich takes this very much to heart, and he has a heart, which he has already proven by the fact that he gets letters from Kolya, and that he even answers these letters sometimes. But aside from this, another curious feature of his character has become known; and as it is a good feature, we hasten to describe it: after every visit to Schneider's establishment, Yevgeny Pavlovich sends a letter to one other person in Petersburg besides Kolya, with the most minute and kindly account of the state of the prince's illness at the present moment. Aside from the most respectful expression of devotion, in these letters there sometimes (and more and more frequently) begin to appear certain frank statements of views, ideas and feelings—in a word, something approaching friendly and intimate feelings is beginning to manifest itself. The person who is in correspondence (though, after all, rather infrequent) with Yevgeny Pavlovich and who has won so much of his attention and respect is Vera Lebedev. We could in no way manage to find out for certain how such relations might have arisen between them; they arose, of course, on account of the same story with the prince, when Vera Lebedev was so struck with grief that she fell positively ill; but under what particular circumstances the acquaintance and friendship came about, we do not know. We have mentioned these letters chiefly with this object—that some of them contained news of the Epanchin family, and, most important, of Aglaia Ivanovna Epanchin. Of her Yevgeny Pavlovich reported in one rather disconnected letter from Paris that, after a brief and unusual attachment to an émigré, a Polish count, she had suddenly married him against the wishes of her parents, who, if they had given their consent at last, then only because the business threatened to end in some extraordinary scandal. Then, after almost half a year's silence, Yevgeny Pavlovich informed his correspondent, again in a lengthy and detailed letter, about the fact that, on his last visit to Professor Schneider in Switzerland, he had run into all the Epanchins (except of course Ivan Fyodorovich, who stayed in Petersburg on business) and Prince Shch. The meeting was a strange one; they had all greeted Yevgeny Pavlovich with some sort of delight; for some reason, Adelaida and Alexandra even considered themselves grateful to him for his "angelic concern about the unhappy prince." Lizaveta Prokofyevna, seeing the prince in his afflicted and humiliated condition, wept from the bottom of her heart. By all appearances, everything had been forgiven him. Prince Shch. pronounced a few felicitous and sensible words of truth on the occasion. It seemed to Yevgeny Pavlovich that he and Adelaida were not yet in perfect harmony, but in the future the perfectly voluntary and sincere subjugation of the impetuous Adelaida to the good sense and experience of Prince Shch. seemed inevitable. Moreover, the lessons borne by the family had a tremendous effect on her, and especially the latest incident with Aglaia and the émigré count. Everything that the family had dreaded in yielding Aglaia to this count, everything had come to pass within six months, with the addition of surprises of which they had never even dreamed. It turned out that the count was not even a count, and if he was in fact an émigré, then with some sort of dark and dubious history. He had captivated Aglaia by the extraordinary nobility of his soul, which was torn with patriotic anguish, and captivated her to such a degree that she, even before she married him, became a member of some kind of foreign committee for the restoration of Poland and, moreover, wound up in the Catholic confessional of some celebrated priest, who took hold of her mind to the point of frenzied passion. The count's colossal fortune, of which he had presented Lizaveta Prokofyevna and Prince Shch. almost incontrovertible evidence, turned out to be completely nonexistent. What was more, within some six months of the wedding the count and his friend, the celebrated confessor, managed to make Aglaia quarrel utterly with her family, so that for some months now they had not even seen her . . . In a word, there was a great deal to tell, but Lizaveta Prokofyevna, her daughters, and even Prince Shch. were so much affected by all this "terror" that they were afraid even to mention certain things in conversation with Yevgeny Pavlovich, though they knew that even as it was he already knew full well the story of Aglaia Ivanovna's latest infatuations. Poor Lizaveta Prokofyevna was longing for Russia, and by Yevgeny Pavlovich's account, she expressed to him bitter and vehemently biased criticism of everything abroad: "They can't bake bread decently anywhere; in the winter, they freeze like mice in the cellar," she said; "at least right here, over this poor fellow, I've had a good Russian cry," she added, pointing in agitation to the prince, who did not recognize her at all. "Enough infatuations now, it's time to give reason its due. And all this, all these foreign parts, and all this Europe of yours, it's all nothing but a fantasy, and all of us abroad are nothing but a fantasy ... Remember my words, you'll see for yourself!" she concluded almost wrathfully, as she parted from Yevgeny Pavlovich.

READING GROUP GUIDE

1. A major theme in *The Idiot* is how goodness leads only to tragedy. Discuss.

2. Another major theme in the novel is the idea that beauty is a redeeming force (see the remark attributed to Myshkin in part III, ch. V that "the world will be saved by beauty"). Discuss.

3. Compare and contrast Myshkin and Rogozhin.

4. Dostoevsky was profoundly affected by the painting *Christ in the Tomb* by Hans Holbein, which he viewed during the fall of 1867, in a museum in Basel, when he began work on *The Idiot*. Discuss the significance of the painting, which is described in detail by Ippolit Terentyev in part II, ch. VI, to the novel's meaning.

5. Discuss the role of money in the novel.

6. Dostoevsky once said, thinking of Myshkin, that humility was "the most fearful force that can exist in the world." What do you think he meant by this remark?

7. Myshkin is supposed to represent the ideal of the most beautiful human being, but in the end, couldn't it be argued that it is his utter lack of understanding about the nature of Aglaia's and Nastasya's feelings that bring about their ruin?

A NOTE ON THE TYPE

The principal text of this Modern Library edition
was set in a digitized version of Janson, a typeface that
dates from about 1690 and was cut by Nicholas Kis,
a Hungarian working in Amsterdam. The original matrices have
survived and are held by the Stempel foundry in Germany.
Hermann Zapf redesigned some of the weights and sizes for
Stempel, basing his revisions on the original design.

MODERN LIBRARY IS ONLINE AT
WWW.MODERNLIBRARY.COM

MODERN LIBRARY ONLINE IS YOUR GUIDE
TO CLASSIC LITERATURE ON THE WEB

THE MODERN LIBRARY E-NEWSLETTER

Our free e-mail newsletter is sent to subscribers, and features sample chapters, interviews with and essays by our authors, upcoming books, special promotions, announcements, and news.

To subscribe to the Modern Library e-newsletter, send a blank e-mail to: **sub_modernlibrary@info.randomhouse.com** or visit **www.modernlibrary.com**

THE MODERN LIBRARY WEBSITE

Check out the Modern Library website at
www.modernlibrary.com for:

- The Modern Library e-newsletter
- A list of our current and upcoming titles and series
- Reading Group Guides and exclusive author spotlights
- Special features with information on the classics and other paperback series
- Excerpts from new releases and other titles
- A list of our e-books and information on where to buy them
- The Modern Library Editorial Board's 100 Best Novels and 100 Best Nonfiction Books of the Twentieth Century written in the English language
- News and announcements

Questions? E-mail us at **modernlibrary@randomhouse.com**.
For questions about examination or desk copies, please visit
the Random House Academic Resources site at
www.randomhouse.com/academic